SEVEN *Brides* *for* SEVEN
Mail-Order Husbands
ROMANCE COLLECTION

A Newspaper Ad for Husbands Brings a Wave of Men
to a Small Kansas Town

SEVEN *Brides* *for* SEVEN *Mail-Order Husbands* ROMANCE COLLECTION

Cynthia Hickey, Susan Page Davis
Susanne Dietze, Darlene Franklin, Patty Smith Hall,
Carrie Fancett Pagels, Gina Welborn

BARBOUR BOOKS
An Imprint of Barbour Publishing, Inc.

Abigail's Proposal ©2017 by Cynthia Hickey
The Kidnapped Groom ©2017 by Susan Page Davis
A Clean Slate ©2017 by Susanne Dietze
Sunshine of My Heart ©2017 by Darlene Franklin
Come What May ©2017 by Patty Smith Hall
Dime Novel Suitor ©2017 by Carrie Fancett Pagels
Louder than Words ©2017 by Gina Welborn

Print ISBN 978-1-68322-132-6

eBook Editions:
Adobe Digital Edition (.epub) 978-1-68322-134-0
Kindle and MobiPocket Edition (.prc) 978-1-68322-133-3

Scripture quotations marked KJV are taken from the King James Version of the Bible.

Scripture quotations marked ESV are from The Holy Bible, English Standard Version®, copyright © 2001 by Crossway Bibles, a publishing ministry of Good News Publishers. Used by permission. All rights reserved.

Scripture quotations marked NIV are taken from the HOLY BIBLE, NEW INTERNATIONAL VERSION®. NIV®. Copyright © 1973, 1978, 1984, 2011 by Biblica, Inc.™ Used by permission. All rights reserved worldwide.

Scripture quotations marked NLT are taken from the *Holy Bible*. New Living Translation copyright© 1996, 2004, 2015 by Tyndale House Foundation. Used by permission of Tyndale House Publishers, Inc. Carol Stream, Illinois 60188. All rights reserved.

Cover Image: shorrocks/ iStock

Published by Barbour Books, an imprint of Barbour Publishing, Inc., P.O. Box 719, Uhrichsville, Ohio 44683, www.barbourbooks.com

Our mission is to publish and distribute inspirational products offering exceptional value and biblical encouragement to the masses.

Member of the
Evangelical Christian
Publishers Association

Printed in Canada.

Contents

Abigail's Proposal

by Cynthia Hickey

Prologue

Kansas, 1865

Abigail Melton entered the kitchen to the sight of her mother slumped over the table, a telegram clutched in one hand. Her shoulders shook from her sobs.

"Ma?" She knelt beside her.

"Oh Abby." She handed over the telegram. "They aren't coming back."

Abby's heart dropped as she scanned the words. Pa and Dan were dead. Killed somewhere in Georgia. Tears blurred the ink on the paper. Whatever would they do? Every day she heard of another man from Turtle Springs who would not be returning home. She put her arms around her mother and joined her in crying.

"How will we tell Lucy?" Ma wailed. "She doted on her pa."

"I'll think of something." She always thought of something.

"You'll have to continue as mayor, dear. At least until the next election. The town can't survive without a Melton running the place."

But Abby was woefully unqualified. So many women already ran ranches, the mercantile, the livery. . .the list went on and on. How could they possibly do it all without their menfolk?

She dried her tears on the sleeve of her blouse, planted a kiss on Ma's head, and headed for the school. Lucy couldn't find out from someone else. She needed to hear it from it Abby or Ma.

Abby waited outside the school until the doors opened and the students barged into the sunshine. Lucy's blond head appeared last, her arms laden with books as she chatted with a friend. Tears stung Abby's eyes again as she realized the smile would soon fade from her sister's face.

"What are you doing here? I was going to walk partway with Mary." Lucy frowned.

"I need to speak with you. Alone, please. You'll have to see Mary another time." Abby blinked rapidly.

"You've been crying. It's Pa, isn't it?" The books fell from Lucy's arms, landing in the dust at her feet with a dull thud. "Dan?"

"Oh sweetheart. They're both gone." Abby reached for her sister as Lucy crumpled to the ground.

Lucy grabbed Abby's shoulders. "Fix this, Abby. You can, I know you can."

"I'll do my best."

Chapter 1

One year later,
Turtle Springs, Kansas, 1866

WANTED: MEN TO AUDITION AS HUSBANDS. TURTLE SPRINGS, KANSAS.
AUDITIONS HELD MAY 25. ONLY GODLY,
UPSTANDING MEN NEED APPLY. CHECK IN AT MAYOR'S OFFICE.

Abby stared at the advertisement in her hand. She planned on posting it to as many newspapers across the country as she had money to do so. But first, she needed to let the women of Turtle Springs know her plan. This was the first step to keeping her promise to her sister last year. The only thing Abby could think of to fix things.

While speaking was a duty of the town's mayor, a role Abby had stepped into when her father failed to return from the War Between the States, it wasn't something she enjoyed. She stared from the church's podium across the sea of mostly hopeful women. A few, such as Maggie Piner, showed mixed feelings. Most likely, some thought Abby a fool for concocting such a plan. Still, caring for her mother and younger sister, in addition to playing mayor, was too much work for her to do on her own. She needed a husband. Plain and simple.

"Thank you for coming, ladies. The fact that you are here means you share, at least in some small regard, an interest in obtaining a husband." She read the advertisement. A few *hmmms* sounded in response. "To make things move more smoothly during your fifteen-minute audition sessions, please have a list of questions available as to what you are looking for in a mate. Are there any questions for me?"

Ma raised her hand, a grin spreading across her face. "Make sure you put in that advertisement that I need a mature man. I'm not too old to start over."

Abby closed her eyes and counted to ten. Ma had been a thorn in her side since the husband-finding plan developed in Abby's mind. "I'm sure we'll have men of all ages and skills."

Another lady raised her hand, concern shadowing her pretty features. "What if we don't take a liking to any of them? I'm quite picky in who I want by my side."

"If you don't like any of them, pray to God to send you someone you do like." Abby gripped the sides of the podium. "I'm doing my best, ladies. Several of you were in agreement when I first proposed this plan. It's too late to back out now."

Jane Ransome, the main benefactor for the ad, stood. "What if more than one of us want the same man?"

Heads nodded in agreement.

"Then we'll have a drawing or pick a straw. Please don't fret. It will all work out."

"What about a sheriff?" Caroline Kane shouted. "With all these strangers coming to town, crime is going to increase."

"I placed an advertisement for a sheriff two weeks ago." Did no one pay attention in this town? "We've discussed this."

Jane stood again. "Shouldn't we have the sheriff hired before all these strangers come to town?"

Abby exhaled heavily. What she'd give for one day of Jane not questioning everything. "It's only a matter of time. Have faith, ladies. Meeting adjourned." Ignoring the rest of the raised hands, she strolled down the center aisle of the church, shoulders squared, face forward. *Oh, Papa, this job isn't for me.*

Rather than wait for Ma, she headed straight home, a white two-story building at the end of Main Street. Once there, she thanked her neighbor for watching Lucy, who at the age of thirteen thought herself much too old to have a sitter. The neighbor, a woman too old to care about training another husband, grinned and waved good-bye. Abby escorted Lucy to bed.

"When are the men coming?" Lucy pulled down the covers. "I hope there are lots. I'm thirteen now and almost ready for a husband of my own."

Gracious. "You're not even close." Abby shrugged out of her gown then hung it in the wardrobe.

"If Ma gets married, and you get married, where does that leave me?"

"With me or Ma. Hush and go to sleep." Abby climbed under the muslin sheet.

"I don't want to live with you. You're too bossy." Lucy flopped onto her back. "I wish Dan were here." Tears ran down her cheeks. "Our brother would make sure you were nice to me."

"I am nice to you. I provide a roof over your head, clothes on your back, and food in your mouth." She could be more patient, she supposed, but after a day of work, exhaustion clouded her mind and coated her limbs. "I'll let you help me pick my husband, how's that?"

"That'll be just fine." Lucy wiped away her tears on the sleeve of her nightgown. "I'll pick a good one, Abby. I promise."

Abby doubted there was a man alive willing to put up with her stubbornness and outspoken ways. Still, she might find some fool willing to look past all that. She was pretty enough, with wheat-colored hair and hazel eyes, or so folks had told her. Sometimes, Pa had said they were as green as the leaves of a tree. She sighed. Surely, God would see fit to lessen her burden.

The front door slammed. Then the sound of Ma's heavy footsteps coming up the stairs. She stopped in the door of Abby's room. "Why didn't you wait? All the interesting conversation went on after you left. Oh the requirements these women are listing." Ma perched on the edge of the bed. "I don't think there's a man out there that can meet them, outside of the Good Lord Himself."

Lucy sat up. "What did you list?"

"As long as he's breathing and standing upright, he's good enough for me. I reckon I can train any man to be a good husband. It worked with your father." She tapped Lucy on the nose. "Go to sleep now."

"I'm sorry, Ma," Abby said, staring at the ceiling. "I'm working very hard for this town and couldn't take the negativity for one more minute. Marry a man good enough to be voted into replacing me as mayor, please. That's all I ask."

"Phooey. You're a fine mayor." Ma patted her leg. "Don't be so hard on yourself." She lowered the wick on the oil lamp and left the room.

Abby continued to stare through the dark at the ceiling long after Lucy's slow, even breaths signaled she was asleep. An advertisement for a husband audition. It was quite possibly the craziest thing she'd ever done, or would do.

Lord, help them all.

Josiah Ingram climbed off his horse and looped the reins around the hitching post in front of the boardinghouse. He only planned on staying one night as he drifted across the country in his search for—well, he didn't know what he was searching for—only that he was a lost man since the war.

The town of Turtle Springs was quiet at 9:00 a.m. Main Street stretched from the church on one end to a two-story house on the other. In between was every type of establishment a man could want. Another road cut across the center, forming a perfect plus. He bet it had once been a bustling little place, where families greeted each other in passing with smiles on their faces. Now, it was as sad as most of the other towns he'd passed through.

He climbed the boardinghouse steps. Only then did he notice a small sign in the window that said WOMEN ONLY. He sighed and glanced once more up and down the street. Surely there was somewhere else to board.

A blond woman, no bigger than a minute, in a blue calico dress, unlocked the door to the mayor's office. Josiah headed her way with long strides. If anyone knew of a place where a man could hang his hat in town, it would be the mayor.

A small sign hung in the window—HUSBAND AUDITIONS HERE. He chuckled. What kind of town had he stopped in?

He pushed open the door and stepped into a small building with two desks, a filing cabinet, a gun rack, and pegs to hang hats and coats. The woman who had entered took a seat behind a desk displaying a plaque that stated MAYOR.

Josiah approached her. "Howdy."

She glanced up, hazel eyes a little too large for her face. "Howdy." Her gaze raked him from the toes of his scuffed boots to the Stetson on his head, settling on the six-shooter at his hip. "Have you ever been arrested?"

Strange question. "No, ma'am."

"Then, you're hired."

"For what, ma'am?" He removed his hat and grinned. Surely, she didn't think he was there to audition.

"Sheriff." She tilted her pretty little head. "I'm Mayor Melton. We're glad to have you." She handed him a sheet of paper and a gold star to pin on his shirt. "Fill this out. You're on a three-month probation period. At the end of that time, the town will decide whether to keep you on. The sheriff's office is across the street. There's a room in back for you to live. But it's small. If you need more space, you could rent a room over the restaurant."

Her eyes narrowed. "I'd like to know which side of the war you fought on."

He opened his mouth to protest then thought better of it. "I fought for a man's right to choose the style of life he wanted. I fought for the Confederacy, although my family never owned slaves. I fought for a world where men could be whatever they wanted to be. I cheered when President Lincoln freed the slaves. Might not make sense to some, but it did to me."

"I understand, sir."

When those amazing eyes settled on him again, he sighed and headed to the empty desk to fill out the application. He pulled a sharpened pencil from a tin can and filled in his name. Why not be sheriff? It wasn't like many job opportunities had come his way. He'd spent most of the year since the war driving cattle, but when that job ended, he'd done nothing more than drift from one odd job to another. It might be nice to settle down for a bit.

He glanced up. "You're the mayor?"

"Yes." Her look challenged him to say something derogatory.

He shrugged. "Guess someone has to be."

Surprise registered on her face.

"What's up with the husband auditions?" He crossed his arms and leaned back in the chair.

"Most of the men of this town didn't return after the war. The women are struggling. It's an answer to a need, nothing more."

"Are you looking?"

Her eyes flashed. "Perhaps. Are you applying for the job?"

"No, ma'am. I don't aim on ever getting hitched." He let the chair return to all four legs with a thud and handed her the filled-out application. "Thanks for the job."

"Once you're settled, meet me back here. We have some things to go over." She handed him a key. "Welcome to Turtle Springs."

He grinned, liking her spunk. Some might call her bossy and abrasive. Not him. He didn't much care for the silly women who fluttered their eyelashes and simpered. He liked a woman who could hold her own with a man. "I'll be back in an hour."

Once outside, he led his horse to the livery, tossed a young man a coin, then slung his saddlebags over his shoulder. For good or bad, Turtle Springs was his new home. At least for three months.

He headed across a street now teeming with women, all of whom cast him appraising glances. *Forget it, ladies, I'm not on the menu.*

He unlocked the door and ducked into the safety of the sheriff's office. A desk, a gun cabinet, and two barred cells made up his office. A small door off to the side led to a one-room living space with a cot and a bureau. He'd slept in worse places. He sat on the cot, which his feet were sure to hang off of once he stretched out, and ran his fingers through his hair. He desperately needed a bath and a shave.

After locating a barber, an elderly gentleman who'd charged too much in his opinion, and getting his first shave and proper bath in weeks, he returned to the mayor's office feeling like a new man. He nodded and smiled at a finely dressed woman with hair the color of a raven's wing and pushed open the office door.

The lovely mayor motioned him to a chair and finished signing a document in front of her. When she'd finished, she looked up with a smile. "Settled in?"

"Yep."

"Good." She folded her hands on the desktop. "We're a peaceful town, but men will be arriving. Strangers. Crime may rise. I expect you to be visible at regular intervals and to be present during the auditions. This will, hopefully, dissuade any man from making improper advances to the women of this town. We'll be having the men set up temporary housing in tents outside of town once the inn is full. You'll need to monitor that, also."

"I can do that."

"Wonderful. I'm sure we will get along famously. If you change your mind about auditioning—"

"I won't."

"But if you do, just let me know and I'll place you in the round up." She laughed, the sound as pleasing as a babbling brook. "The women of this town are going to swarm you, Mr."—she glanced at his application—"Ingram. You clean up nice, you're of marriageable age, and have a job."

He leaned forward. "To keep me as sheriff, Mayor, you're going to have to let these fine women know I'm not interested or I'll be riding out at sunset."

Chapter 2

A bby arrived at work the next morning with optimism in her step. She'd hired a sheriff and moved ahead to find the town's women husbands. Maybe she was a good mayor after all. She inserted the key in the door of her office.

Loud footsteps pounded behind her, followed by giggling. Sheriff Ingram, followed by a bevy of smiling beauties, headed her way. Oh no. She'd forgotten to make the announcement that he was off limits.

Sheriff Ingram grabbed her elbow and dragged her inside then slammed the door. His frown made the cleft in his chin more pronounced. Would her finger fit perfectly in that spot? She raised her hand.

He stepped back. "What are you doing?"

"Oh. Nothing." Heavens to Betsy! She'd almost lost all decorum. Pasting a smile on her face, she said, "How may I help you, Sheriff?"

"Have you already forgotten our agreement? A man can't go anywhere in this town without a gaggle of twittering geese in dresses following him."

"Yes, about that. . . I planned on making the announcement at the next town meeting."

"Which is when?" He crossed his arms, drawing her attention to the muscles bulging under the cotton of his blue shirt. A shirt that matched his eyes, in fact.

She licked her lips. "Next month."

"I can't wait that long. They're driving me loco." He pointed at the women ogling him through the window. "Go tell them now."

"Very well." Chin high, she opened the door and stepped outside. She held up her hands to quiet the group. When they continued chattering, she put her fingers to her lips and gave an ear-piercing, very unladylike whistle. That got their attention.

Multiple sets of eyes focused on her.

"Ladies, the sheriff has informed me that he is not looking for a wife and for you to please leave him in peace, unless you have an emergency or something that requires his expertise." There. Finely said.

"I've got an emergency," one said, laughing. "My heart is breaking. I've a hankering for that tall drink of water."

Abby rolled her eyes. "Madeline Foster that is an inappropriate thing for a lady to say out loud." No need to mention she agreed with her.

"It's the truth. I always speak the truth." The woman motioned her head. "Come on, gals, we'll think of another way to attract that man's attention."

"Wait until the auditions, please. I'm sure you will all find men to your liking."

"I doubt there are two men like that one in the world." Madeline led her troop toward the restaurant.

Abby returned inside. "Done, Sheriff Ingram. It was relatively easy. Something a man such as yourself could have handled."

"I tried. They wouldn't listen." He sat at the desk opposite hers. "Does anything happen in this town that requires me not to laze around?"

"Chicken thefts, disappearing cattle." She sat in her chair. "Nothing too violent. There used to be the occasional fight. . .before the men left. I'm sure your job will be more exciting once men start arriving again."

He glanced out the window. "I hope so. I feel like a rock rattling around in the back of a wagon."

She chuckled. "Not as bad as that, I hope. My mother asked me to extend an invitation to supper tonight. We eat at five."

"I reckon that will be all right, seeing as how I'm not looking for a wife and your family is clear on that."

"Very. My mother is twenty years your senior and my sister much too young. Now, if you'll excuse me, I have work to do." She shuffled some papers, hoping he'd take the hint. She couldn't concentrate with him sitting across from her.

"Go ahead. You won't bother me."

She sighed and glanced over the latest petition. A ridiculous request for a floral shop. Seriously, the women of Turtle Springs did put on airs. She wrote *declined* on the petition and set it aside. The next was for a shoemaker. She had no idea any of the women knew how to. . .wait, they wanted her to find and bring in a shoemaker. Well, an advertisement in the nearest paper should work.

"You seem very engrossed in your work," the sheriff said.

"Very."

"Anything I can do to help?"

"Find the town a shoemaker."

He appeared to be deep in thought. "I ran across an elderly gentleman in my travels that might be willing. I can send him a telegram, if you'd like."

She lifted her eyes. "You'd do that?"

"Sure." He shrugged and plopped his boots on the desktop. "I could use a new pair of boots."

Judging by the hole near his right big toe, he surely did. "I would appreciate the help."

"I'm starving. My stomach is saying hello to my backbone. Let me buy you breakfast and you can tell me what's on the rest of those papers."

"I've already eaten." Mercy. Sitting across the table from him, in public, would start all sorts of gossip.

"Then have a cup of coffee." He gave a lopsided grin.

The grin decided for her. So be it. If the gossip vine said she had her cap set for the sheriff, who was she to stop them? "I'll accept, gladly." She grabbed the stack of papers and followed him out the door and down the street to the diner.

Heads turned as they walked in.

The hostess, a young girl, barely sixteen in age, twittered. "Looks like you found your man."

Abby's neck heated. "We have a strictly business relationship."

"So that means he's available?"

"Absolutely not." The sheriff took Abby's hand. "My fiancée is shy. We're an item." He dragged her to a table, pulled out a chair, and whispered, "I've decided it's best we pretend I'm spoken for. I can't do my job effectively if I'm constantly dodging eager females."

"Don't you think that is something we should have discussed?" Miss Melton glared across the table. "How am I supposed to audition the men if I'm spoken for?"

"Once the men have arrived, we'll have a falling out." What had her dander up? It was a simple solution.

"When I give my word, Sheriff, I keep it." She put her hands over her face. "You've put me in a predicament. The women will think I gave that speech to claim you for myself."

Josiah felt a twinge of remorse. "I tend to speak without thinking. I apologize."

She peered through her fingers. "How will I survive the embarrassment of a broken engagement, real or imagined?" Her hands lowered, and she folded them on the table. "I'm the mayor. I have a reputation to uphold."

"You're a lovely woman, first. I'll act like a total cad. You'll count yourself lucky." He picked up a handwritten menu.

"You have an answer for everything, don't you, Sheriff?"

"Might as well call me Josiah, since we're engaged." He winked, enjoying the bright spots of scarlet appearing on her cheeks.

"Well, Josiah." She tossed her napkin in his face. "I wouldn't marry you if you were the last man on earth." She bolted to her feet and stormed from the restaurant.

He glanced at the women sitting at the closest table. "Lover's spat. Nothing serious." Ducking his head, he hid behind the menu. He had to be the biggest fool this side of the Mississippi River.

By five o'clock, Josiah had worked himself into quite a frenzy. He only had one good shirt and he'd worn it that day. Having already insulted Miss Melton by opening his big mouth, he couldn't show up for supper in a dirty shirt. Sighing, he donned a white muslin shirt that, while clean, had seen better days. He ran his hand over his chin and cheek. Stubble rasped against his palm.

He gave himself a quick shave, nicking himself several times, then slicked his hair back with water. He was as ready as he would ever be. Hopefully, his hostess would accept his apology.

Outside, he headed for the white house at the end of Main Street. Women smiled and waved, falling in behind him. What was wrong with these people? Wasn't a declaration of engagement deterrent enough? He tugged his hat low on his head and increased his pace.

The mayor's house seemed a mile away. When he approached the small path leading to the front door, the women held back. They didn't head away until the front door opened.

A small woman on the round side, but not overly so, opened the door. A big smile graced her unlined face. "You must be Sheriff Ingram. I hope you like beef stew and flaky biscuits. Come on in. I'm Lucille."

"My favorite type of meal. I'm pleased to make your acquaintance." He hung his hat on a rack near the door and smoothed his hair again.

He entered the kitchen to see Abigail setting out bowls and a young girl, who had to be her sister, folding cloth napkins. The resemblance between the three Meltons was uncanny. All three were good-looking women. The youngest had to be setting the hearts of every man under the age of twenty thundering in his chest.

"I'm Lucy, named after my ma. Sit there." The girl pointed at the head of the table. "We're ready to eat."

"Sorry I'm late."

"You're right on time," Lucille said. "Coffee? Tea?"

"Coffee, please."

Once they'd stopped fussing over him, and Lucille said a short blessing, they dug into their meal. It wasn't until Josiah's second bowl of stew that he decided to address the fact that young Lucy hadn't stopped staring at him during the entire meal.

"Do I have something on my face, young lady?" He swiped his mouth with the napkin.

"I don't want you to marry Abby."

"And why is that?" He glanced over at a red-faced Abigail.

"Because I want you to wait three more years and marry me."

He clamped his mouth shut. What did a man say to that? Especially a man who had no plans on ever getting hitched? "Um, well. . . I don't reckon I want to wait too long. I'm only getting older, you see."

"Hogwash."

"Lucy!" Abigail slapped her hand with the back of a spoon. "Your language."

"It's fine, Abigail." Josiah took his time folding his napkin and setting it beside his bowl in hopes of finding just the right words to say. "You see, young lady. . . God has made a man for every woman. I reckon rather than you asking me to wait on you, that you wait for God to bring the right man to you."

Lucy didn't seem pleased with his response, but Abigail's and Lucille's faces beamed. He ruffled Lucy's hair, wanting to remind her she was a child yet, then turned his attention to Abigail. He raised an eyebrow in question.

She nodded and ducked her head.

Good. He'd handled the situation fine.

"Is that truly what you believe, Josiah?" Lucille leaned forward. "I've already had the love of my life, and I'm not against having another husband to spend what's left of my years with. Do you think God has another one for me?"

"Sure. Since the time of Adam and Eve there's been one man and one woman. But I don't believe that means a man or woman should spend their life alone should one pass away." He raised his coffee to his mouth.

"It's good to know this town has a godly man for a sheriff. I'm glad you're marrying my Abby."

"Ma!" Abigail's eyes widened. "I told you it was just a ruse."

Lucille patted her daughter's hand. "We shall see, dear."

Josiah spit coffee across the starched white tablecloth.

Chapter 3

After what Abby considered a disastrous supper with Josiah, she readied herself for another day of approving and disapproving petitions. She was determined to have a quiet, peaceful day in which to get her work done. A quick glance in the foyer mirror to make sure her hat sat straight on her head and off she went.

Her boots clomped out a quick rhythm on the wooden sidewalks. She smiled and nodded at the townsfolk she passed, stopping to give tips to the elderly men who gathered in front of the mercantile, without fail every morning, to play checkers. When the weather turned cold, they sat in front of the woodstove inside. She pointed out a move to one of them, winked at his sputtering opponent, and continued on her way.

As she prepared to cross the street, a commotion outside the sheriff's office drew her attention. Six women gathered on the sidewalk, jostling for position in front of the window. Abby sighed and squared her shoulders, prepared to do battle. As mayor, it was her job to help keep the town in a semblance of control.

"Best get them hens under control, Mayor," one of the checker players called out. "This is a respectable town." He cackled and bent back over the game board.

A year as mayor and still the old timers didn't take her seriously. Ignoring their jests, Abby marched to the sheriff's office. "Break it up, ladies."

"But he's shaving." One of them swooned, actually swooned. "Right where we can all see him."

Silly man. Hadn't he learned anything? "Move along. I won't say it again." She shoved open the door to the sheriff's office and barged inside. "Sheriff Ingram."

"Miss Mayor." He turned, his shirt unbuttoned several buttons and his strong chin covered with shaving cream.

Abby breathed deeply, inhaling its woodsy aroma. "Are you aware of the spectacle you're presenting? Why aren't you shaving in your private room?"

"The light is better out here." He glanced over her shoulder. His eyes widened. "Can't a man get any peace around here?"

"Not in a town starving for husbands. I suggest you take more care in the future."

He grabbed a towel and wiped his face, then buttoned his shirt, hiding a fine chiseled chest from view. A pity. Abby hadn't seen anything so fine in ages.

As she turned to leave, the women crowded inside. The poor sheriff looked like a cornered animal. Sweat beaded on his brow. He fell into the chair behind his desk and stared with wild eyes at the chattering group who converged on him like starving dogs, shoving Abby to the side.

"I have an emergency," they all said at once.

Josiah took a deep breath, his chest straining against his shirt. "One at a time, please." He fumbled around his desk.

"Pencil?" Abby pulled one from her reticle. "Or shall I write down the requests?" Which were bound to be trivial and nothing more than an excuse to have the sheriff make an appearance at their homes.

"Please assist. I'm more used to cowboys than ladies." He lowered his voice. "Frankly, they scare me to death."

She nodded then turned to the women. "One at a time, list your needs. The sheriff will attend them in the order he deems necessary."

The women looked at each other. Clearly, they had no idea how to proceed.

Abby raised her eyebrows.

"I'm missing some chickens," said one.

"Someone broke my fence," stated another.

On and on it went with things so trivial Abby thought the pencil would break from her grip. "Does anyone have anything life threatening?"

"There's been a man peeping in my windows." A middle-aged woman spoke up from the back. "It's the gospel truth. If he shows his face again, I plan on giving him a taste of buckshot."

A loud thud reverberated through the room as Josiah let his feet fall to the floor. "You aren't joshing?"

"No sir." She pushed herself to the front of the group. "I've no need to pretend. I'm not looking for a husband."

He grinned and grabbed his hat. "Very well, then. I'll follow you back to your place."

The other women groaned.

"Mayor?" Josiah tipped his head. "Would you like to come along? You know this town better than anyone, I'd wager."

She smiled. "I'd be happy to." While a stack of petitions awaited her on her desk, she'd love to see the new sheriff in action. After all, she'd hired him on sight, with no interview. What if he wasn't qualified, other than wearing a gun at his hip and being handsome enough to charm a badger? Not that a sheriff needed to be handsome, but it certainly didn't hurt.

She followed him to the livery, where she mentioned there was a buckboard for his use. Josiah nodded and hitched a horse to the wagon, then helped her climb onto the seat. "I know the way to Mrs. Wilson's farm. I've sent her ahead," Abby said. "It will take us close to thirty minutes to ride out there."

"It's a beautiful day." He climbed up beside her and took the reins. "Seems a bit strange for a peeping tom in a town with very few men. Wouldn't the women have noticed a stranger in town?"

"Perhaps he hasn't come to town. That's if Mrs. Wilson isn't imagining things." Abby straightened her skirt. "Some of the older women living alone on the outskirts of town are skittish at times."

"Is there anything to the missing chickens?"

"A fox, maybe. Whether it's two legged or four is for you to determine." She smiled and folded her hands primly in her lap.

Every time Abigail shifted position, a breeze carried a delightful whiff of roses to Josiah's nose and teased loose strands of hair from under her hat. He clutched the reins to keep from reaching over and tucking the hair behind her ear. What he couldn't figure out was why she had folks calling her Abby. That was for girls in short skirts. Abigail Melton was all woman.

He didn't know why he'd asked her to come along. The pretty woman was nothing more than a distraction, but he'd once again spoken without thinking. Now, here they sat, him as tongue-tied and clumsy as a newborn calf. Especially after her sister's statement the night before. He really should've thought things through before saying he and Abigail were engaged. Now, all he could think about was what if they really were?

Would marrying a self-assured woman such as her be a bad thing? He studied her out of the corner of his eye. He'd always figured if he were to get hitched his wife would stay home and tend the house and young'uns. He doubted the lovely lady next to him would be content with such a simple life.

"When you find that husband you're looking for, do you intend to resign as mayor?"

She frowned. "Not unless the town votes me out of the position. Why? Do you feel as if I do a poor job?"

"Not at all. I was raised that a woman's place was in the home. What about when the babies come?"

"The war changed many things, Sher—Josiah, including a woman's role. No longer can we sit back and let the men handle things. If we'd done that, Turtle Springs would be nothing more than a ghost town." She glanced across the prairie. "The women own this town now. We're willing to form partnerships with the men we choose to marry, not be their servants."

It was a lot for Josiah to digest. Women who wanted to wed, but not give up their careers. "Doesn't seem natural to me."

She whipped her head around to face him. "Whyever not? Look at the town, Josiah. We've prospered. We're just tired of going it alone. Goodness, do you think all the men will have the same mindset as you?"

He shrugged. "I guess you won't know until you interview them."

"I suppose." She shrugged. "Turn right at the fork in the road." She didn't speak again until she told him to turn left at a barn full of woodpecker holes.

They stopped in front of a cozy white-washed cabin. Laundry flapped on the line. Chickens scurried across the yard. A mule bayed from a corral. The homestead looked well-kept despite the absence of a man.

Josiah set the brake and hopped down, then hurried to help Abigail from the wagon. "Go fetch Mrs. Wilson while I scour the perimeter."

"I'm here." The woman appeared from around the back of the house. "No need to go fetching anyone. I'll show you where the scoundrel has been peeking in."

Josiah exchanged an amused glance with Abigail then followed the plump woman to the back of the house.

"Right there." She pointed to a window. "He watches me cook. It's quite unnerving."

"Maybe he's hungry." Josiah studied the ground, finding the telltale marks of a man's boot in the dirt around some rose bushes.

Mrs. Wilson put her fists on her hips. "Single woman can't go offering food to a strange man at her window, now can she? Should I set him a plate outside like I would a stray dog?" She glared. "I want you to hide in those bushes and catch this person red-handed."

"I didn't bring my horse, ma'am. How do you expect me to get back to town?"

"You can borrow my mule."

The woman wasn't to be dissuaded. "Can you make it back to town all right?" he asked Abigail. "I promised to return the wagon as soon as possible."

She grinned. "I've been doing so for years. I'll come back for you. I'll ride your horse back and lead mine."

"You'll waste your entire day doing that."

"Nothing better to do than watch you catch a scoundrel." She hurried back to the wagon. "See you at sundown." With a saucy grin and wave, she drove off, leaving him standing helpless in Mrs. Wilson's yard.

"Come in and have some tea," the woman said, opening the back door. "Don't worry. I won't make improper advances. I'm old enough to be your mother. I might even fix you a bite to eat."

Not one to turn down a free meal, Josiah bounded up the steps. By sundown, he had a full belly and his ear talked off. Now, he waited on the front porch for Abigail to arrive. When she did, leading his horse, rather than riding as she'd said, he rushed to meet her.

"Your horse is evil. He tried to bite me when I moved to climb into the saddle." She handed him the reins. "We should hide these two, right? It's about suppertime."

"You're staying?" Josiah swallowed, hard. She was going to hunker down in the bushes with him?

"Of course, I am. I thought you understood that." Leading her horse to the small barn, she said, "Come on, now. I can smell stew brewing."

Before he could think of reasons to send her on her way, he and Abigail were crouched low in the bushes opposite Mrs. Wilson's kitchen window. Josiah couldn't remember the last time he was in the dark with a woman.

"Stop fidgeting. He'll hear us." Abigail slapped his arm. "I swear, you're like a child on an ant hill."

He didn't feel like a child. Her presence made him feel very much like a man.

Crunching leaves alerted him to someone else's presence. He stilled as a rail-thin man stepped into the light spilling out the kitchen window.

"I know him," Abigail whispered. "That's Horace. He's been in love with Mrs. Wilson for over ten years. Ever since her husband died, if not before."

"Is he harmless?"

She grinned, her teeth gleaming in the light of the moon. "He's always trying to steal a kiss from her every Sunday after church."

Josiah chuckled and stepped into the yard. "Mrs. Wilson! Come on out." He motioned to the man to stay. "We've found your peeping tom."

"Why, Horace Tindal. What in tarnation. . ."

"I just want to watch you. You're a sight to behold cooking at that stove." He hung his head. "There wasn't any need to call the law."

Mrs. Wilson sighed. "You scared five years off my life. Come on in and have some pie." She turned to Josiah. "I reckon you can go now. I guess the only way to get this man to leave me alone is to marry him."

Chapter 4

Two weeks after the oh-so-romantic gesture of Horace Tindal—Abby's heart still fluttered at the thought—men were swarming into Turtle Springs. One of them might possibly be her future husband. Her heart skipped at the thought.

She caught sight of Josiah entering the restaurant. A pity, really, that he was adamant about not getting married. If he were, she'd choose him. He cut a fine figure and was the handsomest man she'd ever laid eyes on. If only he weren't so. . . well, surly and prone to false tales. She still couldn't convince the townsfolk their engagement was nothing more than a joke.

"Abigail, a moment please," a woman's voice called behind her.

She smiled and greeted Jane Ransome. "Hello, Jane. It's a lovely day."

"I have a question that I want a straight answer for. Are you, or are you not, engaged to the sheriff?"

"We're not. It's a ruse he concocted to keep women from hounding him." Was it possible Jane was interested? "Have you set your cap for him?"

"Perhaps." Jane's dark eyes flashed. "He fits my requirements perfectly."

If Abby did want to marry Josiah, which, if she were honest, she wasn't adverse to, she didn't stand a chance against the beautiful Jane. "He's said he intends to never marry, but I wish you luck." She thrust out her hand.

Jane returned her handshake. "Thank you for your honesty." With a swish of her skirts, she strolled away. Head high.

Abby's gaze drifted back to the restaurant. Still, she was tempted to follow Josiah in order to share a pot of coffee. But, to do so would only encourage the town's gossip. She sighed and unlocked the door to her office, casting a quick glance to the sign in the window that told auditioning men to sign up inside.

She smiled and pushed the door open. Everything was going according to plan.

Before she could sit at her desk, a line of men had formed, all in a hurry to sign a piece of paper agreeing to the terms of the audition. Abby stood behind her desk, her smile never fading, as the men bombarded her with questions.

"How long we got with each gal?"

"Can we kiss 'em?"

"Can we get hitched right away if we're chosen?"

She raised her hands. "Gentlemen. You'll have fifteen minutes with each woman.

No, you cannot touch them in any way. The sheriff will be present at all times to ensure you behave yourselves. The time frame of getting married is up to you and your prospective bride." She guessed several of the women would prefer a time of engagement, but who was she to say?

Satisfied with her answers, the men signed the agreement and drifted away, their excitement filling the town with more energy and hope than it'd had in over a year.

"You look quite pleased with yourself." Josiah leaned in the doorway.

"I am." She looked up from the petitions in front of her. "Or, at least, I was." She waved a sheet of paper at him. "The men just started arriving and already somebody is asking that the saloon be reopened."

"Yeah, so?" He stepped inside and seated himself behind the desk across the room. "Some men like their drink after a hard day's work."

"Very few of them are working, Sheriff." She frowned. "Reopening the saloon will only cause problems. Some of them will drink to excess."

"Then, I'll lock them up." He leaned his elbows on the table. "I don't imbibe myself, but can't fault another man for his tastes. What I can do is make sure no man enters the audition that had even a sip of whiskey that morning."

She sighed. "I'll think about it." She didn't like it, not a bit, but would try to see the good in reopening. She glanced again at the petition and set it aside, taking note of the signature. Mr. Franklin Harper. . .good luck finding a wife in Turtle Springs.

"Maybe he isn't looking for a wife," Josiah said. "Not every man wants to hitch his wagon to a woman."

She wasn't aware she'd spoken her thoughts out loud. "Perhaps." She riffled through the other petitions, setting aside the ones requiring a closer look. "I'm heading out for a few minutes. I'd like to observe the type of men arriving in town from the front window of the mercantile."

"Best snooping place in town?" He stood and crooked his arm.

"The very best. Plus, Ma needs some supplies." Her arm in his, she allowed Josiah to lead her across the street. With men swarming the sidewalks and staring her way, she was more than glad to have the sheriff's assistance. Once safely ensconced inside the mercantile, she handed the clerk her list then planted herself in front of the window.

Men of all ages and sizes strolled up and down the wooden sidewalks. Some wore beards; some were clean shaven. Some wore fine clothes; others wore patches. All were clean and nodded at each group of women who passed. Good. They seemed to be on their best behavior. She could only pray they would remain that way. "Thank You, God, for helping me with this plan."

"Are you sure it was God's idea?" Josiah's whisper, as he leaned close, tickled the hair at the nape of her neck. "Or your desperate attempt at finding a man to help you run this town?"

She really needed to learn to keep her thoughts from escaping her lips. "Of course it was God's idea. I prayed for a solution and this came to me." She glanced up, his face unnervingly close to hers. The scent of his shaving cream, clean and crisp, teased her senses. His blue eyes lured her like a bee to honey.

"Abigail? Mayor?" Josiah smiled, long and slow. She didn't seem to be regretting his impulsive statement about their engagement at the moment. Rather, she seemed enraptured by his charms. His gaze landed on her lips. He chuckled and pulled back before he acted. "Folks are staring."

"What? Oh!" She put her hands to rosy cheeks. "Must you toy with me so?"

"Part of the act, darling." He winked.

"It isn't becoming of the mayor to act like a love-starved girl still in short dresses." She patted her hair in place and moved to the counter. "Thank you, Chardy. How are the boys?"

"Fine. A bit rowdy at times, as boys are." She grinned. "I'll add these to your tab."

"Thank you." Abigail turned back to Josiah. "I've had enough of watching the men for one morning. I'm headed home for lunch, if you'd like to join me. Lucy will be at school, but I'm sure my mother would love to have you."

Josiah glanced at the crowd out the window. He really should be monitoring the town, but the sparkle in Abigail's eyes decided for him. That and the delightful whiff of rose water he'd caught when whispering in her ear. She sure didn't smell like any mayor he'd ever met. "I'd be delighted."

"Wonderful. First, we need to stop by the jail. I want to see firsthand that you are ready for. . .visitors."

"Is that what you call them? Hmm." He guided her to the sheriff's office and opened the door. "Both cells have a cot and a chamber pot. That's all a body needs."

"My mother will provide the meals, if needed." She speared him with a sharp glance. "I'm trusting you to keep the women safe, Sheriff. No tomfoolery with these men. If they break a law, they get locked up. Plain and simple."

"Are the laws posted somewhere?" He perched on the corner of his desk.

"They should be. I'll have a list written up by nightfall." With a tilt of her pert chin, she headed back outside, leaving him to follow as if he were her obedient watchdog.

Shaking his head, he did as she expected. Why? He had no idea. No other gal in all his life had him tagging after her. Ever. What was it about Abigail Melton that had him disregarding his vow to stay away from women? The more time he spent with her, the less he wanted to stay away. The thought scared him more than if he faced three armed men.

"What's wrong?" Abigail stopped and stared into his face. "You've gone quite pale. Are you ill?"

He shook his head. "Just thinking scary thoughts."

Her brows drew together. "Whatever for?"

"No reason. Sometimes, they just come to me."

"You're a strange man, Sheriff. Perhaps it's aftermath of the war."

"Perhaps." He put his hand on the small of her back, guiding her up the stairs to her house. Shock vibrated through his palm and up his arm. Some might think Abigail on the skinny side, and tall for a woman, his hand almost spanned the entire width of her back, but he thought her just right. He stopped and watched her climb the last few steps alone.

She turned, a questioning look on her face. "Are you coming? I seriously think you should see a doctor."

No doctor could cure what ailed him. "I'm fine. Just hungry." He bounded up the steps.

She tilted her head, studying him. "I'm worried about you. We need you now more than ever. We can't have you falling ill."

He quirked his mouth. "I'm ready for whatever this town can throw my way." Almost. He was ready for anything besides the lure of a lovely woman.

She made a noise that clearly said she didn't believe him. "Maybe a good meal will help."

"That must be it. I skipped breakfast."

"No, you didn't. I saw you enter the restaurant this morning." She propped a fist on her hip. "Why are you lying?" She placed a hand against his forehead. "You feel a little warm, and you aren't acting at all like yourself. Come lie down in my bed."

Tarnation, the woman wasn't helping! Her touch and mention of a bed might very well send him into heart palpitations. What he needed was a dunking in a cold creek and a serious conversation with God, who, it seemed, had a sense of humor.

"I, uh. . ." He sighed and followed her into the house. Lies, no matter how small, only got a man into more trouble. Best to keep his head down, his gaze off Abigail, and his mouth shut.

"Josiah." Lucille took his face in her hands and kissed his cheek. "You seem a little flushed. Sit. I'll pour you some lemonade."

"That's exactly what I need."

Abigail sat across from him and shook her hair free from its bun. "Oh how I wish I were young like Lucy and could let my hair hang free."

The woman was pure torture. Josiah ducked his head and closed his eyes. *Lord, what are You doing? We had a deal. No marriage for me.* If war raised its ugly head again during Josiah's lifetime, he intended to fight. A country's freedom should be protected, no matter the sacrifice. He couldn't marry for that very reason. He didn't want to be a man that left his wife behind to possibly become a widow.

Look at Turtle Springs. Dozens of women left behind to fend for themselves. No, it was best he stick to his resolve.

He gratefully accepted the lemonade and concentrated on not gulping it. Anything to keep from watching Abigail put her hair back up. When she moved to help her mother bring the food to the table, he heaved a sigh of relief.

Keeping his heart from falling for Abigail was going to be the hardest challenge he'd ever faced.

Chapter 5

I haven't seen much of the sheriff lately," Ma said, putting two strips of crispy bacon on Abby's plate.

"I guess he's busy with all the new arrivals." Abby sure was. Men tromped in and out of her office all day long. Some skipped the audition sign-up sheet and proposed to her outright. Not one of them met her fancy. What if her efforts were nothing more than a waste of time? What if all she'd done was get the hopes up of the women in town? She gasped and put her hand to her mouth. What if she'd brought nothing but men wanting to take advantage of women? Gracious! What to do?

"Stop fretting." Ma pulled her hand down. "Everything will be fine. In fact, I've set my eye on the man I'm going to choose."

"Already?" Her mother worked fast. "Who is it?"

"I don't know his name, dear. We haven't met, but I like his look. He seems kind." She smiled and plopped eggs onto Abby's plate.

"I've picked." Lucy shoved bacon into her mouth. "The sheriff. Since he isn't auditioning, maybe he'll be ready to get hitched when I'm old enough."

Abby groaned. "Get that foolish notion out of your head right now. The sheriff has made it clear from the beginning he doesn't plan on setting down roots in Turtle Springs." A real shame in her mind. The man was starting to grow on her, and they hadn't had any severe lawbreaking since she hung up the rules on every establishment in town.

After breakfast, she headed down Main Street. She stopped at the sight of Josiah, hat pulled low over his face, asleep in front of the sheriff's office, and slapped his feet off the hitching rail. "Wake up, before I take away every good thought I've had of you."

He peered up from under his hat brim and grinned. "You've been having good thoughts of me?"

"Only in your abilities to keep the law. Which"—she crossed her arms—"I'm rethinking. What kind of sheriff sleeps in the middle of the day where everyone can see?"

"A tired one." His feet fell with a thud to the sidewalk. "I'm kept running hither and yon on foolish errands. I'm starting to suspect that one. . .the women want to spend time with me, and two. . .they're asking scores of questions about the newcomers, none of which I can answer. I'm plumb tuckered out."

"Really, Josiah, I—"

"Madame Mayor." Franklin Harper removed his hat and bowed. "Have you come to a decision about my hopes of opening the saloon?"

"Not yet, Mr. Harper. It's on my list."

"My funds won't last forever, Mayor." His eyes narrowed. "I need a way to make a living."

"I'll get to it soon, Mr. Harper." She forced a smile, nodded at Josiah with a warning look not to go to sleep again, then marched to her office and slammed the door.

Anything could've happened while Josiah had been sleeping. The bank could've been robbed, a woman accosted...anything! Wait a minute.

She stomped back outside and glanced at the window. No list of rules. She scanned the street. No papers tacked to other windows, either. With steel in her backbone, she hurried to the sheriff's office, where Josiah now lounged behind his desk. "Someone took down my rules while you were sleeping."

He shook his head. "Those were down when I woke this morning."

She planted her fists on her hips. "What are you going to do about it?"

"Nothing to do. No witnesses." He leaned back on the chair's hind two legs. "You'll have to put them up again."

"Why are you behaving so obstinate lately?" Seriously, the man was like a child. Ever since lunch at her house a few days ago, he'd become downright lazy and difficult to deal with. If she didn't know better, she'd think he was trying to make her dislike him.

"Look, Mayor." Josiah heaved a sigh. "I'm doing my best. Why, in the amount of time it took for you to head across the street, I've had two women come in here about men picking flowers from their very own gardens and then knocking on their door, flowers in hand. I cannot be everywhere."

She hmmphed and whirled, storming back to her office. The impulsive decision to hire as sheriff the first man who looked the part had not been her finest moment.

She plopped into her chair, choosing to ignore the mound of paperwork on her desk. Instead, she put her head in her hands and felt sorry for herself. The advertisement had brought more than enough men for the women to choose from. The problem was none of them looked the sort to steal Abby's affections. Only one man came close, and he was proving not to be what she'd thought.

Groaning, she let her forehead fall to the desktop. What a ninny. Josiah had made it clear from day one he wasn't looking to get married. He'd also alluded to the fact he might not stay. She glanced out the window to see his long strides eating up the sidewalk.

Was he the man she wanted? Possibly. If so, how could she get him to see reason? Two strong-minded people such as they would get along famously.

She smiled. He'd come up with the idea of them being engaged. How would he react if she suddenly played the part? She could bat her eyelashes and simper

31

as well as the next gal.

Yes. She'd decided Josiah might be the man for her. Of course, she still needed to participate in the audition. No, that would never work. She couldn't toy with him that way. Oh when had matters of the heart gotten so difficult? She couldn't flirt with him then attend the auditions, and she had to go through with her original plan. After all, the women of Turtle Springs were following her lead. *Lord, I could use Your—*

"Mayor?"

She lifted her head to see one of the town's widows, Mrs. Fredrickson, slip inside the building. "Yes?"

"Well, I've a bit of problem, you see, and"—her cheeks darkened—"it's too delicate of a matter to take before the sheriff. It's not in the slightest ladylike, and it's a bit embarrassing."

"What is it you need, ma'am?"

"Me and Irma Bombay have our eyes set on the same gentleman, and we are going to fight for him out by the creek this afternoon."

"Fight, as in fisticuffs?" Abby's eyes widened.

The woman lifted her chin. "If need be."

Gracious.

Josiah hadn't missed the flash of hurt in Abigail's eyes at his behavior. Nor could he escape it, no matter how far and fast he walked.

He stopped at the livery and immersed himself in currying his horse. "You know, old boy, maybe I should stick around after all this nonsense is over. It's been a long time since you and I had a home. In a month or two, all these eager women will be someone else's responsibility and we can sit back and enjoy a peaceful life."

"Josiah! You have to stop them." Abigail burst into the livery, dispelling his fanciful ideas of a peaceful life.

"Stop who?" He set down the curry brush, patted the horse's nose, then turned to the woman who created havoc in his mind and heart.

"Mrs. Bombay and Mrs. Fredrickson. They're going to fight down by the creek."

"Women?"

She stomped her foot. "Yes. You must come with me now."

"Are they elderly?"

"What difference does that make?"

He shrugged, biting back a grin. "How much damage can they do?"

She glared. "Mrs. Bombay is the best shot in town. She might very well pull a gun."

That put a different spin on things. A woman with a gun was never a safe thing. "I'm coming. Lead the way."

Abigail hiked her skirts above trim ankles ensconced in blue stockings, causing a lump to rise in Josiah's throat, then raced toward the edge of town in a manner not at all fitting her job as mayor. Josiah grinned, liking the idea that Abigail Melton wasn't as full of starch as she pretended to be. In fact, petticoats fluttering under a navy hem and flaxen hair falling loose from her bun, she was a wonderful sight to behold. Quite the most beautiful thing he'd ever seen.

She stopped, chest heaving, in a small clearing next to the bubbling brook the town was named after. "Where are they?" She raised eyes the color of a spring meadow.

"Shh. We'll hear them." Josiah cocked his head. Women weren't known for their silence. There. A scream. He bolted through the trees.

Shoving aside branches, he shot into another clearing and skid to a halt. Sitting on a boulder was a grinning older man in a patched suit. In front of him were two plump, elderly women who looked ready to spit nails. Both were dressed in what looked like their Sunday best, complete with hats and feathers.

"The one on the left is Mrs. Bombay. The other is Mrs. Fredrickson," Abigail informed him.

"I saw him first," Mrs. Bombay said. "Now, go away or I'll bean you with my reticule."

"I'd like to see you try." Mrs. Fredrickson narrowed her eyes.

"Do you still think that advertisement was a good idea?" Josiah asked Abigail. "Is this normal behavior for two women of this age?"

"No and no," she groaned. "Do something before someone gets hurt."

Just as he stepped forward to put himself between the snarling women, Mrs. Bombay let loose with her purse and caught him in the side of the head. "Ow! What's in that thing?" He grabbed the ruffled purse and peered inside. "Rocks?"

"As a matter of fact, yes. I wanted her to feel it should I choose to swing." The woman didn't look the slightest remorseful.

Mrs. Fredrickson reached around him and whacked the other woman with a stick. Mrs. Bombay grunted and jumped out of the way of the second swing which caught Josiah right where it hurt the most.

He fell to his knees and concentrated on his breathing. Spots darted in front of his eyes.

Abigail pulled his pistol from his belt. "That's it, ladies. You're both under arrest for assault and intended. . .something. Josiah, are you all right?"

Swallowing back nausea, he pushed to his feet. "I'll take it from here. Ladies, to the jailhouse."

Mrs. Bombay's eyes widened. "Are you seriously arresting us?"

"Yes, ma'am. I have two empty cells ready for two silly women." With his head and groin still throbbing, he wasn't in the mood to be nice or forgiving. "You can stay in there until you regain some sense."

"The creek is always ice cold," Abigail whispered. "Maybe you should. . .uh. . .sit in it?"

"Shut up." He forced himself to walk upright, his face as hot as a July afternoon.

A giggle rose from her. He shot her a sharp glance. "Are you laughing at me?"

"No." She pressed her lips together, her eyes dancing. "What do you want to do with him?" She pointed at the still grinning old man.

"Leave him." He was going to lock these two up and retire to his room.

"You're angry with me."

"A bit."

"Someone would've gotten hurt, Josiah."

He cut her another look. "Someone did. Look." He bent his head. "I'm bleeding from the rocks in her purse."

"I'll tend to that when we return to your office. It's all in a day's work." She grinned. "I make a darn good deputy, if I say so myself. I could have hauled them in."

He shook his head. If she could have, then why didn't she and spare him the pain?

In his office, he locked each complaining woman in a separate cell then sat behind his desk so Abigail could tend to his head. "Yes, you make a good deputy," he said, grudgingly. "Don't interfere with more dangerous folks, though, or I'll lock you up for your protection."

"More dangerous than two women with rocks in their purses?" She giggled, dabbing at his head with a cloth soaked in cool water. "I don't think you'll need stitches."

The fragrance of roses he'd come to expect when she was around swirled around him. Her hair fell forward in a soft curtain. His eyes locked with hers. "Blame this on me getting banged in the head." He cupped her head and pulled her close for a kiss.

He started slow and tender, teasing, but soon kissed her like a man starving when she didn't pull away.

Chapter 6

"Sheriff?"

Abby straightened as Mrs. Bombay called out from her jail cell. She pressed her lips together, her gaze clashing again with Josiah's. "Some knock on the head," she forced through her clogged throat.

He gave a lopsided grin. "Maybe I should get hit with a woman's reticule more often."

She smiled. "Behave. I'll go see what Mrs. Bombay wants." Her heart threatened to burst free as she headed to the back of the office. It wasn't her first kiss, but oh my! No other kiss had come close to making her blood race. She wanted another one so badly she actually glanced over her shoulder and contemplated stealing one.

"Mayor?"

She sighed. "I'm coming."

Each of the women had their faces pressed to the bars, trying to see into the front of the jail. Plump cheeks folded around bars gripped in pudgy hands.

"Is our beau here?" Mrs. Bombay asked, her eyes darting from one corner of the room to the other.

"No, ma'am. I'm afraid he isn't coming." The scoundrel most likely played the two women as fools.

"He'll be here," Mrs. Fredrickson said. "He'll bail me out and leave you to rot."

"Why you—"

"Ladies!" Josiah bellowed from his chair. "That kind of behavior will keep you here for a good long while."

Abby bit back a grin and shrugged. "If I see your gentleman, I'll send him over. Are you hungry? My mother cooks for the prisoners."

"Prisoner?" Mrs. Bombay's eyes swelled with tears. "Is that what we are? Oh, Ruth." She grasped her nemesis's hand.

Mrs. Fredrickson squeezed back. "We must be strong, Irma. Yes, Mayor, we'd like something to eat. A drink of water, too, if it's not too much trouble. I'm sorry to say our escapade in the woods made me parched."

Receiving a heated look from Josiah that sent her heart into palpitations again, Abby headed home to let her mother know about the women requiring food. Her step was light, tapping out a merry beat on the sidewalk.

A hand from the alley grabbed her wrist and yanked her behind the barbershop.

"Look what we have here." The man raked her from head to foot with his gaze. Whiskey fumes washed over her.

She stomped on his foot, causing his grip to loosen. "Where did you get the liquor?" She two-hand shoved him against the wall. The man was too drunk to be much more than a nuisance. "Well?"

"Made it myself in a shack in the woods." He winked. "It's my specialty."

She exhaled sharply. "You are an undesirable, sir! Please vacate Turtle Springs immediately."

"I can't. I done went and got hitched to a woman named Richards. We didn't want to wait for that fancy audition. I reckon she needs me."

Abby seriously doubted any woman needed a foolish drunkard for a husband. "Please come with me." She whirled and marched him back to the sheriff's office. "Josiah, this man is intoxicated."

"You brung me to jail?" The man's eyes widened. "I didn't do nothing but grab ya!"

Josiah shot to his feet. "You touched her?"

Abby held up a hand to stop him. "I'm fine, but this man is brewing liquor in the woods."

"Is that so?" Josiah crossed his arms. "Mind showing me where?"

"I do mind." The man popped his suspenders. "But, seeing as how you're the law, I reckon I should. Otherwise, the missus will pound me. She's a bossy one."

"Aren't you going to lock him up?" Abby frowned. "He's a nuisance and clearly breaking one of the town's laws."

"I don't have another cell, Abigail."

"The women can share."

He shook his head. "They'll kill each other. No, I'll take Mr. . . . ." He raised his eyebrows.

"Watson. Name's Watson."

"Mr. Watson to shut down his still then home. I'm sure his bride will handle him." He gripped the man's elbow. His eyes softened as he glanced at Abby. "I'd like to have supper with you, if you're willing. Maybe a nice one at the restaurant."

"I'd like that."

"Not until we get our food!" Mrs. Bombay screeched from the back.

"Of course." Abby tossed Josiah a smile then headed home, praying nothing else would interfere with her duties for the day. So far, she'd assisted Josiah in arresting two unruly women and deposited a lawbreaker into his hands. Maybe she was cut out to be a mayor after all.

"Ma, there's two women in the jail in need of supper." She stepped into the kitchen where her mother stood, wrapped in the arms of a man. "Ma!"

"Hello, dear. Meet Hank. He's the man I've chosen." Ma caressed the man's face and stepped back.

"Pleased to meet you, ma'am." Hank held out a hand. "Always a pleasure to meet someone in as esteemed a position such as yourself."

"Likewise." She intended to get to the bottom of her mother's secrecy as soon as she returned home that evening. "If everyone keeps finding grooms early on, there will be none left for the audition."

"I can't let someone else grab him." Ma grabbed a skillet from the counter. "Who's in jail?"

"Bombay and Fredrickson. Fighting over a man. It's quite scandalous." Abby glanced sideways at Hank.

"The women of this town sure are spirited." He pulled out a chair and sat down, as if he lived there. "I'm going to like living here."

"What is it you do, Mr., uh, Hank?" Abby leaned back against the counter and crossed her arms.

"I use to be a banker, back before the war. Now, I'm looking to plant a garden and enjoy life."

If he thought he was going to freeload off Abby and her family, the man was mistaken. "Hard to make a living with a simple garden."

"My dear, I've money in the bank. More than enough to care for all of us in the time I have left." He grinned. "Besides, aren't you on the lookout for a husband of your own?"

Abby had forgotten. She was out to find a husband and here she was enjoying Josiah's kisses. What well-brought-up lady behaved that way?

Josiah followed Watson through the woods behind the church. It wasn't too long before he realized the drunken fool was lost. "You did say you'd recently gotten hitched, didn't you?"

"Yes, sir." Watson turned in a slow circle. "We left the church and headed straight out this-a-ways. Maybe we ain't gone far enough yet. It was quite a walk with six young'uns tagging along."

"Where's the still, Mr. Watson?" Josiah's patience floated to the treetops.

"Past the house. I didn't want it too close to town, you understand."

"Of course." Josiah took a deep breath and counted to ten. The day had to be one of his most trying since the war. "Continue."

Another half-hour walk brought them to a dilapidated cabin. Small children in various stages of undress played in the dirt yard. A three-legged dog lifted its head from the sagging porch.

"Home sweet home," Watson said. "Howdy, young'uns. Where's your ma?"

A little girl pointed to the back of the house.

"She's hanging laundry," Watson said. He waved for Josiah to follow. "I reckon you'll be getting hitched soon to the mayor, right, Sheriff?"

"Why do you say that?"

"The audition is next week. If you don't snatch her up now, someone else will." He grabbed a rail-thin woman around the waist and lifted her off her feet. "Like I did my gal right here."

She slapped his shoulder. "What's the sheriff here for?"

"I was bad." Watson shook his head. "I imbibed too much of my own creation and grabbed the mayor."

Mrs. Watson, formerly Mrs. Richards, frowned. "Did you apologize?"

"I didn't have the chance. Now, the sheriff is here to close down the still. I don't know how I'll pay for food in those little ones' mouths."

"We'll manage." She patted his cheek. "Thank you for bringing him home, Sheriff."

"I've got to see the still, ma'am." He hated taking food out of babies' mouths, but it was his job to uphold the law.

"About a hundred yards that way." She took her husband by the arm and led him into the house. "Let me feed him first, then he'll join you."

Josiah nodded and headed in the direction she'd pointed. As he walked, his thoughts returned to something Watson had said.

Abigail could very well be married next week, or shortly after. Josiah sat on a stump, his gaze landing on a crude still. If that happened, he wasn't sure he could stick around Turtle Springs. He hadn't stopped there with the intention of falling in love, yet. . .

Did he love Abigail? He certainly admired her and enjoyed her company. But enough to give up his freedom? What about his vow not to marry in case the country went to war again? Josiah had some deep thinking to do. The thought of Abigail marrying someone else cut to the quick.

Feeling as if life had grown too heavy, he doused the fire under the still and poured out the whiskey. The fumes made his head spin. He didn't find pleasure in destroying the only way for a man to feed his family.

"So, it's gone." Mrs. Watson crossed her arms and glared.

"Yes. Where is your husband?"

"Run off."

Josiah's shoulders sagged. "On his own or with help?"

She shrugged and gave him a defiant look. "I need a job, Sheriff."

"I reckon the jail needs a cleaning lady." He kicked at a rock as he passed her. "Tell your husband to come on home. If he's worth his salt, he won't mind doing some odd jobs for money. I'll put the word out."

She grinned, revealing several missing teeth. "I reckon that is just fine. We'll be there in the morning. I'd appreciate it if you didn't say what happened here today."

"I'd appreciate the same." He didn't need word getting out that Turtle Springs had a soft sheriff. He'd be the laughing stock of the county and riffraff from miles around would converge on the town, if they hadn't already.

❧

Back in town, he paid for a shave and a bath in preparation for his supper with Abigail. When she showed up at the jailhouse a while later in a green dress that set off the same color in her hazel eyes, his resolve to stay single wavered again. What kind of fool didn't want to marry her?

He forced a grin and offered his arm, catching a heady fragrance of lilac this time. The woman was a walking garden!

"What happened with Mr. Watson?" she asked as he held open the restaurant door.

"I hired him to do odd jobs. Him and the missus."

She caressed his cheek. "You're a big softie, Josiah Ingram."

He leaned into her touch and closed his eyes. "I reckon I am. How are the prisoners?"

"Bickering again. I don't think locking them up is having any effect whatsoever on their behavior."

He chuckled. "I'll release them after supper. Lord, help the town."

She giggled, sending his heart soaring. "I think we'll survive. Their beau skipped town. I'm sure they'll find another man to fight over." She shook her head as he pulled out a chair for her. "I had no idea this audition would be such a circus."

"People are funny creatures, Abigail." He took his seat and studied her fair face. "Have you thought of your requirements for a husband?"

"Of course. He must be upstanding, family oriented, a good provider, and a godly man." She spread her napkin in her lap. "That isn't too much to ask, is it?"

"What about love?"

She tilted her head. "Surely, you don't think a man and woman can fall in love during a fifteen-minute interview?"

"No." His heart fell to his stomach. He fit her requirements, at least he thought he did. What in tarnation was he going to do?

"Do you have to go through with it? You can't know anyone well enough in fifteen minutes."

Her eyes shimmered. "I have to, Josiah. It was all my idea. I can't ask the other women to do something I'm not willing to do as well."

Chapter 7

"Why so sad, dear?" Ma wrapped her arms around Abby. "Today is a grand day. It's audition day!"

Abby burst into tears. "That's why it's awful." She slipped free and plopped onto the bed. "I don't want to sit across from strangers. I want to marry Josiah."

"Have you told Lucy?" Ma grinned and sat next to her.

"Don't jest. This is serious. I've created a mess." She fell to her back on the mattress.

"How so?" Ma pulled her back up. "This town needed men and you made that happen. There are already several very happy women because of what you've done."

Abby refused to listen. "He asked me what I wanted in a husband and I rattled off a list as if I were going to the mercantile." She draped her arm over her eyes. "I'm a dunderhead." Not to mention she'd lost any chance of a happy ever after.

Ma sighed and grabbed her hand. "Up. You are not going to miss the audition. You'll put on your best suit, walk in there, do what needs doing, then follow your heart. The same as you always do."

Groaning, she allowed Ma to pull her to her feet. "Hand me the blue suit. It looks the best on me."

An hour later, Abby surveyed the restaurant, where punch and finger sandwiches were being served. Men lined the sidewalk in preparation for the interviews. A reporter, J. R. Lockhart, from *Godey's Lady's Book* shook hands with men near the middle of the line then made a beeline for Abby.

"Mayor, a question please."

"Yes?"

"I'd like clarification on the rumors that you are engaged to the sheriff. Yet, here you are, prepared to take part in the audition."

Abby sighed. "It was only a rumor, nothing more."

"Really? But the sheriff himself started the rumor." He pulled a notepad from an inside pocket of his jacket.

Abby choked back a groan. "I have no intention of marrying the sheriff. Now, please excuse me, I must take my seat." She left the reporter standing in the center of the room. When would the silly statement Josiah made die?

The women took their seats at the tables. Nervous expressions flitted across their faces. Caroline Kane's older sister, beautiful and aloof, picked at a spot on the table. Frieda Lomax, a widow, looked as if she were about ready to lose her lunch. Save for Jane Ransome, none of the ladies looked as self-assured as Abby had hoped. She put a hand over her own nervous stomach and nodded to have the doors open, then hurried to a table of her own.

The first man inside was Josiah, who had taken up position right inside and glared at each man who entered. If he didn't look a bit more pleasant, he'd scare them off.

"Howdy." A handsome man in a threadbare woolen suit sat across from Abby. "You're a fine-looking woman."

"Thank you." She forced a smile and folded her hands on top of the table. "Are you a God-fearing man, Mr—"

"Dixon. Name's William Dixon. Yes, ma'am, I am."

She should have brought the questions she'd written out. "What do you do for a living?"

"Well, I reckon iffen you pick me, I'll take over as mayor. I've a good head on my shoulders and a talent for figuring."

Give up her job as mayor? The thought hadn't occurred to her. "I'm not thinking of giving up my position, sir. I rather enjoy the act of mayor. Besides, it's an elected position. It wouldn't pass to you just because we got married."

His smile faded. "It wouldn't do for a man to run for the office against his wife, now would it?"

"No, I guess not." She sighed and endured his endless chatter until the next man sat, and the next. All of whom thought they'd become mayor should she choose them.

She flicked a glance at the stony-faced Josiah. Would he expect the same? Did all men believe the role of mayor wasn't fit for a woman? She'd thought so herself, once upon a time. Now, she realized the women of Turtle Springs were every bit as capable as men at running the businesses. Would they all have to hand over the reins after marriage?

Josiah met her glance and winked. Immediately, her nerves settled. A smile spread across her face, giving hope to the man sitting across from her.

He prattled on about his dreams of owning his own ranch. She kept smiling and tuned him out. Not one man that afternoon set her heart aflutter. Not one man other than the one wearing a shiny star on his vest, that is. The one in the room who wasn't there to find a bride.

"Are you hungry, ma'am?" A nice-looking man in brown pants and a crisp tan shirt handed her a glass of punch and a plate of sandwiches. "I couldn't help noticing you didn't get up to imbibe in refreshments."

"Thank you." She lifted her gaze to meet the dark brown ones of a man around her age. "I'm Abigail Melton."

"Lawrence Nelson, at your service." He reached out to shake her hand. "I'm pretty sure I have the answers to any questions you might have. I love the Lord, attend church regularly, and until recently spent much of my time as a circuit preacher. Then the war came, and after a stint as chaplain, I realized I wanted to settle down with a wife and family. I've purchased a bit of land outside of town and hope to grow a fine herd of cattle."

He sounded too good to be true. "Are you adverse to a time of courtship, Mr. Nelson?"

"Not at all. I think it quite prudent. Marriage vows are not to be taken lightly, Miss Melton."

"I agree." She toasted him with her glass of punch and sipped the sweet drink as she studied him over the rim. If she couldn't have Josiah, Mr. Nelson came in a close second. "How do you feel about a woman mayor?"

"I reckon I'll be too busy ranching to undertake the position myself." He grinned. "You seem to have done a fine job, so far."

She narrowed her eyes. The man was nothing like the others. She waited for a niggling from the Lord that he was not as he appeared. When none came, she returned his grin. "I'd like to invite you to supper tomorrow night, Mr. Nelson."

"I'm pleased to accept your invitation."

Josiah wanted to shoot the man laughing with Abigail. Especially when fifteen minutes was up and the man waved on the next interviewee. His fingers twitched toward the gun at his belt.

Hold up, pardner. You've no one to blame but yourself. You're the one who told Abigail you weren't looking for a wife.

He needed some air. He shoved through the door, emerging into the dusk. Who knew two hours could seem like forever? The men were all well-behaved. Josiah wasn't needed in there any more than he was needed out here. He fell onto a bench and slumped against the wood. He was a coward. If he wasn't, he'd march in there and tell Abigail what a fool he was, and ask her to forget the grinning imbecile across from her and marry him.

He wanted to leave. Not just the restaurant, but the town. But, he'd given his word to oversee the auditions. Then he'd start thinking about finding a man to replace him as sheriff and drift to the next town. One where the women weren't crazy and man hungry.

The restaurant door opened. "Josiah? Are you all right?" Abigail sat on the bench next to him.

"Shouldn't you be inside laughing with that...sheep head?"

She chuckled. "If I didn't know better, I'd think you were jealous."

"Well I'm not." He lunged to his feet. "I'm just tired of the circus."

Her face fell. "We're finishing up. You're free to go."

He couldn't help but wonder whether she meant to his one-room home behind the jail or free to leave town. He opened his mouth to clarify then snapped it shut. With a touch of his fingers to the brim of his hat, he turned and stormed away.

His walk didn't stop at the jail. Instead, he passed the church, then the shack of Mr. and Mrs. Watson, until he reached the creek. He stooped and chose several rocks good for skipping and skimmed them across the water.

If he left, the Watsons would be without work. If he left, he'd never see Abigail again. Could he bear to stay and watch another man court then marry her? Oh yes, he'd been eavesdropping. He'd heard all the ways the man met her silly list of criteria.

"Hey, mister!"

He turned to see one of the Watson boys, he didn't know the name before the woman remarried, standing behind him in dirty overalls and no shirt or shoes. "What 'cha doing?"

"Thinking."

"About something sad from the look on your face. A girl? They're always making fellas sad."

Josiah laughed. "How old are you, son?"

"Ten." The boy skipped a rock farther across the creek than any of Josiah's had gone. "Am I right about what you're thinking?"

"Yes."

"A waste of time in my mind. Girls are trouble. They don't like to get dirty, and they run and tattle on every little thing."

"I reckon."

"I'm Owen. You're sweet on the mayor. Ain't you engaged to her? Is that what has you so sad?"

How could Josiah have forgotten? The town didn't know he and Abigail were only pretending to be engaged. She couldn't court another man when everyone thought she belonged to him. He started to head back to town then stopped.

She had to have said something. No one seemed surprised to see her sitting in the auditions. He glanced back at the boy. "I think our relationship is dissolved."

"If you don't want it to be then fight for her. That's what my pa would have said. Iffen he were here."

Josiah ruffled Owen's hair. "You're wise beyond your years, son. Thank you." He turned and jogged back through the trees. He'd made up his mind. Forget his vow to never marry. He'd rather spend the rest of his life with Abigail than wait for a war that might never come.

He stopped a few feet from the restaurant as those inside began filing out. Abigail and her new beau were one of the last to leave. Just as Josiah stepped forward, the scoundrel bent and placed a kiss on Abigail's cheek.

Her face turned the shade of pink that was quickly becoming Josiah's favorite color. When he was the one to put it there. He clenched his fists. How dare the man take such liberties?

"Hey! That's my girl." The words burst forth before his mind could register the fact they'd formed.

"Josiah." Abigail's eyes widened. "Our engagement wasn't real."

"Maybe I want it to be."

"What kind of game are you playing? I've agreed to let Mr. Nelson court me." She turned to the man at her side and excused herself. She grabbed Josiah's arm and dragged him between two buildings. "Explain yourself. You've embarrassed me."

He didn't know what to say.

She stomped her foot. "Well? Is it only that you're afraid of losing face? I've dropped hints here and there for the last couple of days that we are no longer together. I've made it out to be all my fault." She glanced toward the street. "Which will probably cost me the next election, but I know how much your freedom means to you."

"My freedom?" he whispered. He didn't want to be free. Not from her.

She turned red-rimmed eyes his way. "Yes. You've made it very clear that marriage is not in your future. You've mentioned not sticking around Turtle Springs for long. Now, you're free to decide what it is you want." With a swish of her skirt, she flounced down the sidewalk and away from him.

He wanted her. Only he was too dense to know how to tell her so.

Chapter 8

Abby sat with her back to a giant oak tree next to the creek and listened to Mr. Nelson rattle on about the different types of cattle, and the pros and cons of each. It's all the man talked about. She pulled a blade of grass and twirled it in her fingers.

"Am I boring you, dearest?" He glanced up from where he reclined on one elbow.

"Of course not." Yes. After three days of agreeing to a courtship and spending every supper hour with him of those three days, she was bored out of her mind. They had absolutely nothing in common. The man was well-mannered, polite, and as pompous as a person could be.

Ma tolerated him, Lucy avoided him, and Ma's beau, Hank Weldon, didn't speak to him, only grunted. It didn't help that at every meal Lucy asked when Josiah was going to visit again. That comment only made Mr. Nelson talk more.

"Well?"

She wasn't aware he'd asked her a question. "Pardon me?"

"You are not with me, Abigail." Mr. Nelson frowned. "I believe it's time I took you home." He stood and helped her to her feet. After folding the faded quilt and tucking it under his arm, he led her past the church and into town. "I do believe I'll be quite pleased when the saloon opens." He peered through a crack in one of the boarded-up windows. "A man needs some pleasurable pastimes."

Her steps faltered. "Wouldn't he find that within the walls of his home? With his wife and children?"

He gave a patronizing smile. "You are sweet. There are things about a man that women simply cannot understand."

It took all her willpower not to groan. He really was insufferable. "I'm going to plead a headache." She stomped away from him.

"I've said something to upset you." He hurried to catch up with her. "Is it the saloon?"

"Partly. We've managed just fine for a year without one. No loose women, no rowdy drunks." Well, until Mr. Watson. "We've enjoyed the peace, Mr. Nelson."

"Dearest." There was that simpering smile she'd thought charming three days ago. "Things are different. Men have arrived."

She opened her mouth to give a sharp retort when she caught sight of Josiah whittling outside the jail. Her heart fluttered. How different he was from the man standing next to her.

A young woman stopped beside Josiah. Whatever she said made him laugh. Jealousy rose in Abby faster than a jackrabbit bolting from its burrow. She squelched the emotion. She had no hold on him. Obviously, he'd decided to stay in Turtle Springs. People *were* going to speak with him, women included.

Mr. Nelson tugged her arm. "We're engaged now. Ogling other men is not proper."

"I'm the mayor. The sheriff and I often need to work closely together."

"Perhaps I'll become sheriff. I've been told I'm a fair shot."

She cut him a quick glance. "You're a rancher."

"I could do both. The man rarely moves from that spot, it seems."

"Because this is a peaceful town. Reopening the saloon will change that." She thought of the petition still on her desk. If possible, she'd never sign it or bring it before the other women in meeting. No, that wouldn't work. Any town meetings would now involve men. Men who wanted a saloon.

"All right, dear. We won't bother your pretty little head anymore with a subject so distasteful to you." He stopped at the bottom of the steps to her home. As he'd done every night since the audition, he tried to steal a kiss. Just as she'd done every time, she turned her head to where his lips only grazed her cheek.

"Good night, Mr. Nelson."

"Please call me Lawrence." His eyes narrowed. "I've asked several times."

She stepped back at the look in his eyes. "I'm sorry. Of course. . .Lawrence."

He smiled. "Very good." Whistling, he headed toward his room above the restaurant.

Abby plopped into a rocking chair on the porch. How was she going to end things with Mr. Nelson? It became more and more apparent that marriage to him was far worse than spinsterhood.

But probably not bad at all, if she were married to Josiah. As if her thoughts had conjured him, he strolled toward her home. He stopped and propped a booted foot on the bottom step.

"Evenin', Abigail." His deep voice cut smoothly through the darkening night.

"Josiah. What brings you here?"

"The town wants to meet on the saloon."

She closed her eyes and exhaled sharply. "I'm sick of talking about the saloon."

"You can't put it off forever."

"Fine. We'll discuss it at the next town meeting." She pushed her toes against the floor and set the chair to rocking.

Josiah bounded up the stairs and sat in the rocker next to her. "What's wrong?"

She rolled her head to peer through the dark. "I don't want to marry Mr. Nelson."

"Then don't."

"I gave my word."

"So?" His teeth flashed. "You broke off with me easily enough."

"Our engagement wasn't real." Pain squeezed her heart.

Josiah reached over and took her hand. "You aren't hitched yet. There's time to back out. Think long and hard, Abigail. Marriage is until death do you part."

His touch burned her, and she pulled away. "I know."

"The tone of your voice tells me you've decided."

Was she imagining the hope in his voice? "I don't want to die a spinster," she whispered.

"Darlin', there is no chance of that happening." He leaned forward and planted a soft kiss on her lips. "Pray about it. I think you forgot that important step when you came up with the audition idea, didn't you?"

She nodded. "I've always been one to jump ahead without asking God whether I should or not. I will pray about it, Josiah. Thank you."

"Make sure you wait for the answer." He chuckled and stood. "I'll be seeing you around, Mayor."

The next morning, Josiah woke with a smile on his face. Not that he wanted Abigail to be unhappy. Not at all. He only wanted her to be happy with him. Which was selfish and unfair, he knew. Still, his heart knew what it wanted. Why else had he stayed away from her? She needed to miss him as much as he missed her. He saw a glimpse of that last night.

Swinging his legs off the side of his cot, he tugged on his boots, splashed water on his face, then grabbed his hat, ready to start the day. As was his morning routine, he got coffee at the restaurant and strolled the two streets before unlocking the jail. Since releasing the two women last week, he hadn't had any overnight visitors. Mrs. Watson kept the place so clean you could eat off the floors, and her husband stayed busy painting and nailing all over town.

Not once had Josiah regretted his decision to hire them. He glanced at the boarded-up saloon, the place of so much discussion and dissension in town. He spotted Mr. Nelson and Mr. Harper in deep discussion in front of the building. What possible interest could Mr. Nelson have in the saloon, other than a place to grab a nip once in a while? The two men didn't appear to be strangers.

Josiah moseyed closer, pretending to be interested in a loose board on the livery.

"I'm telling you, I can control the mayor," Nelson said. "She's wrapped around my finger, completely ensnared by my charm."

Josiah scoffed. If the man only knew.

"I need this saloon to open," Harper said. "I've no other way of making a living, and I'm not inclined to be a traveling man. If we set up gambling tables here, bring in a few soiled doves, we're bound to rake in the coins. Men will be starved for entertainment within a few weeks' time."

Not good, God-fearing men, Josiah thought. There were church socials, the occasional barn raising, the upcoming Founder's Day celebration, all wholesome, clean fun for families. Not that the town had hosted any. . .yet, but he knew they were coming once the weddings commenced.

"What are we going to do about that sheriff?" Nelson asked. "He acts like he's lazy and not aware of his surroundings, but my guess is he keeps an eagle eye on everything that goes on in this town."

Josiah smiled, stepping farther around the corner, out of sight. He moved still closer to the men.

"He might know what's going on around here," Harper added, "but that's nothing a bullet can't put an end to. You let me handle the sheriff. You keep working on the mayor. Use force and threats if you have to." Footsteps sounded, heading away.

Josiah leaned against the side of the building. He needed to warn Abigail. Since she was already adverse to marrying Nelson, anything Josiah said wouldn't affect her decision unless to confirm it. He pushed away from the wall and headed to her office. He peered through the open window.

He was too late. Nelson had beat him there.

The man perched on the corner of Abigail's desk. She stared up, unsmiling, then shook her head and stood. Whatever she said made the man angry.

He bolted over the desk, scattering papers and pencils to grab her arms. He shook her, his voice rising. "How dare you! No woman breaks up with the likes of me. Especially some low-down prairie mayor."

Josiah banged open the door. "Problem here?"

Abigail shook free. "Not at all. Mr. Nelson was just leaving."

"You haven't heard the last of this, Abigail. Mark my words."

Chapter 9

A bby stared over the sea of faces in the pews and squared her shoulders for battle. Her gaze landed on the glare of Mr. Nelson. Let him stare. She wasn't afraid, not with Josiah standing mere feet away.

"Good afternoon, good people of Turtle Springs. So many new faces. So many newly blended families. Welcome to our humble town." She gripped the sides of the podium. "We have only one item on our agenda today, and that is the possible reopening of the saloon."

Cheers and groans filled the church.

She held up her hands for silence. "We will have folks speak their opinion on the matter then place it to a vote. Before I hear any complaints, men *and* women will have the right to vote in this. Is it fair to forbid the women, the very ones who kept this town running, the right to vote on the town's welfare? I think not." She glanced at the papers in front of her. "The first to speak is Mrs. Bombay."

The woman bustled down the aisle, practically shoving Abby out of the way. Mrs. Bombay took her time looking around the room then spoke. "I say no. That building should have been torn down months ago. My dearly departed husband liked his drink, oh yes he did. That caused no small amount of trouble between the two of us.

"I say, we turn the saloon into a meeting hall. A place for social events. Not a place for loose women and whiskey that addles a man's mind."

Abby stepped close and whispered, "Tell us why it's a bad idea, Mrs. Bombay. List the facts, not your personal opinion."

"Very well. Drunkenness, unfaithfulness, rowdiness, that is what will come of reopening the saloon. Good points. . .there are none. Thank you." She stepped down and marched back to her seat.

"Sheriff?"

Josiah took his place behind the podium and tossed her a wink. "Now, folks, I'm an impartial party to this debate, but I'd like to tell you how things will go if the saloon is opened." He met the curious looks of several in the audience. "Yes, crime will rise. Yes, I'll take care of any infractions in a timely manner. Laws will be posted outside the saloon. Anyone who removes those laws will be dealt with severely. This is a God-fearing town, and I'd like to keep it that way. One thing I will forbid, should the saloon open, is prostitution. Should that occur, the doors will be nailed shut immediately. You can have a peaceful place for men to gather. I've seen them. A place where men talk business, smoke cigars, have a drink, and play cards. Loose women are not needed in such a place."

"Thank you, Sheriff." Abby called out the next name. "Mr. Lawrence Nelson will speak on behalf of the saloon."

"Now, my good people of Turtle Springs." He gave a charming smile. "Do not listen to the naysayers. This saloon of Mr. Harper's will be nothing like the passionate Mrs. Bombay described. It will simply be a place for men to gather, play cards, smoke a fine cigar, imbibe in the best whiskey, just as your fine sheriff said. Yes, there will be women, but they are only there to sing and to serve. Nothing more." He placed a hand over his heart. "I swear on my dear mama's grave."

It was all Abby could do not to scoff out loud. The man was as slick as oil spilled across water. All it would take to cause destruction was a spark.

"Soon," he continued, "I will be a prominent rancher in these parts, and intend to run for mayor in the next election, alongside my beautiful fiancée. What a competition that will be!"

Anger, hotter than a July sun, rose in Abby. Her face heated as applause broke out. The man had once been a preacher, he'd said. How could he behave this way if that were true? She cast a worried glance toward Josiah.

He smiled and winked again, reassuring her. All would be well as long as he was near.

Abby took the podium. "Thank you, Mr. Nelson." She lowered her voice and hissed, "We are no longer courting. Remember?" She forced a smile and turned back to the others. "There are ballots in the back for your votes. One says *yay*, the other *nay*. Simply sign your name and drop into the appropriate box. One vote per person, please, or your vote will be discarded."

She stepped next to Josiah. "I think it best to wait until the line dies down a bit, don't you?"

"Go with me to the June social."

"What?" She glanced up.

"I want to dance with you. It'll be the best way to show the townsfolk that you aren't with Nelson."

"But, I'm not with you, either."

He grinned, a dimple winking in his cheek. "They'll think we had a lover's spat and made up."

"Another ruse." She couldn't. Her heart couldn't take another pretend romance with Josiah.

"It doesn't have to be." His eyes darkened. "I meet your criteria, Abigail. Give—"

Shouts erupted from the makeshift voting booths. Josiah exhaled sharply and headed toward the commotion.

Abby eyed the simple cross on the wall behind her. God, please help her deal with Josiah.

With more force than necessary, Josiah yanked the two squabbling men apart. Just as he was about to pour out his heart to Abigail, they had to go and ruin it! "Settle down or I'll haul both your sorry behinds to jail."

"He started it, Sheriff." One man so skinny a strong wind would knock him over pointed at another man as wide as he was tall. "He said that I wasn't capable of voting because I was a few rocks short of a ton."

Whatever that meant. Josiah turned to the heavier man. "Everyone gets a vote."

"He don't even live here. He lives outside the town limits. Only citizens should vote."

"Where do you live?" Josiah crossed his arms. "Above the restaurant? As a guest? Or have you procured permanent lodgings?"

The man's face darkened. "That's what I thought. You have no more right to a vote than this gentleman. Listen up!" Josiah faced the line. "Unless you've made Turtle Springs your permanent home, please leave. If you're only passing through, you don't get a vote."

Grumblings rose at his word, but several men stepped out of line and stormed from the church.

Josiah grinned. Those men would have voted on the side of the saloon, no doubt. He eyed the others. The men still outnumbered the ladies, but there was nothing more he could do to help Abigail's cause.

Withdrawing a telegram from his pocket, he headed back to the front where Abigail kneeled. He stood back and waited for her to finish her prayer, then helped her to her feet when she made to rise.

"I have something for you." He handed her the telegram.

She read it then raised her head, a questioning look on her face. "What does it mean?"

"Nelson is no more a preacher than I am. I had a friend of mine do some checking. That isn't all." He took her by the elbow and led her to a far corner of the room. "I overheard him and Harper talking. Nelson plans on forcing you to agree to the saloon while Harper will take care of me."

"Take care of you?" Her eyes widened. "Does that mean he intends harm?"

"Most likely. Don't worry, Darlin'. I can take care of myself. It's you I'm worried about."

"He wouldn't dare." She crossed her arms and glared to where Nelson stood off to the side watching every ballot that went into the voting boxes. From the pleased look on the man's face, more were going into the *yay* than the *nay*.

For that reason only, Josiah wasn't overly afraid for Abigail. The man wouldn't harm her if the town voted in favor of the saloon. Unless. . .

"Who has final say in the voting?"

Abigail grinned. "I do. It's in the town's bylaws. Of course, I usually side with the majority. I won't allow the saloon, at least not right away. I'm going to do everything in my power to see those two men run out of town."

Concern for her safety rose again. "The saloon will pass by a large margin. Let me handle the men."

"You don't think I'm capable of ridding this town of a nuisance? How do you think we survived the last year? All I need to do is get a group of like-minded women—"

"Some men don't have any qualms about harming women."

"I daresay we'll be fine." She narrowed her eyes. "You do your job, and I'll do mine."

"Abigail—"

She pushed to the front of the line, signed a ballot, and dropped it into the *nay* box with a defiant glare at Nelson and Harper. Then, pretty head held high, she strolled from the church as if they'd just had a service.

Josiah kept a close watch on the two men, following when Nelson left through a side door. Staying out of sight, he watched as the man increased his pace to catch up with Abigail.

She whirled, her cheeks a bright pink. Whatever Nelson said didn't sit well with her. She tossed her head back like a spirited filly and let loose a barrage of words Josiah couldn't make out.

Didn't she see she was only pouring kerosene onto an already blazing fire? When Nelson grabbed her arm, Josiah rushed forward. "What's going on?"

"This man refuses to see reason." Abigail crossed her arms. "He can't seem to fathom that I'm serious about not marrying him."

"She's quite serious." Josiah slipped an arm around her waist, pulling her close. "She can't marry you, sir, because she's marrying me. A week from Saturday."

Nelson stepped back. "So, Miss Melton only toyed with my affections."

"No." Abigail shook her head. "I've come to the realization that we are not a likely couple. It's better to know that now than later."

"You'd marry a drifter over someone with an affluent future?" Nelson glanced from Josiah to Abigail. "You'll regret this decision, my dear." He turned on a well-shined shoe and marched back to the church.

Abigail slipped from Josiah's hold. "Thank you, but you didn't need to tell another falsehood."

Josiah sighed. Why wouldn't she listen to his feelings? "You never gave me an answer about the social. Will you go with me?"

Tears sprang to her eyes, wrenching his gut. "I can't. It's best we let this façade go."

He wanted to tell her it wasn't a façade. That he really did want to marry her and stay in Turtle Springs. But, he held his tongue and let her leave. She'd be at the celebration. He'd get her to dance with him. Then, as the sun set over the prairie, he'd tell her how much he loved her.

He headed back to the church to cast his vote, knowing as he did that it was futile. The saloon would win. The danger to the strong-minded, beautiful mayor would rise.

The hardest part of knowing was the fact he couldn't do anything to change the runaway locomotive heading straight for Turtle Springs. . .and the woman he loved.

Chapter 10

Abby did her best to avoid Josiah, but a yearning to see him drew her regularly to her office window. Every day he sat on the bench outside the jail, pretending to lounge. She now knew he watched everything that occurred up and down the street.

Jane Ransome stopped and spoke to Josiah, the sun highlighting her dark hair. Josiah tilted back his hat and smiled. They made a beautiful couple. Jane was much more suited to the sheriff than bossy Abby.

"Why are you so sad?" Lucy glanced up from where she filed papers. "Is it because your beau was a crook?"

"No, sweetie. It's not because of Mr. Nelson." Abby sighed and turned away from the window. There were too many reasons to load onto the shoulders of a child.

"The sheriff, then." Lucy gave a definitive nod. "You're sad because I want to marry him. Well, you can have him. I'd rather have Josiah as a brother-in-law than nothing at all."

Abby chuckled. "You are the dearest sister, but I'm afraid I've ruined it with him." Her heart lurched. "You'll find the perfect groom when you're of marrying age." Maybe Lucy would have more luck in matters of the heart.

A commotion outside drew both of them back to the window. A man approached Josiah then the men raced toward the saloon, leaving Jane standing on the sidewalk. The woman shrugged and headed for the mercantile.

"Stay here." Abby slapped her straw hat on her head and stepped out to the sidewalk.

Josiah pulled a board away from the saloon window and peered inside. "I don't see anything."

The man, a newcomer in town, said, "I'm telling you I saw a light. Someone's living in there or"—his eyes widened—"I've heard tell of whiskey flowing."

From a closed-up saloon? Abby stepped forward. "Perhaps Mr. Watson is up to his old tricks."

"Oh hello, Abigail." Josiah shook his head. "No, the man has been a regular pillar of society since I helped him find work. If someone is selling liquor, it isn't him."

"What are you going to do?"

"Hang around after dark, I reckon."

"Then, you'd best hang out in the clearing a few yards behind the building." The other man snapped his suspenders. "I see lights here and there. My guess is the men are hanging in the woods but they're drinking."

Abby headed for the clearing.

"What are you doing?" Josiah grabbed her arm.

"Making sure the saloon hasn't moved outdoors. As the mayor, this is something I cannot allow." She pulled free. "I'll just take a peek and then you can come back tonight and arrest the scoundrels, if there are any."

He made a sound deep in his throat. "Lord protect me from stubborn women. Stay behind me, Abigail." His hand on the butt of his gun, he parted the foliage.

Thick muscles rippling under his shirt drew her gaze. The way his hair curled right before brushing his collar. She closed her eyes, pretending for just a moment that she'd accepted his declaration of love as real. But, alas, the man was prone to tall tales, and his words were nothing more than a falsehood.

The silly advertisement in the paper had brought her nothing but heartache. When would she learn to be still and wait for God to act?

"It does look as if folks have been here." Josiah motioned to sawed logs used as seats. Cigar butts littered the ground. He turned back toward the saloon. "There isn't any liquor stored in there. I checked last week."

"My guess is Mr. Nelson and his friend are conducting business whether I approve their petition or not." Abby planted her fists on her hips. "I intend to confront them immediately."

Josiah narrowed his eyes. "You'll do no such thing. This is my job as the sheriff. Go back to your office and sign papers or something."

Her mouth fell open. She snapped it shut. What happened to the kind Josiah? This one was positively cruel. "Hmmph!" She whirled and stomped away. And to think she'd actually had second thoughts about dancing with him at the upcoming social. The man could take a turn around the dance floor with a pig for all she cared.

"What's wrong?" Lucy asked, the moment Abby returned.

"Men drinking in the woods behind the saloon." Abby plopped into a chair. "Nothing to concern yourself about."

"I saw two men carrying crates the other day when I was walking home from school. I heard the clanking of bottles, but didn't think anything of it."

"Really? Where were they coming from?"

"The shed behind the school."

Mercy. Abby dashed back to Josiah. "The liquor is being kept behind the school."

"I told you to let me handle this." He took her by the arm and led her back to the sidewalk. "Abigail, I'm serious. This is dangerous business. These men want that saloon and they'll do anything to get it. Guess who stands in their way? You."

"Surely they won't harm me. The votes favored the *yay* side."

"Have you signed the petition?"

She smiled. "No, I'm not going to either, at least, not for a very long time."

"Stalling will get you killed."

"Stalling will keep down the crime."

"Yeah, it's worked well so far. I've two drunks in jail right now."

She took her bottom lip between her teeth. "So, you knew about this?"

"I suspected, yes. I'll check out the school as soon as you go back to your office."

She shook her head. "I'm coming with you."

"Abigail, please, let me do my job." He turned and marched away from her.

She quick-stepped to catch up with him. "I'm sorry, but you're stuck with me. I'm the mayor, and I insist on accompanying you." She'd do pretty much anything to spend time with him, even if it angered him. How pathetic was she?

He turned to face her, his eyes darkening. He looked so long, so intensely, that she flushed. "Do I have something on my face?"

"No. You're driving me loco." He took a deep breath. "I'd kiss you if I thought it would make you mad enough to go back where you belong." His gaze settled on her lips.

Her stomach quivered. A kiss wouldn't be so bad, would it? Except, she shouldn't encourage him. She'd had her say. The town now knew they weren't engaged. In fact, she'd heard two women gossiping just yesterday that Abigail Melton was fickle and couldn't choose between two suitors. She closed her eyes and took a step back.

Why wasn't she saying anything? Instead, Abigail looked like a beaten dog.

Josiah rubbed his chin. "All right, you can come with me. There's no reason for the long face." He couldn't bear for her to be unhappy.

"I'll do as you say. I promise."

"Wonderful. Now, chin up. Let's find some liquor." He chucked her under the chin and grinned. "You'll need spunk to get through what's coming."

"You really think I'm in danger?"

"Yep." He turned and led the way to the school. Nosing around with him only increased that danger, but crazy as it was, he enjoyed her tagging along. "Where?"

"The shed in back. I have a key." She pulled a key ring from her pocket and fished for one to unlock a padlock. Within seconds, Josiah swung open the wood-slated door.

Inside were piled crates of bottles filled with liquor. Josiah sighed. "Help me dump this out by the creek."

"Where did it come from?"

"It's moonshine, not fine whiskey. Someone is brewing their own."

"Nelson and Harper?"

"Maybe." He glanced around them. Where would they have built their still? Leaving Abby to follow, he hefted a crate and headed for the thick brush. "You can pour while I carry," he told her. "Keep an eye out for two-legged predators."

An hour later, Josiah leaned over the creek and splashed cool water on his perspiring face.

Abby squatted next to him and dabbed her face and neck with a handkerchief soaked in the stream. "It's hot."

He choked as she dribbled water down the neckline of her blouse. "Do you have any idea what you're doing to me?"

"What?" Her eyes widened.

"That?" He pointed at the lace-trimmed handkerchief. Everything she did sent his heart racing like a thoroughbred. The way she walked, tilted her head. . .washed at the creek. It was as if she tried to drive him crazy on purpose.

Before he could think and change his mind, he grabbed her close, entwined his hands in her hair, and kissed her. Not a nice, sweet little kiss, either. He put everything he felt and wanted into the kiss. When she released a moan deep in her throat, he stepped back. "Think about that when you lie down to sleep tonight, Abigail." He tilted an invisible hat and strolled, whistling, to town.

Footsteps pounded behind him. Abigail rushed in front of him, slapped his chest, and head held high, continued before him. "Think about that!"

He laughed, startling a mockingbird from a nearby tree. Oh yes, Miss Melton was definitely going to lose some sleep over that kiss. He rubbed his chest where she'd smacked him. He might lose a few winks himself.

Dusk found Josiah hunkered down near the clearing behind the saloon. Since he and Abigail had dumped the moonshine, he didn't hold out much hope anyone would show up. Then Nelson and Harper strode into the clearing and set a lantern in the center.

Another man barged in behind them. "It's all gone. Every last drop. Someone saw the mayor and sheriff dumping it all out."

"And they didn't think to stop them?" Harper's eyes glittered in the light of the lamp.

"No, sir. They didn't want to get shot."

"Imbecile." Harper kicked at a rock. "Those two cost me a fair bit of change. They're going to pay for it, too. Once we get the treasure. . ."

"Are you sure there is a treasure?" Nelson asked. "I've not seen any sign of it since you told me. Not even a map. What if it's all hearsay?"

"It isn't." Harper shoved him. "My pa told me about it when I was a young'un. We've looked all over this town. It has to be in the saloon. That's the only business that's boarded up. Why else would the mayor be so against reopening?"

Because of lowlifes like you, Josiah wanted to say. He'd never heard tell of a treasure in Turtle Springs. The man was a few nails short of a bushel, and that made him very dangerous.

Josiah shoved back and got to his feet, once he was clear of being seen. He'd searched the saloon himself after being told about a light. Nothing but cobwebs and dust. Not even a single whisky glass left on the shelf. Abigail was in danger because of a fairy tale.

Chapter 11

Abby smoothed the skirt of her deep-green dress and glanced at the buffet table set up in the churchyard. Her stomach rumbled. She couldn't go over there with Josiah filling his plate. Not after the way she acted yesterday. All he'd wanted to do was help.

If she ever hoped to win his heart, she needed to let go of some of her independence and rely on the help of another. Not all the time, mind you, but there were times it was prudent.

Every bit in her wanted to take back that she'd said anything about a façade. Why couldn't she keep her mouth closed long enough to let the man speak?

She'd seen the warmth of his eyes when he looked upon her. Was it fear that kept her sharp tongue from letting him get close? She squared her shoulders. Abigail Melton was a lot of things, but coward was not one of them.

Grinning like a loon, she took her first steps toward the man she was determined to profess her love to. A sharp object in her ribcage stopped her.

"Don't let on there's a gun to your back, Miss Melton." Nelson jabbed her ribs. "Keep smiling and come with me."

Abby met Josiah's gaze across the dance floor, widened her eyes, and nodded, praying, hoping, he could see the fear in them. "What do you want with me?"

"A serious conversation, my dear." He led her around to the back of the church where a buggy waited. "Climb on up and let's go."

This is what she got for barging ahead with a foolish plan without waiting for God to answer. Kidnapping! She pretended to have difficulty climbing into the wagon in her skirts until Nelson grabbed her wrist and dragged her up to the driver's seat, as if she were nothing more than a sack of feed. Her shin banged against the wheel rim. Pain shot through her leg.

"No need to be so rough." She yanked her hand away.

"Hold on tight, dear." He slapped the reins against the backs of the dray horses. They bolted down Main Street, scattering pedestrians like chaff in the wind.

Abby gripped the seat and closed her eyes, certain they'd tip and be crushed. A few minutes later, she peeled one eye open. They'd left town and were continuing at a fast pace away from Turtle Springs. . .and Josiah.

"Where are we going?"

Nelson cut her a sideways glance. "Somewhere private. Harper is waiting for us."

"I have no need to speak with him." She swallowed past the dread in her throat.

"He wants to speak to you all right. The boss is angry that you poured out all his liquor. Took us weeks to make that much." Nelson laughed and whipped the horses again. "Got to make some distance before that sheriff comes looking. When he does, we'll kill him. Whether we shoot you will depend on you."

"All because of a saloon?" She turned her head. The two men were crazy. "Why not go to another town? Turtle Springs isn't large enough to make you rich."

"Harper wants this town. A town full of new men besotted with new brides. They'll be easier to con out of their money."

"Ridiculous."

The wagon slowed then turned down a path through the trees. "Get out." Nelson aimed his gun at her. "We walk from here."

If she got her hands on that gun she'd shoot him herself. Bunching her skirts in her hand, she jumped to the ground. Her dress snagged on a loose nail in the wagon bed. She ripped it free and trudged ahead, Nelson following her.

Night was falling. Without gas lanterns lighting the way, the woods were full of shadows and strange sounds. Her stomach growled again, louder this time.

"Just keep going straight. You'll run into a cabin about the time you see it. If you're good, maybe Harper will spare a bit of beans to fill the hole in your stomach."

She didn't want anything from either of the crooks. There still had to be more to their lawbreaking than a simple saloon. She stopped. "You want my job."

"You're a smart one, you are." He shoved her forward.

"Then run against me. Why go to all this trouble?"

"I also came here to get me a wife. You're the one I picked and you tossed me aside like a dirty rag."

"You kidnapped me because I won't marry you?" She tossed a look over her shoulder. "There are plenty of women in this town. I'm not taking one more step until you tell me the truth."

"We want your father's map, Miss Melton." Harper stepped out of the shadows. "The one with the combination to a safe that is under the floor of the saloon. Now, how is that for a truth?"

"Unfortunately, you've wasted your time. There is nothing buried under the saloon. That's a rumor from ages ago. Surely you understand that many men have searched for the so-called treasure."

He sighed. "Let's get inside before we're discovered. You'll tell us what we want to know soon enough."

"I'll show you if you take me back to town." She planted fists on her hips. "There is no gold." Surely her father would have said something if there was truth to the story.

Harper's eyes glittered in the moonlight. "Let's head back. Only we'll leave the wagon behind. We'll be less likely to be seen on horseback. Once the sheriff finds this place, he'll never think of us heading back."

He would if he spotted the words Abby traced in the dirt under her skirt. Taking care to step over them, she dropped her hair ribbon and walked between the two men to a pair of saddled horses.

"She'll ride with you, Nelson." Harper swung into the saddle.

"Up, Miss Melton." Nelson kept his gun trained on her then mounted the horse behind her.

Abby groaned inwardly. If she could have ridden behind him, sliding off and dashing into the trees would have been a simple task. Now, she was forced to have his arms around her, a bit too snugly for her taste, all the way back to town.

Would they really shoot her once they discovered there was no gold? Her eyes widened. What if there actually was? Would they take it and leave her be?

By the time Josiah fetched his horse from the livery, there was no sign of Abigail or Nelson. Fear choked him.

"They took off like the hounds of Hades were on their heels," Mrs. Bombay said. "That way. Almost knocked me right out of my shoes. My guess is they're eloping."

He doubted that. "Thank you." Josiah swung into the saddle and galloped in the direction the woman had pointed. He sent a prayer of thanksgiving heavenward for the moon and starlight. Without them, he'd be riding blind and putting not only himself at risk, but his horse.

Once he found her, and saved her from Nelson's clutches, he'd make her listen to his proclamations of love. They'd be married right away, before she could change her mind.

He rode for half an hour before he found the wagon. He slid off his horse and slowly searched the ground for sign. A trail of flattened foliage led west. He followed it, spotting a cabin through the trees. No lantern glowed, no smoke from the fireplace. The cabin looked deserted.

He turned in a circle. If not here, where? He retraced his steps, finally spotting a ribbon fluttering low on a bush. His gaze fell on scuffs in the dirt. "Back 2 saloon." At least he thought that's what the markings said.

What if he were wrong and he headed back to town while Nelson took Abigail farther from Turtle Springs? *Lord, I need Your help.*

He felt a nudging to make haste back to Turtle Springs. He raced for his horse, leaped into the saddle, and galloped the way he'd come.

If they'd gone back, which made no sense to him, then Nelson obviously wasn't forcing Abigail to marry him. So why take her in the first place?

Once he hit the outskirts of town, he looped his horse's reins over a hitching post and snuck down the street behind the buildings. At the saloon, a board had been removed from a side door, leaving just enough room for a man to squeeze through.

Pulling his gun from its holster, Josiah slid inside.

"See? I told you there wasn't any gold." Abigail's voice came from the front of the building. "No map, no gold, no treasure. It was nothing more than folklore."

"That's unfortunate for you, Miss Melton." Harper, the snake!

"Just leave me be and go. The two of you can be long gone before anyone discovers us."

"I do believe a lovely hostage will benefit us better." Harper moved into Josiah's sight line.

As he aimed his gun, the man moved away. "Now, where is that sheriff? I'd like to do away with him so no one bothers to follow us." He sat in an old wooden chair and glanced around him. "A pity we can't stay. This town needs a saloon."

Abigail crossed her arms. "I thought you wanted gold then to leave."

"That plan didn't work out too well, now did it." His voice rose. "So, it's on to plan *B*, which is make you disappear and then open this lousy saloon. Or plan *C*, which is to leave and take you as hostage. You've got to be worth something. What we choose to do depends on you."

Her eyes widened. "Plan *B* means you kill me. Plan *C* means you take me as hostage then kill me. I don't like either option."

"Unfortunate."

"Not necessarily." Josiah stepped around the corner. "Drop the gun, Nelson. I'd like nothing better than to shoot you like the dog you are." He motioned with his weapon. "Go stand next to your friend."

"Abigail, darlin', you come stand behind me. There's an extra gun in my waistband. Take it and keep it trained on these two while I cuff them."

"Not me, you ain't!" Nelson pulled the trigger and dove behind the chair.

The bullet grazed Josiah's arm. He aimed and shot, taking Nelson in the chest. He immediately swung his aim to Harper. "Want the same?"

Harper stood, hands in the air.

"That's not one of his plans," Abigail said, with a nervous laugh.

"It is now." Josiah motioned his weapon for Harper to lead the way. "Stay with us, darlin'. You and I have some talking to do."

Once he had Harper behind bars and Nelson's body taken care of, he let Abigail take him home so she could tend to his arm. She sat him at her kitchen table and wrapped a clean bandage around the wound.

She lifted tear-filled eyes to his. "You scared me to death, Josiah Ingram. When Nelson shot—"

"You were scared? What about me? I thought you'd run off with that scoundrel. I chased after you to bring you back."

"Why?" She cupped his face. "Because you love me? I sincerely hope so because, Josiah Ingram"—she planted a tender kiss on his lips—"I'm asking you to marry me. I can't wait on you any longer. My heart won't take it. I know I haven't taken your declarations serious, but I am now. I'm taking my chances on you having told me the truth. I know I can be a shrew sometimes, I'm strong-minded and opinionated—"

He put a finger to her lips. "Shh."

"I won't even be mayor anymore. I'll just be your wife. Every moment of every day. I've prayed long and hard, really I have. This time, I feel certain God—"

"Hush, Abigail." His own eyes filled with tears. "You silly woman. I've been trying to tell you for days that I love you, but you never stop talking long enough for me to make you see reason."

She tilted her head and smiled. "Is that a yes, Mr. Ingram?"

"That's a yes, Miss Melton. I'll be honored to marry you." He cupped the back of her head and pulled her lips to his.

Epilogue

She was getting married! Maybe her silly plan to bring men to Turtle Springs hadn't been so bad after all.

Abby smoothed the bodice of her cream-colored dress. Ma had worked long hours stitching the wedding gown. Josiah hadn't wanted to wait long.

The town was rejuvenated with weddings. Every weekend one or more couples tied the knot. This time, it was Abby's turn. She smiled and twirled in front of the mirror, feeling like a princess in one of the fairy tales Lucy read.

"I really wanted to marry the sheriff." Lucy grinned from the doorway. "But, at least my sister is, so that's second best."

"Oh it is, is it?" Abby drew her sister into a hug. "Your turn will come. Turtle Springs will continue to grow and young men will flock here to see our beauties."

"Sure. Let's go. Ma said she's ready to marry her beau." Lucy heaved a sigh. "He's all right, I guess. Not as fine as your groom, but Ma is happy."

Abby laughed and tucked Lucy's arm in hers. "You can pretend you're marrying Josiah for as long as it takes you to walk up the aisle in front of me and Ma. But no longer." She tweaked her sister's nose.

"It's a deal." Lucy raced ahead of her.

Hank waited next to the wagon. "No sense in my beauties walking on their wedding day," he said, grinning. "Even if it is only a couple of blocks." He helped Ma onto the driver's seat, then Abby, leaving Lucy to climb in the back. "I'm as excited as a child on Christmas." He leaned over and gave Ma a kiss.

Abby knew the feeling. If her heart beat any faster, she'd die.

They pulled up to the church and entered through a back door. Lucy dashed off, only to return moments later. "Josiah looks like an angel." She put her hands under her knees and pretended to swoon.

Abby laughed and took her place behind Ma. This was it. The best day of her life. She took a deep breath as Lucy opened the door.

By the time she'd made her way down the aisle, tears filled her eyes so much she could barely make out Josiah's face. He took her hand, pulled her close, and wiped away her tears.

"I hope those are tears of joy."

She hiccupped a laugh. The words stuck in her throat, so she nodded like a ninny. For the first time in a long time, she was at a loss for words.

Josiah laughed, the sound ringing through the church like bells. Abby joined in.

"I love you." Josiah leaned close, his breath tickling the hair on her neck.

"Oh, dearest, I love you so. I'll try not to be such a ninny in the future."

"I don't want you to change a thing." He tucked a curl behind her ear. "Except. . .maybe let me get a word in once in a while."

"I promise." With her hand tucked in his, they faced the preacher. She hardly heard the words spoken. Josiah filled her every sense. It wasn't until her groom bent her over his arm, and the preacher said he could kiss his bride, did she come to her senses.

She wrapped her arms around his neck and held on while he stole her breath away.

Cynthia Hickey grew up in a family of storytellers and moved around the country a lot as an army brat. Her desire is to write about real, but flawed characters in a wholesome way that her seven children and five grandchildren can all be proud of. She and her husband live in Arizona where Cynthia is a full-time writer.

The Kidnapped Groom

By Susan Page Davis

Chapter 1

Turtle Springs, Kansas
April 1866

Sam Cayford rode into the small town and looked around with interest. There wasn't much to Turtle Springs. A general store, a boarded up saloon, a livery stable, a few other businesses. He tied his horse, Rocker, named for his easy gait, at a rail outside a three-story building with a sign that said TUMBLE INN— MEALS SERVED hanging over the boardwalk out front. The paint was peeling and the windows looked none too clean, but Sam didn't see any other options. As he mounted the step, a sheet of paper tacked to the door caught his eye. HUSBANDS WANTED.

He hesitated. What on earth? All he wanted was a meal, not a wife. Leaning closer, he read the small print: MEN AUDITIONING FOR PROSPECTIVE HUSBANDS SIGN UP AT THE MAYOR'S OFFICE.

He looked down the street, hoping to spot another place he could eat. Other posters looking suspiciously like this one hung on porch posts and walls all down the street. Had this town gone crazy?

His stomach growled, and he decided to risk it and see about getting some food. No telling how long before he came to another restaurant. And besides, somebody in this establishment might know what ranches in the area were likely to hire hands.

Pushing open the door, he surveyed the dim interior. It looked all right. Three long tables filled most of the room, with chairs and benches along the sides. Ten or twelve diners were scattered among them—mostly men, but one couple and a woman with two medium-sized children. The air smelled good—fresh bread and some kind of meat smell. . .stew, maybe—and grease. Over it all wafted a teasing hint of ginger. That was enough for Sam. He strode to the nearest table and took a seat on a stool opposite a man whose tanned skin and rough clothing pegged him as one who worked outdoors.

"Howdy," Sam said with a nod.

Chewing, the bearded man across from him nodded. He reached for his coffee mug, took a swig, and swallowed. "New here?"

"Yeah, just passing through."

"Oh? You didn't come for the mail-order husband doings?"

Sam shook his head, frowning. "What's that all about, anyhow? I saw the signs."

"Women in town who need husbands. They took an ad in some papers, and the men are starting to drift in for it."

"Well, I'm drifting on through with the breeze." Sam looked up as a gray-haired woman wearing an apron came to stand beside him. The apron looked clean, but he noted that she kept her hands in her pockets.

"You want the lunch special, sir?"

"What's on it?"

"Bowl of beef stew, biscuits, coffee, and pie. Only fifty cents."

"Sounds good." Sam reached into his pocket for a half dollar, trying not to think how little cash that left him. He glanced at the man across the table and up at the waitress. "I'm looking for a job. Do you know any ranches that are hiring?"

"Try the Russell place," the woman said. "It's about four miles west of here. You can skip the Martincheks' place. They're full up."

The other man nodded. "I've got my own place, but it's small. I got all the help I need right now. If Russell's don't work out, you might ride on to the Therron place—the T Snake Ranch. They usually hire in the fall. I don't know about now."

Sam smiled. "Thanks."

"I'll get your food." The waitress shuffled away.

"I'm Borden Hanks," his tablemate said, sticking out a sinewy hand.

Sam shook it. "Sam Cayford. Much obliged for the help."

Hanks shrugged. "You seem like a sensible feller. Not buying into this fool husband thing." He glanced quickly at Sam. "Not that being a husband is a bad thing, necessarily. I've got me a wife, and I like it fine. I just think it's an oddball way to go about it."

"Got a lot of spinsters in these parts, I guess?"

"A few. Seems like Turtle Springs might have more'n its share of widders."

"Oh. Too bad."

Hanks raised his chin in the direction of the departing waitress. "She's one of 'em. The owner of this place hired her after her husband died."

"Well, at least she's got a job."

"Yup. Don't think she needs it, though, with that big house of hers. I think she might just be lonely." Hanks shook his head. "Does seem out of proportion here. Some war widders, some from other causes. Rather'n pack up and go East, they decided to advertise for men to come here. Least, that's what my wife says."

"Hard to know what you're getting when you throw out bait like that," Sam said.

"That's what I say. If you don't find work in these parts, try closer to Dodge City."

"Probably good advice."

The woman returned with a tray, one hand balancing it with a curled fist. As she set Sam's food and coffee before him, he saw that her fingers were gnarled. He looked up into eyes that sternly warned him against pity. "That stew looks and smells great, ma'am."

A gentle smile warmed her face. "We have lemon pie or apple when you're ready."

"Apple please," Sam said.

The woman nodded and walked toward the kitchen.

"Well, I'd best push off," said Hanks. "If you find a job, I expect I'll see you again. If not, well, good luck, Cayford."

"Thanks." Sam watched him leave with a pang of regret. Borden Hanks was the friendliest soul he'd encountered in weeks. When his pie came, he'd ask for explicit directions to the Russell and Therron ranches.

An hour later, he and Rocker were a couple of miles west of town. The Flint Hills made up a pretty region, with lots of trees and views that made him long for a piece of land where he could start his own ranch. The afternoon had turned off hot, and when Sam heard the sound of running water, he decided to stop and let his bay gelding get a drink. He watched the side of the trail, and after a while spotted a path through the willows that might lead down to the water. He rode through the trees, appreciating the coolness of the shade.

Sure enough, a brook rippled over the rocky bed below him. From the look of the banks, he decided the water was lower than usual.

Sam dismounted and led Rocker down to where the horse could reach the stream. The gelding stretched out his neck and slurped water. Holding the end of the reins loosely, Sam crouched on his upstream side and cupped his hand, bringing a small amount of water to his mouth. It was cooler than he'd expected, and refreshing. He scooped another handful.

Rocker stepped out into the water, feeling his way in until the stream covered his hooves and eddied around his pasterns. Sam indulged him by stretching out his arm and giving him all the rein he could. Rocker lowered his head to drink again.

"Hold it, mister," a voice said from behind him.

Sam stiffened but didn't rise.

"Put your hands up."

Slowly, he obeyed, tugging Rocker's reins as he did so, making the horse lift his head and step toward him. No way was Sam going to lose hold of his horse right now. Just his luck to get held up. Now he was glad he'd spent fifty cents on a good dinner.

He turned his upper body ever so slowly, until he could see over his shoulder toward the trees.

"What—?" He stared at the two boys standing on the path. The older one looked about twelve years old, not a day older, towheaded and blue eyed, his face set in what might pass for a fierce scowl. A step behind him lurked another lad, younger and even blonder, peeking from beneath the older boy's elbow and the shotgun he held up with difficulty. That one looked scared.

"You robbing me?" Sam asked incredulously as he turned fully toward them. "Boys, if you need money, you picked the wrong person." He took a step toward them, and Rocker came with him. "Hold it," the boy with the gun growled.

Sam stopped. They'd better not be trying to steal his horse. Sam couldn't allow that. The shotgun would hold only one shell at a time. He wondered what the load was and hoped it was bird shot.

"Boys, you know horse thieving is a hanging offense." Sam looked gravely into the bigger boy's eyes.

The younger one tugged his brother's shirttail—Sam had no doubt they were brothers. Same china-blue eyes, same pale hair.

"Fred, you gonna get us *hung*. You heard him."

"Hush," Fred told him. "You get his horse and bring it along home." Still aiming pointblank at Sam's chest, though his arms trembled with the weight of the shotgun, he smiled. "We're not stealing nothing, mister. In fact, you can thank us. This is your lucky day."

"Lucky?" Sam shook his head, his hands still at shoulder height. Could he make the four steps from here to the boy and safely wrestle the shotgun from him? "I don't consider it lucky to be held at gunpoint."

"Oh, you're lucky all right," Fred said. "Today's your weddin' day."

Maggie Piner hurried her steps toward home. She hadn't meant to stay in town so long. Her two boys were generally well-behaved, and she trusted them, but after all, they were boys.

Fred, at twelve, was old enough to be left in charge of his younger brother, Benjy, for a short while. He had matured greatly since they'd learned of his father's death. He seemed determined to be the man of the house and the boss of the fledgling ranch.

But she had figured this jaunt would only take an hour. Wishful thinking. She had left home shortly after noon, and it must be nearing three o'clock now. After the meeting at the church, she had stopped at the general store to see if she could buy a cup of sugar. That was all she needed.

Chardy Stevens had said she couldn't do that, she had to sell sugar by the sack. But in the end, she had offered to loan Maggie a cup from her personal supply. Chardy was a sweetheart. Taking care of her four little brothers, she understood what it was like to try to feed hungry young'uns when the purse was light. But still Maggie had hesitated. She didn't want to be beholden, even for a cup of sugar.

In the end, she had insisted on paying Chardy a few cents for it, a fraction of the cost of a five-pound sack, and Chardy had accepted. If only her friend knew—those pennies were nearly the last Maggie had.

Today was Benjy's birthday, and she wanted to give him a cake, even if she couldn't afford any presents. She wouldn't have splurged on sugar if it weren't for that. Something had to be special for him today. He was turning nine, and his pa wouldn't be there to celebrate.

The house was more than a mile outside town, and Maggie hurried along, hoping the boys weren't up to mischief in her absence. She supposed she ought to have taken them with her, but what could she have done with them during the meeting?

Those ladies wouldn't want two boys sitting in while they discussed the best way to find husbands.

She smiled as she remembered how soberly Benjy had listened at breakfast this morning when Fred had asked her about the mail-order grooms.

"Mama, why are the women in town putting up wanted posters?"

"They're not wanted posters, Fred," she'd said quickly. "It's just a form of advertising."

"What's that?" Benjy asked.

"Well, it's a way of letting other people know if you need something—or if you have something they might want. Like the mercantile advertises when they've got a new shipment of goods coming in, so people will stop in at the store and buy something."

"But they're not buying husbands," Fred said, frowning. "The signs say 'husbands wanted.'"

"No, but the ladies want folks to know they're open to marrying. We had a meeting Sunday afternoon—you remember."

"Yeah. You're not part of the husband thing, are you?" Fred asked.

Maggie had felt her face flush. She wasn't going to tell the boys unless something came of it.

"I told them I'd consider it. I'm supposed to go to another meeting today, as a matter of fact."

And now she was in it, up to her neck. She wondered how the boys would take the news. The women had set a date for a social time, where the ladies seeking husbands could speak to each of the men who had answered their advertisements and come forward as potential grooms.

The women had done their best to sift through the letters that came in. All had agreed that the grooms must be honest and hardworking. In some cases, they must be willing to take on a family—like Maggie's, for instance. She was widowed and had two boys. It might be hard to find a man open to raising Fred and Benjy. A man who was strong and would work hard to pay off the mortgage, so that they owned the property outright, fulfilling Rodney's dream.

She had to make sure he was a kindhearted man, though, before she would let him anywhere near her sons. Maggie was determined not to get into something permanent and then decide it wasn't best for her boys.

But she had to do something, and fast. The bank wouldn't wait forever. When her husband died more than a year ago, near the end of the war, she had been left owing on the mortgage. They had hoped that when Rodney got home, he could get the ranch going and raise enough money within a year. Then the land would be theirs for good and no one could take it away from them.

Only Rodney had never made it home.

Three years, almost, since Rod had left home. Maggie had scraped by, tending to the land as best she could and taking care of the boys, but she hadn't been able to buy the livestock he'd wanted. She had lived for the day Rod would walk up the lane and make the place prosper.

She'd heard the war was over before she got the black-bordered letter announcing his death. Cruel, it was. Downright cruel.

She shook herself as she approached the little house. It wouldn't do to let the boys see her downhearted. Things had been hard enough for them since their pa left. This past year, knowing he wouldn't ever come home, had been rough on all of them.

The bottom step was loose. She ought to fix it—or challenge Fred to fix it. That's what she'd do. He was learning to use his father's tools and take care of their place. She was the only one here to teach him those things now. Unless this wild mail-order husband idea played out well and she found another man willing to help her shoulder the burden.

She opened the door. The house was quiet. The boys normally played outside and met her on the lane. As she stepped inside, she looked toward the kitchen end of the front room, where the cookstove sat—Rodney's pride and joy when he'd presented it to her five years ago.

Maggie stopped in her tracks. A strange man sat at her kitchen table. Her heart pounded. Why had the boys let him in? She had an impression of shaggy, windblown brown hair, a week's growth of beard, and worn, inexpensive clothes.

He started to rise, but Fred said sternly, in his best imitation of his father's voice, "Sit down, mister."

Then she noticed the shotgun. Fred had propped the barrel on the back of the chair she usually sat in, across from the stranger, to help him hold it steady. How long had he stood there, menacing the man?

"Fred, what's this?" She asked, setting her basket on a small stand near the door.

"This here's Sam Cayford," Fred said.

Benjy charged toward her, his face flushed. "Mama, what took you so long? We got you a husband!"

Chapter 2

With a cautious glance at Fred, Sam decided it was best to stay seated. He offered the boys' mother an apologetic smile.

"I'm sorry, ma'am. It wasn't my intention to bust in on your home like this."

She eyed him narrowly then frowned at Fred. "Why do you have the gun out, Fred?"

"To make sure he don't get away."

"Has he done something wrong?" she asked.

She was pretty, and her righteous suspicion made her beautiful, even. Her hair was golden, a shade darker than Fred's. The china blue eyes were the same. She wore a threadbare gray-and-black striped dress. Probably one she made herself, Sam thought, not because it looked poorly made—quite the opposite. But this woman looked smart enough to make nice clothing that fit her perfectly. A brighter color would have done her more justice, but then, she was one of those war widows, wasn't she? That was why her sons thought she needed a husband.

"Nothin'," Fred said. "Not that I know of."

"Then why are you pointing that thing at him?"

Fred shrugged.

"Put it down." When the boy hesitated, she said, "Now."

At last Fred turned the shotgun's barrel slightly away, so that it pointed toward the window, not at Sam's heart.

"Thank you, ma'am," he said in as genial a tone as he could muster. "I tried to explain to the boys that I was just passing through and I meant no harm."

"How long have you been here?"

"I guess about twenty minutes or a half hour. Young Benjamin put my horse in your barn."

She looked down at Benjy, who clung to her arm.

"He's got a awful pretty bay horse, Mama. It's a good'un."

"Why did you stop here?" she asked, still not moving from her position just inside the doorway.

"Well, I didn't, actually," Sam said. "I stopped at the stream, up the road a bit, to water my horse. Young Fred here got the drop on me. He's pretty clever, this one."

She turned her gaping face toward Fred. "You forced this man to come here? You threatened him?"

"No, Mama, I didn't threaten. I just told him to follow Benjy."

"And held the gun on him the whole time," his mother said a bit testily.

Fred frowned but said nothing.

"Mister—sir, I'm so sorry." She stepped toward Sam, her face now all regret and shame for her sons' antics. "Can you forgive them? They're good boys."

"I'm sure they were trying to help." Sam almost smiled, remembering Fred's words about getting her a husband, but the seriousness of the situation restrained him. The boy could have blown his head off without meaning to. And why did he think his ma needed help finding a man, anyway? She was smart enough to take care of that herself and pretty enough to find a man if she wanted one.

She walked around the table.

"Give me that." She took the shotgun from Fred and rested it with the butt on the floor and the business end pointing toward the ceiling. "Now explain yourself."

"We went huntin'," Fred said with a note of stubbornness in his voice.

His mother glanced about the room. "I don't see any rabbits, and besides, you're not supposed to take the gun out without me saying so."

Fred scowled and looked down at the floor. "Well, we bagged us a new daddy."

The woman's cheeks went scarlet. "I don't need you bringing me potential husbands, Frederick Piner."

"But you went to that meeting to—"

"Never mind about that." She threw Sam a quick glance then looked sternly back at her son. "You put this shotgun where it belongs, and while you're in the corner, you see if you can find your manners and put them on."

Relieved that things seemed to be getting back to normal, Sam stood. "Well, I'd best be getting on my way, Mrs—I'm sorry, I don't even know your name."

"I'm Maggie Piner, and I do apologize for my boys."

"Think nothing of it, ma'am." Sam reached for his hat, which rested on the table.

"Would you like something to eat?" Maggie asked. "I think there's some biscuits and gravy left from dinner, if the boys haven't been into it."

"You don't have to do that."

"I wish I could do more. I'd invite you to stay for supper, but I know you want to get to your destination, and there's three hours or so of good daylight left."

Sam couldn't help smiling. She was so pretty, and a tiny bit nervous, he thought. She was trying to seem confident, but he reckoned she was insecure on the inside.

"Well, I . . . I guess I could use a drink."

"Sure. We have good water. I'm sorry I don't have any coffee."

"That's all right," Sam said. Did she dislike coffee, or had she run out and not replenished her supply because money was tight? A cup would sure taste good right about now, before he hit the trail again, but he would settle for water. He wouldn't mind learning a little bit more about this charming woman, either.

She picked up a bucket from the floor beside the stove. "Boys, run out and bring some fresh, cool water for Mr. Cayford."

Fred came reluctantly to take the pail.

"You can get his horse out, too," Maggie said. "He'll be leaving soon. Fred, you do that while Benjy fetches water."

The boys scurried out the door, and she took a thick white china cup down from a shelf.

"They won't be long. I wish I had Benjy's cake made so you could have some." She threw him a timid glance. "It's his birthday."

"Oh? How old is he?"

"Nine today. He's a good boy. But I should start making the cake now."

"Don't let me keep you," Sam said. He was suddenly uncomfortable, but he couldn't very well refuse the water now to get out of her way.

"If you don't mind, I'll start putting it together." She walked over to the stand where she had left the basket and came back with a small paper packet. She threw him a tiny smile. "My sugar's in here. I couldn't buy a whole sack, but I got enough for Benjy's cake."

She got out a large yellow crockery bowl and set it on the end of the table, stooped over a small barrel, and came back with a big measuring cup full of flour.

"A boy ought to have a cake on his birthday," she said, "if nothing else."

Sam wondered if that meant Benjy would get nothing but his cake. How long had Mr. Piner been gone? If he died in the war, more than a year. Perhaps several years. It must be hard for the widow and her kids. And yet, she kept a neat, pleasant house. Her boys weren't chubby, but they didn't look starved either, and their clothes were whole and neat.

The door opened, and Fred entered with the water bucket. He set it down by the stove and set the dipper in it.

"Give Mr. Cayford a drink," his mother said absently. Then, as Fred obeyed, she straightened and eyed him sharply. "Where's Benjy? I told him to get the water while you got Mr. Cayford's horse ready for him."

Fred filled the white mug with water and brought it to the table, setting it squarely in front of Sam before he faced his mother.

"He's gone to get the preacher."

"What?" Maggie dropped her wooden spoon. It clattered into the yellow bowl. "Why on earth did he do that? It's more than a mile to Reverend Smith's house. I don't want your little brother walking that far alone."

"He's not walkin'." Fred raised his chin. "He rode Sam's horse."

Maggie stared at him as though she couldn't believe her ears. "Frederick Daniel Piner! Why on earth would Benjy ride off on Mr. Cayford's horse? And why to the reverend's house? We don't need him."

"Sure we do." A note of defiance crept into Fred's voice. He glanced sidelong at Sam then back at Maggie. "We need him to marry you and Sam."

Sam's stomach did a strange lurch, sort of the way he felt when a horse bucked hard and he knew there was no way to recover, that within a few seconds at most he was going to hit the ground hard.

Maggie whirled around and grabbed another wooden spoon from a drawer. She turned with it raised in her hand. "That's enough of this nonsense, Fred. You get up to your bed, and you stay there until I tell you that you can come down."

Fred drew in a quick breath. He looked at Sam. Sam looked away. He wasn't going to give the boy any help in this escapade.

"I mean it," Maggie said, advancing on the boy. "You may be twelve years old, but you're not too big for a spanking. Not if you're going to behave like this to our guest. And bringing the reverend all the way over here for nothing. If your father was here, he'd tan your hide."

Tears made the boys eyes glisten. "If Papa was here, you wouldn't need a husband."

Maggie gasped.

Sam stood and cleared his throat. "I'd say that's about enough on that subject, Fred. Best do as your ma says."

"Yes," Maggie choked out. "Get up in that loft, right now!"

She brandished the spoon again. Fred threw a look of bitter disappointment Sam's way. *Traitor*, his shining eyes seemed to say. He turned on his heel and marched to the ladder in the corner and climbed up it, his back stiff with outrage.

But he went. That was something, Sam thought. He wasn't a bad boy. He wanted something good for his ma. It made him feel a little warmer inside to know Fred thought he would be a good thing for the family.

"Thank you," Maggie whispered.

"He meant no harm." Sam looked her up and down.

She still stood with the spoon raised at shoulder height, staring after her son. Slowly, she lowered it. Color flooded her cheeks, and she seemed unable to meet his gaze. "I am so sorry. The boys can be a handful, but they've never outright disobeyed me like this. I've taught them better."

Sam considered his words carefully before speaking. He didn't want to insult her or upset her further, but perhaps there was some truth in what the boy had said—or at least, Fred believed it was true.

"He seems to feel there's some great need here."

Maggie's breath squeezed out of her, and her body sank a little, her confident pose collapsing until she stood meek and defeated with the spoon dangling loosely from her fingers. When she looked up at him, tears glistened in her eyes.

"He frets more than he should. A boy that age shouldn't have to shoulder the worries of a whole family. He wants to take his father's place, you see."

Sam couldn't keep his lips from twitching. "That's not such a bad attitude, but it seemed to me that he was mighty anxious for *me* to take his father's place."

Maggie's eyes snapped up to meet his. She looked horror stricken for a moment, but when Sam smiled, she softened.

"I guess he did. He oughtn't to have brought you—or anyone else—into this. I can handle it. If not here, then somewhere else."

"What do you mean?" Sam asked.

She hesitated.

After a moment, he said softly, "Why'n't you go on making your cake, Mrs. Piner? And maybe you can tell me a little bit about your situation. The preacher's coming, and it seems I ought to know what to tell him."

"Oh, I don't know. . ."

He wasn't sure if she was going to crumple or not, but after a moment she seemed to find new strength.

"You can go now if you want. I'll speak to the reverend. You needn't stop to explain anything."

"That's all right. I've got to wait for my horse anyway." Sam sat down and placed his hands on the table. "Maybe you can tell me a little bit about your late husband."

"Rodney." She looked into the middle distance between them when she spoke his name. "He went to fight three years ago. That's the last we saw him. Word came early in '65, not long after the truce." She blinked back tears. "He was a good man."

"I'm very sorry," Sam said.

She dashed away a tear and turned to a cupboard nearby. She came back a moment later with two eggs in her hands. One was plump and brown, the other was smaller and speckled. She gave a rueful chuckle. "Those hens have kept us going when we couldn't get meat. We're down to four now, though." Her brow wrinkled.

Another cause for worry, Sam thought. "How many'd you start with?"

"At one time I had two dozen, but. . .the foxes."

He nodded. "They're heartless."

She met his gaze then. "I'm likely to lose the ranch, Mr. Cayford. I didn't tell the boys, but Fred found out somehow. I think he saw the notice I got from the bank. Or maybe he overheard something. I don't know, but he's taken on this big worry. When I said I'd consider going in on the mail-order husband project, I guess he saw it as a solution. He thinks a man could put this place in order—with his and Benjy's help, of course."

"Is that how you see it?"

"I don't know. I've been to a couple of meetings. Some of the ladies are counting on it. Risking everything, it seems to me. I mean, what if I agreed to it and the man I got was just in it for the property?"

Sam nodded.

"That wouldn't help pay the mortgage or the taxes. And it wouldn't help the boys learn to be men." Maggie cracked the eggs into her bowl and stirred.

He cleared his throat, which seemed a little tight. He heard a small rustling sound from the loft overhead, but he didn't look up. It was easy to see how Fred knew about things, though. If Maggie spilled her heart to a friend in this kitchen, her boys probably heard every word. And if she cried in the nighttime, Fred would know.

"Hard to judge a person's character on first meeting," he said.

"That's what I think." Maggie nodded and added a few more things to her mixing bowl.

"So. . ." She looked up, and Sam continued. "You and Mr. Piner had a mortgage when he left?"

She stopped stirring. "He left me enough, we thought, to keep up the payments. We didn't know he'd be gone so long." She blinked hard. "When he died, I couldn't keep paying. I sold off the livestock, and I picked up a few jobs, sewing and cleaning, but it's not enough. It's gotten to where I'll probably have to let this place go and move into town where I can work steady."

"That's too bad," Sam said. "Your husband wanted to build up a cattle ranch here?"

She nodded. "A hundred and sixty acres. It's not bad land. But Mr. Grant says—"

"Mr. Grant?"

"The banker." Maggie winced as she said it. "The debt is bigger than I knew, or so he tells me."

"And he'll foreclose on you?"

She nodded. "He's making threats." As though suddenly conscious of her son's proximity, she glanced upward. "But we're going to be all right," she said firmly.

"Sure you are." Sam picked up his mug. It was empty, and he put it down again. It sounded like Maggie needed a man with some cash in the bank—not some drifting cowpuncher like him. Fred might have a notion to help his ma, but he'd picked the wrong man.

Movement overhead made them both look toward the ladder. Fred was slowly coming down. When he reached the bottom, he turned to face them.

"Mama, if you'd marry this fella, there wouldn't be a problem."

Maggie's mouth tightened. "I told you to stay up there, Fred."

"But Pa told me to take care of you. And the best way I can see to do that is to find you another husband. I know I can't do the ranching work by myself. You told me that before we sold the herd. We had to do it. I understand that. But if Sam stayed on. . ."

"Freddie." Maggie's eyes had that watery look again. She walked over to her son and put her hand on his thin shoulder. "I know you want the best for our family, and I'm praying every day that God will show us what to do. If things don't work out for us to keep the ranch, then we'll just have to go elsewhere."

"But with Sam. . ."

"No, Son. You don't understand. It's going to take more than hard work. We can't pay the bank, and I doubt Sam could, either." She threw him a rueful glance.

"She's right," Sam said, hating to admit it. "I'm flat broke. That's why I was riding through here. Heading for Dodge, looking for a job."

Sam's eyes brightened. "We could hire you."

Maggie shook her head. "Fred, we couldn't pay him."

Fred opened his mouth and closed it. In the silence that followed, they all heard it—hoofbeats on the lane.

"Sounds like Reverend Smith's here." Maggie sounded more cheerful, but Sam could tell it was an act. She crossed the room and flung the door open then closed it just as quickly. She turned toward Sam, her face white.

"It's not the pastor. It's Rutherford Grant."

Chapter 3

Maggie started to untie her apron, but stilled her hands. Why should she make herself look nice for Rutherford Grant? The man was doing his best to ruin her life. Not that it wasn't already ruined, with Rodney dead, but he wanted to take their home away from her and the boys. She was already poor, but he wanted to take away the land, the garden, the chickens, the little bit of sustaining property they claimed.

It should have been hers by now. Rod had left her with enough money to pay six months on the mortgage. She had paid another eight months by selling off their cattle a few at a time. Somewhere in there, she'd gotten word of Rod's death. She'd managed to eke out two more payments, and after that she knew it was hopeless.

Sam stood. "Do you want me to leave?"

That was a silly question, she thought. He didn't have his horse back yet. But he could go outside while she talked to the banker.

"No," Maggie said quickly. The last thing she wanted was to be in the house alone with Mr. Grant. "Please stay."

He nodded.

Fred ran over to stand beside his mother. "Don't let him send us to the orphanage, Mama!"

Maggie caught her breath. So he had heard that, too. She had hoped the boys had missed out on Grant's latest suggestion—that she send the boys to the orphanage in Kansas City and find employment for herself in the city.

"Hush now, Fred."

He ran to the corner and snatched up his father's shotgun.

"Don't let him in!" He hefted the gun and pointed it unsteadily at the door.

"Here now, son." Sam took a step toward him. "You can't go pointing loaded weapons at folks like that."

Fred backed up a couple of steps and ducked his head as he faded into the shadows under the ladder. The barrel of the shotgun poked out a second later, through the rungs. "I've got you covered, Mama."

"Now, Fred, that's dangerous!"

Before she could say more, a firm knock sounded on the door. She looked at Sam.

"Best open it," he said quietly.

She glanced at the ladder. If she hadn't known Fred was there, she wouldn't have seen him. She hauled in a deep breath and pulled the door open, keeping her body between the opening and Fred.

"Mr. Grant. Is there something I can do for you?" She tried to keep her voice pleasant.

"Not unless you can make a substantial payment on your loan," the banker replied gruffly.

He didn't look any friendlier than he had the last time. He'd taken to coming out here once a week lately, unless she stopped in at the bank in town. His gray hair and fancy clothes were supposed to make him look distinguished, she supposed—and trustworthy. But she wouldn't trust this man farther than she could throw him.

"I. . .I can't," she said. "My situation hasn't changed."

"Well then, you can prepare to move out." Grant reached into his coat and drew out a folded sheet of paper. "This is your eviction notice. The bank will take possession one week from today."

"What? A week? That's not enough time for the boys and me to—" She looked numbly at the folded paper he thrust toward her.

"That's right. And if your things aren't out of here, I'll hire some men to come and throw them out. You'd best make arrangements before then, Mrs. Piner."

"But I—please! Give us more time." A tear betrayed Maggie and rolled down her cheek, and she swiped at it.

Grant shook his head. "More time? I've dealt with trash like you before. You think if you just don't leave and cry a little, you don't have to live up to your contract. Well, save the tears. You'd best be out in seven days, or I'll have you arrested." He returned to his horse and swung into the saddle.

Sam had heard about enough of this. He stepped over to the ladder and grabbed the shotgun's barrel. Before Fred could do more than let out a squawk, Sam wrenched the gun away from him. He strode to the door and stepped out into the sunlight beside Maggie. She looked mighty fine in the light of day, and her scent wafted to him—sun-warmed meadows and baking bread. But he couldn't think about that now. He leveled the shotgun at the banker's fancy waistcoat.

"That's not a very nice way to speak to a lady, mister."

Grant stiffened in the saddle. His gaze flickered over Sam and went back to Maggie's face.

"Who's this?"

"He—" Maggie glanced at Sam. Her eyes were wide, and her face was tightened. She looked plain terrified, and she wrung her hands. "I—he's my—we're going to be married."

Grant's shoulders relaxed a little bit. "Why didn't you say so?" He looked at Sam. "I'm Rutherford Grant, of the Turtle Springs Bank. Do you intend to pay off this woman's mortgage?"

Sam kept the shotgun pointed at him. "I don't do business like this, mister. Go on back to the bank. And don't you ever speak to Mrs. Piner like that again."

Grant scowled at him. "Does this mean you'll come into the bank and discuss it?"

"Get moving." Sam raised the gun barrel just a hair.

Grant got the message. "I'll expect to see you at the bank within forty-eight hours." He wheeled his horse and urged it into a canter. Sam kept his position until the rider was out of sight. Then he slowly lowered the shotgun.

"Thank you." Maggie's voice cracked. "I'm sorry."

"You weren't serious, then." Sam tried to see her eyes, but she wasn't looking at him. She stared down at the flat stone that made the doorstep. Her shoulders quivered beneath the thick green material of her dress.

"I didn't mean to lie," she choked out. "I only thought I could maybe buy us more time. And now I've dragged you into it. I shouldn't have told a falsehood to get out of a bad situation. I'm truly sorry."

Fred charged through the front door. "You did it, Sam! You made him go away."

"Well yeah," Sam conceded. He set the butt of the shotgun down on the doorstep.

"Mama, I told you he was the right one!" Fred seized Maggie's hands. "You said you'd marry Sam."

Maggie sighed. "Freddie, this doesn't change a thing. Now, come on, we have to start packing."

"No! Sam—"

"We still owe the bank," Maggie said tightly. "We're still going to lose the property."

"But you told Mr. Grant that Sam would marry you. Maybe he can pay our bill."

"Now, Fred," Maggie began.

Sam laid a hand on the boy's shoulder. Fred had to quit thinking he could save their home. Maybe Maggie would find someone with deeper pockets than him through this mail-order husband thing. He almost regretted the thought of her marrying someone else—a stranger—just to keep the ranch. But then, he was a stranger, too, and he had no right to wish anything for her.

"I'm sorry, Fred. If I could help you, I would." He knew as he spoke that it was true. "But I don't hardly have a cent. That's why I was riding through here, looking for a job. I told you—I'm broke, and I can't pay off that mortgage."

Fred's face fell then he looked up again, still hopeful. "Maybe you can get a job in town. Maybe—"

"Stop it, Fred," Maggie said sharply. "Mr. Cayford needs to get on his way, and he'll do that as soon as your brother brings his horse back." She looked anxiously down the lane.

She'd said the reverend's house was a mile away. Sam caught her tension. The boy should have been back by now.

"Maybe the preacher had gone somewhere, and Benjy had to track him down." Maggie glanced sidelong at him, and Sam shrugged, feeling useless again. Nothing was going to relieve her anxiety until she was settled with her boys and a steady, hardworking man, preferably one that could pay the bank enough to stop Grant from bothering them about the mortgage.

Maggie drew in a deep breath and turned to face Fred. "I made a mistake, Fred. I lied to Mr. Grant. I've asked God to forgive me, and I know He will. Mr. Cayford says he'll forgive me, too, because I lied about him. It wasn't true, and Sam isn't going to marry me."

"But you said—"

Maggie held up one hand. "Uh-uh. We have to do what's right. What do you think God wants us to do right now?"

Fred's chin sank to his chest, and he wouldn't meet her gaze.

"We have to let Mr. Cayford go," she said, so quietly Sam could barely hear her.

Fred looked over at Sam. "Won't you help us, Sam? Even if you don't have any money, you could—"

Drumming hoofbeats drowned out his words. They all looked toward the lane. Sam recognized his horse, Rocker, first, and then the small boy clinging to the saddle.

"It's Benjy," Fred said.

Maggie gasped. "He'll break his neck."

Sam handed Fred the shotgun and stepped forward to intercept the horse.

"*Whoa*, Rocker. *Whoa*, boy."

The bay gelding stopped so fast he nearly sat down, and Benjy tumbled off, landing in the dust at Sam's feet. Rocker snorted, jumped up, and skittered off a couple of yards toward the side. Sam reached down and picked Benjy up as Maggie ran toward them.

"You all right, kid?" Sam asked.

Panting, Benjy nodded.

"What ails you?" Maggie cried.

"It's Preacher Smith. He's hurt bad."

Chapter 4

Maggie knelt before Benjy and drew him toward her. "What happened?" Still panting, his face red, Benjy gasped out, "I got there and I couldn't find him. I was going to ride over to the church and see if he was there, and I heard something funny. Like a ghost moaning." Benjy paused, a worried frown creasing his brow.

"That must have scared you," Sam said.

Maggie glanced up at him. She didn't know Sam well—hardly at all—but he had a way with boys.

"Yes," she said. "What did you do?"

Benjy swallowed hard. "I sneaked up to the porch and looked in the window."

Fred had come to stand beside them, holding the shotgun with the muzzle pointed skyward, as Sam had. "What'd you see?" he asked his little brother.

"Nothin' at first. But the noise was louder."

"Did you go inside?" Maggie asked.

"I was afeared to. You ain't supposed to go in someone's house unless they ask you." Benjy looked to his mother for approval on this statement.

"That's right, but if someone's hurt. . ."

"He didn't know he was hurt then," Fred said.

"Nope. Didn't." Benjy shook his head. "It was making me shiver all over, and I thought maybe I ought to hightail it back here."

"Why didn't you?" Maggie asked.

"I dunno. Sounded like words, I guess."

"So you could tell it was human?" Sam asked.

Benjy peered up at him, puzzled, as though wondering why the drifter wasn't sitting in the kitchen with Fred keeping him at the end of the shotgun barrel.

"Not sure, 'xactly, but. . ."

"But what?" his mother prompted.

"Went around back."

"And?"

"Louder. It was real loud then." He looked uneasily at Maggie. "I opened the back door."

"That was brave of you," Sam said quickly.

Benjy's eyes pleaded for mercy. "Didn't mean no harm."

"It's all right, Son," Maggie said, patting his arm. "What did you find?"

"The preacher. He was lying on the floor yellin'. He-e-e-elp! He-e-e-elp!" Benjy gave the words a spectral wail.

"He must have been hurtin'," Sam said.

Benjy ducked his head. "I went over to him, and he said, 'Benjamin Piner, I don't know what you're doing here, but thank God you've come.' And he said to get somebody to help him."

"Was he bleeding?" Sam asked.

Benjy shook his head. "Not that I saw. Said he thought he'd broke his leg. Something about his cat."

"He's got a big ol' black cat," Fred said. "To keep the mice down."

Maggie nodded. "Festus. That cat is always underfoot. I've heard the reverend say one day he'd trip over it and break his neck. I guess that day has come. We'd best get over there."

"I'll go," Sam said. "Benjy, will you ride with me and show me where the preacher lives?"

Benjy turned wide eyes on his mother. She stood and gave his shoulder a reassuring pat.

"You go," Maggie said. "Show Mr. Cayford. Fred and I can walk over."

"No need for that," Sam said.

"He might need a doctor."

"We can ride for one, can't we, Benjy?"

The boy nodded uncertainly. Sam picked him up and plopped him on the saddle then mounted and adjusted Benjy in his perch. Sam tipped his hat to Maggie.

"Don't fret now. We'll be back as soon as we can."

"Mama?" Benjy sounded frightened, so Maggie stepped up to the horse's side.

"What is it?"

"We don't. . ." Benjy jerked his chin slightly and whispered, "We don't know this guy."

Maggie smiled. "It's all right. Sam and I are friends now."

Sam rode on the warmth of her words, holding Benjy around the waist. The boy guided him back toward the little town of Turtle Springs and down a side road. When they came to a small clapboard house, he pointed, and Sam turned Rocker into the yard.

"This it?"

Benjy nodded.

Sam swung down and reached up to pull the boy off, but Benjy was already feeling for the stirrup with his foot, so Sam let him dismount on his own.

"Can you watch Rocker? That's my horse's name."

"Uh-huh."

Sam hurried to the front door. The sun had fallen behind the trees, and the shadows were long, but no light shone from within the house. He gave a peremptory knock.

"Mr. Smith?"

No answer came, and he tried the latch. The door swung open. He walked into a small sitting room with an upright stove to one side, a horsehair settee flanked by a small side table, and an upholstered chair. Sam walked on through to the kitchen doorway. Enough light came through the single window at the back for him to see the large man lying on the floor.

"Mr. Smith?"

Still no answer, and Sam's pulse quickened. Maybe the minister was hurt worse than Benjy had thought. And they had wasted a good ten minutes talking about it in Maggie's dooryard!

He strode across the room and knelt by the prone man.

"Sir?"

He touched the man's shoulder, and he moaned. Relief flooded through Sam.

"Mr. Smith, I'm Sam Cayford. I'm—I'm a friend of the Piners. Benjy brought me."

"Thank God," the man choked out. "It's my leg. I think it's bad."

"All right, is there a doctor in town?"

"Yes, Dr. Carter, on the main street, past the mercantile."

"I'll fetch him, but can I do anything first to make you more comfortable?"

"Water."

"Of course. Hold on." Sam rose and looked around. He spotted a lamp and quickly lit it. Then he was able to locate the minister's water bucket, half full, and a cup. He brought the drink to him and helped him raise his head and shoulders enough to sip. Smith let out a yelp on the first move, and Sam paused.

"Easy, sir." He held the cup carefully to the preacher's lips so he could reach it without moving further then he eased him back onto the floor.

"Thank you."

"You're welcome." Sam studied the lines of his legs. "You look mighty uncomfortable, but I don't know as I should move you. They say it can make things worse."

"Please," Smith gasped. "I've been here for hours. If you can just get me a pillow from my bed."

"Surely." Sam rose and carried the lamp with him. The small bedroom opened off the kitchen. He plucked the pillow from the cot and pulled the top blanket off and carried them to the kitchen.

"I'm sorry, we're going to have to leave you again," he said.

"I'm comforted," the doctor managed.

Sam left the lamp burning low and hurried outside. Benjy crouched on the ground in the dooryard, holding the end of Rocker's trailing reins and watching the horse crop grass.

"Come on, Benjy. We're off to fetch Dr. Carter. Do you know him?"

Benjy nodded. This time Sam climbed to the saddle and swung the boy up behind him. He found the doctor's office without trouble. If only little Benjy had realized it, he'd have served the preacher better if he'd fetched the doctor first. Reverend Smith's house was closer to the physician's office than it was to the Piner ranch.

He swung his leg over the front of the saddle and jumped down. Handing Benjy the reins, he said, "Stay here." He ran up the steps to the doctor's porch and pounded on the door. A few seconds later, a dour woman of about forty opened the door.

"The door's always open, young man."

"Oh. Sorry. Is the doctor in?"

"He's eating his supper." Her face looked fierce as a bulldog's.

"Well, the preacher's hurt bad," Sam said. "Broke his leg. He's lying on his kitchen floor. Been there for hours."

The woman's eyebrows shot up. "Reverend Smith?"

"Yes, ma'am."

"Oh dear. Come in." She turned her head and yelled, "Lawrence! It seems Mr. Smith has injured himself." She walked through the outer room, which was set up with several chairs and benches so that people could sit comfortably while waiting to see the doctor.

Sam followed her down a short hall, through a door, and into the family kitchen. The doctor sat hunched over the table, his plate before him.

"Lawrence," the woman said, "this gentleman says Reverend Smith needs you. Urgently, of course."

Dr. Carter glanced up at him. "Pardon me if I eat while you tell me about it. I have to take the opportunity when I can."

Sam nodded. "My name's Cayford. I was at the Piners' place when one of the boys came in and said the preacher was hurt. I rode over there, and he thinks his leg is broken. He's in a lot of pain."

Dr. Carter swallowed. "Sounds like I'll need some help. Can you go back there with me?"

"Yes, sir."

"Good. You got a wagon?"

Sam shook his head.

"Then I'll have to get someone to take one out. Maybe you can step over to the blacksmith's? He'd probably hitch up and go out there with us. We'll have to bring Mr. Smith here, since he has no one living with him to care for him."

"I'll go now, if you like," Sam said. "If the blacksmith's agreeable, I'll go back to the preacher's house and meet you there."

He got directions for the blacksmith's shop and went out. Benjy was drooping in Rocker's saddle.

"Wake up kid," he said, gently shaking Benjy's foot. "We've got more riding to do." Sam mounted and guided Rocker to the smithy, where the proprietor quickly agreed to take a wagon to the minister's home.

"I'll meet you there as soon as I get my team hitched," he said.

Even Sam was tired by the time they reached Reverend Smith's house. Twilight shrouded the yard, but faint light from the lamp in the kitchen on the back of the house seeped out through the front room's windows.

Sam climbed down once more and lifted Benjy from the saddle. He carried him inside and laid him on the preacher's settee. Maggie must be worried sick by now, but he didn't dare take her word until the doctor arrived. He went to the kitchen and found the reverend lying where he'd left him, sleeping fitfully. Sam turned the lamp up a little and went about making coffee as quietly as he could.

Within minutes, Dr. Carter drove up in his buggy, followed by the blacksmith with his wagon. Sam met them at the front door and led them into the kitchen. The doctor quickly assessed Smith's injury, rousing the minister at his first touch. He administered a dose of laudanum, after he proceeded to put splints on the broken leg and bandaged it.

"Let's move him on a blanket," he told the others. "His femur is broken."

"What's that?" the blacksmith asked.

"The long thigh bone."

"Ah."

"Too bad we don't have a stretcher, but we'll work with what we have."

They moved the sedated man onto the blanket. Sam and the blacksmith lifted it and carried Mr. Smith out to the wagon. When they had headed off to town, Sam went back inside. Benjy was sound asleep in the parlor. Sam gulped down a cup of the tepid coffee he had prepared, turned out the lamp, and lugged Benjy outside.

"Is the doc here?" Benjy muttered.

"Here and gone, kid." Sam hoisted him into the saddle and climbed up behind him. Rocker seemed eager to jog back to Maggie's house, but Sam was bone tired. When they reached the little ranch house and he saw a warm yellow light spilling out the front windows, he felt as though he'd reached home.

Chapter 5

Fred must have heard Rocker's hoofbeats. He threw open the front door and ran out to meet them. Sam was glad to see he wasn't toting the shotgun. He dismounted and eased Benjy down. The boy was groggy but stood on his own feet.

"What happened?" Fred demanded.

"Not much," Sam replied. "The doc's got Mr. Smith over to his place now. He'll be laid up for a while."

Maggie was in the doorway, looking anxiously toward them. Sam dropped Rocker's reins and walked over to her. The lamplight behind her made her hair glow softly, like a halo.

"I hope you weren't worried," he said. "It took a while, but I think the preacher's taken care of now."

"Thank you." She gave him a tremulous smile. "I finished the cake. Won't you have supper with us? Fred and I have been waiting on you and Benjy."

"I'd best move on," Sam said, but he had no idea where he'd land tonight. He had no money for lodgings, so he'd probably camp down the creek a ways.

"Please," Maggie said. "It's Benjy's birthday." She reached for the younger boy as he tottered toward her. "He looks beat, but I'm sure he'll eat something."

"Nine years old?" Sam asked, mulling the possibilities if he stayed.

"That's right. It's a day he won't forget, I'm sure, what with meeting you and finding Mr. Smith hurt like that."

Sam crouched and looked into Benjy's drooping eyes.

"What do you say, kid? Should I stay and help you eat that birthday cake?"

Benjy hesitated and then nodded. "You ain't mad at us?"

"Mad? Naw." Sam stood. "I'll just put Rocker away, ma'am, if you don't mind."

"Of course. There's a lantern hanging inside the barn door. Show him, Fred." She put her arm around Benjy and turned him inside the house.

Sam walked back to the horse. Fred had already picked up the reins. He handed them to Sam.

"Mama says if I don't apologize to you, I don't get no cake."

"I see." Sam walked slowly beside him toward the small barn, Rocker trailing them.

"So, yeah." Fred rubbed his hair into a bird's nest. "Sorry. I shouldn't have kidnapped you."

Sam smiled. "That's forgiven. You had good intentions. But a man needs to think things through before he acts."

"Right." Fred opened the barn door and fumbled inside for the lantern. A moment later the light sprang out, filling the enclosed space. Sam led Rocker inside. The barn consisted of two empty tie stalls and a walled-off haymow.

"You don't have any horses," he said, but he'd guessed that already.

"Pa took one to war when he went, and we didn't get him back. Ma sold the other one last fall. She said we couldn't feed him over the winter, but I'll bet we coulda."

Sam rested a hand on his shoulder. "She was protecting you, Fred. She probably used the money to make another payment or two on the mortgage."

"What's a mortgage, anyway?" Fred kicked at a tuft of loose straw on the floor.

"It's when the bank lends you money. Likely your pa took the loan when he bought this place, to help pay for it. But you have to pay it back, a little at a time. And if you can't make those payments when you're supposed to, well, the bank gets the ranch."

"That ain't fair."

Sam lifted the stirrup leather and began to undo the cinch strap on his saddle. "Well, in a way it is, but it's hard to explain."

Fred scowled at him. "Mama didn't think it was fair. After Pa died, she said the bank told her we owed more than she thought."

"More than your pa told her they owed?"

"I think she thought the bill was higher than it should be or something. I don't know really."

"Hmm." Sam lifted the stock saddle off Rocker's back. "Where can I put this?"

Fred showed him the short rail where his father's saddle used to rest. "The bridle goes there." He pointed to a nail in the wall. "We got brushes. Can I help brush him?"

"Sure." Sam wondered if Fred was jealous of Benjy's time riding the horse. "Have you got any feed?"

Fred shook his head. "There's a little hay left."

"That'll have to do, then."

They made Rocker comfortable, and then Sam blew out the lantern. They walked companionably toward the house.

"I wish you really was marryin' Mama," Fred said in the dark dooryard.

"Do you?"

"Yeah. Then you'd stay, and Mr. Grant wouldn't come around and bother her about the money."

"Mmm," Sam said noncommittally.

"And maybe we could get some more cattle."

Sam shook his head. "If I had money for cattle, I'd have my own place and not be looking to hire out to someone else." If only, he thought. It was a nice dream, for a few seconds. And Maggie and the boys being in it made it even more attractive.

They reached the front stoop, and Fred opened the door.

"Sam! Lookit the cake," Benjy cried. The small boy ran toward him and grabbed his hand. "It's got jelly in the middle and powdered sugar on top."

Sam grinned. "Sounds like a fine mouthful, Benjy."

"Stew first," Maggie said sternly, but her smile took away the rebuke.

The stew was light on rabbit and long on potatoes and turnips, but Sam was so hungry he didn't mind. The cornbread was plentiful and tasty—crisp on the outside and tender within. No one offered butter, and he didn't ask for any. The milk cow probably went soon after the beef herd. To his surprise, Maggie brought him a cup of coffee.

The cake was the crowning finish, and Benjy's eyes grew huge as Maggie cut the first piece and set it before him.

"Make a wish," she told him.

Benjy didn't hesitate. "I wish Sam would stay with us."

Sam felt his face heat, and he glanced at Maggie. She was looking at him, too, as though she seconded the wish.

"Thank you, Benjy," Sam said. "That's a mighty fine compliment. But I really can't stay. I've got to find some work soon."

Maggie nodded. "Still, it's late now. It's not much, but you and your horse can bed down in the barn overnight, if you want."

Sam considered that. It made sense, and he'd get to say his good-byes in the morning. He liked the idea. He really didn't want to ride off tonight and leave Maggie and the boys. Truth was, he didn't want to leave at all. If it was within his power, he'd make Benjy's wish come true. But he couldn't do that.

He cleared his throat. "Thank you. I'll just do that."

Fred scowled as he accepted his cake from his mother.

"What's the matter, Fred?" Sam asked. Maybe the boy didn't like the idea of his hanging around so much, since he wasn't marrying into the family.

"I guess Mama'll have to get one of those mail-order husbands after all." He picked up his slab of cake and took a big bite.

"That's enough," Maggie said. "Just finish your cake."

When they had all cleaned their plates, she set the boys to washing up the dishes. Maggie put the food away and brought a cloth to wipe off the table.

"What can I do?" Sam asked.

"You're a guest, Mr. Cayford. You don't need to do anything," Maggie replied.

"I want to. Can I bring in some more water? How about firewood?"

She nodded. "That would be nice. It would save the boys from doing it in the dark, and I'd be ready to get breakfast in the morning, before you ride out."

Sam went about the tasks willingly. They had a well with a sturdy stone wall around it. No doubt Rodney Piner had built it before he went into the army. The wooden bucket splashed into water ten feet below ground. He was glad they had a plentiful supply of good water.

Wood was another question. He surveyed the meager woodpile with misgivings. Of course, it was spring. They'd used up most of their store over the winter, but even if they didn't need to keep a fire at night now, Maggie would need fuel for cooking every day. What was stacked at the side of the house wouldn't last more than a few days, and most of the pieces were small, broken sticks. No good thick, split logs left.

He carried in an armful and went back for another. When he went in, the boys were mounting the ladder to the loft.

Fred looked over his shoulder when the door shut. "Night, Sam."

"Good night, Fred. Benjy."

Benjy paused and turned around on the second rung. "You won't leave without we see you in the morning', will you, Sam?"

"I won't. Your ma said something about breakfast."

"Of course you'll take breakfast with us," Maggie said.

Sam nodded and smiled as he watched the boys continue up the ladder. When they'd disappeared from view, he said quietly, "I hate to eat out of your stores, ma'am."

"Don't you fret about that," she said.

"Well, is there a place where I could cut you some wood? I'd like to repay you, and your woodpile looks a mite sparse."

"Thank you, but I have to pay a neighbor to do that for me. I don't have a draft horse anymore, and it's more than you could do with Rocker. I let the next rancher cut some wood on my place and give me half, all split."

"All right." Sam guessed there wasn't much more he could do.

Maggie lifted the coffeepot and shook it a little. "There's about one cup of coffee left. You want it, Mr. Cayford?"

"Please call me Sam. And not if you usually drink it yourself."

"Not this late at night," she said. "I have to sleep so I can get up in the morning and keep up with those boys."

Sam smiled. "Sure, I'll take it then."

She poured what was left into a mug and handed it to him.

"There's a bench outside, where my Rodney liked to sit in the evening. The stove makes the house too hot sometimes, and he liked to get the breeze."

"Thank you." Sam hesitated. Was she shooing him out so she could retire, too? Or was she offering him a place where they could talk without the boys hearing them? He looked into her eyes. She hadn't gone back to her busywork. "Would. . .would you like to join me for a few minutes?"

"Thank you, I would," Maggie said.

She led him outside. He'd seen the bench before, to one side of the stoop, but hadn't taken much notice of it. It was on the opposite end of the house from the loft, though, and he saw it now as the parents' refuge, but close enough so they could still hear if the children called out to them.

He sat down beside Maggie, very conscious of her nearness. He took a sip of the coffee. It tasted bitter, but he didn't care.

Maggie sat in silence, looking out over what must have been their pasture. It was all overgrown now, and bushes were encroaching on the field. But the view of the night sky was still fantastic. He could almost picture the ranch with a herd of fat cattle grazing out there, along with a team of draft horses.

"This is a nice spot," he said.

"Yes."

They were silent for a few minutes. Sam took another swallow from his cup.

"The boys will miss you," she said.

"They're good boys."

"Yes."

Sam smiled. This conversation needed a boost. He looked over at her and said slowly, "What about this mail-order husband thing? Are all the widows in town supporting it?"

Her chin rose. "Some. I'm not sure about it. I just don't want to risk getting some no-good man. My boys. . ."

"Yes." Sam knew what she meant, even though she didn't finish. She didn't want some bounder in charge of her boys, teaching them bad ways or being mean to them. And what if she got a lazy man who wouldn't haul and split plenty of wood for her? Who wouldn't do the careful work Rodney had to build this snug little house and the barn and the masonry wall around the well?

All sorts of things ran through his mind, but no matter how he looked at it, he needed to get a job and earn some money.

"They told me in town to check at the Russell ranch and the Therron place. Do you know about them?"

Maggie nodded. "You might hire on at one of those."

"I guess I'll try. If they don't take me, I reckon I'll head for Dodge City."

"They'd be foolish not to take you."

Sam eyed her carefully. "That right?"

"I think so. You're honest, and you don't lose your temper easily. You can see what needs to be done, and you do it."

"Thank you." He grinned. "I feel as though I ought to ask you for a reference."

Maggie gave a little chuckle that warmed him. "If they need help, they'll hire you."

"That gives me hope." He drained the coffee mug. "And I hope. . . I hope things work out for you and the boys, Maggie." He held out the mug to her.

She took it. "Thank you. I'd like to know what happens to you—if you get work in these parts or not. I guess that's asking a lot."

"No, I could drop you a line. Does Turtle Springs have a post office?"

"Yes. Send a postcard to Margaret Piner, Turtle Springs, Kansas, if you can spare the penny."

"I'll find one somewhere," Sam said, and he meant every word.

They sat for a few more minutes, not talking, looking at the stars and the pasture, rippling in the light breeze. Sam wanted to look at Maggie, but he didn't dare.

He didn't want her to feel as though he was staring at her, but he would if he could.
Finally, she stirred. "I'd best go in."
He stood and offered her a hand, pulling her up. Her hand was warm in his, and he hated to let it go.
"Thank you," he said. "It was nice being with a family again."
She smiled in the starlight. "We enjoyed it. Good night."
She went inside and shut the door. Sam took a deep breath and turned toward the barn. It was going to be hard, riding out of here in the morning.

Chapter 6

Maggie heard the boys rustling around in the loft before full daylight. She rose, wishing she had risen before them. She wanted time to prepare a full breakfast for Sam before he left.

Just thinking about it made her sad, which was silly. He'd been here for less than a day, and already he'd found a place in their hearts. She would miss him, and she knew the boys would, too.

Benjy had seemed scared of him at first, but after riding to Reverend Smith's and the doctor's with him, and then home again, he seemed to have grown attached to Sam. He'd told her how he'd helped get the preacher the help he needed and how he'd let Benjy take care of his horse.

Fred had wanted Sam for his new daddy from the start, only because he was handy. But the more time he spent in Sam's company, the more that desire seemed to grow.

Yes, they were all going to miss him.

She dressed quickly, in the blue cotton dress she usually reserved for Sundays in summer. She owned three dresses—a warm woolen one for winter, a drab calico for everyday, and the blue one, which was only in slightly better condition than the black-and-gray striped one, but made her feel better. When she pulled the blue dress over her head, she felt this was going to be a good day, which was odd, since Sam was leaving today.

In the kitchen, she swiftly built up the fire in the stove. Thanks to Sam, she had plenty of wood this morning. The coffee was next. That had to be ready when Sam was. Pancakes and eggs for the meal, she decided. She didn't have any more meat.

Fred came down the ladder backward.

"Good morning," Maggie called. "Can you check for eggs, please?"

"Yes'm." Fred grabbed the egg basket and went out, shutting the door none too softly. Maybe he hoped Sam would hear it and come find him. Sam was different from Rodney, she mused. Taller, for one thing, and their features were nothing alike. She had noticed, too, that Sam was left-handed. She wondered if that made some things harder for him, but she hadn't thought it polite to ask. He seemed to do all right with his reins, tools, and the shotgun.

Benjy appeared at the top of the ladder, yawning. He sat down with his feet dangling over the edge, toward the top rung.

"Mama, I can't find my socks."

"Well they're not down here. You had them on when you went up last night, so look again." She took stock of her cupboard. She had a few jars of applesauce and plums left from last fall. She chose one of plums. The boys loved them, canned in a sweet sugar syrup. Maybe Sam would like them, too. And she had no sugar left for his coffee, so they would add a little sweetening.

"Morning."

She whirled around at the deep voice. Sam stood in the doorway with the sun behind him. He wore the same clothes he had the day before, and his chin was nearly covered in whiskers. She wondered if he had a razor. She could offer to let him use Rodney's. Or would that insult him? With or without the beginnings of a beard, he was a handsome man.

"Morning. The coffee will be ready directly."

"Thank you. Can I get anything for you?"

"Uh no, I don't think so." Maggie brushed back a wisp of hair. "I sent Fred out for eggs, and I have plenty of water."

He nodded. "I'll just go help Fred then."

"Mama," Benjy called, with frustration filling his voice. "I still can't find my socks."

Sam grinned. "Or maybe I'll climb up and help Benjamin."

"Oh, would you?" Maggie asked. "That would be wonderful, and it would save me climbing the ladder." She hated climbing up there in her unwieldy skirts.

"Surely." Sam moved to the ladder and climbed it like a cat.

She made herself look away and take out the flour and baking powder for the pancake batter.

Fred came in with his basket. "I only got one egg today."

Maggie frowned. "Are you sure that's all?"

"Pretty sure."

She sighed. "I'll put it in the pancakes, then. We'll just have to eat more pancakes."

"Where's Sam?" Fred asked.

"Helping Benjy find his socks." She looked up at the loft.

Fred dashed to the ladder and scaled it. She heard Sam's cordial greeting and the boys' lower voices then a shrill laugh from Benjy. She hoped that meant the socks were found.

An hour later, Sam saddled his horse, wishing he could put off the parting longer. But it wouldn't be fair to Maggie—she had work to do. He wondered if Rutherford Grant would ride out here again tomorrow if he didn't go into the bank and make a payment.

He had to quit thinking about that. Maggie's situation was no worse than it had been before he came, and he had held the banker off for a couple more days. That was about all he could do for Maggie.

Once Rocker was ready to go, he turned to the forlorn little group waiting by the stoop. Benjy reached up to him, and Sam bent down to hug him.

"You be good, Benjy. Help your ma."

"I will," Benjy said.

"Fred." Sam straightened and eyed the older boy, searching for a clue to what he wanted out of the farewell.

Fred stuck out his hand, and Sam shook it solemnly, like he would a man's.

"Take care."

Fred nodded. "You, too. Ride easy."

Sam smiled and looked at Maggie. Was that a sheen of tears in her eyes? He knew his own heart was aching at having to leave her and the boys behind. That wasn't right. He barely knew them. And yet, he felt like he knew them well. This parting was a bereavement.

"I'll let you know," he said softly.

Maggie nodded. "Thank you," she whispered. There was no need to say more. Talking would just prolong the pain. The sooner he left, the sooner the boys would forget about him and stop thinking he could help them.

Sam held her gaze for a moment longer then turned away. He swung up on Rocker's back. The three dollars remaining in his pocket seemed to burn. He wanted to give it to them. But that was all he had left, and if he didn't find a job today, he'd need to pay for his food while he prolonged his quest. He tried not to think about what Maggie and the kids would eat tomorrow.

He tipped his hat. The boys waved, and Maggie nodded, standing behind Benjy and clutching his shoulders. That was the way he would remember them as he rode through Turtle Springs, toward the Russell ranch. From what Maggie and the man at the restaurant had told him, that sounded like the most likely outfit to hire him right away. He would not think about the odds of Maggie shedding tears for him as he rode away. He blinked hard. He was riding into the wind, and it sure did sting his eyes.

Maggie checked the boys' hands and faces to make sure they were clean. Reverend Smith had agreed to let the boys wait for her at his house while Maggie went into town for the ladies' meeting. He was home now, five days after his accident. He was starting to hobble about on crutches. The deacons' wives went over by turns to check on him and take him prepared meals.

"Now, remember," she told Fred sternly as they walked toward Reverend Smith's house, "you have to be quiet. Mr. Smith needs to rest, and if he's feeling up to it, he'll be studying."

"Is he going to preach next Sunday?" Fred asked.

"I don't know. But if someone took him to church in their wagon, I guess he could. It might depend on how much pain his leg gives him." She put her hand on Benjy's shoulder. "So, either way, you boys need to be quiet and not disturb him. He said he has books you can look at. And you've got your marbles."

Fred nodded. "We'll be good, Mama. Don't worry about us."

"I'll try not to."

"Are you bringing us home a new pa?" Benjy asked.

Maggie's pulse quickened, and she felt the blood rush to her cheeks. "I don't think so. Not today, anyhow. We're just meeting the gentlemen who've applied. If one of them is interested in our family, I'll probably arrange another meeting, so we can get to know each other better. But I hope to be back for you by five o'clock." She almost added, "Can you be good that long?" but she didn't want to imply she questioned their ability to behave.

One of the ladies was at the house when they arrived, and Maggie was glad.

"Hello, boys," Mrs. Sills said. "Pastor Smith is eager to see you. Why don't you go right through to his room?"

"Thank you," Maggie said. "I'll try not to be long."

Mrs. Sills arched her eyebrows. "Well, I expect it might take a while to pick out a proper husband."

An annoying flush crept into Maggie's cheeks. She could feel it. "Well, I'm not sure about this method."

Mrs. Sills patted her hand. "I hope you find someone nice, dear. I've been praying about it. The Lord knows we need some good, dependable men in this community."

"Yes, that's what we're hoping for."

Maggie left and headed for the inn, on edge because of the strangers she would be meeting, and because she wasn't entirely sure the boys would be good. After that stunt they pulled on poor Sam Cayford, she wondered what they would be up to next.

When she came in sight of the Tumble Inn, where the meeting was to take place, several women were gathered outside, talking in small clusters. A few headed inside. Maggie decided she had time enough to dash in and check at Stevens Mercantile to see if she had any mail. If she did, it would be a wonder, as she almost never received anything, but she couldn't help remembering Sam's promise to drop her a line.

He'd been gone five days. If he'd found work nearby, surely she would have heard something by now. On the other hand, if he'd had to ride clear over to Dodge, it might take a while. And he might forget.

Chardy Stevens, the owner, was in the store, but she was taking off her big white apron. "Maggie." She nodded. "Going to the auditions?"

"Yes."

"So am I. I was just getting ready." Chardy hung the apron on a hook behind the counter.

"I thought I'd pop in and see if I had any mail—if you have time, that is."

"I sure do." Chardy's smile widened. "And I have something for you." She stepped behind the post office counter. Hope rose in Maggie's heart.

"Oh, thank you!" A sudden fear hit her. What if it was a threatening notice from the bank? But Chardy handed her a plain penny postcard, address side up, with her name and *Turtle Springs, Kansas* scrawled across it. Her heart pounded.

She managed to stay calm and chat for a moment then said, "Well, I'll let you get ready. See you there!" She went out, holding the postcard against her skirt. She didn't want to turn it over and read it unless she could find a private spot.

Outside the inn, she saw that most of the women had already entered. Maggie didn't want to be the last one. Maybe she should wait for Chardy and they could go in together. She couldn't wait to look at her postcard, though. She glanced around to make sure no one was near, paused at the edge of the yard, and turned the card over.

Dear Maggie, I didn't get on with Russell or Therron, but I've found a place about 20 mi. west. It's not too far. Thinking of you and the boys and hope all is well. S.C.

She felt warm all over. He hadn't forgotten, and he'd found work. Not only that, he wished them well. If only a man like Sam was attending the audition today. She clutched the card to her chest for a moment and then tucked it carefully into her handbag. No one must see that this afternoon, but she could imagine Fred and Benjy's joy when she showed it to them later. Of course, they would be disappointed that Sam had not included a return address, where they could send a reply.

She looked toward the inn. At least a dozen saddlehorses were tied up nearby. A group of four men lingered under a tree across the street. She didn't recognize any of them, but one of them looked her way and seemed to be taking her measure. Maggie jerked her head around and stared straight at the inn's door as she approached it. She wished she had waited for Chardy.

She pushed the door open, walked in, and gasped. There were so many of them! Would they outnumber the single women? What were they thinking when they agreed to do this?

Chapter 7

Abigail Melton, the mayor of Turtle Springs, had suggested the idea of advertising for grooms and had set up the audition meeting at the restaurant. Maggie watched, her heart skittering, as Abby took her place at the front of the dining room and smiled at the crowd.

"Hello, ladies and gentlemen. I'd like to thank you all for coming to this event."

Maggie swallowed hard and found a seat after Abby indicated where she wanted the ladies to sit. Each man, it seemed, would sit down opposite a woman to talk. They would have fifteen minutes to get to know a bit about each other. Then the men would move on to the next lady and begin their spiels all over again. Extra men would have to wait.

How many of these men were prepared to marry a widow with children, Maggie wondered. Over a hundred men had responded to the advertisements. How many were serious about making a lifetime commitment to one of the women of Turtle Springs?

Josiah Ingram, the new sheriff, lounged in the doorway, his eyes scanning the full room as Abigail explained the guidelines she and the other women had hammered out in their meetings. The prospective brides' safety was a major concern. They didn't want any strangers playing up to a lady and then taking advantage of her.

Maggie was glad Sheriff Ingram was here, making the presence of the law felt. He had recently blown into town and been hired by Abby as the town's sheriff. Maggie hadn't met him formally, but she'd seen him around town and knew who he was. So far, she hadn't heard any complaints about him except that he wasn't available in the husband hunt. It seemed he had his eye on Abby.

Between him and Abby Melton, they would see that everything was done in an orderly manner. While Maggie didn't know the sheriff personally, she did know Abby. Mayor Melton would not put up with any nonsense.

She flinched as the first man plunked down opposite her. He grinned at her, exposing tobacco-stained teeth and a gap where one incisor was missing.

"Afternoon." His brown eyes swept over her critically.

"Hello." Maggie felt her face go crimson. "I'm Margaret Piner."

"Henry Swan, but folks call me Jug." The large man's grin, if possible, grew broader.

Maggie wanted to ask how he got his nickname but thought better of it. If it was because of the odd shape of his head, she didn't want to embarrass him, and if it was because he was a hard drinker, she didn't want to know.

"So, Mr. Swan, what made you decide to come to this event?" The women had discussed what to use as opening questions and had come up with a few to get the men talking and perhaps reveal details about their personalities and motives.

"Well, hey," he said, leaning toward her over the table. "This is quite a sight, you know? All these ladies wanting husbands. I reckon some of 'em's got houses already, maybe even some land." He quirked an eyebrow expectantly.

"Yes," Maggie said slowly, "I'm sure some of them hope to find a man who will help work their property."

"Oh I'm a hard worker," Jug said.

"What do you work hard at, Mr. Swan?"

"I can throw a steer or drive a fence post with the best of 'em."

"I see. But I don't have any cattle, or any fences that need mending." She didn't mention the fact that she hoped one day to replace the livestock she'd been forced to sell. "Are you a family man?" she asked.

He sat back, frowning. "Well I h'ain't got one, if that's what you mean. Almost got married once, but she changed her mind."

"I have two boys," Maggie said.

"I see. Are they growed?"

Somehow, Maggie managed to keep the conversation going for the remaining minutes. Why hadn't Abby made the interviews ten minutes, instead of fifteen? She glanced about. Some of the women seemed quite contented with their conversation partners. Maybe she had simply drawn a poor specimen on the first session. She wondered what the schoolteacher would do if she wound up opposite Jug Swan.

At last the bell rang, and Jug stood. "Nice meetin' ya, Miss Piner."

"Mrs."

"Oh right. I'll keep you in mind."

Don't, she wanted to say, but she merely smiled and nodded before turning her attention to the next man, who took the seat opposite.

"Good day," he said, smiling. "Aren't you a pretty sight?"

Maggie's hackles rose, but she only said, "Thank you, sir. I'm Mrs. Margaret Piner."

"Oh, widow lady?"

"Yes, my husband was killed in the war."

He looked a little too polished to her, a little too elegant for Turtle Springs. Eyeing his tailored gray suit, bowler hat, and gold watch chain, she decided he wasn't a cowboy or a laborer of any sort.

"I'm Franklin Harper," he said, extending a smooth, uncallused hand. "Do you live in town?"

"A short distance out," she said.

"I see. I'm interested in starting a business here. Would that fit in with your plans, Mrs. Piner?"

"It might. I suppose it would depend on what kind of business, and what you envision your wife's role to be in it."

Mr. Harper smiled, and Maggie had to suppress a shudder. What was it about him that made her so uncomfortable?

"I noticed as I rode through town on my arrival that there seems to be a gap in the businesses."

"Oh?" Maggie thought about the stores on Main Street. It was true they could use a little more competition where groceries and dry goods were concerned, but it wasn't as if they couldn't get their hands on what they needed.

"My throat was dry and dusty after riding all the way out here," he said. "But I found nary a place where a man could wet his whistle."

Maggie swallowed hard. "We used to have a saloon, before the war. The town's a lot quieter now, and there's not the demand for it there once was."

He cocked his head to one side and eyed her skeptically. "Don't the cowboys from the ranches want to come in town on their day off and have a place to cut loose?"

"I—I don't know. The truth is, I've never thought about it. I was just glad we didn't have all the ruckus and the shooting and having to step over drunks on the sidewalk."

"I've spoken to the mayor about my plans." Harper turned his head and gazed across the room to where Abigail Melton was deep in conversation with another of the prospective husbands.

Maggie stared at him. "And what did Miss Melton say?"

"She hasn't said one way or the other yet. She wanted to wait until after this event was over, but she did have me fill out a form and leave it with her." He leaned over the table toward her. "So how did it happen that the saloon closed?"

"Mike Hapsworth packed up and left town." She brushed a hand through the air in dismissal. "He owned the saloon, but he's long gone."

Harper's eyes narrowed. "I've seen the building. It wouldn't take much to put it to rights and open for business."

"Well, just so you know. . ." Maggie squared her shoulders and took a deep breath. "I would not be interested in working at a saloon, or in marrying a man who ran one."

"I see." The bell rang, and he pushed back his chair. "Good evening, Mrs. Piner. I get the impression we wouldn't suit in marriage, but it was a pleasure speaking to someone so intelligent and knowledgeable."

Maggie just nodded. She didn't know about the intelligence—she felt pretty stupid right now—or the knowledge. All she'd done was direct him away from herself. Was it to go like this all afternoon?

She pulled in a breath as the next man took his place in the chair across from her. He smiled tentatively, and she tried to smile back. He looked ten years younger than her. He might be a nice young man, but Maggie knew instantly he wasn't for her. She sent up a quick prayer for strength and introduced herself.

Sam was weary when he rode into the barnyard at the Pine Tree Ranch. The foreman here worked the men hard. He didn't mind. Hard work was a good thing, and he was glad he'd found a paying job. He would sleep tonight, that was for sure, and a lot better in his bunk than he had on the ground while he'd camped on his search for employment.

He and one of the other cowboys were assigned to taking care of the extra horses from the remuda, which meant they were to be checked over for foot problems and turned out to graze in the pasture. He saw to Rocker first and turned him out then joined Eph—short for Ephraim—at the holding corral, where the extra horses milled about, restless and hungry.

They checked each horse quickly, lifting their feet and running a gentle hand along each leg.

"Find anything?" Eph asked.

"The gray has a shoe loose. It's hanging on by a couple of nails."

"We'd better yank it," Eph said. "The blacksmith can put a new shoe on tomorrow. Do you know where the tools are?"

"Yeah," Sam said.

"Go get the pullers and a rasp. I'll let the rest of these nags out."

Sam hurried into the barn, to the saddle room where they kept their gear, barrels of oats, medicines for the animals, and tools. When he got back to the corral, Eph was at the pasture gate. The limping gray was still in the pen, and a fine buggy was driving into the yard. He nodded at the driver.

"Is Mr. McClure in?" the white-haired gentleman asked.

"I believe he's at the house, sir," Sam said. "I saw him speak with the foreman a few minutes past, when we rode in from our work."

"May I hand off my horse and rig to you? I don't expect to be long."

"Of course, sir." Sam laid down the tools, stepped forward, and accepted the reins. "I'll give him some water."

The gentleman climbed down. "Thank you. I only need to have Mr. McClure sign some papers. Unless he wishes to discuss something, I'll be on my way back to town in a trice."

Sam nodded and led the horse over to a water trough in the yard, where horses could drink without being unhitched. Eph came from the pasture.

"So, the lawyer's here, huh?"

"Is that who he is?" Sam asked. "He says he's not stopping."

"Could be—or could be they'll chew the fat for an hour. I'd best tend to the gray."

"Thanks," Sam said.

Eph picked up the shoe pullers and rasp and went into the holding pen. It took him only minutes to lever off the loose shoe and file the edges of the gray's hoof smooth. When he turned the horse out with the others, Sam was still holding the lawyer's horse.

Eph waved. "See what I mean? Best tie him up and come in. We'll be eating supper any minute."

Sam nodded. "Thanks."

The horse had finished drinking, so he led it in a wide circle to point the buggy back toward town. He was about to do what Eph had suggested and tie it to the hitching rail when the door of the ranch house opened. Mr. McClure, who owned the Pine Tree ranch, and the lawyer emerged, still talking.

"Thank you, but I'd best get back to town," the lawyer said. "My wife invited dinner guests this evening, and she won't like it if I don't appear on schedule."

"All right then," Mr. McClure said. "Thanks for coming out with those papers. I'll see you in town next week." He looked toward the buggy, his gaze landing on Sam, at the horse's head. He nodded Sam's way, shook the attorney's hand, and went inside.

The lawyer strode toward the buggy. "Thank you, young man." He reached into his pocket and took out a coin.

"No need for that, sir," Sam said. "It was a pleasure. You have a fine horse here."

"Well thanks." He climbed up to the seat and reached for the reins.

"Sir, would it be amiss for me to ask you something?"

The man eyed him curiously. "Well, I suppose that depends on the nature of your question. If it's anything to do with Mr. McClure or this ranch—"

"Oh, no sir," Sam said quickly. "It's just that I was told you're a lawyer, and I know someone who has a bit of a dilemma."

"Ask away, then. I can't guarantee I can help you."

"Of course. I wondered, just in general, sir, if a widow can be made to pay her husband's debt to the bank. Seems like I had an aunt in that situation once, and they said she wasn't liable once her husband died and was under the ground."

"That depends. If the debt was solely her husband's, no."

"It's a mortgage, sir."

"Well then, it still depends. If the widow signed for the mortgage with her husband, then she's probably liable. If he alone incurred the debt, then she's not."

Sam frowned, not sure he understood and wishing he knew what questions to ask.

"It's a lot more complicated than that," the lawyer said, not unkindly. "It sounds to me as though the lady in question should get legal counsel. Does she live around here?"

"Not real close, sir."

He nodded. "Tell her to seek out a lawyer. That's the best way to be sure. And the laws vary from one place to another."

Sam let go of the reins at last. "Thank you. And, if you don't mind my asking, is it expensive?"

"What, hiring a lawyer?"

"Yes, sir."

"My fee is a dollar an hour."

Sam gulped. He was only getting a dollar a day.

The lawyer smiled. "Didn't mean to shock you. She might find the matter resolved in less than an hour. If she had to go to court, it might get expensive."

Sam nodded. "Sounds sensible, sir. Thanks again."

"No trouble, son. And good luck."

For some reason, Rutherford Grant had left Maggie alone for more than two weeks. She couldn't fathom it, but she was thankful. She carefully avoided walking past the bank when she was in town. During that time, she had sewn two dresses and four shirts for people in town, and agreed to thoroughly clean the minister's little house once a week for fifty cents each time. It wasn't much, but she could do it easily in a couple of hours while the boys were at school.

The cleaning and the sewing had kept food on the table since Sam left. Funny how she marked events now by when they happened in relation to Sam's visit. Fred had started it, remarking on how he'd killed two squirrels the day after Sam left, but they'd all fallen into it. Fred and Benjy hadn't seemed too disappointed the evening of the auditions, when she had told them she did not meet a prospective husband that day. She had thought it a little odd at the time, but they'd accepted the news quite cheerfully.

A rancher had placed an order with her for two work shirts. She was about to enter the mercantile to buy the material for them, when the sheriff, who had been leaning against the wall, stepped forward and tipped his hat.

"Mrs. Piner, I'm glad to see you. This will save me riding out to your place."

Maggie stopped in her tracks and stared at him. "Oh? What is it, Sheriff?" So far as she knew, he was still pursuing Abigail. He'd stuck around Turtle Springs, anyway, and she considered that a good thing.

"Mr. Grant at the bank asked me to deliver this." He took a folded sheet of paper from his pocket and handed it to her.

Maggie pulled in a deep breath and opened it. It was a formal, official-looking notice with the word *eviction* in large, fancy letters at the top. She felt as though she might collapse on the porch of the mercantile.

"It says tomorrow," she gasped.

"I'm sorry," Sheriff Ingram said. He sounded as though he meant it. "Mr. Rutherford said you promised him two weeks ago to make a payment within forty-eight hours, but you didn't."

"I—I didn't say that."

"Well. . ." The sheriff pushed his hat forward and scratched the back of his neck. "He mentioned a gentleman who was with you."

"Oh. Mr. Cayford."

"I thought maybe you'd met someone at the husband auditions. None of my business, but. . ." He eyed her expectantly.

"Surely he wouldn't have me arrested," Maggie said, ignoring the reference to Sam.

"Well, he could. He'll probably just have you forcibly removed from the property. I'd hate to have to do that."

Maggie's jaw dropped. "You? You'd physically push me and my boys out of our home?"

He sighed. "If it's legal, then I'm required to enforce the law."

"If it's legal?" She looked at the paper again.

"I don't know your business, Mrs. Piner. Do you owe the bank the amount stated there?"

Maggie frowned. "Rutherford Grant says I do, but I've paid him more than this since Rodney went away to war, and he kept saying it wasn't enough—that we owed more than Rod told me."

The sheriff's eyebrows drew together. He was certainly a handsome man, Maggie thought, and he seemed genuinely concerned about her plight.

"Is there someone who could look into it for you? I'm not a lawyer, ma'am. But if you know someone who's up on banking and such. . ."

"No." Maggie thought of Sam, but she doubted he knew anything but cattle.

"This Mr. Cayford. . ." The sheriff's frank gaze unnerved her. "I don't recall his name on the list of aspiring husbands."

She shook her head. "I didn't meet him there. He—he stopped by our ranch on the way to someplace else. He had dinner with us, and we let him sleep in the barn with his horse. He happened to be there when Mr. Grant came by, and I was glad of it. But he's not around here anymore." She looked up at the sheriff quickly. "I'd appreciate it if you didn't tell Mr. Grant that."

Josiah held up one hand. "Not my nevermind, ma'am."

"Thank you."

"Maybe if you could make a small payment. . ."

"I've been doing that as often as I can." She huffed out a breath. "Sheriff, I earned two dollars last week. I spent nearly all of it on food for me and my boys. I just don't know how I can scrape together a payment." She had a dollar and fifteen cents left in coins from what she'd had on hand, and what was left from her pay for the jobs she'd done. That was all, until she got paid for making these shirts, and that would be a small profit. Very small.

"I'm sorry," he said. "If Mr. Grant tells me to, I'll have to come out to your place tomorrow. Is there someplace you can go?"

She shook her head. "I know it's not your doin', Sheriff, but you'll understand if I don't thank you for this." Fighting back tears, she stuffed the eviction notice into her handbag and trudged into the mercantile.

Chapter 8

S am guided his horse in quick turns to head off yearlings trying to escape the
bunch he and two other cowpunchers were guarding. They'd spent the last two
days rounding up the boss's cattle from the hills, and today was branding day.
In the process of marking the new calves with the ranch's brand, they would also
cull out the steers to be sold for beef in the fall and any animals that had something
wrong with them.

"What about them two with the Double T brand?" he asked Buck when the
bunch had settled down for a moment.

"I reckon a couple of us will push 'em on over to Therron's boundary when we're
done with the roundup." Buck spit tobacco on the ground and adjusted his reins.

Sam shifted in his saddle. He was riding one of the ranch's string of cow ponies
today. He rode Rocker every other day, but the hard work tired horses out quickly,
so each man rotated his mounts. Tomorrow was his day off, and he wanted Rocker
fresh when he set out in the morning.

"You going into town tomorra?" Buck asked.

"Thought I go visit some friends, over Turtle Springs' way," Sam said.

"That's a piece," Buck said. He spit again. "They got no saloons there."

"I don't mind."

In fact, Turtle Springs was just about the perfect little town, so far as Sam was
concerned. It had everything the residents needed. And it had Maggie Piner.

"Hey!" Buck spurred his horse off to chase a young steer making a break for
open ground.

Sam calmed his fidgety horse, watching the other cattle. "Don't you think it," he
told one moody old cow. She was getting too old to breed, and they'd put her in with
the culls in case the boss wanted to send her to the butcher.

His thoughts drifted back to Maggie Piner. On payday at the end of May, he
had been working on the ranch less than a week, but the boss paid him for the
days he'd worked. Sam had held back a dollar for incidentals and put the rest in an
envelope. He hadn't had a chance to mail it yet, but he reckoned she could use it. He
hoped she wouldn't be offended.

The foreman rode up just as Buck brought back the two escapees.

"This bunch ready?"

"Yep," Sam said.

"All right, Cayford, you push 'em to the fire, one at a time. The boys are ready."

"What about that old cow?" Buck called, and nodded toward the one in question. She had put her head down to graze, but she sent baleful looks their way.

"Aw, she's good for another year," the foreman said.

"She's not particular who she aims those horns at," Buck said.

"Can't blame her, can you?" The foreman chuckled. "Oh, Cayford, I'm supposed to tell you we'll still be working out here tomorrow."

Sam was pretty sure he knew what that meant. "You mean...?"

The foreman nodded. "The boss says to postpone all days off until we're done branding. You'll get your day off the first full day after we're done here. Could be a few more days, though."

Sam frowned. "Can I send a letter?"

"Sure. The cook's going into town for supplies this afternoon. Send it with him."

Better than nothing, Sam guessed. He cut a two-month-old calf from the bunch and nudged him toward the fire. The calf bounded away from his horse, bawling, and Sam took off after him. He dropped his rope over the calf's head.

"Sorry, little fella, but it's gotta be done."

Maggie had the boys out in the garden a few days later. She hadn't had enough money to buy seeds, but she had planted all she'd saved from last year's garden, along with some for wax beans and turnips that Reverend Smith had given her, and a few tomato plants donated by Mrs. Sills. Maggie had worked with the deacon's wife yesterday afternoon to put in a small plot for Reverend Smith as well. He was recovering from his accident, but still couldn't put weight on his broken leg.

"Benjy, go refill the water bucket," she said, pushing back her hair from her sweaty forehead. The sun wasn't halfway to noon yet, and she hoped they could finish before it got hot.

Benjy picked up the wooden pail. Maggie continued hoeing down the row of tiny bean plants. Fred worked in the next row, pulling out grass and other weeds threatening to strangle the tender vegetable sprouts. He looked like his daddy, bent over and frowning with great concentration, his blond hair spilling down over his forehead.

As she worked, Maggie wondered what the other women were doing today. How many of those who took part in the auditions had started courtships? Some had seemed to enjoy themselves at the meeting. She hoped not all of them had been as disillusioned as she had. Maybe she would get some news at church tomorrow.

"Ma," Benjy called.

Maggie turned toward the house. Benjy stood at the edge of the garden plot, holding the bucket. He pointed toward the lane. A black-clad man rode toward the house. His derby hat and snappy horse gave him away before she could see his face. Rutherford Grant.

She straightened her back and glanced down at her dress. He would catch her out here in her threadbare calico, the one she saved for outdoor chores.

But what did it matter? Maggie stepped over the row of beans and handed her hoe to Fred.

"Here you go. Just keep working. If we're not here to eat these beans, someone else will be." She raised her skirts a couple of inches and made her way carefully to the edge of the garden.

Rutherford had reached her hitching rail and dismounted. He flipped the reins around the peeled log and walked toward her, sweeping off his hat.

"Good morning, Mrs. Piner."

Maggie couldn't see anything good about it. "Mr. Grant."

He looked around expectantly. "Sheriff Ingram hasn't arrived?"

Maggie made herself draw in a breath slowly. "Nobody's come around today but you."

"Ah. Well, I've asked him to meet me here." The banker pulled out his gold pocket watch and sprang open the cover.

"Maybe Mr. Ingram doesn't have a watch," Fred said at her elbow.

Maggie whirled toward him. Fred stood there, nearly as tall as she was, with the hoe at his side, pointed toward the fluffy clouds above them. It reminded Maggie of Sam Cayford's stance with the shotgun the last time Grant had come calling. She bit back her rebuke. Fred saw it as his job to stand by his mother, instead of hoeing beans. She wouldn't deny him that.

"I confess, I expected to find the house empty." Grant surveyed the little building with displeasure.

"I didn't see a point in packing," Maggie said. "This is our home, and we have nowhere else to go."

"We're not goin' anywhere," Fred said. Maggie reached around and laid her hand lightly on his back.

Grant eyed her pensively for a moment. "Frankly, Mrs. Piner, I was torn between that and another alternative. I thought perhaps I would hear news of your nuptials. The, uh—" He coughed gently. "The gentleman who was on the premises the last time I rode out here. I believe you said you expected to be married."

Maggie's heart sank. Why had she lied that day? Now she had to own up to it, and the result would be even worse. True, she and the boys had gained two weeks of relative peace, but she hadn't used it to make any preparations. She had worked every moment she could. To be honest, she had also pegged a slender thread of hope on the husband auditions. But that had come to naught, where she was concerned. She didn't wish to marry a shiftless man or a slick easterner trying to open up a saloon in their town. Maybe some of the men who had come to the meeting were good, honest, and hardworking, but if so, they'd attached themselves to others among the hopeful women.

She opened her mouth to respond to Grant's dig, when Fred spoke again.

"Sam had to go away for a while. He's got a job, and he needed to go and work. But he's comin' back."

"Indeed?" Grant's gaze shifted to Fred then back to Maggie. "Is this true?"

"Well—"

"We've had word from him," Fred said.

"But do you have the money for your overdue mortgage payment?" Grant tucked his gold watch pack into his waistcoat pocket. "That's the question, Mrs. Piner."

Staccato hoofbeats drew their attention to the lane, where a horse loped into sight.

"Well, the sheriff has decided to meet his obligations after all," Grant said. He walked across the dooryard to meet Sheriff Ingram.

Maggie looked at Fred. "Best not say any more about Sam."

"Why not?"

"He's not coming back, that's why not."

Fred's face fell. On her other side, Benjy crowded against her, still holding the empty bucket.

"Are we going to have to leave, Mama? Where will we go?"

She brushed Benjy's tumbled blond curls back from his brow. "I don't know yet. You boys stay here and pray. The sheriff's usually a reasonable man. Just let me talk to him." She looked inquiringly at Fred, and after a moment he nodded, his mouth twisted in a scowl.

Maggie walked over to where Josiah Ingram was dismounting. Grant threw her a glance and then focused on the sheriff.

"Are you prepared to act on your duty, Sheriff?" he asked.

"That depends, sir."

"Mrs. Piner has not made any effort to meet her financial obligation to the bank, so it's time for the eviction. You know that."

"Well, first I need to give you a message from the bank, sir. Apparently the auditor arrived just minutes after you'd set out to come here."

Grant's face froze. "Auditor?"

"Yes, sir. One of your tellers, Mrs. Johnson, ran out just as I was heading this way and asked me if I'd see you this morning. I said that was my plan, and she asked me to please tell you the state auditor had come, and to please return to the bank as soon as possible."

"Heavens, he was just here last— Yes, I suppose it is that time again." Grant strode to the hitching rail and untied his horse's reins. "Ingram, I'll leave you to it. See that Mrs. Piner and her children are out of here by sunset. Anything she leaves behind will be sold to help reconcile the debt."

The sheriff frowned but said nothing. He watched as Grant climbed into the saddle and urged his horse into a trot.

Maggie hauled in a deep breath. "Sheriff, is this really necessary? I don't want to put you in a bad situation, but as you can imagine, if we have to pick up and leave today, it will put the boys and me in a very bad one."

Josiah pushed his hat back and scratched his head. "How much would it take to keep him off your back for another month, ma'am?"

"The payment is ten dollars a month, but it might as well be a thousand. I couldn't come up with it last month, you see, no matter how hard I tried, and now it's overdue for a second month." Maggie shook her head. "I'm afraid there's no way I can raise ten dollars today. I've only managed to set aside three from my work these last few weeks. He would probably insist on twenty, anyway, since I didn't pay him last month." Tears stung her eyes. She hated that. She wouldn't use her femininity or her weakness to gain favors.

"I'm sorry, ma'am." He reached into his vest pocket, and for a moment, Maggie thought he was going to bring out the eviction notice. Instead, he held out a small envelope with her name scrawled across the front in pencil, followed by *Turtle Springs, Kans.*

Her heart leaped. Surely that was the same hand that had addressed the postcard she'd received earlier. She reached for it with trembling fingers. "How. . . ?"

"Chardy Stevens gave me that when I stopped by the mercantile this mornin'. Asked if I was by any chance coming this way. When I said I was, she asked if I could tell you a letter had been sittin' at the post office for you for a day or two. I think she figured you'd want to know."

"Yes, thank you." Maggie could hardly breathe.

"Oh, and another thing."

Maggie's lungs squeezed. "Y–yes?"

"Miss Stevens told me you sew shirts for some of her customers."

"Yes, I do. I charge a dollar apiece, unless you want fancy material."

"So, you have to buy the cloth out of that?"

"Well, most times."

Sheriff Ingram's eyebrows drew down. "How long does it take you to make one?"

"I can make one a day, easy," Maggie said. "Three in two days, if that's all I do."

He nodded soberly and reached in his pocket, coming out with a handful of coins. He picked through them and held out his selection.

"Here's two dollars and four bits. Can you make me two shirts by the end of next week?"

"Certainly. It's too much, though."

As she peered down at the two silver dollars and two quarters in her hand, Maggie realized her boys had come from the garden and now crowded in on each side of her.

"The extra's for the makings," Ingram said. "Oh, and I'm partial to plain cloth and buttons."

"I understand."

"Now, as to Mr. Grant. . ."

Maggie waited, expecting the worst.

"That auditor answered my telegram real quick. He'll keep Mr. Grant busy for the rest of the day. Maybe more than that. Would you like help packing anything up?"

"I—I might be able to make a small payment now. Very small."

He nodded. "All right then. Best stay away from the bank today."

"I'll go to town first thing in the morning to buy your cloth and buttons, and I'll stop at the bank then."

"That sounds fine to me. If Grant's still bound to evict you, I'll get the blacksmith to bring his wagon out and help tote your stuff."

Maggie drew in a shaky breath and met his gaze. "Thank you, Sheriff."

"Thank *you*, ma'am. I look forward to wearing my new shirts." He winked at her and mounted his horse.

"Mama, does he like you?" Benjy asked, his voice laced with suspicion.

"I believe he likes all of us," Maggie said as she watched the man ride off, slouched in the saddle. "But if you mean is he sweet on me, then no. I happen to know he's got his eyes set on Mayor Melton." She pulled her handkerchief from her pocket and wrapped the coins in it. "I shall have to go into town tomorrow, but for now, come. We've got a garden to tend."

"What about that letter?" Fred asked.

"Oh yes, the letter." Maggie patted her pocket. She hadn't forgotten, but she certainly hadn't wanted to open it with Sheriff Ingram looking on. She had about decided to open it tonight, after the boys were in bed.

"It's from Sam, ain't it?" Fred said, his blue eyes staring into hers, demanding honesty.

"I believe so."

"Open it, open it." Benjy pulled at her arm.

"All right." Maggie walked over to the doorstep, drawing out the letter as she did. She sat down on the stoop and tore open the envelope. She pulled out a small piece of paper, and green banknotes peeped at her from between the folds. She gasped.

"It's got money in it," Fred said.

Maggie swallowed hard. She opened the paper carefully and handed Fred five one-dollar bills.

"*'Dear Maggie and boys,'*" she read aloud. "*'I had my first payday, and I hope you'll accept this small token of my friendship and esteem. If you have left the home place by now, or if your circumstances have otherwise changed, then I'm sorry. I don't mean to interfere. Please use this as you see best, with no obligations attached. Yours sincerely, Sam Cayford.'*"

Maggie's voice choked over his name.

"*'P.S. We are having spring roundup on the ranch. Tell the boys I helped brand*

over a hundred Pine Tree Ranch calves today.'"

"A hundred calves." Benjy stared off toward their empty pasture, as though trying to imagine a hundred beef critters frisking about on the Piner land.

"Where's the Pine Tree Ranch?" Fred asked.

"I don't know, but he said on his postcard it was west of here. Twenty miles west."

"Mama," Fred said, fingering the money. "Can you give this to the bank? That's what Sam wants, isn't it?"

Maggie couldn't explain the feelings fomenting inside her. It was daybreak and a rainbow in the middle of a tornado. She stood and took the bills gently from Fred's fingers.

"You boys will go with me, first thing in the morning. If you're late to school, I'll explain to the teacher."

Fred squared his shoulders. "Come on, Benjy. We got to weed that garden real good."

Chapter 9

Roundup was over at last. Sam bathed in the stream that ran through the ranch and washed out his clothes. The shirt—his best of two—was so sadly frayed he nearly cried. He almost wished he had kept another dollar from his pay so he could buy another in town, but no. He had done the right thing. At least he was clean. Of course, a day's ride on the dusty roads would dirty him up again, but Maggie would understand.

He got up at dawn on his day off and dressed quickly. As he fastened his cuff buttons, he frowned. That husband audition thing had come and gone. Had she found a man to take on the ranch and the boys with her? He didn't like to think it, and yet he wanted the best for her. As he saddled Rocker for the long ride, he placed the matter in God's hands. Maggie Piner either needed him or she didn't. She would either be glad to see him riding up the lane or not. When he got down to basics, she would either still be Maggie Piner or not. If she'd found another man and wore his name now, Sam would turn around and ride back to the ranch and try to be happy for her.

He had plenty of time to mull things over on the twenty-mile ride. Rocker moved along, but even so, it was midmorning when he rode up to the Piner house. The yard was deserted except for a couple of hens pecking about near the sagging pasture gate. No smoke came from the chimney. A dread seized him as he walked up to the front door.

His knock echoed through the little house. Empty. He knew it. Cautiously, he pushed the door open. To his surprise, the large room inside looked almost exactly the same as it had when he left it. That was Maggie's furniture, and her dishes, her cookstove. Her yellow mixing bowl on the table. Surely she'd have taken that if she was forced to move out.

Sam stepped out and shut the door. He walked to the corner of the house. Maggie had a small garden, and it had been tended recently. The rows of fledgling beans, corn, and potatoes were weed free. He looked toward the back of the house. The clothesline. A linen sheet, two pairs of boys' pants, and a small plaid shirt that had to be Benjy's hung there, flapping in the light breeze.

He smiled. Of course they hadn't gone. The boys were likely at school, and Maggie was probably in town, seeing to one of those odd jobs she had mentioned. Cleaning someone's house or sewing a dress for a woman with more money than she had. None of the things in the laundry looked like men's clothes, he noted with gratitude. Fred must not have found her a husband yet.

Rocker raised his head and snuffled.

"Yeah, it's time we made tracks, boy." Sam strode to the bay horse, scooped up the reins, and vaulted into the saddle.

Maggie approached the bank in trepidation, even though her boys flanked her solidly. Well perhaps not so solidly.

"Mama?" Benjy's voice quavered as he tugged at her hand and dragged his steps. She stopped and looked down at him.

"Yes?"

"Is Mr. Grant going to be in there?"

"I expect so, dear."

Benjy's lips twitched. "I don't like him."

"I should have brought the shotgun," Fred said.

Maggie stared at him. "Frederick Daniel! Behave yourself. This will be a quick business transaction." She eyed her sons carefully. "I shan't regret having let you come, shall I?"

After a moment's pause, Fred shook his head. "No ma'am."

She looked down at Benjy.

"No," he squeaked out.

Maggie nodded, trying to seem confident. "Right. Let's go and pay our bill."

She smoothed the skirts of her black-and-gray dress and raised her chin. The boys marched beside her up the steps and into the cool, dim lobby of the bank.

She walked to the teller's desk and said to the woman behind it, "I would like to make a payment on my mortgage."

"Good morning, Mrs. Piner," the woman said. "Let me find your account."

Maggie bit her bottom lip and opened her purse. She took out the ten dollars—five from Sam, two from Sheriff Ingram, and three she had managed to save from her work—and laid it on the desk. She wanted there to be no question she could make a full payment this time.

The woman returned carrying a large, flat book and frowning.

"I'm sorry. It seems you've been served an eviction notice and the account has been stopped."

A painful lump formed in Maggie's throat. "But I can make the month's entire payment."

The teller cleared her throat. "I'm sorry. I'll have to ask Mr. Grant. Perhaps he can explain it to you."

She sent a nervous glance toward a closed door across the room. Maggie knew Mr. Grant's desk was behind that door. She had been in his office more times than she wished to remember.

"He's with someone right now. Can you come back later?"

"Well, I. . ." Maggie looked at Fred. "The boys have to go to school. I suppose I can wait."

"We'll stay with you, Mama," Fred said.

Maggie opened her mouth and closed it. Perhaps having her fatherless children beside her would sway Mr. Grant, but she doubted it.

"You can take a seat over there." The teller pointed to a cushioned bench against the side wall. "As soon as he's done with the auditor—"

"I thought the auditor came yesterday," Maggie said.

The woman's face flushed. "He did. He stayed quite late last night and returned this morning. I'm not sure what the fuss is, but I'm sure Mr. Grant will be able to see you after a while. Perhaps you want to take the boys to school and come back in an hour."

An hour. Maggie couldn't imagine Benjy sitting still that long. It was hard enough to keep him quiet during church, and he had trouble staying seated all day at school, too—she had apologetic but firm notes from the teacher to prove it.

"All right," she said.

"Mama—" Fred's eyes pleaded.

"It's best, Fred. It could be a long time, and I don't want Benjy to miss school." Maybe her inference that he could bear it better would mollify him. "Thank you," she told the teller. She picked up her money and carefully put it in her bag. Taking Benjy's hand, she turned toward the door. "Come. Let's get you to the schoolhouse. I'll come back and see Mr. Grant later."

As they walked down the steps outside, a bay horse came trotting up the street.

"Rocker!" Benjy tore down the steps and into the horse's path.

"Benjy!" Maggie couldn't help screaming his name, but the rider was able to stop the horse in time. Sam Cayford dismounted and walked carefully out in front of his mount. He scooped Benjy up from where he had tumbled when he realized the big horse was heading directly toward him.

"Now, son, that's a precarious way to greet a man—or a horse." Sam grinned down at the boy.

Benjy burrowed his head into Sam's shirt front. "Sam. I knew you'd come back. Can I ride Rocker?"

Sam laughed and set him down on the sidewalk. "Maybe later." He gathered the reins and led Rocker over to where Maggie stood, pausing before her and the boys.

"Good morning, Piners. Didn't mean to cause a stir."

Maggie could hardly believe he was standing there in front of her. She had not dared to dream of this moment, telling herself he had remembered them kindly but would never return. She tried to clear her throat. Before she could speak, Fred stuck out his hand.

"Welcome back, Sam."

Sam sobered and shook Fred's hand.

"You been taking care of your ma?"

"Trying to," Fred replied.

"Oh, Sam." Maggie couldn't help the tears filling her eyes. He looked at her, nearly on her level with Maggie standing on the sidewalk.

"You just came from the bank, I take it," he said. "How did it turn out?"

"I went in to make a payment. We—we got your letter, and thank you." Her cheeks felt hotter than the early sun warranted, and she dropped her gaze. "But the teller said she couldn't accept it because Mr. Grant already sent the eviction notice. She wouldn't let me talk to him because the auditor's here."

"Auditor, huh?" Sam frowned. "That's like a bank examiner, isn't it?"

"Yes, it's someone who checks all their accounts to make sure everything's in order."

"Sounds like he might be just the man you need to see."

"What do you mean?" Maggie looked into his brown eyes. The caring she saw there made hope flutter inside her.

"Well, I spoke to a lawyer."

"A lawyer?" That startled her.

"He's my boss's lawyer, for the ranch," Sam explained. "He said—"

The bank's door flew open and a man in a black wool suit charged out. "Does anyone know where the sheriff is?"

Chapter 10

S am jerked his chin up. "I saw him over near the mayor's office. Do you need him?"

"At once. I want him to arrest the bank president, before he gets away."

The auditor, Sam surmised. He laid a hand on Fred's shoulder. "Run to the mayor's office and fetch the sheriff, Fred."

Without a word, the boy took off at full speed.

"Now, I'm assuming you're talking about Mr. Rutherford Grant," Sam said to the auditor.

"That's right."

"Where is he?" Sam led Rocker a few steps to a hitching rail and looped his reins over it.

"He excused himself for a minute, and when he didn't return, I asked the teller. She said he'd gone out the backdoor. I suspect he's making a run for it, after what I found in his ledgers."

"How long?" Sam asked grimly, mounting the steps.

"Five minutes or more," the auditor said as he passed him.

Sam whirled around. "Maggie, does Grant have a wagon or a buggy? Or just that horse he rode out to your house?"

"I don't know," she said. "If he does, he might keep it at his house, on Willow Street, or at the livery stable."

"Tell the sheriff if I don't pick up his trail here, I'll cover the livery. He can go to Grant's house. And get Benjy away, someplace safe."

So Grant was robbing his own bank, or at any rate, the good citizens of Turtle Springs. That didn't surprise him one bit. Sam strode to the bank's door and flung it open.

Behind the teller's cage, a woman in a conservative gray dress was speaking animatedly to a young man in a suit. Sam marched forward.

"Where's Mr. Grant?"

The young man just stared at him.

"He—he went out the back door," the woman said, pointing.

Sam crossed the room, took a quick look into a small office, and continued on to a short hallway. At the end was another door. He opened it on the back lot of the bank that held nothing but a privy and a large wooden barrel brimming with trash. Across and alley he could see the backyard of a house. He went out, checked the

118

privy, and then he walked swiftly along the backs of Main Street businesses toward the livery stable.

The banker stood just inside the barn door, watching the livery owner saddle his horse. As Sam approached, he whirled around, spotted him, and ducked inside.

Chagrined, Sam flattened himself against the outside barn wall, by the big rolling door that hung on a track.

"Grant, the sheriff's on his way. Don't try to leave."

The liveryman looked around at him. "What's going on?"

Grant seized the reins from him and swung into the saddle. Sam wished he had a gun, but he didn't. Instead, he put his shoulder to the heavy barn door and rolled it shut. When only a foot was left in the gap between the door and the jamb on the other side, Grant's horse's head appeared. The animal squealed and tried to draw back.

"Easy now," Sam said. He didn't want to injure the horse, and if he kept it trapped in the gap of the doorway, it would probably start kicking and thrashing. Sam ran over to the horse and put his hand on its muzzle. "Calm down, fella." He peered through the foot-wide gap in the doorway at the rider.

"Mr. Grant, you're not getting away. Get off the horse and wait quietly."

To Sam's surprise, he was looking down the muzzle of a pocket pistol.

"Open the door and get out of the way," Grant yelled.

"No, sir." Sam kept his hand firmly on the horse's bridle.

The report of the pistol echoed in the barn, and the horse went wild.

"Thank You, Lord," Sam said aloud, glad he'd ducked at the right instant, but unable to hear himself because his ears rang with the sound of the shot.

The horse had pulled its head back inside and proceeded to tear about the barn, kicking and shrieking. Sam turned sideways and slipped through the narrow gap. Mr. Grant lay in a heap on the wood floor, and the liveryman approached the horse cautiously with a blanket in his hands. Sam moved in carefully, speaking softly to the animal. The stable owner had just grabbed the horse's cheek strap and was settling him down when the big door rolled halfway open.

"All right in there?" Sheriff Ingram called.

Sam walked over to the door. "I'm glad to see you. Thought you'd headed for Grant's house by now."

"I started to, but I heard the shot," Ingram replied. He peered around the dim barn. The liveryman was leading the horse to a tie-up. The sheriff's gaze landed on Grant. "Is he shot?"

"No, he fired the gun," Sam said. "I don't have one with me. I think the horse dumped him. Went plumb crazy when he fired."

The sheriff walked over to Grant and knelt beside him. He rose a moment later. "Dead. Probably broke his neck, but Doc Carter will tell us. You all right?"

"I'm fine, and I can hear what you're saying, so I guess I'm not deaf," Sam said.

Ingram nodded and called the same question to the liveryman, who was coming out of the stall.

"I'm all right, Sheriff," he said. "I'm glad to see you, though. I don't know who this fella is."

"If I'm not mistaken, he's Sam Cayford," Ingram told him.

"Yes, sir," Sam said.

Ingram extended his hand. "Pleased to meet you." He looked at the livery owner. "I'll vouch for him."

The man looked back and forth between them. "All right, then. We had a little excitement. Your timing is a little off, though, sheriff. I'm going to have to make some repairs in here." He looked sourly at a broken stall divider and a barrel and some tools that had been knocked over.

Ingram looked around and nodded soberly. "Sorry. Since Mr. Grant's not going to be needing that fancy horse anymore, I'll ask the mayor if you can keep it in payment for damages."

The livery owner brightened. "That's a good idea. He owed me for two weeks' board, too."

Chapter 11

S am walked up Main Street and paused outside the bank, near his horse. His heart was heavy as he tried to absorb the fact that Mr. Grant was dead. Could he have prevented it if he'd acted differently?

He looked around, but Maggie and the boys were nowhere to be seen.

"Sam! Over here!"

He turned toward the voice. Maggie stood in the doorway of the freshly painted restaurant, looking prettier than a mountain sunrise. She waved, and he couldn't help grinning, despite what had happened at the livery. He strode toward her, his heart thumping away again, but this time not because of imminent danger. She'd waited for him.

When he walked in, she was seated demurely at a table near the window.

Caroline Kane, the owner, called, "Coffee, Mr. Cayford?"

Sam nodded. "Thank you." He walked over and took the chair opposite Maggie. "I'm surprised she remembers me. I've only ever stopped in here twice."

"I told her about you." Maggie looked as if she couldn't contain herself a moment longer. "What happened?"

"Oh." Sam took off his hat and laid it on the table. "Mr. Grant, uh. . . He fell off his horse."

"What?" She gazed at him with a puzzled expression.

"He was trying to get away from the livery and I shut the door. He shot at me, and the horse took exception. Threw him on the hard floor in the stable."

"And?"

"Broken neck, the sheriff says."

Maggie stared at him.

"I wish it ended otherwise, but—well, it was God's doing, I guess," Sam said.

She nodded slowly. "That man at the bank—he was the auditor."

"I figured."

"He. . .he spoke to me after you left."

Sam fixed his gaze on Maggie's troubled blue eyes. "What did he say?"

"When I told him who I was, he said to come to the bank this afternoon. He said my account is one of several he's been examining closely. What do you think it means, Sam?"

"Could be good news for you."

A tall man with auburn hair stepped to the table. "Might I interest you in a spot of tea? And scones?" His heavy British accent took Sam by surprise.

Caroline elbowed past the Englishman and plunked a cup down beside him. "They want coffee, Barden, good American coffee." She poured the mug full of coffee. "Milk and sugar?"

She shot a glance over her head at the man wielding the teapot and tray of fancy biscuits.

"No, thanks." Sam had learned to drink it black on the trail, where more often than not the fixings weren't available.

Caroline topped off Maggie's cup.

"Here you go." Sam passed her a few coins.

"Thank you. Enjoy, folks." Caroline walked away, and the Englishman followed her with his eyes as she left.

"Hmm." Maggie took a sip of her coffee and met Sam's gaze. "Looks to me like someone has eyes for Caroline, even if she didn't want to look for a husband."

Sam leaned toward her. "Maggie, I came to talk to you about. . .well, I had some notions about the future." He felt his cheeks burn, so he picked up the cup and sipped his coffee as a distraction. It was too hot, and he breathed in quickly to cool it before it scalded his gullet.

"What do you mean, Sam? Are you planning to stay at the Pine Tree Ranch?"

"I thought maybe I could work six months or so. I can live on almost nothing there, Maggie. I could send you most of my pay. And after six months or so, we could buy a few cattle." He clutched the coffee mug between his hands, but it was likely to burn his fingers, so he set it down clumsily.

She stared at him across the table. "Cattle?"

Sam nodded. "Mr. McClure would give me a good price on young stock."

"I—" She seemed speechless. She took a sip of her coffee and put the cup down. "Sam, after the six months, what then?"

"Well, I—I guess it would depend on whether the bank lets you keep your place. I was thinking you, me, and the boys. . ." He dared a glance at her. She was smiling, and he felt encouraged to plunge on, over the cataract. "Maggie, we could get married. That is—I mean—would you marry me?"

In the silence that followed, Sam realized the dozen or so diners in the restaurant were hanging on every word. He glanced around nervously.

A woman at the next table said wryly, "Come on, Miz Piner. What ya waiting for?"

Maggie went scarlet. She leaned over the table toward him and hissed, "Could we please go somewhere else for this?"

"I—uh—yeah." Sam gulped. Was she saving him the mortification of a public rejection?

He stood and waited for her to pass him. Maggie preceded him to the double doors. Caroline stood near the serving counter with a water glass in her hand, staring after them.

When they got outside and the door closed behind them, Sam blurted, "I'm sorry, Maggie. I didn't mean to embarrass you."

She walked on a few steps, around the corner of the building then turned and faced him.

"You didn't embarrass me, Sam, but I was afraid I might embarrass you."

"Wh–whadya mean?"

She stepped up real close and put her hands on his shoulders. Sam felt a little sluggish, but it didn't take him long to realize her intent. He folded her into his arms and kissed her. The shock of it rocked him back on his heels. She was so soft and—

"Maggie!" He pushed her away a few inches and studied her face.

"What?"

"I'll be able to make your regular payment at the end of June, and the one you missed. Then—"

"Sam, would you forget the mortgage, just for one minute?"

He swallowed hard. "Sure." Hesitantly, he bent to kiss her again. When she released him this time, he held her close. "I love you, Maggie. The boys, too."

She squeezed tight against him. "I love you, too, Sam. I know we haven't known each other long, but I feel like this is right."

"What about the husband tryouts?"

She leaned back and shook her head, her face puckered in distaste. "I didn't meet anyone who can hold a candle to you, Sam. I want a God-fearing man, one who'll care for me and the boys and work hard on the ranch. But I want one I can love, too, Sam. And I can love you."

Three kisses later, she whispered, "Now, about that mortgage. Would you be willing to go with me to talk to the auditor later on?"

"Yes, ma'am." He pulled away and eyed her cautiously. "You might not need a husband anymore, if he says Grant cheated you."

"Oh, yes," Maggie said. "I do need a husband. I need you, Sam."

Two weeks later, Maggie stood on the church steps in the warm June sun and straightened Fred's ribbon tie.

"There you go. My, you look handsome."

Fred made a face.

"Aren't you glad, Fred?"

"Awful glad. I'm glad we got the money back, and that we can buy cattle. But mostly, I'm glad about Sam."

Maggie smiled. "Me, too. The auditor was very nice about it, wasn't he?"

Fred nodded. "He even said he was sorry the bank did that to us."

"Not the bank. Mr. Grant did it. No one else at the bank knew he was cheating people and keeping the money himself." She smoothed folds of the new pale-blue dress she had sewn. "I'm glad you left the shotgun home, too."

Fred cracked a smile then.

Chardy Stevens poked her head out the church door. "All ready, Maggie."

"Thanks." They could hear strains of music from the piano.

Fred crooked his elbow and held it out to her gravely.

Maggie took it and walked with him into the church.

It seemed like the whole town had turned out for the wedding. Reverend Smith just had his cast removed the day before, and Dr. Carter had declared him fit to stand and marry them. Maggie smiled at him from the length of the aisle. Caroline Kane's English fellow had preached in Reverend Smith's place one Sunday, but Maggie was glad her own minister was up to performing her wedding.

She turned her gaze on the men at the front of the little church.

Benjy looked very small, standing between Sam and Sheriff Ingram, but he squared his shoulders and stretched as tall as he could.

They started down the aisle, with Fred muttering, "Left, right, left, right."

Sam's gaze drew Maggie's. She couldn't tell at first what his expression meant. Was he going to keel over, burst out in song, or cloud up and rain tears? Then his smile broke out, and she knew it was all right. Sam had just been doing his usual thoughtful assessment, and he had reached an agreeable conclusion. She returned his smile and walked straight toward him.

Sam took her hand, and she sent a mental prayer of thanks skyward. She barely heard Fred's rehearsed "My brother, Benjamin, and I do" when asked who gave her in marriage. But when Pastor Smith asked, "Do you, Margaret, take Samuel to be your lawful wedded husband?" she heard nothing else.

"I do," she said with conviction, and the joy in Sam's eyes echoed hers.

Susan Page Davis is the author of more than sixty Christian novels and novellas, which have sold more than 1.5 million copies. Her historical novels have won numerous awards, including the Carol Award, the Will Rogers Medallion for Western Fiction, and the Inspirational Readers' Choice Contest. She has also been a finalist in the More than Magic Contest and Willa Literary Awards. She lives in western Kentucky with her husband. She's the mother of six and grandmother of ten. Visit her website at: www.susanpagedavis.com.

A Clean Slate

By Susanne Dietze

Dedication

For all teachers who generously and sacrificially give of their time and talents for their students, especially my mom, Virginia Copeland.

Acknowledgments

Gina Welborn, in your quest to be a blessing, you responded to an e-mail from this stranger all those years ago, invited me to join Inkwell, and became my friend. Thank you for your help and support in writing and in life. Hugs and chocolate to you, sister.

Author's Note

Drew's decision to fight for the Union was inspired by my family history. Although I'm a native Californian, my roots in middle Tennessee run deep, and I descend from two families who were neighbors but supported opposite sides during the Civil War. My great-grandfather's family fought for the Union, while my great-grandmother's ancestors fought for the Confederacy.

Behold, I am doing a new thing; now it springs forth, do you not perceive it?
ISAIAH 43:19 ESV

Chapter 1

In her four years as teacher for Turtle Springs School, Roberta Green had never once left the schoolroom at day's end in such an untidy state—until today.

She hadn't erased the long division from the blackboard, replaced the primers on the bookshelf, or swept the floor. The only thing she'd had time to sweep was her students from the congested doorway of the one-room schoolhouse.

"See you Monday, boys and girls." She gently guided them out the door. "No shoving, Opie. Henry, don't forget your lunch pail."

A small hand waved by her face. "My ribbon ith th-tuck."

Red-haired Minnie Lomax had developed a lisp when she lost both her top front teeth last week, but the seven-year-old's habit of removing her bonnet each morning without untying the bow, and somehow tugging the ribbon into a tight knot in the process, was not new.

Take a deep breath, Birdy. It will be fine if you're a few minutes late. Although, she was already several minutes tardy, and who knew what was going on at the Tumble Inn by now. Birdy puffed out an exasperated breath and dug at the knot.

Mary Ann, the middle of the three Lomax girls, fidgeted near the schoolhouse door. "Aunt Birdy, you don't have time. It's already started."

And *it*—the extraordinary event at the Tumble Inn—would change the lives of the three Lomax girls forever. Birdy yanked, hurrying. "I know."

"You forgot the rule-th, Mary Ann." Minnie fisted her hands on her nonexistent hips. "We have to call her Mith Green until we get home. *Then* we can call her Aunt Birdy."

"No one's left in the schoolhouse to overhear, Minnie, and everyone knows she lives with us, anyway." Polly, Minnie's eldest sister, didn't usually sound so sharp. The thirteen-year-old was sweet as shoofly pie most of the time.

But today was a strange day, and it was little wonder they were all tense. Birdy plopped the bonnet on Minnie's head, the ribbon still in a knot. "Sorry, Minnie. I'll fix it when I get home, but Mary Ann's right. I'm late."

Polly preceded her out the door and paused on the porch. "I'll have supper waiting for you and Ma."

"Minnie and I will set the table." Mary Ann dashed out the door. Her boots thumped the three stairs down from the schoolhouse to the street.

"I won't even complain," Minnie promised.

Birdy grinned. She couldn't love this red-headed trio more if she was related to them by blood. She was their aunt in her heart, though, privileged to live with them and their mother, her best friend, Frieda, and she loved them all fiercely. She would do right by them all today.

She brushed chalk dust from the green-plaid wool of her sleeve, shoved a pencil behind her ear—unladylike, perhaps, but she was rushing—and grabbed her leather-bound journal. Resolving to clean the schoolroom tomorrow morning, she hastened out to the schoolhouse's tiny porch where she yanked the door shut, tugging and pulling the door handle upward to get it to latch, since it stuck so badly these days. "I know you're worried, girls, but it'll be over soon. Pray we'll have discernment with all those men."

She twisted around and startled. The girls, her intended audience, bobbed several yards' distant, already headed for home, but someone had nevertheless heard what she'd said. A man in a dark gray coat stood on the bottom step of the schoolhouse.

"I didn't mean to frighten you, ma'am." He removed his hat, revealing straight hair so dark a brown it was almost black. He was young and broad shouldered, if lean, with a hint of dark stubble on his jaw. A stranger to her.

No surprise, almost all the men in town were strangers these past few weeks.

What was surprising was his Southern drawl. Her shoulders stiffened. The South might have surrendered to the Union over a year ago, but the war wasn't quite over in her bruised heart.

She'd been praying for the will to forgive the Confederacy for what it took from her. Perhaps meeting this fellow was a chance to take a step in that direction. At any rate, she should show him common courtesy. This fellow wasn't personally responsible for the sad trajectory of her life.

He was, however, lost. "Come along." She brushed past him, tipping her head in invitation to follow her.

He did, matching her hurried stride. "I beg your pardon?"

"That was the schoolhouse."

"I figured, with the bell on the porch and the swings in the yard. And since you're the one holding its keys, I reckon you're the schoolmarm."

"Correct, but the auditions are at the Tumble Inn restaurant, not the schoolhouse. See it there, ahead on the right?"

It was hard to miss, at three stories tall. The inn looked slightly worse for wear, like the schoolhouse, Frieda's house, and almost every other building in town. Everyone did repairs as they could, but the times were difficult and funds were strained.

Without men, their town was dying.

Little wonder signs were posted at regular intervals up and down the street: HUSBANDS WANTED. MEN AUDITIONING FOR PROSPECTIVE HUSBANDS SIGN UP AT THE MAYOR'S OFFICE.

A thrill of nerves skittered up Birdy's spine. Those auditions were being held right this minute. The man beside her had come for this purpose, of course. All the men had.

Smiling, he looked down at her with eyes as blue as a jaybird's wing. "Thanks for walking me here, ma'am. I confess it's been a while since a schoolmarm escorted me anywhere."

It was hard not to smile back. "If you were escorted, you must have been misbehaving."

"I dunked Audra Colby's braid in the inkwell. Miss Meredith dragged me out back by the ear." His laugh was pleasant. Comforting, too, maybe because she hadn't heard the laugh of a man her age in a long time.

Emory's was the heartiest laugh she'd ever heard, though. Emory—

"Here, I'll get the door." He dashed ahead and pulled open the door to the restaurant on the inn's ground floor. Voices spilled out, indicating the auditions for husbands were well underway. Would this venture produce any matches?

Before entering the restaurant, Birdy paused to nod at this man who, completely unawares, had given her the opportunity to interact normally with a Southerner, a small but significant step toward forgiving the Confederacy. "I wish you the best at finding the perfect wife, sir."

"I don't need perfect. Just perfect for me and chosen by the Lord."

Her estimation of him raised a notch. One of her neighbors would be blessed to have a husband who sought God's will in his life.

She hurried inside, giving her eyes a moment to adjust to the dim. Mrs. Martinchek called *time* and the scrapes of chairs and benches against the wood floor echoed through the space as men of all sizes stood and moved to their next post. Birdy nodded at Abby Melton, the mayor, passed the serious-looking sheriff who provided security during the proceedings, and then hastened to one of the small tables where a strawberry-haired woman in blue stripes sat, her face expectant.

"Sorry I'm late." Birdy perched on a stool beside Frieda's chair.

Frieda patted Birdy's hand. "It's all right. You're here now."

"I wouldn't let you audition husbands alone, unless you wanted to."

"You haven't let me go through anything alone, Birdy. Not losing Hank, not raising the girls, and I know you wouldn't miss this. Not that I've needed much help yet. I met a man named Jug Swan." Frieda shuddered. "We would not have suited—oh hello."

A tall, fine-looking gentleman with a thick blond mustache and neat brown frock coat appeared at their table and bowed. He looked to be in his late twenties, maybe thirty, a few years shy of Frieda's thirty-three. "How do you do, ladies?"

"Well, thank you." Frieda indicated for him to take a seat. "I'm Mrs. Lomax. I've asked my friend, Miss Green, to listen in on our conversation."

He grinned, revealing even teeth. "It helps to have the counsel of a friend in times like these. My name is Sherman Toovey."

Birdy pulled the pencil from behind her ear and scribbled his name in her journal. She also jotted *mustache, brown coat* to help them remember him later.

"Where are you from, Mr. Toovey?" Frieda's voice was sweet, much like her daughter Polly's. Frieda's husband, Hank, had always teased that her voice was sweetened by all the honey she put in her tea.

Birdy frowned. Thinking of Hank always made her think of Emory. And her brother, Lemuel, too. But this wasn't the time to think of fallen heroes, lost in the war. She had an obligation to help Frieda forge a future.

"Maryland." Mr. Toovey crossed his legs. "When I came home from the war, I thought a change seemed in order. I sold the farm and thought I'd try something new."

"You farmed?" Frieda sat up taller. "I have a farm."

Sherman Toovey sat up taller, too. "How many acres?"

"One hundred and twenty, right outside of town. My husband left me the land. He also left me with three daughters," Frieda said, making him aware of her priorities.

"Are they as pretty as their mother?"

Frieda giggled, like she hadn't done since Hank marched off to war.

Birdy wrote *flatterer, but he's right. Frieda is pretty.*

Taking further notes proved a challenge, since Frieda abandoned her list of prepared questions and chatted with Mr. Toovey. They discovered their mutual love of fiddle music and ice cream—which would be served at tomorrow's Founder's Day celebration, to their mutual delight. Everything, in fact, seemed to be to their mutual delight. Birdy was starting to feel unnecessary as Frieda's guide in this whole auditioning-husbands process. She doodled a stick-legged bird on the page and fantasized about supper. Would the girls remember to put out the butter?

"May I escort you to the Founder's Day celebration tomorrow for some of that ice cream, Mrs. Lomax?" Mr. Toovey leaned forward.

"I'd be honored." Frieda giggled again.

While they set up plans, Birdy allowed her gaze to wander to the others in the room. Maggie Piner, mother of two of Birdy's students, interviewed a fellow in need of a shave. Black-haired Jane Ransome stared down the man across the table from her, while Chardy Stevens from the mercantile offered her auditioner a polite smile. Blond Debbie Barker nodded at Virginia Tumbleston, sister of the inn's proprietor, Caroline Kane. Virginia set down a tray of cups near the punch bowl; they'd had their hands more than full at the inn since the men came to town.

Birdy's gaze tugged to the right, meeting the unsmiling gaze of the man in the gray coat from the schoolhouse. He leaned against the wall, watching. Why wasn't he auditioning? Perhaps he waited his turn, or perhaps by arriving late, he'd missed his opportunity.

He pushed off from the wall and strode toward them. He must want to meet Frieda, but just as in school, the men must take turns. He couldn't jump in and—

"Toovey, isn't it?" To Birdy's surprise, his gaze was on Frieda's new friend, not Frieda. "May I speak to you in private?"

Mr. Toovey's eyes bugged out. "I'm busy, fella."

"It'll take a moment, no more." The man from the schoolhouse did not look happy. And now, neither did Frieda.

Birdy rose. "I'm sure Mr. Toovey will be happy to speak with you after the auditions."

"But—"

Birdy had no choice. She took the man's arm and tugged him outside.

Drew followed along, his arm caught in the fair-haired schoolmarm's firm grasp. For a dainty thing, she sure had a robust grip. He could have pulled away if he'd wanted to, but instead, he opened the door for her.

Her hand fell away the instant they were outside. "I don't know what you're trying to accomplish, Mister—"

"Drew Cooper."

"But you're ruining things for Frieda."

He was ruining it? Now that was funny. "Is she your sister, miss?"

"Roberta Green." Her surname was the hue of her dress, although the gown's pastel color reminded Drew more of tender leaves and baby apples than jade or spruce. Her eyes were a shade grayer than her dress, but right now, those eyes narrowed in suspicion. "Why do you want to know?"

"I overheard her making plans with that Toovey character. Did I hear wrong?"

Her arms folded. "It's none of your affair. If you're upset you didn't get a chance to audition with Frieda, there's still time. Speak to the mayor."

This was coming out all wrong. "It's Toovey I need words with, before things go further."

"Why?"

Even though he came to Turtle Springs for a fresh start, he had the same principles he'd always had, so he couldn't stand by and watch someone get hurt. But he didn't need to cause a scene. "I don't like telling tales out of school—no pun intended for the schoolmarm—so I'd prefer to handle this with Toovey."

If she was affected by his unintended pun, she didn't show it. Instead her pale brows rose high on her forehead. Then she positioned her body so he couldn't get back in the restaurant—even though she must be a full eight inches shorter and fifty pounds lighter than he was. She glared up at him. "I don't want you upsetting Frieda. Say your piece and I'll decide if it's worth disturbing her audition with Mr. Toovey."

She reminded him of Aunt Lou, a managing female, but also as upright and loving as they came. And he knew better than to argue with a woman like his aunt. "Fine. Warn your sister before she goes into a courtship with a man who's less than truthful to her."

"Frieda is my friend. But Mr. Toovey likes children, farming, and Frieda, three things she needs in a husband. How can I be certain he's the liar and you're not? No offense, Mr. Cooper, but I don't know either of you."

She had a point. The schoolmarm was as sharp as she was pretty. He'd have to tell her outright, then. "He's misrepresenting himself."

"As what?" She looked up at him with a Schoolmarm Face, disapproving and disappointed, like he'd been the liar, not Toovey.

"A single man, for one thing. I overheard him tell someone on the train to Manhattan that he had a wife back in Maryland, as well as a heap of debt—and he sold shoes."

She flinched. "He's married?"

"If he isn't, he was lying to the man on the train. But if he is a married man, he has no business here."

"Why would he do something so terrible?"

"If what he said about his debts was true, he might be hiding from them." Or maybe he thought if he married a widow with property, he could cash it in and leave her, too. It wouldn't be the first time an unscrupulous man married more than one woman for their money and then disappeared—

Drew didn't like thinking of it. "I don't know what's true with Toovey, but she should be warned in case. I have no proof though, ma'am. Just my report, on my honor as a gentleman, a Christian, and a soldier."

"A *Confederate* soldier."

Ah, there it was—the reason her lips had pursed the minute he'd started talking at the schoolhouse. "I was in the 5th Tennessee Volunteer Cavalry Regiment from Murfreesboro—a Union regiment."

There went those eyebrows again, up to her hairline. "A Tennessean enlisting in the Union army is brave. Almost as brave as being a Jayhawker."

A chuckle escaped his throat.

She shifted. "Pardon me, Mr. Cooper. I'd like to speak to Mr. Toovey."

Oh no. "I should be the one—"

But she had marched inside, and he had no choice but to follow her to where Mr. Toovey shook hands with her friend, Frieda.

Miss Green sashayed between them. "Mr. Toovey, may I ask one thing before you go?"

He sneaked a glance at Drew. "Anything for a friend of Mrs. Lomax."

The schoolmarm folded her hands at her waist, a posture that made her look exactly like a woman of her occupation should. "What did you farm in Maryland?"

A tiny pause. "Vegetables."

"Beans? Cabbages?"

"Exactly. Cabbages and all sorts of beans, from green to skunk." Toovey exchanged grins with Frieda.

Drew folded his arms. Where exactly was the schoolmarm going with this? He'd expected her to accuse him of being married, not ask about the farm he didn't have.

Miss Green blinked up at Toovey. "I haven't done well with skunk beans in our garden. When did you find it the best time to plant them?"

Frieda touched Miss Green's arm. "We can discuss planting another time, Birdy."

"No, I don't mind." Toovey gave the schoolmarm a condescending smile. "After the frost."

"Well, yes, but when, precisely?"

"Follow the *Farmer's Almanac*, I always say."

"I agree." Miss Green nodded. "So the waning moon, then, right before the new moon? Because the dark is good for the seeds?"

Drew pitched his head forward. Had he heard her right?

"Yep. Waning moon." Toovey rocked on his heels. "Maybe your soil is the problem."

She fixed her disappointed schoolmarm expression on him. "Incorrect. I live on a farm, you see, and several of my students will grow to be farmers, so I use the almanac in my schoolhouse, yet most of the children already know above-ground crops like beans are planted in the *waxing* moon. It's a practice as old as agriculture, but science has proven seeds absorb more water during the waxing and full moons than at other phases of the moon."

Drew burst into laughter, but Toovey burst into a sputtering froth. "You tricked me. I wasn't thinking."

"Forgive me for employing chicanery, sir, in my quest to learn the truth."

"Shi-kaner-what?"

"Deception. Flimflam. Underhandedness by purposefully misspeaking to test your response." She sounded like a human dictionary.

Drew liked it. "Come on, Toovey, the jig is up."

Frieda pinked like a ripe berry. "Are you a farmer or not, Mr. Toovey?"

Toovey lifted his hands, but the gesture revealed a fine-looking manicure and no calluses. There was the answer to her question.

"Well, I—I should like to learn to be one." Toovey said it like a question, hoping it was the correct response.

"And so you might have, on my farm, had you been honest with me. A husband with a sound knowledge of farming is important to me, yes, but such skills can be learned if a man is hardworking and eager. And honest, but I could never trust you now." Frieda gathered her shawl, so she didn't see Toovey shove past Drew, out of the inn.

Miss Green put a comforting hand on her friend's shoulders. "He's gone, and his phony farm isn't the worst of it. He might even be married—Frieda? What are you doing?"

Lips clamped shut like she was holding back tears, Frieda dashed out of the inn. Drew rubbed his jaw. Exposing Toovey as a liar was the right thing to do, but if he'd spoken to Toovey privately, he could've spared the ladies hurt or embarrassment.

Shoulders sagging, Miss Green looked up at Drew. "Thank you for the information, Mr. Cooper. You've protected Frieda from a grave mistake. I wish you well finding a bride in the auditions."

"Oh, I'm not here for the auditions." Drew peered down at her. "I'm here for you, Miss Green."

Chapter 2

"I am not seeking a husband." Truer words had never left Birdy's mouth. She might be unmarried, standing in a room full of husband-seeking females, but she was not one of them. Not that way.

She'd had her chance at happily-ever-after. She didn't get another.

Mr. Cooper's dark brows rose. "No, I need to speak to you. Because you're the schoolmarm."

Heat suffused her face. How foolish of her to assume he'd been lost, looking for the auditions. Why, he could be the parent of a prospective student, come to meet the teacher. What must he think of her for dragging him here? "I am terribly sorry, sir."

He gestured for her to precede him outside, a good idea considering how hot the room had suddenly grown. "It was only natural to assume I was looking for the auditions. That's why all the men are here, isn't it? Well, almost all of them."

But not him. Nodding, she preceded him down to the street where she shut her eyes for the briefest of moments, grateful for the tickling of the late afternoon breeze against her nape. "How can I help you? Will you and your wife be enrolling students in the school?"

"Another reasonable assumption, but I don't have any young 'uns. I've never been hitched." He grinned. "I was hoping to borrow some books."

One wrong guess after another, where this man was concerned. Birdy folded her hands tightly together. "Books?"

"For reading." His eyes twinkled.

"You can't read? You said you went to school." The words blurted out without delicacy or discretion, and she shook her head at herself.

"I can read my Bible and my *Farmer's Almanac*, but I'd like to improve my skill and my mind by attempting some literature. Do you have anything I could borrow?"

Birdy's hand flew to her chest. Oh yes, she had literature. What an understatement. "I do not boast a great library, to be sure, but I own several dozen volumes." Her mind searched her collection for titles that might appeal to a man. "What did you have in mind? Dickens? Hawthorne? *The Count of Monte Cristo*?"

"I never read none of 'em, ma'am, but I'm game to try anything." He toed the dirt with his boot. "I've always wanted to get a gander at Shakespeare, though."

Birdy gasped. Except for her schoolmasters, she'd never met a man who actually *wanted* to read Shakespeare. Her fiancé, Emory, had happily tolerated—but tolerated, nonetheless—her sonnet recitations. Pa bought her books without ever wanting to read them himself, and when she tried to share them with her brother, Lemuel, he'd rolled his eyes and told her *"If the hogs have no use for sonnets, I don't either."*

Birdy had teased that, clearly, the same was true in regards to soap and table manners.

But that was before the war, when her house and heart were full.

She took a shaky breath, banishing the memories far away, at least for now. Besides, Mr. Cooper had sought her out because he wanted to read Shakespeare—he really did. His eyes sparked and he had a look of eagerness about him few of her students ever expressed.

"You'll be in town for a while?" The moment she asked it, she bit her lip. What a silly question. If he was auditioning to marry a local woman, there was a good chance he'd be wed within the fortnight.

"I'm at the Tumble Inn now, but yes, I'm looking to buy ranchland here in Turtle Springs."

"Splendid." She hugged her journal to her chest. "Are you able to meet at the schoolhouse tomorrow morning at nine?"

"Yes, ma'am."

"Very well, Mr. Cooper. Tomorrow I shall introduce you to Shakespeare." She held out her hand.

The grip of his handshake was perfect, firm enough to show respect but not so tight she'd be wincing and shaking her fingers to restore blood flow. "Thank you kindly, Miss Green."

"Hey, Miz Green?" Chester Spitts, a man of middle years with a fondness for whiskey and whose farm was as poorly tended as his gnarled, dirty hair, leered at her from across the street.

She took a fortifying breath. "Yes, Mr. Spitts?"

"I thought you were all high and mighty about not auditionin', but you got yourself a new man already?"

She almost blurted, "He's not my man," but she wouldn't dignify his loathsome question with a response. Then she realized she still clasped Mr. Cooper's hand. She yanked it back and prayed for a breeze to cool the heat flooding her cheeks for the umpteenth time this afternoon.

"Good day, Mr. Cooper."

"Thanks, ma'am." Mr. Cooper kept his gaze on her, even though he surely heard Chester Spitts's amused hoots as well as she did. Bless him for ignoring them.

Birdy's farewell nod was curt. Holding her head high while she passed Chester Spitts, she hastened toward the Lomax farmhouse. Poor Frieda. Birdy hadn't realized she'd take Mr. Toovey's deception so to heart. He was hardly even an acquaintance, and the town was full of other prospective grooms who were indubitably more honorable. Frieda should be grateful, not sad.

Frieda lived close to town, so it didn't take more than a few minutes for Birdy to reach the borders of the Lomax farm. Passing rows of young corn, she hurried until she reached the white-rail fence surrounding the house. Frieda had left the gate open, so Birdy shut it behind her and trod the path to the porch steps to the clapboard house.

The door stuck, like the one at the schoolhouse. The white paint around the door peeled and crackled. Once inside, the savory scent of stew mingled with the faint odor of mold, something they hadn't been able to fully eradicate since the roof started leaking this past winter. Although she and Frieda and done their best to fix the roof, the smell lingered along with new drips and a dark circle staining the rag rug in the parlor.

Frieda's new husband, whoever he would be, had quite a list of chores waiting for him.

At once, Birdy was greeted by a knee-high, buff-colored terrier, and she reached down to give him a proper patting. Diggory—named because he was a good digger—might not be a purebred variety, but he was as pure in heart as a dog could be. With a final pat, Birdy rose and dropped her journal and pencil onto the scratched-up table in the vestibule. She hadn't buffed or polished it in a while, and it showed. Tomorrow, she'd get to that and the other chores she'd postponed this past busy week. "Girls? Frieda?"

The only response was the clank of the cast-iron skillet in the kitchen. Birdy passed the dining room table—set for five, thanks to Mary Ann and Minnie—and turned into the kitchen, where Frieda dropped the kettle on the stove with such vigor that the clatter made Birdy jump.

"Frieda? What are you doing? The auditions are still going on."

Frieda didn't look up from measuring tea into the brown glazed pot. "I'm not going back."

Diggory scratched at the kitchen door, so Birdy let him out. He ran to join the girls on the small rise in the yard behind the house, but then they started back down and Mary Ann said something about playing with the new piglets sleeping in a special little pen in the barn. "Don't let them out again, girls!" Birdy turned back. "What do you mean, not going back? Of course you are."

Frieda's head shook.

"Whyever not? You were the first to sign up when this harebrained idea was proposed. You couldn't have been more eager."

Frieda's glare could've frosted the cornfield. "You said auditioning husbands was a fine idea, but now you've admitted what I suspected all along. You think it's harebrained!"

Birdy's big mouth! She chomped the inside of her cheek. "It *is* fine."

"For me, maybe, but not for *you*."

"I don't have three children and a farm to consider." Birdy's spine stiffened. "You have to admit, it's a little extraordinary to audition husbands—"

"You said *harebrained*, not extraordinary."

"Well, I'm sorry I said it." Birdy sighed. "You know I support you in this. If I didn't, I wouldn't have come today to help assess the gentlemen—"

Frieda sloshed water as she filled the pot. "You did more than *assess* Sherman Toovey."

Shouldn't Frieda be grateful? "He lied. Mr. Cooper overheard him say he's married, and while we can't prove it, it's as obvious as his bushy mustache that he's no farmer."

Frieda's shoulders slumped. "I would've figured it out in about a half hour, Birdy. I'm capable. But you made me look like a fool in front of all the men in the restaurant. I can't face them now."

Birdy picked at a hangnail. "That wasn't my intention. I only wanted to protect you."

"I don't need protecting. I need a friend who won't turn me into a spectacle." Frieda sighed. "Mr. Toovey may have been trying to swindle me of my farm—oh yes, I'd expected some men might not be in Turtle Springs for the right reasons—but you and that Mr. Cooper fellow, whoever he is, might have been wrong. You should have spoken to Mr. Toovey privately."

Just as Drew Cooper had intended to do. Birdy rubbed her aching head. "But—"

Frieda held up her hand, forestalling Birdy from speaking. "I don't want the tea anymore. I'm not hungry either. I'll call the girls in from outside and you can eat supper without me tonight."

Birdy gaped. She hadn't meant to embarrass Frieda. Wasn't a brief scene far preferable to a lifetime of pain and remorse? If Birdy was overzealous, well, she hadn't been able to protect or control much of anything in her life, especially since the war started.

Birdy forced a smile as the girls filed in to wash up for supper, eyes wide with questions. They didn't ask them while they ate their stew and cornbread, though. Birdy nibbled, mulling over her conversation with Frieda. They'd never had an argument like this before, and Birdy had lived here since Pa died in the summer of '61.

Before his passing, she hadn't known about Pa's debt to the bank. Within a week of losing him, she'd lost her home, too. She'd been blessed to take the teaching post vacated by the previous schoolmaster, who'd marched off with her fiancé, Emory, and her brother, Lemuel, when the war broke out. The schoolmasters always lived with the Lomaxes as part of their compensation, so Birdy hadn't felt like she was taking charity when she moved into the vacant room. The arrangement helped Birdy and Frieda both, since Frieda received a few dollars for housing the schoolteacher. As an added blessing, they'd grown so close living together, they'd become like sisters.

Then one cool autumn afternoon, when the sky was lead dark and the wind whipped the bluestem grass like waves of water, two letters arrived for her at once, one telling her Emory was dead, and the other stating the same news about Lemuel. The three most important men in her life, Pa, Lemuel, and precious Emory, were gone, and soon thereafter, word arrived that Frieda's husband, Hank, had succumbed to dysentery.

Quickly, Birdy had become aware how little control she had over anything, but she and Frieda held each other together in those dark days. Was it any wonder Birdy wanted to protect Frieda now?

"Ith Ma getting married?" Minnie asked while they cleared the table.

Polly rolled her eyes. "She left the audition, Minnie, so no."

"There are ways to meet gentlemen without auditioning them," Birdy said, trying to inject hope into her tone. The girls wanted a new father as much they wanted a husband for their mother. "Tomorrow, I need your help tidying the schoolroom."

"But tomorrow's the Founder's Day celebration. I wanna go bad." Mary Ann's lower lip protruded.

"You want to go *badly*. Go is a verb, so it must be described by an adverb." They might not be in the schoolroom, but Birdy couldn't stop teaching. "As for the celebration, there will be plenty of time for you to enjoy the festivities."

She'd make sure of it.

They cleaned the kitchen, saw to the livestock, and retreated to the parlor, where the girls played with Diggory and Birdy read. Frieda joined them after a while, but she didn't look Birdy in the eye. It was a relief to retreat to her bedroom to plan each grade's spelling lists and reading assignments for next week. Which reminded her—

She had a new student. She crossed her tiny room to her bookshelf and pulled down the volume of Shakespeare.

Smiling, she wrote the name of the man who would be borrowing it on a page in her notebook.

Library List: Drew Cooper.

The next morning, Drew hurried over his breakfast, hardly tasting the molasses on his hot corn mush.

"You're going to get a bellyache, eating so fast." Drew's companion, Jeb Washburn, had the look of a man who'd worked outdoors for twenty years or more— tanned, muscled, with deep lines around his eyes from squinting in the sun. He was jovial, too, and Drew had found Jeb to be one of the most amiable fellows staying at the Tumble Inn.

"You should talk, Jeb. Have you looked at your bowl?"

Jeb looked down at his near-empty bowl and laughed. "Guess we're both hungry. Say, I'll go with you to look at land, if'n you want. After working cattle ranches since I could shave, I know a thing or two about grassland."

Drew knew a fair shake about cattle. He'd researched ranching and had the funds to buy land, thanks to an inheritance from his mother split between him and his brother, Clement. In many ways, he was well prepared for this new enterprise, but he'd be a fool to turn down Jeb's expertise.

"I'd like that, but this morning I have a meeting with Miss—Nevermind."

Jeb's brows shot up, furrowing his brow. "Miss Nevermind, eh? I thought you weren't doing the auditions like the rest of us."

"I'm not." Drew swiped his lips with his napkin. "I'm going back to school. See you at dinner, Jeb."

Drew paid the bill and ventured to Stevens Mercantile to buy a few items first. His meeting with the teacher wasn't scheduled until nine, leaving him plenty of time to complete some tasks.

Already, townsfolk were decorating for tonight's Founder's Day celebration. He waved to the mayor, Miss Melton, as well as the sheriff who always seemed to be watching her with a possessive eye, and ambled toward the schoolhouse, where he set to work.

Drew had plugged three large holes with a mixture of lime and sand before footsteps—more than one pair—sounded on the gravel path to the schoolhouse.

He craned his neck to smile at Miss Green and her young companions, the three girls with red, braided pigtails he'd seen with her at the schoolhouse yesterday. "How do you do, ladies?"

"What are you doing?" The littlest girl squatted beside him.

"Daubing the wall so no vermin get in."

She leaped back, smack into the middle sister. "Mice-th!"

"Mice are everywhere, Minnie." The sister rolled her eyes. "We don't see 'em at home because Diggory's such a good rat catcher."

Miss Green mounted the porch. "Mr. Cooper, these are the Lomaxes—Polly, Mary Ann, and Minnie. Girls, say hello to Mr. Cooper. Now what's this about mice?"

Drew rose from his haunches for the greetings before pointing down to the holes. "I couldn't help noticing these holes yesterday. Seemed I could fix them right fast, so I did. Hope I didn't set anyone's dander up."

"Certainly not mine. What a clean job you've done of it, too." She glanced down at his daub-work. "It's thoughtful of you, although you have no obligation to earn the borrowing of the book." She smiled and pulled a leather volume from the gold-and-green brocade satchel she carried. Gold lettering on the spine announced the author: Shakespeare. "I brought you sonnets. Do you enjoy poetry?"

"I don't know, but I aim to find out." He added the last bit of lime-and-sand mixture to the hole.

Three pairs of footsteps retreated down the stairs to the yard, toward the swings. The girls must not be admirers of Shakespeare. Drew chuckled.

Miss Green leaned against the schoolhouse wall. "I'm sure you've heard of several of these. Sonnet 18 is quite famous. 'Shall I compare thee to a summer's day? Thou art more lovely and more temperate.'"

Romantic words.

"I'm not sure." Drew tasted the words in his mind. "What does he mean by temperate? Like the weather on a day like today, pleasant and comfortable?"

"Precisely. The object of the sonnet is more pleasant and comfortable than a day like today, when the sun is warm and the temperature fine." She twisted a key in the stubborn-sounding lock. Clearly, it gave her as much trouble now as it had the previous day.

"May I?" He rose and held out his hand.

"By all means." She stepped back.

The locking mechanism was troublesome, all right. He twisted and yanked before the door opened. "I'll fix this for you."

"That's kind, Mr. Cooper, but not necessary. The school board is aware of our maintenance needs, and. . ." Her voice trailed off as she stepped inside the schoolroom and sighed, her gaze taking in the space.

Drew paused behind her. Aside from the slight untidiness of books waiting to be put away, the room was clean and orderly, but there were signs of chronic disrepair from top to bottom. Brown water stains splotched the ceiling. The walls required a coat of paint, and a few loose planks caused potential hazards underfoot.

He removed his hat. "Looks like the school board has been a little busy, Miss Green, but I happen to have a hammer on me." A brand-new one, too.

"Nonsense. You're here for a book. One moment." She swept past him to lean out the door. "Girls? Come help, please, in case of a surprise inspection today. Polly, will you sweep? Mary Ann, put away the primers, and Minnie, clean the blackboard. Thank you."

Did the school board really check in, unannounced, on weekends? From the tight set of Birdy Green's jaw, Drew suspected they did indeed.

Well, he'd help, too. "Hold up on the sweeping for a minute, Miss Polly."

The redhead hadn't even touched the broom yet, but she nodded.

He trotted outside to retrieve the box of tools he'd purchased, returning to squat at the loose floorboards with the hammer and nails. "I'll be done in a jiffy."

"How kind of you. I didn't notice the loose plank until Nancy McGee tripped yesterday." Miss Green set the book of Shakespeare on the desk and moved to the blackboard.

"She wasn't hurt, was she?" Drew pried out the loose nail.

"No, thankfully." She drew a diagram of a corn plant on the side of the blackboard Minnie had cleaned. While Drew worked, he snuck glances at the dainty teacher as she labeled it: Roots. Stalk. Ear. Leaf. Silk. She had impressive penmanship, but then again, she was a schoolmarm. It was probably a job requirement.

Mary Ann, the one putting away primers, paused by Drew's side. "Tell us if you find something underneath. I thought I saw Opie hide something in there."

"Oh dear." Miss Green spun around, chalk in hand.

Knowing boys, it could be anything. Drew snuck a finger under the board. Sure enough, something solid met his touch. He extracted a cream-colored square flecked with bluish-green. "Opie doesn't like cheese?"

143

Minnie squealed. Mary Ann gagged. Polly shuddered, and Miss Green dashed toward him with a dustpan. "Opie is seven. He doesn't like anything except dessert."

"I'm th-even, too, and I eat chee-th." Minnie lifted her chin then eyed the cheese. "But maybe not that kind."

Drew couldn't blame anyone for preferring to hide the cheese rather than eat it. It reminded him of food he'd had to eat during the war.

"The McGees are struggling to eat," Miss Green whispered to Drew while he dropped the cheese onto the pan with a metallic *clink*. "His mother, Jenny, is a widow."

Drew nodded, returning to the task of sealing up Opie's hiding spot. "The war left a bitter legacy."

Finished with the blackboard, Minnie leaned on the desk closest to him. "It took our Pa."

He'd guessed as much. "I'm sorry."

"Are you here to marry our ma?"

The hammer fell out of his hand. Miss Green spun around again. "Minnie."

"Ma is real nice," Mary Ann added. "And you're good with tools. Our house needs fixing, bad." She glanced at her teacher. "Bad*ly*."

Polly clutched the broom. "She's a good cook, too."

"That's enough, girls." Miss Green's usual pale complexion mottled pink, but the girls looked at him, awaiting his answer. Drew screwed the lid on the nail jar, choosing his words carefully. "I met your ma yesterday, brief-like, and she seemed like a fine woman, but I didn't come to Kansas for the auditions."

"Brief*ly*," Mary Ann muttered.

"Why'd you come, then?" Minnie sidled up to him, smelling of something fruity, like she'd had jam for breakfast.

These Lomax girls sure weren't shy. Miss Green opened her mouth, but Drew held up a hand. Some might think children should be seen and not heard, but Drew had never believed that. Instead he thought people who asked honest questions, children included, deserved honest answers.

"The ad drew me to Kansas, all right, but I'm looking for ranch land and a fresh start." Not love. "See, my family isn't as close is yours is. My brother was mad as a hornet when I joined the Union army, like your pa did."

Minnie patted his shoulder in a sweet, gentle gesture. "Did he die, too?"

"No. He's back on the homestead."

Mary Ann frowned, but then she turned her expectant gaze on Miss Green. "Can we go home yet? I want to get ready for the Founder's Day celebration."

"Go play while Mr. Cooper and I finish up." Miss Green tipped her head toward the door. Once the girls were outside, she leaned against her desk. "I'm sorry for the girls' impertinence."

"They're curious, is all. It's all right if you want to ask me something, too." From the way she chewed her bottom lip, it was clear she was as curious as Minnie.

She lasted a whole ten seconds before she cleared her throat. "Did you leave Tennessee because of your brother?"

"Yes." He packed up the tools.

"You couldn't reconcile?"

"I wanted to, but it didn't work out."

"It must have been awkward, with you having fought on opposite sides."

"Awkward isn't the word I'd use." He barked out a humorless laugh. "Clement preferred to see me dead than back at home."

Her gulp was audible. "Dead?"

Drew offered a smile to lessen the sting of his brother's threat, but he couldn't quite meet her eyes. "He said he'd kill me if I didn't leave Tennessee."

Chapter 3

Birdy's hand went to her throat. Mr. Cooper's own brother threatened to murder him? She struggled for words, but none of the usual platitudes seemed appropriate. She settled for the words on her tongue.

"That's horrible."

"It was."

"Surely your brother didn't mean it."

"I'm sure you're right, but at the time, he had a hammer in his hand. I thought it best not to stay and tempt him to sin." Mr. Cooper offered a small smile, as if to lighten the gravity of his words.

His smile didn't fool her a lick. All it convinced her of was he loved his brother but didn't wish to disparage him, just like he hadn't wished to challenge Mr. Toovey and embarrass Frieda publicly yesterday. That spoke volumes for his character—and put her to shame for the humiliating scene she'd caused at the auditions. Frieda had been correct. For all her good intentions, Birdy had been merciless.

Her stomach swooped. She'd set things right with Frieda, but at this moment, Mr. Cooper stood in front of her, unquestionably wounded by his brother's actions. She couldn't dare ignore his pain.

Beyond a handshake, she hadn't touched a man since Pa died, and it felt strange, but she laid her fingers on Mr. Cooper's forearm. "I'm sure your brother regrets his words, but I can't imagine the pain they must have caused you."

"I didn't expect it, after so long. See, I stayed with the army after the war, so I didn't return home until a few months ago. We'd paid neighbors to run the farm in our absence, but it didn't hold up well. Clement came home to a mess to deal with all by himself. After our reunion, for lack of a better word, I stayed in the county, living with my Aunt Lou, hoping to make peace, but he wanted nothing to do with me. Our parents passed a long time ago, and I reckoned it was time to try something new." He lifted the volume of Shakespeare sonnets. "Like book learning and trying my hand at ranching, which I always wanted to do."

She couldn't help but admire his attitude. They weren't so different, in that they were still grappling with the effects of the war. They'd both lost their homes and their brothers, in one way or another.

She was also impressed by his desire to improve himself by studying. She'd do all she could to help him. "I hope you enjoy the sonnets. Shall we meet when you're finished to discuss your thoughts?"

His brows rose. "That's right kind of you, ma'am."

"Write down any questions that cross your mind or words you don't know. Here, borrow a clean slate and chalk. I have a surplus." She handed him a small board and chalk stick. The symbolism of the gesture struck her, since the slate represented his determination to start fresh.

He nodded his thanks. "See you at the Founder's Day celebration?"

She chewed her lip. "I'm not sure. I need to speak to Frieda—Mrs. Lomax—about yesterday. I shouldn't have caused a scene."

"Maybe not, but you love your friend, and she's blessed to have you."

His words were like balm, as comforting as a hug. "Thank you."

How unexpected to have found something like a friend in Mr. Cooper.

Birdy was also blessed to have Frieda. After Mr. Cooper left, she called the girls from the swings and walked the short distance home.

"Sorry we asked Mr. Cooper about the audition," Mary Ann said, walking backward in front of Birdy. "But he knows how to fix things."

"And he'th handthome." Minnie skipped ahead.

"He sure is." Polly giggled. "Do you think so, Aunt Birdy?"

Birdy's stomach flipped over. "Handsome is as handsome does."

"Yes, but don't you think he has lovely eyes?"

Birdy had noticed, not that she'd admit that to Polly. "You're thirteen, Polly."

Polly twirled one of her braids around her finger. "It's an observation, is all, and Ma was fourteen when she starting courting Pa."

True, and Birdy was sixteen when she realized Emory watched her from under his fringed lashes—but Polly seemed so young! "Observing is fine, but he's too old for you."

"Oh, I know he's old." Polly rolled her eyes. "He's probably your age."

Birdy bit back a laugh.

As they turned in at the gate, Birdy could make out the bob of Frieda's wide sunbonnet as she bent in the kitchen garden. Diggory ran up, jumping around their legs.

"Let's see the piglets," Polly beckoned.

"I'm going to help your mother." As the girls and terrier ran around the house, Birdy ambled to Frieda's side, crouched in the dirt, and dug out a dandelion with her fingers. "Are you saving these for tea or a salad?"

"Yes. They go there." Frieda pointed to a small basket. "Careful, though, or you're going to need a bath before the Founder's Day celebration."

At least Frieda was speaking to her, although she didn't look up.

"I'll stay home." Birdy tapped the loose dirt off the roots. "The kitchen floor needs a good scrub."

"Chores aren't part of your agreement with the school board. If they knew you fed pigs and picked weeds, they would disapprove."

"I help because I want to, even when I do more harm than good." Birdy reached for Frieda's gloved hand and clasped it. "You were right yesterday. I'm sorry for embarrassing and hurting you. But please believe me, I support you in this audition process. I didn't participate myself because, well. . ." She shrugged.

"Because of Emory." Frieda squeezed her hand.

Birdy allowed herself a moment of grief. "I miss him."

"I miss Hank, too." Frieda's grip didn't lessen. "But I'm ready to open my heart again. Hank wouldn't mind, I don't think."

Emory might understand Birdy marrying, too, but Birdy didn't dare consider it. It would be a betrayal against her family—

"I don't think your pa would mind, either, Birdy—"

"We are talking about you and finding you a husband. The town is still full of bachelors. Plenty will be at the Founder's Day celebration."

Frieda chuckled. "We'll see."

"You and the girls have fun. You deserve it." And Birdy could use the time to think while she saw to long-overdue chores.

"Thank you." Frieda hugged her and then stripped off her gloves. "You'll need these."

Birdy donned the warm, damp gloves. Talking about whether or not Pa would mind Birdy marrying anyone but Emory soured her stomach, but being in harmony with Frieda again made her happy enough to ignore the ache and sing while she worked.

She was still singing snatches of hymns under her breath three days later when she lingered at the schoolhouse after dismissing the students. The day was so fine, she left the door open to admit a gentle, warm breeze that promised summer. Rather than rushing home to do chores, some of the students remained in the yard, playing and chattering. Birdy paused in the doorway, her heart swelling with affection as they darted over the bluestem grass. Clyde McGee, Opie's brother, appeared to be *It* in a game of tag, but oh! Then he caught Leonard Tumbleston after a valiant chase. The game, which included the Lomax girls, continued off school property and into the street before breaking up as the students headed home.

Birdy retreated inside. She'd told Frieda she wouldn't linger overlong at the schoolhouse so she could attempt to fix the front door at home. First, however, she must compile assignments for the four Stevens boys, who studied at home since the snake incident when the school board suspended them from school. She was stacking the papers when the sound of boot steps ascending the stairs made her turn.

Drew Cooper strode in through the open door, her volume of Shakespeare and the slate in one hand and a tool box in the other. He wore a blue-striped shirt that made his eyes look bright as the summer sky. "I hope I'm not interrupting."

"Not at all. Finished with the book already?"

"I am. I thought I'd return it and fix your lock, too."

"There's no need for an exchange of services, Mr. Cooper."

"My name's Drew, and I'm just being neighborly. Your lock needs fixing."

She'd be a prideful fool to say no to a willing man with tools in hand. "Thank you. . .Drew." Saying his name made her face warm. "I'm Roberta. Birdy."

His smile revealed his dimples and made her cheeks grow hotter. "You sing like a birdie, too. I heard you when I came in. You have a lovely voice."

Oh dear. "I didn't mean to be loud."

"You weren't." He set down the tools. "I liked it. One of my favorite hymns. Believe me, during the war there wasn't much opportunity to hear a lady sing, just a bunch of soldiers singing 'Lorena' over and over."

Birdy laughed. "It's a nice song."

"The first fifty times, maybe." He handed her the slate and the book. "I wrote down a few words I didn't understand, but if you're busy, I'm happy to fix the lock and be on my way."

"I have the time."

The animals at home could wait a few more minutes. She examined his list. "Ah yes, most of these are antiquated words we don't use anymore. Let's consult the dictionary."

She patted the back of the spare chair at her desk and she sat beside him, pushing the thick dictionary between them. The faint, pleasant smell of bay rum met her nose, mixed with dust and grass and a hint of perspiration. He must have spent his day outdoors. "Did you look for land today?"

Nodding, he tapped his thumb beside the dictionary. "My new friend, Jeb Washburn, has experience as a ranch hand, and he's helping me choose land."

"Have you raised cattle?"

"We had a farm, so no, not like this, although I bred mules and horses. I think I can make a decent go of it, though. I have enough cash to make a good start, and I'm eager to settle in, build a house, and make a home."

My, his eyelashes were long. And dark, making his eyes look all the brighter—

Birdy startled. He'd been talking about mules, and she'd been studying his eyelashes. Giving herself a silent scolding, she straightened her posture so she felt more like a teacher than a girl Polly's age. "It sounds to be a promising enterprise."

"I hope so."

Rather than look at his dimples, she opened the dictionary. "Did you have a favorite sonnet?"

"I'm not sure, but each poem made me feel differently. Some are hopeful, and some made me sad. Like Number 33."

"He was but one hour mine, the region cloud hath mask'd him from me now," she said.

A lock of Mr. Cooper's dark hair fell across his forehead when he looked up at her. "It's about a broken friendship, isn't it? Or did I completely misunderstand?"

"No, you're correct, but the tone and words fit many a situation where loss is experienced, doesn't it?" Like Emory, gone from her sight, even though he was in heaven.

"Who'd you lose in the war?"

It wasn't a secret. "My older brother, Lemuel, and my fiancé, Emory, were part of Jennison's Jayhawkers. They both died in hand-to-hand combat in the battle of Mine Creek, a year and a half ago."

"I'm sorry."

"They were best friends. They worked Pa's little farm, but when Pa died, I learned he hadn't made his bank payments and I lost it all. It was a blessing I could teach and move in with Frieda, and then we both lost our men a few years later, like many of the women in Turtle Springs did." Hot tears stung her eyes. "But that's another topic. What's the first word on your list? *Amain.* Archaic indeed."

He looked it up in the dictionary. "To hurry. Makes sense now."

"Good."

"Another thing that makes sense now—you didn't participate in the auditions because of your fiancé." The corners of his eyes creased.

Her throat thickened, so she nodded. Even though Drew's conclusion about her lack of participation in the auditions wasn't the whole truth.

Drew fingered the edge of the dictionary pages, studying Birdy. Her pale lashes fluttered against her cheeks, and he wished she'd look up at him again, so she could read the sincerity in his eyes when he apologized for hurting her. "I overstepped. I'm sorry."

The skin between her brows crinkled with what looked like confusion. "You didn't."

Curious. But he'd pressed enough—and pressing had cost him greatly when it came to his brother, Clement. Casting aside the memories, Drew thumbed through the dictionary for the next word on his list. In little time, they'd finished, and he stood to fix the lock.

He hadn't reached the door when a chest-high whirlwind of brown in too-short pants thundered into the schoolhouse. "I forgot my pencil."

How could the kid not even pant after a run like that? Drew chuckled and started on the locking mechanism.

"Oh dear, Opie. Remember not to run in the schoolhouse, and shake hands with Mr. Cooper."

So this was the boy who'd hid his moldy cheese. Drew shook hands with the boy. "Howdy, Opie."

"Howdy, sir."

Birdy smiled. "Is your pencil under your desk?"

He dropped to his hands and knees and scuttled before lunging. "Found it."

"Wonderful. Before you go, Opie, would you please do me a favor?"

"Want me to clean the erasers?"

"No, thank you. I wondered if you'd take home the extra cornbread from our lunch. We didn't quite finish it."

So Birdy brought food to supplement her students' lunches. She'd mentioned Opie's family had trouble filling the pantry. Drew oiled the lock and smiled at her generosity.

"As long as it's not char-i-tee."

"On the contrary, I can't use it, so you're helping a neighbor, like Mr. Cooper fixing the lock for us."

Drew nodded. "And Miss Green is loaning me books."

Opie's face screwed into a humorous expression. Then he shrugged. "I guess I can help you. It was good cornbread, too."

As she reached into her bag and pulled out a bundled dishtowel and some papers, a young man tromped into the schoolhouse, his steps loud on the stairs. Drew stepped aside, making way for the fair-haired youth to enter. He was as tall as Drew, but lanky, with a fuzz of whiskers atop his lip. "Miss Green?"

"Good afternoon. Mr. Cooper, meet Bob Kent." She waved her hand in introduction and Drew shook the boy's dry, calloused hand as Opie ran out of the schoolhouse. She shut her eyes, muttering, "Walk."

"I remembered something and wanted to ask before I started my chores." His voice was almost as deep as Drew's.

"Sure, Bob."

"It's about the mathematics assignment."

Drew finished the lock and tightened a few loose screws in the door hinge while Birdy and Bob worked on the blackboard. Birdy had a good way, kind and direct. The boy's response to her showed respect for her, which she'd clearly earned.

"Thanks, Miss Green. Nice to meet you, Mr. Cooper."

"You, too, Bob." Drew packed his tools as Bob left. "He seems like a hard worker."

"He is." Birdy erased the chalkboard. "Bob is in eighth grade, about to graduate. His father, Phil, was one of the few men in town who came back from the war, but he lost a leg. Bob has kept up his studies while working the farm with his father, but I heard talk they might be moving to Lawrence with Phil's brother for a fresh start."

A clean slate.

Drew's eye caught on the papers on her desk, which must have come out of her bag when she withdrew the cornbread. One was a pamphlet, the font too large to ignore.

KANSAS EDUCATORS SOCIETY
TEACHER TRAINING AND EMPLOYMENT FAIR

Employment fair? Did Birdy need a fresh start, too?

She spun around, saw the pamphlet, and hurriedly shoved it into her bag. "I must get home now, but would you like to borrow another book?"

"Sure, but I'd like to do something for you, neighbor to neighbor." He didn't try to hide his grin.

"You're not going to let me forget what I told Opie, are you?"

"Nope. The girls mentioned your house needs some repairs. Tomorrow, Jeb and I will be scouting one last piece of land, but afterwards, may I come by your house to do a few repairs?"

She wanted to say no. It was written on her delicate face. But then she nodded. "You've got yourself a deal, and we can find you a book then. But could you start tonight? Right now, in fact."

Really? An evening with her sounded incredibly appealing. Drew's grin widened. "I can do that."

The corner of her mouth lifted. "One other thing. You have to stay for supper."

Chapter 4

You invited a man for supper?" Frieda whispered, but Birdy cringed. Drew would have to be deaf not to notice the hushed conversation coming from the kitchen, even though he was working on the front door with the girls and Diggory for loud, chattering company.

"I didn't invite. I *forced* him, because he's fixing our door and it's almost suppertime. How could I not insist he stay?" Birdy added a dash of cinnamon to the apple-cobbler filling, glaring at Frieda at the same time.

Frieda's strawberry eyebrows knit together. "This isn't a matchmaking ruse, is it? Since I missed the auditions?"

Drew a match to Frieda? Birdy's shoulders stiffened as she spooned the filling into a pie plate, scraping the sides of the bowl clean. "First of all, I won't be interfering in your romantic affairs anymore, not after what happened with Mr. Toovey. You can find your own suitors and determine whether or not they're liars."

"So if I meet a man you dislike, you won't say a word?"

"I'll rejoice in your happiness."

Frieda swiped a finger in the bowl and licked the apple filling from it. "You said *first of all.* What's the second thing?"

Birdy spooned on the topping. "Second, he's lonely. He came to Kansas because his Confederate brother Clement threatened to kill him."

Frieda's brows rose. "Why, I never."

"Me, neither. But now you understand he can use support. Besides, the man deserves a home-cooked meal for all he's done at the schoolhouse."

"I thought he was fixing our door in exchange for borrowing your books."

Birdy placed the cobbler in the oven. "It's not an even exchange, in my opinion. How could it be, when Drew so earnestly desires to grow more learned? I find it admirable of him."

"Oh, so it's *Drew,* is it? Not *Mr. Cooper?*"

Birdy's face heated, and not because she'd opened the oven. "Slice the ham."

"If you say so."

Frieda was still smiling when they set supper on the table. Birdy shot her a warning glare and put Diggory out, so he wouldn't beg while they ate.

"Everything looks wonderful," Drew said after grace, helping himself to a spoonful of redeye gravy.

"We told you Ma ith a good cook," Minnie said.

"Birdy made the cabbage and cobbler." Frieda winked at Birdy.

Birdy shot Frieda another warning glare before offering Drew the bowl of cabbage. "Thank you for fixing the door, Drew."

"No trouble." If he minded being the lone male among five females, he didn't show it.

"The door was stuck so bad this morning we had to go out the back." Mary Ann glanced at Birdy with a guilty expression. "I mean, *badly*."

Birdy nodded at Mary Ann to reinforce her grammatical correction.

"We have baby pigth." Minnie sat up. "Mama Pig is their mama, and they're all pink and black. Wanna meet 'em later?"

"Sure, if your ma says it's all right." Drew forked into his corn cakes. "That reminds me, Mrs. Lomax, I couldn't help but notice a few fence posts could use shoring up. I'd be happy to work on those tomorrow evening."

"Then you must stay for supper tomorrow, too."

"That's right kind of you, Mrs. Lomax." But when Drew set down his water glass, he smiled at Birdy across the table. It was impossible not to smile back.

After supper, Birdy and Frieda cleaned up while the girls showed Drew the piglets, all seven of them. They returned with Diggory as Birdy set a kerosene lamp to the table. "I thought we could all work here tonight."

In a few minutes, they'd resumed their chairs. Diggory lay atop Drew's boots in a contented heap. Frieda crocheted a cap from pink yarn for Minnie, Minnie crocheted a smaller, lumpier hat for her doll from the same yarn, and the older girls worked on their math assignments. After discussing Shakespeare for a few minutes, Birdy set three books on the table for Drew to choose from.

"How about this one?" He held up Paul Bunyan's *The Pilgrim's Progress*.

"It's an edifying choice. Why don't you start reading while I grade papers? That way, if you have any initial questions, we can discuss them now." Birdy refused to look at Frieda, who had better not be smirking.

"Sure, if you're certain I'm not overstaying." Drew couldn't move anyway, not without disturbing a snoring Diggory.

Frieda's lips twitched. "Not at all."

"Nope," Minnie added, popping the *P*.

"Stay as long as you like." Polly blushed.

"I'm checking the door to see if it works." Mary Ann hopped up and headed to the front door.

Drew grinned at Birdy. She grinned back, and they set to their tasks accompanied by the sounds of the front door opening and closing, opening and closing, smooth and unstuck, thanks to him.

Suppers over the next week followed the same pattern. Drew came in the late afternoons to make repairs around the house and see to the livestock, and then he stayed for supper. While there was still much to be done on the property, after only a week, he'd fixed the fence around the house and the pigpen, cleaned the barn, and cut firewood.

Birdy hadn't enjoyed her evenings this much in a long, long time.

Tonight, as they gathered around the dining table, Birdy sketched out the upcoming graduation ceremony, something that didn't require all her concentration so Drew could ask questions as he started a Dickens novel.

At seven o'clock, Drew rose, as was his custom. "Thank you, ladies. I'd best head back to town, but before I go I wanted to tell you my good news. I selected land for my ranch today, and tomorrow I have an appointment to take care of the legalities."

"Congratulations." Birdy clapped.

"Indeed." Frieda grinned. "Where is it?"

"On your northern border, actually." Drew glanced at Birdy. "We'll be neighbors."

"How wonderful." Birdy rose to stand with him. What a blessing Frieda would have such a conscientious neighbor.

"Are you coming tomorrow night?" Minnie shoved the pink cap atop her dolly's head.

"We're having pork roast and apples." Polly batted her eyelashes. That child!

"I'm sorry to say my appointment will keep me out too late to be here in time to make any repairs, and I wouldn't dream of coming for supper without earning it." Drew offered an apologetic smile.

"Neighbors come for supper just because," Polly piped up.

"You've done too much for us already." Frieda smiled. "We'll celebrate another night, and don't you dare bring your tool box."

Birdy shouldn't feel disappointed he wasn't coming tomorrow, but there was no other word for the swirl of discomfort in her abdomen. It had only been a week, but she'd grown accustomed to Drew spending the evenings with them. "I'll walk you to the door."

He bid the others good night and followed her out. She left the door open and stood on the porch, admitting cool evening air into the house, accompanied by the chorus of crickets.

"Tell Frieda I found some coyote tracks a little too close to the yard." Drew's voice was quiet.

Oh dear. "We'll watch for it."

"I have one last question, Birdy." Drew held the book aloft.

About Dickens? "Yes?"

"My appointment is late tomorrow, but I wondered if you'd be interested in joining me for supper at the Tumble Inn restaurant afterwards. I'd like to thank you for all you've done to help me better myself."

Birdy's jaw went slack. Supper, with a man, in public? She couldn't, but when she opened her mouth, the word *yes* popped out.

"I'll call for you at six, if that suits you."

"It does."

But as she shut the door behind him, she covered her mouth with her hand. What would Emory say? Or Lemuel or Pa?

She knew full well the answers. They matched the churning of her conscience.

It's just a thank-you supper, Lord. I hope You understand.

The next evening, Drew led Birdy to one of the restaurant's smaller tables in the back and pulled out her chair. Her flowery fragrance wafted around him as he scooched her chair under the table.

As he took his seat, she shook her head. "It's been a long time since a gentleman held out my chair. I almost forgot what to do."

"It's only been a few weeks since I seated a lady." He placed his napkin on his lap. "Aunt Lou."

"She must have enjoyed your company. I'm sure she was sorry to see you go."

"Actually, she shook her finger at me and said I'd been underfoot for too long." He chuckled. "It was her way of setting me free so I could start over, and it was done in love. When I arrived in Turtle Springs, there was already a letter from her waiting here for me. She must have mailed it while I was still in her house."

Birdy laughed. "She'll love getting the letter about your property."

"I'll write to her tonight—"

The dark-haired younger sister of the Inn's owner, Virginia, stood at the table's edge, clutching a pencil and notepad, her gaze flickering between Drew and Birdy as if guessing their relationship. She couldn't be more than nineteen.

"Ma'am, Mr. Cooper." Virginia's eyes shone bright with unabashed curiosity.

Twin spots of color bloomed in Birdy's cheeks, but she smiled. "Good evening, Virginia. I've been meaning to speak with you about a teacher training and job fair coming up in Topeka." She smiled at Drew. "Virginia has aspirations to teach."

So that explained the pamphlet he'd seen. "Wonderful."

"I look forward to it, ma'am." Virginia smiled and squared her shoulders. "Our supper choices this evening are pork roast with root vegetables, or mutton stew with fresh peas and spring onions."

"I'll have the pork," Birdy said without hesitation.

"Me, too." Drew waited until Virginia was out of earshot before smiling at Birdy. "Thank you for coming tonight."

"Thank you for inviting me out as a thank-you. My, that's a lot of thank-yous." She chuckled.

"I guess we've both got a lot to be grateful for." One thing he was most grateful for was meeting her. Hopefully this thank-you dinner was the first of many evenings out.

"Congratulations on your property purchase. It went well?"

"It did. I'm eager to get started fencing off some areas and building a temporary house so I can move out of the inn. The barn will be next then a real house. I'm not sure what I want, though. A big porch or a small one?"

"Big, of course."

Suddenly he could see it: a wide, long porch offering plenty of space for relaxing at day's end and room for children to play. "You're right."

She smiled. "What about your cattle?"

"Jeb—my new friend—and I already spoke to one of the neighboring ranchers about purchasing some of their stock to get us started."

"Will Jeb be your partner?"

Drew swallowed a sip of water. "He has no interest in partnership, but he's willing to be my foreman."

"So, like you, he came to Turtle Springs to work, not because of the audition?"

"Oh he came to audition, all right, and he's taken a shine to a particular gal, but he won't tell me who she is. All he'll say is she's a hardworking widow."

"What a mystery. I wonder who—"

Virginia returned bearing two plates of fragrant pork roast, and Drew and Birdy said a brief prayer before lifting their forks and shifting the conversation. The meal was delicious, but Drew could have eaten straw and been as content as he was now. Birdy's eyes flashed as she asked questions about the ranch, their green hue almost a match to her grass-green dress. The lamplight played on her hair, making it look golden and bright. A more learned man could find a way to describe how she looked, green and gold like summer, but all Drew could do was appreciate the moment and rely on Shakespeare's words.

Shall I compare thee to a summer's day? Thou art more lovely and more temperate.

He cared for her. He couldn't help it. Would she be open to marrying, even though she didn't participate in the auditions? Drew didn't sign up because he wanted to establish a home before starting a family. Meeting Birdy made him want to rethink his plan, though. He hadn't expected to care for someone until he was settled, but wasn't that love, sometimes? It crept up on a person at inconvenient, surprising times.

Like now, when he couldn't stop staring into her smiling eyes.

She set down her fork. "I am so pleased for you, Drew, starting fresh."

"I feel blessed, although I didn't see the blessing when I returned from the war and Clement threatened me." Drew sat back. He wanted Birdy to know him better, so he didn't mind sharing. "We shared everything, including a love of our home state. It turned out we showed our love in different ways, and even though we fought on opposite sides, I never stopped loving my brother. The truth is, I bear some responsibility for his anger toward me. You see—"

Virginia came back, and he clamped his mouth shut. As she cleared their plates, she smiled. "Dessert tonight is nut cake or mock lemon pie. Which would you prefer?"

Birdy tipped her head to the side. "Nut cake, please, and coffee."

Drew met Virginia's expectant gaze. "Lemon pie and coffee."

Virginia nodded. "I'll return in a moment."

"Drew Cooper?"

The man's voice behind him pulled him out of his chair. All the blood in his body plummeted to his boots. "Get behind me, Birdy."

In a crisp hop, Birdy rose. "Do you know this man?"

The straight, dark hair, the gray-blue eyes, the stocky build, two inches shorter than Drew. The man's hands fell at his sides, but his fingers twitched, like he might pull a weapon.

And Birdy still wasn't behind him. He shielded her with his arm and gave her a quick but impassioned glance.

"He's my brother, Clement."

Birdy stayed still—for a moment. Then she shoved free of the cage of his arm.

Chapter 5

C lement Cooper, here in Kansas?

Birdy marched up to him, hands fisted on her hips, scrutinizing his features. Aside from sharing the same color hair and set of their mouths, the brothers didn't look too much alike. Drew was thinner, his eyes larger, and his jaw more square than his brother's. If she'd passed Clement on the street, she might not have guessed he was related to Drew.

But now she knew who he was, she couldn't sit idly by. "You've got some nerve, mister."

In a shielding gesture, Drew's arm reached to tuck her behind him. How silly of him. She didn't need protecting. Drew did.

She touched Drew's arm. "I'm going for the sheriff."

"Birdy." Drew looked down at her, though he didn't lessen his protective posture. "It's all right."

"It's nothing of the sort." Then she saw it—everyone in the restaurant watched them. There wasn't a single fork clattering or hushed conversation. Virginia stood staring, holding their plates of dessert.

Drew nodded toward the door. "Come outside, Clem. Pardon me, Birdy. I'll be but a moment."

As if she'd stay in her seat nibbling cake while his brother made good on his threat? Pah. She scooped up her shawl and followed them outside.

The evening air was cool against her hot cheeks as she joined them on the porch. Even in the dark, the hard line of Drew's clenched jaw was evident, as was the stony set to his eyes. She didn't know Clement enough to read his features, but at least his hands didn't hold a weapon. She glared up at him. "What are you doing here, Mr. Cooper?"

"My question exactly. How'd you find me?" Drew wrapped his arm around Birdy, but stiffly, as if to keep her safe rather than to hold her close. There was nothing romantic in the gesture, but her stomach swooped at his touch.

Or perhaps her insides wobbled like aspic because a Confederate stood but a yard distant after tracking Drew here from Tennessee. She folded her arms, waiting for his response.

Clement scratched his nape. "Aunt Lou told me where you'd gone."

Drew's head nodded. "I guess I shouldn't be surprised. She never was one for feuding."

Birdy chomped her cheek so hard she tasted blood. "This isn't a feud, Drew. You tried to make peace and *he* would have none of it."

"I see my brother told you the story, ma'am." Clement's shoulders went stiff. "Can we talk?"

"No," Birdy answered for Drew.

"Yes." Drew glanced down at her. "But Miss Green and I have a dessert to finish first."

She couldn't swallow cake if she tried. "Drew, no."

"No dessert?"

"No dessert, and no to him."

"Clement's come a long way to talk to me." He faced her, turning away from his brother. "I'm sorry to end our evening like this. Maybe Virginia can wrap our desserts so you can share them with the girls." He leveled his gaze at his brother. "I'll return in an hour to meet you in the restaurant for coffee."

Clement nodded and left the porch, but Birdy's head shook with such vigor that Drew couldn't possibly mistake her disapproval. "This is an outrage."

"I know. I promised you a good supper and a celebration."

"Not that. Him." She pointed to the dark street.

His face was stoic when he paid their bill, asked for their desserts to be transferred to a borrowed pie tin, and handed her up into his rented wagon. Birdy's arms folded the moment her rump landed on the hard seat. "How can you listen to him, Drew?"

With a flick of the reins, Drew urged the team into the street for the short ride to the farm. "I needed a fresh start. Maybe Clement wants one, too."

"Or maybe he's going to make good on his threat."

"If he wanted to kill me, he'd have been smarter not to announce himself first."

Birdy ground her molars together. "I cannot believe you trust him."

"He's my brother."

"He said he'd kill you," she reminded him.

"He did, but I forgave him."

"Forgiveness doesn't mean forgetting."

"I'm not expecting things will be the same again, but if there's a hope of reconciliation, I need to take it. I can't be the sort of man who holds grudges his entire life. I have to forgive, even when it hurts. And believe me, this hurts."

It hurt Birdy, too. Clement threatened Drew—and he was a Confederate, to boot. Drew might be able to forgive and be reconciled, but why would he want to?

I know I'm wrong, Lord. But it still isn't wise for Drew to be alone with Clement.

Drew turned the wagon onto her road, and when they arrived in front of the Lomax house, Drew set the wagon brake. "I didn't want to leave Tennessee, but if Clement hadn't said what he did, I wouldn't have come to Kansas, and it turns out this is where I'm supposed to be. God used Clement's threat for good."

He'd leaned forward while he spoke, and his breath was warm on her cheek.

She stared into the depths of his eyes, forgetting she was supposed to respond. She forgot everything until he broke the hold of their gazes, hopped from the wagon, and helped her down.

This time when he touched her and her skin and stomach prickled, she couldn't attribute it to confronting a murderous ex-Confederate, like she did in the restaurant.

She had to admit to herself the reason she shivered at his touch was due to something far more dangerous.

Drew's hands lingered on Birdy's waist after he lifted her down. She fit right into his arms, soft and sweet, but he couldn't hold her like this forever. Unwilling to lose all contact with her, though, his hand sought hers in the dark. "I'd like to give you a proper thank-you supper. Later this week?"

"If you live that long." Her mouth turned down at the corners.

She wasn't joking, but her retort made him smile. With a squeeze of her hand, he let go, gave her the desserts, and waited until she was inside before heading back to town.

After returning the rented wagon to the livery, he entered the restaurant. Clement occupied Birdy's spot at the table. Praying for wisdom, Drew moved toward him.

Before he took two steps, Jeb Washburn rose from a table by the door, his eyes crinkled in concern. "I hear tell that the feller there's your brother. Is that him? The one you told me about?"

Word spread fast in Turtle Springs. "Yep."

"Want me to send him on his way?"

The display of support made Drew pause. After all he'd been through, it was a blessed reminder that God provided friends who cared like family. He clapped Jeb's shoulder. "Thanks, Jeb, but I'd like to hear him out."

"Fine, but I'm keepin' an eye on 'im." Jeb returned to his seat, his gaze fixed on Clement.

Taking a deep breath, Drew pulled out the chair across from Clement. "You're a long way from home."

Clement's brows rose, as if surprised Drew had come back. "So are you. But that's my fault, little brother."

Now it was Drew's turn to be surprised. "Do you aim to keep your word by killing me?"

"No, Drew. I came to apologize."

"You could've written."

"Neither of us got enough schoolin' to write *that* well." He bent forward, his eyes damp. "I wronged you, brother. No excuse for what I did, but I can tell you why, if you want to hear."

"I do." More than anything.

Clement fiddled with his mug. "When I came home from the war, there wasn't much left of the farm. Even though you sent money, and I tried for a year, I couldn't salvage it. I knew I was going to have to sell. I blamed the war. I blamed you. I blamed our neighbors for not keeping it up like we paid 'em to. And you didn't come home to help me."

"I didn't choose to stay away. I was needed in Washington. Aunt Lou knew I couldn't come back yet—"

"I know, but I saw it as one more betrayal. I lost the war, and now I was losing my home." Clement looked down. "I sold it to the bank, signed the papers, and the next day, you came back."

Drew's jaw slackened. Clement hadn't said anything about the farm that day. Just angry, bitter words and then, the threat. "I'm so sorry, Clem."

"That proves how much better a man you are than I am. I wronged you, little brother. I'm the sorry one. I'm the one who spent a year stewing in anger at you over the war, and you not coming home, and instead of paying you your half of the proceeds from the farm, I threatened to take my hand to you." He looked at his hand as if astonished that he'd contemplated violence with it. "Since then, I've had plenty of time to come to my senses. I took a long, hard look at myself and didn't recognize the man I'd become."

The truth was Clement's violent outburst had forced Drew to look at himself, too. "I'm not blameless. We had different views about the war, but I provoked you. Challenged you instead of talked to you. Thinking I was right didn't give me cause to act superior to you, but I did, Clem, and I'm sorry. I goaded you."

"Don't excuse what I did." Clem gripped his mug. "I've started going to church, Drew, and I know there's hope and forgiveness, but that won't erase what I did to you."

Clem, in church? Drew swallowed hard. "There's hope for us both yet, brother."

Clem hung his head. "I hope someday, you'll forgive me."

"I forgave you a long time ago. I hope you can forgive me, too."

A ghost of a smile played on Clement's lips as he nodded. "Does that mean we can be brothers again?"

"I'd like to work toward it."

Clement puffed out a large, relieved breath. "That's more than I could hope for."

It was a monumental moment in his life—both of their lives—but Drew wasn't sure what to do next. There was still a gulf between them that they'd have to bridge, and it would take time before they were comfortable with each other again. Drew cleared the thickness in his throat and rubbed the back of his neck. "I don't know how much of the farm money is left—"

"I've got your half, right here." Clement shoved a hand in his coat pocket.

Drew forestalled him with his hand. "That wasn't what I meant. If you need work, I could use a ranch hand."

"That's what you did with your share of Ma's money? You bought a ranch?"

"As of today." Drew laughed. In the past twelve hours, he'd become the owner of a spread of land, got his brother back. . .and took Birdy to supper, too. All in all, a fine day indeed.

"You'll make a fine job of it, little brother."

Drew stood, and though he still ached over the past, he embraced his brother. It was stiff at first, awkward and one-sided, but then Clement returned Drew's hold.

"Do you have a place to stay tonight?"

"Under the stars with my bedroll."

"You can stay with me."

"Naw, it's warm out. I'm fine." Clearly, Clement needed more time.

"All right, then. Meet me here, tomorrow morning at nine. We've got a lot of work to do." But he couldn't start any earlier, not if he wanted to catch Birdy at the schoolhouse before the bell rang.

The moment Clement left the restaurant, Jeb rushed to occupy Clement's chair. "He didn't kill you."

"Not even close." Drew recounted their conversation.

Jeb whistled. "I'll give him a fair shake tomorrow, then. Glad it went well, but it's too bad it messed up your evening with the pretty schoolmarm."

"Oh, you think she's pretty?"

"Sure, but not as pretty as my gal." Jeb shrugged.

Drew doubted it. "Are you going to tell me your gal's name?"

"Not yet, because she wants to keep it quiet on account of her young 'uns. But I think they like me. I took a page out of your book and repaired her fence one afternoon. Hey, that's funny, a page out of your book, since you're always readin' one of the schoolmarm's books."

Jeb guffawed at his unintentional joke, leaving Drew to his thoughts. He didn't consider pressing Jeb as to the identity of his lady, when he didn't want to talk about his burgeoning feelings for Birdy. They were too new, like the baby corn plants on the Lomax farm—but he had a hunch his feelings wouldn't stay small for long. His affections for Birdy were more powerful than any he'd ever felt before.

And they kept him awake most of the night, so by the time he arrived at the schoolhouse at half past eight the next morning, he'd been up for several hours. He straightened the moment Birdy came into view, wearing the blue dress that made her eyes look grayer, with the Lomax girls, their red hair bound in braids, sauntering toward the schoolhouse. He waved.

"Mr. Cooper!" Polly smoothed her hairline.

Mary Ann waved back. "Thanks for dessert last night. The pie was good."

"Mmm-hmm." Minnie rubbed her small, round belly.

"You're most welcome." Drew executed a courtly half bow.

"The nut cake was tasty, too." Polly clutched her books to her chest.

"Aunt Birdy didn't eat it," Minnie reported.

Birdy pinked. "I was full after my pork roast, that's all. Polly, here's the key. Go on in. I'll be there in a minute."

Once they were gone, Drew stepped closer to Birdy. "I'm so sorry about last night."

She met him halfway. "Don't be silly. Tell me what happened after I left."

"I heard him out, and he heard me. Things aren't repaired between us, but we're going to work at it, and I've hired him to help me set up the ranch."

Her eyes darkened. "He's staying in town?"

"Yes, but how about I explain at supper tonight? A nice, uninterrupted meal at the restaurant."

"Oh no. I'm sorry."

"Because of Clement?"

"Because—I have plans."

Maybe she had a ladies' meeting. "Could I drop by your house tomorrow to return your book, though? Maybe Clement could come with me, so you could get to know him."

"Fine." But it was clear Birdy didn't approve.

"We'll come after supper." No working the property, no potential invitation for supper. A short visit might be all she could bear.

She nodded and backed away, toward the schoolhouse. "It's almost time for school. I'm sorry, but I must prepare for the students."

"I understand." About her going into the schoolhouse, at least. Birdy's response otherwise puzzled him. Something had changed since the pleasant start to their meal last night—actually, something changed the moment he told her Clem was staying in town.

She'd been so protective last night, willing to battle against Clement because of his threat against Drew. . .but was there more to it than that? Could she forgive Clement? Or was Clement's status as a former Confederate more than she could forgive?

Drew turned from the schoolhouse, his heart sinking to his boots. He'd come to Kansas for a fresh start. So, it seemed, had Clement.

Kansas was big enough for all of them to start over. But maybe not big enough for Birdy, and if that was the case, her heart might need some healing, too.

Chapter 6

B irdy picked at her supper, although her stomach ached from emptiness.
Minnie leaned into her shoulder. "Can I have your cornbread, if you don't
want it?"

"May I," Birdy corrected without thinking. "Sure."

"So we're really having a Confederate in the house tonight?" Polly toyed with
her ham. "And you're fine with it, Ma?"

Birdy had warned Frieda about their evening callers, but Frieda didn't agree
with Birdy that they should keep the visit brief and formal. Frieda set down her
knife. "The Good Book says to love your enemies. Mr. Cooper's brother is no longer our enemy, though. And when Mr. Cooper stopped by today, he told me his
brother wants a fresh start. Let's welcome him, shall we, girls?" Frieda's question
was for her daughters, but her eyes fixed on Birdy.

Birdy's lips smashed together.

The kitchen was cleaned and the coffee brewed when the knock sounded on the
door. Frieda smoothed her brown homespun dress over her waist and admitted their
guests. "Good evening, gentlemen."

Hats in hand, Drew and Clement stepped inside and were immediately set
upon by Diggory. The group exchanged greetings, although Birdy couldn't quite
smile for Clement.

Diggory's pink tongue lolled over his teeth while Clement bent to scratch him.
"Now this is a fine looking pooch."

"He's a good rat-catcher, too," Mary Ann noted.

"Come into the parlor," Frieda invited. "Sorry about Diggory's excitement."

"I don't mind a bit." Clement's smile was warm.

Minnie grabbed Drew's sleeve. "Opie McGee tried to hide his lunch under the
floor again, but he couldn't becau-th you boarded it up, Mr. Cooper."

"I can't help but pity poor Opie that his hiding place is gone." Drew laughed, but
his eyes crinkled in concern when he looked at Birdy. "Are you all right?"

The truth was, she wasn't sure. Tonight she was confronted by guilt—over not
wanting to forgive a Confederate like Clement, and over being so happy to see
Drew again.

Both of the feelings were wrong.

So she offered Drew a polite smile, even though her innards quaked like a can full of worms heading to the fishing hole. "Tired after a long day, that's all. You must be, as well, working new property. How was it today?"

"There's a lot of work to do, but Clem and Jeb Washburn are helping, and it won't be long before everything's settled."

Interesting, since she felt more *unsettled* tonight than she had in a long time. She stepped backward. "I'll get the coffee and cookies."

Drew took a step. "I'll help."

"No, enjoy your visit. I'll be but a moment."

He looked disappointed at her response, but she needed a moment to collect herself. *Change me, Lord. Help me forgive Clement and not think of Drew as more than a friend.*

From the kitchen, she heard the conversation easily. "Do you girls know how to play jackstraws?" Clement's drawl was sweet and thick as molasses, like Drew's.

"Of course."

"How about Find the Penny?"

"What's that?" Mary Ann's voice went higher.

"You take this penny here, and one person hides it while the others aren't looking. Then the others hunt for it. May we try it now, Mrs. Lomax?"

"By all means." Frieda laughed.

The girls ran into the kitchen, bright eyed and pink cheeked.

"Mr. Cooper's gonna hide a real penny for us to find!" Mary Ann twirled in a circle.

"In the parlor!" Minnie hopped up and down.

"I wonder how hard it will be to find." Polly chewed her lip.

"That's wonderful, girls." It was good to see them happy, even if it was at the hand of Clement Cooper. Birdy held out the plate of cookies to them—

"Ready," Clement called. The girls dashed out, never having glanced at the cookies.

Birdy didn't want to follow, but she'd hidden long enough. She set the cookies with the coffee on the tray and carried it to the parlor, pausing at the threshold. The girls scrambled, laughing and running, with Diggory at their heels. Maybe she should wait a moment, so she wouldn't collide with one of them and drop the tray.

"Found it!" Polly shouted.

"Where?" Minnie was breathless.

"Under Ma's elbow."

"Ma!" Mary Ann fisted her hands on her hips but laughed. "You helped Mr. Cooper!"

"Of course I did, but the penny wasn't all the way under my elbow."

"I saw the glint of copper," Polly added. "That was fun. Can we play again?"

"You *may*, another time. Tonight's a school night." Frieda's tone was indulgent and happy. Happier than Birdy had heard it in a long time.

Birdy chewed her lip as she marched in to set the tray on the table. Drew smiled at her as she sat beside him and started pouring cups of fragrant coffee.

"Only one more week of school, and then we have all summer to play." Mary Ann's voice was joyful.

"And pull weeds and feed animals and help me tend corn," Frieda added.

"How many farmhands do you have, ma'am?" Clement bent to scratch Diggory's neck, and the dog curled atop his feet.

"Only a few. We do a lot ourselves."

"Drew told me he's seen to a few chores around your homestead. I reckon I can help, too, when we're done for the day on the ranch."

"I can't pay you." Frieda looked down, her fair lashes fanning against her cheeks.

"I don't need pay for bein' neighborly."

"Then you must stay for supper when you help us. You and Drew. Tomorrow, if you like." Frieda's voice held no hesitation. "It's the least I can do to thank you."

Birdy clutched the cup she was about to hand to Frieda. Frieda well knew Clement threatened to kill Drew, and that he'd fought against the North. Yet here she was, inviting him to supper?

That was a bit too much to bear.

Right or wrong, she felt relieved for having an excuse tomorrow. "I'll be at the Kents' tomorrow. Bob's parents are helping me plan graduation."

"Oh that's right." Frieda leaned toward Clement. "Four graduates on Friday evening—"

Minnie looked up at Birdy, a sign she didn't wish to interrupt her ma. "Can we look at the piglet-th?"

"You *may*, but be careful." Advice she should heed, the way her pulse thrummed at sitting beside Drew.

He took a cookie. "Isn't Bob the young man I met?"

"Yes, his father, Phil, is an amputee." She glanced at Clement.

"Sounds like a busy week ahead."

"It is. Exams and then fun. Friday we're having a picnic. I'll also be meeting with the eighth graders' families all week. Last night I dined with Leonard Tumbleston's family, and tomorrow, I'll be at the Fosters'."

Diggory abandoned Clement for Drew, and he set down his coffee to attend to the dog. "So I won't see much of you this week."

"Probably not."

He nodded, but he seemed disappointed. She didn't like that, but she couldn't have supper with him at the restaurant again. A thank you was one thing, but a second supper looked like courting, and she was not free.

If she were, she'd say yes to Drew faster than it took to blink. He was honorable, hardworking, and when he looked at her like he did now, he made her stomach turn inside out. Sometimes he even made her forget about Emory and Pa's instructions.

But forgetting was a luxury she couldn't afford.

It was a relief when the girls stomped in. Frieda broke from her conversation with Clement. "Girls, you didn't wipe your boots."

"We saw eyes, Ma. From the brush on the rise, and there were paw prints by the barn."

Drew stood, followed by Clement. "I'll take a look."

"What is it, Ma?" Mary Ann curled by Frieda on the chair as the men hurried out, Diggory dashing ahead of them.

"I'm afraid there's a coyote visiting us. They're normally afraid of people, but this one must be young or curious. No more going outside at night without me or Aunt Birdy."

Birdy hugged Minnie, and they spoke quietly until the men returned.

"Coyote," Drew confirmed. "It's gone now, but I secured the barn. Make sure you keep the animals inside, and tomorrow afternoon I'll ensure there are no loose places where a coyote can get in."

Then Minnie yawned, long and loud, breaking the tension and signaling an end to the evening. Birdy's shoulders slumped in relief, and it wasn't because Clement was leaving, although she was glad for it, or because she had exams to grade, which she did.

It was because when Drew came back in the house after seeing to the barn, he looked at her with such protective compassion she almost hugged him. She cared for him and appreciated his work on behalf of people she loved.

It would be easy to add Drew into that group of loved ones, which was one thing she could never, ever do.

The rest of the week passed quickly for Drew as he cleared land and built a temporary shelter for him, Clement, and Jeb, but the evenings were long when they were spent without Birdy.

He knew she had supper plans each night, but on Wednesday when he and Clement stopped by to see to the Lomax animals—a habit that had become routine—he'd hoped to at least catch a few words with Birdy before her supper with her student's family. She never came home, however, and Mary Ann informed him that Birdy stayed late to tutor the rascally Stevens boys. Thursday night, Birdy decorated the schoolhouse before her supper with the Andersons, according to Minnie.

But he'd get to see Birdy tonight.

She didn't come home after school, but Frieda fed the rest of them an early supper in advance of the graduation ceremony. Drew had donned his Sunday shirt and tie for tonight's event. The sun was low in the sky, but bright, when they arrived at the schoolhouse, where light and happy chatter spilled from the open door.

The familiar space looked different tonight, with a congratulatory banner hung over the blackboard, benches replacing the desks, and the teacher's desk topped with a red-checked tablecloth and plates of refreshments.

While Frieda dashed toward it with a plate of cookies, Drew took his seat in the back row between Polly and Clement, who saved Frieda a seat beside him. Birdy's back was to them as she chatted at the front of the room with a smiling, gray-haired man. She wore the blue dress she'd worn to church last Sunday that swayed around her ankles like a graceful bell.

Her fiancé, Emory, had been blessed to have had her love. Could she ever feel that way about Drew? Even a little?

Polly shifted beside him, drawing him to the present, so he smiled at her. "Next year, you'll be the one graduating."

She pinked. "Maybe I'll be a teacher like Aunt Birdy."

"I won't." Mary Ann sighed. "I don't use adverbs right. I mean right*ly*."

"Correctly," Polly amended.

Mary Ann puffed out a breath. "See?"

Drew laughed. At the sound, Birdy spun, her blue skirt swirling around her at the sudden movement. Her gaze met his and—she blushed. There was no denying it, not with her fair skin reddening from the top of her lacy collar to the tips of her ears.

She may not care for him like he cared for her, but she wasn't indifferent to him. Drew sat up straighter and grinned.

Birdy bent to ring a small bell on her desk, and the crowd went silent. She folded her hands at her waist, looking every inch the proper schoolmarm. "Welcome, one and all, as we honor our eighth-grade graduates."

Drew applauded along with the rest of the audience, but movement behind him captured his attention. Late arrivals tiptoed into seats, including Opie McGee, his siblings, and a woman who must be their ma, escorted by none other than Jeb Washburn. One of Jenny McGee's hands tucked into the crook of Jeb's arms, and the other rested on his bicep—flashing a shiny, new-looking gemstone ring.

Drew didn't know Jenny McGee, but Birdy had mentioned she'd been struggling to feed her family. Jeb wouldn't let them go hungry from here on out, though. Happy for his friend, Drew couldn't hide his grin as he returned his attention to Birdy.

Birdy extended her hand to the gray-haired gentleman she'd been speaking to earlier. "I'd like to invite Mr. Spivet, president of the school board, to open us in prayer and share a few remarks."

After the prayer and a speech about character, Birdy led a choir of schoolchildren, including the Lomax girls, in "The Battle Hymn of the Republic." Even from Drew's spot in the back row, he could make out Birdy's melodious voice as she joined in.

Clement clapped enthusiastically when the choir finished. "The Lomax girls are something, aren't they?"

Drew nodded, but his eyes were on Birdy, who'd gathered four sheaves of paper.

"Now, the moment we've all been waiting for. Ethel Anderson, Gertrude Foster, Robert Kent, and Leonard Tumbleston, will you stand, please? I have been honored to be your instructor the past few years, and you've inspired me by your fortitude and dedication to your studies despite enduring a difficult, challenging time for our nation, our town, and for your families. You have done us all proud."

Minnie wiggled. "I can't th-ee."

"Here." Clement pulled her onto his lap. "Better?"

She nodded, leaning against his chest.

Frieda's damp eyes glowed in the lamplight.

She wasn't alone, as far as damp eyes went. Tears of pride, joy, and yes, even sadness over those who weren't present to celebrate fell as Birdy called the students up for their diplomas. Ethel, Trudie, Bob, and Leonard all shook her hand, and then the hand of the school board member. The ceremony was brief, but heartfelt, and when it ended, Drew hopped to his feet along with everyone else to applaud. Clement hoisted Minnie in his arms.

"Hooray!" Minnie cheered. Clement bounced her in his arms.

Then Bob gestured to Birdy. "To the finest teacher in Kansas!"

The applause swelled. Birdy swiped her eyes.

Folks swarmed the graduates and Birdy, but Drew followed Jeb to the cookies. "Is that a ring I see on Mrs. McGee's finger?"

"You don't mind having a married foreman, do you, boss?" The creases in Jeb's leathery features deepened as he grinned. "I proposed right before supper, not just to her but the young 'uns, too. They all said yes."

"I'm thrilled for you, Jeb. Truly. You all are welcome at the ranch."

"Thanks, Drew, but Jenny's got a good house."

Mrs. McGee glanced up at Jeb, her features aglow. Would Birdy ever look at him like that?

Drew congratulated Jeb, his new fiancée, and the graduates. The sun was setting when Clement nudged Drew's shoulder. "I'm walking Frieda and the girls home. I don't suppose you'd mind staying to escort Birdy home, would you?" He grabbed a piece of fruit from the table and tossed it to Drew. "Maybe you'd like an apple to give the teacher?"

Was he that obvious? "Go on, now." Drew mock punched Clement's arm and waved goodnight to Frieda, who'd retrieved her cookie plate and hugged Birdy.

"G'night, Mr. Cooper." Mary Ann waved at him before taking Clement's hand.

"Good night, all."

When Birdy bid the last of the parents farewell, he started stacking benches. She shook her head at him. "You don't have to do that. A few of the boys are coming back tomorrow to move out the benches and bring back the desks."

"No school board inspection, then?" He kept stacking.

She laughed and unpinned the banner on the blackboard. "No."

"Did you see my friend, Jeb, with Mrs. McGee?"

"I did." Birdy's grin widened. "Jenny is a dear, and so are her children. Jeb seems like a caring man. I'm happy for them."

She looked it, but would she be as happy if Frieda married Clement? They were getting friendlier every day, but she hadn't been around to see it. "It was a nice ceremony, Birdy."

"Thank you. The students worked hard for this."

"You worked hard, too. I've missed seeing you this week."

Birdy froze, gripping the banner. Then she swallowed loud enough he could hear it from ten feet away. "Is it— Do you need to borrow a new book?"

"As a matter of fact, I do." He shoved the last bench to the side of the room. "But I had a question."

She turned away and gathered the red-checked tablecloth from her desk. "About your reading?"

"About Emory."

Her fingers immobilized. After a pause, she nodded.

He wished he could see her face. "Is he the reason you didn't participate in the auditions for a husband?"

"Yes." It was a strangled whisper.

"Because you still love him?"

She spun around, her lips bloodless. "A body doesn't just wake up one day and stop loving someone."

"I know that, especially not someone as special as Emory must have been, for you to love him." Drew licked his dry lips. "Do you feel you'd betray him if you found love again?"

Her eyes dampened. "Not exactly."

Drew reached for her hand. It was cold, soft, the bones tiny. He pulled her to sit on one of the benches, and he dropped down beside her. "Emory can't be replaced, Birdy, but is there room in your heart for anyone else? Like me?"

"Oh, Drew." She shut her eyes. "I can't. I'm sorry."

His gut went hot and his hands numbed, but he willed his voice to stay even and gentle. "All right, then."

He started to withdraw his hand, but she gripped it in both of hers. "My whole life, I heard Pa tell Lemuel and me about all the hard work he had to do to earn the approval of my mother's father before he could marry her. Pa was a man of character, but he had to demonstrate his worthiness to my grandpa, and he was happy to do it, because he said she was a woman worth working for."

"Sounds fair to me." He squeezed her hand, glad she still held his. Did that mean she did care for him?

A sad smile twitched at her lips. "I didn't know it at the time, but all those years when Emory came around as Lemuel's best friend, he was demonstrating his worthiness to Pa. My family chose Emory for me."

Drew's jaw slackened. "Your engagement was arranged?"

"Not like that. He loved me, and I loved him, too." Her chin quivered. So did her hands. "But Pa said a family's approval is more important than the strings that tug the heart. Feelings are fickle, but worthiness and family approval are solid and sure foundations for a marriage. If I'd loved Emory and Pa hadn't approved, I couldn't have married him. I *wouldn't* have married him."

"You honored your pa. I appreciate that—"

"You don't understand. I didn't love Emory until Pa approved. When I was a little girl, after hearing those stories about proving his worthiness to Ma, Pa made me promise I'd trust my family instead of my heart. Every time someone mentioned Ma after she died, or a local gal married a fellow Pa didn't like, I heard the story and made the promise."

A promise she intended to still keep. Then something she'd said sunk to his marrow. "You didn't love Emory until your pa approved. You're afraid of your feelings?"

Her hands shook harder. "Feelings are fickle, Drew. Pa taught me not to trust them."

So she did care for him, but was shackled to her dead pa's admonitions. Drew prayed for wisdom. "He taught you to trust him, and I'd never suggest you disobey your pa, but he's gone. Emory's gone, too. Your promise was made in a different time. The war changed everything."

"I know. Every day I wake up to a life without people I love because of that war."

"We've both got our wounds, don't we? But we aren't alone. I may have fought for the Union, but Tennessee is my home, and my Confederate neighbors and kin are still suffering from the devastation of the war, just like thousands of other Southerners—and they'll suffer for a long time to come. Homes, farms, railroad lines, and businesses were destroyed, and too many husbands, fathers, and brothers didn't come home. I ache for those folks as much as I ache for the Union losses. There's no easy way to heal from this war, not on either side, but recognizing and grieving over the other side's losses might be a step in the right direction."

She stiffened. "I–I'm sorry. I haven't thought of it that way."

"I'm not saying it's easy, though. When Clement threatened me, it hurt me to the bone."

"It doesn't look like it." Her look was sharp.

"Because I'm trying to be reconciled with him?"

"You act like there's nothing between you but goodwill."

He couldn't hold back a snort. "There's a world of hurt between us, but I chose years ago to follow God's ways, even though it's painful as a bayonet in the ribs sometimes. I have to forgive him, and he's chosen to follow God, too, so he wants reconciliation. But the truth is, I bear some responsibility in angering him. Before the war, I pestered him about my opinions on federal rights. He agreed with my abolitionist views, but I thought if I preached at him enough against secession, he'd see things my way, when all I accomplished was to make him dig in his heels. That wasn't brotherly love; it was condemnation. How can I not forgive him for his threat when I need his forgiveness, too?"

"I'm so angry at him, though. I don't *want* to forgive him for threatening you. And I'm sorry the war caused so much suffering, but I can't blink and forget a

Southern soldier killed Emory."

When her eyes squeezed shut, he rubbed her fingers with his thumb. "I can't imagine how losing him feels, but I hope you start at least *wanting* to forgive the South, for your own sake. And as much as I appreciate you wanting to protect me from my brother, you'd do well to forgive him, too. It'll be good for you, body and soul, and it'll make life a lot easier for you, what with him and Frieda sweet on each other."

Birdy's head dropped. "When I saw you all come in together tonight, I wondered. I hoped I was wrong."

"Did you see him take Minnie on his lap? Or carry her home?"

She shook her head.

"Even Diggory likes him."

"Diggory likes everyone."

"Well, I aim to be more like Diggory, less judgmental and friendlier."

"So you're saying I'm judgmental." Her tone was tired, not angry.

He pressed her now-warm hands in his. "No, I'm saying you're human. And I'm not challenging your pa either. I don't know how you feel about me, or if you want to be friends, even, but you're an adult with good mind and a beautiful heart. If your pa was alive, I'd do all I could to prove my worthiness for your hand, but he's not. Only you and the Lord together can decide what's worth fighting to keep the same, and what you're free to change."

One final squeeze, and he let her hands go. "I'll walk you home."

She nodded and gathered her things.

Drew had a hunch it would be a long, silent walk home.

Chapter 7

Birdy didn't trust herself to speak during the walk home. What could she say to Drew, when he had asked if there was room for him in her heart? When he said he'd prove his worthiness to Pa if he could?

She cast him a quick glance as he walked beside her, hands loose at his sides. No matter how she felt, she owed him better than to talk about the weather or another inane topic after his heart-stopping revelation. But she couldn't very well talk about their relationship either. How could she, when she didn't even know her own heart?

It was such a confusing muddle. She cared for him, too. Being around him was restful, yet invigorating at the same time, appealing to her mind as well as her heart. Oh yes, how she cared for him.

But was she wrong? She'd thought she was a confident person, but Pa's well-intentioned insistence that she couldn't trust her feelings made her feel foolish and inadequate. And what she'd been taught to trust—her family's judgment—was no longer with her.

Drew was right that the war had changed things. He was also right about forgiveness. She needed to at least want to try forgiving Southerners and even Clement—and maybe even herself for having feelings for a man other than the one who'd worked to earn Pa's approval.

She glanced at Drew again, walking beside her in the twilight, and she let her imagination wander for an instant. She could take his hand and choose to be with him. But was it worth the guilt and shame she might feel later? Was Drew worth the risk?

Trudging up the path to the house, she wished she knew the answer.

Little squares of light shone from the windows, a welcoming sight as dusk deepened to dark. Birdy looked up at the pinpricks of stars beginning to shine through the sky. "Would you like a lamp?"

"Nah, thanks." He shoved his hands into his pockets. "I live next door, remember? And there's a moon to see by."

She couldn't hold back a snicker. "It's a good quarter mile to your shelter, according to Frieda—and copperheads are out at night, sometimes. That's not much of a moon either. It's only been three days since the new moon."

"It's waxing." He looked up at it and smiled. "A good time to plant skunk beans."

Laughter bubbled up her throat. "I'd almost forgotten Mr. Toovey and his skunk beans."

Drew's smile changed. It was almost sad. "It was the day we met."

"And I'm so glad we did." Even though meeting Drew seemed to be breaking her already fractured heart. "Good night, Drew. Thank you for seeing me safely home."

"Good night, Birdy."

When she reached the door, she waved, and for a minute, she watched him walk away.

Inside, the girls were energetic, stirring Diggory into a jumping, barking frenzy. Instantly, a headache started pounding in Birdy's temples. Birdy offered Frieda a tight smile. "I'm tired. I think I'll go up to bed early."

"Of course, after such a busy week. Would you like me to bring you some chamomile tea?"

"Thanks, but no. Good night, girls." She bent for kisses, patted Diggory, and prayed for escape from her contradictory, perplexing thoughts.

Pity she'd decided against the chamomile, because she didn't sleep much. Maybe that accounted for her sour mood the next day, despite the air of festivity surrounding the wedding day for the mother of two of her students, Fred and Benjy Piner. Watching Maggie and Sam exchange vows, Birdy was happy for them, but she still felt...blue.

All around her, the maids and widows of Turtle Springs were pairing off with gentlemen. Romance carried on the June breeze, and Frieda hadn't stopped humming all day, except for the moments when she brought Clement into the conversation by sharing something funny he'd said, or how she needed to have fresh cream for his coffee tonight, or how Minnie almost fell asleep when he carried her home from graduation last night.

After the whole debacle with Mr. Toovey and his skunk beans, Birdy had promised to keep her mouth shut about Frieda's suitors. Her tongue was raw from biting it all morning.

It was a relief to part from the Lomaxes after the wedding to go open the schoolhouse for the boys. It didn't take long for them to replace the benches with the desks, and once they'd finished, she locked up and returned home. As she retraced the steps she and Drew took last night, she repeated their conversation in her mind.

Pa. Emory. Promises. Forgiveness. It hurt Birdy's head as well as her heart.

Once she'd returned to the house, the smell of onions cooking in hot fat met her nose and made her stomach grumble. She hurried to the kitchen, where Diggory curled on the rag rug while Frieda and Minnie worked, still in their Sunday dresses from the wedding, just like Birdy was. After saying hello, she pulled her yellow gingham apron over her head.

175

Minnie stood at the sink, drying a spoon with a dishtowel. "Want me to tie your bow, Aunt Birdy?"

Minnie could tie a bow? Birdy nodded her assent and turned her back for Minnie. "When did you learn how to tie bows?"

"Mr. Cooper taught me yeth-terday." Minnie's little fingers were gentle against Birdy's spine. "I'm good at it now."

"Yes, you are." Frieda stirred the onions. "But you, Birdy, are awful quiet today." Then she giggled. "I mean *awfully*. Sorry."

Was she that bad? Shame crept up Birdy's chest. "I'm sorry for correcting you on something so unimportant, Frieda."

"Adverbs are always important, Miss Schoolmarm." Frieda adopted a mock expression of shock, and then sighed. "I guess I'm not funny."

"Yeth you are." Minnie stacked the utensils.

"You're uproarious." The hyperbole came out glum, and recognizing the irony, she chuckled. "Very well, you found me out. I'm a gloomy goose today."

"You must be exhausted, after graduation." Frieda's concerned expression vanished when she caught sight of something out the window. Birdy turned. Two male figures strode past toward the barn. The Cooper brothers had arrived to see to the animals. Frieda waved, and they waved back.

Minnie patted Frieda's backside. "May I go?"

"Yes, but be a help, not a hindrance," she called, even though Minnie and Diggory were already out the back door by the end of Frieda's sentence. Frieda sighed. "What was I saying? Oh yes. Graduation. How nice it will be to have a rest from teaching this summer."

Birdy shut her eyes for a moment. The girls weren't in the room, so she could speak freely. "I've decided to attend a teacher training and job fair in Topeka this summer."

Birdy counted to five until Frieda's face changed. "A job fair? What does that mean?"

"It means I might not come back to Turtle Springs."

"But why?" Frieda's voice was soft with hurt. She abandoned the pot on the stove and took Birdy's hands. "You want to leave us?"

"I think I need a clean slate, and I'm not sure I can stay in this house if you get married again."

"But we discussed this when I told you I planned to participate in the auditions—oh. This isn't about me marrying. It's about me being friendly with Clement."

"When he walked past just now, your eyes lit up like roman candles. I know I said I'd trust you to make your own decisions, but he's—"

"A nice man."

"Is he? I said I'd be quiet, but as your friend, I must remind you he told Drew he'd kill him. I'm not at all sure that's the sort of man who should be around you and the girls."

Frieda's grip tightened on Birdy's hands. "He and I have discussed his hideous threat against his own brother. Twice, for a few hours at a spell. I told him I wouldn't marry a violent or angry man."

"You've already talked about marrying him?" Oh dear.

"Marriage in general. He said his actions grieve him to no end. He also suggested I talk to Drew, so I did. He said Clement never lifted his hand against anyone before the war, and Drew explained that he'd had a part in goading Clement. It's no excuse, but I've made mistakes, too, Birdy. I'm watching carefully, but I truly believe Clement regrets his threat, and he's truly a gentle man—with the girls, Diggory, me. The cow kicked him on Thursday, and he didn't get angry. So I'm going to give it time and let him demonstrate that he's a man of honor and peace now. He's found God, and he's willing to confer with the reverend with me over the matter."

"Even if that threat was a one-time occurrence that he regrets, he was a Confederate. Hank's enemy."

Frieda's head shook. "The war is over. Clement isn't my enemy. He's the man who's taken care of my livestock and helped Drew fix my house and played with my girls and looked at me like I was the prettiest thing in Kansas and made me feel alive again. I think I love him, but it's awful—I mean *awfully*—soon to tell for sure."

Birdy sniffled back tears. "I love you. I want to protect you."

"Love me enough to trust me, Birdy." Frieda pulled her into a hug.

Birdy remained tucked into Frieda's shoulder, reveling in her friend's comfort. "Do you think Hank would mind you loving Clement?"

"Hank was a gem, and while there isn't a day that goes by that I don't miss him, or feel a twinge because I see him in the girls, I am so grateful he didn't place the horrible burden on me that your pa placed on you."

Birdy pulled back and swiped her damp cheeks. "What do you mean?"

"It's a loving thing to make sure the man who marries your daughter is worthy of her. But it's another thing altogether to shackle her to a life of singleness because he's not here to be in charge. In fact, I think he'd agree with me. He always struck me as a gruff sort of fellow, but he loved you, Birdy. He'd want you to be happy."

Memories flashed through Birdy's mind, of Pa's laughter and teasing and hugs. Yes, he'd want her to be happy. But he'd thought only he knew best what that was. Frieda could be trusted to make up her own mind. Could Birdy?

God, would You and Pa mind—

A scream from outside pierced the late afternoon air. Birdy and Frieda broke apart and dashed out the back door to the yard. Red faced and crying, Minnie waved her arms as she ran from the barn toward the house.

Frieda met her daughter halfway and scooped her up in her arms. "What's wrong?"

"I'm th-orry." Minnie sobbed. "It's my fault. The piglet-th."

Birdy patted Minnie's back. "What happened to the piglets?"

Polly and Mary Ann ran from the house. "What's the matter?"

A yell Birdy recognized as Drew's came from behind the barn, accompanied by Diggory's barks. And then Birdy understood.

The barn door yawned wide open. The pen doors within must have been opened, too, because livestock scampered free in the yard, including little lumps of pink and black—the piglets. All watched by a lean coyote on the edge of the yard.

Drew marched away from the yard toward the coyote watching them from the edge of the brush. Usually coyotes were scared of folks, but the lure of a pork supper must be too strong for him to resist, since he didn't run off despite the noise and activity, and even Diggory barking and running circles around Drew's legs.

Unless the coyote was rabid.

Muttering a prayer that it wasn't the case, Drew waved his arms and charged at the coyote. "Git! Go on, now!"

"Careful, Drew!" Birdy's voice was tight.

"I am. Get the piglets. And Diggory." And every other animal Minnie had let escape by opening the pen doors inside the barn. Drew glanced at the ground for a stick to brandish to make himself look bigger, but couldn't find one, so he continued to wave his arms. "Git!"

The coyote twitched then stepped to the side but stood its ground. Stubborn thing. Young, too, by the looks of his paws. Drew marched forward as Birdy dashed up to him to scoop Diggory into her arms.

Maybe it was the sight of two humans coming close, but at last, the animal turned tail and disappeared into the brush. Drew waited a moment, and sure enough, the coyote appeared on the small rise a few yards distant. Drew jogged after it, waving his arms and shouting. This time when the coyote ran, it didn't stop, and Drew watched until the coyote's brown coat melded into the scenery.

Satisfied, Drew hurried back to the barnyard. Each of the girls lunged after a squirming piglet while Frieda tethered the skittish horse and Clem chased the dairy cow, who'd pranced off into the grass, as if it ran from the coyote. Diggory barked, but was now securely tethered to the pump, and Birdy beckoned Mama Pig with her hand, nodding. "Come on, Mama. We've got good slops for you tonight. Pie. You can have my piece."

Drew chuckled. Oh, how he loved that woman.

Out of the corner of his eye, he saw Clem go down, like his ankle had given out. He'd stumbled upon an uneven spot, perhaps—

Clem's arm shot up. "Stay back!"

Frieda hurried toward him anyway. "Are you hurt?"

"Stay back, Frieda; I mean it. I disturbed a snake." Clem's authoritative tone couldn't disguise the slight shaking in his voice.

Drew ran down the slope, considering the tools in the barn he could use as weapons, or to push the snake away long enough for Clem to retreat. The hoe might serve both purposes.

"Girls," Frieda beckoned, her voice loud over Diggory's barks.

"But the piggies!" Mary Ann clutched a miniature porker to her chest.

"Coyote's gone," Birdy insisted, coming alongside Clement, the hoe clutched in her hands like a sword. Her steps were so smooth, the bell of her skirt didn't even wobble. "Hold still, Clement."

Drew reached the yard, scooping a piglet on the way and handing its muddy little body to Polly without looking. "Excellent idea, Birdy. Give me the hoe."

"Not enough time." She gripped the business end of the hoe and lowered the handle to the ground, prodding the snake's body, gently, gently.

A few more prods, and then she stepped closer to Clem. Then closer. Drew stepped behind her, slowly. "Is it a copperhead?"

"This fellow's coloring is right, and copperheads can become nocturnal when the weather warms up, but I don't want to kill a snake that doesn't mean us any harm—and I could be wrong, but I think this is a harmless fellow. I don't see venom pockets on either side of the head. Remember the shape of a venomous snake's head, girls?"

"Triangle," they said together.

"And nocturnal means what, Minnie?"

"Awake at night," Minnie announced.

"Always the teacher." Drew took her gently by the shoulders, surprised to feel them trembling under his hands. The snake slithered away into the grass. "I think you can stop now. It's gone."

He took the hoe from her shaking hands, wrapped his arm around her, and turned back to his brother—the brother Birdy jumped in to save from what could've been a venomous snake. "Do you need help?"

Frieda was already pulling him to his feet. "Did it twist? Let's get you inside."

"I'm fine." Clement shook out his limbs.

"You could've been—"

"But I wasn't. I'm fine. We're all fine." Clement's look for Frieda was so tender, Drew had to look away. A glance assured him Birdy had seen it, too, because she stared at the ground.

Clement shifted beside Frieda. "Besides, we still have work to do. I'm guessing no one shut the door to the pigpen after putting the pigs back inside the barn."

Drew gaped. Clem was right. Piglets snuffled around the barn doors and trotted in the grass. "Let's get to work then." He leaned down to Birdy. "Do you need to go in the house?"

"No, I need to work off some of these jitters." With a tremulous smile, she slipped from his arm and strode after a piglet around the edge of the barn. "Where are you off to? Are you trying to get eaten by that coyote?"

A loud squish caught Drew's attention. Mary Ann slipped and landed on her rump in the mud by the water trough. The pig she'd been reaching for skittered away.

Frieda burst into laughter. "I guess you won't be wearing that to church tomorrow."

"Me, neither." Minnie pointed to her smeared bodice.

"I tried, Ma." Polly's Sunday dress was dotted with dirt, too, but she was laughing.

"Ah well." Frieda tapped her muddy finger on Polly's nose, leaving a streak of mud. Polly shrieked. "Mother! I'm shocked at you!"

Frieda responded by flicking more mud on Polly, and somehow everyone started laughing and flicking mud while they worked.

Shortly, they gathered in the barn, and Birdy lowered the last of the piglets into the pen, which Clem latched with a loud click. He double checked it and nodded. "I'll get the cow."

"What happened?" Drew leaned against the pen, brushing dirt off his hands.

"I let 'em all out. They wanted to play." Minnie shrugged.

"Oh, did they? Well, they're going to play in their pens from now on. We keep them penned inside the barn to keep them safe until they're larger, and now you understand why." Frieda snorted. "If you could have seen yourselves, leaping over the yard like bullfrogs. I've never seen anything so funny in all my days."

Polly giggled. "And Aunt Birdy, beckoning Mama Pig with the promise of pie—"

They turned their heads to look at Birdy, but she was gone.

Drew had a pretty good idea where she'd gone. He waited a minute before stepping outside.

Birdy and Clem stood with the cow about six yards away, their expressions serious. Then Birdy nodded and extended her hand to Clem. He took it and they shook, a businesslike transaction, but it was a start.

Drew leaned against the barn door, half indoors with the female conversation behind him, half outdoors, with Birdy and Clem in his sights, although he kept his gaze up at the sliver moon appearing in the darkening sky.

"Oh no, supper!" Frieda shrieked, hurrying past him out of the barn. "Wash up, everyone."

"What about our dresses?" Mary Ann held out her skirt.

"Change and then, oh, I don't know. Dunk the ones you have on under the pump. But you, Cooper brothers, can eat in your dirty shirts. Just wash your hands."

"We will," Clem answered. He nodded at Birdy and led the cow into the barn.

Birdy watched Drew, and a faint smile tipped her lips when he drew alongside her. Ever so slowly, they ambled to the house. He looked down at her dirt-streaked face. "Everything all right?"

"I apologized to Clement for holding a grudge. I want to forgive him for being a Confederate, and I want to forgive him for threatening you, but that doesn't mean I should trust him if he's violent. Do you truly think he's changed?"

"He was never violent, beyond that threat. He was angry at me, broken by the war, and he lashed out in an inexcusable way. But I do think he's different now. Some people say they've found God, but Clement means it. He came all this way to make peace, and what you saw tonight, his concern and affection for Frieda and the girls? That's all real."

She looked about to say more, but Frieda returned from the house. "You spoke to Clement?"

"I did. He accepted my apology, gave me his own, and said he truly wants Frieda's best friend to approve of his suit."

Frieda blinked back tears—happy ones, from the look of it. Drew's heart swelled at the knowledge that his brother cared about Birdy's opinion, knowing it would make Frieda and the girls happy.

Birdy nodded. "I'll pray about it, all right?"

"I can't ask for more. I'm so happy, Birdy. I don't want anything between us when you leave for the job fair in Topeka."

Drew stiffened. The pamphlet that was for Virginia from the restaurant... Birdy was going, too?

"Oh, you didn't tell Drew?" Frieda's fingers covered her mouth. "I'm sorry."

"Not yet." Birdy's furtive glance told him enough. She'd managed to change her mind when it came to giving Clement a chance, but she couldn't give Drew one.

As he trudged in to supper, he couldn't help wishing more had changed in her heart and mind than her resentment against Clement.

Chapter 8

Birdy's heart thumped hard and fast all through supper, all night long, and through the worship service the next morning, and it had nothing to do with the snake or the coyote, or even Clement.

She was afraid, plain and simple. Scared enough to gather her things and run off to Topeka tonight, and the job fair didn't even start for a few weeks.

But you're no coward, Roberta Green.

So after church, while the congregants gathered on the lawn and Clement hoisted Minnie in his arms and Frieda asked if they should have a picnic, Birdy moved to stand smack in front of Drew. "There's something I need to attend to at the schoolhouse. Would you come with me, Drew?"

Drew stared, his eyes wide and blue. "I'm happy to help you."

Polly pushed forward. "Me, too. What do you need?"

Frieda's head shake at her oldest daughter was not in the least subtle.

"What?" Polly asked.

"Um, let's check the piglets and make sure that latch is secure before we have our picnic." Clement tipped his head toward the wagon, but his gaze was on Polly. "If Aunt Birdy and Drew are finished in time, they can meet us. He and I found the perfect spot on his new land for a picnic, where the cottonwoods give just the right amount of shade on a fine day like this."

Birdy nodded at him. He winked at her.

Drew's brows pulled low as they walked the short distance to the schoolhouse. "Did the board do a surprise inspection after all?"

"No." Oh, this was horribly scary. When they climbed the steps to the schoolhouse, she reached into her bag and handed him the key with trembling fingers "Would you get the door for me?"

"It's stuck again?" He frowned and used far more force than was necessary for a perfectly working door.

The schoolhouse smelled of chalk, paper, and familiarity. It was her home, in a way, a place where she felt safe among well-ordered items. She strode to her desk, where the pamphlet for the Topeka fair lay, inanimate but practically screaming at her. She turned her back on it. "Thanks for coming with me, Drew. The truth is, the matter I wished to attend to is you. Last night, there was too much going on for us to have any privacy."

Exuberant girls. Five dresses to scrub so the mud stains wouldn't set. The fierce, loud pattering of her heartbeat in her ears and her thoughts swirling in a confusing jumble.

Drew stood still as a signpost in the center of the schoolhouse. "Talking to Clement couldn't have been easy for you."

"It wasn't, but you were right. I wasn't just protecting Frieda. I was angry at him for threatening you and for his part in the war."

His gaze rested on the pamphlet on her desk. "I don't like how we left things Friday night. Or last night either. The truth is, I care about you. Enough that I want you to be fulfilled and happy and whole. So I think your trip to Topeka is a good idea. Learn some new things, make friends."

"I'm not going to Topeka after all."

"Why not?" Rather than sounding happy about it, he seemed frustrated. "You should do something for yourself, Birdy. You should get a clean slate if you want one, just like the rest of us."

"The clean slate I need is within me, not outside of me." Birdy's palms dampened. "Since my family died—including Emory—I've been stuck in a pit of grief. Fear, too. I've struggled to forgive the soldiers responsible for killing Lemuel and Emory, but my father wouldn't have forgiven them either. He held a grudge, and I doubt he would have shown any kindness to a Confederate. I feel like I'm disappointing him by just listening to Clement. But making peace with him? I know Pa wouldn't have liked it. But you're right, God calls us to something different."

"I'm glad you're closer to peace, Birdy. But Topeka—"

"Yesterday I spontaneously decided to go because I wanted to escape my feelings. Leaving town seemed the best way to do it. I don't want to escape anymore." Although her pulse contradicted her, so fast it could probably keep time with a hummingbird's. "My father wanted me to have a worthy man who'd earned my family's approval. I have that man."

His brows knit in confusion.

"Last night, somewhere between you chasing off the coyote and me getting up this morning, I saw the truth, and I couldn't believe my blindness. How could I not see that you proved time and again that you are diligent, hardworking, fair, righteous, and kind? You repaired the schoolhouse and my home. You've demonstrated the sort of man you are, Drew, and I can trust my feelings. If I'm afraid to, though, I can look to my family."

"But I never met your family, Birdy."

She smiled. "Not Pa or Lemuel, no, but I realized last night that I have a new family now. Frieda and the girls. They don't just approve of you, Drew. They think you hung the waxing moon."

Still, Drew didn't move. Didn't he understand what she was telling him?

Then her thoughts hopped backward to his words just now. He'd said it was a good idea for her to go to Topeka.

Last night, while she was realizing the Lomaxes and Coopers were her family and she could trust her heart, Drew must have realized something, too. He didn't care for her like that anymore.

Birdy's mouth went dry.

Drew thawed from his frozen pose and hurried toward her—no, her desk. "I need a slate."

"Did you lose the other one?" Her voice was thick with embarrassment and shame.

"No, but I need to know how to spell something." He reached to the blackboard for a stick of chalk.

Now? Couldn't he leave her to wallow in private? "Just tell me what the word is. You don't have to write it—"

"My teacher taught me that writing helps me retain knowledge better, and I don't want to forget this."

He scrawled. Then turned the slate around.

Thou art more lovely and more temperate than a summer's day. A reference to Shakespeare's 33rd Sonnet, the first thing they studied. Her insides swooped low. "Drew."

"Did I misspell *temperate?*"

"No, it's correct, but—"

"I'm not done." Tugging his handkerchief from his pocket, he snapped it open and erased what he'd written. The words disappeared into white particles of chalk dust. He scribbled again and then turned the slate.

I know I can't replace Emery.

She wouldn't dare correct his misspelling. Her hand went to her mouth. His hanky went to good use erasing the slate again, and he wrote.

But if there's any room left in your heart. . .

Her eyes prickled with wet heat.

Even though I'm no Shakespeare. . .

She chuckled, which was clearly what he'd intended, because he laughed and, oh, his eyes were crinkled with something that looked suspiciously like delight. Since he was being funny, she fisted her hands on her hips to tease him. "This is a very long sentence."

"Almost done." He was still grinning, but when he turned the slate around, there was fear in his eyes.

I will love you with all I am and all I have for all my days.

He was as scared as she was. Somehow, that gave her more strength. She held out her hand. "Chalk, please."

"What did I misspell?" He said it like a joke.

"Nothing." She took the slate, wiped it properly with an eraser, and wrote on it, producing the squeaky sounds chalk always made. Then she turned the slate.

You are correct: you are not Shakespeare.

He burst into laughter. "Yep, that's for sure."

She wrote, took a breath, and turned the slate around.

I don't want Mr. Shakespeare, however. I want you.

He waited for two heartbeats, maybe three, before removing the chalk and slate from her hands and setting them on the desk. "But?"

"There's no *but*. I ended my sentence with a period, not a conjunction."

His hands took hers, and he stood before her, lowering his head until his forehead rested on hers. "That would be grammatically incorrect, I s'pose."

"It would." Her pulse skittered, but no longer from fear. Drew's breath was warm against her cheeks.

"I don't want you to miss out on teacher training in Topeka. I'll be here when you get back."

Her head shook against his. "I don't want to go. I'm staying here because this is my home, and I—I love you, too. I fought it, but I didn't need to."

"We're both finding our way. Starting over is never easy." Then his lips brushed hers. He pulled back to look at her, and then—oh, he was kissing her. Soft at first, but then something changed. He let go of her hands to take her waist, and she wrapped her arms around his broad shoulders.

Starting over might not be easy, but *this* was as simple as her ABCs and 123s. Kissing Drew was bliss.

Too soon, he pulled back and enveloped her in an embrace. "It hasn't been long, but you need to know, I aim to marry you."

She smiled into his chest. "You want to get married? Wait, why am I the one asking?"

"Because I didn't raise my hand?" He laughed and kissed her forehead.

"Very funny, Mr. Cooper."

He took her hands again and dropped to his knee. "I don't have a ring for you yet. All I have is my heart and the ranch next door to your family. I'll love you every day God gives us together. Roberta Green, my darling Birdy, will you marry me?"

"Yes." Her voice was as clear as the school bell.

He rose to his feet and sealed their engagement with a kiss.

The late August morning was hot and sultry, but Birdy shivered as Polly, Mary Ann, and Minnie left her and Frieda in the vestibule to precede them up the church aisle. After waiting a few seconds, Birdy nodded at Frieda.

"Ready?"

"Almost." Frieda, pretty in her new apple-green dress, bent to kiss Birdy's cheek. "Thank you for getting to know Clement these past few months. I'm so glad you've seen that he's changed."

"And next week, you'll be the bride." Birdy squeezed Frieda's hand.

Grinning, Frieda slipped from Birdy's hold and took her turn up the aisle.

Alone in the vestibule, Birdy took a steadying breath. She'd always imagined

Pa giving her away on her wedding day, smiling his approval. He wasn't here, but she felt nothing but peace today, as well as an eagerness for further healing in her heart, and for the nation in the future. Choosing forgiveness had helped her choose hope, too.

She moved into position.

Drew waited beside Rev. Smith at the end of the aisle, handsome in a new dark suit, his near-black hair neat and his shoes shiny. But Birdy liked his smile best, and was certain hers was as wide as his.

Her students watched from the pews. So did newlyweds Jeb and Jenny Washburn. Clement, the best man, smiled from his place by Drew's side.

When she reached the end of the aisle, Drew took her hands and smiled down at her. They promised to love, honor, and keep one another until parted by death, and then Rev. Smith pronounced them man and wife.

Drew leaned down for a kiss that curled her toes. She was so blessed to love and be loved by him.

To think, she'd almost let him slip away.

Even teachers needed to learn a lesson or two, sometimes.

Susanne Dietze began writing love stories in high school, casting her friends in the starring roles. Today, she's the award-winning author of a dozen new and upcoming historical romances who's seen her work on the ECPA and Publisher's Weekly Bestseller Lists for Inspirational Fiction. Married to a pastor and the mom of two, Susanne lives in California and enjoys fancy-schmancy tea parties, the beach, and curling up on the couch with a costume drama and a plate of nachos. You can visit her online at www.susannedietze.com and subscribe to her newsletters at http://eepurl.com/bieza5.

Sunshine of My Heart

By Darlene Franklin

A time to weep, and a time to laugh; a time to mourn, and a time to dance.
ECCLESIASTES 3:4 KJV

Chapter 1

D ebbie Barker spotted an empty seat at the long table between Alanna Radle and another lady she didn't know. She made her way through the throng who had arrived to watch the interviews. Had there ever been a town like Turtle Springs, in such need of marriageable men they'd invited strangers to audition to become mail-order grooms?

And Debbie was one of the women desperate enough to seek her husband using this gambit. She understood the widows, who struggled to keep their businesses or ranches running. There were other homesteader daughters like herself. What kind of wife would these men be looking for?

A few of the potential husbands had entered the restaurant and were munching on the finger sandwiches provided for the event. What kind of man would leave his life behind to gamble on this audition? A man with no strings? No money?

How could a man like Papa gamble on Kansas when he'd left Maine after the war claimed his only son and his two older daughters had married? "We've decided to start over," he'd told his youngest daughter a year ago. "I spoke with your sister, Heather. If you wish, you can stay and have a home with her for as long as you want."

A spinster aunt spending her day helping raise four children, with another on the way? No thank you.

"Or you can come with us to Kansas."

Kansas, definitely.

Were all the men from Kansas? How far had Miss Melton, the acting mayor, sent letters?

Could any of them even be from Maine? The thought made Debbie want to giggle. Her hometown would never have held an audition for potential husbands. Something so audacious just wasn't done.

The minute hand on the clock moved toward four, and the remaining men entered the restaurant and took seats at the back wall. She studied the possibilities. Practically, she needed a strong man who knew something about farming. Hopefully he'd have broad interests, say, in politics, or someone who liked to read. Someone who knew the Lord but not someone who did nothing but preach every time he opened his mouth. The audition ads had specified God-fearing men, so she wouldn't spend too much time on that issue.

Was it vain to want someone who was good-looking, who tickled her insides just by looking at her? That was the first thing a gal might notice. A quick glance identified a few men good-looking enough to run for office.

She caught Papa's gaze; he pointed to the sky. She'd done nothing but pray since she signed up. She'd be listening to the man answering her questions with one ear and tuning the other to that still, small voice.

The men studied the women with equal interest. A few looked down on their luck, but by and large, they looked like a decent lot. One young lad caught her eye and tipped his hat to her. She blushed and turned away. What if he was the one? That would make an interesting story to tell their children.

The number of men outnumbered the ladies. A blessing for the women, although the men might disagree.

Miss Melton called the people together and explained the process. Each woman would have fifteen minutes to talk with each man. The men's reactions were noteworthy. If a man appeared amused by the process, was he serious about seeking a wife? Most of them simply nodded.

Debbie removed a small notebook and pencil from her reticule. Note-taking—how unromantic. Did she want a man who treated the audition as a business transaction or as a social event? Charm or honesty? Mama had known Papa all her life. Debbie wouldn't have that advantage.

But God knew every man here, Debbie reminded herself for the hundredth time. He would guide each potential couple, as long as they were seeking His will.

The young man who'd caught her attention earlier locked eyes with her again. This time she decided he was too young for her.

Another man's gaze passed over Debbie. He had the erect bearing of an ex-soldier. He'd probably experienced painful losses, either on the field of battle or at home or maybe both. His expression intrigued her—not one of speculation. Not flirtation. Something—something almost like—hope? Peace? She wanted to hear his story.

At the sound of the bell, the first twenty men took their seats across from the ladies. Debbie felt bad for the men who had to wait until the next round started. Did they think they would have lost their chance before their first interview?

The man with a Union cap had a seat in the second row. He didn't seem worried.

The interviews flew by. Three of the candidates were named John. Confusing, but she didn't think any of them were possibilities. One was older than she wished. Another looked too young to marry anyone except his childhood sweetheart. The third John frowned when she mentioned he would help her Papa prove up on their homestead. Even after she added, "Which will belong to me—and my husband—someday."

The remainder of the first line brought one more John, three Williams, and a pair of Georges. Three had answered all her questions well. Assuming they were Christians, she'd asked, "What did you talk to God about this morning?" She wanted a man who made God a part of his daily life.

John Brooks—John number four—had said, "Do you mean in addition to whether I would meet my helpmeet today?"

His comment brought a smile to her face, and she nodded.

"I prayed I could encourage the women in Turtle Springs. The war hit a lot of communities hard, but not many of them have taken the extreme measure of looking for grooms." He allowed himself a smile. "Although the strategy will prove to be a blessing to both parties, God willing."

John Brooks was her favorite so far, even if he was on the far side of thirty. She shouldn't let unimportant details like a balding head and short stature bother her, but was it wrong to want someone who fit her definition of handsome?

No one had answered her trick question to her satisfaction yet.

The first line of men had finished their interviews. Debbie looked at the woman to her right, Alanna Radle. She wiggled her fingers in a wave.

The second row of men stood and headed in their direction.

This was his last chance to back out.

The thought slipped through Zack Gage's mind but he ignored it. He hadn't traveled over fourteen-hundred miles from Connecticut to Kansas to change his mind now. If God didn't have a bride for Zack in Turtle Springs, he'd find a job. A town looking for husbands could probably use hard-working men in other capacities. God had brought him here for a reason.

Since he'd landed toward the end of the line, he thought it was possible no one would choose him. By now they must be tired and the men would start to blur together. Did any of the woman interest him?

Some of the brides were barely out of the schoolroom. They wouldn't want a war-weary soldier. Good-bye, Betty and Lizzie. Some of them were widows, a bit older than he was. No thank you, Mary and Martha. He wanted someone closer to his age, someone who might have married in the past five years if the war hadn't interfered.

Someone like that strawberry blond ahead, whom he had caught looking at him before the auditions started. What would she ask? Her questions. They would reveal more about her than her pretty looks.

He reached the blond's spot at the table. "Hello, I'm Zack Gage."

Her eyebrows went up. "Zack—that's the first Z I've encountered today. My name is Debbie Barker."

The way she pronounced her surname as *Bah-keh* told him something important. "We have something in common. We hail from the venerable part of the country known as New England. I'm from Connecticut."

She closed her eyes as she listened to him talk. When she opened them, their deep blue depths startled him.

Zack found his voice and said, "Your voice lands like music on my ears. Folks all across the country are kind and God-fearing, but I expect heaven to sound like New England."

Debbie laughed. "I have to agree. We came here from a farm in Lincoln County, Maine, last fall." She spread her hands but didn't explain. She didn't want to talk about it yet. That was all right. He'd rather not discuss the home he'd left behind either. The pain of his past mustn't define these few short minutes.

"So is your father farming out here, or did he take up a different occupation?"

Miss Barker's eyelids fluttered, as if surprised he was taking over the direction of the questions. "Yes, he's hoping to prove up a homestead." She hesitated. "It will belong to me and my husband, one day."

A farm. He could live with that. "Before the war, my family used to make farm implements. But I've never used them myself."

She tapped the paper in front of her. "So you have a mechanical bent?"

"I suppose."

She made a note and glanced at the clock. "Tell me, what did you talk with God about this morning?"

No one else had asked a question anything like that. "Mostly I thanked God I got here on time. I know God has a purpose for me here. I want to start over."

He couldn't believe he'd just said that. What about this girl made him open up and say something so revealing?

Because she's the one?

Miss Barker tilted her head, a smile lighting her face. "One last question. What do you consider lovely?"

You. That answer wouldn't satisfy. "Sunrise, especially over the sea. Birds flying through the air. A moose's bugle on a spring morning. At least, I used to find those things beautiful, once upon a time."

Her lips remained slightly parted, and she didn't respond.

His heart pounded quickly. "Miss Barker, I haven't said this to anyone else, and I don't know if it's appropriate, but I hope you'll accept my audition."

The bell rang, and he went to the next spot on the long table. A lot of men were probably interested in Debbie. She had both beauty and brains, with a dowry for any man willing to apply himself. Zack told himself to keep an open mind for the remaining ladies.

Miriam was pretty enough and a good conversationalist. Widowed within a month of her wedding. Which was worse—to have loved and lost your soul mate or to never have found them at all? After Debbie, Miriam was Zack's next choice.

How strange the next step in the courtship dance lay in the hands of women. At least no immediate marriages were expected. Zack would never have come otherwise.

What if no one chose him? The possibility hurt, since he'd met a fellow New Englander who asked unusual questions.

With the questioning over, the men were invited to enjoy the food tables while the ladies deliberated. Although he wasn't hungry, he filled his plate. It gave him something to do while he waited. He took a seat by the wall. Debbie was talking with an older couple—her parents? Miriam chatted with a few of the other widows. What if more than one woman was interested in him or one of the other candidates? How would they handle it? He'd trust God to sort that one out.

The mayor gathered papers reflecting the ladies' choices and tallied them. The men drifted back to their seats.

More people arrived for the announcements than had watched the auditions themselves. He studied the newcomers. One of them might be his employer, if no bride chose him.

The mayor began with the bride at the head of the table—she asked for someone else. No surprise. When it came to Miriam, Zack sucked in his breath.

"Miriam Webb has requested John Brooks."

Polite applause broke out.

When they reached a young lady who seemed greatly interested in Zack's war experiences, he tented his hands and held his breath. "Alanna Radle chooses Sidney Anderson."

Next came Debbie. "Debbie Barker chooses—Zack Gage."

He jumped to his feet. "Hallelujah!"

Chapter 2

Applause rang out after Zack's shout. Debbie buried her head in her father's shoulder, but she kept one eye open, searching the crowd for Zack. They found each other. A grin rippled across her face—she couldn't help it. He grinned back.

Miss Melton brought the crowd under control. After all, everyone wanted to hear the remaining matches. Even if Debbie wanted to run to Zack's side right that minute.

Debbie heard the names, saw the disappointment of the men who would leave without a potential bride. But she could only bring herself to care about Zack. *Hurry up!* She wanted to introduce him to her parents and begin the process.

Miss Melton introduced Mr. J.R. Lockhart, a journalist who wanted to write about today's audition. He asked the couples to come together for a picture. The men stirred from their chairs. Zack fixed his eyes on Debbie, and she remained in place, waiting for him to claim her—the first official act of their courtship.

As he walked toward her, her heart fluttered. Had she made the right decision? Although he was only of average height, he carried himself with military precision. His legs ate up the ground between them. Confidence marked his every move. "Miss Barker."

"Such formality." She giggled. "Debbie, please. You are halfway toward becoming my fiancé."

"Indeed." Hope flickered in his eyes. "I am more honored than I can say that you chose me, Miss—Debbie. I look forward to getting to know you better. But now shall we join the others for the portrait?"

He offered his arm, and she slipped her hand around his elbow. They made a good pair physically. She wouldn't mind looking into that face every morning when she woke up—provided he had a character to match. That was the point of the audition, though, wasn't it? To give potential couples a head start.

"Did they say which magazine is publishing the article?" Zack asked.

"Lady Godey's," Debbie answered. The one magazine every woman in America read or borrowed whenever she had a chance. Her sisters were bound to see it.

The couples stood in two lines, the men behind their ladies. What a pity the illustration wouldn't be in color, with all the lovely dresses the women had worn. Of course, none of them wore the kind of fashions which normally made their appearance in the pages of the magazine.

As soon as the photograph was finished, Debbie's parents rushed toward them. Papa extended his hand. "Mr. Gage, I'm Charles Barker, Debbie's father. You can call me Charles."

Zack grabbed the proffered hand in a firm handshake. "Pleased to meet you, Charles." He turned to Debbie's mother. "And you must be Mrs. Barker."

"Kathleen, please."

After that, conversation stalled. "Zack, we need to head home before it gets dark. Our homestead is at the end of the road, and we have evening chores to do." Debbie was uncertain how to proceed. "Do you have any objection to returning home with us tonight? Where shall we pick up your belongings?"

"I was hoping to go back with you. The sooner I can get to work, helping out around the place, the better I'll feel." He pointed down the street. "I left my horse and my saddle bag at the livery." He smiled at them, revealing teeth in better shape than most. "Why don't I meet you back here in fifteen minutes?"

He disappeared so quickly Debbie didn't have a chance to answer.

"I believe God is at work in bringing the two of you together," Mama said. "He seems like a fine young man."

Papa grunted. "We'll see what he's made of, come tomorrow."

Debbie wanted to protest, but they had already argued the point and Papa had won. She'd wanted at least one day to get to know her potential groom better before he started working.

Papa contended there'd be plenty of time for talking at the end of an honest day's work. If the fellow couldn't help around the farm, he might not be the right man for her, no matter what other qualities he had.

Remembering that conversation, Debbie's heart stuttered. "Papa, remember his background is in mechanics and manufacturing before the war. I'm praying he'll have an aptitude for farming, but don't expect him to know it like you do."

Papa grunted. "I know, girl. I just hope he can help us get enough sod broken to get a crop planted for a harvest. Enough to help us survive the winter."

The ladies of Turtle Springs had decided against discussing finances during the audition. They didn't want money to be a factor in the decision. If it was God's will, He would provide. As Miss Melton had pointed out, the men spent money and time just to come to the audition.

Once again Debbie prayed Zack was the right one for her.

When he rejoined them, as comfortable on horseback as a Kansas cowboy, she couldn't hold back a smile. Oh my, he embodied everything she'd dreamed of. He resembled a war-weary knight returning from battle to protect his family and his castle. A proven leader, one ready to confront whatever challenges lay within his realm. His saddlebags and blanket roll held everything he'd need to confront and conquer his enemies.

Once again she felt certain she'd picked the right man. She said a quick prayer before urging her horse to step forward. "Are you ready to get your first look at the Barker Family Homestead?"

Silence reigned during the trip from Turtle Springs to the homestead. Zack scanned the area they passed through. The land was as different from his Connecticut home as he'd expected—hoped, even. After the war had turned his life upside down, he wanted a place to make a new life for himself.

So far he saw farm country. Small buildings indicated the transition from prairie to acres plowed under and animals straining against their yokes to plant the year's crops.

Zack had hoped to see miles of grassland, as endless as the ocean with the wind blowing through its waves. The Flint Hills got in the way. Hills rose and fell wherever he looked. In between farms and up the hills and filling the valleys, he glimpsed grass tall enough for a horse to pass through unnoticed. He hoped that meant rich farmland.

Debbie noticed his interest. "I could tell you the names of most of the families along this road, but I thought that would be overwhelming."

"You can entertain me later with their names and stories. Were any of them involved in the audition today?"

"Yes." Debbie's pretty pink cheeks looked nice with her golden hair. "The lady seated to my right, Alanna Radle. She chose Sidney Anderson." She glanced over her shoulder. "I believe they're about half a mile behind us. We're coming up on their farm."

The Radle homestead marked the end of the farms clustered close together near the town. After that, the distance between the homes grew and the smaller the cultivated plots became.

The abundance of flint Zack saw glittering in the mountains—the reason Zebulon Pike had dubbed the region the Flint Hills in his journal on his journey west—interested him as a mechanic and inventor of practical machinery for agriculture. Zack squelched the thoughts. From today on, Zack Gage was a good ol' farm boy. And he'd learn to like it.

When the Barkers shifted in their seats, Zack looked around for the home they would share. Only a thin path led between the blowing grass; he didn't see any buildings at all.

After a few minutes, they arrived at the most basic of homesteads Zack had seen so far. Housing for humans—a small dirt soddy, probably one compact room. Housing for animals—the same, across a small patch of cleared land. A trodden path allowed them to access the nearby river. In the distance, he saw evidence of a field being prepared for planting. A rope fence indicated the extent to which Mr. Barker—Charles—hoped to finish plowing. He hadn't even reached the halfway point yet.

Debbie pulled her lips over her teeth before forcing a smile on her face. "Welcome home, Zack. It's actually quite nice inside. Just a little snug." She held her hat in front of her, at her waist, expecting—what?

"It's fine. Impressive. You told me you arrived late last fall. You've come a long way in a short time." He hesitated. "If accommodations inside are crowded, I'd be happy to sleep outside. I even have a tent, if it rains."

Debbie opened her arms wide and gestured around her. "I know it's not much. But after your years of service to the Union, I hate for you to sleep on the ground. Why don't you check our setup and then decide?"

After such a heartfelt invitation, Zack would sleep inside, whatever the condition. She took him by the hand and through the door. A reminder of their old home greeted them as soon as they entered, a small framed watercolor of a boat on the Atlantic on a sunny day.

Although Zack was of average height, the ceiling only cleared his head by six inches. Every inch was neat and organized. Blocks of soil accomplished what rough logs had for the colonists in New England, creating a single rectangular room. The furniture was rough but functional. Mattresses were rolled and stacked in the corner.

In spite of his promise, Zack would prefer to sleep under the open sky. Solitude would allow him to wrestle with the situations that had brought him to Kansas. He didn't know how well he would sleep, resting only a few feet away from one of the prettiest creatures he'd ever laid eyes on. During the long hours of the night, his thoughts might stray where a Christian's shouldn't go before marriage. But he had promised.

"You've organized so well." His voice sounded hoarse, and he took a drink from his canteen. "This will work." He nodded to Mrs. Barker—Kathleen. "I love the picture of the ocean."

She pointed to Debbie, who had raised her right hand. "Guilty. We brought that one painting with us." Tears glistened in her eyes. "When I look at this picture, I ask God to help me see the Flint Hills differently. The hills remind me a little of the Appalachians, but I miss the ocean."

"And not a maple tree in sight."

Debbie laughed out loud. "I wish I had pressed a perfect red leaf to carry with us. But it wouldn't have survived the journey."

What could he say? "I traveled long distances in the Army. I learned one thing better than everything else: wherever we are, God is there—and He doesn't change."

She nodded in appreciation. "Amen. And now I'd better help Mama prepare supper. She wants to make your first meal with us memorable." She chuckled. "Another time we'll prepare baked beans New England style. We weren't expecting a fellow New Englander."

"That sounds good." He rubbed his hands together. "Where can I find your father?"

"Taking care of chores."

"Then I'll join him until you sound the dinner bell." His saddlebags could stay on the wagon bed for a little while longer. He wasn't sure where they would fit in the soddy.

They might be glad he didn't own many possessions. Where would they put them? The Barker homestead was such a blank slate, it certainly provided the new beginning he wanted.

With a spring in his step, Zack looked around until he found the spot where Mr. Barker—Charles—was currying the horses after their trip to town. He'd already tied down the wagon under a tarp, safe and snug.

"What can I do to help? The ladies are busy with dinner."

Charles chuckled. "I stay outside as long as I can. Not enough room for a man to turn around inside that place." He sighed. "I'm sorry I don't have a better home to offer you."

"I'm not afraid of hard work." Zack grabbed a curry comb and started on the second horse.

The homestead did lack one thing, what he hungered for more than anything else. Beauty. *Whatever is lovely, think on these things.*

If there was loveliness to be found on the Barker homestead, God would have to lead him to it.

Debbie's head appeared in the doorway. Then again, God had already showed him the greatest beauty of all. Now to discover more details of God's gracious creation.

Chapter 3

They did extra wash on Saturday. Debbie peeked into Zack's personal belongings. He couldn't have worn these in the war. They would have been more worn out. He also didn't have his army uniform. Was he ashamed of something that happened during the war? No. She shook her head. More likely, he wanted to forget about it.

His clothes were of good quality, but not suitable for farming. The next time they went to the mercantile, she would buy material to make him something suitable. She studied him in the distance, imagining him in his new clothes.

Mama saw her looking at Zack. "It's kind of nice to have them where we can see them, isn't it?"

Unlike during the war when families didn't hear from fathers and husbands, brothers and sons for months at a time.

Debbie nodded. "I was thinking of making him farm clothes." She held her breath, waiting for Mama's reaction.

Mama shook her head. "Not yet. He might feel beholden to you."

Mama was right, as usual. "I want to do something for him. To thank him for—"

"Auditioning?" Mama smiled. "He's here. You chose him, and he accepted. That's the best thank you of all, in my opinion." She shook her head. "I never heard of such a thing, but we've never lost so many young men like the war took from us."

Mama stared at Zack as if she were imagining her son Robert. They were of a similar height, the same ease of standing, but there the similarities ended.

Mama and Papa wanted the son they had lost. Debbie wanted love, a family of her own—the ordinary life every schoolgirl dreamed of until the Confederacy fired upon Appomattox.

Zack appeared to swing his arms with ease, as if he knew everything about breaking up sod, and tossed it on the waiting wagon.

"Stop staring at Zack so we can finish hanging the wash," Mama said.

"Let's change sides, then."

Mama looked at her as if she were a crazy fool but they switched places. With Debbie's back to the field, her fingers flew to the clothespins and she hung the clothes straight to avoid extra ironing. At her height, she blocked Ma's view of the field as well. "From what I could see, they made great progress this morning.

We're gathering enough sod to add an extra room if we want to." A pleading note crept into Debbie's voice. She might not miss the vast ocean so badly if she could see more than the tiny soddy threatening to close in on her.

"That's a girl. Keep working hard, and maybe you'll wear yourself out enough to sleep tonight." Mama said in a singsong voice.

At least the sheet between them prevented Mama from seeing the heat in Debbie's cheeks. So Mama had noticed her sleeplessness. With Zack so close, so real, she struggled to keep her eyes closed at night.

Her presence didn't seem to trouble him. His snores alone might have kept her awake even if she'd been able to still her wandering heart.

Silence fell between them. Papa and Zack worked well together, but did they get along? Could they imagine living side by side, here in Kansas? She wished she could eavesdrop on their conversation. If only she could shrink small enough to ride on a bird's back and listen to them talk.

An unexpected sound reached across the fields, and she strained her ears to listen. "They're singing hymns." As quickly as it started, the music ended.

Too soon, Debbie and her mother finished hanging the laundry and headed inside to fix the meal. She rang the cowbell and waited for the man of her prayers and dreams to come home. Her hands covered her heart, as if she could protect herself from falling in love with a man who might still choose to leave.

His smile widened when he noticed her, and she relaxed. So far, he had chosen to stay, in spite of working so hard.

Mama dished out food, which the men devoured in a few bites. Zack answered Debbie's questions with single words, and neither one said much before they finished.

When Debbie spied Zack at the pump, she ran out to him with a towel. His angry red hands brought her to a halt. "Oh no."

"It's nothing." He grinned as if they didn't hurt. "They'll toughen up. I'll wear gloves this afternoon. Don't know what I was thinking this morning."

"Let me get some bag balm for your hands."

He left before she reached the door. "Tonight." He joined Papa and they headed for the field.

At least he pulled gloves over his hands.

Debbie marched into the soddy, wanting to hit something. Instead, she pounded hard on the sod. "I didn't expect Papa to work him so hard. If he keeps this up, Zack might decide he'd get better treatment somewhere else."

"Oh, Debbie." Mama pulled her close. "He's not working any harder than your father."

"Maybe not." Debbie had hoped having two men working the farm would help Papa slow down. Maybe in time. She hurried through her afternoon chores. If she couldn't get them to slow down, maybe she could work by their side.

What were they going to do with all the sod they had removed today?

Build a house for when Zack married Debbie—if they wed?

Charles hadn't told Zack his plans for the extra sod.

When Debbie wanted to tend to his hands after lunch, Zack called on all his willpower to follow Charles. His hands hurt. Cleaning out the ground-in dirt had sent firebolts raging up his arms, but leaving it ground in could have created problems later. The gloves that had seen him through four years of war should suffice until the sun went down.

Charles seemed oblivious to Zack's discomfort. "If we finish our plot today, tomorrow we can start preparing the land for planting." They were about two-thirds of the way down the roped-in area. His shoulders sagged. "Maybe tomorrow."

"Tomorrow would be tremendous progress." Zack closed his eyes and called on God's strength to keep going. He lifted his arms high overhead. What did God tell Adam? He would earn his food by the sweat of his brow? Thanks, Adam. Wonder what his workweek was like before the fall? Pruning a few branches every now and then?

Since Charles wasn't talking much, Zack asked questions. Singing hymns this morning had brought them together, dreaming of the day they'd be "bringing in the sheaves."

"What made you decide on Kansas? It's a long way from Maine." Zack kept working. Charles might scold him if he slowed down.

Charles broke his rhythm while he considered the question. "When my son didn't come back from the war, I wanted to start over." His mouth pulled into an expression as much grimace as smile. "And I wanted something as different from Maine as possible."

"So, no ocean. Not California or Oregon or Washington."

Barker shook his head.

"You could've headed for the desert. I hear it's high and dry in places like Arizona and New Mexico."

Barker looked shocked. "But how could I farm there?"

Okay, Charles was a farmer at heart. He wanted to farm wherever he went.

Zack placed the latest block of sod in the wagon. The bed groaned. He could fix the wheel if necessary, but he hoped his hands would heal before he had to prove his mechanical skills. "These Flint Hills remind me a little of the Taconic Mountains in Connecticut."

Charles grunted. "We got misdirected along the way. I think it's flatter when you get farther north. Or south. But when we reached Turtle Springs, we liked the people and decided we'd stay put."

"Seems like a nice spot. The people I've met so far are fine Christian folk," Zack said.

"Glad to hear you say that. Guess fighting in the war, you've gotten more used to the thought God is everywhere." Charles chuckled. "What a thing to say. What did God have to do with that terrible conflict?"

There was no good answer to that question. They fell back to working in silence. Didn't Charles have any questions for the man who might marry his daughter?

Although it had only been one day, so far Zack felt more like a hired hand than a guest. Rather, make that a soldier obeying the orders of his commanding officer. His lips twisted as he finished digging out yet another square of sod. How open would Charles be to suggestions? Zack could think of other uses for this land than farming. Would he be willing to listen? After the first crop came in, maybe. Zack had known he was playing for the long haul before he arrived.

When Zack felt like he couldn't break the crust of top soil one more time, he saw a mirage of Debbie walking through the meadow in his direction. Wind caught her slate-blue skirt, rounding it as fashionably as any hoop. Her delicate beauty could preside in the salons of high society, but she also possessed the strength to survive New England's harsh winters.

It was Debbie in the flesh, of course. The war had made women like Debbie stronger, not weaker. Every sinew, nerve, and lovely curve filled with purpose.

Charles's eyes narrowed, as if he were ready to speak.

Zack shook himself. Stop daydreaming and finish the slice, he commanded himself. His cut was sloppy. If it went in a house, they'd need twice as much mud daub to cover the cracks. Maybe a peace branch was in order. "You can't blame a man for looking. You've raised a beautiful daughter, sir, both inside and out."

"Is that so?" Debbie's voice carried across the grass.

Zack threw his scythe wide again. The piece ended up looking like some geometrical shape.

The corners of Mr. Barker's mouth twitched. "You'll do better on the next one."

Zack doubted that, not as long as Debbie was around to distract him.

"I wasn't expecting to see you. Did Mama offer to finish the laundry by herself?"

Debbie shrugged, unconcerned about her father's gruff tone, as if used to it. "We finished early. The sunshine and a stiff breeze beat all the dampness out of the clothes in no time at all. Besides"—she tilted her head back so Zack could see her eyes, the color of the sky—"it's later than you think. I thought you'd like a drink before you dried up like apples for pie."

"Water." Zack's throat constricted. "I'd like some."

Debbie had walked across the field under the broiling soil, carrying a heavy pail—just for him. The haze of late afternoon light bathed her in sunshine like the angel she was.

Chapter 4

D ebbie tapped her toes, thankful they didn't make a sound on the dirt floor. Papa wouldn't like it. Quiet, that's what he craved. No idle chatter beyond "please pass the potatoes" marred their evening meals.

Zack didn't speak either. Was he taciturn, like Papa? Maybe he was just tired. He did compliment Mama on her cooking.

"Debbie cooked most of it."

Debbie tucked her chin in, hiding her face. "Only because you were preparing the beans for dinner tomorrow."

"I'm looking forward to it." Zack's smile radiated from somewhere deep within. He might be bone tired, but his mind seemed to be far, far away. From what Debbie could tell, he was strong enough to withstand the trials life would hurl at them.

After dinner, Papa reached for their family Bible, one of five treasured books, sitting on a shelf next to the kitchen. He opened to the eighth chapter of John.

"And ye shall know the truth, and the truth shall set you free." Zack's voice echoed the familiar verse. "That's one of my favorites. I thought on it a lot during the war."

"But what is truth? During the war it didn't seem as clear," Debbie said.

Zack brightened. "You're quoting Pilate."

Debbie reviewed the accounts of Jesus' trials. "I guess I am."

Zack drummed his fingers on the table. "Jesus didn't answer, so take my answer with a grain of salt. Here's the easy answer: Jesus is the way, the truth, and the life. Jesus, the truth, will set us free. We're to speak the truth. Don't tell lies. Honesty."

Papa nodded his head, and Debbie basked in his approval.

"But other times we are told to live the truth, to be true," Zack continued. "Or God makes us true. That's when I scratch my head." He took another helping of potatoes.

Debbie liked what she heard. "Integrity." She had wanted a man who loved God, a deep thinker.

Zack nodded as he ladled gravy onto his potatoes. "What I claim to be should match what I do. The war turned everything upside down. Christian men on both sides believed they were doing God's will, but we disagreed about what that truth was."

"Traitorous slave holders." Papa had no patience for the enemy, who'd caused the death of his son.

Zack said no more. A wise move, but Debbie was sorry for the discussion to end.

After dinner, Zack scrubbed his hands clean, and Debbie brought out the bag balm. The more dirt disappeared, the more she saw of his swollen, angry fingers and palms. Tears pushed against the back of her eyelids. "How did you get through the afternoon?" She kept her voice to a whisper. From their spot near the fireplace with the fire crackling and the noise of Mama washing dishes, she doubted they could be heard. Still, Papa had the hearing of an owl when he chose to listen.

Debbie rubbed balm over the center of Zack's right palm.

"By thinking about the meaning of truth?" His lips turned into a grin. "It helped when I remembered the pretty strawberry blond I happened to meet at the audition."

Her finger slipped across his hands, laying a strip of balm on his shirt cuff. "I'm sorry."

"I'm not." He bent his head near her ears and whispered, "I meant what I said."

A tall shadow loomed over them and they sprang apart. "Do you think we'll start plowing under tomorrow?"

Debbie's lips formed a protest, but Zack spoke first. "There's a good chance we will." He pulled his gloves over his tell-tale hands. "I don't know much about farming, but I do know the planting season waits for no man."

"Now, Papa. Zack traveled all the way to Turtle Springs to meet Debbie at the audition. Give them some time together." Mama joined them by the fireplace. "Zack, you should see a Kansas sunset. Nothing beats sunrise over the ocean, but sunset here gives it a run for the money. Check it out." She pushed the young couple out the door.

Debbie swallowed a giggle, but Zack seemed at ease. He meandered around the yard. "Without the sun or a compass, I'm not sure if I could tell directions." He spoke loud enough for Papa to hear. "Let's check out that sunset."

Grabbing her hand, Zack led her farther away from the soddy. "I wondered if we could talk for longer than five minutes without an audience."

Debbie giggled. "Perhaps I should have warned you yesterday, but other things seemed more important."

"And I could say, you deserve someone who doesn't need instructions in every step of growing crops. But here we are, and I'm not sorry." A grin flit around his face. "Not yet."

Debbie laughed again. Something about Zack helped her to laugh. "Then I will work twice as hard, so you won't change your mind."

His hand tightened over hers as they watched the sunset. The bare soil he and Papa had uncovered shivered beneath its halo, a tiny piece of the vast prairie before them.

"Did you ever want to be a farmer?" Debbie hoped and prayed he'd say yes.

Zack twisted a blade of grass between his fingers. "Part of me thought a life surrounded by animals, along with a troop of boys to wrangle with, might be fun. But farming as a career? I didn't really consider it, no."

A troop of boys. So like a man to want sons. "What do you think of farming after one day?"

"I don't judge anything after only twenty-four hours. Even pretty girls can be ugly inside." His eyes slid in her direction. "Although, so far you keep getting prettier."

Heat like the slanting rays of the sun rose in her cheeks. "Be serious."

"I am serious." He pointed in the distance. "That patch of land represents a new beginning. Everywhere I've been since the war started, things got changed around. Fields and houses burned to the ground. Factories and businesses abandoned. Some had it better, some had it worse. After all that, growing crops and raising cattle—putting food on the table—seems like a good place to start."

Zack plucked a sunflower and handed it to her. "And what about you? Did you ever want to try city life?"

Debbie accepted the flower—tall and sturdy like the grass, a splash of yellow against the green carpet. "I can't imagine not having a garden. Every summer, we gathered bouquets of wildflowers, arrowheads and asters, doll's eyes and bluebells, and so many more. I don't know the names of the flowers here, and they don't seem as pretty, at least not to me." What a petty thing to complain about. "We'll have a garden here, if we can get Maine's flowers to take root. Maybe next year." She gestured across the fields. "Or maybe not until we've proved up the home-stead." A garden, a few rows of fleeting beauty, for no other reason than to bring joy and celebrate God's creation.

"You'll have that garden before then." Zack's face was set in grim lines. "I promise you that. If I do nothing else for you during this audition." He pulled Debbie close. She laid her head against his shoulder, their hearts beating as one, until the first stars appeared in the sky.

Zack woke before sunrise in the morning. He meant to start on his promise to Debbie immediately. Hopefully he could squeeze out a few minutes before Charles wanted to leave.

During the war Zack had nailed the art of moving silently. No one heard as he stepped outside and checked the stall for a rake and hoe. He didn't rightly know the best place for a garden. His mother had groomed a vegetable patch on the south side of the house, near the kitchen door. Of course, the soddy only had one door, but the land on the other side of the stove faced the growing clearing. They had their laundry equipment on that side, since it was closest to the river. They might eventually plant a vegetable garden on that side, but not flowers.

In front, traffic would trample anything underfoot. That left the sleeping end of the soddy or the back. The beds, he decided. What point was a flower garden where Debbie would rarely see it?

"There you are." Charles sounded irritated. "Come inside. Breakfast is ready."

Zack stood in the doorway for a brief second, studying the angle of the sunrise. Unless the clouds deceived him, Charles had arisen earlier today than yesterday. Disappointment took hold, but Zack held his tongue.

Zack loved watching Debbie. He did more looking than eating during breakfast, spooning food in mindlessly.

Debbie caught him staring at her and blushed lightly. "It's simple fare today." Flapjacks and sausage didn't weigh down the table like yesterday, but a bowl filled with a heap of fluffy, scrambled eggs more than made up for it. "We've packed some ham biscuits for you to take with you." A lunch basket waited for them. "But I thought you might enjoy a buttered biscuit with blueberry jam before you leave."

The dark purple jar tempted Zack like a saloon to a cowhand at the end of the trail. "Don't tell me they have blueberry bushes in Kansas."

Debbie giggled. "I haven't found any. They have something called elderberries. We brought two jars of blueberry jam with us, but we'll run out soon enough."

Maine was famous for blueberries, strawberries, and other fruits. Zack took a bite of the biscuit and closed his eyes. That single taste carried him back to a time before the war, when he'd spent a day picking raspberries. The sweet aromas of fruit and sugar simmering down to jam had teased him all day long. A small piece of home encouraged him to start the new day. "It's perfect. Don't waste any more on me today. That's enough to keep me going until sunset."

Debbie smiled. "I'm going to pick some of those elderberries when they're ripe. A new home, new flavors. I'm sure they'll be delicious."

Charles had remained quiet, quickly devouring the food. "Finish up so we can get started."

Debbie's lips straightened in a thin line. "Zack's going to finish eating a proper breakfast and then I'll take care of his hands. The sun's barely over the horizon. You continue what you're doing. Zack will be ready in a bee's minute."

Zack might have protested—he did have his pride, after all. But he loved Debbie's spunk. After her outburst, he chewed his biscuit slowly before plowing through a second helping of eggs. He reached for his hat.

"Not so fast." Debbie guided him to the fireplace. She went to work quickly, drawing in her breath when she peeled off his gloves.

"Are you going to get high-handed with me, the way you did with your father?" Zack managed to keep his tone light.

Her head popped up so fast that her fingers pressed down hard on one of his blisters. "Only if you're as stubborn as he is." When she returned to the task at hand, her touch softened. Hand in hand, she looked him straight in the eye. "Do you want a quiet wife who always says 'yes sir, no sir'?"

"Maybe you should've asked that question at the audition." His eyebrow lifted and he grinned.

A small smile lifted her lips. "That's all I can do." She handed him the gloves, words hovering on her lips. "You don't have to prove anything to me." Her eyes flickered toward the door. "Or him."

He pulled on his gloves. "Maybe I have to prove it to myself. Can I homestead, make a home for my wife? Don't worry, I'm tough." He reached the door in two strides. He closed his eyes to recall the blueberry jam then looked to burn Debbie's image into his memory to get him through the day.

Charles didn't speak as they walked to the field, content to keep up with Zack's pace, but his shoulders sagged. Maybe Debbie should've used some liniment on her father.

"We should've celebrated last night, since we finished breaking the sod," Zack said. "It takes a strong man to accomplish everything you have this year."

"You sped up the process. Thank you for your help. But let's wait to celebrate until we can start planting the seeds."

If Charles kept postponing celebration, would Zack still be there? He hoped so. The more time he spent with Debbie, the more he liked her. A woman like her could adapt to life anywhere. But he didn't have any other life to offer her. If he couldn't make it as a farmer, he didn't know what he'd do instead.

Ladies willing to audition for grooms might not wait for a groom who dragged his feet. And Debbie shouldn't have to wait. She was a woman, full grown, ready to create a home away from her parents.

They tore through the soil with rakes, dragging up rocks. They'd have enough to build a wall, maybe even a house. German settlers in Texas had built half-timbered houses, but had anyone in Kansas tried it? Might as well try. He placed the smoothest rocks in the wagon.

Charles watched the growing pile with interest. "What are you doing with the rocks?"

Zack shrugged. "A wall, maybe? A fireplace, part of a house?" He loosened the dirt around another rock he'd run into.

His partner looked at him, sharply. "A house? Have you already made up your mind?"

Zack wanted to bite his tongue. "Charles, Mr. Barker, sir, that question lies between your daughter and me."

It was a good thing Charles couldn't read Zack's mind, couldn't see the image in his brain, of two figures sitting in front of a cheery fireplace—himself and Debbie.

Chapter 5

Saturday, eight days after the audition, Debbie and Zack rode in the back of the wagon while her father drove them into town. She welcomed the chance for a private conversation.

"What are your plans for the day?" Zack asked.

Debbie tucked a few stray hairs into her braid. She hoped to see at least a few of the other brides, and maybe the mayor, who had helped put the audition together. How was everyone doing with their grooms? Did anyone else feel as strange about the experience as she did? "I'd like to see some of the other brides." Her cheeks grew warm. "What about you?"

Zack scratched his head. "I don't care about the other brides."

Debbie laughed in response. "I should hope not."

"I was hoping you'd show me around town. Maybe I could meet your friends?" His eyebrow lifted.

How lovely and sweet. She couldn't say no. "I'll ask Mama to make sure we have time to explore. There's the church—we'll be there tomorrow. And the school, although no one will be there today. Birdie Green is the teacher. As nice as can be. We'll be at the mercantile, too." Maybe she could chat with Chardy Stevens. She might know how things were working out with the other grooms.

"Maybe I could treat the family to a meal at the restaurant where they held the auditions," Zack said. "To thank you for your hospitality this past week."

Debbie's stomach rumbled in response. "That would be lovely." And Carolyn, the restaurant owner, would have heard gossip, too.

The town came into view. How quickly the trip had passed with someone to talk with.

Papa parked the wagon by the church. "Zack, I'll leave you on your own until we're ready to load our supplies. Does an hour give you enough time for your errands?"

Before Debbie had a chance to ask for more time, Zack spoke. "That sounds good. And I'm treating your family to a meal at the restaurant."

"It's not necessary." Papa turned away.

Don't worry. Zack mouthed the words to Debbie. "I insist. I want to thank you for everything you've done, and I can meet more of my neighbors."

Debbie held back her grin. He had Papa in a corner.

"Thank you, Zack. That's a kindly thought." Mama put her arm through Pa's, as if ready to keep it there until lunchtime. "We'll meet you at the restaurant in an hour."

Sixty minutes didn't give them much time. For now, they'd stroll to the mercantile. Children played on a nearby lawn. A ball landed at her feet. Debbie picked it up, ready to lob it back, when a young boy came up to her. "Kin I have it?"

She looked at the ball, hefted its weight in her palm. "Go over there and get ready to catch it."

"But, ma'am."

Debbie drew her arm back, and the kid's eyes opened wide. He ran to the others, managing to yell "Thanks" over his shoulder.

She waited a moment then threw the ball into the boy's waiting hands. He whooped.

When Debbie turned around, Zack was grinning. He waved to the children across the street. "Maybe she can play on your team next time."

They giggled and ran away.

"My secret is out," Debbie whispered.

"I'm impressed," Zack said. "Where did you learn to throw like that, with all those sisters?"

"That's easy. My brother needed someone to play with, and I was the only one younger and smaller than he was. We played ball and went fishing and played hoops. . ." She stopped. "And I had two sisters ready to teach me how to be a girl, so I got the best of both worlds."

They moved as if of one mind, strolling down the street. "You must miss him."

"I did, terribly, especially when he first went away. Then I grew up. I miss the memory of him—but if he were alive today, our relationship would have changed."

They nodded at passersby. "Did you pester your sister mercilessly? You do have a sister, right?"

He went still. "I had two sisters. Lanna died during childbirth during the war. I hadn't seen her since she married. Dolores is happily married. I was able to see her before I came to Kansas."

"I'm so sorry."

He shrugged it off. "Things were so ugly by then, her death almost seemed like a blessing. Now I wish I had seen her again, to say good-bye, but someday, in heaven. . ."

They walked for a few minutes without speaking. "What did your other sister—Dolores?—think of your destination?"

Zack spread his hands apart. "The war came between us. She didn't like my leaving, but she didn't like all the other changes either. She closed her eyes to a lot of things. She's not strong like you, Debbie. She could never come to Kansas and start over with a soddy for a home."

"I didn't have a choice." No, that wasn't true. Either of her sisters would have taken her in, and she could have grown into an old maid. She shivered.

He caught her reaction.

"At least not a choice I wanted. And here's the mercantile." She sped up. The conversation had become uncomfortable. "I love coming here. Every visit is like a trip to another world."

He cocked his head, and she wondered if he doubted her. He'd seen so much more of the world than she had. Never matter. It was a fun place. "Let's head inside."

When the doorbell announced their arrival, a loud voice called, "Debbie Barker, come over here and let me meet your man."

Chardy Stevens was a friendly sort. She took over running the store after her father's death and had four younger brothers to raise on her own. Debbie shook her head. God had been so good to her, sparing her the tragedy Chardy had endured. She had no reason to complain, the pampered baby sister instead of the eldest stepping into the role of mother to her brothers and sisters.

And Chardy had taken part in the audition. Whom had she chosen? Debbie glanced around the mercantile quickly, hoping to spot him, but she didn't see the candidate.

Chardy's customers stole glances at Debbie and Zack for the same reason, no doubt. The whole town had watched the audition. "Shall we get this over with?"

"Oh, I think I got over the embarrassment when I hollered, 'hallelujah.'" Zack grinned from ear to ear and winked. "Let's see what Miss Stevens wants."

Zack studied the mercantile owner. They had met during the audition, of course. Between work and family, she had an immediate need for a husband. Wanted one, too, which wasn't always the same thing.

But she wasn't the one for Zack. He'd known that as soon as they interviewed, and apparently she had agreed.

"Hello, Miss Stevens. I'm—"

"Don't tell me." She closed her eyes. "You're Zack. I remember because of the Z. Unusual."

"That's right. Zack Gage."

"You have a winner here in Debbie. The Barkers haven't been in Turtle Springs very long, but we've all fallen in love with her."

"She's a fine woman." Zack shut his mouth before he said more than he should.

"Oh good. I'm glad things are working out between you." She smiled broadly as if she could guess all their secrets.

"And your gentleman?" Zack wished he could remember the name, but he had been so focused on Debbie's choice, he missed most of the other pairings.

Chardy blushed, and looked to the floor. "We're making plans."

Ah. He decided not to pry. "Debbie tells me I can find the world in this store."

Chardy laughed, a hearty sound. "We try to provide whatever our customers may need." She leaned forward and winked. "Or desire. Go ahead, look around. If there's something you want and I don't carry, I'll try to get it for you."

Hopefully they had satisfied everyone's curiosity. Zack returned his attention to Debbie and guided her to the far corner, where a few shelves might protect them from the curious glances. "Let's start the tour back here. I believe I can identify the equipment."

Debbie giggled. Large farming implements filled the floor, and wall posters featured other items available by special order. "Some of these would come in useful on the homestead." He walked around, checking the machinery and workings of each piece. "They're well made."

"There's half a dozen things we'd like to have right this minute. But Papa wants to stretch out our funds until we start making money again. He refuses to go into debt."

"A good quality." If his own father had paid more attention to sound financial management, they might not have lost the factory. But Zack didn't know for certain, and he was blessed with a fair-sized inheritance.

"Besides, we're Yankees." She grinned and shook a finger at him. "'Use it up, wear it out, make do, or do without.' It's in our blood, and that makes us good homesteaders." She flashed an uncertain smile in his direction. "At least, we hope so. Perhaps we trust in our strength more than in the Lord's."

"Well, you know what Jesus had to say about farmers, both good and bad. He sends sunshine and rain on both sides in equal measure. No special treatment for good Christians." Too many good men had died on the battlefields for him to take automatic protection from all of life's problems for granted.

He studied the equipment and gave up his wish list, for the time being. "Whatever equipment your father has, I can probably keep it going. And I might be able to make some things if we can get ahold of the lumber. I hear I can order it here, that there's no lumberyard." He tapped the plow he was leaning against. "Our factory made a plow a lot like this one. I have the know-how."

"Did I hear you say you can fix a plow?" A woman Zack didn't recognize came up behind them. "I'm sorry, I didn't mean to intrude. But I wanted to introduce myself. We're neighbors. I'm Susan Terry, and here's my husband."

"Pleased to meet you. Mrs. Terry, Mr. Terry." Zack extended his hand to the husband. "If I can get away this afternoon, I'll take a look at it." Adding money to the family pot would make Zack feel better. He had no illusions. His potential father-in-law was more concerned about proving up the homestead than his daughter's marital happiness. Zack would have to figure that out on his own.

While Zack chatted with the Terrys, Debbie had slipped away. She was visiting with a bride he'd met at the audition. Anna? Alma? No, Alanna, that was it. The two of them were giggling like schoolgirls. Giggling.

Zack scanned the store, searching for the source of their amusement. Nothing seemed out of the ordinary. Men, women, and children wandered the aisles, exploring the goods the store had to offer.

Not just families. Men, on their own. The grooms from the audition? He recognized one face—Sidney Anderson, who headed in Alanna's direction.

Ah. Sidney had been Alanna's choice. Zack decided to join the trio. Debbie smiled at his approach. "I told Chardy you can repair farm equipment. She'll spread the word—you may have more business than you want."

"I appreciate that." As long as Charles gives me time to make the repairs. Maybe if Zack slept only two hours a night, he could accomplish everything on his list of chores. Maybe if he was lucky, he could get four hours. "I hate to interrupt, but Debbie promised me a tour of the world in this store."

They responded with a polite laugh. "I'll see you later," Debbie promised as she slipped her hand around Zack's proffered arm. "First stop. France. Pay attention, in case you ever decide to buy me a gift."

Goodness, she was flirting with him. "Lead me away."

She stopped in front of toiletry supplies, generally of more interest to the ladies than to a man. "Fancy perfume?" He hazarded a guess.

She shook her head. "Scented soap. A real treat compared to the lye we're reduced to so much of the time." She lifted one bar. "Rose." And another. "Lavender."

Zack joined the game, sniffing a package. "Lilac," he said, surprised.

A stronger scent tickled his nose and he tracked it to its source. *Pine.* He made a note of the soaps Debbie had requested before he went in search of the homey smell of the evergreen. A little further along in household products, he found two-inch square bags sewed around all four sides.

Debbie giggled. "I prepared sachets before we left Maine, to keep the scent of home in my belongings. Chardy asked about selling a few."

Zack lifted the sachet to his nose and inhaled deeply. He was transported back in time to childhood memories, like hiking through the woods surrounding his grandparents' home. The towering trees, the flickering sunlight, the soft calling of a chickadee. . .

When he opened his eyes, the cowboy hats and sunbonnets hanging on the walls reminded him he was in Kansas. "I want to buy one of those things," he said.

She smiled, as if she knew exactly what he was thinking.

Chapter 6

Cornhusks rustled as weight shifted on one of the mattresses in the soddy. Debbie stirred to wakefulness. The door opened, letting in a spit of fresh air, but she couldn't see who opened it.

Even so, she had no doubt: Zack. Twice this week the same sound had awakened her, but she hadn't caught him yet.

What was he doing outside in the middle of the night? She worried about him. In a couple of hours, he'd come back into the house, and the same sounds would wake her up again. Didn't her parents notice his nighttime wanderings?

She flopped on her back and wondered what had changed. Maybe she could go with him when he returned their neighbor's plow, and they could talk, the way they had after he first auditioned. Didn't the man know a girl wanted to be courted, to be sweet-talked, even if it started with an audition?

Unless he'd changed his mind. That possibility hurt more than Debbie could have guessed. She wanted to be married. She wanted to know a man's love, the joy of bearing children, of creating a home to bring laughter and beauty and culture to this Kansas frontier.

She tried to go to sleep, but her mind kept working. *God, was I wrong to take part? Do You have other plans for me?* She thought of the Proverb she was memorizing. "Commit thy works unto the Lord, and thy thoughts shall be established." *So, Lord, I guess I just need to wait for You to establish my works and my thoughts.*

She heard sounds outside the soddy. Pa's gun lay out of reach, by the door where he could grab it before heading out. In case it wasn't Zack she heard.

Curiosity overcame her, and she decided to check things out. At the doorway, she waited for her eyes to adjust to the nighttime sky. With hardly a cloud and a thousand dots of light, the sky sparkled like a house after spring cleaning. She could see almost as well as in daytime.

Holding the shotgun steady, she padded quietly on her bare feet around the corner—and poked Zack in the stomach with the rifle barrel.

Shivers ran up and down her body. "I could have shot you. I should have left it inside."

He held his finger to his mouth, reminding her not to wake up her parents.

"What are you doing out here?" They asked the question simultaneously.

"Ladies first." Zack's grin stretched widely, as if he held the winning hand. Perhaps he did.

"I heard you go outside. At least, I thought it was you."

His eyebrows went up. "And so you came after me with a gun?"

Her eyes flickered in dismissal. "I wasn't sure."

His mouth worked. "Have you checked this side of the soddy recently?"

"Only to see that all the sod in the prairie has taken up residence there. If we keep it up, soon we'll have a grass-covered mound. We can call it Barker Hill." She slid her eyes at him. "Or Gage Hill." The sod was stacked up nearly as high as in the soddy, forming three rough walls as though they were adding an extra room.

"Barker-Gage?" He suggested, and they both laughed.

"So, what's your secret? Why are you out here? Making plans for Gage Hill?" She walked around the walls. "Adding another room?"

He shook his head. "None of those. Come and see." With a small smile, he led her to narrow entry in the wall she hadn't noticed before.

It took a few minutes for her eyes to adjust to the shadows. But once she did, she couldn't believe the sight.

More slices of sod were piled in one corner, along with dirt and rocks. The ground had been torn up. The walls weren't erected well enough for habitation, and the open sky overhead suggested this wasn't meant to be another room.

Maybe Zack couldn't do any better quality work in the middle of the night. "So tell me. What is so important that you are spending half your nights working out here?" She'd let him speak for himself.

"Not half the night." A smile tugged at his lips. "Only an hour or two."

She waited for his explanation.

"You'll think I'm crazy. I'm doing it for you. I know how much you're missing your flower garden. And you're afraid you might not get one here for years."

Debbie's mouth opened and closed, as if she couldn't picture it. "What are the walls for?"

Her less-than-enthusiastic response dampened his joy, and his smile dimmed. "To keep my real reason secret for as long as I can. I'm afraid if your father finds out I'm doing all this for a flower garden, he'll tell me to stop."

Her nightdress rustled as she sank to the ground. She ran her hand over the soil. "This is so well tilled, it's almost ready for planting right now. And you did this all for me?"

Wonder filled her voice, and his heart swelled. "Yes, ma'am." He grinned. "You deserve flowers and every other kind of beauty surrounding you. And you shouldn't have to wait for it. Maybe you can't have fancy French soap every time you go to the store, but you should be able to pick a flower every day."

He stepped closer and clasped her hands. "You're right. It's almost ready." Leaning forward, he whispered. "And I bought a few of those flower seed packets you've been eyeing at the store. A day to till the rows, get them straight and ready, and then I'll plant the seeds."

She couldn't stop smiling. "No. *We'll* plant the seeds. I'll follow you outside tomorrow night and the next night until we get them all planted." She looked overhead. "And pray for rain."

Uh-oh. Doing it by himself, he had been able to sneak in and out. Even so, Debbie had discovered his secret. If they both left, Mr. Barker would find out. Quickly.

But how long could it take to plant the seeds? One night? Two? Surely God could close the man's eyes long enough for them to finish the job, to do the work Zack had promised to accomplish for Debbie. To honor her, and the Lord, who created the flowers.

"I can't wait. But I think we'd better get back inside. Let me go first." She slipped around the corner and inside the soddy. He waited five minutes, giving her time to get settled, and later than he usually retired. When he crept onto his mattress, he couldn't relax enough to sleep. When he did, he dreamed of lilacs and roses, swaying in the breeze. That kept him asleep until Charles hollered to wake him up.

Debbie must have shared the same dream. She hadn't stopped humming and smiling since she started cooking breakfast, flapjacks with honey. Only last weekend they had found the honey. The soddy had rung with the scent of sweetness and joy on the day they had purified and jarred the sweet goodness.

Dark circles under her eyes matched his own, hinting at the lost sleep. But joy flowed from her like water, hiding traces of anything else. Her happiness could have torn a hole in the roof.

Maybe he felt it because of what they had shared the previous evening. Her parents didn't seem to notice.

Charles allowed five extra minutes at breakfast before he dragged Zack to the fields. Debbie walked with them to the edge of the yard, waving slowly as they trudged through the grass. Zack's heart beat fast, eager for the day to pass and for the evening to arrive, so they could work together on their journey to joy.

If he needed more evidence God was smiling on him, by midday they had turned over the last of the soil and removed the last rocks. They would make a handsome fireplace, a thing of beauty in the house he planned to build one day.

Charles only had eyes for the field. "This afternoon we'll turn the soil over once more. Twice if we have time. And then tomorrow." He breathed deeply.

Zack let Charles finish the thought.

"Tomorrow we can plow the land. Get the rows ready for planting." Charles beamed the same kind of happiness that had Debbie flying around the kitchen in the morning.

God was good. Both the field and the garden, ready for planting at the same time. And like God promised the Israelites, He intended for the Barkers to enjoy the fruit of the land.

Did that promise include Zack, on this patch of land?

Charles clapped Zack on the back. "God blessed us the day He brought you our way."

The satisfaction the man felt traveled down his arms across Zack's back and reached his heart. Their hearts beat together, the joy in seeing the impossible fulfilled, the first step of the promise God had given them for the land. For that moment, Zack felt like a member of the family.

When Debbie called them to lunch, Charles stepped away, but the smile remained on his face.

Debbie spread a quilt on the grass and anchored it with the lunch basket before joining them. Instead of calling them to eat, she walked to the clearing. With a single hand, she touched the rakes standing at attention at the corner post with reverence. Bending over, she let the dirt run through her fingers. "Oh, my. It's nearly ready, isn't it?"

Zack let Charles make the announcement. "We should start plowing the day after tomorrow at the latest."

Debbie clapped her hands together. "We must celebrate."

The two men exchanged glances. "Your father thinks we should hold off until we've got the seeds in the ground," Zack said.

Debbie shook her head. "I think a special dinner would be good. We'll dedicate our work to the Lord, for it to take root and for Him to give the increase."

Charles's jutted out his chin. "We will discuss it tonight."

Debbie joined them in their luncheon meal, as had become their habit. Some days, Kathleen joined them as well. Other times, only Debbie came. When that happened, Charles finished early and left the two of them alone for a few minutes.

Zack's mouth twitched as he walked away. "Our chaperone."

Debbie giggled. "I can't stop thinking about last night. And tonight. And look, you and Papa have the fields ready for planting." Debbie lifted her hands to the sky. "I want to stand to my feet and dance and shout hallelujah. Before you got here, I didn't know how much Papa would have been able to plant this year."

She shaded her eyes. "Oh dear. That sounds like I asked for a groom only to have someone help out on the farm."

He smiled. "That's all right. Anyone with an eye in his head can see you're a lovely young woman who is ripe to be wooed and wedded. Ours may be an unusual courtship, but I don't mind earning your favor by the work of my hands."

Nothing was enough for his Debbie. She deserved the fruit of his labor, of the fields, the earth and sea and sky. . .

God willing, it would happen.

Chapter 7

They're ready to start plowing and planting. The day after tomorrow at the latest." Debbie announced as soon as she entered the soddy.

The news erased weary lines from Mama's face, "That's wonderful news." She lifted her hands from the butter churn and rubbed them together, easing the weary muscles.

"Let me take that." Today Debbie had enough energy to do all the chores and make a quilt. The plunger slipped through her hands with ease. "I think we should have a party. Invite our neighbors. Make a special meal, pray over it, make some kind of monument? Something like that. Years later we can look back and say, 'That's the day our homestead became a farm.'"

Mama laughed. "Sounds like something your sisters would like to do." A wistful look crossed her face. "Too bad they can't join us."

"This Saturday. And we could invite the Terrys to join us, since they're at the closest farm. And maybe the Radles." As soon as Debbie spoke, she shook her head. "But Papa said he wants to wait until the crop is planted before we have a party."

"He's right." Mama sighed. "But nothing can stop us from frying up some ham and baking beans and brown bread."

"And an apple butter cake," Debbie added.

Mama blinked. "Sounds good." Even though their stores of canned foods dwindled by the day. "What kind of marker do you have in mind? Something you're working on inside those sod walls outside the house?"

Debbie's mouth opened. Zack's project was a secret gift from him to her, and she didn't want to share. "Do you know what he's been working on?"

"I'm not deaf. I don't know what he's doing, but I've heard him going out while we're sleeping, but last night was the first time you joined him." Mama waited, her steady eyes daring Debbie to disagree.

She hung her head, not denying it.

Mama took back over with the churn; the steady movement of the plunger worked in rhythm with her words. "I don't know what Zack is up to, but he has behaved with perfect decorum, and Lord knows Papa doesn't give him time to do anything by himself during the day."

Debbie relaxed. If Papa made Zack stop, she didn't know what would happen. Zack shouldn't have to choose.

"But you, young lady, can't be out there with him, alone, in the dark. That's the kind of behavior can get a girl into trouble."

"Mama." Debbie's face heated as if she'd sat too long at the hearth. "I would never—"

"And I'm sure Zack wouldn't either. But you don't know the temptations being alone places on you. Either of you."

Debbie stood, so angry she wanted to walk out. "I know what happens between a husband and wife, Mama. You told me some of it when I started my monthlies, and, well, my sisters told me more."

"Oh, darling girl." Mama set the churn aside. She patted the seat for Debbie to sit down again. "Knowing in your head is different than being close to the man you love in the dark. Trust me. Don't put yourselves in the way of temptation."

"But Mama. I promised I would help him finish."

Mama kept her hand on Debbie's knee, but her face fell into set lines. "You must not. You don't want to involve your father, do you?"

Debbie shook her head.

"Besides, I believe Zack wants this to be his gift to you."

Tears crept into Debbie's eyes. "I want to be part of it, Mama. I didn't get to court before the war started. Is it wrong for me to want some semblance of romance for myself?"

"Of course not." Mama smoothed Debbie's hair. "Which is why we agreed to this strange concept of an audition for grooms, and why we have accepted Zack into our home. But you cannot meet together secretly in the night-time hours."

Mama hugged her close. "Trust me. It will happen, in God's time. And if Zack is the man God has for you, he will understand as well."

Debbie had to agree, or she feared she'd lose everything.

When they presented their party plans, Papa reluctantly accepted them. They decided to invite the Radles, with Debbie's friend, Alanna, and prospective fiancé, Sidney, as well as the Terrys. But Mama's prohibition dampened Debbie's excitement over the occasion.

Preparation day, the day before the party arrived, and Debbie grew excited as they took out the last of their stores from Maine for their feast. Blueberry and strawberry jam, maple syrup, dried apples, apple butter and applesauce, and the northern beans needed for Boston-style baked beans. Last fall they had enjoyed the last of the cider. She would miss it this year.

God had blessed them in allowing them to arrive in Kansas with all the jars intact. Debbie reached for the dry ingredients first, then she put together items which would make it swim in New England goodness. Three-quarters of a cup of apple butter—which was more like an apple jam and not buttery in the least, but that was its name—made from McIntosh apples, the best variety God had ever created.

Debbie glanced across the clearing, where they had planted apple cores last fall.

Would they grow here in Kansas? Her stomach rumbled in hope.

About half the jar remained full. Good. A half-a-cup each of dried cranberries and pecans. The nuts were a nod to their new home; they grew naturally out in Kansas, whereas walnuts couldn't be found.

As the cake baked, familiar aromas filled the soddy. Memories wrapped around Debbie. Would the time ever come when the smell of the prairie, of the wind over the grass, cedar trees and tall pines, bison and beef, be as welcome as salty air, spruce trees, and the fishermen's dock?

"It smells good," Mama said. "You have a good hand with baking."

Debbie allowed the rhythms of cooking to push aside her worries about Zack. She'd hoped he'd be home by now. When the beans took a little longer to reach the right softness, they were glad the men delayed in coming home.

The food cooled, taken from the fire, and the sun passed completely from the horizon and the moon began to climb in the sky. Still the men hadn't come home.

When the North Star climbed in the sky, Debbie had had enough. "I'm going to check on them."

"But in the dark. . ." Mrs. Barker rarely ventured far from their home plot.

"I walk there every day. I could probably draw a map, including every gopher hole." Debbie headed for the door. Should she carry the gun? Yes, as well as the horse. Her familiarity with the ground should get her to the field safely.

When Zack had suggested they could finish preparing the ground before the party, he hadn't realized how much was left to do.

Sundown had passed long ago, and they worked under a night sky. Sharp edges cut into his fingers. Although they had already removed large rocks, an abundance of stones and flint littered the soil. Zack tossed them into a growing pile. Perhaps they could sell the flint as fire-starting material.

Conversation had dwindled up as their mouths grew dry. They drank the last of their water supply by their normal dinnertime. Each shovel hurt, his throat constricting with thirst.

Charles had slowed down, his movements sluggish and sloppy. Zack held saliva in his mouth for a long moment then swallowed it, and he could pull his tongue away from the roof of his mouth. "I know we intended to finish tonight. But it's time to stop." He didn't dare say the man looked ready to drop. "One more day. It's not worth making ourselves sick for."

The man tensed to protest, but his knees shook from exhaustion. When he grabbed for his tools, he stumbled. With one hand on his heart, he slipped down to the earth.

"Charles!" Zack barked.

"I'm fine. Help me up." But instead of standing, he sank to the earth.

Zack grabbed his hand. His skin burned as hot as the mid-day sun in spite of

221

the night sky overhead. Overheated, his muscles had worn out. His heart? Something else? What could Zack do?

The Bible talked a lot about living water. They could use some about now. But no water spouted out of the ground, and Zack didn't feel right to leave Charles alone while he went for help.

Scratching for remedies learned during the war, he rushed through common sense tactics. First, he took off Charles's shirt and undid his long johns to his waist. He removed his own shirt and rolled all the clothes into a ball, then placed it under Charles's feet. Not high enough. A rock instead, softened by the fabric.

Charles breathed in short gasps.

"Breathe in, breath out." Slowly, too slowly, his breathing came under control. What to do next? Stay there until morning? Build a fire and hope someone at the house saw it?

While Zack was deciding, the ground shivered and horse hooves pounded across the dirt. He grabbed his gun and went into sentry mode, watching for an unexpected animal or stranger to come upon him—hoping it might be help.

A cloud floated away from the moon long enough for the familiar pattern of the family's paint to appear, as well as Debbie's figure on horseback. She urged the horse forward at a slightly faster speed and jumped into his arms a moment later.

"Thank God, you're all right." She hugged him and kissed him quick on the lips. "Papa. What's wrong?" Terror spread across her face.

"Heatstroke's my guess," Zack said. "Most of all, he needs water. Then something to help him cool down, and probably rest."

"You sound sure of yourself." Debbie poked her hands around her father's prone body.

Charles's eyes fluttered open. "My girl." He clasped her hand. "I'm ready to go home." He pushed on his arms to stand.

Zack sprang to his side. Charles made it to his feet, but bent over. With Debbie on his other side, they held him erect.

"I'm glad I brought the horse." She nodded at Zack. "I'll get on first, and you put Papa in front of me. Or should you ride with him?"

"You. I'll walk along beside you, to make sure he's okay." He turned to Charles. "Do you think you can sit up in the saddle?"

The fire defining the man made it possible. "Who do you think you're talking to?"

"The commander of the cavalry, sir." Zack saluted. Charles returned a weak salute, and Zack relaxed. Soon they both sat astride the horse, the pommel in Charles's hand and Debbie's slight form hugging his sides while she took hold of the reins. "Let's go."

Their slow pace allowed Zack to keep up. After a couple of minutes, she stopped. "Stupid. I filled the canteen we had at the house and forgot to give it to you." She unscrewed the cap and handed it to her father. "Here you go, Papa."

Charles's left hand trembled while he drank one, two, three long gulps. Zack held his thirst to two sips. That should keep him until they got to the house. He checked Charles's arm—still too hot. He would need a sponge bath. "Drink some more, then we'll get to the soddy."

He drank more than half of the contents, but at last his posture straightened. The break lessened the strain on Debbie's arms. An eternity later, they arrived at the soddy.

Mrs. Barker ran to meet them. "Praise God. I've been so afraid, praying all the time."

Zack helped her husband from the horse.

"Dearest! What happened?" Fear-filled eyes turned to Zack.

"A heatstroke, I guess. We ran out of water several hours ago." Guilt hit him hard. "I should've gone for water. We were just so eager to finish."

"Just fifteen more minutes. If I had a penny for every time he says that, we'd be rich." Charles leaned heavily on his wife, but together they made it to his mattress.

This was worse than the nights he had watched his friends sicken from bullet wounds and die. Mr. Barker was almost family, and Zack felt as though he'd shot the fatal bullet himself.

Chapter 8

D ebbie's worries subsided as she watched her mother guide her father inside the house. They were a matched pair, their strength holding the other up in difficult times. While Mama got him settled, Debbie looked for things that would help. They could use more water; cooking the beans had drained the pails they brought up each morning. It had to be enough.

"I'll go for water." Zack reached for the pail.

"Eat first." She slapped food on the table. "We don't want you sick, too. Give me a few minutes to reheat the beans." She pulled out a pan of sliced ham from the now-cold oven. The edges had begun to curl. "I hope the ham is edible. It might taste better in a sandwich." She used the remainder of the day's bread to make two thick sandwiches.

When he struggled with swallowing his first bite, she handed him a glass of water. "Would you rather have milk or tea, instead?"

He shook his head. "I need water. I should've known better." After he swallowed half the glass, he finished the first sandwich without any additional coughing.

Debbie watched him closely, afraid he might turn into a second patient. When he finished the last bite and started on the second sandwich, she dished out a bowl of beans.

While he ate, Debbie took a bowl of beans to her parents. "Do you feel up to eating some baked beans?"

Papa nodded. "Give them to me."

Debbie relaxed and went back to Zack. He took his time with the beans, the extra syrup and chunks of pork fat mocking tonight's emergency. "A meal fit for a celebration. I'm sorry we got so caught up in finishing." His elbow caught the edge of the table and he winced.

"You must be exhausted."

"Nothing a good meal and a few hours of sleep won't cure." He glanced at her parents, who were busy in conversation. "I'm heading to bed after I get the water. The garden will have to wait."

Debbie nodded. She hadn't told him about her mother's stern warning, didn't know how to bring it up. Zack must have caught her hesitation. "What's wrong?"

He stopped eating. Without the sound of his spoon scraping against the bowl, the soddy fell dangerously quiet. *I can't talk about it.* She mouthed the words, hoping he would understand.

He tilted his head as if trying to figure out what she was saying, and then nodded. His eyes snapped and burned like sparks from a fire, full of questions and impatient for answers. When would they have the opportunity to hash matters out?

She put Zack's dishes in to soak, then sat down with him. "I'm so thankful you were with Papa tonight. Mama worries about him when he's alone. But we need time together, too. I miss our visits." An idea popped into her head, and she grinned. "I'm going to write about it in my journal."

She maneuvered around her parents to the small stack she kept by her bed: her Bible, journal, and stationery. When she returned to the table, she took a sheet of stationery instead of her journal. She scribbled as quickly as she could. *Mama knows about last night. She doesn't want it to happen again.* Instead of explaining more, she folded the page, slipped it in an envelope, and slid it to Zack.

Zack read the short lines and spread his hands as if to say, "Why not?"

She took the paper back. The explanation came more easily than she expected. *Appearances. Temptation. A man and a woman alone in the middle of the night.* Warmth crept up her neck. She glanced at her parents, but they weren't paying attention.

His eyebrow rose, and a faint smile lifted his lips. In his softest voice, he said, "She might have a point." His hand traced her face, then he grew serious. "I know farmers don't work at night, but I've heard some interesting stories. There was a war widow during the Revolutionary War—somewhere in New England. Vermont, maybe. When the Tories claimed her land for the king, her family took refuge in a cave and farmed their land at night."

"That's about as believable as Paul Bunyan." At least the two of them both had heard the tales of the lumberjack and his blue ox, unlike most of the farmers here in Kansas.

"Somebody told us the story when we were children. During the summers we'd hide in a cave and pretend to be brave Patriots defending our land from the bad Tories." His smile faded. "It was fun as long as it was pretend."

"That horrible war." They both stayed quiet, staring into the flickering lamp. History lessons at school focused on wars and battles, dates and armies and generals. But this most recent conflict seemed the worst of all, with brother fighting brother, a country so divided they had to fight each other. The Union won, but would the states that seceded ever feel like part of the United States again?

"I'll tell you one good thing about the war." Zack traced his fingers over the back of her hand. "I don't think I would ever have answered an ad for brides in a small Kansas town looking for potential grooms." His smile widened into a grin, and they both burst into laughter.

"And I might never have placed the ad," Debbie agreed. "You could say God used the war to bring us together. And that's a good thing."

"That's a very good thing." Zack stood. "I'd better get the water before it gets any later."

The single day Zack had expected to finish preparing the fields—both the crops and the garden—stretched out for nearly a week. Charles recovered from the heat stroke, but they all insisted he take things easy for a few days. So he worked only in the cool morning hours.

Zack felt duty bound to make up the difference. Turning the soil took an additional day. Then he rested on the much-needed Sabbath. In spite of the break, Zack couldn't force himself to work on the flower garden at night.

If only Debbie could help him, he might finish it. Zack kicked himself for even thinking that way. Why did he feel as helpless as a ship without a sail, now that her mother forbid their working together? He had come so far on his own.

Come Monday morning, satisfied they'd prepared the ground as much as possible for planting, they harnessed the steer to the plow and began dragging the rows.

"You watch how it's done," Charles said. "We want the field planted in rows as straight as the seams on your pants."

Zack watched, but he'd learn better by doing it himself. It looked simple.

Of course it wasn't. Even Charles struggled. The plow drifted and he wrestled the steer back in line. Sweat poured down his face. Before Zack could call a halt, Charles dropped the reins and leaned over the plow.

Zack reached his side in a second and offered the precious canteen along with a wedge of cheese. "It's hotter than a forest fire today. Take a rest."

"I'm okay." Charles stumbled to one knee, and something close to a sob came from him.

He had to stop. "Let me try. Tell me what to do. Every mistake I make, you can laugh, and you'll be ready to work again in no time at all."

"Good-for-nothing city gentleman." Humor lightened Charles's grumble. "Show me what you've got."

As soon as the harness settled on Zack's shoulders, its weight told him it would be different from anything he'd ever done before. It reminded him of the knapsacks he'd carried during the war, heavy enough to form grooves in his skin. Maybe Debbie could rub some of that bag balm onto his back to ease it into toughness, the way she had helped his hands.

He hadn't even gone a quarter of a row, and already they were veering to the left. He pushed himself against the plow, forcing it in the opposite direction.

The steer bellowed. The ropes and plow probably hurt its muscles as well. "Sorry, fella." They moved two more yards. Glancing behind his shoulder, the line wobbled like a toddler's trip across the floor, but at least it didn't slither like a snake.

Half an hour later, he finished the first row. Sweat had soaked the brim of his hat.

Charles ambled over with the canteen. "Drink some water." He studied the row Zack had plowed. "Not bad. Keep your eye on where you're headed."

Zack nodded. He took his neckerchief and poured water onto it before tying it beneath his hat. If it helped in the southern swamps, it should work under the Kansas sun.

The steer didn't want to leave his feast of prairie grass to go back to work, but Zack forced him to plow the third row. Charles stood at the end of the row to give him a visual. Good idea. Zack tipped his hat. If he stayed focused, maybe he'd finish the field by the end of the day. He glanced up at the sky. Maybe half the field.

"Yoo-hoo," Debbie called.

Zack kept his eyes fixed on the end of the row, only three feet ahead. She kept calling, and he kept ignoring her, until she reached the field as he finished his sixth row.

Luncheon called him to a halt. Zack felt about as strong as jelly in a jar. "Aren't you a sight for sore eyes?" He sat down carefully, hoping he could hide his exhaustion. Debbie handed him a jar of milk, while her eyes wandered between the two men. Her gaze returned to Zack. "So today you became a farmer."

He reached up to rub his shoulder. "Perhaps you should ask old Babe over there. He might have a different opinion."

The steer lowed, as if he knew he was being discussed then grabbed another mouthful of grass. "I wish we had it that easy to find food," Zack said.

"You can. Just eat grass," Charles said.

Zack enjoyed Charles's quiet humor. "I tried it once. Didn't like it. I blame it all on Eve."

Debbie's eyes widened at his words. "Oh, you can't blame Eve for everything. God told Adam the ground was cursed because of what he did."

"Yeah. He listened to Eve."

Charles cleared his throat, and Zack stopped talking. That didn't stop him from smiling at Debbie and imagining her as his Eve. Did women realize how much influence they had over men, how far a man would go to win a woman's affections?

To stop his mind from wandering too far in that direction, he grabbed a sandwich. Before he took his first bite, he said, "So what do you think of my farm?"

Instead of answering, she walked up and down the rows. The direction her feet wandered demonstrated how crooked they were. He stifled a groan and forced himself to eat. Charles ate at a leisurely pace, quiet amusement lighting his features.

By the time she finished, Zack was ready to return to work. He met her at the corner of the field. "So what do you think?"

"Our farm is in good hands, Mr. Zack Gage."

A goofy smile spread across his face while she packed up lunch and headed home. Zack waited until she disappeared from view. If he had started before, he would have kept his eyes on her and run the plow off the field in his pursuit.

The break had done him good. Her approval of the job he had done that morning spurred him to finish the field by the end of the day.

Chapter 9

The Barkers had rescheduled their celebration dinner, after Papa recovered and they'd finished the planting. Mama's checklist ran longer than when they lived in a house, complete with fancy china and linens.

Debbie's immediate task was to sweep the yard and make it level, ridding the area of excess chicken feed and droppings. Zack had built a coop, so their chickens wouldn't wander around. The poor hens kept running against the wire, their claws scratching at the dirt just out of reach.

When Debbie reached the garden enclosure, she couldn't resist checking the progress. Her heart sank when she saw no change. It shouldn't have surprised her; she hadn't heard Zack's movements at night. He had taken over Papa's burden of getting the crops planted.

Debbie snapped her fingers. If Zack wasn't working at night, she could. It wouldn't break Mama's rule. A gift to him for all he'd done for her family—for all he meant to her. Delighted with her plan, she skipped out of the room before Mama discovered her dawdling.

Soon she would see Alanna again. She was eager to hear about her mail-order romance. Even more, she wanted to show off Zack.

Zack had fashioned a couple of plank benches for their guests. They didn't have enough chairs for everyone, but few homesteaders would. Food they had aplenty. In a few months, they would have fresh vegetables. Hope bubbled up in Debbie. When they left Maine last year, her spirits had dragged until the day she met Zack. A thread of hope had stitched itself into her life every day since.

Papa and Zack disappeared to the creek to clean up. Mama called to Debbie. "I have bath water ready for you." She held a clean towel and a bar of soap in her hands.

Debbie threw her arms around her mother. "It will have to be quick."

"I'll help with your hair."

When Debbie took the soap from her mother's hand, she saw it was one of the bars of fancy French perfume. "When did we get this?"

Mama's face grew pink while she shaved a few flakes of the soaps and set them aside for Debbie to wash her hair. "You told a certain gentleman you liked these fancy soaps."

"Zack?" Debbie dipped herself under the water, holding her breath, amazed he would buy the soap for her.

"It seems like a strange topic to discuss with a man." Mama soaped up Debbie's long hair. The head massage relaxed her. "What kind of soap you prefer."

Looking back on it, Debbie giggled. It had seemed natural at the time. They were sharing things that brought them joy. Certain aromas stirred memories in her. From now on, this soap would bring Zack to her mind—the same way his masculine scent alerted her to his return at night before he'd set a foot inside the soddy. "I also showed him the pine sachets."

Mama shrugged as if she didn't understand. "It's sweet." Debbie dipped beneath the water to rinse out the lather from her head. The soap felt luxurious on her body, cleaning out the ground-in dirt on her feet while smoothing her arms. She emerged from the tub, wrapped in a blanket. "I feel glorious." She hadn't taken such care since meeting Zack, not even on the day of the audition—thanks to the soap he had provided.

Her dress slipped on easily enough, but she encountered unexpected tangles in brushing her hair. Mama took another brush and worked on the opposite side of Debbie's head. "Your hair is worth every brushstroke. It's a woman's crowning glory. And yours shines like the sunrise, especially when it's clean. The summer sun brings out the highlights."

Debbie's hand went to her face. The sun also brought out a few freckles.

By the time they'd finished, they'd looped her hair into a simple bun, adorned by a braid on top of Debbie's head. She tugged at her shirtwaist, a pretty shade of yellow, which paired well with her green brocade skirt. The only thing lacking was the bustle featured in nearly every dress advertised in Godey's lady's magazine, but bustles were no more practical on the Kansas prairie than they had been on their farm in Maine. Even without the bustle, the white buttons, lace cuffs, and the frill showing around the edge of her skirt—a new addition—could grace a ballroom. All she needed to complete her perfect summer outfit was an umbrella.

Tonight she wouldn't even use a sunbonnet, so her hair would be visible. Was she daring the sunset to a duel? The fanciful thought brought another smile to her face, one of many.

"Debbie." Ma's voice reached her where she sat, putting the finishing touches to her toilette together. "Our guests are almost here."

At last the field was tilled and planted. A few clouds ran across the sky, suggesting God would bless them with rain to encourage the seeds to grow.

Both men took a bath in the river. The water was surprisingly warm, easing Zack's muscles when he scrubbed the dirt out of his skin. What did Debbie think of her new soap? After tonight, he'd dedicate the time to her that she deserved. He'd work on the garden.

Tonight he wore blue wool slacks that made him itch just to look at them, but they matched his shirt, ironed with sharp creases. Kathleen chose it for him, saying they brought out his eyes, and Debbie said he looked good in blue. Zack took his time clearing his chin of whiskers.

Charles finished first and watched his efforts. "Do you want to get rid of some of that hair?" He lifted a pair of scissors. "It looks like it's been a while."

A poor hair cut was better than hair so long it slipped under his shirt collar. "I'd appreciate it."

Charles's hair didn't need cutting. Maybe Kathleen took care of it for him. Zack ran his hand around his neck, imagining Debbie doing the same for him. Such small things made him long for the comforts of a home and a wife.

Charles took his time. When he reached Zack's ears, he stopped and surveyed his work. "Maybe we should have left it long. Your neck is white." He chuckled.

Zack felt the back of his neck, his hair hadn't been cut shorter since his enlistment. Hair would always grow back, unless he went bald. "Thank you." His shirt and belt fit well. The steady flow of solid meals offset the long hours of work. His chest expanded under the shirt a bit more, his muscles more defined. He dared hope Debbie would notice.

"Stop admiring yourself," Charles said. "The ladies are waiting for us."

In the distance, puffs of dust announced the approach of their guests. "We'd better get back to the house."

When he saw Debbie, dressed in all her splendor after her bath, Zack became as speechless as a schoolboy. Her skin looked like tinted porcelain, her clothes belonged on the pages of a fashion magazine, and her hair—her hair was on fire, the red-and-gold highlights reflected on her sun-kissed cheeks, a few freckles spread across her nose and cheeks.

She stared at him, seemingly as speechless as he was. She found her voice first. "Who cut your hair?"

"Your father." He ran his hand across the back of his neck. "How did he do?"

She walked around him, studying the cut. Her gaze tickled his skin as surely as the edge of a razor. "He did a good job." She swallowed. "And I don't believe I have seen that outfit before. You look even handsomer than before."

He waved that aside. "I have no words to describe how beautiful you are this evening."

"It's the French soap I used." She winked at him.

The arrival of the Radles—Debbie's friend Alanna with her parents, Michael and Earlene—kept Zack from getting more tongue-tied. In his opinion, Alanna couldn't hold a candle to his Debbie, in spite of her freckles. Alanna would make a good schoolmarm, with a bit of severity to give her authority. Good-looking in her own way.

Sidney made a beeline for Zack and shook his hand as if they were the best of friends. They looked each other in the eye, each asking about the other's progress in the mail-order audition business.

"Miss Barker looks as happy as a firecracker on the Fourth of July," Sidney said.

Zack stifled a laugh. The way Debbie tossed her head about in eager conversation, red sparks did appear to fly from her hair. "She's glad to have company. From what I've seen since I arrived, they haven't taken time for much other than work since the ground thawed."

"Except show up in town for the audition." Sidney grinned.

Zack's face warmed, but Sidney was in the same situation. He wouldn't share his suspicion—Mr. Barker welcomed him more as an extra farmhand than as a potential suitor. "I'm grateful they did." He tilted his head in Debbie's direction. "You see, I like firecrackers."

Sidney laughed. "I prefer brunettes myself."

Alanna's long, dark hair reminded Zack of his sisters. "They seem to be good friends," he said. "How long have the Radles been homesteading?"

"They just proved up this year. They're hoping Alanna and I will take the claim next to them."

Zack raised his eyebrow. "So have you settled your mind to marry the girl, then?"

"Of course," Sidney said. "I assumed you had, too. That's what we're celebrating tonight, isn't it?"

His words hit Zack like a punch to the stomach. Is that what everyone was expecting?

Was Debbie hoping for a proposal tonight?

O Lord, what do I do?

Chapter 10

A s soon as the Radles arrived for the party, Sidney had headed for Zack. Good. She was glad Zack had made a friend in Turtle Springs outside of her family. Debbie and her mother had finished setting up for the meal already, so she welcomed a chance to chat with Alanna. They found a spot across the clearing from the men.

"They're looking at us." Alanna spoke too low for anyone else to hear. "Our mail-order grooms."

How did Alanna stay so calm while Debbie felt her own face warm like bread in the oven? "Of course they are. We're taking about them, after all."

"So." Alanna moved even closer, so her mouth was right next to Debbie's ear. "What do you think of your Mr. Gage? Sidney hasn't asked yet, but we've talked about it. I expect him to propose soon."

"Congratulations." If only Debbie could say the same.

"Now we've proved up on the homestead, nothing could make Papa happier, except maybe a grandbaby next summer."

"Alanna." Debbie laughed. Proposal, marriage, children—Debbie wanted the same things, but she was less certain about her parents.

"How about you? How are you and Zack getting along?" Alanna elbowed Debbie. "We wondered if tonight's party had a special reason."

Debbie backed away a few inches. "What? No, tonight we're just happy we got our first field planted this week. We're praying God will give us ideal weather conditions and enough of a crop to keep us through the winter." She sighed. "And then, I suppose they'll break up more ground." She rattled off a list of improvements to the farm, speaking faster with each word.

Zack took Sidney into the extra space he had added, where they wanted to plant a garden, and she wanted to follow. Even now, seeds should be below the soil, reaching for the sunshine, and small green stems ready to appear. She stopped, ashamed of her jealousy over such a selfish request.

Alanna hugged her friend. "It will get better. The first year is always the hardest." She looked at the men. "Judging from the way Zack looks at you, you have nothing to worry about. He's smitten. He's working as hard for you as Jacob did for Rachel."

Debbie choked on a laugh. "Let's hope he doesn't take fourteen years."

"No. Five years, tops, until you prove up on the land."

Alanna's silliness broke the crust of Debbie's gloom, and she laughed out loud. "Not even Papa would make us wait that long. I almost made old maid status waiting for the war to end."

Mama dashed into the soddy, and Debbie decided to head inside to help with last minute tasks. "If you'll excuse me, I'd better help Mama. The Terrys are coming."

"Let me help."

Debbie didn't refuse. Mrs. Radle joined them. They formed a line like volunteer fire fighters, passing pans from the stove to the yard. The final bowl landed on the table as the Terrys' wagon arrived.

Clark Terry swung his wife, Susan, around easily. Debbie imagined Zack's arms around her waist and shivered. Give it time, she reminded herself. Like the garden-to-be, showers of patience and hope mixed with the sunshine of joy should bring about the desired result.

The Radles, who'd lived in Turtle Springs the longest, praised Papa and Zack so much their heads could have floated across the sky like balloons. "But don't expect a lot from this first crop," Michael Radle warned. "It takes a year, sometimes two, for the ground to be properly ready for a crop."

Zack helped himself to more ham. "I think the Flint Hills might be better suited to cattle ranching than farming." He chewed a bite of the ham. "But I don't know much about either occupation."

Did Zack mean he thought the farm might fail? Debbie's insides sickened.

The Radles' glance gave weight to Zack's suspicions. "It depends on what you want. Ranching's a good option. We have plenty of grass growing around here, plenty of cattle fodder."

Debbie enjoyed watching the wind ripple through the fields, like waves crossing the ocean. They were blessed. Papa wanted enough of a crop to feed themselves for the next year, but they had money from the sale of their family farm to tide them over. But what about Zack? They hadn't discussed money in detail. All she knew was his family's factory had closed.

"So tell me, gentlemen." Mr. Terry looked up and down the table then leaned forward, as if the serious business of the night had started. "I'll confess, I'm curious as to why you came to Turtle Springs for our 'audition.'"

Silence fell around the table. Debbie hadn't expected such a direct question from their neighbors.

Mr. Radle broke the silence. "The missus and me are happy as peacocks to have them here. They each have their own story. And regardless of Mr. Terry's question, most of the menfolk of Turtle Springs are mighty pleased to have our numbers increased. Sidney's told me his reasons, but I'll let him tell it."

"Clark. I'm ashamed of you. Leave the poor men alone." Mrs. Terry bought a few minutes quiet from her inquisitive husband. "There's a newspaperman in town from Godey's Lady's Book interviewing the couples. You can read his article." She winked at Debbie. "It's plain to anyone with a female sensibility these two couples have chosen well. Pretty soon our little church might have so many weddings scheduled, we'll have to hold two in a single day."

Weddings. Debbie focused on the one word from Mr. Terry's question that registered. She looked down at her dress, imagining it with a bustle, barely narrow enough to pass down the center aisle of the church. Such a thought was impractical—no one would wear a dress for only one day. That she couldn't wear in the future. No, the outfit she had on would make a fine wedding dress as it was. That dark blue looked grand on Zack, but a vest and a tie would be nice additions for a wedding...

Conversation fell into a lull as they dug into the feast. After the ladies had finished cleaning up, Debbie searched for Zack and spotted him inside the garden room he'd made for her. She untied her apron. "Let's join the men. I have a particular interest in that spot."

Alanna looked at her with questions in her eyes, but Debbie didn't explain. Instead, she sauntered in Zack's direction, lifting her dress high enough to show a glimpse of her ankle, her hips swaying as softly as dandelions gone to seed.

Zack and Sidney stopped talking to watch her approach. Debbie held back a grin. Men were such predictable creatures. Her sisters had schooled her in how to catch their interest. Apparently their suggestions worked as well on the Kansas prairie as they did back in Maine.

Before Debbie had taken two steps, she drew Zack's attention as if she were a snake, mesmerizing its prey. He couldn't take his eyes off her. When Alanna joined her, the two of them prettier than any flowers in God's creation, both men were lost. Zack crossed his arms over his chest and left them there, maintaining his resolve to reach his goal before he gave in to Debbie.

Alanna spoke first. "What's going on in here? Why don't you have a roof?"

The yard went silent, and Zack feared his secret plans would become the latest gossip around town. He looked to Debbie in a silent plea, but her face held no expression.

Support came from the most unlikely place—Charles. "He hasn't even told me why there's no roof. But I understand it has something to do with my daughter."

"Then I'm even more curious." Alanna moved forward. He had to move before she ran into him. She stepped away from the threshold, Debbie at her heels.

Alanna walked the perimeter, studying the misshaped squares of sod. "You're not building a room over here. No floor, no roof."

Debbie headed to the wheelbarrow in the corner. She peeked inside the burlap sack Zack had hidden in it.

He counted: one, two three—she smiled. Zack took a breath.

"No, he's not adding to the soddy. He's planting a flower garden." She crossed the space between them and stopped, only a few inches separating them. "For me." She leaned closer and whispered, "But when have you been working on it?"

"My secret," he whispered. There hadn't been enough time. He felt guilty for not finishing it, for not yet fulfilling his promise to her. "I hoped to have it planted by now, at the same time as the crops, but. . ."

"He's been working hard enough for both of us," Charles said. He didn't mention his own illness, and Zack didn't blame him. Who wanted to reveal his weakness?

Sidney grabbed the nearest hoe. "Then let's get the job done. We can get this planted this afternoon, if we all help out." He winked. "Anything to help a fellow mail-order groom, after all."

Zack had never seen a dinner party turn into a work party so quickly, women included. Debbie, Sidney, and Alanna grabbed the tools standing in the corner and worked on turning over the sod. Zack's heart turned in admiration as he watched his Debbie kneel, dirt scattering across her skirt and up the bright yellow sleeves of her blouse.

Today she looked like a flower herself, a green stem pushing up from the ground with yellow leaves and flowers, a full-grown tree, with the sunshine of her hair radiating warmth in every direction.

If he didn't stop staring at Debbie, he wouldn't get any work done. He turned his back on her.

Hardly any time passed before Charles clapped him on his back. "What do you think? Are we ready to furrow the rows?"

Debbie ran to Zack's side. Dirt clung to her hands and smudged her face, but her smile rewarded him in full. "I think it's ready. Don't you?"

Zack was no more an expert than he had been when he arrived in Turtle Springs. This didn't look like the field where they'd planted the crops. It looked better, and that was good news for the small plants. "Let's do it."

The Barkers and the Terrys took the rakes and hoes and worked on creating their first row. Zack, who'd partnered with Debbie, took her by the hand. "Come with me." He tugged her away from the garden plot.

She turned around, confused, but he smiled and pulled her toward the corner where he'd left the burlap sack. "This is a job only you can do. The mercantile owner has promised me all of these will grow well in the soil here, but I want you to choose which varieties." He dug out a sample of the packets he'd purchased during their last trip to town.

Her smile faded a smidgeon. "I brought seeds with me from Maine."

He had anticipated that. "I know you did, but—this year's garden is an experiment. I don't want you to waste those precious seeds on your first attempt. Next year we can try planting all the lilacs and roses you want."

"Next year? Will there be a next year for us, Zack?" Her soft voice, the uncertainty it carried, broke his heart.

When she looked at him like that, the whole expanse of the sky swimming in her blue eyes, his heart jumped into his throat. He swallowed before he tried to speak. "God willing, I sure hope so, Debbie."

She grinned and twirled about. "All right then. Let me see what seeds they recommended. I want to use them *all*." She studied them seriously, separating them into four piles.

"Let's start with these." She handed him the first pile, which included flowers like Missouri goldenrod and Maximilian's sunflower. "These are supposed to be yellow, and that's my favorite color." She tapped her mouth and picked out three more. "With some purple thistle and red verbena and white aster for variety. Let's show them what we've chosen."

Charles bumped into Zack's arm. "What are you two up to while the rest of us are hard at work?"

"Choosing the seeds." Debbie waved them over her head. "These seeds are Zack's love letters to me. So treat them carefully, because I want to read them, all summer long."

Titters ran across the group, but Alanna led in clapping. "Then let's get started."

Zack stood still for a moment, face burning with heat. If Debbie called them love letters, then she must like them. His heart singing, he rushed forward to finish the afternoon's work.

Debbie sat on a stool by the door, directing where each group of seeds should be planted. The rows seemed too close together, but their helpers probably had more experience than he did. Was planting them so close to the soddy a mistake? While they planted the seeds, all the things that could go wrong raced through his mind. What good would his "love letters" do if they couldn't be seen?

He looked up at heaven. *Lord, please let some of these flowers bloom. Especially the yellow ones. And maybe some red, too, since that's my favorite.*

Before sunset, every last seed was in the earth.

"One final step." Sidney raised his eyebrows at Zack, as if asking permission.

"Go ahead." He grinned.

Sidney reached up for the highest block of sod. "Let's tear down the walls so the sunshine can reach these plants."

"Leave the first layer." A smile hadn't left her face. "Maybe it will help discourage little critters from chewing on the plants."

With that, they tore down the walls, adding to the stacks of sod Zack had already had accumulated at the edge of the clearing.

They said a prayer, dedicating both the fields and the garden to the Lord and asking for His blessing. Full of satisfaction and goodwill, their neighbors left, and Zack took Debbie's hand in his, rubbing his thumb across her knuckles. *I love you.* The words stuck in his throat. It was too soon.

Hopefully the flowers would say it for him.

Chapter 11

Oh what a glorious Saturday morning, this last day of June. After she finished her chores, Debbie went outside for a few minutes in the sunshine. Her first stop, the garden. She visited it the first and last thing each day, waiting and hoping for the plants to push through the ground.

Papa reported on the corn each day, while they continued to weed the fields and prepare new ground. She'd never seen anything more beautiful than the first green shoots which broke through the day before yesterday. Now a dozen or more shoots had sprouted down every row. She couldn't wait to the see the riot of color.

God created life to go on. He put all the potential of another stalk of corn, another cedar tree, another daffodil, in a seed. Like the mustard seed in the Bible. God took from a man and a woman, in ways she didn't quite understand, to create a new human being.

Out of the death caused by the war, whether in Maine or in Kansas, life would go on. And that was beautiful. God willing, Debbie's new life would include Zack. Her stomach tumbled in excitement at the prospect.

He'd worked so hard. He'd made his feelings clear, but he hadn't said anything to her about a proper courtship. Maybe he'd talked with Papa. Maybe they had some sort of agreement. But why hadn't he said anything more to her?

Zack's hand landed on her shoulder. "They should bloom soon. In a week, two at the most."

"That sounds wonderful." Today might make up his mind. More than shopping took them to town. One of the mail-order grooms was marrying his bride, Emma Mason and Liam Logan. She was happy for the couple, but it made her long for her own possible marriage even more.

Determined not to bemoan Zack's lack of courtship, Debbie wondered about the bride's attire. Would she wear a special wedding dress? It was unlikely.

Of all her sisters, Debbie had always been the most interested in fashion. They teased her, saying she belonged in New York, if she wanted to dress like Lady Godey and not like a proper Maine Yankee.

Even less like a prairie homesteader. She tied on her prairie bonnet for practical purposes. Zack liked the way the sun struck her hair, but she had given in to the necessity of protecting her face. Sunburns were painful.

Like the blisters on Zack's hands? They had hardened into callouses over time, and all the fieldwork had led to strongly muscled arms. Oh, he was a handsome man.

And he deserved to see her at her best. That decided for her—no bonnet. If her skin did burn, she would rub ointment on it later.

Before long the four of them had climbed on the wagon. Debbie tucked the tea towel she had stitched for the bride into her bag. She understood why Emma and Liam had married quickly; a widow and a widower with children, they had good reason to start their lives together as soon as possible.

After all, some mail-order brides married as soon as they met their prospective grooms. Maybe that was better than an ongoing delay that raised more questions than answers.

Debbie shook her head. The ladies of Turtle Springs had done the mail-order process in a sensible manner, and giving women some of the control appealed to her. If she decided to, she could ask Zack to leave. But how she wanted him to stay. She woke up in the mornings and checked for his well-worn Bible and his service revolver. When they were by his bedroll, she knew he hadn't left.

The wagon rolled over a bump, and she grabbed Zack's arm. He put his arm around her shoulder. When he held her close, she felt like they could run into the biggest rock in all of the Flint Hills and it couldn't make her fall out. She relaxed in the shelter of his embrace.

His eyes sought hers, tender and strong at the same time, and she melted into a puddle of hot spring water. When she was in that shape, she couldn't hold two thoughts together. Instead she admired him. Today he was wearing a green shirt that suited him as well as the dark blue she liked so much. Even if he wore something the color of swamp water, she'd still think he was handsome.

As they entered the church, she told herself they looked like a couple. People watched the mail-order pairs eagerly. They gaged the way he escorted her down the aisle, how he saw to her every need at the reception.

They clearly passed the test of public opinion. So why didn't he ever say anything about it?

"He that is hasty of spirit exalteth folly." Debbie had memorized the verse from Proverbs to help her stay patient, but it just made her mad. Sure, it was best to wait for God's timing.

She just hoped Zack didn't take as long to make up his mind as it took Noah to build the ark.

Zack had plenty of experience sitting still. Four years in the army involved a lot of marching and fighting, mixed with days of boredom. He'd passed those hours fighting sleep, to keep watch and stay alert.

All those years of practice did him no good today. He couldn't stay still. Every rustle made him want to look to see if another auditioning couple was enjoying an intimate moment. If they looked happy, he felt jealous. He could only blame himself.

Could he hurry things along by going to a larger town or the county seat? Probably not. He expected his order to arrive shortly. Waiting was just too hard.

Zack ached while he watched Emma and Liam exchange vows. He wanted to study Debbie's face, to picture her lips repeating those words.

But if he did, he'd give in to the temptation to propose then and there. And it wasn't the right time. Not quite yet. He needed a fortnight to prepare. A month at most. He clamped his teeth together and feared she could hear them grinding on each other.

From the periphery of his vision, he saw her face in profile, focused on the tableau in front of them. People said women dreamed of their wedding day all their lives. How much more so for Debbie, who'd watched two older sisters get married. She probably had her wedding dress planned down to the buttons on her sleeves, the most beautiful bride in the world.

He studied Charles and Kathleen. Charles would like to see the crops in before he had to worry about a wedding. Zack suspected a part of Charles wanted to postpone the wedding of his youngest daughter as long as possible.

But Zack wasn't Jacob, working for the right to marry his daughter. Kathleen had let slip Debbie's twenty-fifth birthday was coming up in July. If all was right in God's world, the first flowers would have bloomed.

And Zack knew just what he'd do to celebrate her birthday. The years might make Debbie feel uncomfortable, but as far he was concerned, her quarter century was a perfect match to his own three decades. Since the war, he'd felt as old as his grandfather. Debbie helped him feel young again.

After they left the reception, he went with the Barkers to the mercantile. He asked Kathleen to keep Debbie occupied while he attended to business. When everything came together in a few weeks, Debbie couldn't say no. He'd start with something as beautiful and as strong as she was.

Now to engage the clerk who was helping him without Debbie's noticing. Half the couples from the audition milled through the store's displays, and Debbie talked with each one. Once she was in deep discussion with Alanna, Zack excused himself.

Debbie's dazzling smiled stung him with a moment of guilt. Ever since he'd seen her absolute delight with the French soap, he'd purchased some small thing for her every week. Today he had bigger projects to undertake.

Kathleen waved to him, and Zack slipped into the storeroom, where he found the man who ordered supplies for the mercantile. He'd gone to him for help when he learned the town didn't have a lumberyard.

"Mr. Gage. I was hoping to see you today. The wood you ordered came in."

Zack ran his hand over the black mahogany. He couldn't wait to get started.

"What do you plan on making with that wood?" The clerk asked, as Zack paid him.

Zack smiled mysteriously and unrolled his sketch. "We don't have much room in the soddy, so I figure this is a good size. I plan to fill it with mementos of our memories."

"Your lady will like it." He nodded. "How are things working out between the two of you?"

Why did everyone in Turtle Springs feel they needed to know his personal business? "Well, I hope." Zack rewrapped the paper around the wood. "She deserves so much, and I have so little to offer." He tucked the package under his arm. "Except myself, which, God willing, will be enough."

"She did invite you—well, all the mail-order groom candidates—here. Such an upside-down way to do things. I bet your character is the most important thing. You'll be fine. We're rooting for all of you."

"I'd better get on to my next order of business." Zack took the back exit, set the wood in the wagon, and headed down Main Street. He prayed, pleaded, with God the parcel he wanted would be available. If farming wasn't profitable in the Flint Hills, Zack had some other ideas—and he wanted it in his hand before he proposed.

Half an hour later, with storm clouds gathering overhead, he ran to the mercantile, grinning from ear to ear.

Debbie met him at the door. "Where have you been? Papa's after us to get home before the rain breaks."

Zack entered the store just as Charles joined Debbie outside. He called over his shoulder. "I need another minute. I'll be right out." He went straight to the clerk. "Do you have it?"

"Will this work?" The young lady held up a slim yellow ribbon, about ten inches long.

Zack breathed in deeply. "That's it. Thank you." He slipped it in his pocket and headed for the door. "What are you all waiting for?" He grinned at Debbie.

She put her hand over her mouth to hide her giggle.

"Let's go. Don't want to get caught in the rain."

Clouds rolled in, colors ranging from pale gray to water-laden black, pushed by the wind toward Turtle Springs. The farm might escape the worst of the approaching storm.

The groceries were already in the wagon. The gentlemen assisted the ladies onto their wagon, and within minutes they headed home.

One advantage of dry weather was hard ground, and the horses made good time.

"What's that?" Debbie had located his package of wood and was pulling at the paper.

He lifted the package and settled it next to him. "That's for me to know and you to wait for. No peeking."

She wiggled in her space. "I'll look forward to it." She looked across the plains, at the rain falling in sheets to the west. "I was disappointed you didn't stay to visit with the other couples. Everyone was asking for you."

"I had business to settle."

"What business?"

He shook his head. "Look. I know I disappointed you today, but I hope to make it up to you soon. Will you forgive me?"

"I suppose." She accepted his arm, but it lacked the pleasure they'd shared on the ride into town.

He knew she wanted more from him. And she would have it, soon. If only she would wait.

Chapter 12

Today was her birthday! And perhaps another special day, too? Debbie lay on her bed, awake, excited, and eager to start the day. A year ago she'd dreaded the arrival of her year five-and-twenty. But Zack's recent behavior hinted today was *the* day, the day she had looked forward to since they'd met at the audition. Had only two months passed?

The door inched open and Zack entered the soddy. He tiptoed to her mattress and knelt. "I know you're awake." His whisper was barely louder than a cricket's song.

She giggled.

"Happy birthday, dearest Debbie." Nothing more—he returned to his bed, the corncobs rustling under his body. A few minutes later, his light snore announced he'd gone to sleep.

Sweet, as if Santa Claus had stopped by her bed on Christmas Eve. She wished he had kissed her, on her forehead at least. Now, if only she could go back to sleep. She hadn't been this excited since. . .since Christmas, 1860, when the entire family gathered at the family home and five children, under the age of ten, ran around underfoot.

Lord, thank You for my sisters and their husbands. Bless them today. Susanna and Robert, Heather and Norman. . . She drifted to sleep, dreaming of her family—and children of her own.

The next thing she knew, someone was shaking her shoulder. "Daughter dear, you'd better get dressed. I let you sleep as long as I could."

Sunlight gleamed through the window, set high in the wall. "It's late. Why didn't you get me up earlier?"

"It's your birthday. How do biscuits and blueberry jam sound?"

"I can't wait." Debbie reached for her dress. The blue-and-green gingham held up to the rigors of daily life. She added a green ribbon to her hair.

She touched her Bible. The yellow ribbon Zack had given her sat in its place in Ecclesiastes 3, the subject of last week's sermon. Today was her time to dance.

"Sit. Enjoy a cup of coffee. I'll have everything ready before the men come in." Mama handed Debbie a fresh cup of coffee in one of their good china cups. She tried to dredge up guilt for letting her mother do all the work, then decided to enjoy the special treatment.

244

Hot coffee, with sugar and a dollop of fresh cream. Sometimes Debbie thought the beverage alone was enough for breakfast. But not today. Not with blueberry jam available.

Mama continued cooking something Debbie couldn't quite identify by the aroma. Debbie peeked into the skillet. Flour, milk, salt, and pepper swirled in the frying pan.

"I had this at the eatery in town a couple of times," Mama said. "Their cook shared the recipe. It should make a filling breakfast."

"Biscuits and gravy. I remember." Debbie did remember the conversation. *"But if you don't put gravy on your biscuits, what do you eat with them?"* Meat. Eggs. Butter, jam, honey, molasses. . .a long list entered her mind before gravy.

Zack stepped aside to allow her father to enter first. "Happy birthday, little girl."

Debbie closed her eyes. Papa was the only one allowed to call her little girl—his youngest child. He put his hands on her shoulders. "I would never have been brave enough to come to Kansas if I couldn't have brought one of my girls with me. You, and the family you'll have some day, give me a reason to plan for the future."

"Oh, Papa." Tears gathered in Debbie's eyes, and she hugged him. "You've got lots more years to come. You and Mama."

"Of course we do, you old fool," Mama said. "Sit down before I scorch this gravy."

Debbie pinched herself when Zack sat next to her. She never expected him, or anyone like him, when she moved to Kansas. But in some ways, she felt like she had known him forever.

"Happy birthday, Miss Barker. You grow prettier every year." He lifted her hand to his lips.

Laughing, she swatted his hand away. "You can't say that. You haven't known me for a year."

"I don't see why not. You've grown prettier every day since I met you."

"Are you sure that's not the eyes of love talking?" Papa asked.

Silence reigned around the table while Mama poured gravy over open biscuits, and goodwill seeped from the scene until Zack laughed. "Love might put the portrait in a gold-gilded frame, but she'd be just as beautiful to a blind man in a cave."

Debbie's cheeks felt as hot as the steaming gravy on her biscuits.

"Don't let this breakfast fool you," Mama said. "From now until supper, it will be an ordinary day. Working dawn to dusk."

"And then we'll party from dusk to dawn." Zack winked, and this time warmth spread from Debbie's head to her toes.

Papa cleared his throat. "You've got to sleep sometime, son."

When they'd finished eating, Debbie told her mother she'd be right back to help with the dishes. She wanted to check the garden. The flowers looked so close to blooming she thought God was going to send her a special birthday present only He could provide.

But before she reached the garden, she stopped, stymied in her pursuit. Instead of the single layer of sod for a barrier, tent canvas hung from tall poles around the perimeter. A flat board blocked the door, painted with No ENTRY. She couldn't see inside.

Zack. Her cry came out half laughter, half frustration.

"No peeking until tonight," he said.

"This is what you were doing last night."

He grinned more widely than ever. He'd continued taking time away from the soddy in the middle of the night. Now the garden was planted, what had he been working on? She didn't have a clue. If Mama did, she wasn't sharing.

He came close, close enough they would touch if either one of them moved half an inch.

He wanted to kiss her, she knew it. *Go ahead, it's my birthday*. But he didn't.

"Don't work too hard today. Take time to dream."

Dream. About tonight? She held her apron up to her face while the men walked off. Oh, it was going to be a *long* day.

Every weed that grew in Kansas had decided to poke through the ground on Debbie's birthday. They needed pulling for the crops to grow properly. With each plant, Zack wondered how to approach Charles. When they stopped for lunch, he searched for an opening. "Today is Debbie's birthday."

"I know. I was there, waiting for three hours to learn I had yet another girl, or a boy so I'd have two of each." He grinned. "People thought I'd want a boy, but I couldn't be happier God decided to bless me with a bundle of beauties." He took out their luncheon and patted the ground next to him. "Sit down. We can afford to take a few extra minutes today."

Zack accepted the offered sandwich.

"What do you want to talk about? You've been as skittish as a cat running away from a dog all day."

The bite in Zack's mouth turned to sawdust, and he chugged it down with a gulp of water. "Yes, sir. It's about Debbie, sir."

Charles nodded and smiled, as if encouraging him to go on.

"It's no surprise to you I'd like to marry your daughter. After all, I came to Turtle Springs in answer to an ad for mail-order grooms." Gazing over the fields of growing wheat and corn, the meadows waving in the wind, with a good man sitting next to him, Zack knew he had gained even more than a bride. "After the war, I was ready for a fresh start. A new wife in a new part of the country seemed like a good way to go about it."

Now he had started, it wasn't so hard. "I didn't expect to meet someone like Debbie. So pretty, so intelligent, hard-working, so accomplished. Someone who loves the Lord like she does. I fell for her almost the first time I met her."

Charles scoffed. "I know that. We've been wondering when you'd get around to talking with her about it."

Zack drank from his canteen, but no amount of water could keep his face from heating up. "I wanted to give her time to get to know me. You, too." There was more, but those things he wanted to share with Debbie only. "I guess I'm asking if I've proved myself to you yet. Do you trust me with your daughter's hand in marriage? The best present I can give her is myself."

Charles set his sandwich down and clasped Zack's right hand. "If I didn't, I would have kicked you out of here a long time ago."

Zack jumped up and whooped. Charles chuckled. "Something tells me you may not get much accomplished this afternoon."

Instead of more backbreaking, sod-clearing work, they spent the afternoon weeding the crops. While they worked, Zack explained his plans for his future with Debbie, which met with Charles's surprise and approval.

Since a rainstorm threatened, they wouldn't water the field. "Do you mind if I go back? I'd like to change before tonight." Zack couldn't get a bath, but a change of clothes, a fresh shave, and water to get his hair to behave would help.

"I'll join you. If a man can't celebrate his own child's birthday and engagement to a fine man, when can he?" Charles wagged his finger in Zack's face. "But be prepared to work twice as hard tomorrow."

"Yes, sir." Zack grinned. Triply hard, now he had something to work for.

Despite their early departure from the fields, gentle rain sprinkled them on their way to the soddy. Farmers seemed to live on a razor's edge between too much water and too little.

"Tell Debbie I'll be in shortly," Zack said, and he swerved away to the little stall he'd created to have some privacy to work on Debbie's present. Early that morning he'd set up his shaving equipment. The bowl of water had warmed nicely in the midday heat. Not quite a hot shave but better than the river-cold water they used in the mornings. He changed from his workday shirt into Debbie's favorite blue one then slicked down his hair. The reflection in his tiny mirror showed he had done the best he could. Not that she was marrying him for his looks.

Next he gathered the object he had made for Debby, along with a packet of letters. Last stop, inside the garden, he found a single, perfect sunflower. He clipped it carefully and slipped it in with her other presents. He looked to the sky in silent thanksgiving—and the sky let loose with a deluge of water.

"Zack, there you are." Debbie opened the door and let him in. "I was about to send a posse hunting for you."

"I had some preparations to finish," he protested. "I wanted to freshen up—but the rain undid most of my efforts." He slipped his bag next to his bed, where she couldn't snoop.

She handed him a towel. "You look fine to me."

"As do you." She had done something different with her hair. He'd seen his sister heat iron rods in the fireplace and use them to curl strands of her hair. Maybe that's what Debbie had done. Whatever it was, her hair curled around her face and dangled down her neck like angel feathers. She had twined a few blue-and-green ribbons in her hair. "Your hair is different."

She touched it self-consciously. "You like it?"

"I do." His heart lurched.

"Supper's ready," Kathleen called.

Food filled the table. "You outdid yourself on this meal."

"It's not every day your baby girl turns twenty-five," she said.

Zack loved the way red slammed through Debbie's face. "Mama." He wondered what bothered her more, being called a baby—or the reminder she was twenty-five.

The fare was plain, but plentiful. A feast, a celebration, which her parents dragged out when Zack wanted to rush. He was too excited to eat more than a few bites.

Thunder rumbled throughout the meal. When at last they had finished eating, he laid down his silverware. "Do you mind if we wait until later in the evening to enjoy the cake? I would like to take Debbie for a walk in the rain." He grabbed the umbrella where it waited by the door. "You might want to put on your coat."

Debbie blinked and flushed again. "Outside? In this weather?" She smiled coquettishly. "Or do you just want time alone with me?"

"I'd check before you go out." Charles nodded at the high window. The sky had turned dark gray, lightning flashing in the near distance. Small white balls, the size of peas, peppered the dirt.

Hail.

"No." He ran to the garden in two strides. Half of the new blooms had been snapped off, others crushed to the ground. The lovely, beautiful garden—his birthday present and engagement gift—ruined by a capricious storm.

"What is it?"

Debbie, his Debbie, stood at his side.

"The garden. Most of the flowers finished blooming today, as if they knew it was your birthday. And the hail—the hail."

"Broke the plants." She picked up the bruised stalk of a peony. "We didn't have hail in Maine." She sighed.

"I wanted to give you something beautiful—something lovely—something to make up the years the war stole from both of us. And now it's as ruined as my family's factory."

"But the flowers will grow again." She took his hands. "We've already made a new beginning, right here. You're part of it. You make me feel lovely, inside and out."

The rain had flattened her curls, but she couldn't look any prettier. He refused to wait longer. "Let's go inside before we get soaked enough to catch a cold." They dashed inside the soddy. The rest of his plan should go as hoped.

The destruction the hail had caused increased the importance of his other gifts. "I have two more gifts for you." He retrieved his bag from his corner and brought out a miniature dresser he'd carved from the mahogany wood he'd bought in town. Its tiny drawers could hold a ribbon or a necklace and other knickknacks.

"It's beautiful. Where did you get it?" She examined it, each curve, each carefully fit drawer and knob, all beautifully polished.

"I made it myself. The first of all the furniture I hope we'll need." He felt his face heat, but who cared? "Look inside."

She opened the two top drawers—the right size for a ring or earrings, but empty—then the second drawer. It held a multifolded sheet of paper.

"I've spent this summer helping your parents' homestead get a good start." He nodded at Charles, who sat at the table with Kathleen over coffee, smiling and nodding their approval. "But I've been thinking about our future. I want a place of my own, for myself and my wife." He held back a grin, ignoring the question on her face.

"This is paperwork for another homestead," she said. Confusion clouded her eyes. "The plot to the west of this one," he said. "Ready for whatever we decide to do with it. Myself, I think a cattle ranch might be a good idea."

Her hand went to her mouth.

"There's one more gift." He hoped she would understand its significance.

The bottom drawer revealed a bloom. "A sunflower," she said with wonder.

"I picked that one flower when I came back this afternoon. Maybe you can dry it and keep it as a reminder." He stepped closer to her. "Of our future. Of all the lovely things God has for you and me, together. Debbie Barker, will you be my wife?"

"Oh, Zack, I can't wait for the day we start every beautiful day together as husband and wife. Yes, yes, yes!"

With Charles and Kathleen smiling approvingly, Zack pulled Debbie close for a kiss.

They pulled apart. "What do you think about a wedding after the harvest? Maybe your sisters can come. Mine, too."

The joy in Debbie's face told him she liked his idea. Kathleen and Charles hugged each other.

"A new beginning—keeping the old with the new. I'll wait as long as it takes—because of you." Debbie leaned close. "One more kiss. Make it good enough to last until October."

Charles and Kathleen laughed as Zack and Debbie shared a very satisfying kiss.

Bestselling author **Darlene Franklin**'s greatest claim to fame is that she writes full-time from a nursing home. She lives in Oklahoma, near her son and his family, and continues her interests in playing the piano and singing, books, good fellowship, and reality TV in addition to writing. She is an active member of Oklahoma City Christian Fiction Writers, American Christian Fiction Writers, and the Christian Authors Network. She has written over fifty books and more than 250 devotionals. Her historical fiction ranges from the Revolutionary War to World War II, from Texas to Vermont. You can find Darlene online at www.darlenefranklinwrites.com.

Come What May

By Patty Smith Hall

Dedication

To my grandson, Carter Adam Valentine. May the Lord bless you and keep you, and may His face shine upon you always, my sweet boy.

Chapter 1

The school board has decided your brothers are no longer welcomed at our school."

Desperation stiffened Chardy Stevens's back as she sat up in her chair. "You can't do that!"

Emily Peabody, the school board president and a perpetual thorn in Chardy's side, glanced over the rim of her glasses, her features unperturbed. "We certainly can, Miss Stevens. Your brothers are a bunch of hooligans who have no place in the classroom."

Chardy forced her jaw to relax. It wouldn't help the situation to get angry no matter how much she felt like spitting fire. "My brothers can be a little rambunctious at times, but they're good boys."

"A little?" Henrietta Watson shuffled through a pile of papers in front of her before finding the one she needed. She showed it to Emily and Louise Doolittle, the other board member present. "Your brothers, Thomas and Emmett, almost burnt down the schoolhouse!"

"Not intentionally." The sinking feeling that had plagued Chardy since news of her father's death at the Battle of Atlanta had reached them, weighed heavy on her now. "I'm just saying they aren't the first boys to smoke rabbit tobacco behind the schoolhouse."

Emily sniffed her petulant nose. "What about the snake they let loose in the schoolroom?"

"That was Neil." Her youngest brother, who at six had discovered a love for anything with scales or a tail. "He usually keeps his snakes and lizards in jars, but that day, he fell and the jar broke. He didn't have any place to put Mathilda, so he slipped her in his pocket." She shrugged slightly. "Sometime during the day, she slipped out."

Emily's mouth puckered as if she'd bit into a sour persimmon. "And I suppose you have an explanation for the fighting and the stealing?"

Chardy's gaze dropped to her fisted hands in her lap. Her oldest brother, George, had been tight lipped about the black eye he nursed. And the stealing—well she didn't have an explanation for that. If only he would tell her what was troubling him. But no matter how much she pleaded and bullied, he refused to talk. Papa would know now how to handle the situation, not that there would be anything to handle.

The trouble with her brothers had only started after their father had died.

"Miss Stevens?"

Chardy drew in a deep breath. "I don't have an explanation for George's action, though he did replace the girl's ribbon."

"Not really a punishment when his sister owns the local mercantile," Emily replied with a smug look on her face.

"I'm sure George worked to repay the merchandise," her friend, Caroline Kane, said as she gave Chardy an encouraging smile. "Isn't that right?"

"Still," Emily interrupted, a rough edge to her voice, "George came to school the next day and attacked my son during recess."

"Maybe Rupert deserved it," Chardy muttered under her breath. The boy was known around the schoolyard as a pest. Just like his mother.

"Did you say something, Miss Stevens?"

Chardy lifted her head to meet Emily's beady little eyes. "I was just wondering how Rupert is doing after his ordeal."

The woman scowled. "He's no worse for wear, just a few little scratches." Leaning over to Henrietta, she said, "My son knows how to use his fists when need be."

Chardy couldn't do anything but nod. Truth be known, she wouldn't have known who George had fought with if Neil hadn't let it slip while they were feeding the animals. Why hadn't George told her about it himself?

What did it matter now? She was going to have to fall on the mercy of the school board if she wanted to keep her brothers in school. Chardy drew in a deep breath. "I sincerely apologize for all the trouble my brothers have caused and promise to keep a closer eye on them in the future."

"And how do you plan to do that?" Henrietta asked.

Chardy blinked. "I'm not sure I understand."

"Dear, you run the mercantile and the farm your father left you." Louise's sympathetic smile made her cringe. "Where do you plan to find the time to watch your brothers, too?"

The other ladies on the board looked to her for an answer. "Well, I. . ." She understood their concerns. She'd lived those same worries since her father's decision to leave her in charge of four little boys while he went off to the war. Papa was supposed to be back before her brothers needed his help to become men. She just never counted on him dying.

But he had, and now, it was her responsibility to raise her brothers. Chardy lifted her chin. "I'll figure out something."

Emily glanced at her then turned to the other board members. "What she needs is a husband."

"Emily," Caroline admonished her. "Don't."

But the woman stormed ahead. "I thought you had a beau, or did your brothers scare him off?"

Chardy felt her cheeks go hot. Everyone in town knew Luke Collins had been courting her before he enlisted in the Union Army. But the war had a way of changing plans. "It's not my future we're discussing here, but my brothers'. Are you going to allow them to stay in school or not?"

Emily and Louise exchanged glances before the chairwoman spoke. "Until such a time that you can prove your brothers can behave in class, this board has no other choice but to suspend them indefinitely."

Chapter 2

The sound of a door slamming shut caused Luke Collins to flinch. Too much like the gunshots that whizzed by him during the war. The doctor had told him it would subside eventually, but he didn't hold much credence in the man's word. After all, he said he'd save Luke's leg...

He turned away from the harness he was working on to see who was making all the ruckus, and stilled. Chardy. Even from this distance, he could see she had worked herself up into a fury. Odd, really. The woman had the sweetest disposition he'd ever known. Only one thing could ruffle Chardy's feathers.

What kind of mess had her brothers gotten into now?

Not that it was any of his business. That right had been robbed from him by a sniper's bullet just outside of Atlanta. Why hadn't she accepted his offer when her father had enlisted? He wouldn't have joined up then, not with the responsibility of four boys, the mercantile, and the farm. But she hadn't, and Luke enlisted the next day.

Now, any hopes of winning Chardy's hand were gone.

He watched her walk down the sidewalk. He couldn't be her friend, could he? Luke stepped back and grabbed the crutch that was now his constant companion, the jab of pain in his left knee a reminder of all the reasons he should walk the other way. If only Chardy hadn't looked as if she might crumble under the weight of her problems.

Instead, he headed down the sidewalk after her. By the time he reached her, she had untied her horse from the hitching post.

Maybe a good ride was all she needed to clear her thoughts.

"Luke?"

No way out of this now. He leaned on his crutch. "Chardy. How are you?"

"Fine." The word had come out with a sharp edge. Chardy was never curt. Whatever her brothers had done, it must have been bad even by their standards.

Well, that wouldn't deter him. "Are you all right?"

She didn't look at him, instead concentrating on her horse's saddle. "Why would you ask that?"

He'd forgotten how protective she was of her brothers. "I don't know. Maybe it's because you popped out of the schoolhouse like your skirts were on fire."

Her shoulders slumped slightly but she didn't stop working. "Nothing I can't handle."

That was the truth. Chardy had handled her fair share of troubles over the last few years, including their broken engagement. But a body, even one as strong-willed as Chardy, could only stand so much. "You might feel better if you talked about it."

She stopped fidgeting with the stirrups then leaned her head against Sassy's chest. "No, it won't."

Luke lifted his arm to put around her shoulders then stopped. He'd given up his right to hold her anymore. "You'll never know until you try."

She thought for a long moment then turned to face him. "The school board has decided my brothers are no longer welcomed in school."

This was worse than he thought. "Isn't every child entitled to an education?"

She shook her head. "Not when they almost burn down the schoolhouse."

"I see." He remembered the Stevens boys as being high spirited, but fire here on the prairie was serious business. "How old are they now? The little one was just a baby when I left."

"Neil is six now."

That meant Emmett was eight, Thomas ten, and George was thirteen years old. They'd grown up in the time he'd been gone. If the boys were as rambunctious as he and his brother were, Chardy had her hands full. "What are you going to do with them while you're working in the mercantile?"

She shrugged. "I don't know. Maybe they can help me out around the store."

Luke laughed. "Four boys underfoot all day? You might as well run cattle through it. Isn't there someone who might need extra workers? Maybe a rancher or farmer nearby?"

"I couldn't inflict them on somebody else." She shook her head. "If only Papa had lived. He'd know what to do."

Luke nodded. George Stevens, Sr. had been a planner, especially where his children were concerned. The war had changed everything. Now, Chardy was raising her brothers, and the future Luke had planned wasn't possible anymore. Still, he might be able to help her. "What about the farm?"

"Didn't seem to be any reason to stay out there with the boys in school and me working at the store. Why do you ask?"

"It's just that your papa once told me he wanted to grow fresh vegetables and sell them at your store."

She gave him a weak smile. "Papa was always thinking up new ways to bring in business. And he was right. Folks loved our fresh produce. The boys loved that place." She hesitated. "I should have sold it by now, but I just didn't have the heart to do it."

She'd kept the farm? That didn't sound like the practical woman he'd known. "Why?"

Chardy thought for a second. "I don't know. We had so many wonderful memories there. Emmett and Neil were both born there, and you and I." Her gaze dropped to a button on his shirt. "It just seemed wrong."

Luke nodded. Some of his favorite moments happened at the Stevens' place.

Cool evenings swinging with Chardy on the front porch, talking about their future and making plans. Holding hands in her father's parlor. Luke had fallen in love with Chardy there.

Now those memories were of a life he couldn't have.

Still, he might have a way to help Chardy out with her siblings. "Have you considered letting the boys work the farm until they can go back to school?"

"You're not serious." The look she gave him told him she wasn't crazy about the idea. "They're children."

"They're a lot older than I was when I started working in the fields." He waited for her rebuttal but there wasn't one, so he continued. "If they're old enough to get booted out of school, they're old enough to pull weeds and plant seeds."

"I don't know." She worried her lower lip. "They've been through so much in the last year."

So had she, Luke thought, but she kept moving ahead. "Work will be good for them, Chardy. It'll keep their minds busy rather than thinking on everything that's happened."

"They're so young."

He cocked his head to the side, studying her. "Didn't you once tell me your papa had you dusting and sweeping out his store when you were barely old enough to hold a broom?"

"True, but I can't leave them out at the farm by themselves, and riding back and forth to the store every night is just not possible." She thought for a moment then her eyes widened as she stared up at him. "What about you?"

"I don't understand the question."

"You're looking for work, aren't you?"

He shifted his gaze to look beyond her shoulder, anything to keep from looking her in the eye. She knew the answer to that question. Nobody wanted a cripple working for them, no matter how hard he might work. "The inn told me to come back in a few weeks, once the men start arriving."

"That's perfect! You could teach the boys about farming while I'm at the store." She stared up at him in expectation. "You know everything there is about running a farm, and the boys like you. Tell me a reason why this wouldn't work."

There was one very good reason. "What about my leg?"

She glanced down then back up to meet his eyes. "What about it?"

Luke cringed. This had been her same argument when he'd broken off their courtship. Why couldn't she see that he wasn't the man he once was? That he never would be again? Time she got a dose of reality. "Not much call for a crippled farmhand."

She shook her head. "Not a farmhand, a foreman. I reckon you can do that on one leg with your hands tied behind your back."

"You mean a babysitter."

"I'd think you'd need both hands if you were babysitting my brothers." Her lips twitched.

Luke wanted to yell, but he kept his emotions in check. "It's not funny."

"No, it's not. And I would never insult you by offering you a babysitting job." She poked her dainty finger in his chest. "Do you think I know how to plant corn and beans so that we get the best return? Or how to teach the proper way to cultivate the plants? Do you?"

He rubbed the sore spot. Lord, when this woman got a head of steam, it was best to get out of her way. Without thinking, he put a hand on her shoulder. "I'm sorry."

She stilled then lifted her gaze to meet his. He'd always loved her eyes, their pale, peaceful shade of blue had soothed him to sleep many a night after a day filled with cannon fire, fighting, and death. Only now, there was a hint of sadness that comes from hardship and heartache. "I really think you could help my brothers, Luke."

It was useless to fight her. Maybe if he took this position, she'd begin to understand that he wasn't the man for her anymore. And maybe he'd finally stow away his dreams of a life with this woman. "All right, Chardy. I'll do it."

Chapter 3

The ride to the Stevens farm a couple of mornings later was longer than Luke remembered, but then he hadn't been riding in a wagon. He'd rode Skeeter, his stallion who had been as gentle as he was fast. The horse had been shot out from under him at the Battle of Kolb Farm, the last time Luke had saddled up and rode. He'd almost forgotten the feel of horseflesh beneath him, the taut muscles straining against his thighs as he gave the horse his head. How many times had they traveled this road in anticipation of seeing Chardy? A hundred? Maybe two?

He flicked the reins. Best he leave those memories behind. He'd only taken this job to prove a point. When she realized he couldn't do the work that needed done, she'd finally understand why he'd broken things off with her and move on with her life.

The old path leading up to the house had grown over. Wild grass as tall as the wagon wheel waved softly in the early morning breeze. Luke turned off the road and stopped. First thing he'd do is get the two oldest boys to work cutting this mess down. It wouldn't do for Chardy's horse coming across a rattler in the weeds. Besides, the tender green shoots would make good feed for the cow, if they had one.

Drawing closer to the house, thoughts about livestock faded. Luke pulled up in the yard and stared at the place for a long moment. Chardy hadn't exaggerated. The house was in bad shape, far worse than he expected. The wide front porch her father had been so proud of sagged to one side, the front steps pulled away from the center of the porch, making it easy to trip over. Some of the shingles were missing, as were several panes of glass. The white paint Chardy loved had turned to a dull gray, and in some spots was peeling so badly the boards were exposed.

Luke took off his hat and scrubbed a hand through his hair. Lord only knew what the fields looked like. Well, that's why Chardy had hired him, to set this place to rights and get a crop in the ground. After pulling his wagon close to the house, he set the brake, then jumped down, holding on to the side of the wagon until he could grab his cane.

"Chardy said you were coming, but I didn't believe her."

Surprised, Luke turned to see a tall, lanky boy walking toward him, a bucket of fresh milk sloshing over the rim. "Good to see you too, George. You've grown up quite a bit since the last time I saw you."

"Never expected to see this place again." The boy shrugged. "I didn't have much choice. They kicked me out of school. Chardy moved us out here." He stretched to his full height, though he was still a few inches shorter than Luke. "I'm man of the house now that Papa's gone."

Luke nodded. Both Chardy and George had bigger responsibilities now that their father was gone. "I was sorry to hear about your father, boy. He was a good man."

"Foolish, if you ask me." The boy started toward the front porch, his body tense. "He should've been here, taking care of his family, not running off to play soldier and getting himself killed."

Luke didn't blame the boy for being angry. Too many good men had died during battle, not to mention those left maimed or broken. But George had always been even tempered, so easy to get along with. What had happened to that boy? "Where's Chardy?"

"She's in the kitchen fixing breakfast."

He scoured the grounds. "And the other boys?"

"Probably still in bed," George said. "Which is where I'd be if Daisy didn't needed milking."

Luke didn't like the sound of that. All of Chardy's brothers were old enough to be doing their own chores. Well, he'd take care of that soon enough. "I'll meet you inside."

He'd barely made it up the stairs to the porch when George called out, "Luke?"

He turned. "Yes?"

The boy's gaze drifted to his leg. "Does it hurt much?"

It was inevitable the boys would have questions about his injury. He just hadn't expected it this soon. Might as well be honest with George. "Sometimes, when I get a blister on the stump."

The boy didn't ask anything else, just nodded. "Go on in. She's expecting you."

Luke waited until George had rounded the corner of the house then hobbled over to the front door and knocked. George might have given him leave to enter, but Luke didn't think it was such a good idea just to walk inside. It reminded him too much of the past when he was courting Chardy, and he'd thought of this family as his own. But when several moments passed without a response, he opened the door slightly. "Hello?"

"Luke? Is that you?" There was a gaiety in her voice that always made the corners of his mouth turn up. "I'm back here in the kitchen."

He stepped inside, clicking the door shut behind him, then turned. The parlor looked the same as the day he'd left to join the army, though the chairs looked more worn and the curtains faded by the sun. He'd dreamed such big dreams in this parlor, of owning his own farm and making a good living. A future that had always included Chardy. He could have stayed here in this place forever as long as she was with him. Then war was declared, and he couldn't sit by while others fought and died for the freedom for all men.

Oh how he'd paid dearly for that decision!

Leaving the parlor, Luke hobbled toward the kitchen. No sense dwelling on the past. What was done was done. He was here to help Chardy with her brothers, to help them get their garden planted. Nothing more than that.

At the kitchen door, he stopped to watch her for a few moments. Since the minute he'd met her, she'd bounced around like a tumbleweed in a windstorm, always moving and working on something. This morning was no exception. "Something smells good."

Chardy threw a smile over her shoulder at him. "I couldn't decide what to fix, so I cooked a little of everything. I hope you like it, Luke."

He shouldn't like the way she said his name with a kind of breathless quality that made his muscles clench. "Morning."

"Still a man of few words, I see." She nodded toward a chair at the table. "Sit down and I'll bring you some coffee."

"I'd appreciate that." Taking a seat, he glanced over all the different dishes Chardy had laid out on the table. "Who are you expecting? Grant's army?"

She chuckled softly as she forked a piece of ham out of the frying pan. "You haven't seen my brothers eat in a while. You'd think, by the way they act, I starve them to death."

"I doubt that." He watched as she laid down the fork and removed the pan from the fire. "I guess it helps that you cook when you're nervous."

Chardy stopped and stared at him. "You remember that?"

"It's hard not to when every breakfast dish known to mankind is sitting on this table right now."

"Oh." She glanced around as if seeing all the steamy dishes for the first time then shrugged. "I didn't realize I'd cooked so much."

"If you're worried that I can't handle your brothers, Chardy—"

"No, that's not it at all." Her cheeks went a delicate shade of pink. "It's just so much has changed since the last time you were here."

Luke stiffened. He wasn't ready to talk about what had happened between them, but he wouldn't back away from it either. "Yes, it has."

She shook her head. "What I mean to say is. . .it's kind of hard thinking of you as a friend after," —she pressed her lips together—"what we meant to each other."

A sharp ache started under his ribs. Had he being foolish, thinking they could be friends? Yet, the thought of being out of her life completely made him feel empty inside. Anything more was out of the question. "I'd like to be friends, but if it's going to be hard. . ." He glanced out over the table again. "I don't want you to cook yourself out of house and home."

"Well, nerves are not the only reason I cook." Wrapping her hand in a thick cotton square, she picked up the coffee pot and walked toward him. "Remember the boys."

"You'd better get used to that." He chuckled as she poured him a cup. "My mother had to buy more hens to keep up with the eggs my brother and I put away every morning."

"How is Matthew?"

"You know he's a papa now. He and Johnna have a little boy, Clay." He caught her up on his family as she poured herself a cup. When she sat the pot down and walked over to the counter to grab six plates, he couldn't keep his question to himself any longer. "Why aren't the boys helping you?"

She scoffed as she passed out the plates on the table then went back for the silverware and tin mugs. "Nobody expects boys to help out in the kitchen! It's just not done."

"My parents must have missed that piece of news."

Her lovely eyes stared at him in wide-eyed wonder. "Your mother let you in her kitchen?"

His heart thumped against his chest. Chardy was so adorably pretty. Would he ever get used to the affect she had on him? "When I was too short to reach the washtub, Pa stood me on a chair so I could help Matthew wash the dishes. When we were older, Ma taught us how to cook a few things. It helped out when we made camp during the war."

She pulled out the chair beside him and sat down. "That's a lot of work for a little boy."

He shrugged. "Maybe, but a little hard work never hurt anyone."

"I know." She released a tired sigh. "Papa would be so disappointed in how I've handled the boys. But I don't know what to do between working at the mercantile and trying to keep them out of trouble."

Luke couldn't stand to see Chardy whooped like this. He reached over and covered her hand with his, warmth traveling through his fingers and up his arm. "Don't worry. I've got a few ideas on how to change that."

She gave him a slight smile. "I knew you would."

The trust that shone in her eyes when she looked at him made Luke sit up a little taller. Chardy always had the ability to make him want to be a better man. It was one of the things that had attracted him to her. What if he failed her? What if he made things worse with her brothers?

What if they refused to take orders from a crippled man?

Chapter 4

Luke had a plan to tame her brothers!

Praise the Lord! Because she was at the end of her very last rope where they were concerned. Between the fighting and the stealing and Neil finding every slimy creature under the sun, she was ready to throw up her arms in surrender.

Chardy picked up the pot and freshened his coffee. "I'd like to hear about it."

He studied her for a moment, as if he were weighing the pros and cons, then took a sip. "It might be better if you don't know all the details."

His answer startled her. What exactly did he have planned? "As their guardian, I think I have the right to know what you're going to do with my brothers."

"You're going to have to trust me on this."

Chardy hurried over to the stove and wiped down the iron surface as she thought. She'd trusted Luke with her heart and he had broken it into so many pieces, she wasn't sure she'd even find them all again. If he wanted her trust again, he'd have to earn it. "I want to know what you're planning."

If he was upset by her statement, he didn't show it. Instead, he sat back in his chair, his arms crossed over his wide chest. "You're not going to like it."

She hated when he tried to think for her. "You don't know that."

"All right." He leaned against the table, his hands fisted together as if in prayer. "Your brothers need a firm hand, and with everything you have to do, you can't do that."

She blinked. "Excuse me, I'm very strict with them."

"Then why are they fighting and stealing in school?"

She hated it, but he was right. "I told you I wasn't good at this."

Luke shook his head. "It's nothing against you. You're spread so thin, trying to run the mercantile and manage this place, that the boys take advantage of you."

Chardy jerked back. If she wanted to be berated about her parenting skills, she'd give the ladies on the school board another go, but not Luke. She couldn't bear his disappointment.

"You think I'm that weak."

His gaze was filled with sympathy and respect. "The truth is you're so sweet and love them so much, you can't be the tough person they need right now."

"It's just that they've lost so much in the last year."

"You have, too." His voice was low and comforting. "You've been both mother and father to them. You need help."

She nodded. Luke was right, but was he the help she needed? Just sitting here in the kitchen, talking through her problems with the boys, reminded her of why she'd fallen in love with him in the first place. Could her heart withstand being his friend? She didn't know.

She hadn't even realized he'd stood until she felt his strong hand resting on her shoulder. "Let me carry this burden for you. Please?"

The way he said it, low and soothing, made Chardy's heart melt. Being this close to him and not being able to share her love for him would be so painful. Why was the man being so stubborn? Didn't he realize how much they needed each other?

"Will you trust me with this, Chardy?"

She stared up at him. There were so many reasons not to believe him, but silly woman that she was, she did. Luke was throwing her a rope, and she would grab it with both hands. Chardy drew in a steadying breath. "Of course, I trust you."

"Good." He moved away and she instantly missed his touch. If Luke had ever had any tender feelings for her, they'd been blown away by his time in the war.

Maybe Emily Peabody was right. Maybe Chardy did need a husband. She couldn't deny the boys needed a father figure; Luke had just as much as said so. Maybe if she married, she'd be too busy with her new family to think about Luke and the feelings she had for him. Grabbing a dishtowel, she pulled a pan of biscuits out of the oven. "Maybe, you're right."

"Right about what?"

"That the boys need the steady presence of a man in their lives." She rubbed a knife across the butter and slathered it on the bread. "You can handle the boys while I get ready for the groom auditions."

Luke glared at her as if she'd lost her mind. "What are you talking about?"

"You heard about the ad the mayor put in the newspapers back East? About needing men for marriageable young ladies?"

"What's that got to do with you?" he growled.

She gingerly picked up a hot biscuit and moved it to a plate. "I was thinking maybe one of them might suit me."

His mouth fell out then he slammed it shut. "I didn't think you wanted to get married now."

"I don't." She snatched her hand from the hot pan and blew on her fingers. "But my brothers need a father to teach them how to become good men. I have to think about them."

Luke walked to the other side of the room like a caged animal. "That's a sorry excuse for getting married."

Chardy pressed her lips together. He had some nerve, judging her. Well, he'd given up any right to have a say in her life when he'd broken off their courtship. "It's not just for the boys." She grasped her hands together. "The truth is I'm ready to settle down, maybe start a family of my own." Her laugh held no humor. "Can't do that without a husband."

"I see."

Blast him! He didn't have to sound so angry. Did he expect her to live out her days alone simply because he had chosen to?

Or was it the idea of another man in her life that upset him?

"You don't like the idea of me interviewing for a husband."

"It's just. . ." He stumbled for the words. "You deserve to marry for love."

Chardy sighed. Dear goodness, this was getting them nowhere. "Who knows? Maybe it will turn into a love match. It's been known to happen."

He shook his head. "Right."

But he didn't sound convinced. She must've been daft to have asked Luke for help. Just sitting across from him, even arguing with him, reminded her of all they had lost. Years of building a home together, having children. Hard times, yes, but good times made all the sweeter by sharing them with him.

Only that wasn't going to happen now, and her brothers needed help. Chardy wiped her hands on a dishtowel then brushed at her skirts. "I need to go over the ledgers before I open the store. There's biscuits and ham you can have for lunch." She glanced at the table. "And I'm sure there will be leftovers from this."

As she rounded the table, Luke grabbed her hand. "Are you really going to interview for a husband?"

There wasn't any anger in his question, just a vague kind of acceptance that felt like a punch to her stomach.

If only Luke could see himself as she saw him. Until he did, it was hopeless. "Can you give me a reason why I shouldn't?"

He didn't say anything, just shook his head and let her go.

Chapter 5

Chardy was hunting for a husband.

The door to the kitchen clicked shut, startling Luke out of his shocked stupor. He glanced around, half expecting to find her bustling around or washing dishes at the counter. Only her mug sat on the kitchen table.

He picked it up. It was still warm from the coffee, and her touch. Maybe it was best if Chardy found herself a husband. If ever a woman was meant to be a wife and mother, it was her. He'd known that almost since the moment he'd laid eyes on her at the church social four years ago. She'd been barely seventeen then but already a mother to her brothers after the loss of their own. It was one of the things that had attracted him, the way she took care of her family. Well, that and the sweet smile she'd given him when he'd asked for a second helping of her blackberry cobbler.

But interview for a husband? The thought made his head throb. Chardy deserved so much more than some mail-order groom. She needed someone who would love and respect her, who could make her laugh after a hard day at the mercantile, and hold her when she needed a shoulder to cry on. Someone like. . .

Luke shook his head. No. Any thoughts he'd had of marrying Chardy had been destroyed the day his leg had been ripped to shreds by a rebel's mini ball. If only he'd followed orders instead of going after that rebel sniper. Maybe then. . .

"Where's Sister?" a sleepy voice asked from the kitchen door.

Luke looked up to find a small boy, his blond hair rumpled from sleep. The younger boys called Chardy *Sister*, so was this Emmett or Neil? "Your sister has gone to the mercantile, so I'm staying with you today."

Another boy joined the first one, then seeing Luke, launched himself across the room into his arms. "Mr. Luke! It's been a long time since you've come to see us. I was beginning to think you forgot where we lived!"

"Good to see you, too, Emmett." He hugged the boy, tousling his hair before letting him go. "You're not a little kid anymore."

The boy puffed up his chest, a snaggletooth smile splitting his face. "No sir! I'm almost ten."

"No, you're not." The younger boy scowled as he sat down at the table. "You just turned eight."

"You don't know math." He glared at his little brother. "I was rounding up. Just like Miss Green taught me."

"Sounds like you lied to me," Neil mumbled as he grabbed a handful of bacon.

Emmett jerked the boy back by his nightshirt. "I ain't no liar!"

Luke had to stop this before a brawl broke out. "Sit down, the both of you. Or there won't be any breakfast."

Both boys stopped and stared at him. Finally, Emmett spoke. "But Chardy fixed breakfast for us. It would be rude to let it go to waste."

Oh the boy was a smooth one. Luke leaned forward. "Just because she made it don't necessarily mean you'll get to eat it, especially if you start another fight at the table. Is that understood?"

Both sat meekly in their chairs. "Yes, sir."

"Good." Luke dished some eggs onto a plate then handed it to Neil. "How are you, this morning?"

The boy eyed him for a moment then took the plate. "Why don't I remember you?"

"That's because you were just a baby when Luke left to join the army." Emmett forked a stack of pancakes onto his plate then grabbed some sausage as he sat down. "As far as I can tell, you're still one."

"I am not a baby!" Neil swiped a cake from the other boy's plate and stuffed it in his mouth.

"That's mine." Emmett yelled. "You little baby."

Neil reared back his hand, but Luke was faster, grabbing his balled fist in his hand. He pointed the boy toward the door then turned back and grabbed Emmett by the back of his shirt as he tried to escape.

"Breakfast is over."

"What? But I'm hungry!" Emmett struggled like a wildcat but Luke wouldn't yield.

"I told you it would happen if you fought at the table. Now, you're going to do without." With his free hand, he gripped his cane and hobbled to the door. "Come along, Neil. Time to get dressed for work."

"I don't think I like you," the smaller boy mumbled.

"That's okay, because right now, I don't like you much either."

The boy stopped and stared up at him. "Really?"

"He don't mean it," Emmett answered. "Right, Luke?"

Luke looked from one boy to the other. "I don't like the way you behave."

Both of the boys nodded. "We'll do better."

"Sounds good." Still, he'd guard the kitchen door to make sure they didn't try to get back inside. "There's work to be done."

"But Chardy says we're not old enough to work," Emmett protested.

No wonder there wasn't any joy in Chardy's expression, what with these two. She had trusted him to help her brothers, and he wouldn't let her down. "Your sister left me in charge, and I say we work."

Emmett rolled his eyes. "I should have stayed in school."

At least Neil seemed more enthusiastic. "What are we going to do?"

Luke thought for a moment. What chores could he give these two runts that would keep them out of trouble? "The barn needs mucked out and new straw laid out for the animals." He leaned on his cane slightly. "You think you can do that?"

The youngest boy nodded, his face shining with excitement. "Maybe I'll find a lizard, or maybe a rat snake."

Luke seemed to recall hearing the boy collected reptiles.

"What do you put them in when you catch them?"

"Chardy gives him old tin cans to keep them in," Emmett answered.

"As long as you keep them away from the house." He riffled the boy's head. "I can't imagine your sister would be happy to find a lizard in her room."

"Oh that already happened!" Emmett's lips twitched.

"She found a field mouse in her bag of knitting and like to screamed to high heavens. I swear, sometimes Sister can be such a girl."

Laugher bubbled up in his chest. Poor woman! She'd never been one for creepy-crawly things. Her brothers needed to learn to respect that. "Your sister is a lady, and you need to remember that," Luke said, and then turned the conversation back to their chores. "Do either one of you know how to ride?"

"Chardy won't let us."

"I know how to ride." The last Stevens boy, Thomas, hesitated for a moment then spoke. "I go down to the livery every day after school to help. Mr. Clarkston taught me."

"Does Chardy know about that?" George asked, obviously annoyed that his younger brother knew how to ride and he didn't. "Maybe we ought to tell her."

Thomas shook his head. "I was waiting until I got really good then I was going to show her."

"Not if I tell her first," George muttered.

For Pete's sake, didn't anyone want breakfast? Luke needed to stop this bickering before it escalated into fists. "That's neither here nor there. We've got a farm to tend, so all of you are going to have to do jobs you've never done before. That's how you learn." He turned to Thomas. "I'm putting you in charge of the animals. Is that understood?"

"But that's my job," George exclaimed. "What am I going to do?"

Luke walked over to the boy and patted him on the back. "As the oldest, it's your responsibility to learn how to run this farm." He laid out his plans to get the ground ready for planting, as well as teaching them how to ride and shoot, so they could protect their home.

When he was finished, Neil raised his hand. "Will you teach me how to milk a cow?"

Luke chuckled. "If that's what you want to learn." The boy seemed satisfied with his answer. "Any more questions?"

George stepped forward, his gaze shifting to Luke's missing leg. "What are you going to be doing?"

It was a question Luke had pondered deep into the night. One thing was for certain, he couldn't afford to look weak in the boys' eyes. "I'll put in a full day's work just like the rest of you."

The older brothers exchanged a skeptical look. He'd just have to prove himself to them. Using his cane, Luke pointed down the hallway to where the boys slept. "Get dressed. We've got a lot to do today."

Chapter 6

"Fifty, sixty, seventy." Chardy pushed the coins onto her palm then put them back into the cash register. It had been a good day for a Wednesday, as a steady stream of ladies had come to see her fabrics and notions. Word was getting around about the groom auditions as well as the social the next day, and the ladies of Turtle Springs wanted to make a good impression. If that meant a new ribbon for their bonnet or a pretty new dress, Chardy was more than happy to help them in their quest.

She sat back in her chair, her booted foot rocking her back and forth. What had she done, telling Luke she was signing up for the interviews? The man had practically goaded her into it with all those questions about trusting him. Whatever it was, it had backfired on her, because not only had Luke basically agreed with her, he acted as if it would be for the best.

Or had he? Chardy went back over their conversation as she had done every day. Luke hadn't really said how he felt about it, one way or the other, though she did sense he was angry. What did that mean? Did the thought of her being with a husband bother him more than she'd thought?

The bell over the front door rang. "Chardy?"

Birdy Green. Probably here to deliver the boys' class assignments. "I'm back here in the office."

Moments later, the schoolteacher stood in the doorway.

Chardy stood and brushed the wrinkles out of her skirts. "How do you look so starched and proper after a day at school? You don't even look like you have a hair out of place."

"I've never really thought about it. It must come from experience."

"And the fact that you had four less hooligans to make you want to pull out your hair today."

Birdy's lips twitched slightly. "I thought the classroom was a bit too quiet today."

"Then remember the snake crawling out of your desk drawer or having to break up a fight. That should help." Chardy picked up a jar of peppermint sticks she kept on her desk and offered it to Birdy.

"Your brothers aren't that bad." Birdy picked one out and popped it into her mouth. "Thank you."

Chardy replaced the lid then put it back where it belonged. "I appreciate you saying that, but I know how difficult they are to handle. I think they're still mourning Papa."

"Possibly. It's only been about a year since he passed, hasn't it?"

"Almost." She'd read Papa's name on the casualty list two days after General Lee had surrendered, but he had been gone for a lot longer than that. "The boys hadn't seen him in almost five years."

"I'm surprised the younger boys even remember him," Birdy said.

"I don't think Neil does." Her youngest brother was barely a toddler when Papa had left. But Emmett remembered, though how much, Chardy wasn't certain. "Emmett talks about him at times, but not that much anymore."

"Maybe that's why the boys are fighting, because they think they should remember more about their father than they do."

"That's a possibility." But how could she help them, when she was still dealing with her own loss?

She felt Birdy's hand come to rest on hers. "Give them time, Chardy."

"Patience has never been my strong suit. And Papa wanted them to get schooling."

The teacher patted her hand. "I understand, and I agree. But education is not restricted to the classroom. Life experiences teach us a great deal, too." She glanced around. "Where are the boys? I thought they'd be helping you here in the store."

Chardy shook her head. "They're out at the farm, putting in the vegetable garden with Luke."

"That's an excellent idea!" Birdy's smile lit up her entire face. "The boys are not only learning the basics of farming, they're learning what's expected of them as men. That's so much more important."

Chardy hadn't thought of it that way, though it made sense. "Luke is a good man. One of the best I've ever met."

Birdy hesitated for the briefest of moments then asked, "Does he still believe you'd be better off without him?"

Chardy turned the key on the register then put it in her desk drawer, anything to avoid the pity in the schoolteacher's eyes. "I told him this morning that I was going to sign up for the groom auditions, but it didn't seem to bother him one way or the other."

The prim schoolmarm scoffed. "Has this town gone mad? Why would anyone audition a man to be your husband? It's not like we've not seen a man before."

Chardy swallowed a laugh. "I think it's that we haven't seen very many unmarried men around here since the war was over."

"Well, that's just my opinion." Birdy patted her hand then released it. "This situation with you and Luke will work itself out with time."

Chardy nodded, but she wasn't so certain. Luke could be stubborn when he thought he was right, and he was positively convinced he wasn't worth having as a husband anymore. How could she change his mind? Convince him that she would love him, come what may?

"I should be going." Birdy placed her hand on top of the schoolbooks she'd set on the corner of Chardy's desk. "I took the liberty of gathering up the boys' schoolwork, for when they have some free time."

"That was mighty nice of you, Birdy. I'll get them back to you as soon as they are finished."

"No need to rush." She glanced at the dainty gold watch on her lapel. "I really need to go. Frieda will start to worry."

"I closed up early so I could go out to the farm for a little while." And see what Luke and the boys had been up to these last few days. She just prayed the house was still standing.

"I shouldn't keep you then." The teacher walked over to the door then paused and turned back to Chardy. "Don't give up hope. God has a plan for you and Luke."

Chardy sure hoped so. Just as long as it didn't include saying good-bye.

By the time Chardy replenished her stock and ordered more fabric, the afternoon was almost gone. The sharp shards of sunlight from early in the day had softened, bathing the world in a warm, rosy glow. This used to be her favorite time of the day. Only now, instead of picnics by the stream near their house, or long rides on Sassy, there were socks to mend and supper to make.

Still, she enjoyed these moments. They were precious, almost sacred to her. Once she was out of town, she pushed Sassy into a trot then lifted her face to the heavens. The fading sunlight warmed her skin, and she closed her eyes and breathed deep the scents of wildflowers and earth that always settled her thoughts.

Had Birdy been right? Did God have a plan for her? She didn't see it, but she hadn't been on the best terms with the Lord since word of Papa's passing had reached them. Probably before then, if she were honest. In the days leading up to her father's departure for the army, she'd prayed he'd change his mind, so certain God would hear her and make Papa stay. After all, her prayer was an unselfish one. Her brothers needed their father.

But Papa left, and Chardy hadn't prayed much since.

Maybe it was time she tried again. *Lord, I'm sorry it's been so long since we talked. I guess I was kind of mad at You for taking Papa away. Please forgive me. Help me do what's right for the boys and with Luke.*

"Do you always ride with your eyes shut?"

Chardy's eyes flew open. Coming toward her on the biggest stallion this side of the Mississippi was a man she didn't recognize. His clothes were worn and dusty, as if they hadn't seen a cake of soap in weeks. The cowboy hat he wore sat low on his forehead, casting a shadow over most of his face. But he had an honest smile and a gentlemanly way about him that put her at ease. "I was praying."

He slowed his horse as he came alongside her. "This is a mighty unusual place to be praying. But, then again, the Bible says we should pray without ceasing."

"Yes, it sure does." Chardy laughed. "Are you heading toward Turtle Springs?"

"Yes, ma'am. Answering an ad from a paper back East. Something about the town needing grooms."

She hadn't expected men to start arriving so soon. "You're in the right place, then. Chardy Stevens. I run the mercantile."

"Pleasure to meet you, Miss Chardy." He tipped the brim of his hat. "I'm William Carter, but my friends call me Will."

"Are you staying in town?" She stopped. Really, what business was that of hers? For all she knew, he could be an outlaw planning to rob her. "There's a lovely inn right on Main Street, if you're looking for a place to stay."

"Why thank you, ma'am."

Chardy tightened her grip on her reins. "I'd better get moving before my family sends out a search party to look for me."

"Of course. You wouldn't want to worry your husband."

"I'm not married." Chardy regretted the words the moment they were out. Will Carter seemed like a nice enough man as a friend, but she didn't want him getting any ideas about her. "I have four brothers."

"Then I'd better get you home so they don't worry." The man tugged his horse around then pulled up next to Chardy. "Shall we?"

Irritation welled up inside her. "Thank you, but I'm perfectly capable of getting home by myself."

"My mama would roll over in her grave if I didn't escort a lady home." He flashed her a lazy smile. "You wouldn't want that on your conscience, now would you?"

Chardy pressed her lips together. She didn't give two shakes of a lamb's tail what Will Carter's mother thought, God rest her soul. But she was tired and hungry, and didn't feel like arguing with the man.

"Suit yourself," she answered then kicked Sassy in the side. The horse responded like a shot, leaving the lumbering cowboy in a cloud of dust.

Chapter 7

Where could Chardy be? Luke paced to the end of the porch and looked out toward the road, his leg tired and aching from working the plow today. It was a good feeling, one he'd never thought he'd experience again, after his time in the hospital. He hadn't done much. He had worked one row, but it was enough to make him wonder what other things he could do, once he built his muscles up for the demanding work.

He scanned the freshly cut field in front of the house and smiled. Surprisingly, the boys had taken to their new chores like ducks to water, waking up early every day, ready to learn how to turn their father's homestead into a proper farm. George had a way of repairing tools that would give the blacksmith a run for his money. Thomas had not only learned to ride but had developed an eye for solid horse flesh. The younger two, especially Neil, had a gentle way with the animals. And Emmett? Well, he hadn't figured out that boy yet, but he was still young. Chardy was in for a huge surprise.

If only she'd get here.

He pulled his watch from his pocket. He'd give her fifteen more minutes then he'd ride out to find her.

"She's running late."

Luke turned to where George stood in the doorway, the dirt that had caked his shirt and arms gone. Funny what a little soap and water could accomplish. "Does she do this a lot?"

The screen door slammed shut as the boy came to stand next to him. "Sometimes she gets a customer in late or she needs to restock the shelves." He looked off into the distance. "But there are times I think she just doesn't want to come home."

That didn't sound like Chardy. "Why do you say that?"

"I don't know." The boy suddenly seemed younger than his thirteen years. "It's just she doesn't kid around or tease us like she used to. She's so serious all the time. I miss how it used to be."

"I know." Luke put a hand on the boy's shoulder. "I do, too."

"You do?

"Of course, I do." What he would do to go back to those days before the war, when he and Chardy had their whole future ahead of them. He heaved a deep breath. "What we've got to do is find the good in the here and now."

George looked up at him. "Is that what you do, Luke?"

Luke glanced over the field. How did he answer that? With the truth, that he'd found nothing good about his life since the war? But that wasn't necessarily so either, at least not since he'd come to help with Chardy's brothers. Teaching the boys how to farm, preparing the fields for a new crop, filled him with a contentment he'd thought he'd lost with his leg. He'd even caught himself praying again. He tuned to the boy. "I'm trying."

George didn't answer, just nodded. "Sometimes, I'm so mad at Papa for doing this to her. If he'd stayed home, Chardy wouldn't have all the worries that she does."

"Maybe what we ought to do is figure out ways to lighten her load."

The boy snorted. "You know how she is. She won't let anyone help her."

Luke had noticed. "That doesn't mean we should stop trying. She may squawk about it some, but in the end, she'll be thankful for the help."

"Even if Neil milks the cows?" George asked with a mischievous grin.

Luke chuckled. "Okay, so Chardy might have a hard time dealing with that one. I'll talk to her."

"Good. She listens to you."

Warmth spread through Luke like honey heated in the sun. Chardy had always listened to him, as he had her. Some men might scoff, but he'd like hearing her thoughts and ideas. If he'd been the head of their relationship, she had been its heart. Still, the idea that she listened to him now, after all they'd been through, humbled him.

He didn't have a chance to respond before the sound of hooves pounding against hard dirt drew his attention toward the two clouds of dust hurtling down the road.

George leaned over the railing. "Why is that man chasing Chardy?"

Luke's jaw tightened. He should have taken the wagon to pick her up, but she'd balked at the idea. His inaction had put her in danger. "Go inside and keep your brothers occupied. I'll handle this."

"But. . ." George started.

He understood the boy's need to protect his sister. "I won't let anything happen to her. I promise."

"Yes, sir." The boy walked over to the door then turned back. "I'll be watching from the window if you need me."

The screen door slammed shut as Chardy rode her horse into the yard. She jumped down and raced up the stairs, grasping to fill her lungs with air.

"We were getting worried about you."

"I'm sorry." She leaned against the railing to catch her breath. "Birdy came by with the boys' schoolwork."

His eyes shifted to the man coming up the path to the house. "Did he give you any trouble?"

Chardy glanced at the man then shook her head. "No. He is a mail-order groom who decided I needed an escort home, whether I wanted one or not."

Luke nodded. She didn't sound too happy about it, but she didn't seem annoyed either, which bothered him to no end.

Chardy straightened as the man rode into the yard. He must not be much of a horseman if he couldn't beat Chardy with that stallion. Or maybe he let her win.

"As you can see, Mr. Carter, I managed to get home all by myself," Chardy said a little breathless.

The man pulled off his hat and swiped his brow with his shirtsleeve. His soft chuckle grated on Luke's nerves. "I can see that, ma'am. Still, I'm glad I could see you home safely." He nodded toward Luke. "I'm sure your brother there appreciates that."

Luke stretched to his full height. "I'm not her—"

But Chardy interrupted him. "I'm sure he does. Now if you'll excuse us, I need to get supper started."

"Wouldn't want your brothers to starve." He gave them a crooked grin. "Maybe I'll see you at the interviews."

Chardy didn't respond. Instead, she gave him a polite nod.

Luke's hand tightened on his cane as the cowboy shoved his hat back on his head, and with a tilt of his brim, turned and rode off.

"I don't like him," Luke said.

Chardy watched the man disappear down the road. "You don't know him. He might be a nice man."

At that, Luke turned toward her. "How do you know him?"

"I met him on the road coming home. He seems like a nice enough fellow. Talkative, though."

"I don't like him," Luke said again. "He doesn't even know you and he's sniffing around your skirts."

She jerked around to face him. "That's a terrible thing to say."

"It's the truth. You could have been hurt, him chasing you down the road like that." The more Luke thought about the way Chardy had rode down the path, as if her life depended on it, the angrier he got. "You aren't going to let that man court you, are you?"

Loose curls of glorious blond hair shook against her shoulders as she glared up at him. "That is the purpose of the groom interviews. So if Mr. Carter wants to court me, I should at least give him an opportunity."

Her words punched Luke in the gut. If only things had been different, if he'd come back from the war whole, he could be the man Chardy needed. He could tell her how the thought of her was the only thing that kept him alive, how she'd been his first thought in the mornings and in his dreams at night. How he would have lost his mind without the memory of her love to push him forward.

Chardy deserved better than being tied to a cripple. No, she deserved the marriage of her dreams, but only with the right man, not some wily cowboy. Maybe he could help. "I've been thinking. Maybe you need someone to help you pick out a suitor."

She blinked. "What?"

"I said maybe. . ."

"I heard what you said. I'm just wondering why you'd think something like that."

Luke wasn't sure. Maybe it was the predatory look in Carter's eyes that got him thinking. "Some of the men answering the ad might be coming here with less than noble intentions."

Fire sparked in her eyes. "And you think I'm not intelligent enough to figure that out?"

"That's not what I'm saying at all!"

"Well, it sure sounds like it."

Maybe he did, but he was just worried about her. He had to defuse the situation. "I'm sorry. I didn't mean it that way."

The lines around her mouth eased. "Then what did you mean?"

Good, she was listening to him again. "They could be good, honorable men for the most part, but the truth is we don't know them from Adam's house cat. What if some are here for something other than marriage?"

Her brows furrowed slightly. "Why would a man be here if he had no intention of following through with the wedding?"

A faint smile pressed against his lips. Chardy always saw the best in people. It might be a bit naive, but he loved that about her. In this case, she needed to know the truth. "Some men get what they want then leave before honoring their promises." The questions in her eyes made him continue. "Usually, that's property or money."

Chardy's lips flattened into a taunt line. "You think a man would only want me because of the store or this farm?"

"Of course not." Luke didn't know whether to shake some sense into her or pull her into his arms. He didn't do either. "There are so many reasons why a man would want you, Chardy. That sweet heart of yours. The way you take care of your brothers." He could name a million more but it only reminded him of what he could never have. "I just think it would be a good idea to have someone with you at the interviews."

Her shoulders slumped a little as she thought. Then she glanced back up at him. "Maybe you're right."

Good, at least they were on the same page now.

"Maybe I should ask George if he would sit in on the interviews. He's the oldest of the bunch and would know what the other boys would like in my husband."

"George," Luke scoffed. The boy was barely out of short pants. "What would he know about the ways of men?"

She chuckled. "Not much, but I've always thought he was a very good judge of character."

Luke drew in a deep breath. Good grief. But what had he expected? Of course,

Chardy would want her brother involved. She didn't have an older male family member to consult.

In this situation though, Chardy needed someone older and wiser than a thirteen-year-old boy, a person who could judge these men on their merits.

Someone like him.

Was that what he wanted, to help the woman that held his heart find a suitable husband? Luke shook his head. He wasn't that unselfish. Just the thought of her walking down the aisle to another man made his stomach turn. But she needed a husband, and if anyone deserved to be loved and cherished, it was Chardy.

Pain rocked through his chest as the realization set in. "I'll help you find a husband if you want."

Chapter 8

L uke was volunteering to find her a husband?

Chardy hadn't thought she could hurt any worse than she had when Luke called off their courtship, but she'd been wrong. This was much worse. Was Luke that anxious to be rid of her?

She stole a glance at him. The man had never worn his emotions on his sleeve, but there was something in his eyes, a slight hesitation, as if he wasn't convinced this was the best course of action. Could he still have feelings for her? What would she give to ask him?

For now, she had to consider his offer to help her. She'd been asking God to find a way through the wall Luke had built around himself. Was this really a blessing in disguise? Chardy plastered a smile on her face. "I might just take you up on that."

If she'd surprised him, he didn't show it. He simply nodded then hobbled over to the screen door. "Guess I'd better finish up dinner before the boys declare a mutiny."

Chardy hurried over to where Luke held the door open for her. "You made dinner?"

"Don't get too excited." His mouth quirked up at the corners. "I just fried some ham up, put on a pot of beans and some cornbread."

Still, she could spend the next hour relaxing with Luke and her brothers rather than cooking. "I don't know what to say."

He followed her inside. "It didn't seem fair, you having to cook after working all day. So me and the boys came up with a schedule. We'll cook during the week while you work, and you can make Sunday dinner. Of course, I could help you with that."

She watched him as he passed her on his way to the kitchen. No one had ever cooked for her before. Since she was old enough to stand, she'd helped out in the kitchen. When her mother had died in childbirth, it was expected that she would prepare all the meals on top of her other responsibilities. That Luke would do this for her touched her more than she could say.

She walked quietly into the kitchen. Thomas was busy laying out their plates and silverware while George manned the stove, occasionally stirring the contents of the large soup pot. But it was the two little heads resting on the table that garnered Chardy's attention.

She glanced at Luke then walked over to her youngest brothers. "Emmett? Neil?"

No answer.

She stared at Luke. "Are they asleep?"

He gave her that familiar lopsided grin that always set her heart to fluttering. "They had a busy day."

"We all have," George added as he grabbed a dishtowel and moved the steaming pot to the middle of the table. "But it was a good kind of busy."

That was an odd remark, considering George usually balked at work. She walked over to the chair Luke had pulled out for her and sat down. "What have you been doing?"

Thomas stopped and looked at her. "You didn't notice the front field?"

The pot landed with a thud against the table. "Or the front porch?"

She glanced up at Luke. Obviously, she'd missed something.

Luke looked at the boys. "Your sister was too preoccupied by the man following her to notice the front yard, boys."

"Who was it, Sister?" George slipped into his childhood name for her, an indication he was worried. "You were riding hard when Luke sent me inside to check on the boys."

"Just someone riding into town." She picked up a napkin and laid it across her lap, anything to keep from looking at Luke. She hadn't told her brothers she planned to sign up for the husband interviews, and now wasn't the time. "He's thinking about moving to Turtle Springs."

"He ain't planning on courting you because of that ad the mayor put in the newspaper, is he?" Thomas asked.

Chardy glared at Luke. "Did you tell them about this?"

"Luke didn't do anything," Thomas said before the man beside her could respond. "All the kids at school know about it. I'm just glad you're not going to interview for one of those husbands."

Now she'd have to tell them, whether she wanted to or not. Chardy sipped her water then spoke. "I am signing up for the interviews."

"You're not serious!" George exclaimed, a scowl on his face. "Why would you do something like that?"

"George." Luke's voice was low and comforting. "Your sister has her reasons."

Thomas stacked the remaining plates on the table, his gaze moving from Chardy to Luke. "I thought you were courting Sister."

Chardy felt her world tilt. She should have told them she and Luke had parted ways, but she still struggled with it herself. She needed time to get her thoughts together before she had this talk with her brothers. She gently shook her youngest brother, but the boy slid away from her, slumping deep into his chair, as if settling in for the night. She glanced up at Luke. "Could you help me put these two to bed?"

He nodded, leaning over to rouse Emmett, helping the boy get to his feet.

Chardy picked up Neil and followed Luke and Emmett to the door. Eyes closed, Emmett breathed deeply and, in a drowsy voice, asked, "Where are we going?"

"To bed," Luke whispered, glancing over his shoulder at her. "Then me and your sister need to have a long talk."

Ignoring Luke, Chardy held Neil close. She wouldn't be able to carry him much longer, he was growing so fast. An emptiness she'd never felt before flooded through her. She'd miss his little boy cuddles, the way his head rested in the nape of her neck when he gave her a hug. She sighed. It was time she held a child of her own.

First, she had to find a husband.

With Neil's warm body cuddled against hers, Chardy moved through the kitchen door and down the hall to the boys' bedroom. She nodded to the bed against the far wall. "If you'll take Emmett's boots off, I'll get them into their nightshirts."

"I think I can manage that," Luke whispered as he led the older boy to a nearby chair. "Just let them sleep in their clothes. Better than waking them up."

She stood after laying Neil on the bed. "I've never heard of such a thing. Won't they be uncomfortable?"

"What do you think?"

Chardy studied her brothers. Emmett's head leaned back against the wall, his eyes closed. As Luke pulled at his boot, Neil had already turned on his side, his hands tucked under his cheek. "They look dead to the world. What exactly did you do today?"

His warm chuckle made her stomach flutter. "Nothing that I didn't do myself at their age."

"Oh." When they were courting, Luke had told her stories about working his father's farm. Though it had sounded like a hard way to live, Luke had seemed to enjoy it. It was one of the reasons he'd wanted a place of his own. And now, he was sharing his love of the land with her brothers.

They worked quietly over the next few minutes, Chardy stealing glances when she could. Luke was so gentle with Emmett, patiently working the boot off so as to not wake up the boy. She could see him with sons of his own, strong boys, with his broad shoulders and gentle ways. Maybe a daughter or two who would wrap their papa's heart around their tiny fingers.

If only he wouldn't deny himself the opportunity.

"When did you start sleeping in the loft?"

"How—" She started then stopped. Of course, he'd remember. That window over by George's bed was where he'd come to say good-bye the night before he left to go east to the war. She'd been so terrified at the thought of never seeing him again, she'd stayed up late into the night to pray. The sharp ping of a pebble against glass had drawn her to the window. How tall and strong he'd looked standing there, telling her everything she wanted to hear. That he loved her. That he was coming back to make a life with her.

Then he'd kissed her for the very first time.

Chardy placed the boys' boots underneath the bed. That was done and gone, Luke's promises unfulfilled. "This room is larger than the loft. It didn't seem right to have all this room when the boys were tripping all over each other upstairs."

He gave her a soft smile as he helped Emmett into bed. "Most ladies wouldn't have given up their room. But then, you've always been a practical woman."

Yes, she supposed she was, not that she liked it much. Raising four boys had forced her to become even more so, to the point Chardy didn't recognize herself at times. Is that why she signed up for the groom interviews? Had practicality over-ruled her heart? Because her heart still belonged to Luke.

Minutes later, Chardy shut the boys' bedroom door. "So what exactly did you do to those two today?" Luke leaned on his cane, and she wondered if was he as tired as the boys.

"We started clearing out that place behind the barn for the vegetable garden."

"That big old field?" No wonder the boys were exhausted. That field hadn't been cleared for years! "Papa usually kept a small spot here behind the house."

"George thought—and I agreed—that with the increased population in town, you would need a bigger growing area."

"I hadn't thought about that," she replied as they walked slowly back to the kitchen. Before they reached the door, she turned toward him. "And you say George thought of this?"

Luke nodded. "The boy has a good head on his shoulders, and he's good with his hands." He must have seen her confusion because he continued, "George likes to work with metal."

"You mean like Mr. Clarkston, the blacksmith?"

He nodded. "I was thinking we could ask him if George could work as his apprentice in the afternoons after school."

She mulled that over for a moment. "I guess so. I always thought George would want to take over this place."

"No," Luke said as they entered the kitchen. "That would be Thomas, though he'd probably turn it into a horse ranch."

Thomas, a rancher. Why the boy had never even ridden an animal. How could Luke know that? Or maybe the better question was why didn't she? She sat down at her place at the table while Luke retrieved the coffee pot. "Why do you say that?"

He poured her a cup. "Because he likes horses. Did you know he can ride?"

"That's not true." She poured a good portion of cream into her coffee then grabbed the sugar bowl. "He's never been on a horse."

"About that." Luke placed the hot pot on a dishtowel then sat down beside her. "It seems he's been visiting Mr. Clarkston in the afternoons. Or should I say, he's been visiting the horses."

She sank back into her chair. "Why didn't he tell me that?"

"I think he was afraid you wouldn't approve."

"He's probably right." She felt his gaze resting on her. "Papa was trampled on by horses after he was shot. That's what killed him. I haven't allowed the boys to ride since then."

Luke's hand closed over her forearm, his touch sending warmth up her arm and across her chest. "I'm so sorry, sweetheart."

She gave him a slight nod then drew in a breath and smiled. "So what do you think Emmett and Neil will turn out to be?"

"Emmett, I'm not sure yet." He released her and sat back, taking his coffee cup with him. He took a sip. "But Neil? That kid's going to be a snake charmer. Have you seen the collection of snakes and lizards he's got out in the barn?"

"I'm hoping he grows out of it. Just the thought of those"—she shuddered slightly—"*things* makes my skin crawl."

"Then you'll be happy to know he let them all go."

"He let them all go," she mimicked, too stunned to react, much less come up with something to say. She blinked. "How did you manage that?"

Luke leaned over slightly, the scent of soap and hard work making her head spin just a little. "We made a trade."

She leaned in toward him, until the world had narrowed down to just the two of them. Luke really was the most handsome man she'd ever known, yet now, with his eyes dancing in little boy mischief, she glimpsed the joy that had won her heart. "What kind of trade?"

He came closer, and for the briefest of moments, she thought he might kiss her. But then the joy seeped from his gaze and he sat back. "He wanted to learn how to milk a cow."

"What?" She jumped back, glaring at him. "You taught him how to milk Daisy?"

Luke cut a slice of cornbread and put it on his plate. "He's pretty good at it, too, though he did slosh most of the milk out of the bucket."

"Why did you do that?"

He stopped buttering his cornbread and looked at her. "Do what?"

"Teach my six-year-old brother how to milk a cow!" Chardy huffed out her frustration. "She could have kicked him."

"But she didn't."

"But she could have. . ." Her voice rose a notch.

"Do you really think I'd leave your brother on his own the first time he milked a cow?" Luke's annoyed gaze bore into her.

The question rumbled in Chardy's ears. Put like that, it's no wonder Luke looks ready to bite a bullet in half. The man had never been one to skirt his responsibilities. But accidents happened in a brief moment, and they'd lost so much all ready. "I know you wouldn't but. . ." She mashed her lips together to keep them from trembling. "I couldn't bear it if something happened to any one of them."

Some of the anger left his expression as he reached out and took her hand in his, the warmth of his caress giving her strength. "Chardy, you can't wrap them up in cotton and hope nothing happens to them. It's not fair to them or to you."

"But what if. . ." She couldn't bear to say the words. What if one of her brothers died like Papa?

"You trust the Lord has a plan for the boys' lives, don't you?"

Her head snapped up. "Of course, I do. It says so in the Bible. Jeremiah 29:11."

His thumb stroked the inside of her wrist in comforting circles. "What if by being so overprotective of them, you're getting in the Lord's way? Not letting them discover who God wants them to be?"

"But I'm only trying to keep them safe."

He nodded slightly. "I know, but you can't stop them from growing up. It's how life is."

It felt as if Daisy had kicked her in the gut. But there was truth in what Luke said. Was she the reason her brothers had acted out in school? Had she held the reins too tightly and caused them to rebel? "What if I can't raise them the way Papa wanted? What if I mess up?"

He chuckled as he pushed a loose curl behind her ear. "Everybody make mistakes, even parents."

"They do?"

"Everyone I've met so far does. And as far as your papa goes, you need to raise those boys as you see fit."

She met his gaze. "Do you think that will be enough?"

"Honey, you love those boys." He let go of her hand and sat back. "As long as you do that and pray, I think they're going to turn out just fine."

Chardy nodded, though she still had lingering doubts. No wonder the Lord gave a child two parents! It was so much easier when there was someone to share it with. If this little talk had taught her anything, it was that her brothers needed a father. There was three weeks until the interviews. In less than a month, she could be married and settled, the boys with the papa they needed. Who would it be?

She glanced over as Luke spooned some beans onto her plate. Her heart knew who she wanted.

She could only pray Luke changed his mind before then.

Chapter 9

Coffee in hand, Luke stepped out on the front porch for a moment of peace before morning chores started. April had turned into May, bringing with it bright green shoots of new life across the prairie. The section of earth they'd plowed over the last week had warmed and stood ready for the seeds Chardy had brought home from the store last night. Soon, tiny spouts of beans, corn, and wheat would spring up and the real work would begin. But for today, he would enjoy this moment.

Chardy moved into view, humming a church hymn as she worked at the stove. Since Will Carter had followed her home almost two weeks ago, he hadn't let her ride alone, picking her up in the afternoon after she closed up the mercantile then returning her back to town after supper. Oh how he looked forward to those rides. They talked about almost anything, and for those few moments, he wasn't an amputee, but a man with dreams and needs.

He loved her. That had never been in question, though he supposed he should try not to care for her so much. But in the last two weeks, he'd come to realize how much he needed her. Needed her smile to brighten the darkness surrounding him, her strength helping to shore up his own.

Luke walked over to the edge of the porch. It would have been best for both of their sakes to stay far away from her because someone was going to be hurt when this job with her brothers' ended.

"Is something wrong?"

Luke startled slightly. How long had she been standing at the door? "Just thinking about today. We should get a good bit planted if the weather holds out."

She closed the door quietly and came to stand beside him. "Are you sure it's warm enough to plant now? There's still a chill in the air."

"Are you cold?"

She wrapped her arms around her waist. "A little."

He shucked his flannel shirt off and wrapped it around her shoulders. "I wouldn't want you to catch a chill."

"Thank you."

Luke lifted his gaze from the button he was fumbling with and froze. She was so close. The light scent of wildflowers hung in the air around her, and he leaned closer to take a deeper breath. A couple of inches and he could press his mouth against hers.

286

"Luke."

He lifted his gaze to meet hers. Love reflected in her eyes, a mirror image of his own feelings. But this was wrong. Chardy deserved so much more than he could offer. He started to step back but before he could, she pressed a kiss to his lips and he was lost.

Luke wrapped his arms around her and pulled her closer. She felt so dainty, like a piece of fine china he'd seen in store windows back East. Holding her like this made his world feel bright, made him feel he could do the impossible as long as she was by his side. She gave a little sigh and he deepened the kiss.

If only...

He lifted his head. What was he doing? He was no better off than he was when he'd broke off their courtship. Work was hard to come by without depending on others, and he wouldn't be beholding. He had nothing to offer Chardy.

Except for his love.

"We would find a way, Luke. Come what may."

He glanced down at her, still so achingly close it hurt not to kiss her again. But he couldn't. He had to be strong for her sake. "I need to get those boys moving, if we're going to put in a crop today."

She stepped away from him, but the pain in her expression tore his heart into shreds. "I think I'm going to go in to work."

He reached out for her but she moved away. "Chardy, I never meant to hurt..."

She stepped past him and hurried toward the stairs. "Would you tell the boys I'm sorry and that I'll come back to see them on Saturday?"

"Chardy..."

"Don't worry about giving me a ride," she threw over her shoulder as she stepped off the porch. "I'm sure Sassy could use the exercise."

"I just don't want you to get the wrong idea about us."

It was the absolute worst thing he could have said. She turned, her eyes blazing with anger as she walked toward him then stopped. "Don't."

The word ripped through him like a knife. He hadn't meant to hurt her. She needed to know that. "Chardy, I..."

She stiffened. "Don't worry about it, Luke. I finally understand. You won't marry me. Now if you'll excuse me, I need to get to work." She hurried down the steps and across the yard to where Sassy stood grazing.

He shouldn't leave things like this. It hurt just thinking of what she must feel, but it might be for the best. Chardy could move on with her life now, marry, and have that houseful of kids she wanted. She'd never have to suffer because he couldn't provide for their family. He couldn't even dance with her at the town social in a couple of days, and he knew how much she loved to dance.

Luke hobbled back to the screen door and threw it open, banging it hard against the wall. This was what he'd wanted, to give Chardy a life without his disability. Then why did letting her go seem so wrong? It might be best if he got the seeds planted then left. The boys could handle the farm and what they didn't know, they could ask one of their neighbors.

With his decision made, Luke walked into the kitchen to find Thomas, Emmett, and Neil digging into their breakfast.

He glanced around. "Where's George?"

The brothers gave each other a look before glancing up at him. They were hiding something, but what? He leaned on his cane. "What's going on?"

"I'll tell you," Emmett answered. "If I can ask you a question."

Luke didn't like the sound of that, particularly if they'd heard him arguing with Chardy, but he needed to find George.

"Fine. What's your question?"

Sitting on his knees, Emmett leaned across the table, his gaze trained on Luke. "Why won't you marry our sister?"

Chapter 10

He should have guessed the little runt would ask something like that. Luke pulled a chair out and sat down across from the boys, feeling as if he were facing a hangman. "That's between me and Chardy."

"I think we should be the judge of that," Thomas said. "We're her brothers."

"Yeah," Neil added, punching the air with his fork. "We the ones who've had to listen to her cry every night."

Chardy crying. That little jab struck him right in the heart.

"Sister's eyes are red all the time," Neil continued.

Emmett glared at Luke as if he'd like to poke him in the eye. "Don't you love her?"

"It's not a question of love." Why had he told these little runts that? Now he'd have to explain. "The truth is your sister deserves better than to be saddled with a cripple for the rest of her life."

Neil leaned over toward Emmett. "What's a cripple?"

"It means you can't walk," Thomas said.

"But Luke can walk," Emmett said matter-a-factly. "I've seen him."

"Me, too!" Neil cried out.

Luke gritted his teeth. This was getting out of hand. "Losing my leg makes it harder for me to find work. A farmhand needs two legs."

Maybe now they would understand why he couldn't marry Chardy. The boys exchanged glances. "You've been working with us for the past few weeks. Isn't that farming?" Thomas asked.

For Pete's sake, the Stevens' were a stubborn bunch. "I haven't done that much. . ."

"You taught me how to milk a cow."

"And showed us the best place to plant our garden and how to sharpen a plow." Emmett stopped to take a breath. "And what feed gave us the most eggs."

Thomas gave him a half smile. "You've been working a lot for a cripple."

When they put it that way, it sounded like he'd done quite a bit, but they didn't understand. "A farmer has to be able to work his land, not just boss everyone around."

"But isn't that what Mr. Walters did when you worked for him?" Thomas sat back in his chair, his arms folded over his chest.

The little runt, but he did have a point. Everything Mr. Walters had taught him about the land and the animals, he was now teaching the Stevens boys. And they had so much more to learn. For the first time in a long time, Luke felt a stirring of hope. He had a lot to think about. "All right, I answered your question. Now, it's your turn. Where's George?"

Emmett grabbed a biscuit from the plate. "He left while we were doing chores. He wanted to get to town before school started."

"Why would he do that?"

The two older boys stared into their plates, but Neil was almost doing a jig in his chair. "George has a sweetheart."

Emmett punched his brother in the arm. "You promised not to tell anyone."

"Luke isn't just anyone," Neil answered, rubbing his arm. "He'll be our brother when he marries Sister."

Luke ignored him and got right to the point. "Who is the girl he's sweet on?"

"Nancy McGee, and she is sweet on him, too," Thomas answered.

He was confused. "Isn't that the girl he stole the ribbon from?"

Thomas shook his head as he bit into a piece of bacon. "Nancy gave it to him. But Rupert Peabody saw it in one of George's books and made a stink over it. Nancy gets embarrassed easy, so George told Miss Green he stole it to make it easier on her."

That explained a lot. "So why did George go to town?"

"He wants to ask Nancy to the social in a couple of weeks," Thomas answered. "Said he was going to wait for her at the school."

"But he's not allowed anywhere near the school." Luke stood, grabbing a piece of toast and shoving it in his pocket.

If the boy was caught, no telling what the school board would do to him. "Planting is going to have to wait. We've got to find George."

Chapter 11

A plume of dust rose from the shelf as Chardy furiously worked the feather duster. It may have only been a week since she'd tackled the shelves, but with the dirt and grime that was tracked through the store every day, it looked more like a year.

Why did he have to go and kiss me like that?

Her hand stilled. The question had been on her mind all morning, yet she wasn't any closer to an answer than she was when she'd stormed off on Sassy. Luke wasn't the type of man to kiss a woman unless he had deep feelings for her.

She touched her fingers to her lips. Still, they tingled from his touch, as if he'd just kissed her. In that moment when he'd pulled her into his arms, she'd felt safe, cherished. Loved. Even now, she could hear little bells going off in her heart.

"Chardy, what are you doing up there?"

Her eyes flew open, and for a moment, her world felt out of balance. She grabbed the ladder's railing and steadied herself. "Millie! You scared the living daylights out of me."

"By walking into your store during business hours?"

Her lips twitched. "Did anyone ever tell you that you're a smart aleck?"

"All the time." Her friend tilted her head to get a better look. "Now, what are you doing on that ladder?"

Chardy waved her feather duster. "It's been a while since I dusted, so I thought now was as good a time as any." She started down the ladder. "What are you doing here? I thought you did your shopping on Tuesdays."

"Don't come down on my account. I just thought I'd look at some fabric for a new dress."

That was surprising. Millie wasn't one to waste money, and she'd just made herself a dress for Christmas. "What's the occasion?"

The woman touched a teddy bear on a nearby shelf then dropped her hand to her side. "I signed up for the mail-order groom auditions this morning."

Millie had said the ocean would have to freeze over before she considered interviewing for a mate. "What changed your mind?"

"I don't know." She sighed. "I guess I figured it was time for me to move on with my life. Lance wouldn't want me to be a widow forever."

"You're right. He wouldn't," Chardy answered quietly. Lance and Millie had been childhood sweethearts but only married the week Lance joined the army. He was gone six months later.

But at least, they had been married. Sometimes Chardy wondered if she shouldn't have married Luke before he'd left. She would have been his wife and they could have faced his injury together.

"So this morning, bright and early, I went to Mayor Melton's office and signed up." She took a step forward and looked up. "That's when I noticed your name on the list."

Chardy nodded. "I signed up this morning, too."

"But I thought you had your heart set on Luke. That's what you've always told me."

"I do." Even more so after these last few weeks. Watching Luke with her brothers, spending time talking with him, laughing with him, had reminded her of why she'd fallen in love with him in the first place. But after this morning, it was time to face the truth. "I can't keep expecting he'll change his mind about us. I have to think of my brothers."

"I'm so sorry, Chardy. I know how much you care for him."

"It's better this way." She didn't sound convinced. Her eyes began to sting. She'd make a puddle on the floor if they didn't change the subject. "I've just got a lovely mint green calico that might match your eyes."

"Oh I love that color," Millie said as she walked toward the back of the store.

"Maybe," Chardy answered with as much enthusiasm as she could muster for someone with a broken heart. A few minutes to collect herself and she'd be fine. If not fine, then functional.

She turned around and eyed the shelf. Might as well finish what she'd started. As she reached the top of the ladder, a door slammed behind her. Chardy glanced at Millie, who gave her a questioning look. "That sounded like the door to my office."

"What would anyone be doing in there?" Millie went to the door, but as she reached for the knob, it flew open, knocking her to the ground. The intruder tore down the aisle toward Chardy. He was almost underneath her before she realized who it was.

"George!"

She'd barely gotten out his name when she felt the jolt. George must have hit the ladder without realizing it. The ladder lurched away from the shelf, momentarily balancing on two legs then falling toward the open floor, shaking her free. She hung suspended for a second, like a blue jay taking flight, then she fell.

"Chardy!"

Luke! She only had enough time to register his voice before the floor reached up and grabbed her. She heard a sickening pop then pain rushed up her arm like a hot flash of lighting. A whimper escaped her lips as she tried to sit up, but her arm refused to support her weight.

Strong arms came around her. "Don't move, sweetheart."

She leaned her head back against Luke's shoulder. "My arm."

"All right." He instructed Millie to fetch Dr. Carter then turned back to her. "I'm going to sit you up slowly but it'll hurt some, okay?"

"Okay."

Gently, he pulled her upright, holding her against his chest. Her stomach lurched. She'd never hurt like this before in her life. Was her arm broken? Lord, she prayed not. She had too much to do.

"You're going to be okay, sweetheart. I promise."

She leaned into him more. "It hurts."

"I know it does. Doc Carter will fix it right up."

Chardy relaxed. If Luke thought she'd be okay, she'd be fine. She trusted him.

"Is she hurt bad?"

She turned her head slightly and found George staring down at her, fear imprinted on his young face. "George."

The boy dropped down on his knees beside them, "I'm so sorry, Sister. I didn't mean for you to get hurt." His voice broke. "I wanted some of those peppermint sticks you keep in your office. I thought I would give one..." He slammed his mouth shut.

Chardy wasn't sure what hurt more, her arm or that George wouldn't confide in her. She closed her eyes, the tears she'd tried hard to hold in check rolling down her checks. She'd failed her brothers, Papa, even Luke.

"George," Luke said. "It's time you told her the truth."

She opened her eyes in time to see George nod then look down at her. "The truth is..." He hesitated, glancing over at Luke. He nodded, and George continued, "I like Nancy McGee."

Chardy tried hard to concentrate through the pain. "Is that why you stole her ribbon?"

"I didn't steal it!" He exclaimed then calmed down. "She gave it to me, only she was too shy to admit it. That's why Emmett and Thomas got into a fight at school. Rupert was making fun of Nancy."

Chardy tried her hardest to smile. "You were looking out for each other."

"I guess." George's expression collapsed into guilt. "I never meant to hurt you, Sister. Never."

"I know you didn't." Another stab of pain shot through her, stealing her breath. When she finally could speak again, she asked, "Did you get the peppermint you wanted?"

"Yes, but..." He hesitated. "I don't think I should go to the dance. Nancy will understand."

"I think that's very good of you, George," Luke said, bracing her injured arm between his strong hands. "Now, do me a favor. Go find out what's taking Doc so long."

"Yes, sir." The boy didn't waste a second, jumping up and running toward the door. The bell clanged as he opened it, followed by muffled voices and the door slamming.

Luke looked up. "Who is George talking to?"

"I don't know. Maybe Doc. . ."

Boot steps echoed against the hardwood floor as the cowboy drew closer. She yelped as Luke tightened his hold.

"Mr. Carter," she grimaced.

The man crouched down beside them. "Miss Millie said you hurt yourself real bad. Thought maybe I could help."

"Unless you're a doctor, we won't be needing you," Luke growled.

Carter glanced over the two of them then took off his hat and sat it next to her. "Then why isn't Miss Chardy at my brother's office getting fixed up right now?"

"We're waiting on him to come here," Luke reasoned. "I don't want to move her until I know it's okay."

"Then you'll be waiting until the cows come home, at the rate Miss Millie is moving." He flashed Chardy a gentle smile. "If I carry you, Doc can get you fixed up lickity-split."

Even as much as she was hurting, she wished Will Carter would leave them alone. Luke would take care of her. He always had.

"I'd be much obliged, Carter."

Chardy glanced up. "Luke?"

But he didn't answer. Instead, Luke stared at the cowboy then nodded his head.

He couldn't even carry Chardy down to the doctor's office.

She was in pain, much more than she was letting on. Her arm was broken, though the bone hadn't punctured the skin, thank God. Less chance of infection. He wouldn't wish that kind of sickness on anyone, not even Will Carter.

The cowboy was right about one thing. The sooner Chardy saw Doc Carter, the better. Luke had seen his share of men suffer from bullet wounds, have their limbs amputated. He'd lain in the bed beside them. But nothing had prepared him to watch Chardy suffer. It felt as if his own arm had been broken along with hers. Seeing her like that, and knowing there wasn't much he could do, made his stomach roil.

But Will Carter could help her. If it meant her finding relief, Luke could swallow his pride and make it happen.

"Luke?"

His eyes met hers. Pain glossed over her pale blue eyes, but also something else, a kind of hurt only another person could inflict on someone. "I can't carry you, sweetheart."

"But I don't want to go without you." The tears were coming faster now. "Maybe I can walk."

Luke didn't doubt it, strong, stubborn woman that she was. But he didn't want to take any chances of injuring her arm more than it already was. He kissed her on the forehead. "Let Carter carry you before that break gets any worse."

"But..." She pleaded with him.

"No arguments, sweetheart. That arm needs to be set."

She nodded with a sniffle. The bodice of the pale blue waist shirt had blotches from her tears. Luke glanced over at Carter and nodded. The man shifted his arms under Chardy and waited.

Luke glanced back at Chardy, who'd turned pale as a sheet. "We're going to try our best not to hurt you, but we might not be able to help it."

She stiffened in Luke's arms. "I know."

Luke shifted her weight slowly into the cowboy's waiting arms, stopping only once to make sure Chardy was okay. She'd been biting her lip so hard, he expected to see blood. What he would give to bear the pain for her!

By the time Carter held her securely in his arms and stood, she had passed out. "Poor little thing."

"Probably for the best." Luke grabbed his cane and stood. "I'll be there as soon as I close up the store and find her brothers."

Carter gave him a slight nod. "I'll tell her when she wakes up."

"Thank you." The words tasted like dust in Luke's mouth. As the man turned and walked out of the store, Luke stopped to pray. *Lord, take care of my girl.*

But Chardy couldn't be his girl or his wife, could she? She needed someone who could take care of her and protect her. He couldn't even carry her to the doctor next door. This was just a broken arm. What if they married and had children? She could die because of him. Maybe now she'd understand the truth of their situation and open her heart to someone else.

But was he strong enough to let her go?

Luke hurried down the sidewalk as fast as he could. Closing up the store had taken longer than he'd thought. Even with the boys helping, the mercantile stayed busy with people coming in for groceries or whatnots, and some who'd dropped by simply to check in on Chardy. It had been over an hour and no one had sent word from the doctor. Had he been wrong by letting Will Carter carry her there? Had she suffered because of him?

Luke stood on the outside of Doc Carter's two-story house and looked through the window at the empty waiting room, then waited for someone to step inside. Following them in, he swiped off his hat, nervously holding it in his free hand.

Footsteps coming down the hall caught Luke. A slight woman with a dour look on her face stood in the doorway. He nodded. "Mrs. Carter."

"Luke." Her mouth tightened into a straight line. "I suppose you're here to check on Chardy."

"Yes, ma'am, though I'd like to talk to Doc first. If that's all right with you."

She scowled as she turned and walked back down the hall, mumbling as she went. "Poor man missed his breakfast, and now his lunch, taking care of folks.

People expect too much from him."

Not sure what to do, Luke waited outside the doorway. Finally, the woman turned then stared at him as if he'd lost his head. "You want to speak to my husband, don't you?"

"Yes, ma'am." Luke hurried to the woman who paused next to an office door down the hall. Opening it, she glared at him. "Be quick about it. My husband needs to eat before his lunch gets cold."

"Yes, ma'am." He nodded as he entered the doc's office.

Doc Carter glanced up at him from behind his desk. He nodded to his wife as she closed the door. "You'll have to forgive my wife, son. While it's my duty to provide care for the citizens of Turtle Springs, my lovely bride considers it her duty to take care of me."

Sounds like Chardy. "A good attribute in a wife."

"Yes, it is." The man's smile widened as he leaned back in his chair. "Have a seat."

Luke sat down. "I want to know how Chardy Stevens is doing."

"She's fine, son. I had to give her some laudanum for the pain. She's resting at the moment. It was a clean break, so I was able to set and plaster it without any problems."

Luke released the breath he'd been holding. "Praise the Lord."

"She'll need to stay here for a couple of days just to make sure she doesn't run a fever, but after that, she can go home, just as long as there's someone to help."

"I'll move her brothers back to town so we can take turns with her." He'd have to get a room at the hotel, but he didn't care as long as he was close by.

"There is one thing, son." Doc leaned forward, his elbows on the edge of the desk, his fingers set in a steeple. "My examination revealed some numbness and tingling in Chardy's fingers and the palm of her hand. Sometimes, this happens because the swelling from the break puts pressure on the nerves in the arm." He met Luke's gaze. "Or it could mean there's nerve damage."

"What does that mean?" Luke asked. It sounded a great deal like what the army doctors had told him before gangrene had settled in his leg.

"It could mean nothing, but it bears watching. There's no sense asking for trouble just yet. Let's get her back home. No activities for at least two weeks, then we'll see how she's doing."

He could handle that, though Chardy might not like it too much. "May I see her now?"

"Of course." Doc rose and walked around his desk to where Luke stood. "You know, she wanted to wait until you got here before she'd let me set it."

That was his Chardy. Stubborn to the bone. "She's a might determined."

The man laughed as he led Luke out into the hallway. "Those are the best kind of wives. They don't turn tail and run when times get hard."

It was true. Not once had Chardy ever faltered in her love for him, not even when he'd come home in pieces. How would she handle it if she lost the use of her hand? It would be a blow, but Chardy would do what she'd always done and make the best of it.

What did that say about himself?

Doctor Carter opened a door to their left before Luke could ponder on it very long. "She's still asleep."

"I'll just stay for a minute."

The man studied him for a moment then nodded. "Remember, she needs her rest."

"I understand." Luke moved deeper into the room, his gaze fixated on Chardy. She looked so pale and fragile, curled up on her side, her good hand balled up under her cheek. Her plastered arm rested on a pillow, her fingers pink and rosy against the snow white case. He leaned down and pushed a loose curl out of her face, his fingers lingering over the softness of her cheek. Without thinking, he pressed a kiss to her forehead. "Rest, my love."

He heard someone at the door. "How's our girl?"

Luke pivoted around. Will Carter. "What are you doing here?"

"I'm staying here with my brother." The cowboy gave him a crooked grin. "So how is Miss Chardy doing?"

Luke took a step toward him. "Why didn't you stay with her? She shouldn't have been left alone."

"She ain't." Will pushed his hat back on his head. "At least, not yet."

And she never would be if Luke had anything to say about it. Chardy needed more than a rambling cowboy who'd leave her for weeks or months on end. "Get out."

Will seemed taken back. "What?"

Planting his good leg, Luke shoved the man toward the door. "You heard me. Visiting hours are over."

Will tugged at his vest. "We'll see who Chardy picks at the interviews." He glanced down at Luke's cane then and met his gaze. "I'm pretty sure it won't be you."

Luke gritted his teeth as the cowboy turned, his boots heavy against the wood floor. He may not like Will Carter, but the man was right about one thing. Chardy wouldn't pick Luke.

Because he wouldn't even put himself in the race.

Chapter 12

Chardy stared out the window of her bedroom above the mercantile, watching the hustle and bustle below. Today was the day of the interviews, and the street below was filled with people hurrying about their day. There were new faces in the crowd, mostly men who'd answered Mayor Melton's ad. This afternoon, everyone would meet in the hotel's dining room and the auditions would commence.

But she had only one person on her mind.

Luke.

Where was he? In the ten days since she'd returned home after the accident, he hadn't visited her once. He still came to pick up the boys every couple of days to go and check out the garden. But this chair beside her window offered her glimpses of him, driving his wagon down the street, going in and out of the hotel during the day. Still he hadn't been back to see her since he'd brought her home from her stay at Doctor Carter's.

"Sister? Someone here to see you," George called from the doorway.

Her heart fluttered in anticipation. "Who is it?"

"Doc Carter and that brother of his." The boy stepped into the room and closed the door. "That cowboy has been by here every day since you came home." He eyed her curiously. "You're not sweet on him, are you?"

Chardy chuckled. George had grown up in the days following her fall. He'd begun to confide in her again, and she was surprised at some of his well-thought-out plans for the store. She'd felt confident enough in his behavior to share some of her worries. Of course, he relished his role as chaperone most of all. "We're just friends."

The boy breathed a sigh of relief. "Good, because Luke doesn't think much of him."

"I don't doubt that," she said, remembering the animosity between the two men. "Still, Luke doesn't know Will that well."

"He knows him well enough. Told me just yesterday to keep an eye on that cowboy."

Yesterday? "When did you see Luke yesterday?"

"When he dropped by here." George rolled his eyes. "He comes by every afternoon to check on you."

That gave her some comfort. "Then why hasn't he come up to see me?"

"I don't know." The boy walked over to her bed and grabbed her shawl. "I think he feels like he let you down."

"Why would he feel like that?"

He draped the shawl over her shoulders then sat across from her. "You remember when I got in that fight with Rupert Peabody?"

She wasn't sure how that had anything to do with her and Luke, but she'd let him finish. "Yes. He was picking on Nancy."

"I don't know why, but I couldn't let him do that. Nancy is important to me, so I feel like I need to take care of her and protect her from bullies like Rupert. I think that's how Luke felt after you fell. But he couldn't, at least, not how he wanted to, because of his leg."

"But that's not what happened. Luke did take care of me in all the ways that mattered," Chardy protested. The man had held her and comforted her in the moments after she'd fallen. He'd been there every time she'd come out of the laudanum-induced fog, giving her sips of water, whispering words of comfort. How could he ever believe he'd let her down?

Chardy glanced over at her brother. "When Luke comes by this afternoon, would you tell him I'd like to see him?"

"I don't know. You might be poking the snake."

"Well maybe it's time to poke him a bit." She pulled the shawl over her injured arm. "Besides, I need to thank him for everything he did. Please?"

"I'll do my best." George gave her a cockeyed grin as he rose to his feet. "I'd do anything for you, Sis, but do me a favor, will ya?"

"What's that?"

"Don't tell any of the other boys. They'll give me what for about it."

She pressed her lips together to keep from laughing. "I promise. Your secret is safe with me." She grabbed the pillow on the floor beside her, set it on her lap, and placed her injured arm on top of it. "Would you send the doctor in now?"

"And that cowboy?" George smirked.

"Tell him I don't feel up to having company today."

"Yes, ma'am!" He slammed the door behind him.

Chardy simply shook her head. Will was a nice man, even if he did go a little overboard with the cowboy route. He'd asked to court her almost as soon as she'd been released, but she'd told him right then that she wouldn't entertain any romantic offers from him. She thought that would be the end of it, but he'd come back the next day with an offer of friendship. Since then, she'd been helping him narrow his list of potential brides.

There was a knock at the door. "Come in."

Doctor Carter poked his head around the edge of the door. "Are you decent?"

She chuckled. "I wouldn't have asked you to come in if I wasn't. Millie came by this morning and helped me get dressed. I didn't realize how tiring it was to lay in bed all day."

He set his black bag on the table then joined her by the window. "Don't try to pull the wool over my eyes, young lady. I've seen you sitting by this window for the last couple of days."

Chardy felt her cheeks go warm. "I'm sorry. I just couldn't sit still anymore."

"That's all right. I'm just glad you felt up to it. Any problems since the last time I saw you?"

None that the doctor could solve. "No, I feel fine."

"Good." He took the hand of her injured arm and examined her fingers. "Any more numbness or tingling?"

"A little, but not as much as before."

The doctor completed his examination then sat back. "I believe you're well enough to take part in the auditions this afternoon."

Chardy recovered her arm with her shawl. "That's nice."

"You don't sound very enthusiastic about the prospect."

No sense lying about her feelings. "I'm not excited about it at all."

He nodded toward her arm. "You're not afraid of reinjuring it, are you? Because I can make arrangements with Mayor Melton if you want to participate."

"That's not it." She hesitated then figured she had nothing to lose by asking the doctor some questions. "Some folks aren't very kind when it comes to those with physical impairments."

Doc Carter's expression cleared. "You're talking about Luke."

She nodded.

"Well yes," he started. "There are people out there who aren't kind at all when it comes to someone being different than them. Some act on those prejudices."

Her heart trembled. "You mean by not hiring him."

"Or worse, by treating him like he's not quite a person anymore. When I witness such, I wish I had a medicine that could heal a person's soul." The doc gave her a soft smile. "Then I have to remind myself that that's the Lord's job, not mine."

"I just worry about Luke." She played with her cuff. "He seems to be struggling since he got back from the war."

"I don't doubt it."

"But what can I do to help. . .him?" Her voice broke.

Doctor Carter's expression softened as he took her free hand in his. "Dear, you have to understand. It's hard for a man like Luke, someone who's been active all of his life, to have restrictions placed on him. But he seems to be adjusting well. I heard he's taking care of your papa's place."

Chardy nodded. "He'd been teaching my brothers how to farm."

"That's just what he needs, work that gives his life purpose. It makes it less likely that he'll fall into a depression that's common among soldiers after a traumatic injury. He's not drinking, is he?"

"No! He'd never drink around me or my brothers."

"That's a good sign. Some men find comfort in a bottle, anything to ease their pain."

Her stomach twisted into a knot. "Is Luke in pain?"

He patted her hand. "It's not a physical pain. Remember, he's having to mourn the loss of all the things he can't do anymore while discovering just what his place is in the world again. But Luke's a strong man. He'll figure this out. Until then, just be there for him."

Chardy nodded, still trying to take in everything the doctor had said. "Thank you for answering some questions for me."

Doc Carter stood. "So I guess this means you're not going to be my sister-in-law."

She wasn't sure how to respond but decided the truth would be best. "Your brother is a good friend, but I've loved Luke since I was barely out of the schoolhouse. I can't give up on him now."

"You're going to make him a fine wife, once he realizes what he has." He grabbed his bag off the table and headed toward the door. "I'll see you in a couple of days."

"Thank you." But Chardy's thoughts were on everything the doctor had told her. She never considered all that Luke had lost when they'd taken his leg, only been thankful that he'd survived and come home to her.

Doc Carter was right. Luke was a strong man, one of the strongest she'd ever known. Losing a part of himself must have been a horrific blow to him, both physical and mentally. She needed to be strong for him, and patient. Give him a chance to work through this new part of his life. Let him find his place in the world again. And he wouldn't have to face this alone.

Chardy bowed her head and prayed.

Chapter 13

"A re you sure you're okay with peeling potatoes?" Mrs. Reed asked as she followed Luke to the alley outside the inn's kitchen. "It don't seem right to have a guest fixing his own dinner when I could get Virginia to do this."

Luke set the full bucket of potatoes down then lowered himself onto the bench. "I don't mind at all, Mrs. Reed. Besides, I like to have something to work on while I'm sitting out here. As my papa use to say, a person can't get into any trouble when his hands are full."

She chuckled. "Like you'd be any trouble. You're one of the nicest men I've ever met. And I've met quite a few."

Her compliment felt good to his battered self-esteem. "You're just saying that because I'm peeling these potatoes for you."

"Possibly." She handed him a clean bowl and a knife. "Can I asked you a question?"

Questions seemed to cause him trouble these days, but Mrs. Reed had been so kind to him, he couldn't deny her. He picked up a potato and started peeling it.

She sat down beside him. "Why aren't you in the dining room looking for a wife?"

As questions went, he hadn't expected that one. "I'm not ready to get married yet."

"Oh. Well, I guess that makes sense." She hopped up from the bench quickly for an older woman. "Maybe Mayor Melton will run another ad when you are."

"Maybe." He finished one last swipe at the potato then tossed it in the bowl. Better to be vague than to open the door to more questions.

"I'll be back in a little while to check on you."

"I'll be here," he called out as she bustled through the kitchen door.

Finally, he was alone, a rarity these days with the town bursting at the seams with newcomers. Men from every corner of the country had invaded Turtle Springs hoping for the chance to win a bride. But here in the alley near the center of town, the constant noise of people and livestock drifted away, and Luke could think.

And his thoughts always turned to Chardy.

He dropped another bare potato into the bowl and retrieved one from the bucket. What was he going to do about her? He'd tried to stay away, but every day he always ended up at the mercantile, listening for her movements overhead, anxious for any news about her. George and Thomas had invited him to visit the family rooms upstairs, but he'd begged off. He wouldn't raise his hopes or hers until he knew what he would do.

Luke glanced up at the sky. "What am I supposed to do, Lord?"

But there was no answer, just this feeling that she might already be lost to him for good.

"I see Mrs. Reed's got you working."

Luke lowered his gaze to find Doc Carter strolling toward him. "She's got enough on her hands with the groom auditions this afternoon."

"There's a mighty big crowd out front," he said, taking the woman's place beside him. "I suppose they'll be getting started soon."

"I guess." Luke jabbed a small potato so hard, it broke in half. He'd seen the cozy little table for two Chardy had been assigned. She was probably sitting there right now, watching as the men queued up to have a moment of her time. Will Carter would probably be at the head of the line, pawing all over her. The thought made Luke sick.

"Chardy will have a good view of all the action."

Luke glared at the man. Was he trying to rub salt in his wounded heart? "I don't know. Her table is off in the corner a bit." That was his doing. The men would have to work a little harder to find her.

"No, I'm talking about the view from her bedroom window."

Chardy wasn't coming? Luke stopped peeling. "There's nothing wrong, is there? She's not running a fever or anything, is she?"

Doc put his hand on Luke's shoulder. "No, son, nothing like that. I just got the feeling the groom interviews weren't her top priority this afternoon."

Luke didn't understand. "But she needs a husband. Someone who can take care of her and the boys."

The doctor leaned his head back and stared up at the sky. "Do you have any brothers or sisters?"

"A brother, Matthew."

"I have a younger sister, Clara. I don't talk about her much because she's quite a bit younger than myself." He took a deep breath. "When she was around five or six, she had a bad fall from the top of the staircase. It was touch and go for a few days, and the doctors were all certain that she would never be the girl she once was. My parents were told it would be best to place her in an institution."

Luke had seen some men so badly scarred by battle, they were admitted to an institution. But a little girl? "What happened?"

Doc smiled slightly. "My parents happened. They felt like the doctors wrote off Clara, but they refused to have her admitted until they had used all of their resources." He stole a glance at Luke. "Papa worked with her every day to build her muscles so that she could walk, and Mama read to Clara every chance she got."

"Your parents sound like pretty remarkable people," Luke said. "Where is your sister now?"

"She lives a few miles away from my parents with her husband and children, and if my last letter from her is any indication, she's blissfully happy."

Luke sat up a little straighter. "So the doctors were wrong about her?"

"I don't know if it was that the doctors were wrong as much as my parents refused to give up on her." Doc leaned back again. "Kind of like how Chardy will never give up on you."

Luke went back to peeling. "I didn't ask your opinion, Doc."

"Maybe not, but when I see people suffering, I try to help when I can." He gave Luke a brief grin. "It's part of the job."

"It's just that. . ." Luke hesitated. He'd already lost his independence, his self-esteem. What would this man say when he learned Luke couldn't even take care of the woman he loved? "What if something happens to her or the boys? What if they get hurt, and I can't even carry them to your office?"

"I'd imagine you'd do what you did with Chardy. You take care of them by getting someone to help you."

"You mean like your brother?" He snorted. "He's the one who took care of Chardy."

"That's not how Will tells it." Doc leaned forward, resting his elbows on his knees. "He said you were the one who stabilized her arm and kept her calm. That you made the decision for him to get her to my office. You put aside your own feelings to see to her care."

His knife slowed. Luke desperately wanted to believe him, but after everything he'd been through, he wasn't certain he could. "They told me at the hospital that no one would want me like this."

"There are those who call themselves physicians who do more harm than good." Doc looked Luke straight in the eye. "Let me ask you something. Do you believe that God has a plan for your life?"

The same question he'd asked Chardy concerning her brothers just a few weeks ago. He nodded. "Jeremiah 29:11."

"Do you remember the rest of that verse?"

Luke stilled as he recalled the scripture. *For I know the plans I have for you. . . plans to prosper you and to not harm you, plans to give you hope and a future.* "Hope and a future," he whispered.

The doctor's hand rested comfortingly on Luke's shoulder. "What happened to you in the war was evil, son. Don't let it rob you of the future God has promised you."

Doc was right. Losing his leg wasn't a part of the life he'd planned for himself. But God hadn't given up on him; He simply had a different dream for Luke's life, a better plan that he would have never followed if he'd come back from the war whole. Luke had let his pride stand in the way of making a new life.

A life with Chardy and the boys.

Luke tossed the knife and the half-peeled potato into the bowl and reached for his cane.

"Where are you going?" the doctor asked.

He stood up, rolled his sleeves down, then turned to the man. "Could you button these for me?"

"Certainly." A few seconds later, the task was done.

Luke scrubbed his free hand across his face. If he had any sense, he'd go upstairs, change his shirt, and run a comb through his hair, but he was in too much of a hurry to get to Chardy and start the future God had promised.

But first, he needed to ask the doctor a question. "Why did your parents decide not to listen to the doctors and just put your sister in an institution?"

The man smiled. "Because they believed that God's plan for Clara was so much bigger than any diagnosis. They were right. She's now a testimony to what a great God we serve."

Luke nodded. Joy he hadn't known was possible flowed through him. The dingy world around him felt lighter, and for the first time in months, he saw things clearly. "Thank you."

Doc Carter stood. "You're welcome. If you ever need to talk, drop by my office. My wife has always got plenty of her homemade cookies on hand."

"I might just do that."

Doc pulled out his pocket watch and glanced at it. "I'd better get going. I have one more appointment before I need to get home for dinner. My wife will be upset if I'm late again." He winked as he passed Luke. "I'll be praying for you."

"Thank you." Luke turned and hurried down the alley toward Main Street. Doc hadn't been kidding when he said there was a crowd. Hordes of men blocked the sidewalk, pushing and pressing their way toward the inn's entrance. Mayor Melton would be pleased by the turnout, but all Luke felt at the moment was irritation. Well, he wasn't going to let a bunch of bride-hungry men keep him from Chardy one more second.

Luke backtracked down the alley and went in through the inn's kitchen door, then up the back stairway. At the top of the stairs, he took a deep breath, doubts darting through his thoughts. He closed his eyes. *I know You have a good plan for my life, Lord. If Chardy is a part of that, please let me know.* A peace he couldn't explain settled over him.

As he reached the lower step, he glanced out over the dining room. For all the chaos outside the front doors, the atmosphere seemed no different than Sunday lunch after church, though instead of families, couples sat talking quietly. The new sheriff guarded the front door, much like a sentinel at the gate. Luke shifted his gaze to where Chardy's table was, then stopped.

Chardy.

She'd promised to meet him so that they could meet the groom candidates together, but after talking to Dr. Carter he'd wondered if she'd remembered. She looked so pretty in a calico dress that was the same pale blue of her eyes, the tiny pink roses on the material a perfect match for the bloom in her cheeks. Her thick blond hair was barely held back by a dainty ribbon at the nape of her neck.

She laughed, and he could hear the sweet melody of it deep down in his heart.

He loved Chardy, more with each passing second. He was stubborn and prideful, yet God had given him such a precious woman. If it took the rest of his days, he'd try to prove himself worthy of her faith in him.

The man with Chardy turned slightly, and the room turned a misty shade of scarlet. Luke balled his free hand into a fist and plowed across the room.

The man was none other than Will Carter.

Chapter 14

"Thanks, Will, for coming and keeping me company, but you didn't have to," Chardy said, fixing the sash of the sling Millie had sewn to match her dress. She'd only come because Luke had said he would help her in the interviews, but now she was tired and just wanted to go home.

"Simply following my brother's orders to keep a close eye on you." He smiled, but there was some difference in his expression as he glanced around the room and saw Millie. "You were right about her. Millie is something special."

"So I take it the interview went well."

"I think so." He almost seemed bashful when he glanced up at her. Not like Will Carter at all. "She's agreed to have dinner with me after the auditions are over."

"That's wonderful, Will. I'm so happy for you!"

"Thank you." He sat back in his chair and studied her. "What about you? Meet anyone who tickled your fancy?"

"I'd like to hear about that myself."

Chardy's heart fluttered as she looked up to find Luke staring down at them. She hadn't realized how much she'd missed him until he was standing there, inches away from her, and looking so tall and handsome, it took her breath away. "I was hoping you would come."

He glanced at Will. "You were?"

"Of course, I was."

"Well, I'd better go claim my date for this evening." Will stood and offered Luke his chair. "I was only keeping the seat warm until you showed up anyway."

"What did he mean by that?" Luke stared after the man then took his seat.

"Will probably thought he was being funny, but I don't want to talk about him." She leaned across the table as far as her cast would allow. "How are you?"

His face relaxed slightly. "I've been better."

She nodded. "Me, too."

They sat quietly for a moment. Some of the men had worn suits and cravats for the interviews, but she much preferred Luke in his blue cotton work shirt that matched the flecks of midnight in his eyes, or the blue jeans that molded to muscle made strong by hard work.

"Chardy," he started, his hands clinched together in front of his chest.

She'd never seen Luke so nervous. Reaching out, she covered his big hand with hers. He looked up then, and what she saw in his face made her heart sing. "I'd like to audition for the role of your husband."

She could barely breathe from the joy of it. But she couldn't be hurt again. She needed to know exactly where she stood. "I thought you didn't want to marry me."

"Oh no, honey." Luke threaded his fingers through hers. "I wasn't sure that you should want to marry me. I'm still not."

"Then why. . ."

"Because I'm a hundred percent certain that I can't live my life without you." He rubbed his thumb against hers. "I just wanted you to know what you were getting into."

Chardy couldn't contain her smile any longer. "I know exactly what I'm getting. A good, decent man who I'll be proud to spend the rest of my life with."

He lifted her hand to his lips. "Chardy, I just. . ."

A bell tinkled behind them. "All right, gentlemen. It's time to move on to the next lady."

"The mayor might not like it, but I'm not going anywhere." Luke squeezed Chardy's hand. "It took me long enough to get here as it was."

"Does that mean you intend to court me?" Her insides shook as she waited for his answer.

Instead, he stood, moved the chair until it was next to hers then retook his seat. Before she knew what he intended, Luke cupped her cheek in his hand and tilted her face up to his. "I love you, Chardy." He kissed the tip of her nose. "But I don't want to court you."

"You don't?" She breathed out the question.

"No, I want to marry you." He brushed his lips against hers. "Do you accept my hand?"

Chardy wound her arm around his neck and pulled him close so that only he could hear her answer. "With all of my heart."

Patty Smith Hall is an award-winning, multi-published author with Love Inspired Historical and Heartsong/Harlequin. She currently serves as president of the ACFW-Atlanta chapter and is active on Facebook, Pinterest, and Twitter. She calls North Georgia her home which she shares with her husband of over thirty years, Danny; two gorgeous daughters; a wonderful son-in-law; and a new grandson who has his grandma's heart. Visit her website at www.pattysmithhall.com.

Dime Novel Suitor

By Carrie Fancett Pagels

Dedication

To Joan Carol Belsky Pagels and Donald R. Pagels.
Thanks for supporting your daughter-in-law's writing!

Acknowledgments

Thank you to Cynthia Hickey for thinking of me for this collection! Cheryl Baranski blessed me by brainstorming this project with me early on. Also, thank you to Kathleen L. Maher, my critique partner, who is such a blessing. Grateful for Regina Fujitani, my professional beta reader for this project, and kudos to Gina Welborn for her helpful suggestions. Vicki McCollum's edits are much appreciated. Thank you, Joyce Hart, my agent, and Becky Germany, our editor and publisher. A group hug to the Pagels' Pals and to my fellow *Seven Brides for Seven Mail-Order Husbands* authors!

"For I know the plans I have for you," declares the LORD, "plans to prosper you
and not to harm you, plans to give you hope and a future."
JEREMIAH 29:11 NIV

Chapter 1

P*a had some kind of nerve, up and dying like that—just when I'd gotten used to Frank being gone.* Adjusting her somber bonnet, Caroline Kane exited what was now her inn, onto the boardwalk and then stepped down to the hard-packed dirt street. She needed to visit her parents' graves before the busy day began. With a breath of frustration, she waited for the dairy wagon to pass. Young Jake Miller waved as he drove by. Would his widowed mother find a husband in the upcoming auditions? What a hare-brained notion. Mrs. Miller sure could use extra help, though, that a husband would provide. As for Caroline, she was fine. Perfectly fine.

"We'll manage just fine," she mumbled to herself.

"Caroline!"

Caroline pivoted to spy Mrs. Reed emerging from the alley alongside the Tumble Inn. The older woman shuffled toward her, bent forward as usual, rubbing her gnarled hands.

"What are you doing up so early, Mrs. Reed?"

"I wish you'd just call me Mae, child." She lifted her chin, and her pale-blue eyes glimmered.

"Doesn't seem natural, ma'am, but I'll try." She smiled at the widow, who'd only recently joined the inn's staff. "So you're an early bird today, too?"

The worry over all the incoming men to the inn had Caroline tossing and turning. Not only would she have to put the men up but they'd have to be fed, and somehow she'd have to keep her two younger sisters from being accosted by any of them.

Mae cringed. "I couldn't sleep. My rheumatism tells me a storm is coming." The silver-haired widow flexed her right hand and grasped her left one, massaging her swollen knuckles. "But I wanted to ask if you think we've got enough biscuits put aside for this morning?"

"I think Deanna did the count last night before she went to sleep." Caroline sighed. "I hate to serve cold biscuits, but with Pa gone, I'm still trying to figure out how to make everything work."

"We'll get help. The Lord never fails us." Mae turned to go back to the inn.

Caroline crossed the street, a wind gust ruffling her skirts, and headed south, past the town green, toward the field behind the church. A rosy glow hovered over the far tree line, the sun determined to rise, despite all that had happened. Life would go on, regardless. She swiped at her wet face and continued on to the cemetery, her laced boots chafing her heels.

He's not there. Caroline slowed her pace. Pa was in heaven now, albeit all too soon, like Frank. "Every day is a precious gift," Pa had often said. With her mother deceased now, these past five years, and Frank gone too, Caroline was truly alone.

Alone?

Caroline drew a breath of fresh morning air, full of the promise of rain. With five younger siblings, an interfering older sister, and an inn filled with Turtle Springs castoffs as workers, she was hardly alone. But with her feelings cracked open like eggs ready to be scrambled, she'd never felt lonelier.

Kansas City, Kansas

How ironic that Barden Granville's first foray into the world of cowboys was in an establishment called The Empire, with its overdone velvet and damask upholstery, and wallpaper a laughable imitation of the grand salons of Europe. His older brother, who would inherit the title and Cheatham estate, would have referred to the decor as Agony in Red, with all the vermillion in the room. Blue smoke hung overhead like a dark cloud in the crowded tavern. Barden coughed as yet another of the cowboys at his card table lit up a cigar.

Chairs scraped the filthy wooden floor, competing with the noise of the serving girls' laughter. Some of the scantily clad young women were no older than his youngest sister. The clergyman within him yearned to take the girls aside and ask if they knew what a slippery slope they were on.

The pock-marked youth adjacent to him threw down a coin. "Who'll match me?"

Barden examined his cards as the other men either folded or plucked a coin from pockets grimed with road dirt. He placed his wager, a niggling of guilt convicting him that this wasn't a good idea.

When the cards were all spread atop the table, the stunning realization hit him. "Criminy, I won!"

The largest of the men, with silver edging his temples, pushed his pile of silver coins toward Barden. The others glanced at the older man before slowly sliding their money across the table.

The man with the filthy red bandana around his thick neck squinted at Barden. "We'll see who wins next time."

None of them had shared their names. Maybe cowboys didn't do that.

A waitress passed, and one of the men flung out an arm and tugged her closer. "Stop that!" She slapped at his hand.

Barden pushed his chair back. "I say, unhand her."

"Or you'll do what?"

He was an excellent pugilist, although his father would have chucked Barden from the house had he known he'd taken up bare-knuckle fighting while at Oxford. "I fear I'd have to teach you a lesson."

Laughter erupted. The men mocked his words, repeating them with an exaggerated British accent, making him sound like a fop. His opponents could confirm he was no such thing, had they been present. Which they were not.

The silver-haired man shoved the table over. Barden's fists took on a life of their own as shouts and screams ensued.

Then Barden descended into darkness.

Head pounding in agony, Barden lay against dank earth that seeped moisture through his clothing. He blinked up at a pale blue sky tinged with golden light. Sunrise. *Where am I, exactly?* Brick walls flanked him left and right. A brass band playing American tunes seemed to occupy his brain. He pressed his eyes closed, which seemed to quiet the noise in his head.

A door slammed shut nearby. Barden flinched.

Quick footsteps neared. "Lawd, have mercy. You all right?" Compassion tinged her words, making him all the more sorry for his plight.

A groan was all he could manage.

"Oh my." She gasped. "I be right back."

The woman hurried off. Barden tried to move, but every body part screamed in agony. Slowly, he flexed his feet. Those cowboys had stolen his new boots. He never should have sat down with them at the card table.

If this was his dream come true then what would a nightmare be like? *Oh, Lord, sovereign God, why me? Why now? I've waited all my life for this. Am I being punished?* Was it for being an ungrateful third son who would never inherit?

Barden bent his knees. His legs still worked—there was something to be grateful for. At least they could bend. He tried to raise his head, but everything seemed to spin. When he lowered his head back onto the dirt, the stench of alley odors suddenly predominated. He'd been tossed in a back alley like refuse.

The door slammed again and quick, heavy footsteps thudded toward him. "He gonna need a doctor, Uziah."

"I'll go get him." The man's deep voice rumbled from his chest.

"First help me get him inside."

"But where we gonna put him, Mary?" The affection in his voice suggested this woman was special to him. His wife?

"That little alcove in the kitchen." Mary pressed a hand to Barden's head. "Go and put that pallet down on the floor, Uziah, and come back out and help me."

Soon, Barden found himself laid out on a thin mattress, covered with a threadbare blanket. And before he could say, "Thank you," he was fast asleep again.

Turtle Springs, Kansas

Looking up from her dishwashing, Caroline dried her hands on her apron and glared at her older sister. "You forgot to tell me what?"

Lorraine batted her pale blond eyelashes. "I contributed to the mail-order husband ad."

"Are you crazy? You're already married."

"For you, you ninny! Now that you seem to realize Frank is gone." Lorraine's words slapped her.

Caroline could only stare, gape-mouthed. Truly, only since Pa's death had she even accepted that she was indeed a widow.

"Well, aren't you going to thank me?"

"No!"

Alvin looked up from where he sat by the door, peeling potatoes. Their seventeen-year-old brother smirked. "How's it feel having other people making decisions for you?"

"Just hush, Al!" Caroline glared at him. Would he still be alive had their father allowed him to go fight?

Picking up a torn dishtowel, Lorraine tut-tutted. "Ma would never have let the inn get so run down like Pa did." Or like Caroline was her inference.

"You don't even live here, and Pa left the inn to me, so you've no need to bother yourself with such details." Caroline yanked the stained cloth from her sister. "What are you doing by going behind my back and putting my name in on that husband-auditioning thing?"

"You'll thank me later."

"I won't do it."

"Then I'll pick someone for you." Lorraine's smirk promised she would. "Trust me, Caroline, you'll be happy once the inn starts making money from new customers in town for the auditions." She averted her gaze and picked at her lace cuffs. "On that note, I should mention I volunteered for the auditions to be held here, in the dining hall."

"What!" Both Caroline and Alvin shouted at the same time.

When her younger brother jumped up from his chair, Caroline held out a staying hand. "Lorraine, you had no right!"

"They'll pay well for the privilege of using the restaurant from four to six that afternoon."

"And will expect food, no doubt."

Twin circles of red appeared on her sister's fair cheeks. "Yes, but something simple."

"Well I'm not going to be participating, and I'll not even be here. . ." Not now that she realized her interfering sister had gone in on the ad in Caroline's name. "So you better figure out a way to serve them."

Lorraine merely shrugged.

If Caroline were ten years younger, she'd be rolling around on the floor with Lorraine like they used to do when her older sister would try to hide her Jane Austen novels. "Did it not occur to you that we'll have to serve an evening meal to our guests, too?"

"Pooh! Most of the men will be staying here, and if they are full up on sandwiches, cookies, punch, and coffee, you can give them stew and biscuits for dinner."

She would have argued, but that rationale actually made sense. "I don't want Deanna or Virginia involved in this either. I don't need any of those men thinking they're looking for husbands."

"I'm much happier married, and I know you would be, too, if only you'd open yourself up again to the possibility."

"Wonderful! Then you and Joel can take Henry and Leonard in at your ranch and share your happiness with them—like you first promised Pa." Then reneged on the promise as he drew closer to death.

Eyes widening, Lorraine opened her pale blue silk reticule. "That reminds me! I just got a letter from Grandmother."

"Grandmother Tyler?" Pa's people had died in South Carolina, years earlier. Ma's folks in Virginia were too prideful to associate with them.

"Yes. Grandmother Tyler."

"What did she say?"

"Read it." Lorraine shoved the cream-colored missive at Caroline. "I have to run. Need to see the milliner about my new hat."

Caroline didn't even bother to wave good-bye as her sister fled with her usual rapidity. Lorraine was good at running away from conflict. That was how she'd become Mrs. Martinchek.

"What are you gonna do?" Alvin set another peeled potato into the crockery bowl. "We could use the extra money, and I'm willing to help. Henry and Leonard can help, too."

Caroline pulled a stool out from beneath the work counter and sat down. "She just makes me so angry. She has no right to interfere."

"Kinda hurt us boys' feelings when she wouldn't let us come out to the ranch."

"Yes, well. . ." She didn't need sensitive Alvin dwelling on these thoughts. "She's newly married."

Mrs. Reed entered from the dining room, waving an empty breadbasket. "Our guests are awfully hungry this morning."

What would they do when the men arrived for the auditions? Surely many would cram into every available space at the inn. They'd be working around the clock. Caroline needed help. . .and fast.

Chapter 2

Telegrams to Father's British rancher friends in the surrounding area went unanswered. Time came for Barden to move on.

Mary Freeman had told Barden, "Our friend, Mr. Tumbleston, send word to us this past winter that they needed help at his inn. He's passed on, Lord rest his soul, but I reckon his daughter, Mrs. Kane, would take you on—like she did with us when we first came to Kansas."

Uziah had given Barden a true compliment: "I reckon you competent to give her some relief, now you learned the ropes."

Competent wasn't a word he'd often heard ascribed to himself, other than at seminary. At the estate, he'd always been the ignored third brother. But his valet recognized Barden's proficiency in reading and had supplied boxes of American dime novels. Through that paperback tutelage, Barden realized he'd been born on the wrong continent. Before he settled down into his ministry in pastoral northern England, he'd live the cowboy life. Although how he'd do that at an inn, he didn't know.

Now, traveling across Kansas, his back ached worse than any hunt he'd been on, riding and jumping over hill and dale in chase of an elusive fox. And his stop at the Martinchek's ranch failed to procure Barden a spot as a hand. The rest of the drive into Turtle Springs was a blur of green as he silently vented at God for His failure to help him in his quest to enjoy cowboy life, even if for only a few months.

The drayman pulled to the side of the street, by a painfully plain building, much like one back home in England—a large ordinary in Leeds. The Tumble Inn, a whitewashed wooden structure, stood three stories high, as did few others in this small borough. No shutters, no protective portico, nothing decorative on the front. The windows bore evidence of street grime, failing to reflect back the sun's impressive glare. Still, he wasn't here to pass judgment.

Barden grabbed his bag and hopped down. Although he had few coins to spare, he pulled one from his pocket and offered it.

The driver shook his head. "No, sir, Uziah pay me good to get you here."

"Well then. . ." Barden tucked the coin back in his vest pocket. "Thank you."

"I can't be lingerin'. God go with you." The man's soulful eyes were gentle, unlike Barden's father's accusatory ones.

If Father knew he was here... This wasn't how Barden had planned to spend his American holiday. He was supposed to be on a ranch, enjoying a bit of cowboy life before settling into the remote northern village that was to be his home and into a stone-walled vicarage that could have fit into this inn several times over.

Couples emerged from the inn, chatting, followed by some solitary men and women. A middle-aged woman attired in a sapphire-blue damask dress held fast to the arm of a red-haired man whose smile could not have been any broader.

Love was a beautiful thing, regardless of age. Too bad those young women interested in him had viewed him only as Lord Cheatham's third son, one who'd inherit nothing.

The front double doors were centered in the inn. Choosing the brass handle on the right, he held fast, hesitating. Should he go around to the back? Like the common servant he'd become?

Before he could choose, the door opened out on him, propelling him backward. He'd almost lost his footing, but recovered, a credit to his cotillion dance instructor, no doubt.

A beautiful young woman, with dark blond hair coiled atop her head, frowned at him. Her flashing brown eyes surveyed him from head to toe. "The auditions are over. The restaurant is closed while we prepare dinner."

He raised his hands. "Auditions?"

Turtle Springs was, indeed, an unusual place. He should pull out his glasses so he could clearly read what was pasted to the door, but before he could do so, the pretty Kansan swiveled away and yanked the placard from it.

"Darned nuisance."

"Pardon me, I'm..."

"You're not here for a room, are you?" She crossed her arms over her black bombazine-covered chest.

"No, I fear not, Miss—"

Her chin lifted slightly, and her winsome features relaxed, but she didn't offer her name.

Barden cleared his throat. "I'm here for Mrs. Caroline Kane."

She eyed him warily. "Why?"

Was this Mrs. Kane? "I'm answering the advertisement."

"Well, you're a bit late."

Uziah and Mary had said the inn owner needed assistance as had the Martinchek ranch owners, where he'd stopped outside of town. Barden's bag seemed to grow heavier. What would he do if he found no work here?

"Did my sister send you?"

Was Mrs. Martinchek her sister? He couldn't remember the Freemans saying so. "Looks very much like you, only a paler version?" He'd spoken briefly with the owner's wife as he was leaving the Martinchek ranch. She'd just arrived home, and looked to be in a huff. But she had spoken with him briefly, encouraging him to seek out Mrs. Kane.

Guilt assailed Caroline at the flutters this stranger was bringing to her bruised heart. His delightful British accent was one Caroline had dreamed of when she'd read her mother's stash of Jane Austen novels. And now he seemed to indicate he considered her to be the prettier sister, not Lorraine. She'd even overheard Frank confess that he considered her older sister to be loveliest of all the girls in town. Caroline ran her fingers along her buttoned-up collar, which suddenly felt too tight.

Would Lorraine carry through with her threat that if Caroline wouldn't pick a suitor from the auction, she'd pick one for her?

"So someone sent you over here then?"

"Yes." He averted his gaze. The sun illuminated the red in his auburn hair, but his gray eyes were what caught her attention. They were so clear, and fathomless as the deepest of still waters.

Exhaling in a *whoosh*, Caroline gestured to the side of the building. "Let's go around to the bench and talk about this."

"Indeed."

He offered his arm to her. Caroline pulled back, surprised by the gesture. The last time she'd linked her arm with a man's had been when Frank and she walked down Main Street for a final good-bye before he was to leave for war. When the man kept his arm extended, she gently rested her fingers atop his flannel-covered arm. Beneath the cloth she felt the sinewy strength of his muscles. He led her toward the wrought iron bench, a gift shipped from back East to her mother years earlier. They sat, each at the corner of the seat, angled in toward one another.

"What's your name?" Would he have a dreadful last name that she'd have to take, if she caved in to Lorraine's wishes?

"My pardons. Barden Granville the—" He clamped his mouth shut.

"Are you ashamed to admit your profession?" What type of job was he not wanting to admit to? Or was it some characteristic? Barden the criminal? From what she'd seen of the "audition men" who were staying at the inn, a few seemed to be ne'er-do-wells.

Mr. Granville rubbed his hand over his chin. "I most recently have been working as a chef, well, as a cook rather, at an establishment in Kansas City."

"I see." She couldn't help smiling. This could be promising, if he really could cook. "Are you a sober man?"

His eyebrows rose. "Other than Eucharist wine, I don't partake."

"Good. And since you mention communion, I assume you are a Christian."

Eyelashes a tad too thick for a man closed over his pale eyes for a long moment, almost as though he was praying. "I am."

This man was too good to be true. But Caroline wasn't about to jump into a marriage with a complete stranger. Frank and she had grown up together—but he'd not made her stomach do the strange things it was doing now. Maybe it was the punch. She smoothed out some creases in her dress.

"I fear I've taken you by surprise, Mrs. Kane. Please accept my apologies for arriving after the auditions." His rich baritone voice warmed her.

Her sister must have coached this man in his lovely, but fake, British accent, knowing that would appeal to Caroline. But she'd find out. Give it time and the truth revealed itself. "You're here now, and we'll see what needs to be done."

"It has been my every intention to aid you in any conceivable way that I might." He nibbled his lower lip and frowned.

Was he lying about something?

"What exactly do you mean?"

"I spent some time working at the Freemans' place."

"With Mary and Uziah?" Such good people.

"Yes. They are well and send their greetings." When he grinned, an adorable dimple formed in one cheek.

She mustn't stare. "Well good. I haven't laid eyes on them in far too long."

"If I say so, myself, I've become a jolly good cook under their tutelage."

Who spoke like that? "How long have you been in America?"

"Not long."

That could be a good thing, because if he became homesick for British soil then Caroline could in good conscience send him packing. Something about him fascinated her and had her breath seemingly stuck in her throat.

"Fortunately the Freemans took me in when I came upon some misfortune."

Oh no, was this some kind of song and dance he did? Was Barden a swindler? But Mary and Uziah wouldn't have sent him on if he was.

"Both send their condolences as well." His voice dropped and held genuine sympathy.

Caroline blinked back unshed tears. "Well then."

Goodness, the ladies must have paid a pretty penny to even place an advertisement in Kansas City. For Mary and Uziah to have seen the ad for the auditions and thought of Caroline touched her. They must have thought highly of this man—if he was telling the truth. She'd send them a missive to find out. But she had her sisters and brothers to protect, too. She mustn't let her hammering heart direct her brain. "Let me tell you how this will work."

"Pray do." His lips twitched. From the way he sat erect at the end of the bench, Mr. Granville reminded her of one of those portraits of lords of the manor. But this wasn't his manor. This was her inn.

"How do you feel about sharing responsibility for my five siblings? Granted, they aren't young children, but they do yet require oversight."

His features tugged in puzzlement. "I will certainly pitch in. Mary didn't mention them."

"I would think that would be rather important in you making your decision." And why had he claimed to not be there for the auditions? Puzzling. But likely Joel had told him he was too late, and then her sister probably jumped on the chance to send Mr. Granville their way. How triumphant she must be feeling at this moment.

"It doesn't deter me in the slightest." He beamed in such an angelic way, she believed him.

"And there will be no decisions made until at least six weeks have passed." She wasn't about to jump into marriage with a stranger, even if he was handsome and spoke with an accent that sent thrills through her. Not even if he had clear gray eyes that one could disappear into. Not even if that dimple near his perfect lips was completely adorable. Not even if he might chase off the memories of her beloved Frank.

"That suits me fine, Mrs. Kane."

Mrs. Kane. The way he said her name, so stiffly, certainly didn't imply any lascivious intent, but she should make things clear. "You'll have a room on the top floor. You'll not reference yourself as anything other than our hired man."

She would not be made a laughing stock. She'd said she wouldn't audition a man for husband and she hadn't. *Then what do you call this?*

"Of course." His brows drew together, forming a line on his smooth brow.

He was taking things well. A good sign for a potential spouse. Perhaps there was hope after all. Frank hadn't been malleable at all. He'd always been the kind of boy who would do exactly what he wanted, when he wanted.

"I need the most help with dinner. Especially with all the men here in town for the auditions and the coach now stopping here more frequently."

"Glad to be of service, Mrs. Kane."

His voice was softer this time, and he leaned toward her.

How would *Mrs. Granville* sound on his lips? Her cheeks heated at the thought. "I could use a hand with the wood throughout the day, keeping the stove going, too."

"I am at your beck and call." He raised his hands as though in surrender and smiled in a slow, satisfied way, his eyelids slipping to half closed.

Caroline's heartbeat raced. No man had ever had this effect upon her, not even her husband. She stood and wiped at her skirt. "Follow me and I'll show you to your room."

Before he could respond, she turned on her heel and headed to the back entrance.

Lord, I don't know what You're up to, but it better be good.

Chapter 3

B arden followed Mrs. Kane's shapely form up narrow stairs for two flights, stopping at a dusty landing with cobweb-strewn windows at each end. "Don't the cleaning girls tidy up on this floor?" Nor on the other landings as far as he could see.

"Mrs. Reed isn't able to reach that high, nor is Mr. Woodson." She didn't offer to explain who Mrs. Reed or Mr. Woodson were.

Barden trailed her down the stuffy hall. First chance he had, he'd open the windows to let in fresh air.

A scream erupted from down the hall. "Give that back!" A chestnut-haired youth ran down the corridor toward them, clutching a stuffed rabbit and laughing.

"Stop!" Mrs. Kane expertly snatched the toy from the miscreant's hands.

"Pa gave me that!" A young lady dressed in a coffee-colored calico dress covered with a white ruffled pinafore, raced toward them, her light brown braid bobbing against her back. "I'm going to kill him if he does that again."

Barden stepped between the boy and girl. "No, you shan't. The Lord frowns upon murder."

The dark-haired youth came alongside Mrs. Kane. "You a preacher, mister?"

Before Barden could reply, his new employer shook her head. "No, Leonard. He's our new—"

"Did you get him at the auction, Sis?" The green-eyed young lady grinned up at Barden.

"No! And it wasn't an auction, Deanna. You make it sound like buying cattle." She made a motion as though swatting away a fly. "I'll talk to you all later about this."

Auctions, cattle, *getting* him—it all sounded rather Alice in Wonderlandish. And they even had a rabbit, albeit stuffed with sawdust.

"I'm Barden Granville, and I'll be responsible for dinner preparations here." He gave them what he hoped was a winning smile. "For the next six weeks at least."

Leonard scratched his cheek. "Where are you from, Bardy?"

He winced. His eldest brother, who would one day inherit Father's title, often teased him with that name. "I prefer to be called Barden, or if you must Americanize it, please call me Bard."

"Bard? That's what they called Shakespeare, ain't it, Sis?" Leonard tapped the side of his head. "I'm soon to be graduated, and some of Miss Green's teaching must have stuck."

"How about you all address me as Barden?" He checked with Mrs. Kane who gave him a noncommittal shrug.

Deanna rolled her eyes at her brother. "What town in England are you from, Barden? Are you from London?"

"Please, Deanna, let the poor man get settled. Leonard, go show him where the water pump is."

"Quite all right. I saw one."

"Good then." She opened the door to what was to be his room.

Dust covered almost every surface. "And I expect I shall require a great many trips up and down the stairs to put this room to rights."

From her shocked expression, he knew he'd been impertinent. If one of his servants had spoken to him in such a manner at home. . . "Please forgive my lack of manners."

"Since Pa died. . . I regret the deplorable condition of this room."

She was apologizing to him? To her new servant? Things certainly were different here in America.

Saturday night was their family meeting time, after the restaurant had closed for the evening. With the auditions over, the cleanup done, coping with all the guests, and introducing their new worker, the inn had been busy. Caroline and her siblings pushed the four middle tables together, grabbed their favorite chairs, and arranged them. Henry and Leonard had theirs close together and slumped into them. Virginia and Deanna chose seats far apart, and they began to arrange their skirts so they could sit.

Alvin still stood, solo, peering down at her. When had he gotten so tall? "You sure you trust that Englishman back there in the kitchen by himself?"

"Someone has to cover for us." Virginia shrugged. "With all these extra folks here."

Grimacing, Alvin slumped into his chair. "Luke's been helping out an awful lot. We ought to hire him on."

"I agree." Caroline sank onto her oak chair. "We have a lot more to discuss, too."

Deanna beamed. "Yes, like how Barden is handsomer than anyone around these parts."

"What about me?" Leonard feigned a slap across the table.

The fifteen-year-old swatted at the air near him. "You're my brother."

Caroline cleared her throat. "Before we discuss Mr. Granville. . ."

"He said to call him Barden." Deanna squared her shoulders.

"Yeah." Leonard lifted his chin.

"Told me that, too." Eighteen-year-old Virginia examined her fingernails.

Alvin simply grunted.

Was it really worth arguing over?

"Besides—don't you mean we'll discuss your future husband?" Virginia drawled. When she batted her eyelashes, the others laughed—except Caroline.

Deanna rested her head on her hands and sighed. "Mrs. Barden Granville has a nice ring to it."

"A ring." Henry slapped the table. "Is that a pun?"

"A good one." Leonard clapped.

Giggles erupted from the girls.

"A big gold ring with an English crest on it, I bet." Virginia's face took on a dreamy expression.

The sound of dishes clattering in the kitchen quieted them all.

Alvin groaned. "Wonder how many more this Barden fellow just broke?"

"He hasn't broken anything." Not yet. And especially not Caroline's heart. "Anyway, let's discuss the letter first."

Deanna scowled. "Why did Lorraine have it anyway?"

Good point. Caroline shook her head as she opened the missive. She hesitated, something niggling at her soul. "First, let's pray."

Although they all bowed their heads, she knew Henry would likely poke at Leonard, and Alvin wouldn't keep his eyes closed. Deanna likely wouldn't listen to the prayer. But God knew all these things. "Heavenly Father, we ask Your guidance as we discuss this letter from our"—did she refer to them as grandparents? She'd never even met them—"kin. May our hearts hear what You wish for us to know. Lord, guide us. We trust You and love You. In Jesus' name, amen."

Alvin had one eye pressed closed and the other fixed on her. "Just who are these kin?"

A lump formed in her throat. How would she manage if they all wanted to go? She'd be alone. She'd have no help. And Pa had wanted her to do right by her brothers and sisters. Wouldn't letting them go, if they wished, be disregarding Pa's wishes? "Our grandparents in Virginia."

Deanna's brown eyebrows rose to her bangs. "In Virginia?"

"Yes."

They all looked at one another before fixing their gazes on her. Alvin assumed an air of nonchalance, leaning one arm around his chair back.

Leonard shoved a hand through his dark hair. "We don't know them."

"This would be one way to do that." Caroline hoped her tone of voice conveyed a conviction she lacked.

"Pa hated them." Virginia may have spoken the truth, but it sounded so harsh coming from her pretty sister.

Caroline cringed. She didn't want to sugarcoat things, but. . . "Pa didn't exactly hate them. They'd cut off relations with Ma after she married Pa."

"He very much didn't like them then." Virginia's lips curled into a pout, as though she was challenging Caroline to refute that.

"Pa didn't like what they did. It hurt Ma real bad." How many times had Ma said she wished she could have contact with her family but she knew it would upset Pa? Too many times to count.

All at once her sisters and brothers began chattering on top of one another, and Caroline couldn't make out words other than the repetitive "Ma said" and "Pa said."

"Hush!"

"Do you want us to go?" Moisture pooled in her youngest sister's eyes.

"Of course not, Deanna. But some of you are getting to the age where you might want more than I. . .than life can give you here in Kansas."

Alvin muttered an oath.

"Alvin!"

"Sorry." The tone of his mumbled apology was anything but sorrowful.

"Let me read the letter to you. How about that?"

She surveyed the table as, one by one, they nodded in agreement. Alvin crossed his arms over his chest. The buttons strained. Not only was he getting taller but he was putting on more muscle. Soon he'd need to make decisions for himself about his future, regardless of where he lived.

Caroline opened the letter and read. When she'd finished reading, all sat in stunned silence.

Henry rocked slightly in his chair. Leonard tapped his index finger on the ging-ham-covered tabletop.

"They have a large home on the James River." A former plantation that they indicated was fairly intact because they'd been occupied by the Union army.

Virginia squared her shoulders. "Of course I'm too old to go. But are they going to put Deanna and the boys to work in the fields? I've read in *Ladies Home Newsletter* that some Southern women are doing that."

"Oh my!" Deanna's cheeks flushed pink. "Will we have to pick cotton?"

More protests went up. "I don't believe so." But she didn't know these people at all.

"But I'm almost out of school." Leonard scowled. "If they want to do anything for me they can send me to medical training."

The kitchen door squeaked.

"I don't want to go." Henry slapped his hand down on the table, so much like Pa used to do that Caroline could only stare at the boy. Truth be told, her youngest brother was her favorite. She didn't want him away either.

Barden wheeled Ma's coffee-service cart into the room. "What's a family gathering without some treats?"

"Yeah!" Henry clapped his hands.

"Why don't we ask Barden his opinion?" Virginia fluttered her eyelashes as she peered up at him.

"Got somethin' in your eye?" Leonard reached across to poke at Virginia, and she swatted him away.

Mr. Granville cleared his throat. "Ask my opinion about what?"

As he expertly poured Caroline her evening tea, she looked up at him. This was a family matter. But what if he was to become her husband? "It seems that my maternal grandparents have come forward to request my brothers and sisters. . ."

Virginia arched an eyebrow. "*Sister*, as in Deanna. I'm eighteen and have no need of grandparents to watch over me."

As he set the teacup down into its saucer, Barden leaned in close. "And what say you of this agenda?"

"She's agin it!" Henry affected a deep drawl and made a comical face. "*Agin* it, I say!"

The others laughed.

"I dare say, if you purport that she's against this dastardly plot, then why would you accept it?"

"I don't." Alvin rolled his eyes. "I'm enlisting in the army first chance I get."

"I'm not going anywhere." Virginia pointed at Caroline. "She's promised to send me to Normal School in Emporia to be a teacher."

"I did." Caroline muttered the words softly, although how she'd ever secure the funds she didn't know.

Barden pointed at the other three siblings in succession. "And how far away are said Grandmama and Grandpapa?"

"Over a thousand miles." Henry sank his head onto his hands. "I don't wanna go anyhow."

"Me, neither." Deanna wrinkled her nose. "I'm almost grown."

Barden set a tray of golden cookies on the table. "Mrs. Freeman's sugar cookies."

As he continued to pour tea, Caroline watched in amazement as her brothers and sisters dug into the cookies. Had Frank been there, he'd have insisted each person take a turn and discuss the pros and cons of the decision to be made. Yet here, in under five minutes, Barden had convinced her brothers and sisters to see things her way. Caroline blinked back tears.

Having another husband might not be so bad after all.

Chapter 4

W ho'd have thought the image of a man washing dishes could be so attractive? Caroline stood slicing potatoes at the work counter behind Barden, watching him. With a white linen towel casually draped over one shoulder, he stood erect, humming as he scoured dishes at the dry sink. Then he transferred those he'd washed to another tub and poured rinse water over them. His blue cotton shirt was tucked neatly into his work trousers, his leather belt shone from a recent polishing. Yesterday he'd brought in tightly woven cotton and linen toweling material purchased from Stevens Mercantile. Mr. Woodson had cut the rectangles and then Mae had sewn them up on the treadle machine she had at her house. They did look nice. But why was Barden trying to change everything?

Mr. Woodson whistled off-key as he carried a load of wood to the pile beside the stove. "Your older sister must be mighty bored to be fraternizin' with us workers again."

"Why is Lorraine here anyway?" Caroline always marveled at the older man's way of getting straight to the point.

Barden turned to face the workman. "We're grateful for the relief she offers us—Mrs. Kane in particular."

Mr. Woodson gaped, and Caroline could only blink. But, it was true that Caroline had been allowed to sleep in that day because of her older sister's presence.

Noisy footsteps announced Lorraine's return to the kitchen. "There's a dozen soldiers out there, Caroline!"

"Soldiers?"

Virginia rushed in, her cheeks flushed, her ebony hair trailing ringlets around her ivory neck. She fanned herself with her hand, eyes wide. "A passel of handsome army men are out there!"

"For the inn or the restaurant?" They had a business to run.

"They're on the move to Fort Mackinac." Lorraine squirreled a handkerchief from her apron pocket and dabbed at her forehead.

Caroline had never heard of this place. "Where is it they're going?"

Virginia batted at the air as if waving something away. "It's far away from here."

Raising his index finger, Barden interjected, "I believe I read about that fort in one of my *Beadle's*. We Brits took Mackinac back from the Americans in the War of 1812."

Mr. Woodson scowled at him. "Better watch yerself, young fella, my Pa served in that war."

Again, Virginia waved their comments away. "But there are a dozen soldiers out there, and all but the commander is single!"

Barden crossed his arms over his chest. "We just sent out your application for the Emporia Normal School. And letters asking for a teaching post that doesn't require additional training. Certainly, you don't entertain the notion that you'll be running off to a fort somewhere?"

Caroline gaped at the man. He'd taken the very words from her mouth, albeit spoken with a heavy British accent.

"Well they are here, and I've no position, do I?" Virginia scowled at them, her face settling back into its usual expression. But oh, what a delight to have seen her beautiful smile again even if for that moment.

Lorraine went to the stove and grabbed the coffee pot. "I'll be needing more coffee right away to keep up with them, if they're anything like our ranch hands."

"As I've offered before, madam, I'm completely at your disposal, if you ever need an extra pair of hands at the ranch."

Lorraine, Virginia, Mr. Woodson, and Caroline all stared at Barden as the room fell silent, save for the sound of the stove and its contents bubbling.

Barden dried his hands and removed the heavy canvas apron. "Let me handle this."

First he'd offered to run off to her sister's. Now he acted like he was the man of this place. She should have objected. Caroline should have insisted it was her duty as owner to ascertain the needs of the military passing through. Instead, she sank onto the stool by the counter and stared at the pitiful pile of potatoes. If a dozen soldiers supped with them tonight, she'd need her efforts multiplied like the fishes and the loaves. Mercifully, funds from the auditions' rental had replenished their coffers. After school the previous day, Henry and Leonard had toted home flour, sugar, coffee, bacon, and more from the mercantile.

Mae Reed entered through the back door, carrying with her the faint odor of liniment and spearmint. Her usual slow shuffle had improved to a steadier gait, with her back straighter, too. "Good morning! How're you all doing this fine morning? You sound well."

"Slept better than I have in a while, thanks to Barden's suggestion."

Caroline stiffened. Barden's list of *suggestions* for the inn and restaurant now topped fifty items. "And what was that?"

"He had me substitute chamomile tea for my evening coffee. That seemed to make a difference. Didn't wake up at all last night."

"Well, good. . ." What else could she say? It was wonderful news. If only his ever-lengthening list of ideas were good. Some were downright ridiculous. Number 20 was *Make the evening meal one of charm and grace;* 21—*bring in more candles to supplement the lamps;* 22—*set out tablecloths.* Caroline had snorted over that idea.

And who did he expect to launder all those table coverings?

Barden re-entered the kitchen, a soldier in a federal blue uniform trailing him. What in the world? Caroline pushed aside her potatoes and smoothed her apron, all the while fixing a glare on Barden that she hoped would convey her dissatisfaction with his behavior. Guests did not belong in the kitchen.

From the crimson blossoming on his cheeks, Barden evidently sensed her ire. The officer appeared nonplussed however. He held his hat tucked under his arm as he stepped forward and nodded curtly. "Captain John Mitchell, Company B, 43rd Regiment of Infantry, honored to make your acquaintance, ma'am."

His gaze settled on Mae, who looked up at him in expectation. "How many men do you have, Captain?"

"Fifty-seven total."

Caroline felt her eyes widen.

"Only twelve are being allowed to stay in town, though."

Although they could use the extra income, she, her family, and the staff were plum worn out from the influx of men for the audition. She exhaled a sigh of relief.

Barden lifted his chin and caught Caroline's eye. "The captain asked about baths for his men, and I believe we have a way to accommodate them."

"Those here will have fresh water, soap, and clean towels in their rooms."

The captain cleared his throat. "Mr. Granville thought all of my men might bathe."

The kitchen seemed to be getting as hot as her temper. "We have only one tub here at the inn."

Barden grinned. "Well, the saloon could be used, if Sheriff Ingram would allow us access."

Not a bad idea, if it wasn't one of so many brilliant notions the Englishman had. The tavern had at least two man-sized steel tubs in the back room and a stove as large as the inn's.

"I think you'd best ask our mayor, Abigail Melton, first."

Barden's smile wobbled. "I purchased the extra wood, already."

"Oh?" Another action he'd not discussed with her. He was beginning to remind her more of Frank and of the things he'd done that had irked her. Things she'd not thought of in the past two years.

"I was certain you'd not mind. It was, after all, needed and an act of Christian charity."

She wasn't running a charity but a business, but they'd have to have a discussion later.

Lorraine not so subtly eyed the captain. "The barber could help—he has a good-sized tub."

"Wonderful notion." The commander stroked his moustache, which looked in need of grooming.

Who'd heard of army men wanting a soak and scrub? "Don't your soldiers simply bathe in the river, Captain Mitchell?"

"Not all are able, ma'am. You see, while I have an infantry unit, most of my men are wounded, some severely."

"Oh." Caroline sank back onto the stool. "Injured, yet they are traveling to another fort?"

The man's ruddy complexion became redder still. "Yes, you see many wish to serve out their commission. The Michigan fort is a light duty fort where my men can recover from the war."

Embarrassed at having questioned the officer, Caroline's lips parted to apologize, but she couldn't manage what to say. She exchanged a glance with Barden. No wonder he'd immediately sought to do something to help the men. One thing she'd learned about him, right away, was his compassion for others. It was touching.

Barden winked at her and then waved toward her, Mae, and Mr. Woodson. "Captain Mitchell, I know I speak for all when I say we are quite happy to meet the needs of your men. Furthermore, tomorrow night you and your officers staying at the inn will be our first guests to experience our new evening dining menu. Suffice it to say, it shall be more suitable for the officers than what we normally offer. And we hope soon to provide this service to all our guests."

Caroline fixed a smile on her face. Had the cat gotten her tongue, wound it up like a ball of yarn, and then unrolled it to the next county over? Just when she'd been admiring his compassionate nature, Barden Granville dumps this surprise on her? *This will have to be nipped in the bud!*

Barden opened the back door of the restaurant for Mae then turned and called over his shoulder, "We'll be right back, Luke." As he escorted the widow to her home, he hummed an American Stephen Foster song one of the soldiers had earlier played on his banjo.

"That was one of my husband's favorite tunes, bless his soul." She carefully took the three wide steps up to her porch.

The two-story brick home featured a wraparound porch. Large mullioned windows fronted the house on either side, with a wide-paneled center door. Maybe Barden had gotten ahead of himself in suggesting they improve the evening meals both in substance and appearance. In the future, when he settled in his new church, would he be forced to ask matrons to share their household goods if there was a parish-wide event?

"Are you sure you feel comfortable with this, Mrs. Reed?"

"Of course, dear. My china and silver are sitting unused." She patted the side of her hair, twisted up and held in place with a large tortoise comb. "Using fine things makes a meal more special, don't you think?"

"I do." He rubbed his chin. "I thought my conversation went rather well with Mrs. Kane earlier, don't you?" He'd laid out all the reasons why the Tumble Inn might wish to spruce up not only its appearance but try to attract a more refined crowd.

Silence, other than the sound of a key turning in the lock, met his ears, much like Mrs. Kane's had earlier. Mrs. Reed tucked the large key back into her apron pocket and pushed open the door. Inside, the cozy parlor, on the left, looked like the place a cowboy would love to come home to. A sturdy velvet-covered chaise rested before a wall of books ensconced in a splendid walnut case. An overstuffed arm chair was matched by a stool, upon which a man might rest his feet after a long day rounding up cattle. A tea table held a silver tea service. He could picture his wife bringing in afternoon tea for him after a hard day on the trail. Why did that image suddenly include a lovely young woman whose caramel-colored hair begged him to bury his face in it every time she drew too near? He could picture a roaring fire glowing in the fireplace on a chill autumn night. Peyton Shiloh, the hero of one of his favorite dime novels, would surely applaud this parlor as perfect. It wouldn't be, though, without the American woman who'd begun to give him more reason to love America than any of his books had.

"Are you all right, Barden?" Mae crossed the hallway to another front-facing room. Barden followed her.

An oval cherrywood table was flanked at each end by shell-backed armchairs. Two matching armless chairs faced another pair across the table. Such furniture would only be found in a wealthy rancher's home. "What did you say your husband did?"

"He was a surgeon." She wiped something from her eyes and turned her back to him as she faced a glass-fronted hutch filled with plates, bowls, and saucers.

She began to remove some of the plates, but the deformity in her hands caused her to struggle.

"Let me help."

Soon they had three sets of complete china place settings. "I had my mother's china, mine, and my grandmother's. I was the only daughter. When we came to Kansas, we had this all packed and shipped. Nary a piece was broken."

Although not nearly as fine as those at the Cheatham Hall estate, the three patterns were of high quality. "They're lovely. Are you certain you wish to engage in this dining experiment with me at the inn?"

"I would flat out love to see these dishes get some use. Life is short, Barden. No use storing up our treasures here on earth. Like the Good Book says."

"Indeed." What earthly goods he had brought with him to America had been taken from him. But God had provided in most unusual ways.

"And I should tell you Caroline is a creature of habit. Not much for change. But she needs to do so if that inn is going to make it."

He had only a short time he could help. And Caroline hadn't yet mentioned when he'd be paid for his duties. "We'll get her off to a good start."

The petite woman's eyebrows wove together. "What do you mean *to a good start?*"

Perhaps it was wisest not to disclose when he must return to tend his flock. And he still wished to fulfill his goal. "Well, you see I really wished to experience the cowboy life before I settle down."

"Ah. . ." Her lower lip drooped. "So you would hop on a chance to work at a ranch if you had the opportunity?"

"I'm afraid so. As you said, life is short. This has been a lifelong dream of mine." He offered her what he hoped was a charming smile.

"Well I'm sure Mrs. Martinchek would be happy to have you provide relief help if you must fulfill your cowboy yearnings before. . ."

"Hello!" Caroline's older sister entered the house. "I could have sworn I heard my name just now."

"You did, dear. It seems Barden wishes to try cowboy life before settling down."

"Yes, before I assume my vocation, I wish to learn more about ranching."

Both women eyed him.

A smirk twitched at Mrs. Martinchek's lips. "Vocation? I've never heard it put that way."

He prayed they didn't question what his vocation was. That had been a deal between himself and God when he'd come on this journey. Not that the Lord made deals, but Barden had offered one. He'd not share he was a vicar, and when he returned to England, he'd be the best parish priest he could be. Oh but how he'd been tempted, though, to tell Caroline. *Lord, guide me.*

Chapter 5

Caroline crumpled Barden's note about the painting crew he'd hired and the cost incurred and then stuffed it into her pocket. Standing outside the inn and peering up, she'd have to agree. Yes, the paint was peeling. Yes, it needed to be done. But it seemed as soon as the Englishman tackled one idea, he'd moved on to the next.

Lord, this cannot be the kind of man You'd put me with. Leastwise on a permanent basis.

The new sheriff, a handsome man, rode by and tipped his hat at her. She offered him a tight smile. Abigail and he made a mighty fine-looking couple, even if those two were like she and Barden were—oil and water.

She wadded the note in her pocket into a tiny ball. If the auditions were ridiculous, then his fancying up the dinner was even more so. To allow their new cook, and her future husband, to sweep in and begin changing up things would have been something Pa would have put a stop to. But Pa wasn't here. Frank wasn't someone who had grand ideas. His one big idea had been serving in the Civil War. And he'd died before he could enlist. Poor Frank. But at least he'd been spared that horror.

Opening the front door to the restaurant, she went looking for Barden. He wasn't in the dining room, which had been swept, mopped, windows cleaned, walls scrubbed, and new tablecloths laid down. But no meal had been started yet and Mae was lying down, so she didn't wish to disturb her. Caroline wove through the kitchen. The back counter was covered with the new dishtowels, presumably over top the rolls they'd be eating that night.

"Barden's outside."

She exited the building. She needed to know what to have the boys and Deanna do when they arrived home from school.

She found Barden sitting at her mother's bench, head bent as though he was in deep thought. "What all do you have for tonight?"

"Oh! Yes. Looks like several of the soldiers are amputees, a few with sword wounds, two with minie balls still inside them. . ."

"No! I meant the meal." For someone whose primary purpose was to feed customers, Barden seemed awfully preoccupied with their life situation. "What are you serving them?"

"Oh." Barden grinned, sending a warmth through her. He stood and took her hand and her heart began beating harder. "I'd rather keep it a surprise."

She despised surprises. All of the surprises she'd had in her life had been hor-rid, up until now. She pulled her hand free. "Seriously. What are you feeding those soldiers?"

Cocking his head at her, Barden eyed her carefully. "You don't trust me to make a good decision, do you?"

Caroline placed her hands on her hips, the plaid material bunching there in a wave of turquoises and blues. "You're making many changes and decisions."

Barden laughed. "Well then, I'm making one now. Go up and rest milady, before your feast is served this evening."

Henry and Leonard walked up carrying a crate, each holding a loop of rope that extruded from each side.

Her soon-to-be-husband turned and held out his hand. "Stop right there, gen-tlemen. We don't want to have Caroline guessing my menu, now do we?"

A small cart pulled by a brown-and-white pony stopped in the alleyway. Deanna called out, "Come on, Caroline, I'm taking you for a ride!"

Barden gestured for her to go on. "Don't fret."

Why on earth she was caving in so easily to this Englishman's demands, Caro-line couldn't articulate. But she soon found herself in the cart with her dark-haired sister whisking her away.

"I'm to get you a new hair bow and I'm purchasing ribbons for myself and I would for Virginia, too, if she wasn't being such a fuss budget this morning."

"What do you mean?"

"She was ornery toward me. Said I was a little girl and she was a young woman and that she no longer wore ribbons in her hair nor did she wish for Barden to buy her anything."

"Barden?"

"Yes. He gave me some money to get us something." Deanna clucked her tongue at the pony to urge her on. "He was so sweet. Said he wished he could purchase us all a whole new wardrobe, but he couldn't."

A whole new wardrobe. Wouldn't that be something? Why would such a notion even cross his mind? Perhaps because he knew he brought nothing to the marriage. Caroline drew in a slow breath. She really should ask him more about himself. He'd said he'd grown up in England and had older brothers. His father did something for the government and his mother stayed at home, presumably taking care of the fam-ily. What kind of parents allowed their educated son to run off to America, though? Truth be told, with knowing Frank all his life, it hadn't been until they'd married that she really understood him better. And it would likely be the same with Barden. He'd tell her more when he was good and ready—like most men.

Three hours later, dressed in her best apricot-colored sateen church dress, Car-oline descended the stairs. Her hands brushed over the freshly waxed banisters, the scent of lemon oil still lingering in the air. Pa wouldn't have wanted Caroline to have continued in what he called her *widow's weeds*, and it was time to give them up regardless of convention.

Virginia's eyes glowed tonight. For the first time since her sweetheart had died, a year earlier, she'd changed out of solid dark clothing and into a floral-patterned dress of icy yellow, soft pinks, and cream. She led Caroline to a white cloth-covered table. Although most of the candleholders in the restaurant didn't match, the glowing candles added a festive light to the lamps that hung from holders on the walls.

Captain Mitchell stood, bowed from the waist, and pulled Caroline's chair from the table. The other two men attempted to rise. Lieutenant Andrews, she'd been told earlier, was missing one leg. The other man was weak from an ongoing sickness from the injuries he'd received in the war.

"Please, gentlemen, remain seated."

Both nodded as Mitchell helped her. Caroline accommodated for the stiff crinoline beneath her skirt as she settled into the chair.

"A great idea, ma'am, of fancyin' things up for the men." Andrews removed the cloth napkin from the table and spread it across his lap.

"It'll lift their spirits." The captain scanned the room, filled with men all attired in their uniforms, all clean and neat.

Caroline laughed. "I think it is already cheering me up, too."

Barden strode through the entrance from the kitchen, dressed in a close-fitting suit that she recognized as being one of Dr. Reed's. The dark wool jacket and matching trousers made him appear taller, and if possible even more handsome. He carried a massive silver platter covered with roast beef slices. Amazing how displaying it in that way made it appear so much more appealing. The beef ranged from a reddish rare to a fully browned well-done. Steam rose from the platter as he approached their table. "Madam, choose your slice."

Caroline pointed out a piece with just a hint of pink. "How on earth did you manage this?"

Captain Mitchell tapped the side of his temple. "Let's just say the mayor was a charming woman and that the tavern smells strongly of roast beef."

"That explains it!" She'd wondered why there'd been no scent of meat cooking.

Her sisters brought gravy boats into the room, while Henry and Leonard served rolls with crocks of fresh butter. Alvin carried around bowls of whipped potatoes.

"We're trying to offer our guests a lovely dinner but with a family feel." Barden smiled down at her. What would life with this man be like? Would he always be coming up with ideas?

Virginia lingered near one table in particular, and her brother, Alvin, at another. Her sister stared, in rapt attention, at a handsome private with dark wavy hair and a moustache. He resembled the sweetheart she'd lost in the war. Caroline averted her gaze. So many of their town men gone, never to return.

"I understand your brother, Alvin, wishes to enlist, Mrs. Kane." Captain Mitchell paused in slicing his almost-red rare piece of beef.

Caroline stifled the urge to gag. Somehow the image of the almost raw meat, a military captain, and the mention of her brother as a possible soldier contrived to make her feel ill. "Alvin is quite young, and he's of much help to us here."

Lieutenant Andrews swallowed the half roll he'd shoved into his mouth. "I reckon he's older'n I was when I enlisted."

"Older than David, too." Captain Mitchell gestured with Mrs. Reed's silver fork toward a smooth-faced boy huddled at the far end of a table, focused only on eating his food. "He's sixteen."

"Sixteen?" Caroline stiffened.

"He'll learn a lot at a fort like Mackinac—with all these seasoned veterans there."

She glanced at the corner table, where Luke Collins conversed with his fiancée. If there was another war, would young David suffer what her newest employee had? "What of his parents? His family?"

Andrews and Mitchell exchanged a brief glance before both shook their heads.

Best not to pursue that topic. Caroline shifted the conversation to the weather and travel, and soon they were discussing the difficulties of a cross-country trip. Alvin and Virginia continued to linger at their respective stops as the soldiers passed the potatoes themselves and poured their gravy.

When Barden strolled through the room, Caroline tugged at his elbow. As he bent near, she inhaled his spicy sandalwood scent. A little lightheaded, she managed to get out her request. "Can you please check on Virginia and Alvin? They're spending excessive time at those tables."

He nodded then straightened. After circling the room, he discreetly stopped to talk with each sibling, who then moved back to the kitchen.

"Have you ever been to Michigan, Mrs. Kane?" Captain Mitchell grabbed another roll and dipped it into his gravy.

"I've never lived outside of Kansas." Other than in her fantasies, where she lived in late eighteenth-century England surrounded by servants and in love with a man who was the epitome of gentlemanly courtliness. No wonder poor Frank Kane couldn't live up to her expectations.

"I hear it is a beautiful place where the fort is situated, but winters can be brutal."

"The lakes are as large as seas." Andrews lifted his chin, a dab of potatoes dotting his cheek. She resisted the urge to wipe it for him and touched her own face in the same spot hoping he'd take the hint. He didn't.

"But the straits around the island freeze in the winter—it's that cold!" Captain Mitchell feigned shivering.

"So you can walk to the mainland." The lieutenant, finally sensing something, wiped his face with his hand.

Mitchell frowned. "If you dare."

What did she dare do? Barden strode toward them, his eyes fixed on her, his smile doing something that launched butterflies in her stomach.

He touched her shoulder and leaned in. "Are you ready for coffee to be served?"

"Or tea?" She resisted the urge to cover his hand with hers. How could such a simple touch set her heart racing?

He grinned, a dimple appearing in one cheek.

"A shame there's no spirits served." Captain Mitchell scanned the room. Was he looking for a liquor cabinet? "The men prefer their beer or liquor."

"Shame there's none to be had." Andrews patted his chest, as though feeling for a bottle.

Caroline straightened in her chair. "Coffee or tea will go well with our dessert." Not that she knew what Mae and Barden had come up with, but there had been a tremendous amount of whipping cream, crumbling of stale cake, and a pan of pudding prepared, plus jars of jelly opened.

"It's a trifle." Barden beamed in apparent self-satisfaction.

Kitchen work wasn't trifling. It was hard. Bone wearying hard. "I beg to differ, as I viewed the results of that dessert preparation."

Captain Mitchell laughed. "I believe Mr. Granville means it's called *trifle*—a kind of English cake and custard concoction."

"Oh. What an unusual name for a dessert. Especially when the mess in the kitchen from preparing it was no trifling matter."

The men laughed, but she'd not meant to be funny. Caroline's cheeks heated. Barden withdrew his hand from her shoulder.

Mr. Woodson emerged from the kitchen, a huge glass punch bowl in his arms. From across the room she spied the pretty layers of white for the cake, red for the jelly, pale yellow for the custard pudding, all topped by a cloud of whipped cream.

The men clapped and a few whistled, making Caroline's ears ring. Someone suddenly strummed on a banjo.

Barden leaned back in, his face so close to hers, she could kiss him if she swiveled toward him. "Do you approve?" His murmur stirred a longing in her.

Did she approve of kissing in public? No, he couldn't read her mind. He meant the trifle. Caroline turned toward him, grasped the back of his neck, and pulled his face closer, choosing at the last minute to plant a kiss on his cheek.

"Thank you, Barden."

Hoots ensued. But the raucous laughter didn't surprise her as much as did Barden's reaction. For his face turned several shades paler as he hastily departed the room.

Oh no. Barden had seen that look before in the eyes of a young lady in one of the parish flocks he'd visited as a priest in training. When he'd gone to put his vestments away, in a backroom of the country church, the girl had popped out like a jack-in-the-box and grabbed him and kissed him before he could stop her. If the parish priest hadn't been only steps behind him, Barden could have been in a world of trouble. As it was, he returned to school and had been warned of the strange proclivity some young ladies had toward men of the cloth. But he wasn't in England. And he wasn't a vicar. Not yet.

Barden pressed his fingertips to where Caroline had kissed his cheek, leaving him wanting more yet knowing he'd be leaving soon. He had to lay his cards on the table, figuratively speaking. Although, look where that had literally gotten him last time he'd done so. Thank God for the Freemans, who'd sheltered him.

Leonard, Henry, and Mae had cleaned up almost all of the pots and pans and bowls and were starting on the soup bowls.

The kitchen door swung in and Caroline joined them, frowning. But when she looked beyond him, at the orderly kitchen, she beamed. "You all have done so well at getting things washed and cleaned."

Leonard tapped the pot he was drying. "Barden promised us a ride out to Lori's ranch if we did a bang-up job."

Barden drew closer to the youth and tapped his shoulder. "Which you did!"

"You promised what?" His employer's voice held a warning.

"Mrs. Martinchek said I was welcome to come out on my day off. . ."

"Day off? I don't get a day off." Caroline's scoff almost sounded like she was holding back tears.

His eyebrows tugged together. She was the owner and could choose whether she'd take a day to herself. "But I do receive time off, like the others. Do I not?"

Her mouth agape, Caroline cocked her head at him, reminding him of a beautiful canary from the hotel where he'd stayed in New York, upon arrival. "I suppose you do."

Now didn't seem like the time to ask about his wages. He clapped his hands. "There. Righto. It's settled then."

Her eyes took on a misty sheen. "I wish you'd ask me first."

He'd never been much on asking. Barden simply did and often paid for the consequences later. Not a very priestly trait, but it was how God had made him. Or perhaps his privileged upbringing had brought this about. "I. . .could start doing that." It might kill him, but he could try. Especially since he'd be answering to a board and to his superiors come autumn.

"I'll go with you all." Caroline's lips formed a perfect pout. "It's time I had a day off, too."

Mr. Woodson carried the empty trifle bowl into the kitchen. "Ya'll goin' somewhere?"

Mae took it and set it into the dishpan. "They're going out to the ranch tomorrow."

The handyman turned toward Caroline. "I'll hold down the fort, ma'am. No trouble at all, as long as Mae helps me."

"Sure thing." Mae beamed at Woodson and then winked at Barden. "If I were younger, I'd want to come out there myself and watch our very own Englishman on the ranch."

Their own? How would she and the others feel when he departed? Yet he, too, had begun to think of these people as his own. He'd felt more a part of these Turtle Springs residents than he had in all his life at Cheatham Hall. It was as though he'd finally gotten where he was supposed to be.

Home.

Chapter 6

Muffled voices from the hallway woke Barden. Alvin and Virginia's tones were an odd rush of excitement mixed with anger.

"Let's ask Barden if he'll put in a word for us." Virginia's voice was clearer now, as though she stood immediately outside his room.

The sharp rap on the door was clearly Alvin's, which was confirmed when he slipped into the room holding a lamp then closed the door behind him. "Sorry to disturb you."

"What is it?" Barden shifted onto his elbows as the iron-framed bed groaned in protest. "Anything wrong?"

In the lamplight, a dozen emotions flickered over the young man's angular face. "No."

"So you're accustomed to entering bedchambers uninvited?"

"No." Alvin ran his tongue over his lower lip. "I just wanted to ask before you and Caroline leave for the ranch."

"Which isn't for another hour or two."

"Yes, well. . ." Alvin shifted his weight side to side, reminding Barden of a pupil about to be disciplined by the headmaster.

"Out with it then."

"Virginia and I, we could use a day off, too, maybe even a couple of days to go visit some of the places that have teacher openings."

What a thoughtful brother. Although he hated to admit it, Barden would not have thought Alvin harbored much interest in anyone beside himself, which was entirely normal for a boy that age. "Commendable."

A strange smile tugged at Alvin's lips. "Someone has to look after her."

"Right you are. I'll put in a good word for you."

This time only unfettered glee lit Alvin's face. How long had it been since any of the Tumblestons had left Turtle Springs for an outing? "Thanks."

"At your service." Barden made a whisking motion with his hand. "Now be off, so I can get ready."

After Alvin left, Barden quickly dressed, stopped in at the kitchen for breakfast, tossed scraps to the two stray dogs in the alley, and washed up. Then he grabbed the coffee pot and carried it into the restaurant.

Barden caught Virginia's eye. Hard to believe such a lovely young lady had already lost her beau. Back in England, they had heard about America's warring upon itself, but he'd never imagined the toll in human lives it had taken. Truly shocking. Perhaps that was why she had such a great interest in the young soldier she stood near. "Why don't you sit for a moment, Miss Tumbleston, while I pour for our guests?"

The private jumped to his feet and pulled out a chair beside him. Virginia blushed but sat, arranging her skirts around her.

Alvin lingered by Captain Mitchell and his officers, seated at the center table, plates piled high with food.

Caroline's brother spoke with more animation than Barden had observed during the weeks prior, his broad hands punctuating his words. The officers nodded.

When Barden approached the table, they became silent. "Good day, gentlemen."

"Mornin', pardner." Andrews chuckled. "Hear you're going to be a ranch hand today."

"I reckon I'll try." Barden's attempt at a cowboy accent was dreadful.

Alvin rolled his eyes. "And I reckon I'll get back to the kitchen."

Andrews tapped his index finger on the oilcloth covered table. "We'll speak with you later, young man."

Alvin ducked his chin and headed off, his step rather bouncy as he went.

"Maybe we can help you out, too." Lieutenant Andrews held up his mug for a refill of coffee.

How were they helping Alvin? It wasn't his place to ask. "Oh how so?"

"We're not cowboys." Captain Mitchell chuckled. "But our sharpshooters can give you some training on firearms."

Barden stifled a laugh. "Very kind of you. But unnecessary."

"No, no, we insist." Lieutenant Andrews shoved an entire biscuit into his mouth.

Captain Mitchell tugged on his now neatly trimmed moustache. "You've treated us so well."

"Here's a tip—try to keep your behind in the saddle, too, when you're riding." Andrews laughed, sending biscuit crumbs onto the napkin covering his blue uniform.

"We'd like to help you with at least one cowboy skill." Mitchell was obviously used to having his commands obeyed.

"No use wasting your time." Barden glanced around, making sure no one was within ear shot, and bent in to whisper. "I'm a crack shot."

From their wild guffaws, they mustn't believe him. He waited a moment.

"Good one!" Mitchell offered his cup to Barden for a refill. "An Englishman who cooks and obviously is accustomed to being a servant. We'll be over in the green, if you'd like some target practice before you go."

Hands shaking, Barden finished pouring coffee and then left the room, wishing he could punch something.

In the kitchen, Caroline packed a small basket with jars of lemonade and ham biscuits. "Mr. Woodson is bringing the wagon around. Do you mind heading out early?"

He set the pot where it could be refilled and rubbed his forehead.

"Are you all right, Barden?"

"I don't know. But I am well, if that is what you mean."

Her features tugged, as though she was working something out that perplexed her.

"Are all employers so thoughtful as you are, Mrs. Kane?"

Her mouth gaped open but then she closed it again. "You're right. We did have an agreement. Six weeks."

What that had to do with cordiality, he didn't know. As those six weeks began to draw to an end, though, he couldn't imagine how hard it would be to tell her he was returning to England. But without a paycheck from her yet, and no word from Father's rancher friends, might he not be extending his stay? Unless he humbled himself and asked his father for the fare. "Well, I thank you for your thoughtfulness."

Before long, they were on their way to the ranch. He drove the rig, with Caroline nestled beside him. She remained quiet until they were just outside of town. Overhead, thick clouds bunched up, and their dove-gray underbellies cautioned him that they might have rain.

"Did you live in the countryside in England?" Caroline bunched a lace-trimmed handkerchief in her lap.

"Yes, I did. There were vast swaths of fields and forests and farmland."

"Sounds lovely."

Not as lovely as she was.

"Why did you leave? Did something bad happen?"

"Oh no, certainly not." But if he left America, something bad would happen to him—he'd be leaving Caroline behind.

"When you were living there, did you ever imagine what it would be like to be a mail-order groom?"

Barden began to laugh. What a notion! "Never!" Not that those men who'd just auditioned and found wives were to be mocked. He bit his tongue.

He took his eyes from the road to glance at her. Her face pinked up, making Caroline look even prettier, her lips inviting him to take his eyes fully from the road and kiss her. With that little copse of maple trees ahead, he could pull over to the side of the road, take her in his arms and. . .

"Barden?"

"Hmm?"

"But you did imagine that you would one day be married, didn't you?"

"Oh yes, of course." And to one of the feisty heroines in a Beadle's novel. An American woman. At least he was finally admitting the truth of his fantasies.

He'd mulled over the notion that he would marry whatever proper Englishwoman who'd accept life with the third son of a nobleman. He and his wife might, on occasion, be invited to visit Cheatham Hall. Some ladies might be satisfied with such an arrangement. And there was the one professor's daughter who'd told him plainly that if his brothers both died and produced no heirs, then Barden would inherit and she'd be interested in being courted. His face flushed at the recollection. How a properly brought up young woman, the daughter of a religion professor, could make so light of his brothers' lives had repulsed him. He'd never spoken with her again.

Caroline sighed. "Marriage wasn't quite like I thought it would be."

He slowed the pair of bays as they crossed a deep rut. Caroline clutched the side of the seat.

As they emerged from the depression in the road, she sighed. "I'd known Frank all my life, but I didn't really know him—if that makes any sense."

With regret, Barden contemplated his valet, Sinclair, who'd asked to come with him to America. Barden had been so taken aback. Perhaps he should have known that the man, whom he'd known all his life, and who'd fed his interest in American fiction, albeit of a questionable quality, would want to go to America. "I know I let someone down, who I'd known since I was a child. I truly hadn't known his wishes. And I wasn't in a position to fulfill them." Perhaps if he'd been more thoughtful, more considerate of other's needs, then perchance he'd have realized and could have better planned.

"Frank didn't get the chance to fulfill any of his wishes. He wanted to go off and fight in the war, but he died of a terrible fever before he could enlist."

"But he had married you. That wish was met. God gave him that."

Soft sobs were accompanied by sniffs. He wanted to pull over and wrap his arms around her and comfort Caroline.

"God...has taken my mother, my husband..." She hiccupped. "Then He took Pa."

Barden exhaled a big puff of air. "I don't know why that happened, Caroline. But I do know that regardless, He loves you. He loved them."

"Doesn't...feel like it."

Barden passed the reins into one hand and pulled his handkerchief out from his vest pocket and pressed it into her hands. "I believe God knows all things. He loves us all. We are in a war with darkness. God knows the devil's plans. He'll take us to the heavenly realms when our life on earth no longer is the place for us to be. We're here but an infinitesimal time, compared to His eternity. We have to trust that God knows why and when we must join Him in glory."

Caroline sniffed then gently blew her nose. "My father used to read us a passage that talked about God sparing us further difficulties that we couldn't bear up under."

"Yes, I believe that's in Isaiah."

Drawing in a shuddering breath, Caroline met his eyes. "I guess I just thought once Mama died, that I'd already done without enough."

Throwing all caution aside, Barden wrapped an arm around her and pulled her closer, kissing the top of her head. "I'm sorry you've gone through this, Caroline. I truly am. And I pray that the Lord will bless the rest of your life in abundance."

He was surprised when she didn't resist but leaned toward him, as though this was the most natural thing in the world.

And it surely felt like it was. He could hold her like this forever, drawing in the sweet scent of lemon soap mixed with vanilla and sugar. Barden couldn't help smiling. This rush of emotions, of wanting to protect her, yet at the same time wanting to kiss her silly had his senses roiling. Could he bring her back with him to the parish? Was there some way they could be together?

Pulling away from him, and looking up with wide eyes, Caroline exhaled a loud breath. "I think we best continue on."

"At your service." Barden kept Caroline close by his side, not wanting to release her, until he needed the use of both hands to steer the horses toward the turn to the Martinchek ranch.

When they got there, Joel jogged out from the barn to greet them. He assisted Caroline down and she rewarded him with a peck on his cheek.

He waved for one of the men to move the wagon. "Water the horses, too, while you're at it."

"Yes, sir!" The blond man saluted Martinchek then turned and winked at the rancher's wife, who had joined Caroline.

When Mrs. Martinchek scowled at the ranch hand, Barden felt a check in his spirit.

Caroline muttered under her breath, "Scotty better watch himself."

So she sensed it, too.

Barden jumped down onto the hard-packed earth and handed off the reins to the cocky cowboy, who wasn't quite as tall as him, but with a thick neck and muscles bulging his plaid cotton shirt.

Barden, wearing his only clean pair of trousers, a vest, and a broadcloth shirt probably didn't look as out of place on the ranch as he felt. But standing next to this ranch hand, he felt the fraud he was. Had he arrived in his clerical attire, or even in his casual clothing from home, he'd have appeared as foreign as he felt. But would he not, then, have been genuine?

Scotty directed the horses to pull the wagon to the side of the barn.

Beyond him, in fenced pastures that extended for acres, cattle munched on grass. In the barn loft, a ranch hand forked hay down below while others, outside, hauled buckets full of water to the troughs. Barden inhaled the fresh scent of the hay, longing to run and join them. This was the sole reason for his jaunt across the ocean. But at every turn he'd been frustrated. Why, Lord? And what had happened with Caroline back there? Something between them had shifted, had deepened into a friendship he didn't want to abandon. But he'd spent a lifetime awaiting this chance.

If he couldn't find a cowboy experience in Turtle Springs, perhaps his godfather or his father's friends, who ranched in a small cow town many hours south, would finally reply to his telegram. Perhaps before he left, he'd visit there, despite his father's wrath, which would surely be invoked if he ever heard.

Several massive dogs burst from the barn and headed straight at the wagon. Joel whistled, but the dogs ignored their master. Barden stepped between Caroline and the animals as he assessed the situation. The oncoming dogs ranged from a yipping beagle to a wolfhound who might weigh more than Barden did.

"Jojo, stop!" Still the rancher's command had no effect.

When Barden perceived all three wagging their tails, he rummaged in his vest pocket for one of the treats he offered the stray dogs back at the inn. All three stopped and sat at his feet, reminding him so much of a hound pack after a hunt. After rubbing each of their heads, Barden divvied up the hard biscuit amongst the trio.

"Well played, old chap." Martinchek's attempt at a British accent was almost as dreadful as Barden's fake drawl. "I hear you've adopted several of Turtle Springs' strays."

"Even the least of God's creatures deserves some care."

"As one of the church deacons, I'd agree." The rancher jerked his thumb toward the hands, several sitting atop a fence rail. "Just don't be speaking too much of that around them. I don't like them thinking about what happens to all those cattle we drive to auction."

"I understand. And, Deacon Martinchek, I'm continuing to pray for the pastor." Especially since the inn's gossip was circulating that Reverend Smith might be retiring after he'd suffered his recent injury. At home, they'd send a supply minister if the vicar was ill or must travel. But apparently not in this part of America.

Joel looped his thumbs into his waistband. "The boys have been wanting to have a little fun. Do a shooting match. Are you up to it?"

Between the army officers and now this rancher, men were pushing for him to prove his mettle with a gun. Granted, such a skill was necessary with the number of rustlers around.

"I'd welcome the opportunity." If given the proper equipment.

"Well then, let's get our crew out here."

Caroline and Lorraine stood behind the row of men. "I can't believe Joel would allow Barden to humiliate himself like this."

"He wouldn't." Her sister patted the side of her flaxen hair, upswept, with a dozen ringlets dangling from her neck.

"What do you mean?"

"I trust my husband. He's not that kind of man. I think he knows exactly what he's doing."

Had her sister gone plum loco over her husband? Lorraine certainly wanted to be alone with Joel. She'd had Caroline and their siblings out to the ranch only a handful of times since the wedding. From the corner of her eye, Caroline watched Lorraine surreptitiously pull at the waistband of her robin's-egg blue skirt.

"Joel is the best rancher in these parts." Too bad he couldn't see what a dolt Scotty was.

"Do you even know what Barden did before he came to Turtle Springs?"

"He worked at Mary's place for a while."

"She sent me a letter. Someone has been looking for Barden. A big man. English, and older, but she wrote that he had meaty fists like a boxer."

Uziah Freeman had boxed for a while to earn his living before they'd bought the restaurant.

"You still have Pa's rifle in the kitchen, don't you?"

Caroline's heartbeat hammered in her chest as the men loaded their guns.

Lorraine removed a small pistol from her skirt pocket and handed it to Caroline. "Some of the men who've come to town have turned out to be criminals."

"Not Barden. If anything, he sounds more like a. . ."

"A what?" Lorraine's lips turned downward in irritation.

"A preacher."

Her sister laughed. "A fine looking man like that? I think not."

Joel took aim at a line of cans and began to fire. Caroline flinched as her brother-in-law shot repeatedly, knocking over three of the seven cans.

"Gotta do better'n that, boss!" Scotty ambled across the yard and set up more cans.

When he returned, he shoved his broad hand through hair that matched Lorraine's color, and he winked up at her. "Watch this ladies!"

Didn't Joel even care how the man acted toward his wife?

Five of the seven cans went down.

When Scotty laughed and began to jog toward the hay bales, Barden called out. "I say, old chap, have you got something smaller?"

Lorraine frowned. "Smaller?"

Barden glanced in her direction. "Some small potatoes, perhaps?"

"What?" Caroline cocked her head.

Within minutes, Lorraine had retrieved potatoes from the root cellar and Scotty had set them up, mocking Barden as he placed them on the haystacks.

Both Caroline and Lorraine sat on the edge of the wooden bench as Barden began to fire.

Every tiny potato had been struck.

Joel strafed his hand along his neck. "Maybe our mayor should have hired you for sheriff."

"Sheriff Ingram got here first," Lorraine called out.

She turned to Caroline. "You better find out more about him and what he's up to."

Yes, she had better.

"I think you'd make a right fine cowboy, and if Caroline ever cuts you loose from the Tumble Inn, you'd be welcome over here, Granville!" Joel clapped Barden's shoulder.

"Splendid!"

"As long as you can ride like you shoot."

Chapter 7

The kitchen gleamed, all the supper dishes had been put away, and the Tumbleston siblings had gone to the Town Green to listen to some of the soldiers play banjo and some of the other instruments they had.

Barden wiped his hands on one of the towels and rehung it from its wooden bar. "I'm heading out, Mae." Not to listen to the delightful American music be played, but to practice a Western style of riding.

The older woman reached for the bottle of Dr. Williams's Best Liniment, one the Granville's butler swore by. "I think this is helping me. Thank you for having the mercantile order it."

"No trouble at all. Just glad it is helping."

"Between this awful smelling stuff and the chamomile tea, I feel better. Maybe not as good as you young people, but much better than I had been."

He grinned and grabbed his hat from the wall peg. "I'm strolling down to the stables."

Mae cast him a sideways glance. "You don't need to prove anything to those rowdy cowboys out at Martincheks'. From what I've heard, your shooting skills had them swallowing their tongues."

Laughing, Barden nodded at her and took his leave. Outside, the sun was climbing into the periwinkle-blue sky. Forevermore, when he thought of Kansas, he'd think of Caroline Kane, her hair the color of the wheat that grew back home, and the beautiful clear skies. And he'd never forget the people. Already, he'd begun to think of them as his flock. He chuckled as he rounded the side of the inn. Luke Collins sat peeling potatoes, his bad leg supported by him sitting sideways on the bench.

"Good job old fellow. You keep us in eats, don't you?"

The man's shaggy hair flopped down over his eyes. He squinted up. "Sometimes it feels like all I ever do is peel potatoes."

Barden discerned a check in his spirit. "You're spending half your days at the farm with the Stevens boys. And taking good care of Chardy."

From Luke's thoughtful expression, Barden addressed the right things. Although he was in a hurry to go ride and learn the proper Western seat on a horse, this man needed him more. He sat down at the end of the bench and turned toward Collins.

The former soldier exhaled a long puff of air. "Sometimes I still struggle over my..." He gestured toward his injured leg.

Barden ran his hand over his raspy jawline. With all the work in the kitchen, he'd not taken time for shaving, and he certainly didn't have a valet to assist, like at home.

"Sometimes we need our...friend—" He was this man's friend, wasn't he? "We need our friends to remind us of things of the eternal. Don't you think?"

"I reckon so."

"Do you think less of Mae because of the limitations her earthly body has?"

Collins dropped the potato and knife into the pan. "No."

"And I've never heard you tell her she ought to be doing more than she's doing. Am I right?"

"Right."

"If we're to treat others as we'd wish to be treated ourselves, why would you not treat yourself with kindness?"

His lips pulled in. "Good point."

How Barden wanted to pray with this man. Right here. Right now. But something held him in check. He'd pray for him as he walked. He rose. "Sometimes we're hardest on ourselves."

"True." The new part-time hire resumed his work. "Can't say I'll ever learn to love peeling potatoes, though!"

As Barden headed down the alleyway he heard Luke whistling. He recognized the tune as "The Ship that Never Returned." Prickles coursed up his arms and to his neck. He paused and listened, trying to remember some of the words to the new song. Was his ship fated to never return? He looked upward to the sky as clouds bundled between the sun and earth, dimming the light. Shaking off foreboding, Barden strode on toward the stables.

As he walked down the boardwalk, he paused to greet some of the inn's customers, giving each an encouraging word. At this rate he'd never get his riding time in.

"This is what I made you for."

Barden stopped and glanced around but didn't see anyone who could have spoken to him. A trio of ranch hands rode in, one lifting his hat and the other two nodding in what he could only think of as a respectful acknowledgment. He nodded in return, immediately recognizing it as the curt gesture he'd seen so many times at seminary among his professors. Not the slow nod of respectful acknowledgment. But it was too late now.

Ahead, by the saloon, Melissa Lee and Alan Henderson stood glaring at one another.

The couple was supposed to be married soon. They'd been coming into the restaurant regularly for lunch and always loved to chat with him. The Lees owned a prosperous farm out near the Martinchek's ranch. None of the Lee men returned from the war, and Mrs. Lee had died shortly before Barden had arrived, apparently of the same fever that had brought about Mr. Tumbleston's demise.

Mr. Henderson seemed embarrassed that he'd been one of the men who'd auditioned for a bride. But Miss Lee had always reassured him. Never had they seemed angry, as they did now.

"Miss Lee, Mr. Henderson, what's wrong?"

"It's him!" Melissa Lee poked a finger in Alan Henderson's chest.

Henderson captured her hand in his. "It's you and your fool way of thinking!"

A dray rolled down the street and paused to turn.

"Why don't we go inside, out of the street?"

"Here?" Miss Lee frowned and looked up at the sagging saloon sign.

Barden fished around in his pocket and opened the door. "We've permission to use it while the army is in town. And they are still here."

He grinned and pointed across to where one of the privates was opening a banjo case.

"All right then." Miss Lee followed him in, trailed by her fiancé.

Henderson gawked at the gaudy interior. "Well don't that beat all? Never seen nothing like this where I come from."

"I should hope not, Alan! A God-fearing man wouldn't be found in a place like this."

"We're here now, aren't we?" Henderson gave his sweetheart a cheeky grin.

Miss Lee crossed her arms over her chest. "That's exactly what I mean. You are always making light of everything I say!"

"Everything? I didn't just now."

Barden shook his head and gestured for them to sit in heavy oak chairs nearby at what looked like a gaming table. "All right, how about I ask you a few questions that I believe are basic to any marriage?"

The couple exchanged a long glance.

"What do you say, Melissa?" Henderson raised the pretty brunette's fingers to his lips and kissed them.

She giggled. "Your moustache tickles. But yes, I agree."

"All right then."

"Tell me what you think a God-ordained marriage looks like?"

"God ordained?" Henderson squared his shoulders.

"Yes, for if he's not in your marriage you surely shall have hard times ahead."

Miss Lee tilted her head, a light brown curl trailing down her neck. "I believe in God. And I love Him."

"Me, too." Henderson brushed his fingertips along his cheek. "But I hadn't really thought about what He means in our marriage."

"We go to church regularly." Miss Lee locked eyes with her betrothed.

"Anyone could go into a church." Leaning into the table, Barden steepled his fingers together. "It's what happens in the rest of your life, including in a marriage, which matters."

Henderson's lips pressed into a thin line. "My ma and pa said the same thing."

"Well, they were right, weren't they?" Barden squirmed. If he remained much longer he'd never get a chance to ride.

"How about we go for a ride together out into the countryside and let's talk about this." They could do that while he practiced his Western seat in the saddle skills.

The two exchanged a glance. "Can't we just keep talking right here?"

Lord, if You needed me in this capacity, You could have kept me in England. Yet He hadn't.

"Indeed. Why not?"

She shouldn't have followed him, but Caroline couldn't resist. The Englishman had shown up in her dreams again last night, this time offering her a lush red rose bouquet and begging her to marry him. She shook her head at the remembrance. Especially since with his gun slinging skills and someone pursuing him, she needed to know more.

Sheriff Ingram lifted his hat as she approached. "Anything wrong, Mrs. Kane?"

Nothing he could fix. It wasn't illegal to steal someone's heart without their consent. "No, thank you."

He was always friendly to her. Poor man had been inundated with females vying for his attention.

"You sure you're all right, Mrs. Kane?"

She needed to find out if Lorraine had spoken with the sheriff about her suspicions. But if she lingered, she'd lose sight of Barden. "Fine. See you!" With that she lifted her skirts, stepped from the boardwalk, and after waiting an interminable time for a slow carriage to pass, crossed the street.

Instead of heading to the stables, where he'd said he was going, Barden had stopped to chat with Melissa Lee and Alan Henderson by the saloon.

Keeping close to the shops, she peered through the mercantile's window. With the money from the suitors and from the army, the inn could afford to buy a few things. What was Virginia doing in there? She should be cleaning her room. Her sister bent over a black leather trunk with brass fittings. Poor thing didn't even have a cedar chest. Maybe a trunk like that did make more sense. Especially if she ever did get a teaching position. Which she didn't currently have. *"Never hurts to look"* Mama used to say, and Caroline refrained from entering the store.

On the drive back home, the previous day, Barden regaled Caroline with the multitude of reasons that Virginia and Alvin should have a day off. And for them to go scouting out teaching positions for in the autumn. Truth be told, Caroline had been so flustered by the news of someone pursuing Barden and by his shooting skills, to focus very well. He had her more confused than she'd ever been in all her years.

Drawing in a breath of cool late-morning air, Caroline continued down the boardwalk. But Barden and her friend were out of sight. She continued on, hoping she'd find them. As she neared the saloon, she heard Melissa's voice raised in anger.

"You do so!"

"I don't." Alan's gruff voice was adamant.

A softer voice interrupted them but she couldn't make out the words. It had to be Barden. She smiled in satisfaction and, glancing around, went around to the side door, opened it, and went in. Carefully she maneuvered behind the elaborate black Chinese fan, located just beside the long bar.

The voices became louder and clearer as she crept closer.

"I think you just want to marry me because of the farm."

"That's part of it."

"See!" Melissa sounded almost hysterical.

Caroline resisted the urge to charge in and try to help.

"Wait," Barden interrupted. "Let's try establishing a few imperatives for a God-ordained marriage."

What kind of outlaw talked like that? Caroline stiffened. He'd spoken the same way to her. Surely no gunslinging criminal would speak in such a way, would he?

"All right." Melissa sniffed.

"Fine by me."

"Good. First, you have to have committed this upcoming marriage to the Lord. Did you do that?" Barden's deep voice held an authority that she'd not heard before, and she stiffened.

"Of course."

"Not sure what you mean. If we get married won't God bless that?" Alan sounded like such a typical man, which tickled her.

Barden's chuckle matched her own suppressed laugh. Yet even though she knew it was silly to think God would simply bless a union because you stood before a preacher, she'd not sought out God's approval of hers and Barden's upcoming nuptials. Nor had they even spoken of it. Hadn't she been dead set against this whole notion of advertising for a groom, anyways?

"The Almighty wants to be in on everything. Especially in a marriage." Chills coursed down Caroline's arms and she rubbed them.

"I reckon I'd not pondered that much."

"Well you should." Melissa's shrill voice promised another argument.

"Please, you two; yes, you should both seek God's will instead of rushing into a union simply for the sake of having a spouse." Barden sounded remarkably like her father, when he was in one of his sermon moods. But unlike Pa, she decided to not tune Barden out.

"He's not getting just a wife, Mr. Granville, he's getting a farm too."

"How does that factor into your decision, Alan?"

"Well, I ain't gonna lie. . .it sure don't hurt." Again, his practical, matter-of-fact, response had Caroline holding back a laugh.

"Well, I never!" Melissa huffed.

"It also don't hurt that she's the purtiest gal I've ever laid eyes on."

Caroline peered between the cut-outs on the elaborately carved screen. She spied Alan leaning in to kiss Melissa's cheek, while her pretty friend leaned away from him.

Although she couldn't hear Barden's sigh, she could imagine him doing so. "Those aren't requirements for a marriage. When you enter into holy matrimony you must consider if your love will last through the bad, maybe even the worst, life has to bring."

Barden sounded like he really meant this. He sounded awfully much like a. . . preacher, like he had the previous day. Caroline sucked in a breath.

"Well, I reckon I'd want to marry Melissa and protect her even if she lost that lovely figure of hers and if her pretty face got covered in wrinkles. Preacher, I do know that she's gonna get old one day, just like me. I ain't dumb, even if I am a cowpoke."

Preacher. Alan had called him preacher.

"And I'd still marry Alan if all his beautiful hair fell out." Melissa raised a hand to her mouth and chuckled. "Well, maybe not."

For a moment there was silence. Caroline moved closer. Alan's loud laughter carried and was joined by the other two's.

"Perhaps the Lord had a reason for sending me here." Barden lowered his head.

"So you really are a priest?" Melissa gasped.

"Don't that mean you can't marry?"

"I'm an Anglican priest. The Church of England allows marriage."

A minister? A crack shot, being tracked down by someone, who'd turned their inn upside down improving it.

Caroline rubbed her head and turned on her heel. There was no way she was going to be able to sort this out by herself. God was going to have to help. Tears of frustration coursed down her cheeks.

Nothing made sense anymore.

Chapter 8

Sleep had come in fits and starts for Barden. Caroline had barely spoken to him that previous evening. He awoke early and began his morning in prayer, all the while disturbed in his spirit.

Downstairs, he stopped first in the restaurant, which was empty of all the soldiers, as the others went on into the kitchen. Besides the military and the two traveling Tumblestons, something else was absent. Laughter. That was what was missing. Neither Virginia's new-found bright laughter nor Alvin's booming voice carried through the room.

Caroline emerged from the kitchen, tugging at her apron with one hand and carrying a pot of coffee in the other. "Well, Virginia and Alvin set off bright and early. I hope you're happy now."

"Happy?" Indeed, he'd been much happier in America.

"Well, you got your way, didn't you? You wanted them to have time away."

"Caroline, surely you don't begrudge your sister a chance to pursue her dreams?"

When her eyes welled with tears, Barden gently took her hand and led her back through the kitchen, the air heavy with the scent of dough rising, biscuits baking, and coffee brewing. Luke grinned up at them as Barden pulled her out the back door. He led her to the bench.

The bright blue sky, dotted with puffs of thin clouds, contrasted with his apprehensive mood. But he'd not let Caroline see that. She dabbed at her eyes with her apron and sat down.

"I don't want to lose Virginia, too."

"I know you don't." Barden squeezed her hand. "But Caroline, your sister is eighteen years old. She's a young woman, and God is directing her path toward teaching."

"And she can't teach here. Not unless Birdy marries Drew."

"Right. She had a wonderful teacher with Miss Green, but there is no position at this time." There had been no clergy position in Kent, mainly because Father wanted him far away. He flinched at the memory of learning that fact from the local bishop. Well, right now, he couldn't be much farther away. "Miss Green left her a pamphlet about a teacher training and job fair in Emporia."

"Really?" Caroline frowned. "She hasn't said anything to me about it."

355

Barden exhaled a puff of air. "Perhaps she was waiting until after Leonard's graduation next week, and the army's departure, to make plans."

She sighed. "With all those army men here, Alvin can talk of nothing else. What will I do if he insists on enlisting?"

"You'll pray. And continue to speak with him about his decisions."

"Father's words fell on deaf ears. If anything, when I caution Alvin, he wants military life even more."

"Either he's going through the normal rebellion of youth or perhaps he, too, is called to the vocation."

"How can you say that?"

"Some men are meant to protect."

"And to abandon their families? Their loved ones?" Caroline narrowed her eyes. Why was she so angry with him?

She plucked at her cotton apron, forming little folds in the fabric. "At least Luke came back. Why don't you and he go fishing today?"

Why did he sense she wanted him away from her? He stood and feigned removing a hat, then bowed from the waist. "At your service, madam."

If Henry and Leonard behaved like this all summer, maybe she would send them to their grandparents after all. Ever since they'd called out, "We're home!" the two had been at each other in the kitchen.

Mr. Woodson grabbed a wooden spoon from Mae and aimed it at Henry and Leonard. "I can't abide by fractious children, so stop all that bickerin'!"

"It ain't fair that Luke and Barden got to go fishin' when I'm the best around." Henry scowled.

Caroline stopped slicing carrots. "You'll practically be living down at the creek the rest of the summer."

Mae cast her a sympathetic look.

Caroline took the spoon from Mr. Woodson and handed it back to Mae. "Henry and Leonard, we're sending you on errands, and if you're still arguing when you get back then you'll each get to chop wood."

If there was anything the boys hated worse than the kitchen, it was chopping wood, stacking it, and bringing it in. They quieted. Then she gave them each a list. "If you fill your list successfully, then you may go fishing."

"Hurrah!" The two boys raced out the door.

Now with Mae, Mr. Woodson, and Deanna, the large kitchen became hushed.

"Tea, anyone?" Caroline went to the tea tin and opened it. Amazing how she'd come to enjoy the beverage so much since Barden had arrived.

Woodson looked up from paring some carrots and shook his head.

Mae smiled from where she sat kneading bread. "I had mine after we finished cleaning up from lunch."

The clink of a large spoon against the side of a crockery bowl accompanied Deanna's, "Yes, please."

A tray of cookie dough circles, ready to be placed in the oven, bore evidence to Deanna's productivity that afternoon.

"You've certainly earned it." Caroline smiled at Deanna, who averted her gaze. "I've never seen you work so hard."

Suddenly her younger sister burst into tears and then ran outside.

"Better go after her." Mae cast Caroline a sympathetic look.

She found Deanna seated on the bench, head bent over, sobbing into her uplifted apron.

"What's wrong?"

Deanna sniffed, and lifted her face. "They. . .aren't. . ."

"Who?"

"Virginia. . .Alvin." A shuddering sigh shook Deanna's shoulders.

"They aren't what?"

"Coming back." Deanna resumed sobbing.

"What do you mean?"

"They're not coming back here!"

Caroline stiffened. "What do you mean? They're only gone until tomorrow night."

Deanna shook her head hard and then closed her eyes, tears streaming down her face.

Grabbing her sister's arm, Caroline gently squeezed. "Deanna, tell me what you're talking about."

"Army."

"The soldiers left."

Her sister nodded vigorously. "With them."

"Virginia and Alvin went with the army. I knew that, but it's because they were all traveling in the same direction."

"No!"

Dizziness suddenly blurred Caroline's vision as understanding dawned on her. "They intend to go with the army then—to the fort?"

"Alvin is joining the army." Deanna fished a handkerchief out and blew her nose. "I don't know what Virginia intends."

Oh dear. Anger and concern pummeled each other for her attention. "Our sister off with all those men? How could they do that?"

"I'm—not sure the captain knows." Deanna wiped her cheeks with her hand. "I should have told you earlier, but Virginia told me not to. She called me a baby and said I spoil all her plans, but you know I don't!"

"It's all right. It's good you told me." Caroline stood, heart hammering. "We've got to go after them."

"I don't know about that. They may hate you if you drag them back here."

Caroline crossed her arms. "Why do you say that?"

"They just want their own lives, Sis, not what Pa wanted for them. Or what you want. Which is basically just what Pa said to do."

What about my heavenly Father? What would He say? Barden was beginning to rub off on her.

"Let's find Barden and ask him to ride after them with Joel and some of his men."

"What if they won't come?" Deanna brushed her tears away.

"We'll have to leave that to Barden and the men to help decide." And to God.

The long ride back, alone, gave Barden new respect for men who spent most of their days in a saddle. But he had nothing to complain about. He'd tried, and he'd failed. But Barden did have a peace about it. Not that he'd blame Caroline for being furious. And hurt. And a multitude of other emotions. Those two siblings had manipulated Barden and lied to Caroline. At least they'd apologized for those two sins. Lorraine, on the other hand, justified her actions, stating that she was the eldest sibling and should be making family decisions.

Sheriff Ingram rode up to him as Barden neared town. "Just you?"

"Afraid so."

"Abigail has been consoling Caroline all afternoon."

"Thank the mayor for me."

"What happened?"

"Those two think they are sufficiently grown up, and apparently the army agrees." And their eldest sister. Barden ached from head to toe, but mostly he hurt for what this would do to Caroline.

Ingram exhaled loudly. "That boy has been talking of nothing else but soldiering since I met him after arriving in town."

Barden gave a curt laugh. "Mrs. Martinchek signed off for him."

"Did Joel know?"

"Nope." Barden was beginning to sound like a Yank.

"And Virginia?"

"She's offered a teaching position at the fort. And she has a young private besotted with her."

"Sure was good to see that girl smiling these past few days. Wasn't sure she could crack a grin." Sheriff Ingram's eyebrows knit together. "Abigail has been concerned for her."

"Keep us all in your prayers." Us. He had begun to see himself as a part of the Tumbleston family.

"You know it." He wheeled his horse around and accompanied Barden back to the inn, the horses' hooves producing the only sounds.

Town was closed up for the night, with a few shop proprietors straggling home. The two men split at the alley beside the inn. Barden would take the horse back to the stables after he'd spoken with Caroline. He directed the mare to the trough, dismounted, and tied her to the hitching rail. After taking a few steps onto the boardwalk, he paused at the inn's front door. He surveyed the property and then scanned the street before entering the building, which held the lingering scent of roast pork. His stomach rumbled.

One couple sat at the table in the middle of the room. Birdy Green and her suitor, Drew Cooper. Wouldn't that be something if the two married, leaving the town in need of a teacher after Virginia had already departed? Barden nodded to the couple as he passed. He rubbed his neck.

Woodson lingered between the kitchen and stairs, worry lines clouding his brow. "Caroline is upstairs. Mae brought her up some more chamomile tea."

Deanna rushed out of the kitchen. She looked at Barden and then beyond. "Where are Virginia and Alvin?"

He shook his head. "Would you kindly request your sister's presence?"

How many stories had this old bench heard? Caroline ran her hand over the dark metal scrollwork, cool to her touch. Barden's handsome face held regret, concern, and something else.

"Thank God my brother and sister are all right." When a tabby cat chased a mouse down the alley, she flinched. "I can't believe they left like that."

"A thousand pardons."

"It's not your fault, Barden." His explanation of what had happened assured her that he'd done all in his power to convince Virginia and Alvin to return, as had the two notes he'd carried with him.

"I wonder, though, why you thought I'd have encouraged such behavior, Caroline?" He rubbed his thumb over the soft flesh of her wrist, distracting her from her sorrow and disappointment. "Not even giving you a fare-thee-well." His brow crinkled, and he frowned, leaning forward, elbow on knee.

"For one thing, what you said about following God's will. And that perhaps this was what was right for them."

He straightened. "The other reason?"

"I. . .I heard you with Melissa and Alan yesterday." She nibbled her lower lip.

He frowned. She turned to face him, her skirt pressing against his knees.

Barden's eyes darkened, and he leaned toward her, a look of longing coloring his face. How she wished he'd take her in his arms and comfort her.

"I don't see how you could have heard us. We were at the old tavern."

"I snooped." A brave expression fought with her tears as she lifted her chin. "I heard you telling them to have God direct their path, and I wondered if you'd told Virginia and Alvin the same thing."

He grasped her hands, his warm and work chafed. "I'll admit, I may have in one of our conversations."

Caroline tried to tug her hands free, but when he resisted her disengagement she relaxed. "But what if that isn't what's best for them?"

"When wouldn't God's will be best?"

"They're young. They probably don't even know what is best. My father wanted us all together. He wanted me to keep this inn going and to take care of them."

He released her hands and moved closer. She needed his comfort. Never had she felt so forlorn, so distressed.

⨋

Barden pulled Caroline into his arms, the softness and warmth of her surging protective desires through him. He tucked her head beneath his chin and patted her back, feeling her ribs beneath the threadbare cloth. She needed more. So much more than he could offer. It was already the middle of June and he would need to depart within a month. How could he leave her now that he loved her so?

"What did you say, Barden?" Caroline pulled back and looked up at him.

Had he uttered the words aloud that groaned in his soul?

He pressed his lips to hers. Yes, he loved her. But he had nothing to offer her. Somehow with her sweet kiss it didn't seem to matter. Barden embraced her and held nothing back as he covered her mouth, her soft cheeks, and her neck with kisses. The scent of sugar and vanilla mixed with floral undertones as he pressed his face into her upswept mass of caramel hair. The silky sensation exceeded his wildest imaginations. When he kissed her again, she returned the kiss with fervor and he pulled her closer.

Trying to catch his breath and still his battering heart Barden pulled away. "We must stop."

Caroline blinked up at him, her lips swollen, her breath ragged. She pressed a hand to her bodice.

"I'd never imagined a preacher could kiss like that."

There. She'd reminded him. Had God used Caroline to convict him of the promise he'd already made to the church? "Caroline. . ."

She pressed a finger to his lips. "Don't say anything right now."

Chapter 9

C aroline couldn't repress the smile tugging at her lips all morning. Barden had whispered he loved her. And the thrill of his kisses had traveled clear down to her laced-up boots. She unlocked the front door of the restaurant, opened the gingham curtains. The window panes sparkled thanks to Barden's and the boys' efforts. Without Virginia there, she now had to make sure the restaurant was ready to receive diners in the morning. With only ten inn guests upstairs, it should be a fairly slow morning. *God, please watch over Virginia and Alvin.* And may the Lord help her forgive the way they departed.

After tying back the last curtain, she strained to look out at the street, where a trio of men rode into town. Peculiar how they seemed to lift slightly from their saddles. That was the same manner in which Barden rode. Unease dribbled through her like hot sorghum syrup on pancakes, especially when one of the men pointed toward the inn.

Caroline hurried to the back and called to Deanna. "I think we have customers."

Mae looked up from cracking eggs into a bowl. "We'll be ready. Barden has the coffee going and the biscuits are baked."

Barden swiveled away from the stove and winked at her, sending her heart skittering down some happy lane where she longed to go. "Deanna will be down in a moment, she had some distress with her ribbons."

"Probably slept with them in her hair again." Tugging at her apron until it was perfectly straight and the ruffles aligned, Caroline headed back out to the restaurant as the front door swung in.

The first two men removed their tan dusters and handed them to the third man, who carried them back out the door. *Odd.*

"May I help you?"

The taller of the two men, with silvery mutton-chop whiskers, turned to the other man, whose round face was cleanly shaven. "Let's partake of breakfast first, eh, before seeking out the lad?"

The man's British accent was thicker than Barden's yet also crisper, as if this was a man used to being in command.

"Capital idea."

Caroline gestured toward the center table. No guests from upstairs had yet come down. "You have the place to yourselves, gentlemen."

"Jolly good." He didn't look jolly at all, as a frown formed between his white eyebrows.

"What are you serving, this morn, madam?" The round-faced man's ruddy cheeks sported a hint of missed whiskers, a sign of haphazard shaving.

"Fried potatoes, ham, scrambled eggs, and biscuits with gravy." Pretty much the same every day. "And coffee."

"Tea?"

"Yes." Only since Barden had come.

"Marvelous. We'll start with a pot of tea and take all the rest of the breakfast offerings."

The third, and younger man, reentered the building. The two dusters now appeared a shade lighter in color so he must have beaten the dust from them and from his own jacket, which he'd removed. He hung each one on a peg and wiped his hands. He turned toward her. "Do you have a water closet on this floor, miss?"

"Water closet? Oh, we do have a wash bowl, soap, and water in that room beneath the stairs." She pointed to the back.

"Much obliged." Although his response was a typical cowboy thank you, the man's intonation was a more guttural version of Barden's accent.

Caroline gestured toward the younger man as he headed back. "Will he be joining you?"

"Jonathan will want his own table." The dark-haired man pointed to the far wall. "And a newspaper if you've one handy."

"Last week's *Kansas Collective* is here."

The older gentleman arched an eyebrow. "That'll do."

"Will he want tea?" She thought she should ask. But what kind of cowboys ordered tea? Thick black coffee was their lifeblood.

"Indeed, and plenty of sugar."

"I'll have everything out shortly."

A niggling feeling continued in her stomach as Caroline headed to the kitchen where Mae, Mr. Woodson, and Leonard were working. "Where's Barden?"

Leonard gestured out back.

Deanna walked in, her hair covered in some kind of turban. It wasn't worth asking about.

"Deanna, I need three breakfast plates brought out, please."

After grabbing a tray, Caroline placed the sugar bowl, three cups, three small plates, and a basket of biscuits atop. She took one of the butter crocks and set a knife on it, then retrieved utensils and napkins.

"Coffee?" Mr. Woodson held the pot aloft.

"No, I'll need tea—make enough for three men."

Mae's eyes widened. "Who are they?"

"They're English but they look like ranchers."

The back door opened, and Barden carried in a basketful of wood for the stove.

Her heart skipped a beat as her lips burned with the memory of his previous night's kiss. Barden's eyes locked on hers, and his cheeks reddened. He'd said he loved her. And if thinking of him all the time, dreaming about him, and feeling like her world had turned upside down was love, then she, too, loved him—but this was such a different kind of love than she'd had with Frank. She was falling in love with her own fiancé. Except he'd never actually spoken to her about marriage—only the future. Were these Englishmen here about Barden?

"You all right, Mrs. Kane?"

Mrs. Kane, *not* Caroline. But when he smiled at her, her heart wobbled in her chest.

Everyone returned to their work. Barden patted his vest pocket. "I almost forgot; I have a letter that Mrs. Freeman sent for you."

"I've got to serve these men and I'll be right back." She didn't want to stay, afraid of what Barden might tell her. But there were many British ranchers in the West. "They're Englishmen."

"Oh?" His voice sounded strained. "Did you catch their names?"

"No. They seem much more interested in their food."

"Ah. Very good." But his auburn brows drew together, and he turned away from her.

As Caroline carried the heavy tray out to the table, her unease built. First she served the two men at the table.

"We're strangers in town, as I imagine you've discerned." The younger of the two men opened his napkin and laid it across his lap.

She couldn't help the smile that tugged at her lips. "I figured as much."

"We're looking for my godson." The older man's voice took on a formal tone. "Barden Granville IV, the son of our good friend, Lord Cheatham."

Thank goodness her tray had been considerably lightened or the tremor in her hands would have toppled everything onto the men.

What they said didn't make sense. Why did Barden have a different last name from his father? Was he an illegitimate son? Was he hiding in America? If so, why would these two men be seeking him out?

"Uncle Drayton!" Barden called out from behind her.

Caroline turned and set the tray on the adjacent table.

"Good to see you, old chap."

When the men didn't rise, Barden bent and hugged Mr. Drayton, and then straightened and shook hands with the other man. Caroline headed over to check on the third guest.

"Sorry it took so long, old chap, but we're here now." Uncle Drayton leaned back in his chair and gestured to the seat adjacent him. "Have a sit down."

Barden raised his hands. "I'm afraid I can't. I've work to do."

The two men exchanged a glance and Chesterfield guffawed. "You've taken over a Church of England parish here, then lad?"

"That's a good one." Drayton laughed.

Not a bad idea, now that they mentioned it. The nondenominational church he attended with Caroline was shepherded by a frail, elderly minister. And the reverend had recently confided that he wished to return back East. "No. I am employed here at the inn."

"Here?" Drayton pressed a hand to his chest.

The younger man, in the corner, glanced their way as Caroline left his table, her shoulders stiff. What had his uncle's valet told her? Hopefully he maintained the same level of discretion as he did in England. But Barden had changed since leaving. What he used to think of as proper or refined seemed superfluous and a way of avoiding dealing with feelings. On the other hand, the gentleman cowboy he'd read of in his dime novels seemed scarcer than a farthing in these parts.

"We received some news from your father just before we left." Drayton steepled his fingers together. "Seems you are to be an uncle soon."

"Excellent." Barden could imagine the delight his brother would have. Granted, the future Lord Cheatham's happiness would be tenfold if his wife produced an heir.

"But Peter"—Lord Chesterfield's pronunciation, like Barden's own, drew out his brother's name and omitted the *r* sound, unlike the Americans did—"has taken ill with a cough."

Uncle Drayton waved a hand dismissively, but the tension in his features belied his casual gesture. "Don't worry yourself. You're going home. You'll see him soon."

"And Father?" The physician had said it would be only a matter of time before his heart condition worsened.

The two men exchanged glances.

"See what you make of the missive he sent." Chesterfield was as pragmatic as ever.

"Must have had his valet write it. Cheatham's handwriting always was atrocious."

Barden's voice stuck in his throat. "Was he too ill to write it himself?" Too weak?

"Apparently he was too distressed about his missing son to write the letter." Drayton's tone held a bite of accusation.

"Maybe I am the Prodigal Son after all." Shame brought heat to Barden's face. He swiped a hand across his cheek.

"Tut-tut. We've sent a transatlantic cable to London to be delivered to him." Chesterfield tapped his thick fingers atop the table. The last time Barden had seen the man, he'd been dressed for dinner in his finest attire, the table covered with layers of starched linen tablecloths, all the silver on display, the crystal gleaming, and the early eighteenth-century French china shining at his country estate.

"If it gets through." Which Barden doubted.

Chesterfield lifted his double chin. "There have been vast improvements now, and by all reports, this attempt at the telegraph cable is expected to succeed."

"Regardless, we've also dispatched a letter to him. And we indicated we'd get you home posthaste." Had Drayton's long, thin nose always seemed raised so high?

Barden splayed his hands. "I'm not ready to leave." He loved his father, but he'd been preparing him for years to be an independent thinker and to always weigh matters. "Did he request my presence at home?"

"No," Drayton grudgingly admitted. "He seemed more bent on getting some word from you."

Uncle Drayton opened a small leather bag that hung from his neck by rawhide. How incongruous to see this man, the son of a peer, dressed not in silks and ready for the *ton*, but with skin dark as rawhide, attired in a cotton shirt and dungarees—granted, they were perfectly tailored to his build and he still sported a white cravat at his neck instead of a handkerchief. "Here you go." He passed Barden the envelope.

Barden recognized the handwriting immediately, and he exhaled in relief. "This is Mother's script."

"Not in the habit of corresponding with her, I dare say." His father's friend raised his bushy eyebrows high.

Barden jabbed at the bottom of the page. Unlike the rest of her handwriting, Mother's signature was, as usual, indecipherable, and next to it she'd carefully written Father's name. "She probably asked Father to write you and when he refused, she took it upon herself to do so. Which means he wasn't expecting to hear anything from me until I arrived back in England to assume the vicarage."

"Mother's intuition, my boy." Chesterfield had a half-dozen sons, four of whom had traveled with him to America.

"Indeed." Drayton had left his wife across the ocean, as well as his children.

Chesterfield's eyes gleamed. "So. Will you rush home to England?"

Trying not to eavesdrop, Caroline sought to focus on Jonathan, presumably their servant. But she couldn't help watching the others from the corner. Bits and pieces of her British novels flew at her. An aristocrat often went by the name of his estate but would have a different surname. So perhaps that was Barden's father's case. Which meant that Barden was the son of a British nobleman.

"You all right, miss?" The young man cocked his head at her. "You look like you've witnessed something skilamalink."

She blinked at him.

"Sorry, miss. You look like you can't believe your eyes. I think that's the expression." Jonathan was a handsome man, and his grin might have sent flutters through someone else, but in her current state, she simply wanted to collapse out of view and cover her face with her apron.

But she couldn't waste this chance to find out more about Barden and these strangers. "I'm fine. I—I forgot to bring the gravy."

He laughed as he slathered butter on his biscuit and reached for the strawberry preserves. "Don't bother yourself, miss. That'd be like butter upon bacon."

"So sorry, I don't have bacon today, simply ham."

Again he chuckled. "I meant no need for gravy for me; this is fine."

Barden tilted his head toward them and paused in his conversation. Was that her imagination or did his narrowed eyes look jealous? She patted the curl that trailed over her shoulder. She leaned in closer. "What brings you gentlemen out to Turtle Springs?"

"Bringing money to old Bardy to get him home again."

From Barden's table, she caught the words of the one gentleman asking if Barden would be going there, which reaffirmed this man's words. Dizziness washed over her, but Caroline forced herself to keep breathing.

"You sure you're all right, miss?"

She positioned her back to Barden, who had not only concealed his background but that he planned only to swoop in here, steal her heart, and then run back to England. All with not so much as a fare-thee-well—just like he'd accused her siblings of doing.

"What's that, miss? Fare-thee-well?"

Now she was even picking up Barden's recent habit of talking under his breath. She poured a cup of tea for him, her hands trembling. "Oh sorry, I meant he'll need a fare as well, won't he? On a ship."

Jonathan gave her a sharp look. "I'm not openin' my sauce-box about all that."

"Sauce box?"

He pointed to his mouth. "Not my place to comment, even if Lord Cheatham is a right old. . ." He glanced toward the others. "Cheatham ain't like them at all. They're what you call *real gents.*"

Jonathan shoved half a biscuit in his mouth, and Caroline retreated to the kitchen.

She grabbed the Freemans' missive from the counter and then strode out the back and around to the side of the inn, to Mama's bench. She sank onto it, arranging her skirts around her. Unfolding the light tan paper, she read Mary's flowing script.

Caroline, how we miss you, girl! God bless you for all you done for us. And we pray Barden has brought the help your father thought you'd need after he died. I'm sorry we took so long findin someone. We got busy and plum forgot about your father's request to place the ad for him. But when Barden came to us, we thought God had provided. So we sent him on. We're sorry he can't stay too long with you, but we pray he's been of help this summer.

The letter fell into her lap. *He can't stay too long.* This was all a misunderstanding. She pressed her fingers to her lips. That kiss was no misunderstanding. Those kisses had been full of passion that had bespoke marital commitment. Heat singed her cheeks at the recollection. He'd just been toying with her affections.

And soon he'd be gone. Back to his father.

Chapter 10

Tears streamed down Caroline's face, unimpeded, as she strode through the grassy field to the cemetery. If Pa was here, she'd tell him all about it. She would have talked with Mae, but the older woman seemed so taken with Barden. Huffing out a sigh, Caroline wondered how Alvin and Virginia were doing, on their way to Fort Mackinac. Barden had come into their lives and had shaken things up. But Lorraine had been trying to do that for so long that it was as if Barden had simply taken over her job. No—it wasn't like that. She sniffed. And she knew Lorraine meant well, in her own meddling way.

Caroline strode to her father's grave and sank onto her knees. *This is so hard. I was just getting used to the notion that I might be able to run the inn by myself.*

"You have never been alone." That assurance came from God. Her earthly father may be gone, but her heavenly Father still remained.

God, I don't know what to do with all these feelings. She let out a sob that grew into a moan. She had not grieved her father, but with the upcoming loss of Barden, who'd not been a husband candidate after all, the dam burst loose inside her. Bending over, she raised her apron to her eyes and caught the tears that should have been shed months ago. *You left me. You left us. You, Frank, and Ma are gone.* Caroline glanced at her parents' headstone, and then beyond, several rows, to Frank's.

Birdsong carried from nearby willow stands. Their cheerful tweets and warbles seemed so at odds with the painful stuttering of her heart. *Why me, God? Why this pain?*

Because she'd finally opened herself up to real love. Not a safe love—one that her friend, her husband, had sought to leave almost as soon as they were wed. He'd confessed as much during his fevered state.

She sniffed.

Real love means wanting what was best for the other person.

Barden was a priest. He'd said so. Which meant he had a flock to tend to in England. She swiped her eyes with her sleeve.

Caroline fished her handkerchief out of her pocket. Anger burned within her. How dare Barden make her fall in love with him? Tears began anew. Now she was really becoming ridiculous. She hiccupped a laugh at herself as she walked back to the inn.

How she wished to go back to her room and have a good long rest. Caroline rubbed the side of her aching head. Both Leonard and Deanna had sat in her bedroom with her into the late hours, sharing how they missed Pa, and now Virginia and Alvin. They'd launched into a reverie about Frank and about Ma, too. When they'd begun discussing whether they should reconsider their grandparents' offer of a train ticket, Caroline had finally sent them off to bed. She'd told them, "If I let you two travel across country you'd both kill each other before you ever arrived."

The two, for some reason, could not resist teasing one another, poking one another, and in general bedeviling one another's lives. Yet they were still grieving, like she was. And they rose each morning to help, instead of running off to the creek or to a friend's home, or a quilting bee. Tears pricked her eyes. They were a blessing, and she was failing them. If only she could rest. Then she'd think more clearly.

When she reached the inn, she walked around to the alley and entered through the back door.

Mae looked up from where she was transferring strawberry jam from a large crock into smaller dishes. "The evening coach should arrive soon."

The quilts atop Caroline's bed seemed to be calling for her to return.

"What is on the lunch menu today?" Barden joined them and stood at the counter, drying glasses as Mr. Woodson washed and rinsed them.

"Whatever Deanna and Henry cook," she retorted. Barden would be leaving soon. The others needed to get used to cooking again.

Mrs. Reed chuckled. "I've yet to see them prepare an entire meal."

Eying the pot of leftover beans and the biscuits nearby, Caroline shrugged. "They can throw some ham on the stove and serve that with the beans."

Auburn eyebrows inched upward as Barden blinked at her. "Surely you don't intend to inflict that slop upon your guests."

Planting her hands on her navy-calico-covered hips, Caroline stared at him. She was too weary to argue. "You have any better ideas? Because I'm going upstairs for a lie down."

"You do that, dear." Mae nodded at her. "You look worn to the bone."

When tears threatened to spill, Caroline swiveled on her heel and headed to the stairs.

Leonard, stirring the mashed potatoes, chewed on his lower lip and frowned. "Sis never naps this long."

A niggling sensation began in Barden's spirit. "I sent Deanna up several minutes ago to check on her."

"Dinner's gonna get cold." Henry lifted the cover and peeked into the pan of pork chops Barden had fried.

Father's friends and their servant had chosen to rest and had gone up to nap earlier.

Deanna, face flushed, bounded into the kitchen. "She's not waking up."

"What do you mean?" Barden narrowed his eyes at Deanna. "Couldn't you rouse her?"

"Well I wasn't about to go slapping her awake or anything."

"Nor would I wish you to do so."

Mrs. Reed removed her checkered apron. "Let me go check. You all go ahead, sit down and eat your supper."

"I'm coming, too." Barden followed her.

Mrs. Reed grabbed one of the stairway lamps and held it aloft. When they reached the upper level, Barden heard footsteps thundering up. He turned to see pools of lamplight illuminating the stair treads as Henry and Leonard pounded up to the landing.

Mrs. Reed scowled. "Well if she was asleep and just resting, she'll certainly be awake now!"

"Sorry," the two mumbled.

The older woman rolled her eyes, slowly swiveled around, and went to Caroline's door. She held the lamp aloft. Even from this distance, Barden could see that her long hair was damp with fevered perspiration. Mrs. Reed pressed her hand to Caroline's brow. "Caroline, do you hear me?"

There was no response.

The boys elbowed past Barden, whose breath seemed to have been sucked out of him.

"Get the doctor." Leonard barked the order at his younger brother, and Barden flinched.

Henry went to the door. "We ain't waiting."

Leonard wiped a tear from his eye as his younger brother departed. "Sorry. I shouldn't have yelled."

"It's all right. You've been through a lot. Too much." Mae gave the boy a quick hug. "I'll get some cool water and make up a willow bark tea while you get Doc."

"I'll stay." Barden pulled the lone chair in the room closer to the bedside as Mae lit another lamp and set it on the side table.

"I'll wait with, Sis." Leonard placed his hand possessively on the chairback.

"No, it's my pleasure." Not quite a pleasure but not a duty either. The only thing Caroline and he had connecting them was a nascent love still burgeoning. But oh how that love was beginning to flame.

Mrs. Reed paused in the doorway. "This is just how Frank died, poor dear. And there was nothing Caroline could do for him."

A sick feeling swelled in his gut as Barden bent over the bed and Leonard slunk into the chair.

"Water?" Caroline's raspy voice jarred Barden awake.

How long ago had he nodded off since he'd displaced Leonard in the chair? He rose, his legs stiff from being bent in place so long. "Coming."

He adjusted the lamp's wick higher, the light illuminating Caroline's hair, strewn across her pillow like strands of molten gold.

"Water."

Lifting the blue-and-white pitcher, his hands shook. He poured a matching cup half full then set it and the carafe down on the bedside table. "Let me help you sit up first."

Gently he lifted Caroline's head, which still burned with fever. He gathered the pillows, plumped them, and then placed them beneath her shoulders.

"Thank you." Her voice was low and strained.

"You are most welcome." He grabbed the water and pressed it into her hands. She wrapped both around the cup before raising it to her lips. Sweat glistened on her beautiful face.

"What time is it?"

He pulled out his pocket watch, which he still had set at Greenwich Time. Calculating the difference from that and what the locals in this town used, he arrived at a number. "About two in the morning."

Caroline handed him the cup and pushed her head back into the pillows. "When will you go?"

"Go?"

"Home."

He took her hand in his. Hot and limp, she barely squeezed his fingers in return. "I don't know."

She shuddered out a sigh. "Sorry."

"For what?"

"I thought. . ."

"I'm sorry, too. I didn't realize, but I should have." He'd walked right in upon the auditions of the town women. She'd not participated in the event. "And I should have told you why I'd come to America."

"Cowboy?"

"Yes." He leaned in and kissed her forehead. "You need to get well, so we can make a proper cowgirl of you."

"Indian maiden."

"Ah, those are some of my favorite stories, but you are entirely too fair for that."

"Cowboy preacher?"

Not a bad idea.

In the stupor she fought against, Caroline could barely manage to speak. "Love you." Barden's parishioners would love him regardless of whether he showed up in clerical garb or in cowboy clothes with a lasso.

"I love you, too." He pressed a kiss to her hand. It felt so good to have him with her.

"They need you." Barden had people waiting on his return.

"I need you more." His raspy voice seared something inside her.

"Go." She had to let him go and fulfill his promise.

"Go get Deanna and the boys?" Through her half-opened eyes she saw him frown. "Please don't leave us, my love."

"No." She couldn't be alone. Not with the way she felt. This tugging, this pulling of something carrying her like an ocean drawing her out into a hot sea. "Don't. . .leave me."

"I won't." Barden sat down next to her on the bed, gently pressing his lips to her cheek.

"You're never alone." The words were spoken into her heart. Caroline sensed the presence of others in the room, but she couldn't see them, although she knew they beckoned her on.

I want to stay. Let me stay for Barden.

Barden's footfall rumbled down the stairs even louder than the boys' had done coming up the night before. He rushed into the kitchen. "Her fever has broken!"

He swept Mrs. Reed into his arms and twirled the woman around.

Mr. Woodson stopped stirring the potatoes he was frying in the skillet. "Glory be!"

Deanna rushed into his arms just as Barden released Mrs. Reed.

"You really love Caroline, don't you?" Deanna's eyes took on the dreamy gaze he'd often seen in females enthralled with the notion of romance.

"Yes, I care deeply for your sister."

"And I can tell she loves you, too."

She did. He knew it in his very being. "I believe so."

"So when ya gonna get hitched then?"

"Hitched? You mean married?" He lowered his head. *What are Your plans, Lord?*

"Ain't that what you came here to Turtle Springs for?" Woodson pushed the potatoes around in the frying pan again.

"Actually, no. I came here at the behest of the Freemans."

"Mary and Uziah?" Deanna looked up at him.

"The Freemans felt I could help with the work here."

"So you weren't here for the auditions?" The girl tossed her braid over her shoulder and backed up. *"Whew!* Good thing we listened to Sis and didn't tease you about being a mail-order groom!"

"No. I'm afraid I was here on a bit of a jaunt. Thought myself a holiday cowboy. . . but that didn't work out."

Now what to do about his obligations. "I'm ordained by the Church of England. . ."

"You ain't in England, anymore." Woodson quirked an eyebrow at him. "In case you haven't noticed."

"I have taken note. In the meanwhile, I have a hungry inn owner upstairs who I'm the very willing footman for. What do you have for me to take upstairs?" To the woman he couldn't live without.

Chapter 11

Late June, 1866

D espite the drizzle, Caroline sat outside on the bench, an umbrella held over-head and pillows propped around her. After being abed for over a week, recovering, the fresh, cool air lifted her spirits.

Someone turned the corner into the alleyway. Steel-gray hair curled beneath a bowler hat as a stranger strolled toward her. The powerfully built man must have been a fearsome sight when he was younger, but as he neared his kind, dark eyes urged Caroline to welcome him.

He removed his hat and tucked it under his suited arm, despite the rain's increase. "Are you the owner of the inn?" The man's accent was heavy, but much different from Barden's, with a roll to it, unlike Barden's clipped tones. "Are you Mrs. Kane?"

"Yes, I am."

"I'm looking for. . .a friend."

Movement from behind her caught her attention. Head down, Barden rounded the corner, wiping his hands on a dishtowel, and surged toward them. "Good heavens, woman, it's raining out here. You'll catch your death yet!"

Her beloved almost reached her when he stopped.

The stranger beamed at Barden. "Mr. Granville, I am here."

"Sinclair!" Barden opened his arms and the two embraced each other like long lost friends. "What are you doing here?"

"It's a rather convoluted tale, but—"

"Let me get this misbehaving lady inside before you tell me all."

As Caroline rose, she swayed, and Barden caught her. He lifted her into his arms.

"What did I tell you, Caroline?" He shifted her weight in his arms, the scent of his clove shaving soap teasing her senses. "Don't push yourself."

"Have you been ill, Mrs. Kane?"

"Indeed she has; we could have lost her. But praise be to God she's with us yet."

Sinclair glanced between the two of them, his brown eyes seeming to take in everything. He followed them into the kitchen and then on to the restaurant, where Barden finally lowered her into a chair.

"Thank you."

"Sinclair was my manservant in England, Caroline."

Mr. Sinclair patted moisture from his face with a creamy handkerchief. "*Was* is the operative word. Lord Cheatham wasn't at all pleased when he'd learned I'd encouraged your interest in the Beadle's books. Nor that I knew you'd taken holiday in America to try your hand at cowboy life."

"Outrageous!" Barden's face twisted in an anger she'd never seen before. "How could he simply dismiss you?"

Bowing his head briefly, Barden leaned against the back of his sweetheart's chair. His little cowboy venture had cost his valet his position. "How did you get here, Sinclair?"

"I actually came in search of you, sir, to ensure that you were well. I didn't hear from you after that message from your hotel."

"After I was attacked. . ."

A muscle in his valet's jaw twitched. "If only I'd been here to help you."

Barden motioned for his friend to sit. "You're here now. How did that happen?"

"I'd put aside funds for my old age, and I appear to be in it now."

"You're hardly in your dotage." Barden laughed. "In fact you look to be in remarkably good condition."

Sinclair patted his midsection. "American food agrees well with me thus far!"

Mrs. Reed wheeled the teacart in. "I understand we have guests."

"Indeed." Barden waved a hand toward his former servant. "May I introduce John Sinclair, an old and dear friend."

Sinclair shot him a look of gratitude. "And responsible for him taking this lark by coming to America and scaring the wits out of us back home."

Mrs. Reed's cheeks flushed. Was she blushing? "What will you do here, Mr. Sinclair?"

"I'm hoping to go for a land grant." Sinclair's cheeks, too, took on a rosy hue. "Perhaps out here or back further east."

Caroline leaned in, resting her elbows on the table. "To become a farmer?"

"Own my own bit of land. My father was a tenant farmer. I only took up the life in service when we'd had two droughts back to back."

"I see." Mrs. Reed's wide eyes seemed to be taking in much.

"I met your friends the Freemans." Sinclair rapped his fingers on the table. "Good people."

"Indeed. They saved me." In more ways than one. He gazed at Caroline. What would life have been like without her in it?

Mrs. Reed served them each tea, her hands a bit unsteady as she poured for Sinclair. Thank God her rheumatism seemed to have improved enough for her to hold and tip a teapot again.

"Thank you, madam." Sinclair's dark eyes took on a gleam as he looked up at Mrs. Reed.

"Call me Mae."

"Delighted to do so." Sinclair gave her a cheeky grin.

Caroline turned to Barden. "Have a seat."

After pouring in milk, Sinclair used the sugar tongs to drop two chunks of sugar into his tea.

"I should have let you pour your milk first, like Barden does." Mrs. Reed blinked down at Sinclair.

As Barden settled into his chair, Caroline beamed up at him, her face still wan but just as beautiful. Thank God she'd soon fully regain her health.

"No trouble at all. Thank you." Sinclair drew in a deep breath, exhaled, and fixed his gaze on Barden. "I have a bit of news I felt you should hear directly from me, since it is my fault you are here."

Barden sipped his tea, eyeing Sinclair over the top of his teacup. "What might that be?"

"The parish has rescinded their offer of a position."

He gulped the hot tea. "What?"

"When your father heard what you had done, he wrote to the bishop and told them he wouldn't sponsor the living for you."

Ire rose up in him, quickly chased by confusion and then relief. "I never realized Father had anything to do with the position—it was so far from home."

"Yes, that horrid man. . ." Sinclair raised his hand and then lowered it. "My apologies, but he never deserved a good son like you."

And Barden had never deserved a companion as faithful as John Sinclair. A man who would follow him across the ocean to check on him, who was a better father to him than his own had been.

Caroline laughed. "I guess you don't have to write that letter to them after all, do you, Barden?"

Squeezing her hand, Barden leaned closer to the woman he'd spend the rest of his life with. "But what then shall I do?"

Caroline cocked her head at him. "Besides marry me?"

"Have you decided?" Barden chuckled. "I believed you'd hired me on a temporary basis, but now I understand you had something else in mind."

The door to the inn opened, and the mayor and her new husband, the sheriff, entered, trailed by Melissa and Alan and the preacher.

"We're married!" Melissa, dressed in a pretty pale blue dress with lace-edged flounces, moved past the others to Caroline's table. "I'm Mrs. Henderson now."

Barden and Mr. Sinclair stood.

"Congratulations!" Caroline grinned up.

Melissa pressed a quick kiss to Caroline's cheek. "How're you feeling?"

Barden cleared his throat. "She's going back upstairs to rest soon. Congratulations on your wedding."

Reverend Smith nodded to them. "You still going to substitute for me next Sunday, when I visit my daughters?"

"Yes, sir."

"I assume you won't be utilizing the Book of Common Prayer." Sinclair's droll expression made Barden chuckle.

"No, indeed."

Sheriff Ingram moved forward and shook Barden's hand. "Think about my offer, too."

Caroline narrowed her eyes at him, in question.

Mrs. Reed tapped his shoulder. "Would you like me to pull these tables together?"

Instead of a country parish council meeting, Barden found himself in Kansas, surrounded by people trying to put their village back together again after a terrible civil war. And he had perfect peace that this was where he belonged.

After Caroline awoke from her nap, Barden brought her to the saloon, protectively steadying her on the boardwalk.

"I want to show you what I was telling the mayor about. . .before you nodded off earlier." He ran his thumb over her chin, sending a delicious thrill through her. "I should have carried you up to bed sooner."

Her cheeks heated. Very soon they'd be married and sharing a bed together. She stepped away from him and scanned the main floor, spotless and serene. . .so unlike the place had been when formerly occupied.

Barden squared his shoulders. "Can you imagine your American veterans coming to a place where they could not only recover from the ravages of war but be retrained?"

"Mayor Ingram says we need more men, more businesses. Why not try?"

"I hope she's right—that the council might donate the building."

"If not, perhaps there's another way." Upstairs, in her room, was a bank check that Barden's rancher friends had sent as a wedding gift. They were off on a cattle drive and wouldn't make it back for the nuptials. Nor would Alvin and Virginia be there to attend, but the Freemans would be.

She took two steps toward him and pressed her hands against his chest. "With more people coming to Turtle Springs, the sheriff said he might need a deputy."

"I'm a good shot, but Caroline, I did not pursue ministry simply because I wasn't going to be Lord Cheatham. I want God to direct my path."

She leaned her head against him, and he tucked his chin down. "Do you think substituting for Reverend Smith will be enough?"

"I'm not sure. But if I can meet the needs of men, like those who came through here and headed off to the fort, and men like Luke Collins, then I'll have served well."

Caroline snuggled in, turning her head, listening to his heart beat out a steady booming rhythm. "You're a blessing to everyone who comes through the inn."

Barden stepped back. "I don't know what I'll be doing for certain, my love, but

I do know that wherever and whatever I am doing, I want you there by my side."

"How about in your arms?" Caroline grinned up at her fiancé, and moved closer, lifting her face up for a kiss.

Barden's lips covered hers. Mail-order husband or not, this Englishman's heart belonged to her.

Author's Notes

The Civil War, with its use of the minie ball, resulted in death or devastating injuries. So many soldiers lost their limbs or were otherwise injured. While researching the history of Fort Mackinac for my upcoming Barbour release, *My Heart Belongs on Mackinac Island: Maude's Mooring*, I was struck by the fact that when the mainly empty fort was reoccupied after the war, the men were mostly injured veterans. In the protected and isolated fort, high above the Straits of Mackinac, these men (who were, on average, the oldest soldiers to occupy the fort) had lighter duties than elsewhere. Phil Porter, director of Mackinac State Historic Parks and author of the book, *A Desirable Station: Soldier Life at Fort Mackinac, 1867–1895* (available at the Fort Michilimackinac store, online at Barnes & Noble, and elsewhere), included information about these disabled veterans occupying the fort. Company "B" of the 43rd Regiment of Infantry, whom I included fictionally in this novella, occupied the fort in 1867. I had the fictionalized company coming through Kansas for the purposes of this story. Although some of the names are of real soldiers, their portrayal here is pure fiction. For a nonfiction account, I suggest you read Mr. Porter's wonderful book.

I'd also like to say that while I often "borrow" the names of real-life people, such as Caroline (Caryl Kane—a reader/reviewer friend) and childhood neighborhood friend Joel Martinchek, their portrayals in the story are, of course, fictitious. Granville, for my hero, was borrowed from Pagels' Pal, Chris, not from *Downton Abbey*; and Barden was my friend Libbie's maiden name. There really was a Tumble Inn near where I grew up. My mom used to like to say *"Tumble Inn and roll out!"*

My grandfather, Lloyd E. Fancett, Sr., was a ranch hand, or "cowboy," out West as a young man. His parents had immigrated to Michigan from Maidstone, Kent, England. Although I never got to know him, I've often wondered what it must have been like for him to come from that British background, yet to become a cowboy! He certainly wasn't alone, as there were a number of British ranchers on the American frontier.

Carrie Fancett Pagels, Ph.D., "Hearts Overcoming Through Time," is an award-winning Christian historical romance author. Carrie's Amazon Christian Historical Romance bestselling novella, *The Fruitcake Challenge*, was released September, 2014. Her short story, "Snowed In," appears in Guidepost Books' *A Christmas Cup of Cheer* (2013). She's the Amazon bestselling and top-rated author of *Return to Shirley Plantation: A Civil War Romance* (2013). Her short story, "The Quilting Contest," will appear in Family Fiction's *The Story 2014* anthology. Carrie is a finalist for the 2014 Maggie Awards for Excellence for her unpublished novel *Grand Exposé*. She's a former psychologist (25 years) and is a mother of two.

Louder than Words

By Gina Welborn

Dedication

For my sister-in-law Cené Burrow.
Because you like Gone with the Wind. . .*which this story is nothing like. But still.*

Acknowledgments

Special thanks to my ISTJ sister who happily decided which Kansas museums this ESTP writer (and her daughter) needed to visit, found the addresses for said museums, and then drove us to the said museums after seeing how I parked at Sephora. To my thirteen-year-old ENTP daughter who, as I drove home, happily explained the Meyers-Briggs personalities in words I could understand. Mostly. Somewhat. Not really. But it was exciting!

Do know, in light of how you two laughed at my parking skills, this special thanks is only 88.4815162342 percent sincere.

Build a fire under them; when it gets hot enough, they'll move.
—President Andrew Jackson, who signed into law the Indian Removal Act of 1830. The US Supreme Court overruled this law, yet Jackson defied the Court's ruling, thereby forcing 16,000 Cherokees to march over 2,000 miles west to Oklahoma Territory. Four thousand died.

Such cold-blooded butchery was never before seen—such deliberate, hellish cruelty.
—Sarah Fitch, survivor of Quantrill's Raid (the Lawrence Massacre)

Marriage is an adventure, like going to war.
—G. K. Chesterton

A tree is known by its fruit; a man by his deeds. A good deed is never lost; he who sows courtesy reaps friendship, and he who plants kindness gathers love.
—Saint Basil

What good is it, dear brothers and sisters, if you say you have faith but don't show it by your actions? Can that kind of faith save anyone? Suppose you see a brother or sister who has no food or clothing, and you say, "Good-bye and have a good day; stay warm and eat well"—but then you don't give that person any food or clothing. What good does that do? So you see, faith by itself isn't enough. Unless it produces good deeds, it is dead and useless.
JAMES 2:14–17 NLT

Chapter 1

The greater the obstacle, the more glory in overcoming it.—Molière

Philadelphia, Pennsylvania
Tuesday afternoon, May 15, 1866

E very editor wanted the same thing: tragedy, triumph, bring our readers to tears. None could—or would—define what they were looking for beyond the usual we-know-it-when-we-see-it.

With a growl of frustration, J.R. Lockhart tossed the letter from the editor of the *Daily Alta California* onto the basket of responses from the *San Francisco Morning Call, San Francisco Chronicle, Sacramento Daily Union,* and *Marysville Daily Appeal.* To name a few. To name the rejections that pained him the most. None of his accounts of soldier life during the war, abolitionist pamphlets, or exposés of post-war reconstruction, nor any of his ballads, essays, or short stories published in the last year at *Godey's Lady's Book* engaged the West Coast editors enough to prompt an offer of employment, or even a simple request he come to California for an interview.

J.R. looked to the continental map tacked on the wall, over the spot where a portrait used to hang of George Washington crossing the Delaware. An inky line stretched from Philadelphia to Cleveland, Chicago, and Omaha. By the end of this year, the Pacific Railroad between Omaha and North Platte would be completed, putting the East Coast—putting him—one state closer to California.

Twenty-eight hundred miles separated him from his future.

A future as bleak as his gray suit.

"I'm never going to leave," he muttered.

A soft *rap-a-tap-tap-tap* drew his attention to the opened door.

J.R. stood and forced a smile. "Ma'am."

Sarah Josepha Hale, in her usual black gown that made her silver hair more striking, stood there bearing a mug and a luncheon plate. "Do you have time to talk?"

He tipped his head in acknowledgment.

Mrs. Hale stepped inside his office and, to his shock, closed the door. J.R. tensed. Not once in the eleven months he'd worked here had she closed the door, or asked him to when he'd visited her office. Why did she feel the need for privacy? She rested the plate with two buttered slices of bread and the mug of coffee in the center of his desk and then sat in a chair across from him as if she were an interviewee instead of the editress of the most popular publication in the country.

"Your mother was a dear friend," she began, "and one of the finest poets I have ever been blessed to work with."

SEVEN *Brides for* SEVEN *Mail-Order Husbands* ROMANCE COLLECTION

J.R. settled back against his leather chair's high back. Mrs. Hale had known him since his birth. In the twenty-seven years since, he'd learned never to interrupt her until she'd had her say, especially when she began a discussion with mention of a *dear friend.* The woman had more dear friends than anyone in all of creation.

"The artistry of Ann Maria's ballads—" Mrs. Hale rested her hands in her lap and sighed. "My dear boy, she is greatly missed. Your father, too. The college will never be the same without his leadership."

Based on the tears in her eyes, one would think his parents had passed away last week, not over two years ago. Then again, this was the same woman who mourned her husband's death every day. . .for the past forty-four years! Now that was devotion.

J.R. sipped his coffee as he waited for her to speak.

She stared absently at his wall of books, a frown growing. "War is hell, as much to a man who fought it with a pen as the one who used a sword." She looked back at him. "Those of my sex also know, for a young man, war is dangerous and exciting."

He tapped his fingers on the chair's armrests. "I didn't join the war because I thought it would be exciting. I went to tell of the horrors—"

She held up a hand, and he fell silent.

"A man's nature is to attack something. To conquer. This is why we have war. It is why we have rifles, boxing, and even cricket. It is why my great-grandson last night felt compelled to thrash a tree in my yard with a stick." Her troubled gaze flickered to the letters in the basket. "A man's nature also calls him to adventure, not to sit behind a desk and write stories that appeal to women." She looked at him. "I've written numerous letters of recommendation on your behalf, and you have yet to tell me what you are seeking in California."

"It's more of what isn't there."

She nodded for him to explain.

"War. Half a million Philadelphians bear scars from it, and yet"—J.R. grabbed a copy of this month's *Lady's Book* atop the stack on his desk—"we print recipes, sentimental songs, household tips, and the latest fashion plates in hopes of keeping war from permeating our daily conversations."

"Do you want us to publish stories about the war?"

Shaking his head, he laid the magazine on the other eleven containing his writings. "When I was fifteen, I started writing abolitionist pamphlets to end slavery. This morning I finished a three-page ballad about a butterfly. 'She was happy and fair, graceful and gay, sporting the summer of bright youth away—'" J.R. groaned, unable to continue reciting the words he'd forced himself to pen. "I'm tired of writing about butterflies in hopes of temporarily distracting readers from the horrors none of us can forget."

"I see." The longer Mrs. Hale studied him, the sadder she looked. "I have not reached the age of six-and-seventy years without learning that deep in a man's heart are fundamental questions which cannot—simply cannot—be answered at a lady's magazine. Who is J.R. Lockhart? A writer? A crusader? A Quaker who must have a good reason why he has yet to set foot inside a church since returning from war?"

J.R. chose to presume her questions were rhetorical.

Her gaze shifted to the neatly stacked piles of papers and magazines on his desk. "Or is he simply a tamed man content to be confined to a chair...in an office...with a lone window overlooking a busy street?"

He took a gulp of coffee to ease his taut throat.

"Life here bores you. Worse, it has turned you into a boring man. I miss the carefree, charming rapscallion that you were." Mrs. Hale eased forward in the chair. "Do you think by moving to California you will find out what are you made of and what you are destined for?"

He returned the mug to his desktop. "I need change, ma'am, not self-enlightenment."

"Then change is my gift to you." Her lips tipped up at the corners. "Before you leave for the day, stop by the clerk's office and pick up your final pay."

J.R. sat up straight. "You're sacking me?"

"Indeed I am."

"Why?"

"You have no family in Philadelphia."

Her reasoning made no sense. "Thus I should lose my employment?"

"You are independently wealthy, thus I can only conclude limited finances are not the cause for you becoming a stick-in-the-mud who gave up even the mildest flirtation. Gloom is not effective bait to hook a lady." She gave him a don't-argue-with-my-assessment-of-you smile, and then said, "Therefore, the only conclusion is...you won't seek your *change* in California until you have nothing to cleave to here."

"You're tossing me out of the boat and hoping I will swim."

"Or I am hoping you won't drown."

"There's a difference?"

Her brows rose as if to say *that's your question to answer*. She withdrew a folded slip of paper, tucked in the wristband of her sleeve. "A dear friend of mine in Memphis thought this might interest me."

J.R. leaned across his desk to take the narrow, rectangular slip of paper. He unfolded what clearly had been cut from a newspaper's advertisement section.

WANTED: MEN TO AUDITION AS HUSBANDS. TURTLE SPRINGS, KANSAS. AUDITIONS HELD MAY 25. ONLY GODLY, UPSTANDING MEN NEED APPLY. CHECK IN AT MAYOR'S OFFICE.

He met her guileless gaze. "Godey's Lady's Book has never mentioned the war. Not even a vague reference. I suspect these desperate women are war widows. Any story about them cannot be written without mentioning why their husbands died."

"This story isn't for me," she said primly. "Since Godey's owns the copyright on the work you've written for us, I advise you to pen something new to sell to other editors. Something filled with pathos and joy."

"These women may not want their stories told." Not that he expected the men would either. Sensationalism was not his cup of journalistic tea.

She seemed to think on that for a moment. "If the ladies of Turtle Springs don't want their names published, then turn their stories into fiction. And write it in installments. Since the serial success of *Uncle Tom's Cabin*, the best American writers first publish their work in serial form. I expect the best from you." She stood.

He stood, too.

"Take care, J.R. I'll send Norville Owens to help you pack your"—she glanced about the room and clearly realized his belongings were limited to—"books."

At the pitying sound of her tone, he could feel the muscles in his face tightening. "Why are you doing this?"

"You need permission."

"To go to Kansas?"

"To go west, young man. Manifest destiny and all."

He coughed a breath.

She smiled, the expression on her face more patient than placating. "Young men need more than adventures. They need beauties to rescue. You may find what you are looking for in Turtle Springs." She paused. "Find the man you once were, J.R. Find your heart."

As Mrs. Hale strolled out of his office, she left the door open. He could see into the sitting room where a handful of writers and businessmen sat while waiting for an audience with the formidable woman who had swayed, at the time, the most powerful man in the world into proclaiming Thanksgiving a national holiday. The same woman who took away J.R.'s job because she thought he needed permission to leave Philadelphia.

He shook his head. He never needed permission. And yet—

With each twist, with each turn, the iron snake consumes its prey. Land ho!

He looked to the map, a smile growing, a poem forming. He could go west. Nothing held him back now. Thanks to Mrs. Hale. A mere twenty-eight hundred miles, and a short stop in Kansas, separated him and his future. A beauty to rescue?

He was a writer, not a warrior.

The only thing he needed to find in Turtle Springs was a story to hook an editor. He'd look for a dark-eyed beauty once he was settled in California.

Chapter 2

Unreasonable haste is the direct road to error.—Molière

Turtle Springs, Kansas
Six weeks earlier...

J ane Ransome stepped out of the telegraph office and breathed in deep. Spring. Change was in the air. She looked across Main Street to the barbershop that rarely saw business anymore. An unfamiliar man stood outside. He ran a hand down one clean-shaven cheek and then the other before tucking his hat onto his head. His index finger swiped across the brim. Were his eyes blue? Possibly green. Maybe gray. They could even be brown. From where she stood, she couldn't tell.

The color of his eyes didn't matter. All that did was—

"He's not married," she whispered, knowing with all certainty she was right.

"What was that you said, Jane Ransome?" Mrs. Olinger called from inside the telegraph office.

Even though Jane had lived in Turtle Springs for three years, the older towns-folk still referred to her by her full name, a common practice when talking about (or to) any native—full blooded or mixed. Never Mr. or Miss So-and-So. Always the full name and sometimes with the preface *that injun* or *that half-breed*. If she said something about how belittling the practice was they'd feel shame and be apologetic. To be sure, she knew they never intended offense. No one in Turtle Springs was mean-spirited or a supremacist. For her to overlook the slight seemed the kindest response. Or so Papa said.

Being a white man, how could *he* know for sure?

Jane looked over her shoulder and smiled across the opened door's threshold. "It was nothing, ma'am. I'll see you Sunday." She looked back across the street.

The man headed west on the boardwalk. Toward the Tumble Inn? That seemed most logical.

Jane quickly stuffed the receipt for the telegram she'd sent to her parents into her reticule that matched her blue-checkered silk day dress. She had a man to track, the most exciting thing she'd done since—

She thought for a moment. Nothing. Not a thing came to mind.

Unless she counted last month when she'd caught her neighbor's children climbing onto the roof of their house to watch the full moon rise. Their mother, Jenny, had been more shocked at seeing Clyde, Nancy, and Opie up there than with seeing Jane sitting with them. It'd been cold. And the trio had looked like they could use pie and hot cocoa and an adult to keep them from jumping to the ground.

That's what her life had come to—supervising children on rooftops.

With a resigned sigh, Jane headed west, paralleling the man's pace, the modest crinoline under her skirt swishing against her legs as she hurried. How could he know about the husband interviews already? Last night at the church meeting, Abby insisted she'd place the advertisements this morning—the first Monday of the month. That gave potential husbands seven weeks to arrive in time for the husband interviews. Even if this man had been at the telegraph offices in Omaha, Dubuque, or Memphis when Abby's telegrams to the newspapers arrived, he wouldn't have had time to ride to Turtle Springs. That included time saved riding the train to Topeka.

So why was he here already?

Curiosity piqued, she kept walking.

He stopped at the intersection where First Street crossed Main, the two major roads dividing the town into the shape of a plus sign. As he looked around, he didn't appear bothered by the numerous boarded-up buildings and homes, nor the number of women teeming about with interest in the handsome stranger.

She didn't fault any of them for admiring him. Was that a dimple in his chin? Other than the seven Turtle Springs men who'd returned from the war, the town hadn't seen the arrival of a stranger—male or female—in the year since Robert E. Lee surrendered the Confederate Army of Northern Virginia to Ulysses S. Grant at Appomattox Court House.

Being handsome was icing on this stranger's bachelorhood cake.

Jane snorted under her breath. Not the best analogy but a fitting one. She reached the mayor's office the same moment their new arrival did. They were near the same height. His brown hair with its golden streaks reminded her of the raccoon fur lining her winter cloak.

Sunlight glinted off the gold star pinned to his shirt. Sheriff?

He smiled at Jane, who smiled back. She started to introduce herself, but he opened the door to step inside.

"Settled in?" came Abigail Melton's matter-of-fact voice.

"Yep," he answered.

The door closed, hindering Jane from hearing their conversation. Settled in? Abby had insisted upon hiring a sheriff before men began arriving for the interviews.

Jane turned from the wooden door and looked to the other women peering her way. No telling how many ladies had decided—upon first sight—they wanted to marry the new sheriff. The hastiness of his appointment to sheriff seemed odd. Even though Abby had placed an advertisement for sheriff two weeks ago, and even though she'd stressed the necessity of hiring a sheriff before men began arriving for the interviews, this man had *just* arrived. And now wore the star. In Jane's initial estimation, there hadn't been enough time to determine if this man met all the requirements.

Decisions of this import shouldn't be made hastily.

What was Abby Melton up to?

Determined to find out, Jane entered the mayor's office.

"Riding out at sunset," their new sheriff was saying. He looked angry and annoyed.

Abby, sitting behind the mayor's desk, looked ready to laugh. Her amused gaze shifted from the sheriff to Jane, and her smile fell. "Oh no, Jane. Don't tell me Doc Carter refused to be our main speaker. If you couldn't convince him, no one can."

Main speaker? What in the world was Abby— Oh!

Jane stepped to desk. "I promised he would agree, and he has."

"That's a relief."

The sheriff's gaze shifted back and forth between Jane and Abby.

Jane turned her smile onto him. "This Sunday we're having a One-Year Remembrance Service for those who fought in the war and for those who lost someone. The anniversary is actually Monday," she clarified. "April 9th. It seemed more prudent to hold the service on a Sunday morning."

His brow furrowed. "Some things are worth forgetting, ma'am."

"As sheriff," she said, "you will be expected to attend, regardless of your personal—"

"Where are my manners?" Abby jumped to her feet. "Sheriff Ingram, this is Miss Jane Ransome. Jane, this is Josiah Ingram."

Jane shook his hand. Strange. She'd expected him to have a firmer grip. Was this limpness natural, or an intentional attempt to convey weakness? To un-impress her?

He cleared his throat then grabbed his hat off Abby's desk. "Ladies, it's been a delight in speaking with you. I need to get going. I have, uhh, sheriff things to do."

Abby gave him an odd look. "Such as. . .?"

He rubbed the back of his neck where his hair curled over the collar of his blue shirt. "Uhh. . .such as introduce myself around town and see if anyone needs sheriff things done." And with that he all but dashed out of the building.

Suspicion growing, Jane turned to Abby. "Where does he hail from? Did you ask if he was a secessionist bushwhacker?"

"Mr. Ingram is from Little Rock, Arkansas, and fought for a man's right to live as he pleased. His family never owned slaves."

"And you believe him?"

"I do."

"Does he have any experience being a lawman?"

"He wears a six-shooter."

"What!" Jane stared at Abby. Another instant decision Abby made based off emotions instead of thinking through all the details first. Much like the advertisement for mail-order husbands. If Jane hadn't been so desperate to find a husband of her own, she wouldn't have helped finance the advertisement. "Abby, please tell me you did not hire him solely on the basis of a gun attached to his hip. Do you even know if he is skilled in shooting it?"

The Abigail Melton known for being bossy and opinionated looked unsure.

Looked worried she'd made a wrong decision. Looked so unlike herself.

"He's on a three-month probation period," she offered in defense. "After that, if we are pleased with his performance, he can continue on until the election in November."

Jane strolled to the front window. Mama often insisted Jane should have been born a male, for then, even with mixed blood, she would have made a mighty Shawnee chief like her uncle Black Bob. To Mama's chagrin, Jane bore no inclination to be the leader of anything. She preferred to serve in the shadows and let others have the governance glory. . .and the stress that came alone with it. That wasn't to say she would turn down any opportunity to be in on the decision-making process, to the benefit of all.

Hiring a sheriff without a lengthy interview process was a mistake waiting to happen. He could be a shark, a villain, a thief. He could have a wife and a bushel of starving children back in Little Rock. Without confirming his references, they would never know.

Jane focused on the view. Through the dusty panes, she could see three ladies blocking the sheriff's entrance into the mercantile across the street. "Did you consider he may be *too* handsome for the job?"

Abby sighed loudly. "I didn't expect him to clean up so. . ."

When Abby didn't finish, Jane turned around to face her, but Abby seemed lost in her own thoughts. Oh, to be in her confidence. To be in anyone's! Not a single lady in town had ever invited Jane over for tea and intimate talks about hopes and dreams. About fears. About why Jane and her family had moved to Turtle Springs. Or how she felt about her younger brothers' delayed return from the war or about her parents' work with the Agency of Indian Affairs. Or if Jane minded living alone.

Even with their lack of confidences, she knew Abby would rather be tending to a husband instead of tending to a town. Jane felt the same.

A husband. A home. Her family together again. Their home brimming with laughter like it used to be before the war. The latter would only happen after Jane married. Or at least became engaged. Learning she had a fiancé would send her parents, her brothers, her sisters, and their families running to Turtle Springs.

Marriage to a lawman—what an intriguing notion!

While she felt no emotional connection with Mr. Ingram, and she wasn't ready to trust him, she was adaptable. Israel Kemp being a missionary had not caused her to question accepting his marriage proposal. The work Reverend Pingree and his wife had done at the Shawnee Mission had led Jane to faith in Jesus as her Savior. So to be a missionary alongside her husband. . .well, she had been willing.

Marriage was the fertile soil in which love grew.

Of course, it was quite possible God had brought Mr. Ingram here for the sole purpose of being sheriff, and not to marry anyone. Or he could be a swindler.

As if suddenly uncomfortable with the silence, Abby grabbed a sheet of paper off the desk, furrows in her brow deepening. "I probably shouldn't have hired him without additional interviews or checking references, but"—she looked to Jane—"Josiah Ingram arrived the moment we needed a sheriff. I. . .you. . .this town. . .we all need to give him a chance to prove his merit."

Because it needed to be asked—"If he doesn't?"

"I'll let you scalp him," Abby said in a deadpan voice, and then she smiled.

Jane chuckled. "All right, I'll give him a chance."

"What matters most is his presence will dissuade men from making improper advances to the ladies of this town."

Into Jane's mind popped the image of the three ladies blocking the sheriff from the mercantile. "What will you do about ladies making improper advances toward him?"

Abby sank back in her chair, the realization of that clearly sinking in. "As mayor, I suppose it's my duty to find him a wife. Can I count on your help?"

Jane restrained her smile. "Always."

The next morning

"Jane Ransome, what has you so chipper?"

Jane stopped in front of the mercantile where Mr. Underwood and Mr. Quimby, in their second-best suits and derby hats, sat on weather-beaten rockers, playing checkers as they did every weekday. She tipped her head so the brim of her hat shielded the sun from her eyes. "Why, Mr. Quimby, I'm always chipper in the morning."

The elderly men exchanged glances.

Mr. Quimby laughed.

Mr. Underwood gave a sad shake to his head.

Cantankerous yet amusing, they reminded her of her cousin, Cyrus.

Jane shifted her kerchief-covered basket to her other arm. "I will admit there have been a few mornings when I haven't been at my most congenial."

"A few?" Mr. Quimby whistled. "Jane Ransome, that there's an ee-zag-ger-ation, if I ever heard one. Every morning you show up here with pastries and a complaint of how the sun rises too early and shines too brightly. Every gray cloud you vow brings rain."

Jane grinned. "We can all agree I am faithful and consistent."

Mr. Quimby snorted and turned his attention to the checkered board. "Not sure how someone who abhors sunrises can see only her own virtues and none of her vices."

"Pay the ol' fool no mind." Mr. Underwood picked up a black disc and jumped it over a white one. He smiled at her. "We're always happy to see you. What's in the basket?"

"Apple fritters."

Mr. Quimby's studious gaze shifted to her basket. "Fresh?"

"Fried this very *chipper* morning," she boasted.

Mr. Underwood leaned back in his rocker. He withdrew a pair of wire spectacles from inside his suit coat. After sliding them on, he looked up at her. "Well now, Quimby, how right you are. Something's gotten into our Jane Ransome. Her cheeks are red."

Jane laughed. "I'm a quarter Shawnee. My skin is always red."

He shook his head. "That's a blush if I ever seen one."

Good heavens, was she actually blushing? "Mr. Underwood, I know full well the only way you'd see me better with those spectacles on would be if I were a book."

"You don't need to be a book for me to see what's making you chipper."

"What do you see?"

He lowered his reading spectacles to the tip of his nose. "What I *know* is the early-bird-you-aren't didn't fry those fritters to impress a pair of meddling old men. And, unfortunately for you, I *see* our new sheriff escorting Miss Melton to breakfast."

Jane swirled around. Sure enough, the couple stopped at the door to the Tumble Inn. Sheriff Ingram opened it then followed Abby inside. Jane gritted her teeth. She should have headed straight to the sheriff's office instead of allowing this pair to distract her.

Mr. Quimby tugged the basket of fritters off her arm. "You'll run faster without these."

"Get on over there," Mr. Underwood said, before he accepted a fritter from his compatriot. "We'll keep your secret."

"Well, now I don't know about—"

Mr. Underwood kicked Mr. Quimby.

"Don't eat—" She bit off her words knowing full well they'd eat them all anyway. "I'll be back for the basket."

Leaving them to enjoy the fritters, Jane hurried down the boardwalk to the best and only restaurant in town. She slipped inside Tumble Inn's dining hall and found a seat at a table behind Abby. Sheriff Ingram's attention didn't flicker from the woman he was exchanging glares with.

"You have an answer for everything," Abby seethed, "don't you, Sheriff?"

"Might as well call me Josiah, since we're engaged."

Engaged?

Jane glanced around the dining hall. The handful of other townsfolk didn't seem to have heard the sheriff's pronouncement, but none were sitting as close as she.

"Well, Josiah"—Abby tossed a napkin in his face—"I wouldn't marry you if you were the last man on earth."

Jane felt her mouth gap.

Now *that* was the spunky Abigail Melton she was familiar with.

Abby bolted to her feet and stormed from the restaurant, drawing the attention of everyone in the dining hall. In the far corner, Chester Spitts cackled with laughter. Everyone had to be all thinking the same as Jane. Engaged? Not engaged?

Which was it?

Sheriff Ingram's sheepish gaze shifted to Jane. "Lover's spat. Nothing serious."

Jane nodded, although he didn't see her. Couldn't, not with how he hid his face behind the menu. Because he felt remorse over embarrassing Abby? Over putting her in an awkward position? Jane hoped so.

She motioned to Deanna Tumbleston, who hurried over. "Could I get a couple mugs and a pot of coffee to take to Misters Quimby and Underwood? I'll also pay for a meal for Chester Spriggs." The poor farmer needed more than coffee after a night of whiskey.

Deanna leaned close and whispered, "The sheriff says Abby is his fiancée. Did you know about that?"

Jane shrugged.

"Interesting." Deanna hurried off, presumably to find someone besides her sister, Caroline, to tell the news. While Jane didn't know Caroline Tumbleston Kane well, she'd heard how Caroline avoided gossip like the plague. An admirable trait.

"Don't forget the coffee and mugs," Jane called out.

Deanna waved over her head before continuing into the kitchen.

Jane *did* know that no one—not even one as handsome as Josiah Ingram—could force Abigail Melton into marrying him. But what did it say about his character in that he would claim Abby was his fiancée when she wasn't? Or was she? He had to have had justifiable reason for saying they were engaged. What if he didn't? Jane shook her head, unsure of what to think. Abby had asked her to give their new sheriff a chance to prove his merit. Give him a chance, Jane would.

If she were a fanciful person, she'd think she heard his scalp saying thank you.

Chapter 3

*Every good act is charity. A man's true wealth hereafter is the good
that he does in this world to his fellows.*—Molière

Wednesday, April 18

Jane shifted on the rocker Misters Quimby and Underwood had placed between
their chairs two weeks ago after she'd returned to the mercantile bearing coffee. . .and the news of Abby and the sheriff's maybe/maybe-not engagement.
Instead of teasing, they invited her into their "overseeing" the town. Their version of
overseeing always began with her reading whatever newspaper Miss Chardy Stevens had in the mercantile. Some papers were dated. Some were nothing more than
political posturing. This one, fortunately, had only been published three days ago.
Whatever the editor's political leanings, he kept them subtle.

Or maybe Jane thought his leanings were subtle because she agreed with them.

She looked over her shoulder at the sheriff's office next door to the mercantile.
The unopened door and the empty chair under the porch signaled the sheriff was
still out and about. Doing what, Jane didn't know.

"This town needs its own newspaper again," Jane grumbled, turning to the second page of the *Kansas State Record*. "That way we know what events are happening
in everyone's lives. Births. Engagements. Things for sale. Relatives from afar visiting." When Mr. Quimby didn't offer a "here, here" for Mr. Underwood to second,
she laid the paper in the lap of her crimson plaid skirt. Both men were studying the
checkerboard. "Are either of you listening to me?"

"I listen when yer reading," Mr. Quimby retorted.

Jane narrowed her eyes at them. "I have better things I could be doing."

"Hmmph." Mr. Underwood moved a piece. "If you leave now, you will miss the
excitement."

"What excitement?"

Mr. Underwood's gaze stayed on the checkerboard. "The school board is sus-
pending Miss Chardy's brothers."

"Booting 'em all out," Mr. Quimby added, "for being hooligans."

Jane stared at them, incredulous at the news. How did they know these things?
She'd presumed their "excitement" to be in regard to any of the twenty-something
men having arrived in town a month before the husband auditions. At this rate, by
the time May 25 arrived, there'd be six eligible men to every unmarried lady. Jane
didn't need six men. She needed one.

A horse and buggy slowed as it approached the mercantile from the east. Maggie Piner and her boys waved. Jane waved back.

The trio continued on to the schoolhouse, where Miss Birdie Green stood on the porch, ringing the bell. If any lady in Turtle Springs needed a husband, Maggie Piner topped the list. Twice Jane had privately offered the bank president the funds to pay off the mortgage on Piner Ranch. Twice the man refused. Jane was at the point of believing that greedy man Rutherford Grant enjoyed making Maggie suffer. The loaves of bread and the elderberry jam Jane had left on Birdie's desk this morning would supplement the little food in the Piner boys'—in many of the students'—lunch pails.

Today, at least.

"Is this suspension supposed to happen today?" she asked Mr. Quimby.

"To-day, to-mar-ree"—he shrugged—"next week. Who's to say?"

"Apparently you two are who's to say."

Mr. Underwood's laughter drew the attention of several pedestrians walking toward the mercantile. "We report the news, Jane Ransome. We can't predict the weather."

Jane looked heavenward. "Oh, dear Lord, why do I suffer these men?"

Mr. Quimby patted her knee. "Good to hear you keeping current on yer prayer life."

"I—" After an unladylike growl she didn't try to hide, Jane looked to Mr. Underwood for support, but his attention was back on the checkerboard, so she lifted the newspaper. "The title of this article is 'Big Cities,'" she said before reading. "It is amusing to read, in the Atchison and Lawrence papers, the glorification of their respective town and of the daily obituaries they write for Leavenworth. Lawrence has a railroad running—"

Mr. Quimby whistled. "Would ye look at that?"

Jane lowered the newspaper. The first thing she saw was Abigail Melton standing at the door to the mayor's office, directly across the street. She and Sheriff Ingram weren't engaged—according to Abby. All a joke—also according to Abby. Jane had yet to meet a person in town who didn't believe the pair were engaged because Josiah Ingram kept saying they were. A man's word was again more credible than a woman's.

The unfairness of it vexed Jane incessantly.

She believed Abby's word over the sheriff's. Abby had no reason to lie. What nagged at Jane's soul—at her conscience—was why the sheriff said they were engaged. Everything else Jane had seen or heard regarding him testified to his honor, to his noble character.

Except the rumor.

Jane felt her head tilt as she studied Abby. Instead of the tight bun she usually wore while attending to her mayoral duties, her wheat-colored hair was in her fancy Sunday chignon, wispy curls framing her face. Her green dress looked like she'd spent an hour ironing it. And with starch! Jane had never known Abby to take this much care on her appearance when there wasn't a special event occurring.

No matter what Misters Quimby and Underwood thought, the expulsion of the Stevens boys from school would never be a special event, even if the school board declared otherwise.

But instead of entering her office, Abby stood there. She stared at something farther down the street.

Jane looked to her right, in curiosity of seeing what had caught Abby's attention. There, where Main and First intersected, Sheriff Ingram stood talking to a man Jane didn't recognize. The sheriff stepped back, and the stranger rode off. Sheriff Ingram looked to the mayor's office then jogged to the Tumble Inn for breakfast, like he did every morning since arriving in Turtle Springs, although this morning was later than his usual time. Not once did he glance Jane's way.

Jane looked back to where Abby still stood. Still staring in the direction of the Tumble Inn with an indecisive look on her face.

No wonder the sheriff had seemed appreciative yet apathetic about the occasional baked goods Jane had brought him in the last two weeks. His feelings were otherwise engaged. Did he realize Abby's feelings for him? Jane had certainly missed noticing them.

Something needed to be done.

While Jane had no power to put an end to the rumor, she could help it into becoming truth. For Abby's sake.

And a little for Jane's as well.

Jane stood and laid the newspaper in her chair. "Guard my spot, men."

"Choose wisely," muttered Mr. Underwood.

"Jane Ransome, don't you do anythen foolish," warned Mr. Quimby.

"I hear you both." Leaving them to their game, she strolled across the dirt-packed street to the mayor's office. "Abby, can you spare a moment?"

Abby's smile wasn't quick enough to cover the panicked look one has when caught doing something one shouldn't. "It's such a lovely day, isn't it?"

Jane eased between Abby and the door to keep watch for anyone approaching. This conversation was one she didn't want overheard. "There's all sorts of rumors going about town regarding you and Sheriff Ingram. Are you engaged?"

"We're not. It's a ruse he concocted to keep women from hounding him."

Jane nodded in understanding. Since his arrival, he'd been hounded all right. Truth be told, *hounded* was an understatement of what Madeline Foster had done to him after the Remembrance Service. Inside the church! What type of woman kissed a man engaged to another? Didn't Madeline have standards?

"Have you set your cap for him?"

Abby's soft-spoken question jerked Jane out of her thoughts.

She couldn't help but notice the way Abby intently studied her face. Too curious to look away? No. Abby's question wasn't born out of curiosity. It came from apprehension. Maybe a little fear. Abby clearly bore fond feelings for Sheriff Ingram. What held her back from encouraging his attentions? Some sleeping dogs—not that Abby was a dog—needed to be woken.

"Perhaps," Jane said without flinching under Abby's scrutiny. "He fits my requirements perfectly." Which wasn't a falsehood. There wasn't a woman in town whose requirements he wouldn't fit perfectly, save for Abby's mother who'd been quite vocal in her desire for a *mature* man.

To Jane's surprise, jealousy didn't flicker in Abby's eyes. Instead, her shoulders drooped. "He's said he intends to never marry, but I wish you luck." She thrust out her hand.

Jane shook it. "Thank you for your honesty." With a swish of her skirts, she strolled back across the street, head held high. She stopped in front of the barrel holding the checkerboard. "Is Abby looking at me or at the inn?"

"The inn," answered Mr. Quimby.

Good. "Is she walking over there?"

"No, she's unlocking the door and"—Mr. Underwood squinted as he looked to the mayor's office—"wait, she stopped. I think she's looking at the sign in the window about the husband auditions. Now she's going in her office." His gaze shifted to Jane. "I thought you wanted to marry our sheriff."

"He was under consideration." Jane grimaced. "Love seems to have gotten in the way."

"I suppose you'll be leaving us now."

The dejection in Mr. Quimby's tone warmed Jane's heart.

"Of course not." She strolled around Mr. Underwood, snatched the paper, and retook her seat. "I need to find an honorable man to marry, and I can't think of two better helpers."

Mr. Quimby slapped his thigh. "By golly we'll find you a good'un."

"You may regret this," warned Mr. Underwood.

Jane lifted the paper to hide her smile. "I already am."

Chapter 4

One ought to look a good deal at oneself before thinking of condemning others.—Molière

Saturday, late afternoon, May 19

Like a cradle on wheels, the stagecoach slowly rolled past the plethora of canvas tents before making its way into the quiet town, drawing no one's attention, as far as J.R. could tell through his window view. Were new arrivals to Turtle Springs now an everyday occurrence? The wooden population sign staked on the outskirts listed 223 residents of this tiny town in Wabaunsee County. Considering boarded-up buildings, that had to be a postwar number. Yet close to thirty men of all ages and sizes strolled the boardwalks on either side of the main thoroughfare, or they loitered under wooden awnings of businesses, nary a woman in sight.

The stagecoach stopped in front of the livery.

J.R. released a tired breath. Four more men to join the throng invading the town.

Ebenezer Zumwalt, the shoemaker from Nashville, leaned forward to shake J.R.'s hand. "Good luck with that article, Lockhart. I doubt you'll have any trouble convincing the ladies here to agree to an interview."

"I hope you're right." J.R. released the older gentleman's hand. "Best wishes on opening your business."

"The world runs faster on well-shod feet." The deep wrinkles around his eyes and mouth were as much from his tendency to smile as from sixty-two years of living. J.R. was as much impressed with the man's handlebar mustache as his willingness to answer the sheriff's telegram request for a shoemaker. Zumwalt had agreed to move here, knowing full well the town's tiny population.

Zumwalt shook hands with the other two men in the coach, exchanged a few words, and then climbed down. The coach shifted with the lightening of his weight and as the driver, his shotgun, and liveryman unloaded luggage. The men bellowed orders at each other while unhitching the team in order to replace the six horses with fresh ones.

Liam Logan, the shy forty-year-old widower from Omaha, nudged his equally shy ten-year-old daughter sitting between him and J.R., who immediately felt sorry for the little redhead who looked to have as many freckles on her arms as on her face. The woman-sized bonnet drooped over her forehead.

"Your papa is blessed to have you helping him," J.R. said, and she smiled, exposing a missing bottom tooth.

As the two left the coach, J.R. noted, except for the cloth doll Miss Beatrice carried, their belongings filled a lone carpet bag. Becoming a mail-order groom was the best opportunity for a penniless widower to improve his and his daughter's lot in

398

life. Desperate certainly described Liam and Beatrice Logan. They also seemed like good people. Not once had either of them complained about the open windows or the breath-taking speed at which Charlie had driven the coach over the hilly roads. Instead, they found white-cloud animals in the azure sky. J.R. didn't need to be a gambling man to wager more than one woman in Turtle Springs would be happy to join their little family.

He made a mental note to check on the Logans following the husband auditions. Joy and pathos described them well.

The fourth man sat across from J.R., unmoving still.

William Dixon stared out the window, a deep furrow in his brow, his affable mood replaced with this saturnine one.

Unlike the Logans, who sparingly answered J.R.'s myriad questions, Dixon had been verbose during today's long drive from Topeka. Twenty-nine. Orphan since the age of nineteen. Hailed from Lebanon, Tennessee. Threadbare suit. Finished his war-interrupted degree from Cumberland School of Law. Twin brother Vincent died a Confederate prisoner-of-war at Camp Douglas in Chicago, Illinois. Of all Dixon's war stories, J.R. itched to write about how fellow Confederates had invited Dixon to join them in burning Cumberland University for no other reason than because it had been barracks to colored Union soldiers. What caused Dixon to refuse? J.R.'s question was never answered.

Pathos, yes, but where does one find joy in that story? Mrs. Hale didn't have to be present for J.R. to hear her editorial rejoinder.

"Something on your mind?" he asked Dixon.

"Doesn't seem right."

"What doesn't?"

Dixon turned away from the window to meet J.R.'s gaze. "Auditioning to be a husband."

"Consider it as a job interview," J.R. suggested. "Being a husband *is* work."

"You ever been married?"

J.R. shook his head.

"Me, neither." Dixon let out a sigh...or maybe a groan. "Engaged?"

"Almost." Feeling pity for the man, J.R. added, "Her parents didn't approve. She married a lieutenant in the Philadelphia Brigade. He died at Gettysburg, and by Christmas of '63, she'd married a banker twice her age. Last I heard they had three children."

"Gents," came a gruff voice.

J.R. looked to where Charlie the driver stood, holding the door with one hand and pocket watch with the other. "Sorry to dally," J.R. said while noting the Colt revolvers on Charlie's hips and rifle strapped to his back. Knives in boots? J.R. didn't doubt it. "Could you recommend lodgings?"

"You could see if there's room at the Tumble Inn."

"How apropos," muttered J.R. before climbing out.

He walked around the stage with Dixon in step. Two main streets divided the town into quadrants. The main street, though, was wide enough for a wagon to turn around. Every one of the businesses was brown and dirty. The houses scattered about had been white-washed, some more recent than others. At one time, it'd had been a pretty little town. Diagonally across from the livery was their destination and, presumably, where the Logans had already taken a room. Several men, though, clustered next to the hitching posts in front of a three-story building with a TUMBLE INN sign. Paint peeling and windows looking none too clean, the inn had seen better days.

After paying the liveryman to keep watch on his and, upon his insistence, Dixon's trunks until they found lodging, J.R. struck out across the street. The group of men turned to look their way. Their gazes narrowed. To size up additional competition? In his tan three-piece suit and matching Derby, J.R. was well aware how he didn't look like a man suited to life on the plains. Certainly not life in a tent.

"Evening, gentlemen. J.R. Lockhart of Philadelphia." He shook hands with the nearest man. "I'm here doing a story on the husband auditions." He shook a few more hands.

"You aren't here to get a woman?" said a younger man wearing a Union cap.

"No, I am not." J.R. looked at each man in turn to assure them of his truthfulness. "I'm passing through on my way to Sacramento."

The door to the inn opened.

Every man in J.R.'s line of sight looked in that direction. An attractive blond exited, wearing a navy-blue dress plainer than any of the ones in the fashion plates *Godey's* published. Two steps behind the blond was the sheriff.

"Abby," he said, "hear me out."

She shook her head. "How we wish to hold the auditions is our decision to make. Do what you were hired to do," she ordered and continued walking, passing J.R. and the group of men at the hitching post.

The sheriff followed. "Slow down."

"No, I need to see what Reverend Smith needs while"—was all J.R. heard before they crossed the dirt-packed street.

He looked back to the inn. More women were filing out. All ages. All sizes. The dated styles of their gowns the only consistency. Over thirty women exited the inn. Within moments, men approached, clamoring for attention.

"I should've arrived sooner," Dixon said, and J.R. noticed his coach mate was the only other man still standing at the hitching post.

"Nothing's stopping you from talking to one of them."

Dixon said nothing. Like a man who'd had the fight beaten out of him, he strolled to the inn.

J.R. withdrew a notebook and a stubby pencil from inside his waistcoat. He jotted down the names of everyone he'd met and key details, along with a list of people to talk with tomorrow. The first being the sheriff, and then he'd find the mayor. *Find out who the blond is. Follow up with Logans,* he added, *Zumwalt shoemaker, and Dixon lawyer.* After a glance to the blue-and-gold horizon, J.R. withdrew his pocket watch. Almost seven. He'd wager there was about forty-five minutes before sunset. Pocketing his watch, pencil, and notebook, he looked around. The streets had emptied. The door to the inn had closed, and lamplight glowed in windows on every floor. No sense milling about. He may as well try to book a room inside and—

A woman's scream pierced the silence.

J.R. took off running east in the direction of the sound. He passed several businesses, most of them boarded up.

"I repeat," a sweet voice said, "let her go."

J.R. stopped at an alley between a business and a prim, one-story house. Halfway down the alley, a woman with raven hair stood with her back to him, her hands on the hips of her shiny green-check dress, her attention on the man pinning a weeping blond against the wall of the butcher shop.

A second man stood next to the couple, glaring at the raven-haired woman. "An' if we don't?"

"This town has rules against molesting women," she replied, and J.R. would swear she was smiling. "It is in your best interest to do as I've requested."

The man laughed, and his friend did, too, which only made the blond cry more.

"Calm your britches, missy," said the second man. "We just wanna little kiss from your friend like she gave the sheriff."

"I baked a cake!" the woman abruptly yelled.

"What—"

With another earsplitting scream of "Cake," the woman lunged forward, knocking him backward. He managed to grasp her left arm. Using the heel of her right palm, she struck up, under his nose. He released her arm and cursed. Palm flat, she jabbed her hand into the base of his throat. He choked. She then thrust her foot into the side of his knee. Nose bleeding, the man crumbled to the ground.

She stepped to the side, out of his reach. "Now please release Miss Foster."

Hurling curses about her *injun* blood, the other man did as she requested.

The blond dashed to her friend. "Oh Jane, I—"

"Madeline," the woman ordered as she ripped the bottom ruffle off her petticoat, "find Sheriff Ingram and tell him where to find us."

"I don't know where he is."

The woman sighed loudly. "Go to Doc Carter's. Abby wanted to see if he was going to plaster Reverend Smith's leg or leave it in a splint. And don't you tell anyone—*anyone*—how I helped you."

"I won't. Stop looking at me like that! I won't tell a soul." The blond looked to the two men. "What about them?"

J.R. stepped into the alley. "I'll keep them from running off."

The blond took one look at him then lifted the front of her skirts and darted past.

The raven-haired woman turned her head enough to see him over her shoulder. Her dark-eyed gaze traveled the length of his body, obviously noting with disappointment his lack of weaponry. Lips pursed, she offered him the torn fabric. "Use this to tie"—she nodded to the man standing—"that one's hands behind his back. Use the other end to do the same to his colleague. Tight, please." And then for a reason J.R. was sure he ought to take offense to, she added, "Like a noose."

Four minutes. That's how long had passed since J.R. finished binding the two men back-to-back with the most secure knots he'd ever made. Miss Warrior Princess stood there, utterly quiet, with the serene expression of a woman selecting a ribbon to match her newest gown. February's issue of *Harper's Weekly* had featured an amusing short story about a pretty Cherokee maiden who'd impressed Louis-Philippe, the Duke of Orléans and later the King of France, with the coquettishness of her manners.

Despite how true the author had claimed the story to be, J.R. knew this maiden would find the story more degrading than humorous.

And yet she had been at the inn with the other ladies. Why would a woman as beautiful and fascinating and able to drop a man to his knees as this one *want* to participate in the husband interviews? He couldn't imagine she had a *need* to participate. If the quality of her clothes were any indication, she wasn't destitute. Nor could he imagine any of the other women in town wanting to compete against her staggering beauty.

Dark eyes, almost as ebony as her hair. Prominent cheekbones. That peculiar tint of complexion found only in one of mixed blood. Comparatively, she must view him somewhere near the vicinity of bleached linen.

> *Vanquish! Charge! Free the captives of the night—*
> *To her army railed the queen of liberty, the queen of light.*

"J.R. Lockhart," he said, snapping closed the lid to his watch, "of Philadelphia." No response.

"I'm a journalist, author, occasional poet."
No response.

"I write—well, I wrote for Godey's Lady's Book."
She did nothing but stand there and massage the heel of her right palm.

"I'm on my way to Sacramento to write for a newspaper there."
Her mouth pinched in at the corners like one did when tolerating an annoyance. She looked at the street and sighed. And that's when he knew. She wasn't irritated. She was bored.

And not merely with him. She was bored with her life, the reason she was participating in the husband auditions. Did she actually want a husband, or was she merely looking to be entertained by the process? If the latter, he didn't fault her. He understood. Life in a 223-people town couldn't offer many amusements. Not like Philadelphia did. Yet life in the country's second-largest city had bored him.

Go west, young man was a more viable option for the man—or woman—seeking adventure than war.

J.R. tucked the watch in the pocket of his waistcoat. "Have you found one you like?"

She gave him an odd look.

"Potential husband," he supplied.

Her lips parted. . .and then her head tilted as she studied him. As she *really* looked at him. And then, when he'd given up on any response, she said, "Why do you want to know?"

"I'm writing a story on the husband advertisement."

She resumed massaging her palm. "So this is an interview?"

"If you want it to be."

"I don't."

The two miscreants on the ground shuffled to face J.R. "You can interview me," said the one without the bloody nose.

"He's not interviewing either of you," came an angry voice.

J.R. turned to the man with a six-shooter on his right hip, a gold star on his chest, and a scowl on his face. The blond standing next to him, and wearing a matching scowl, was the very one the sheriff had followed out of the inn. Unlike the other blond, whose flaxen hair was the same vanilla shade as J.R.'s hair, this one had locks the color of a wheat field.

She looked at J.R. with interest, yet instead of introducing herself, said, "Jane, what happened?"

"That one"—she pointed at the man without the bloody nose—"thought himself above following the rules posted about town. After he accosted Madeline Foster, I nicely explained to him how ladies are to be respected."

"I see. What did the other one do to earn a bloody nose?"

"His face—"

"She broke it!" he wailed.

"—was in the way of my hand," she finished as if the man hadn't even spoken.

Unlike the sheriff, the blond didn't seem the least bit surprised or shocked. She looked at J.R. "Did you witness the. . .accosting?"

"Wait right there!" The man without the bloody nose scooted his hindquarters and legs in order to face the blond and the sheriff. "I didn't do any accosting. I was doing nothing but responding to the lady's flirtations."

"I've heard enough." The sheriff grabbed both men by the arms and hauled them to their feet. He led them away, explaining how they could pay a hefty fine and leave town.

The blond walked over to J.R. "Miss Abigail Melton, acting mayor."

"J.R. Lockhart," he said, shaking her hand.

Her hazel eyes glinted with amusement as she looked up at him. "Welcome to Turtle Springs, Mr. Lockhart. The sign-up for the husband auditions is my office."

"I'm not here for the interviews. Not here to participate," he amended. "I'm a journalist, formerly of Godey's Lady's Book. I'm here to write a story about the advertisement."

She looked at the woman called Jane, whose one-shoulder shrug told him nothing of her thoughts. She turned back to J.R. "As I told the reporter who arrived before you, I can't guarantee any lady will agree to an interview, but I wish you well. And I warn you—the inn is filled to capacity. There's space for you in Tent City."

"I don't own a tent." After four years of sleeping in a tent during the war, he vowed never to sleep in one again.

"This could be a problem." Miss Melton thought for a long moment. "Jane, would you find Mr. Lockhart somewhere to stay? Try the Kassels first. They have a spare bedroom. I need to see how Madeline is faring."

Miss Melton strolled off, clearly expecting the woman called Jane to comply.

He smiled. "That was rather exciting, wouldn't you say?"

She rolled her eyes. "Follow me."

As she strolled past, he caught of whiff of her perfume. The classic smell of violet with a mysterious hint of vanilla—a fitting scent for her. This confident yet mysterious Indian maiden had a story to tell.

Before he continued on to California, he'd find out what it was.

Chapter 5

I have the fault of being a little more sincere than is proper.—Molière

Sunday afternoon, May 20

Jane was no more Sacagawea than Mr. Lockhart was Lewis or Clark, and yet here she was escorting him down the vast terrain called Main Street, because after the morning worship service, Abby Melton had invited him to tea to discuss her participation in the husband auditions. . .and then invited Jane to join them. She couldn't exactly decline. She'd longed for this day. For three years! Never had she imagined a dandified journalist from Philadelphia joining their *tête-à-tête*.

Mr. Lockhart knew full well where the Meltons lived. Abby had been sufficiently clear in her directions on where to walk from the Kassels' home to her house. . .right next door! Yet at precisely 3:42 p.m., Mr. Lockhart had arrived at Jane's house, at the opposite end of town from Abby's house. How did he know where Jane lived? She'd not told him.

She wouldn't have told him.

Unlike the baggy clothes of the other men in town, his black suit, like his tan one yesterday, looked to be perfectly tailored to his lean frame. People feared the unfamiliar. If Mr. Lockhart wanted townsfolk to feel comfortable with him, he needed to *look* like he was one of them. For that very reason, even in the privacy of her home, unwilling to be discovered by a surprise visitor, she continued to forsake her comfortable moccasins for constricting, lace-up boots.

"You look vexed," he said, breaking the delightful silence.

Jane stopped in the middle of Main Street. The strong south wind blew, billowing her skirts and sending dust down the road. Traffic, not that there was any, could pass going either direction and not touch her. By keeping to the middle of the street, none of the men loitering on the boardwalk would hear their conversation. Emily Peabody and Louisa Doolittle stepped out of their dressmaker shop, and a good dozen men swarmed the widows. All businesses in town were closed on Sunday, so what were they up to? Work? Or a chance to be swarmed by men?

Mr. Lockhart cleared his throat, drawing her attention.

Jane tilted her head so the brim of her straw bonnet would shield her eyes from the sun. . .and the dusty wind. "Mr. Lockhart, I have no desire to aid you on your quest for a story. I have better things I could be doing."

"Such as?"

"Baking a pie for Reverend Smith"—was the first, and only, thing that came to mind.

With the tip of his index finger, he eased his hat up. "I get it. I understand. You are embarrassed over what I saw, and you think I view your actions as unbecoming for a lady."

Jane stared at him, at his winkling gray-green eyes conveying the assurance he felt over his judgment. He was wrong, though. "I'm not embarrassed. And I have no care about what you think of me." She resumed walking. "This first building on our right is the church."

"That explains the cross on top."

He grinned.

Jane didn't.

She continued. "The lush green next to it is where the town often hosts socials, such as the upcoming Founders' Day Celebration a week from today."

Mr. Lockhart fell into step next to her, jotting into his small black notebook. His writing—those strange marks—looked like bird tracks.

As he wrote, Jane caught sight of Emma Mason strolling next to a man who held hands with a little girl, who, based on their matching carrot-colored hair, had to be father and daughter. Where were Emma's children?

"Turtle Springs," Jane said, "was founded in '55 by a group of emigrants from Connecticut wanting to join the Underground Railroad. Abolitionist Henry Ward Beecher provided the funds to purchase rifles which were then smuggled through pro-slavery areas in crates marked BEECHER'S BIBLES. The town's free-state founding fathers used these rifles to protect themselves from Missouri Bushwhackers."

"An abolitionist tract was the first thing I was paid for writing."

Jane turned away from watching Emma and the stranger. "You're an abolitionist?"

"Was." He drew a deep breath then let it out. "The fight is over. Slavery is now unconstitutional."

Him an abolitionist. She would have never guessed. "Are you a man of faith?"

"I am a member of the Society of Friends."

She jolted to a stop. "A Quaker?" The second after he nodded, she asked, "Is that why you did not attend worship service? Denominational differences?"

He looked away, and his green eyes grew distant. "No," was all he said. His gaze fell to where she rubbed the heel of her right palm. "Let me see your wrist."

Jane clasped her hands together. "It's nothing."

"You started massaging it yesterday while we waited for the sheriff. You've been massaging it since you stepped out of your house."

He'd noticed?

"It's not broken," she told him.

"I know." His smug grin grew. "If you'd fractured a bone, your hand would be too swollen for a leather glove to fit. You wear gloves today so no one will notice the bruise. If they noticed, they would ask." He leaned forward, his eyes filled with kindness, his voice with concern. "Miss Ransome, why are you embarrassed for anyone to know how you protected your friend?"

She wasn't embarrassed. He had no idea the expectations society placed on women, even more so on one with savage and civilized blood.

Jane resumed walking, and to no surprise, Mr. Lockhart kept pace with her. Several tumbleweeds blew past, and yet only puffy, white clouds dotted the sky. No storm in sight. The stone cellar cave on the Lomax farm could hold most of the townsfolk, but with the number of men in town for the husband auditions—Jane sighed. The odds favored a moderate spring, as usual, with the worst being high winds and dust clouds like today. She doubted a fairer, more genial climate could be found on earth. When a storm did hit, one thing always happened.

The heavens rained down wrath.

If a cyclone dropped, J.R. Lockhart of Philadelphia would not know what to do to survive. Jane would have to lead him to safety in the Lomax cave.

"You look vexed again," he said all-cheerful.

Why wouldn't she be? She had so many better things to be doing with her time.

Jane refocused her thoughts. What had she been discussing? Ah yes, Turtle Springs' history. "After the vicious pro-slaver W.C. Quantrill attacked the peaceful town of Lawrence, slaughtering 183 men as old as ninety and boys as young as fourteen, *and* burning all but two businesses"—she drew in a breath—"the men of Turtle Springs enlisted out of righteous indignation over the unjust massacre of their Kansas brethren. Of the eighty-three men who enlisted to fight, seven returned. Doc Carter is the only one unscathed."

"Physically," he muttered.

The gravity of his tone caught her attention. He knew war. He'd lived it. Like the men who fought and the women who stayed behind, he bore scars. Ones that couldn't be seen. Were they as deep as hers?

"Did you fight?" she said, the question rushing from her mouth.

"Only with words." He scribbled in his notebook. "Did you lose anyone?"

Jane paused until she knew her words would convey no emotion. "I have no connections to anyone in Turtle Springs, either dead or living." Needing a change of topic, she motioned to the red-winged blackbirds perched atop Tumble Inn's roofline, from one end to the other. "Here is where the husband auditions will take place this coming Friday, in the dining hall from four to six in the afternoon. Interviews will last fifteen minutes each."

He cast a glance at the inn before focusing on her. "And then?"

"All men leave for the ladies to deliberate. Once finished, Abby will announce a lady's name and that of the suitor she's chosen."

"To marry?"

"No," Jane sighed. "To permit to court her. A woman would be a fool to marry a man she knows all of fifteen minutes. Some men wrote letters prior to their arrival. Each lady has had an opportunity to read and discuss these letters with their confidantes."

"Have you read the letters?"

"Certainly."

"Who did you discuss them with?"

"This is not information you need to know."

"Ah. So no one then."

Jane let out an inelegant snort.

He scribbled something into his notebook. "Is there a list of set questions the ladies will ask in order to compare answers to see if any man's story changes?"

Jane opened her mouth in defense. . .then closed it because, in this, his point was fair. No one had considered testing the men's honesty, not even her, and she was the one most wary of this husband-hunting process. "The only way that would be feasible would be if Mr. Kassel were still alive and able to print copies on his press." To give herself some credit, she added, "Someone, however, purchased diaries for each lady to take notes."

"That's generous of you."

"Why do you presume it was me?"

"For the same reason you don't deny I'm right."

Jane let out another inelegant snort.

He chuckled then gripped her elbow, guiding her out of the street and onto the boardwalk in front of the mercantile. Neither Mr. Underwood nor Mr. Quimby were there to see Jane walking with Mr. Lockhart, yet she knew come Monday morning, they would have a wealth of questions about him.

Movement inside the mercantile caught her eye. She stepped to the window and noticed all four Stevens boys and Luke Collins, who waved at her. As soon as Jane waved back, he took the broom from Emmett. Whatever Luke said caused the boy to nod repeatedly.

"What's going on in there?"

"I think he's making them clean the store," Jane answered. "Luke used to court their older sister, Chardy, who owns the mercantile. The leg he lost in the war keeps him from seeing how much Chardy still loves him. . .and how much he still loves her. She broke her arm earlier in the week."

"How?"

"Her brother George." Really, it was enough of an answer. Anyone male, or who had at least one brother, should understand.

Mr. Lockhart nodded, clearly having fit the first (if not the second, too) distinction.

"Do you have siblings?" she asked, walking next to him.

"None. You?"

"Six—seven." His brows rose, so she explained, "My oldest brother was massacred in Quantrill's Raid. My two younger ones are exploring Texas." Last she knew.

"Ah." He wrote more in his notebook.

As they walked by the Kassels' home, Millie Kassel Kurtz, her mother, and her brother Oliver were sitting under the covered porch. Jane waved.

"Mr. Lockhart," Mrs. Kassel called out, "you do like pork roast and potatoes?"

"Yes, ma'am." He pointed at Oliver. "I expect a rematch."

To Jane's shock, Oliver—the man, to her knowledge, who hadn't smiled since returning from the war with his left arm sawed off and the bodies of his father and brother in boxes—smiled. Not a little one either. Where was Lizzie Roth to see this? "The cards are shuffled and ready," Oliver answered.

As they walked on, Jane studied Mr. Lockhart. What had he said to bring Oliver out of the woe-is-me muck? Whatever he'd done now explained the teary-eyed hugs and the "thank you for thinking of us" Mrs. Kassel and Millie had given Jane before worship this morning. But she hadn't thought of them. Abby was the one who'd ordered Jane to ask the Kassels to house Mr. Lockhart. Abby should be receiving the gratitude.

They reached the Meltons' two-story white home at the tail end of Main Street. Mr. Lockhart handed Jane his notebook and pencil. He then propped his left foot up on a porch step. As he re-tied his shoe, Jane looked through his notebook. Chicken scratch described his writing. She flipped until she reached the last page with marks.

"See something that interests you?"

Pages of interest, actually. Curiosity piqued, Jane looked from the notebook to his amused gaze. "There's not a single word in here."

"Of course not. There's thousands."

"Thousands?"

He nodded. "It's a form of writing called shorthand. May I?" Instead of taking the notebook, he stepped closer, enough that she could smell his pine cologne. He touched the first line of scratch on the left page. His warm voice in her ear said, "Here I wrote, *Find a pretty maiden to stroll through town with.*"

Jane could feel her cheeks grow warm and her pulse increase. He was flirting. Why? He'd insisted he was here for a story, not to marry. But if he were, there were far more suitable women. Ones who would be thrilled to leave a tiny town a hop, skip, and a throw south of the Kansas River. As she felt his gaze on her, she focused on the notebook, because wisdom counseled her to. So did self-protection and cowardice.

"Mr. Lockhart, is this your attempt at flirtation?"

Chapter 6

There are pretenders to piety as well as to courage. —Molière

Miss Jane Ransome was stunningly direct. *When she wants to be,* J.R. silently amended. She was the sort of woman he would court were he gainfully employed. And in California. He wasn't averse to her beauty or charms, not that he believed she'd attempted to charm him. On the contrary, she seemed intentionally standoffish. He'd wager she didn't want him to be attracted to her. But he was. No sense denying it.

He couldn't remember a time he felt a stronger attraction to a woman. But he was leaving for Sacramento after he finished his article. Wisest thing to do was maintain distance, which was why J.R. stopped admiring the curve of her neck, those inches of skin between her bonnet ribbons and the black lace collar of her emerald-and-white-striped dress.

He looked up. A fat lot of luck it did him. As he took a step back, he noticed the rosy hue infusing her cheeks.

Miss Jane Ransome wasn't averse to him either.

"It is my attempt at a *mild* flirtation," he clarified, because he saw no reason to deny it. Surely she'd engaged in a few innocent flirtations of her own.

His honesty earned him a disapproving shake of her head. "Sir, I have no inclination—"

"To fall victim to my charms?" he supplied.

"No—yes, to *that.*" With a troublesome pucker to her brow, she handed him his notebook and pencil, which he didn't take. "Sir, I intend to choose a suitor during the husband interviews. My potential suitors would not view me respectably should I entertain the flirtatious whims of a man passing through on his way to California."

"That man may wish to find a bride to take with him."

Her look told him her exact thought: *You have no wish at all to do that.*

She was right.

Except she wasn't.

Until this moment, he hadn't considered taking a bride west with him. He never expected or hoped to find one in Turtle Springs. He wasn't obligated to go alone. The thought of having a partner on the journey—now that he entertained the idea—tempted him. Especially a partner he enjoyed talking with. And looking at.

As the sun breaks the dawn, so my heart awakes anew.

Perfect words for this moment. As much as he wished to continue the poem, and he would later, he focused on Miss Ransome. His muse.

"A man has the right to change his mind," he said with conviction.

She looked stunned—except, the look was so fleeting J.R. second-guessed seeing it. Her lips curved enough to convey pained tolerance. Such a beautiful mask in an attempt to hide her lack of immunity to him.

J.R. smiled.

"What's that for?" she asked.

"I can't help it. I like it when you look at me that way." Heaven help him, he did. "Your loveliness breathes words to life in me. We shouldn't keep the Meltons waiting." Giving her no time to rebuff his remark, J.R. placed a hand on her lower back and tried not to dwell on how natural the action felt. He nudged her up the steps.

Miss Abigail Melton opened the door.

Within minutes, introductions had been made and greetings paid to Mrs. Lucille Melton; her youngest daughter, Lucy; Miss Lucy's friend, Nora Mason; and Miss Nora's brothers, Ethan and Orrie. Miss Ransome took it upon herself to explain how the two youths and three-year-old were the children of a widow who owned a goat farm south of town. From the description she gave of the woman and the man and little girl who'd walked with her, J.R. guessed his stagecoach mate, Liam Logan, had already begun courting Widow Mason.

Miss Melton touched her sister's shoulder. "Treats for you four are in the kitchen. Be sure to take Orrie to the outhouse *before* you head across the street to the schoolyard." She gave a warning look to the older Mason boy. "Do not leave him in the outhouse again."

"Yes, ma'am," came from the three older children.

As the four dashed down the hall, Mrs. Melton followed. "Have a seat and start without me," she called out. "I'll bring tea."

"Thanks, Ma." Miss Melton led J.R. and Miss Ransome into the parlor. Blue calico curtains framed the corner windows. She pointed to the settee against a wall and then to the small table in the center of the room. "Please, sit wherever you would like."

Miss Ransome placed J.R.'s notebook and pencil on the table and then settled in a rocking chair near the unlit hearth. J.R. eyed the second rocker beside the hearth. Not the best for sitting and writing. Instead he sat at the table, in the lattice-back chair, enabling him an easy view of Miss Ransome. With each backward movement of her rocker, the floorboard underneath creaked. *Squeak.*

Miss Melton moved the oil lamp from the table—*squeak*—to the desk under the window. *Squeak.* She sat at the table. "Jane, there's an extra chair. You can join us."

Squeak.

"Please"—Miss Ransome waved at nothing in particular—"don't mind me."

Squeak.

Miss Melton hesitated. Then she shifted in her chair to face J.R. *Squeak.* "Where would you like to begin?"

Squeak.

J.R. looked at Miss Ransome, contentedly rocking. Miss Melton didn't seem to notice the annoying sound, or, if she did, she didn't let on she was bothered by the—*squeak.* Both ladies were content. Content with the sound. *Squeak.* Content with the seating arrangement. *Squeak.* Content for Miss Ransome to be *not quite* included.

Squeak.

"This won't do," he muttered. Ignoring the women's confused frowns, he lifted the table over the chairs then placed it in front of Miss Ransome's rocker, hindering her ability to rock. He added two chairs, while Miss Melton moved hers. "There. Much better." Smiling, he opened his notebook and looked at the mayor. "Why the advertisement?"

Miss Melton glanced from him to Miss Ransome, thought for a moment, and then looked back to him, a furrow in her brow. "Of the eighty-three men of our town who went to war, seven returned, including Oliver Kassel. That left many widows struggling even more to provide for their families. The advertisement is an answer to a need, nothing more."

Made sense.

J.R. added her words to his notes.

"That's not true," Miss Melton mused, something causing her to rethink her statement. "Mr. Lockhart, the husband auditions are *more* than to answer a need. They are an opportunity to move forward. We need something to focus on besides our losses. We need a reason to believe tomorrow will be better than today."

J.R. stopped after writing *reason to believe.* Unlike Mrs. Hale, who refused to include any mention of the war in *Godey's,* the ladies of Turtle Springs were not ignoring the scars of war, or pretending the war never happened, or content to numb their pain with poems about butterflies. Their dissatisfaction with their struggles was what pushed them to take such drastic risks to change their futures. They chose hope. They chose to keep living.

He quickly jotted his thoughts before he lost them.

"Well now, I hear you're writing a story about our town," Mrs. Melton said, walking into the parlor. She rested the tea tray on the table then sat at the fourth chair around the table.

"Indeed, ma'am." He laid his pencil inside his notebook. "During the war, I traveled with the Philadelphia Brigade, writing stories of the men who served. Afterward I took a position as a staff writer at Godey's Lady's Book—"

"You write for Godey's?" Before he could answer, Mrs. Melton glared at her daughter. "I cannot believe you didn't tell me." She then dashed from the room.

Miss Melton looked heavenward and shook her head sadly as if to say, "You should have never mentioned Godey's."

J.R. eyed Miss Ransome. She stared absently at the tea service. The desire to know what she was thinking gnawed at him. That she wasn't massaging her bruised palm had to mean something. *I'm sorry.* He wasn't sure why he felt the need to apologize. But he did. He wanted to cheer her up, make her laugh, help her believe her tomorrows would be better than her todays. Why? His pulse quickened. Because he cared.

He shouldn't.

Jane Ransome was the least needy woman he'd ever met. She could take down an attacker with her bare hands. Not to say she didn't wear a weapon somewhere on her person. A knife strapped to her calf, most likely. Possibly a revolver. Even if she wasn't a perfect shot, he was certain she knew how to load, shoot, and hit a target. He'd never held a gun in his life.

A man could be a hero to any woman in this town. In this country, for that matter.

How could any man be a hero to *her*?

Jane Ransome, the beauty she was, didn't need a rescuer. She certainly didn't need a man whose personal belongings fit into two categories: luxurious clothes and books.

Mrs. Melton returned carrying an armful of magazines J.R. recognized instantly. She pushed the tea service across the table; an inch more and it would have toppled into her daughter's lap. "Theodore bought me a year's subscription of Godey's in '33 as a wedding gift. These seven are the ones I received last year, in the months following his death. Spending three dollars on a subscription for this year seemed..." She blinked at the tears in her eyes. "Is your writing in any of these?"

"Let me see." J.R. shifted through the pile, pulling out the ones she'd asked for. He didn't need to check the dates. He'd studied every page of every edition published since he began working for Mrs. Hale. He could describe the covers by memory.

"Would you sign them?" she asked.

He blinked. Sign his work? He looked at Miss Melton and was glad he hadn't laughed. She was serious. "Of course," he said with a smile.

A good thirty minutes passed before he finished autographing the magazines and obliging her myriad questions. Misses Melton and Ransome had finished their tea, poured refills, and were discussing what days they'd each signed up to take meals to Reverend Smith.

J.R. opened his notebook. He cleared his throat to draw their attention. "A town often has a handful of women who—" How to say this without offending them?

"Who rule the roost?" Miss Melton supplied.

He nodded. "Their willingness to share their stories will sway others into talking. Who do you recommend?"

"Emma Peabody and Louisa Doolittle," answered Mrs. Melton. She leaned close and patted his arm. "Be on your guard around those two. A handsome bachelor is a tempting prize that has destroyed more than one friendship. Trust me, I know."

"Ma!"

"Abby, don't be so shocked." Mrs. Melton's chin rose. "The moment I saw your father I knew I wanted him more than any other woman could possibly want him. Once I found my sister a husband of her own, she forgave me for being more alluring."

Miss Melton's cheeks pinked, and yet she smiled. "I swear you say things solely for the sake of embarrassing me."

"Oh, I would never." Mrs. Melton's lips twitched. She sipped her tea. "Unfortunately for Mr. Lockhart, he is too young and adventurous for me to try to impress with my wit. You, on the other hand, need to stop waiting for Sheriff Ingram to come around to your way of thinking and consider how you can woo Mr. Lockhart."

"Ma," groaned Miss Melton. She looked at J.R. "Please ignore her."

"Can't." He winked at Mrs. Melton. "Venus isn't possible to ignore."

Miss Ransome, once again, stared absently at the tea tray. For a woman who had been so talkative during the walk here, she was strangely quiet.

Mrs. Melton fluttered her lashes at J.R. "Call me Lucille."

"What on earth! Ma, stop flirting with Mr. Lockhart." Miss Melton looked at J.R. "You should talk to Maggie Piner. She's about ten years older than I am, has two boys, and lives a mile out of town. Her husband died the same day Pa and my brother Dan did. She's the kindest lady you'll ever meet."

Mrs. Melton nodded. "And pretty, too. Maggie's not as gregarious as Emma or Louisa, but, J.R.," she said, because clearly a mild flirtation put them on first-name basis, "I don't know a soul who doesn't admire how Maggie's worked to keep her land. Frieda Lomax is another good one to interview. And Caroline Kane, but she is so busy with the inn and managing her siblings, she may not have time to tell you her story."

"Same with Chardy Stevens," Miss Melton put in.

J.R. added these names to his list. "Anyone else?"

The Meltons sipped their tea. Exchanged glances with one another. Sighed. "Debbie Barker."

J.R. watched as both Meltons turned their heads to look at Miss Ransome.

"Who?" Miss Melton asked, her confusion matching her mother's.

"Early twenties, deep blue eyes, strawberry blond." When the Meltons shook their heads, Miss Ransome set her teacup and saucer onto the table. "Debbie and her parents live on a homestead a couple miles past the Radles, near Antelope Creek. The Terrys are their closet neighbor."

The Meltons continued to frown like they had no idea who she was talking about.

Miss Ransome looked at J.R.—more precisely, at his notebook. "Debbie wasn't happy about the move to Kansas. They don't come into town too often, so she hasn't made many friends. They were here for the Remembrance Service.

When they make it to Sunday worship, I like to sit near them because all three of them have beautiful singing voices. Debbie says God has been softening her heart about life here, which is why she decided to participate in the husband auditions. Her talking to you won't convince anyone else to agree to an interview, but I would want to read her story."

J.R. looked down at his notes. He hadn't written a thing about the Barker family because he'd been so focused on listening to Miss Ransome talk. The woman was a walking city—perhaps even county—directory. Yet she'd never spoke of anyone as if the woman was an intimate friend. Did she have any? Or was she alone?

Miss Melton turned to her mother.

Mrs. Melton shook her head. Her eyes flickered to Miss Ransome and then to J.R., who then looked at Miss Melton, hoping for her to say something. She released a soft hmmph.

"Uh huh." From her mother.

Another hmmph.

J.R. tapped his notebook with his pencil. This was awkward. Some strange conversation was going on and he was certain it involved him. And not in a good way.

"You sure?" Miss Melton finally said.

Her mother exhaled. "Once you know what to look for, it's obvious."

Miss Melton let out a little laugh. "No wonder Josiah runs from you."

Miss Ransome's eyes widened. She looked back and forth between them. "No. Absolutely not. I have better things to do with my time."

"Of course you do." Lucille Melton stood. She gathered the cups and saucers. "J.R., dear, you are welcome for tea anytime. You, too, Jane Ransome." She strolled out of the parlor, leaving her daughter alone to glower at Miss Ransome.

Miss Melton turned sharply to face her. "What are these better things you have to do?"

After a few moments, Miss Ransome cleared her throat. "For starters, I have to settle upon my list of questions to ask during the husband interviews. Not any simple question will do. That's, at minimum, two full days of work." She rested against the back of her rocker. "I also have to plan and cook a meal for Reverend Smith. Another full day of work."

"Really?"

"Real-ly." Complete conviction laced both syllables. Miss Ransome smiled smugly. "On Tuesday my cousin Cyrus will arrive with the wagon of goods from my father. I have to inventory it, stock my pantry, and then see what Chardy wants to buy. I should take a meal to her, too." She turned to J.R. "Chardy has a broken arm. Her brother's fault."

J.R. started to say, "I know," but he didn't need to be King Belshazzar to see the handwriting on the wall warning him to stay silent.

"Of course," continued Miss Ransome, "I need to also see what assistance Miss Loretta needs with the Founders' Day Celebration." She cast an apologetic glance at J.R. "It's the Saturday after the auditions. Ice cream will be served, but you aren't obligated to attend."

He gave her a nod of understanding. This had to be the strangest conversation he'd ever been a part of. And one of the most enjoyable.

Miss Melton rapped her fingers in a slow yet continual motion on the table. "I like you, Jane," she said in a measured tone. "I do. Which is why I am appointing you as my special hostess to the press."

Miss Ransome's eyes narrowed. "There is no such thing as a hostess to the press."

"There is now." In an abrupt motion, Miss Abigail Melton swiveled in her chair. She gave J.R. a bright smile. "Jane will drive you out to the Barkers' homestead tomorrow. And to the Piner Ranch at your convenience. Let her know who else you need to be introduced to, and she will arrange it under the authority of the office of the mayor."

Chapter 7

The trees that are slow to grow bear the best fruit.—Molière

Friday afternoon, May 25

"Yep, there she goes, she's lookin' again."

Jane turned away from the river of men in front of the Tumble Inn, shifting in her chair to face Mr. Quimby, who studied the checkerboard as if it were a work of art. "Tease all you wish. I am not embarrassed to be caught looking. Abby has the names of over a hundred men on the husband audition sign-up list."

"Over a hundred men!" Mr. Underwood jumped his black piece over two of Mr. Quimby's. "King me again."

Mr. Quimby grumbled. But did as he was told.

Mr. Underwood frowned. "Jane, that's a lot of men for only eight fifteen-minute interview sessions. How's this going to work anyway?"

Jane glanced down the street to the inn. Her heartbeat increased, to her annoyance. Mr. Lockhart, now outside, shook hands with those in line. How little she'd accomplished during the last four days because of all the times he needed "hostess to the press" assistance.

She spent an hour driving him in the buggy out to, and another hour back from, the Barker homestead. She took him to visit the Piner Ranch, only to discover no one was home. She helped him deliver Mrs. Kassel's meal to Reverend Smith. She escorted him to the Lomax farm and, after Frieda's girls told him about their stone cellar, endured his sudden insistence that she, along with Frieda's girls, take him out to see it. She, not Millie, had to sit in a chair in the Kassels' parlor and smile as he and Oliver adjusted the lens on the camera they'd dug out of the newspaper office that hadn't seen the light of day since Oliver and Millie's father marched off to war.

Only—*only*—because she was a nice person had she agreed to dinner last night at the Kassels in order for Oliver and Mr. Lockhart to help her and Millie polish their interview questions, despite the fact no one asked for their bachelor opinions.

She'd even tolerated Mr. Lockhart's constant chattering as he aided her cousin Cyrus in unloading the wagon, and as Mr. Lockhart insisted upon helping her inventory the food, furs, cloth, and seed Papa had sent from his trading posts. And then Mr. Lockhart helped her sell what she didn't need and what Chardy Stevens didn't wish to buy to the men living in Tent City. Actually he did all the selling for her. . .at a greater profit, too! Mama would want to adopt him.

Or insist Jane marry him.

She laughed silently at the ridiculousness.

Point was, her life had been much more peaceful before J.R. Lockhart arrived in town.

He had, she must admit, willingly helped her choose items from her excess to add to the abundant food given to Reverend Smith, which he wanted distributed to those less fortunate. Food they were able to leave at Piner Ranch without Maggie knowing who brought it. Food they also left on the McGees' porch before sunrise this morning.

Mr. Lockhart found enjoyment in busyness and in sitting on the Kassels' front porch watching the sunset, another thing he insisted he needed a *hostess to the press* for. Happy as a puppy he was. Which was no wonder it seemed everyone in town, even in Tent City, was on first-name basis with him. How did he do that? How was it he made friends so easily while after three years, her closest confidants were two elderly men?

With an irritated growl under her breath, she turned back to see Misters Quimby and Underwood smiling at her. "I do not care if you know I was thinking about Mr. Lockhart. Abby ordered me to help him arrange his interviews. What was the question?"

"The interviews?" prodded Mr. Underwood. "Too many men, too little time."

A fitting analysis.

Jane rested her hands atop the journal in the lap of her purple suit. As often as Abby had explained the order of events in last week's meeting, the logistics of it never made complete sense. But Abby said to trust her, so Jane chose not to fret the details. "A good number of men," she explained, "sent letters for us to read. If a lady favored a letter, the author is given an automatic interview time with her, regardless of where he is in the line. No man is required to speak to a lady if he doesn't feel inclined."

"You mean iffen he doesn't think she's pretty enough?"

Jane grimaced. "As cold-hearted as that is, Mr. Quimby, yes. This is why several of the ladies have engaged the interviewees prior to today, to weed out the riffraff. Every man who signed up for the interviews will be given a notecard. If a lady has written her name down on a man's card, he earns an automatic session with her."

"And the tides turn," muttered Mr. Underwood. "If I were a lady, I'd be clever and pick my eight interviewees ahead of time. This way I could talk to whoever I wanted."

Jane smiled and boasted, "Then we shall agree I'm clever."

Mr. Underwood applauded. "That's our girl."

Mr. Quimby merely curled his upper lip. "Is Locky on yer card?"

"Of course not. He's leaving for Sacramento once his article is finished."

Both men stared at her as if she'd spoken another language. For her own personal amusement, she repeated the statement in French. And then in Shawnee.

"Lemme see who ya picked over our Locky."

"Your dear Locky is not an option for any lady to choose." Feeling satisfied about the names she'd written down, she withdrew the list from inside her journal. "I've only met five of them. The other three are highly recommended."

He ripped the card from her hand. "Don't you know better than to take a recommendation from someone yer competing against? They ain't gonna share the good'uns with—*oomph*."

Jane jerked her gaze to Mr. Underwood. "Did you kick him?"

With the tip of a finger, he slid a black checker forward on the board. "He earned it."

"*With an injun* is what you was thinking I was thinking," Mr. Quimby grumbled at his friend. "But I was fixin' to say *with their competition*."

Mr. Underwood dipped his head in apology. Why? He had nothing to apologize for. She could not change what she was. . .or how she was viewed by some people because of what she was. This was why she'd left the Shawnee Mission. Why she'd left Kansas Half-Breed Lands. Why she didn't stay in Lawrence after the massacre. She had a home here. In Turtle Springs. She had people she could help, could love, and do kind things for.

People here needed her.

And as soon as she was engaged to marry, her whole family would come here to evaluate the man she'd chosen. Once they approved him—and they would approve—she'd convince them to stay. Convince them this could be their home, too.

For the first time in years, they could be together again.

Laughter drifted down the boardwalk.

Jane again looked. Mr. Lockhart had made his way to the middle of the line in front of the inn. Even if his hair weren't such a pale blond or if his handsome features didn't have such a pleasing symmetry, he'd stand out in a crowd. He drew people to himself. Because they wanted to hear him speak, but also because they knew he listened to them as well. She'd seen the way the other ladies in town looked at him—a silent, wistful *if only, if only he were an option*. Yet none had hounded him like they had Sheriff Ingram until he convinced all he and Abby were affianced.

Several whistles from the men pierced the air.

Abby wore her lovely blue suit with the scooped neckline. Not too daring. Neither too modest. No wonder the men whistled.

Mr. Lockhart met her in the middle of the street. As he withdrew his notebook from inside his impeccably tailored brown suit, he said something to Abby which made her glower at him. He held his hands up in an apologetic manner. Then he stepped back and gave her room to pass.

When he straightened, he looked right at—

Jane's breath caught. He watched her with such open admiration. With confidence and intensity. And with the knowledge others were noticing. Why? Save for that one comment about *a man has a right to change his mind*, he'd neither done nor said anything to insinuate he was pursuing her. He'd treated her like her brothers used to. Whenever they'd been out walking and he saw someone he knew—and he *always* saw someone he knew—he'd introduce her.

One would think he was a resident of Turtle Springs and she the visitor.

Stop, she mouthed, swiping the air with both hands. He had to cease this or people would misunderstand, and then all of the diligence she'd put into preparing the interview questions would be wasted. All for naught! Because no man would come to her table as long as he believed the man he admired so much had chosen her as his bride. Mr. Lockhart, the flirt he was, hadn't chosen her for anything but to be the subject of his next story.

As soon as he'd accomplished that, he'd be off seeking a new muse. A new adventure. All without her. Like Mama and Papa had done. Like her brothers.

Because no one needed Jane Ransome.

Why should they? She was perfectly capable of taking care of herself. Besides, she didn't *need* anyone anyway.

Mr. Lockhart grinned.

Or at least she thought he did. Her vision had blurred too much for her to tell. He tipped his hat. . .then strolled back to the line.

"Shouldn't you go inside with the other ladies?" asked Mr. Underwood in a soft, fatherly voice. "You deserve to find a mate as much as they do."

"I will in a minute."

"Jane, what's wrong?"

She shrugged. "It's nothing. I'll be fine. I always am."

They looked like spooked owls. Or debutantes at their first ball.

"Excuse me." J.R. slid past Sheriff Ingram, who'd decided the best place to oversee the noisy crowd was right inside the door. Not sure how much overseeing of the crowd he was doing, in light of the fact he rarely looked away from Miss Melton. The women sat patiently at the dining hall's center table, listening to the second group of bachelors.

Poor Mrs. Lomax looked a tad green as a man twice her age—and weight—talked and talked and talked. Where was her friend, Miss Green?

J.R. scanned the dining hall. He didn't see the schoolteacher, but he did see William Dixon talking to Miss Ransome. She wore a simple yet elegant amethyst suit lacking adornment. As if she sensed someone watching, she looked up. . .and their eyes met. A tightness settled in J.R.'s chest, and for the second time today, after looking at her, he had difficulty drawing a breath. Dixon said something, snatching her attention away from J.R., but he couldn't move his gaze off her.

He'd had opportunities to court other women after Sybil's father refused J.R.'s request to court his daughter. He'd attended cotillions. He'd attended more than a few match-making teas his mother forced him to. A year of attempted courtships that never worked out. Fruitless searches. The war gave him an excuse to stop. No more wasting time on shallow conversations and women who viewed him as a dear friend. He could wait until he found the right girl.

And now, Jane.

With her ebony hair twisted into a smooth bun at the top of her head, Jane was as set-apart as a longtail widowbird in a room of hummingbirds, blue jays, and golden pheasants. He smiled, knowing her exact response to his appraisal.

Mr. Lockhart, a lady doesn't take kindly to being compared to a bird.

Jane wouldn't take kindly.

She was the type of woman who lived on good soup, not fine words. He would say them, though, if he knew she'd believe him. If he knew that's all it'd take to convince her to come to California with him. He had to prove to her that what was growing between them would be the foundation for something wonderful.

The mist of love descended on lovers and fools alike—
Both joy and pathos, both heartache and bliss,
For all are equal in hope this rapturous night.

What would she do if he shared the words he wrote for her? What would she do if he strode up to her table and said, "Marry me"? Or knelt at her feet and said, "Marry me"?

Or drew her into his arms, kissed her senseless, and then said "Marry me"?

Some women, even after such short a time of meeting, would relish such a grand proposal. Widows Peabody and Doolittle would. Lucille Melton would. Her oldest daughter would, too.

J.R. eyed the sheriff. The man looked too troubled, too unsure, and too angry to do any proposing tonight.

Ding, ding, ding.

At the tapping of the bell, chairs scrapped against the floor. Men moved about the room, a few leaving as a new set entered. J.R. looked at Jane, just as the lawyer from Tennessee kissed the back of her hand. Her cheeks pinked. Pinked! Fifteen minutes was not enough time for any woman to develop feelings for a man she'd just met. Love at first sight? Jane was too practical to play Juliet to Dixon's Romeo.

Or was this not their first conversation?

During J.R.'s discussion with Miss Melton after worship service, he vaguely remembered seeing Dixon exit the church. Not with Jane, though. She'd walked out alone. And then she'd walked directly to where J.R. and Miss Melton were talking. Dixon would have had no time to court Jane this week because Jane had been J.R.'s hostess. She'd been with *him.* Practically from sunrise to sunset.

As men changed seats, Dixon still held Jane's hand. Her lips froze in a tight smile, her countenance strained enough for J.R. to read her unspoken request for distance.

Dixon held firm. If he saw her discomfiture, he didn't care.

Fury boiled up in J.R. No woman, not even one as capable as Jane, should be forced to endure a man's attentions.

Even as Dixon spoke, Jane's gaze flickered to J.R. He took a step forward, empowered by her silent plea, ready to—

At the touch of a firm hand on his shoulder, he turned.

"Some women think it's romantic to be fought over," Sheriff Ingram said in a chilly tone. "Not that one, Lockhart. She will be mortified to be made the subject to a scene." His bright blue eyes narrowed. "So if I'm right about what you're intending, then you'd better head on outside and decide if you want her. . .or if you just don't want someone else to have her."

"There's a difference?"

His gaze flickered to where Miss Melton sat. "Unfortunately, there is."

Chapter 8

Reason is not what decides love.—Molière

Later that evening

"Care to share your troubles with an old woman?"

J.R. shifted on the porch's top step to look over his shoulder at Gretchen Kassel standing on the door threshold, not looking a day over forty, which pleased her greatly since she'd passed her fiftieth year. She held two mugs. "Is that coffee?" he asked in anticipation.

"If I said yes, would that make you agree to bare your soul?"

"Only if you added milk and honey."

"Then coffee it is." With that perceptive smile of hers, she stepped forward. "The sweet, mucky-colored one is yours." Once he took a mug, she sat next to him. "Beautiful moon."

"It is." He glanced down the boardwalk to the chairs in front of the mercantile, the very ones Jane's elderly protectors occupied most mornings and afternoons. "Will Carter seems to have a problem walking. He and Millie have been sitting there for the last hour. Are you concerned?"

"Oliver is keeping an eye on them from the upstairs window."

"He's a good brother."

"I noticed you talking with Ebenezer Zumwalt while I photographed the couples."

"A lady is always in need of a good shoemaker." She studied him for a moment before smiling mischievously. "Especially if she's in a race with her daughter to the altar."

J.R. laughed, unable to help it.

They sipped their coffee, listening to crickets and the hushed voices of Millie and her new suitor. The young widow had surprised J.R. with her choice. Since the night the Kassels offered him use of the spare bedroom next to Oliver's, J.R. noticed the half-heartedness Millie had for participating in the auditions. Lingering grief over her husband-of-six-month's death? Or guilt over her decision to move forward?

It'd been three years. The time to mourn had passed.

Even her mother realized that.

"I hope things turn out well for them," he said in sincerity.

Mrs. Kassel nodded. "Mr. Carter seems like good man." She rested her hand on J.R.'s forearm. "I appreciate all you've done for Oliver. You're a good man."

"I haven't done much."

"You reminded my son how to smile. That's the first step in learning to live again."

J.R. sipped his coffee. "The biggest credit goes to you for the suggestion to take pictures of the ladies with their chosen suitors. Considering what little experience I have with cameras, I couldn't have managed it or the darkroom, without Oliver's help. You should sell the printing press and convince him to turn the newspaper office into a photography studio."

She held the mug with both hands, staring down into the inky liquid. "He used to love photography and helping his father with the newspaper. After he lost part of his arm. . ." She shook her head and sighed. "He won't consider it unless *you* are the one who suggests it. You remind us all of his father, not because you share the same pale coloring. Bert was warm and fun and had such a positive outlook people loved being around him. You have that same vivaciousness, that same enthusiasm for life."

"Jane isn't impressed."

"Jane doesn't impress easily." Her head tilted slightly, her expression inscrutable as she studied him. "Did she choose a suitor tonight?"

He nodded, hoping she didn't see the annoyance he felt. "William Dixon, lawyer from Tennessee. Good man," he admitted, although the jealous part of him wished it wasn't true. "He's taken out a loan on the empty law office across the street."

"A woman seeking security will find that quite alluring."

"You think Jane doesn't feel secure?" When she didn't answer, he said, "I don't think she favors Dixon's suit. If she did, why refuse to have her photograph taken with him? Every other lady jumped at the opportunity to have a photograph with the man she chose."

"Maybe Jane is waiting."

He stared at her in shock. "On what?"

"I don't know." She shrugged in the manner of one who was guessing, but he knew she was sure of her answer. "Maybe. . .on you deciding if you are going to court her."

"*If* I'm going to court her? What do you think I've been doing this week?"

"I think you've been having a lovely time dangling Jane along as if she's a child-hood playmate."

J.R. winced. "She looked like she was having fun. Do you think she was playacting?"

"I would be surprised if anyone in this town knows Jane well enough to answer that." She set her mug on the step next to his. "What do you know about her, besides the fact she's a beautiful woman who intrigues you?"

He shifted on the step so he could face Mrs. Kassel, crossed his arms, rested his elbows on his knees. "Jane's father, Wellington Ransome, married Victorie Pappan, the fourth daughter of a French trapper and a widowed Shawnee squaw. In '33 the couple left the Ohio Valley and settled in Kansas Territory near what's now the town of Olathe. Ransome built taverns and trading posts near forts. He put ferries at river crossings." J.R. paused. Considering Ransome sent his only unmarried daughter a wagonload of goods every month, J.R. had no doubt her family was far wealthier than anyone in town knew. Some information, like Jane's older brother's murder, was also hers to share.

"Jane's mother, Victorie," he went on, "knows seven languages and speaks with a French accent. Eight of her ten children lived to adulthood. Jane and her two younger brothers are the only ones not married. Ransome and his wife serve as translators for the Agency of Indian Affairs."

Mrs. Kassel nodded. "So that's why they never visit. I heard Indian girls are betrothed, sometimes sold, by their parents when they are very young. Jane is twenty-six and has never been married, that I know of."

"I don't think she has either."

"With all the time you two have had to talk, how is it you don't know?"

"Jane is free with facts." To J.R.'s admiration and frustration, her cousin, Cyrus, had been as stingy with personal stories about Jane. Good man, though. "Her feelings, her fears—she keeps hidden."

"Interesting." Silence lingered. "Don't you think it strange Jane's parents would build that house and then leave her there alone?"

J.R. rubbed at the growing tension in his forehead. He did find it strange.

"Do you want to marry her?" came softly.

"I've entertained the idea." More than entertained. He'd imagined their lives together in Sacramento. He looked at Mrs. Kassel. "Unfortunately, Jane has given me no indication she would welcome my attentions. She doesn't respond to flirting."

"Why should she?" she said with an overt edge in her tone. "You've known her for six days. Women generally need more time to decide if a man is worth a life-long commitment."

"I don't have time to waste waiting for her to decide. I'm leaving for California as soon as I finish writing my article."

"And that, J.R., is why she selected Mr. Dixon."

Saturday afternoon, May 26,
Founders' Day Celebration

Jane held her eyes closed as she waited. . .and *waited* for Clyde McGee to finish the prayer he'd begged Reverend Smith to allow him to give. Was he finished? Was he thinking of another rhyme? She peeked out of the corner of her eye. The youth stood next to her on the top of the church step, head bowed, hands folded together. She tugged the tail of his untucked shirt.

"Aaaaaaaa-men!" he yelled.

Another roar of amens and several whistles followed.

Once the noise quieted down, Jane cupped her hands around her mouth. "If you haven't placed your bid on a quilt," she yelled to the crowd, "then hightail it over to the bidding booth." She raised an arm in the air, holding up three fingers. "The auction ends at three. Madeline Foster has the list. Madeline, wave so everyone sees where you are."

One by one, the crowd turned from where Jane stood on the church steps and looked to the wooden booth between the cemetery and the Fosters' two-story home. Madeline Foster stood on an upside-down crate next to the booth, waving. To her left, the colorful array of quilts, buffalo hides, and fur pelts attached to her mother's clothesline fluttered in the warm breeze.

"Thanks, Miss Jane, for organizing this." Clyde grasped her around the waist and held tight. "You're the best neighbor."

"Uhhh. . ." She patted his back. "You're welcome?"

He darted down the steps. Raising his hands in the air, he stopped in front of his friends. They all patted him on the back.

Slowly the crowd spread out. Some headed to peruse the quilts, hides, and pelts being auctioned to pay for the school's repair fund. Some headed to the tables spread with pastries and hand-cranked freezers of ice cream. To be sure, Mrs. Bombay's strawberry and cream would be the first consumed. It always was. Of course, she refused to serve it to children.

"I bet she uses liquor," Jane muttered.

"I wouldn't say that too loudly."

Jane looked to Mr. Lockhart standing at the bottom of the steps, wearing that fancy tan suit of his. "Where have you been? You missed Reverend Smith's oral presentation on the history of the town."

He leaned against the wooden bannister. Slid his hat back with the tip of his finger, and a lock of white-blond hair fell across his forehead. "I've been helping Ebenezer Zumwalt persuade the guests abiding in his soon-to-be residence above his soon-to-be-open business to find habitat elsewhere."

"You've been there all day?"

"All day," he said with a smug grin.

"I see." Jane tried—and failed—to school her smile. "You must have a twin, for three people informed me you were loitering about my house while I was here setting up tables." She descended the steps. "Truthfully, Mr. Lockhart, what shenanigans are you about?"

"Do I have to answer?"

She laughed. "Well now you do."

He held his arm out, a silent request for her to take a stroll with him.

Jane nervously looked around. "Mr. Dixon is—"

"Busy," he cut in. His gaze shifted to where Mr. Dixon held the medicine chest Doc Carter had loaned them to use to collect auction money. Madeline, still standing on the upside-down crate, touched his shoulder. Somehow he managed to hold the chest and use both hands to lift her to the ground. Instead of giving him a flirtatious smile, she started talking to Mr. and Mrs. Watson. Since the altercation in the alley, Madeline hadn't been the same.

"She skipped the husband interviews," Jane said, looking to Mr. Lockhart.

"Are you jealous of your friend?"

"What for?"

"You chose Dixon, and yet he is there, not here."

"Ah." Choose him she did.

Mr. Lockhart looped her arm around his and led her away from the church. "Jane, my dear, this is where you are supposed to bat your lashes at me and say,"—his voice pitched falsetto—"why, sir, *you* sound jealous."

"I'm supposed to do that?"

He nodded.

"Why?" she asked, feeling a tad mortified.

"Didn't your sisters teach you the art of flirtation? It's a useful skill, or so I read every month in Godey's."

Jane opened her mouth then closed it.

"I take that as a no," he said softly, his breath warm against her cheek. The very air around them felt different. She felt different.

She wanted. . .something.

She wanted to be someone so bold, so daring, so confident in who she was that, like Ma Melton had, she could say to other women, "I want this man more than any of you ever could." Doing that was no guarantee the man she wanted would reciprocate her feelings. If a man truly cared for her, he would not want her to be clingy. Or needy. If a man truly cared for her, he would ensure she knew his feelings *and* he would know hers without her needing to speak or allure him with batting her lashes.

"I know I'm not good at flirting," she said. When she saw that all-it-takes-is-practice-to-be-good-at-something look in his eyes, she added, "I am fine with that."

"*You* are," he murmured. "I'm not sure I am."

"Why would you not be fine with me not being a flirt?"

With an "Oh, Jane," he stepped onto the dirt-packed street.

Jane happily left him to his thoughts. If her sisters had taught her the art of flirtation, she would understand his comment. They hadn't. Thus she didn't. And yet the strange—whatever *that* was—feeling that had come over her had, thankfully, faded. All was right in her world again.

Of course, she still didn't see how flirting was a useful skill. Mistaken intention would be lessened if one were honest with emotions. Why did society consider it too brazen to say, "I regard you fondly"? Why make courting rituals so complicated?

"Mr. Lockhart, did you know *The Handbook of Good Society* lists ways to flirt with a handkerchief, with gloves, a parasol, a fan, and even a hat? Even the movements of one's eyes has flirtatious meanings." Jane released a weary sigh. "I am supposed to remember dozens of actions and eye flutters *and* the meanings for them, and yet I cannot remember if the correct past tense of *kneel* is *kneeled* or *knelt*."

"For me, it's *sneaked*, *snuck*, or *snelt*." He groaned. "And I'm a writer."

"Now you are being silly."

"Then you must call me J.R."

"I don't see the connection."

"There isn't one"—he winked—"but be adventurous and do it anyway."

Jane stopped walking upon reaching the boundary of her property, but he tugged her onward, leading her down the dirt path that ran alongside her house. "Where are we going?" she asked, feeling out of breath. From the pace. Certainly not from his nearness.

"You'll see."

They continued on. Past her garden. Past the well. Past the small corral with her horse, Lady, and goats—Chief Fish, Baby, Nana, and Fawn, all instantly bleating for her to bestow upon them some attention in the form of a treat. Past the carriage house and—

"What's this?" she asked.

Mr. Lockhart stopped on the south side of the building. "Congratulations! It's our own private Founders' Day Celebration." There on the ground was a blanket, a covered basket, and someone's hand-cranked ice cream machine.

She gave him a wary look.

In response, he blinked both eyes repeatedly at the same time.

"What are you doing?"

"Flirting"—he grimaced—"I think."

Jane laughed aloud at that.

"It's the best I can do, sweetheart, for I am sorely lacking fan, gloves, and parasol."

"You do have a hat," she reminded him. Then pointed at it.

"Ah." He rested it over his heart…and stood there like a soldier…saying nothing.

Jane stepped closer. She leaned forward until her cheek was parallel with his and whispered, "I am afraid I don't know what your hat is conveying."

He leaned toward her, just the tiniest bit. His smile faded. "Why didn't you ask me why I'm jealous of Dixon?"

She started to say he wasn't jealous of Mr. Dixon and that this was no joking matter, but her argument might not withstand the seriousness in the depths of his gray-green eyes. He *was* jealous of Mr. Dixon. Her heart pounded anew. She wanted to believe—hope, even—that he cared for her. If he did, they could court. Maybe marry.

If he cared.

No, her heart cautioned. It was too much to hope…and yet she had to know. She needed to, which was why she could not stop the soft words from escaping.

"Why are you jealous of him?"

"Normally I wouldn't be so forward"—his gaze fell to her lips, and her heart skipped a beat—"but when he kissed your hand, and you blushed, I realized my subtle courtship this week has been lost on you."

Jane felt her eyes widen. "You were courting me?"

"Mrs. Kassel kindly pointed out that courting does not count if the admired lady fails to realize her suitor's intentions." He tilted her chin, angling her face to his. "I intend on remedying that beginning now. I think I'm falling in love with you, Jane Ransome, if I'm not there already. Will you allow me to court you?"

She did not say anything right away. Not yet. She had never felt so treasured, so desired, so chosen. J.R. could have had his choice of any lady in town—in all truth, he *did* have his choice, and he chose her. If he would have participated in the interviews, she would have chosen him. Oh my. She had to let this moment stretch and grow and take root in her heart. The most wonderful man in town was falling in love. With her. *If I'm not there already.*

If. Her cheeked warmed. *If* was such a mighty big word.

"J.R.," she whispered, and for a moment he leaned closer, as if he was about to touch his lips to hers, "I think I'm falling in love with you, too."

"If you're not there already?"

Jane smiled at the hopefulness in his voice. She nodded. "*If* I'm not."

He smiled.

And then he released her. "I hope you like plain vanilla, because that's all I have."

Chapter 9

The more we love our friends, the less we flatter them;
it is by excusing nothing that pure love shows itself.—Molière

With the last of the ice cream eaten, J.R. stretched out on the blanket and rested one ankle atop the other. He folded his arms behind his head, using his palms for a pillow. The sweetness of the ice cream paled against the beauty who blushed as he'd recited to her his favorite William Wordsworth poem.

She was a Phantom of delight
When first she gleamed upon my sight;
A lovely Apparition, sent
To be a moment's ornament;
Her eyes as stars of Twilight fair;
Like Twilight's, too, her dusky hair. . .

No more truer words described how he'd felt when he first saw Jane in the alley between the butchery and what was now a soon-to-be shoemaker shop.

"You never told me why you chose Dixon?" he asked, studying the white clouds dotting the sky.

"He asked for my help."

J.R. turned his head, just enough to see her sitting, legs tucked to the side. She'd moved the basket and ice cream bucket to the edge of the blanket. Her bare hands—gloves removed so she did not soil them with ice cream—rested in the lap of her blue-checked dress. Her lips curved. He'd slay a dragon for her. He wanted to, at least. Surely that had to count. Thankfully dragons had been vanquished by men who had known how to wield swords.

He was more apt with wielding a pen.

"And?" he prodded. "There's more to your story. There has to be."

She drew a deep breath then let it out. "Prior to the husband interviews, I spoke with Mr. Dixon upon two occasions. He is a reserved man, who desperately yearns to find a God-fearing woman to marry, but women have told him he is too nice. So as I overheard his interview with Abby, I wondered why the brash demeanor. During our session, I questioned him, and he admitted he thought by adopting a more vibrant—his words, not mine—persona, he would interest a lady."

"With what did he ask your help?"

"After expressing shame for his attempting to be untrue to his character, he thanked me for being a true friend. He suggested the ease with which we had in communicating would make an excellent marital foundation." Her gaze looked to the field, to the carriage house, to the blanket. To anywhere but him. "I considered Mr. Dixon's words then offered to choose him, thereby relieving him of any further interviews."

"Jane Ransome, you are a strong woman with a soft heart."

"He'd embarrassed himself in hopes of impressing a lady. I hated to see that continue."

"You agreed to court him out of pity."

"Yes." She looked unsure. "Do you fault me for coming to his aid?"

J.R. rolled onto his side, using his elbow to prop himself up. "If I hadn't pursued you, confessed my feelings, would you marry Dixon for the sole reason you hated to see him agonize over courting a lady?" His heart pounded in his chest as he saw the answer on her face. "Why, Jane? Why would you marry a man out of pity?"

"Because I want a husband." The answer was obvious. In *her* mind.

Not in J.R.'s.

"Why do you want a husband?"

"One is beneficial if a lady wishes to have children." The words were said in such a calm manner J.R. knew she was being truthful about her desire to be a mother. But that wasn't the deeper reason. That wasn't the real reason. She turned her head, listening. "I hear fiddles. The dance is about to begin. We should go back."

He reached over to lay his hand atop hers. "My life is an open book. I've been honest about my feelings. You don't have to be afraid to tell me what you think or feel. I want to know your fears. I want us to tell each other those things we've never told another."

Her eyes widened.

And then she laughed. "You are drunk on your own hypocrisy."

He blinked. It took him a moment to understand what she meant. "I answered openly every question you've asked."

"Then I have a new question for you." She leaned forward. "You refuse to join fellow believers in worshipping the very God you say you thank daily for saving you from hell and damnation and giving you new life in Christ. Why do you avoid churches?"

He hadn't expected her to ask that.

J.R. shoved himself off the ground and stood. So he was a hypocrite. He strolled out into the field, staring out at the gently rolling landscape, blanketed with tall grass waving in the soft breeze. In the distance, a herd of bison roamed freely. Going where they wished. They may die tomorrow, but that did not stop them from living today.

He didn't hear her approach.

He didn't know she stood there until he felt her fingers lace through his. She tightened her grip. Or maybe they both did.

"I haven't stepped inside a church since I returned from the war. I can't." J.R. paused. "My pulse races, and I feel like I will lose what is in my stomach."

"Why not?"

"Before his death, my father had been a college president. The war started, and Father cancelled classes. He said God ordered the trumpets to sound, calling all young men to battle." J.R. turned to Jane, but she was staring out at the prairie. "All men. . .except me."

This drew her attention. "He couldn't risk losing his only child to war."

"Exactly."

"You sound bitter."

"Father swore he knew that if I went to war, I would die. He couldn't live with himself knowing he'd sent his son to his death."

"People cannot see the future."

"My father didn't have to see the future." His voice choked. "He saw *me*. I've never chopped down a tree. I don't know how to handle a team of horses or plow a field. Instead of riding horseback, I prefer to walk or ride in a carriage. I can't load, shoot, or clean a gun. I don't know anything about bows and arrows or spears or nets or how to use them to hunt. I've never been hunting. My father knew I didn't have what it takes to be a soldier."

"But you did go to war, and you didn't die."

"I didn't die," he repeated.

Physically, he didn't. Emotionally, he died every battle.

J.R. took a breath then let it out in a lengthy exhale. The influenza that had taken his parents' lives while he was away interviewing soldiers forever prevented him from proving to them that he had what it took to survive a war. He could fight using a pen as a weapon. The man he'd become returned with every body part intact. That same man learned to compose vignettes and ballads for a lady's magazine in hopes of forgetting what he saw.

"J.R.," she said softly, cutting off his mental rambling, "I don't care if you've never chopped down a tree. God doesn't care if you can't use a net to catch a fish. No one in Turtle Springs cares that you can't shoot an arrow."

"I care." Now that he'd uncorked his past, the words spewed forth. "I'm ashamed at what I never learned to do because I chose to stay inside and read a book. I'm ashamed of hiding out in my tent and pleading with God to keep me alive. I interviewed Unions and Confederates who swore they'd been called by God into battle, as if that justified taking another man's life." He released her hand. "I feel like I'm drowning in fear and shame. Every morning I wake and wonder if I step inside a church again, will God call me into another battle? I can't, Jane. My father was right. I don't have what it takes to be a warrior. I'm a writer."

"You've limited God's grace to man-size proportions. . .and allowed your fear to grow into God-size proportions."

He winced.

She looked from him to the horizon.

Moments passed. Then minutes. Her lips twitched like she was trying to form coherency out of her jumbled thoughts. He felt the same.

"When I was a child"—her words came slow, measured—"we lived with my mother's people. They taught me to fast during the day, to go from sunrise to sunset without saying a word or making a sound, to walk long distances without complaint, to track animals, and to stop the white man from taking what doesn't belong to him." The corners of her lips twitched upward. "I was happy. . .until I heard one of the missionaries talking to God as if he knew Him, as if God was his father and his friend. Our tribe's shaman counseled the squaws to teach their half-breed children to not want colored dresses, not want cooking pots, not want a wheel to spin yarn, or a loom or a candlemold, or a wagon, a buggy, a lantern, a book."

For a moment she seemed lost in thought, caught up in memories.

She cocked her head to the side and looked at him. "I didn't want any of those things. I just wanted the white man's God. I wanted a friend who would never leave me."

He gave her an understanding smile.

She released a puff of breath. "Mama said I could not be a child of both worlds, so I was sent to live at the Shawnee Mission."

J.R. tensed. "By yourself?"

"There were other half-breed children there. Mama said I would be fine," she said, and it hurt J.R. to hear acceptance in her voice. "I wasn't a needy child like my siblings all were. I was the fifth daughter. I could take care of myself, and this way I could talk to the God I loved and not bring shame upon Mama."

"How old were you?"

"Twelve. And now you know why my sisters never taught me the art of flirtation. The Reverend and Mrs. Pingree taught modesty in manners." She turned from the field and strolled back to the blanket. Sitting, she drew her legs to her chest, smoothing her skirts over them.

J.R. found a spot next to her. "I suddenly feel more thankful for the parents I had."

She wrapped her arms around her legs. "My uncle Chief Black Bob says that seeing the past makes a man wise, living in the past makes him a fool." As she rested her chin on her knees, a furrow deepened between her brows. "I was engaged once."

"Why didn't you marry him?"

"My family must approve my groom. All of them," she stressed.

"How many is that?"

"Not counting children and youths. . .sixty-seven."

J.R. thought about Dixon and imagined him in the Tumble Inn dining hall being interviewed by Jane's relatives. All sixty-seven! If Jane had thought this through at the husband auditions, she would have never agreed to allow the reticent lawyer to court her. The man was likely to suffer apoplexy after five minutes just in the intimidating presence of her cousin, Cyrus.

"And if they don't approve of the man you wish to marry?" *Me. What if they don't approve of me?*

She released a little hmmph, as if being approved was a given. Then she smiled, and his doubts flittered away. "Oh, J.R., once they see how wonderful life is here in Turtle Springs, they'll decide to stay." She pointed at the field spreading east. "Most of this is my land. I own some up by Antelope Creek."

As her joy grew, his faded.

She'd made plans to reunite with her family. She'd made plans to build her future here. He liked Kansas well enough. The genial climate surpassed Philadelphia's. Even if he waited a decade, the state's population would not reach that of Sacramento alone. California had readers. Thousands of readers.

Kansas had farmers.

"Once I finish my article, I'm going to Sacramento." He tucked a loosened strand of hair back behind her ear. "Come with me."

"This is my home."

"It's a house, Jane. It's land. You can sell it and start over."

"This is my *home.*" Tears pooled in her dark eyes. She pushed away and stood. "People here need me."

"Do they?" he said, scrambling to his feet. "Or is this what you tell yourself because you want to feel needed?"

Her mouth gaped.

"Sweetheart," J.R. said quietly, and as the tears slid down her cheeks, his heart broke. "Your parents deserted you. You've lived here for three years, and if any of the sixty-six other people in your family besides Cyrus wanted to see you, they would have visited. Yet you think if you become engaged, your family will rush over here to render judgment on your fiancé. You may want to consider they don't care who you marry."

"You sure are full of vinegar," she snapped. "But I hear you. I'm not someone people crave to be with. There's always going to be someone or somewhere everyone wants more."

"I want to be with you," he said—begged, really. "I'm leaving for Sacramento, and I want a wife, a partner, to join me on the adventure. I want you. Come with me."

Her mouth tightened, and she looked away. "I'll think about it."

"Thank you. I—"

She grabbed the ice cream bucket and strode away, in the direction of the church. By the time she was out of sight, J.R. knew full well she'd finished thinking. She wasn't going anywhere with him.

Chapter 10

Love is often the fruit of marriage.—Molière

Four weeks to finish an article," Zumwalt said as J.R. hammered a nail into the loosened, ornate tin square securely it onto the ceiling. "You sure do write slow. Or is it you keep looking for a reason not to leave?"

"I keep getting interrupted. When the army arrived"—J.R. stopped hammering and looked down at the shoemaker—"I couldn't *not* interview them. It's my patriotic duty. Just as I couldn't *not* write something on those English chaps."

"I suppose you couldn't *not* miss Millie's wedding."

J.R. leaned against the top of the ladder, his mood as bright as the morning sunshine. "Certainly not! She's my sister."

"Sister?"

"Practically speaking. She's done my laundry since I arrived, and only charges me a quarter an item. . .*and still* only charges me a quarter, even after I moved into the inn. Only a sister—practically-a-sister, in her case—would be that kind."

"Your perception of sisters is astonishing."

The moment J.R. said, "Thank you," Zumwalt remarked, "I thought you were an only child."

"I really don't see how that's relevant."

Zumwalt laughed.

As thunder rolled in the distance, J.R. descended the ladder. He grabbed his gray suit coat off the workbench and deposited the hammer in its place, anxious to leave before the storm came in. Less because he didn't want to have to run through the rain, and more because it was only a matter of time before Zumwalt mentioned Jane. He always brought her into their conversations. Especially when she was in the same room as J.R. Whether it was hearing her name or seeing her about town or sitting near her during whatever afternoon tea they'd both been invited to, his heart faithfully catapulted in his chest. How sure—how calm—he would strive to seem, while inside he fidgeted like a love-struck schoolboy trying to put his feelings in a rhyme.

A mute confession is his glance, her blush a mute replying.
You read my soul, you know my wish; oh grant me its fulfilling.
She answers low, "If heaven smiles, and if my father is willing."

Therein lay the crux.

J.R. could ask her father and all sixty-seven members of her family for permission to marry her. As sure as rain (fittingly, another crack of thunder rolled), the answer would be yes. *Take her to Sacramento. Take her wherever. She's capable of managing without us.* J.R. would be given his heart's desire. . .and Jane would continue believing the lies that no one needed her. She was unneeded. Unwanted. Unloved.

Here he was. Stuck. Unable to leave town without her. Unable to be with her because she refused to leave behind her past.

J.R. shoved one arm and then the other into his suit coat. "Besides," he said to Zumwalt, "how often does a man's practically-a-sister get married in a joint service with her mother *and* her mother's best friend? Three couples hitched in one wedding is a news story, *and* one I've sold to every paper and journal in the state, plus ones in Kansas City and Omaha."

Zumwalt's face scrunched as he slowly nodded. "Seeing how one of the couples included me, I should get two-sevenths of the money."

"Two-sevenths?" J.R. chuckled. "How do you arrive at that number?"

"Lucille and Hank—two-sevenths, Millie and Will—two-sevenths, me and Gretchen—two-sevenths, and one-seventh to the writer. You wouldn't have a story if we hadn't married. Think of it as a finder's fee."

"You have a point there." J.R. folded up the ladder. Instead of carrying it to the back room, he gave the shoemaker his most ponderous, most I'm-taking-this-serious look. "Although. . .a better division is ninths."

Zumwalt's silvery brows rose. "Ninths?"

"Sheriff Ingram deserves a percentage because you wouldn't have married Gretchen if he hadn't telegrammed you to come to Turtle Springs, *and*," J.R. stressed, "he wouldn't have known the town wanted a shoemaker unless Abby hired him to be sheriff. Two-ninths to the happy newlyweds."

With a soft grumble, Zumwalt lifted one end of the ladder, leaving J.R. to carry the other. They stowed the ladder in the back room.

J.R. strolled back into the shop, his good mood sinking. A sheet of rain now cascaded over the wooden awning and onto the boardwalk, blurring the view of the street despite the bright sunlight. "Even if I wanted to leave town today, it's raining. Again." He sat on the nearest stool then swiveled to face Zumwalt. "Did I tell you Liam Logan asked me to stand up for him at his wedding?"

"I hadn't heard he proposed."

"Emma wanted to wait until they had all the Logan and Mason ducks—*umm*, children—in a row."

Zumwalt sat next to his workbench, laid a partially constructed shoe in the lap of his white apron, then studied his tools. He picked up a pair of pincers that looked like four other pincers on his workbench. "Tenths is more like it."

"So who else are you whittling my earnings out to?"

Zumwalt frowned at the pincers then at the shoe in his lap and then at his pallet of tools. "Who do you think?"

Jane.

Everything came back to her. In a town this size, avoiding someone was near impossible. Not that he was the one doing the avoiding. If anything, she ought to pay him for all the time he wasn't writing because he was thinking about her.

J.R. checked his pocket watch. "I wonder how long this rain is going to last. I need to get on over and help Oliver finish typesetting."

Zumwalt looked up, confused. "That press is for sale. Does his mother know about this?"

"I didn't think to ask." J.R. pocketed his watch. "Oliver and I were talking over breakfast, about how much I abhor writing multiple copies of my work to send to editors. I wouldn't have to do that if I owned a letter copying press. Since I don't, I decided to be a Scrooge and hire myself a Bob Cratchit to overwork and underpay."

"That's kind of you," remarked Zumwalt.

"I know. Unfortunately, your stepson couldn't catch my vision. He suggested we use the printing press. Why are you smiling?"

"The parent in me likes hearing my stepson is not following in your rapscallion ways." Zumwalt's smile abruptly fell. His expression grew serious. "It's time to move on, J.R. Pack your trunks and get on to Sacramento. Delaying the inevitable isn't fair to you or to Jane."

There was an awkward moment of silence, and then J.R. whispered, "I can't leave."

"*Can't* is an interesting word choice. Why can't you?"

"She needs me to rescue her."

Zumwalt's lips parted in surprise. "Not what I was expecting you to say, but I'll entertain your thinking. What are you supposed to rescue her from?"

"I don't know."

He didn't—and it plagued him. What was he missing? What didn't he see? It was there. He could feel it, sense it, know he needed to act, but couldn't. He was a man standing waist-deep in an icy lake, neither swimming nor drowning, frozen immobile. As bad a feeling as staring at a blank sheet of paper and having no idea what to write.

Muttering under his breath, Zumwalt tossed the pincers and shoe onto the workbench. He gathered his stool and moved it next to J.R.'s. "You know the answer"—he tapped J.R.'s chest—"in here. You come into my shop every day, wanting to know what you can do to help me, but all the while you are wanting me to tell you why you can't act. Why you can't move."

"You're not the first person who's told me I'm a stick-in-the mud."

"You can't be the man you want to be until you face it."

"Face what?"

"I don't know." Zumwalt tapped J.R.'s chest again. "Fight the battle, son."

J.R. swallowed, but his throat still felt tight. He tipped his chin in acknowledgment of Zumwalt's challenge, but he wasn't going to battle anything. There was nothing to fight. The war was over. He didn't need to fear that anymore. He didn't.

But he did.

As Zumwalt returned to his workbench, J.R. stared out the window. Rain pounded and thunder continued to roll, and yet the sun shone bright. He'd never seen a storm like it. Fascinated, he walked to the window for a better look. Leaving his hat on the rack, he strode outside. Into the street. Into the rain. Into the sun storm. Not a dark cloud overhead, but a line of dark clouds crawled across the western horizon. Lighting danced. Thunder crackled. As rain soaked his clothes, as mud oozed into his shoes, he stood there. And then he took a step. Then another. J.R. kept walking. One destination in mind. By the time he reached the church steps, his hands were shaking, his lungs tight.

It'd been five years.

"You've limited God's grace to man-size proportions. . .and allowed your fear to grow into God-size proportions."

Jane had been right about him. He had to face his fear. He had to for himself, and a little bit for her, too.

With an indrawn breath, J.R. gripped the door handle and walked inside.

Wednesday noon, July 4

"In a letter to his wife, on July 3, 1776, John Adams wrote that Independence Day should be commemorated"—Jane lowered the newspaper to see if Misters Underwood and Quimby were paying attention to her more than the checkerboard, and they were—"and I quote, 'with pomp and parade, with shews, games, sports, guns, bells, bonfires and illuminations from one end of this continent to the other from this time forward forever more.' Unquote."

"So that explains why we shoot fireworks," remarked Mr. Underwood as Mr. Quimby studied for his next move. "Too bad we didn't have the parade. I've always like parades."

"There's always next year." It was the best response Jane could give without lying. Unlike Mr. Underwood, she didn't like parades. The last one she'd attended spotlighted the newly enlisted soldiers marching off to war. Their standards raised. The trumpets blew. Everyone in Lawrence—in Douglas County, for that matter—had lined both sides of Massachusetts Street, cheering. She hadn't seen her younger brothers since that day.

The band changed tunes.

While several townsfolk strolled up and down the boardwalk, visiting the businesses that were open for a few more hours, most of the town and homesteaders in for the celebration were congregating over on the green, enjoying the day's entertainment. Games. Music. Reenactment "shews" put on by the schoolchildren. Upon popular request, the Ladies' Handbell Choir would perform a prelude to the fireworks display.

If J.R. were in town, that's where he'd be. Surrounded by people.

But he wasn't in town.

His return, however, was eminent, or so everyone said. How could they know? He'd left eight days ago without telling anyone where he was going or when—*if*— he would return.

Mr. Quimby breathed deep. "Mmm-mmm. Doc Carter's roasting us a good pig this year."

"Indeed." Jane scanned the rest of the paper for something of consequence. "There's a story here on the railroad and one about last month's flooding. Gentlemen, your pick?"

"Hmmph," came from Mr. Quimby.

Jane lowered the paper again. Both men were standing and looking in the direction of the church where the music had stopped. People lined the boardwalk. Unable to see what garnered all the attention, Jane stood. Still nothing.

"What's going on?" she asked.

"Dust storm, I reckon. Come here, gel. Ya gotta see this." Mr. Quimby grabbed her by the arm and pulled her out to the middle of Main Street. They stood there, with Mr. Underwood moving to Jane's other side.

Dust rose in the air above the road leading into town. Over the hill came a couple-dozen riders on horseback. All men, it looked like. Next came buggies and wagons and more single riders, some of these looked to be females, their colorful skirts fluttering.

"I'll wager we aren't about to be attacked by a gang of thieves," she said in hopes of lessening their scowls. "Or the army. Everyone is in civilian clothes. Look, there's even a few ladies riding shotgun on some of those wagons." As the lead riders neared the outskirts, Jane squinted. If she didn't know better, that one in the middle without a hat covering his white-blond hair looked like—

A resounding cheer went up on the far end of the town.

"Well, I'll be," bellowed Mr. Quimby. "That there's ol' Locky. Did ya know he knew how to ride a horse? He's sittin' as high in the saddle as them others."

Jane pursed her lips to hide her smile. She didn't know J.R. knew how to ride, but riding a horse wasn't all that difficult to learn. The real question was, what was he doing wearing buckskins? And where did he find all these people? Not to mention, why was he leading them into town?

She gasped.

Her chest tightened and vision blurred, the moment she recognized the gray-haired man riding next to J.R. "Papa," she whispered.

"Those yer kin?"

Mr. Underwood reached behind Jane and slapped Mr. Quimby's hat right off his head for asking such a dunce question.

Upon reaching the town, the riders slowed their horses to a trot. People on either side of the street waved at J.R. and those with him. A few cheers rose up. The band burst out in a rowdy march.

"Mr. Underwood," Jane said, smiling, "I believe that's about as close to a parade as we'll get today."

"Indeed, Miss Ransome, indeed."

J.R. reined his horse to a dead stop. Cousin Cyrus stopped next to J.R., an amused grin on his handsome face. One by one, the other riders and those driving buggies and wagons stopped, too, all in a cluster in the center of the street. It'd been years since Jane had seen her sisters and their families, her aunts, uncles, and other cousins. Mama drew her horse up next to Papa, he in his trapper clothes and Mama in her beaded tunic and leggings. None of the women wore hats. Their hair hung unbound or in braids down their back. Chief Black Bob, leaner and grayer than she remembered, wore tan trousers. No shoes. No shirt. Just trousers, the most clothes she'd ever seen on him during a summer month. Her family was a beautiful mix of savage and civilized. And they were here. In Turtle Springs.

Jane straightened her shoulders and stepped forward. She didn't know what to say to J.R. or to Papa, especially since they all sat there watching her walk to them.

She finally came to a stop a few feet from J.R. He was covered in dust and dirt and clearly hadn't shaved since he left town eight days ago. He looked wonderful.

They stared at each other for several long seconds.

J.R. dismounted. That's when she saw the bandage around his left hand. He handed the reins to her father, said something too low for Jane to hear, and then smiled. At her. She was so happy she could weep. *Please let this be what I think.* If it wasn't, the heartbreak would be too great to bear.

He strolled forward. "Hello, Jane."

"Hello, J.R.," she said with more calm than she felt. "Why are you dressed like that?"

"Chief Black Bob wanted to trade."

"So you traded him your fancy suit? Or just your trousers?"

He gave her a sheepish grin. "It was the only way to convince him to agree to come with us."

"And your hand?"

"Accident. I was cutting an apple."

"Why did you bring my parents here?"

"I love a girl who is direct. They're here because I asked them for permission to marry you." J.R. pointed over his shoulder. "All of them. All sixty-five of them."

Her chest tightened. Who died? She couldn't bring herself to say the words. Quintus? She didn't see him among the riders. Her baby brother hated riding in buggies or wagons or anything with wheels. The motion made him queasy. Where was Dexter? Her younger brothers never went anywhere without the other.

"Your brothers are"—he scratched his bearded jaw—"truth is, they're in a Fort Worth jail cell and will be until one of them agrees to marry the judge's daughter."

Jane looked to her father. "Is this true?"

"Sure is," he grumbled. "And I'm not sending bail. Now stop your yammering and listen to this man's proposal. He earned our approval. There's a pig that smells about ready to eat."

Mama shook her head. Not surprising. She'd never had many words to spare for Jane.

"Lockhart," Cyrus put in, a warning edge in his deep voice. "I advise you to be about your business. Hungry folk tend to get restless quick."

"Jane, would you mind. . . ?" J.R. motioned toward the school.

They walked in silence.

He led her around the building, shielding them from anyone's view.

Jane curled her fingers around his hand. "How did you earn their approval?"

"First things first. I'm not a hero," he said. "I write poems about butterflies and own more suits than I need and cost more than I should've spent. I fought a war with words. I've read *Uncle Tom's Cabin* seven times and cried every time. There aren't many things I can rescue you from. But there is one."

Jane's heart pounded fiercely. "There is?"

He cupped her cheek. "I *can* rescue you from being alone. I don't need California. I need Jane Ransome." Leaning close, he brushed his lips across hers. "I need you."

"Is this where I'm supposed to say yes, I'll marry you?"

He winked. "Not yet."

"Not yet?"

His lips claimed hers, and Jane didn't mind waiting a little longer for answers to how he earned the approval of her family or for his proposal. Not that she needed an official one. His actions spoke louder than any words ever could.

Apple Fritters

The New Household Receipt Book (1854) —*Sarah Josepha Hale*

Pare and core some fine large pippins (apples), and cut them into round slices. Soak them in wine, sugar, and nutmeg, for two or three hours. Make a batter of four eggs, a tablespoonful of rosewater, and a tablespoonful of milk. Thicken with enough flour, stirred in by degrees, to make a batter. Mix it two or three hours before it is wanted, that it may be light. Heat some butter in a frying-pan. Dip each slice of apple separately in the batter. Fry them brown. Sift powdered sugar and grate nutmeg over them.

Prior to *The Boston Cooking-School Cook Book* by Fannie Farmer, published 1896, recipes (formerly called *receipts*) had vague, if any, measurements. "A teacup of milk." "A piece of butter the size of an egg." "One wine-glass of wine." In *The New Household Receipt Book,* Mrs. Sarah Josepha Hale's recipe for sponge cake calls for the cook to "take the weight of the eggs in sugar and half their weight in flour." Large eggs? Medium eggs? Thank you, Miss Famer, for revolutionizing the industry by introducing the concept of using standardized measuring spoons and cups. You've made us better cooks!

Author's Note

Truly we know not the horrors of war till peace has fled.—Pvt. Elijah Beeman, with the Union Army, to his sister Ann, April 26, 1862

Despite the US government's extensive plans to settle Indians in Kansas, by 1850 white Americans were illegally squatting on their land and clamoring for the entire area to be opened for settlement. Several US army forts, including Fort Riley, were soon established deep in Indian Territory to guard travelers on the various western trails. From 1855 to 1858, Kansas Territory experienced extensive violence and some open battles. This period—known as "Bleeding Kansas" or "the Border Wars"—directly presaged the Civil War. In the 1860s, Kansas experienced war, the beginning of the cattle drives, the roots of Prohibition in Kansas, and the start of the Indian Wars on the western plains.

Turtle Springs is a fictionalized version of the unincorporated community of Wabaunsee, Kansas, nestled in the Flint Hills. The fourth new town in Kansas Territory (after Lawrence, Topeka, and Manhattan), Wabaunsee was named after a Pottawatomi chief, who, strangely enough, never actually lived in Kansas. Next time you are in the Sunflower State, be sure to visit Beecher Bible and Rifle Church, the oldest community building in the county, located on the corner of Chapel and Elm Streets, in Wabaunsee, Kansas.

ECPA-bestselling author **Gina Welborn** worked for a news radio station until she fell in love with writing romances. She serves on the American Christian Fiction Writers Foundation Board. Sharing her husband's love for the premier American sportscar, she is a founding member of the Southwest Oklahoma Corvette Club and a lifetime member of the National Corvette Museum. Gina lives with her husband, three of their five Okie-Hokie children, two rabbits, two guinea pigs, and a dog that doesn't realize rabbits and pigs are edible. Find her online at www.ginawelborn.com!

Dear Reader,

Turtle Springs is a fictional town with fictional characters. We sure hope you enjoyed your stay. So many times we've read wonderful stories of mail-order brides. But in this collection, we wanted to show what might happen if women put out a call for men to audition as husbands. We had a lot of fun writing these stories.

After the Civil War, many women were left without husbands, fathers, and brothers. They fought to eke out a living. Many succeeded greatly. Still, they yearned for a helpmate, a partner in life's trials. I don't figure it was too far of a stretch for a woman to find a man she fancied and propose to him. Then, after having had to be independent, the women struggled to fit back into the traditional roles of housewives and mothers. More and more, women were seen running businesses and working outside the home.

In Turtle Springs, they had no choice. It was either stay and work, or leave for the unknown. Our ladies chose to stay and forged a plan to make their town prosper.

Sincerely,
Cynthia Hickey

If You Liked This Book, You'll Also Like...

The Blue Ribbon Brides Collection
Nine inspiring romances heat up at old time state and county fairs. The competition is fierce when nine women between 1889 and 1930 go for the blue ribbon to prove they have something valuable to contribute to society. But who will win the best honor of all—a devoted heart?

Paperback / 978-1-63409-861-8 / $14.99

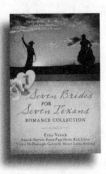

Seven Brides for Seven Texans Romance Collection
G. W. Hart is tired of waiting for his seven grown sons to marry, and now he may not live long enough to see grandchildren born. So he sets an ultimatum for each son to marry before the end of 1874 or be written out of his will. But can love form on a deadline?

Paperback / 978-1-63409-965-3 / $14.99

The American Heiress Brides Collection
Nine young American women between 1866 and 1905 have been blessed by fortunes made in gold, silver, industry, ranching, and banking. But when it comes to love, each woman struggles to find true love and know who to trust with their greatest treasure—their hearts?

Paperback / 978-1-63409-997-4 / $14.99

JOIN US ONLINE!

Christian Fiction for Women

Christian Fiction for Women is your online home for the latest in Christian fiction.

Check us out online for:

- Giveaways
- Recipes
- Info about Upcoming Releases
- Book Trailers
- News and More!

Find Christian Fiction for Women at Your Favorite Social Media Site:

 Search "Christian Fiction for Women"

 @fictionforwomen